A Beauty So Rare

Center Point
Large Print

Also by Tamera Alexander and available from Center Point Large Print:

Belmont Mansion Novels:
  Lasting Impression

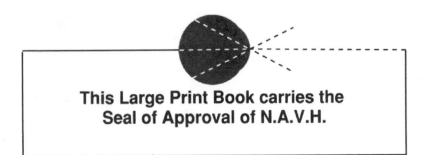

A BELMONT MANSION NOVEL • 2

A Beauty So Rare

Tamera Alexander

CENTER POINT LARGE PRINT
THORNDIKE, MAINE

This Center Point Large Print edition is published
in the year 2014 by arrangement with Bethany House
Publishers, a division of Baker Publishing Group.

Scripture quotations are from the Holy Bible,
King James Version.

This is a work of historical reconstruction; the
appearances of certain historical figures are therefore
inevitable. All other characters, however, are products
of the author's imagination, and any resemblance to
actual persons, living or dead, is coincidental.

The text of this Large Print edition is unabridged.
In other aspects, this book may vary
from the original edition.
Printed in the United States of America
on permanent paper.
Set in 16-point Times New Roman type.

ISBN: 978-1-62899-077-5

Library of Congress Cataloging-in-Publication Data

Alexander, Tamera.
A beauty so rare : a Belmont mansion novel / Tamera Alexander. —
Center Point Large Print edition.
pages ; cm
ISBN 978-1-62899-077-5 (library binding : alk. paper)
1. Architects—Tennessee—History—19th century—Fiction.
2. Women and war—History—Civil War, 1861–1865—Fiction.
3. Orphans—Tennessee—History—19th century—Fiction.
4. Upper class—Tennessee—Fiction. 5. Large type books.
6. Southern States—History—1865–1877—Fiction. I. Title.
PS3601.L3563B43 2014b
813'.6—dc23
                                            2014003993

For my readers,
who not only take these journeys with me,
but who add such joy and beauty to my own.

"It is only with the heart that one can see clearly, for the most essential things are invisible to the eye."

—Antoine de Saint-Exupéry

Preface

Most of the novel you're about to read is fictional, though there is plenty of real history and people woven throughout. For instance, there really is a Belmont Mansion in Nashville, built in 1853, that still stands today and that welcomes your visit. And Mrs. Adelicia Acklen, a character in the novel, is the dynamic, born-before-her-time woman who lived there.

In addition to Adelicia Acklen, many of the other characters in the novel were inspired by real people who lived during that time—people who lived and worked at Belmont. But the characters' personalities and actions as depicted in this story are of my own imagination and should be construed as such.

The first time I stepped across the threshold of Belmont Mansion and learned about Adelicia and her extraordinary personality and life, I knew I wanted to write stories that included her, her magnificent Belmont estate, and this crucial time in our nation's history. I invite you to join me as we open the door to history once again and step into another time and place.

Thank you for entrusting your time to me. It's a weighty investment, one I treasure, and that I never take for granted.

Tamera

Prologue

December 15, 1864
A Confederate field hospital some distance
    from the line of battle
Nashville, Tennessee

Eleanor Braddock startled when the soldier grabbed her hand, his grip surprisingly strong, his palm slicked with blood, sweat, and war. With eyes clenched tight, he held on to her as though she were the last person on earth. Which for him . . . she was.

From habit, she searched the left pocket of the soldier's uniform for his name, but the material—bloodied gray and soaked clean through—had been ripped to shreds by a cannon blast, much like the rest of him. She was grateful he'd been unconscious moments earlier when the surgeon examined him. He'd been spared the brusque shake of the doctor's head.

"Nurse . . ."

His gaze sought hers, and against the distant barrage of rifle and cannon fire, Eleanor steeled herself for the question she knew was forthcoming. No matter how many times she was forced to answer, it never got any easier to tell a man he was about to die.

And neither did watching it happen.

"Yes?" she said softly, not bothering to correct his

misassumption about her medical training, or lack thereof.

"Could you tell me—" He coughed, and his bearded chin shook from the cold or pain, likely both. A gurgling sound bubbled up inside his throat. "Did we . . . take the hill?"

Surprised that he asked of the battle and not his life, and touched by the strained hope behind his query, a tender knot formed in Eleanor's throat. "Yes," she answered without hesitation, having not the least clue which army held the upper hand in the battle. All she knew was that countless men— fathers, sons, husbands . . . *brothers*—were being slaughtered a short distance away. And this man deserved to die with a semblance of peace, believing that his life had counted for something. "Yes . . . you did." She tried to smile. "And General Lee will be so pleased."

Traces of pride but mostly relief shone in the soldier's eyes before they drifted shut. He fought for breath, each one exacting a price, and she prayed that his struggle would soon cease. But she'd seen men with similar wounds linger for hours, drifting in and out of agony.

He was no mere youth—into his thirties, at least—and his feet overhung the cot by several inches. Both boots were worn clean through at the toe. She'd detected the hint of a brogue in his voice, an accent from far away, something she'd always admired.

She studied him, wondering what his life had

10

been like before the war, and how he'd come to be on a bleak battlefield in the middle of Tennessee. His cheekbones were especially prominent, and she wished she had some of the beef tea she'd made for the men last evening, as she did nearly every night. No matter that she watered it down to stretch as far as possible, the men always made quick work of it. *"We ain't tasted nothin' this good in months,"* they'd say, draining their cups.

She'd always enjoyed cooking, but seeing her patients eat, even that little bit, did her heart good in ways she couldn't have imagined before serving injured and dying men.

She shifted her weight, and the soldier's grip tightened.

He grimaced and clenched his jaw, moaning, as though determined not to cry out like the others.

Empty bottles of laudanum on a nearby table caught her eye. She wished she had something to give him, but the last of the pain medication, including the morphine, chloroform, and ether, had been administered that morning, prior to them learning that the expected shipment of medical supplies wouldn't be arriving—thanks to the Federal Army.

She could make sense of the interception of ammunition and currency, or even provisions—but medical supplies? Even war should have certain rules.

Cannon fire thundered in the distance, and an icy wind knifed the canvased confines of the hospital tent. The moans and cries of the wounded and dying rent the air, and Eleanor shivered against the chill of it all. Though it was absurd, she was certain she could feel the earth groaning, straining beneath her feet, wondering, as she did, how much longer this insanity could continue. Surely, this was what hell was like. . . .

And yet, as she thought of the dark calamity of madness occurring just over the hill, she knew she'd only seen the outskirts of hell in these tents.

How had she lived for twenty-six years without realizing how precious and fragile life was? And how tenuous its peace. She'd never considered whether she'd squandered her life to that point. But when contrasting the experiences of her whole life with what she'd seen and done in recent months . . . *squandered* seemed a painfully appropriate term.

Her focus moved down the row of soldiers lining both sides of the tent. How many more would die before the two sides determined enough blood had been spilled?

When she'd first read the advertisement in the Murfreesboro newspaper soliciting "plain-looking women between the ages of 35 and 50" to volunteer in field hospitals and surgical tents, she'd wondered whether her age would prevent them from accepting her. But with the need for volunteers so great—and the first requirement met without a doubt—she'd quickly been accepted.

The only other point that had drawn a raised brow from her was the line "no specialized medical training or experience required." But it hadn't taken her long to understand why, and to realize that she'd grossly underestimated the task for which she'd volunteered.

She'd only known that after seeing her brother enlist along with most of her male relatives and friends, she couldn't sit at home and do nothing—especially with their aging father championing the Confederacy as he did.

She briefly closed her eyes, fatigue and worry joining forces. With stinging clarity, she imagined her younger brother lying somewhere on a battlefield, wounded, cold, and alone, the precious lifeblood pouring out of him. And a chill stole through her.

If anything happened to Teddy, she didn't know how she would bear it. Or how their father would hold up beneath the weight of such a loss. Though he possessed the physical strength of a man half his age and at six foot four—only five inches taller than she—still stood ramrod straight, her father's mind was slipping. Her mother's passing, nearly a decade ago—God rest her soul—had been especially difficult for him. He'd endured a long period of grief, mourning her passing. But in the past few months Eleanor had noticed a marked change in his memory and in his ability to recall recent details.

A sudden gust of wind thrashed the tent, and for a second, Eleanor feared the force would uproot it at the stakes.

Above the distant rumble of battle, the stomp of

horses' hooves and the creak of wagon wheels announced the arrival of another ambulance.

The other two volunteers in the tent moved to assist with unloading the wounded men. Eleanor knew she needed to do the same—and would receive a reprimand from Dr. Rankin if he saw her lingering overlong with any one patient. But thinking of Teddy, of the possibility of him being somewhere like this—frightened, wounded, and alone—she couldn't force herself to leave the soldier's side.

Even if he were to let go of her hand—which he hadn't.

"Most of what a person fears never comes to fruition, Eleanor." Her father's counsel returned from years past, and she knew if he were there, he would tell her not to be worried about imaginings. *"The mind can be a deceitful thing. You must be sensible, daughter, not given to the worrisome nature that so often befalls your gender. Focus on what you can see, not on what your imagination tells you is there."*

She knew from experience he was right, but her imaginings were sometimes so powerful they were hard to resist. And knowing a tiny percentage of fears actually *did* come true fed the seed of worry. Surely this makeshift hospital ward bore proof of that.

"The doc . . ." came a gruff whisper.

She looked down to see the soldier watching her again.

"Would you be knowin' wh—" He gritted his teeth, his already pale complexion growing more so. A moment passed before he spoke. "When will he . . . be comin' by?"

Despising her helplessness, Eleanor forced a steadiness to her voice. The training she and the other women in her group had received had been brief but clear, especially in regard to the dying. *"Don't ply a soldier with questions when he's near the end. You're there to be a solace. And above all, if he asks about his condition, always tell him the truth."* Eleanor wholeheartedly agreed with that last principle—in theory.

But theory and practice were two very different things.

"Actually . . ." She tried to frame the truth gently. "The doctor already has been by." She squeezed his hand. "I'm so sorry, but . . . nothing can be done."

Slowly the soldier's gaze narrowed. Then with effort, and a hint of disbelief, he lifted his head and peered down at his battered body. Reality forced the air from his lungs, and Eleanor gently eased his head back down.

A single tear slipped from the corner of his eye, and his shoulders began to shake. Yet he didn't make a sound.

She wanted to tell him it was all right if he cried out, that there was no shame in it. But something kept the words from forming, told her that whispering such a thing wouldn't be a comfort to him. And she wanted to be of comfort.

15

If only there were something she could give him to ease his passing, something to help cut the—

A pitcher of water and a tin cup on the tray beside the empty medicine bottles caught her eye. And an idea formed.

Swiftly, before reason could dissuade her—or her conscience could offer argument—she removed her hand from his, poured some water into the cup, and tipped an empty bottle of laudanum into it as though mixing the two. She made certain the soldier could see her—hoping no one else did—and swirled the contents of the cup, then held it to his mouth.

"Here," she whispered, summoning a cautious tone. "But only a little. It's mighty powerful."

His effort to gulp the contents tugged at her heart. Gasping, he worked to swallow every drop. Too quickly, though, and he coughed some back up. She wiped the residue from his mouth and beard. The cloth came away bloodied.

"Oh, thank you, lass. Thank you," he whispered, over and over, as though she'd given him the elixir of life.

For the longest time, he stared overhead, his breathing labored, his body racked with shakes. Eleanor stood close beside him, waiting for a telling flicker in his eyes that would reveal he recognized what she'd done. Or had tried to do.

Then gradually . . . the sharp lines of pain in his features began to relax, and to her amazement and disbelief, the tension in his body eased. How right her father had been—the mind could be a deceitful thing.

The soldier took a breath, holding his chest as he did, and emotion glazed his eyes. "I wish . . . I'd done better," he ground out. "I w-wish that—" His voice broke, and he reached again for her hand.

"Shhh . . ." Eleanor leaned close. "It's going to be all right."

"No . . ." The muscles in his neck corded tight. "I need to be sayin' this, lass . . . while I still have me breath."

Giving him the silence he needed, she brushed the hair back from his forehead in a manner that would have felt far too intimate months earlier. But war had a way of rewriting etiquette.

"I . . . I wish . . ." Tears traced his temples. His expression grew more intent, purposeful. "I wish I'd . . . done for you . . . like I said I would, Mary girl. Like I promised . . . 'fore I left." His sigh held longing. "Every day . . . in my mind, I been—"

He choked on a sob and reached out as though trying to touch her face, but Eleanor knew she wasn't the woman he was seeing anymore. She cradled his hand between hers, and his tears came afresh.

"What?" she gently coaxed, seeing the pain in his features and thinking that if he stated his regret aloud, it might be lessened.

He fumbled with the hem of his coat, and when she realized his intent, she helped him pull a small bundle from his pocket. Carefully, she unwrapped it.

An embroidered handkerchief, damp with blood. A rose pressed between its folds.

"I been carryin' this with me, my sweet Mary," he whispered. "Just like you asked." His lips trembled. His blue eyes smiled. "I still can't believe you're mine, darlin'. That you said yes . . . to the likes of me."

Eleanor blinked, and only then did she feel the moisture on her lashes. She'd never minded the sight of blood. She'd assisted in the surgical tent, where the large wooden table ran red for days on end, and she'd watched wagon after wagon lumber away, loaded with amputated limbs. But this . . .

Listening to final whispers, to the contents of a man's heart poured out to a stranger . . . this she couldn't do without crying. Whoever this woman— this *Mary girl*—was, she prayed the woman knew how well she was loved.

Or . . . had been loved.

Not doubting herself at all now, Eleanor leaned close so he would be sure to hear her. "I'm *proud* to be yours, and always have been," she said, trying to imagine what it would be like to be so loved by a man. But she couldn't.

She looked again at the handkerchief, thinking about how brief life truly was and about all the things she hadn't yet done—she'd never been kissed, much less married or given birth to children. She'd never traveled outside Tennessee or seen the ocean's tide roll in and out. Growing up, she'd never held a boy's hand, other than Teddy's, and she'd never lain awake all night beneath the stars to watch the sun's journey begin again. Countless other *never had*s flitted through her mind, and yet . . . how distant and unimportant they seemed now, in comparison to the world closing in around them.

"You're proud to be mine," he whispered, as if relishing the thought even while struggling to accept it. "It's too late, I know, Mary girl, but . . ." Deep furrows knit his brow. "If I could, I'd . . ." He grimaced and sucked in a breath.

Her chest aching with the weight of this man's regret, Eleanor pressed the handkerchief into his palm. "What?" she whispered, squeezing his hand, feeling him slipping away. "What would you do?"

He peered into her eyes. "Oh, my precious Mary . . . I'd do like I promised you and—"

A blast of winter shook the canvas walls of the tent. Only, Eleanor felt the ground shake this time too, and she realized it wasn't the wind.

"Miss Braddock!"

She turned to see Dr. Rankin racing toward her, chaos in the tent behind him.

"Quickly!" he shouted. "Get to the ambulances! Federal troops have taken the hill!"

A high-pitched whistle pierced the air over-head, and in the brief second it took her to place the sound . . . the world exploded. Dr. Rankin grabbed her shoulder to steady her. Smoke filled the tent. The acrid burn of gunpowder thickened the air.

"Go, Miss Braddock! All volunteers to the ambulances. Now!"

"But . . . we can't leave the men!"

"We're moving those we can." He turned. "But if we don't leave soon, we'll be dead alongside them!"

Only then did she realize . . . the soldier had let go of her hand.

She looked back at him, saw his slack jaw, the dissonant peace in his expression. . . .

Hearing the volley of gunfire, she hastily touched his cheek, hoping his regret over whatever it was he wished he'd done in this life would somehow be lessened in the next. She turned to go—

And remembered.

Frantic, she checked the soldier's hand for the handkerchief. A volley of gunfire made her flinch. His hand was empty. Wanting to keep the handkerchief made no sense, but knowing how much it had meant to him, it seemed wrong to simply leave it behind to be trampled and forgotten.

Finally, she spotted the bloodstained cloth on the floor and grabbed it. But the rose was gone. Never partial to flowers, she dismissed it at first, but quickly thought again of the soldier having carried his Mary girl's rose into battle.

Heart racing, and hearing the blast of cannon fire explode outside, she knelt in the dirt, feeling foolish as she searched, telling herself it was useless. She needed to be—

There. Her palm closed around the delicate pressed flower, the petals coming loose in her grip. She positioned the flower carefully into the handkerchief and then into her pocket. As she turned to leave, she saw the remaining wounded in the tent.

So many . . .

She spotted a soldier struggling to stand—a man Dr. Rankin had scheduled for surgery—and with strength she didn't know she had, she pulled him to his feet, draped his arm around her shoulders, and half dragged, half carried him to the ambulance. Someone from behind picked her up and shoved her into the wagon beside him just as a second shrill scream sounded overhead.

Eleanor covered her head and braced for the impact, thinking of Teddy and praying he wasn't dead, and promising herself that if she got through this alive—if this wretched war ever ended—she would get as far away from death and dying as she could, and she would do a better job at living than she'd done before. She would make her life count for something.

And she would find that soldier's widow, his Mary girl, whoever she was, and tell her what he'd said. And ask her what he'd meant.

1

September 2, 1868
Nashville, Tennessee

Eleanor knew in her heart that what she was doing was right—so why was her heart fighting her on it *now,* when the day had finally arrived.

Seated across from her in the carriage, her father stared out the window, solemn, hands clasped in his lap, so different from moments earlier when they'd first entered the city of Nashville. He'd seemed almost childlike in his enthusiasm as the carriage carried them through the heart of town.

She'd asked the driver to stop by the post office first. It wouldn't take her but a moment inside. She preferred to have the signed contract in hand for her *meeting* later that afternoon, and the building owner with whom she'd corresponded in recent weeks had indicated he would leave it for her there.

"I'm going there to rest," her father said softly, his tone bordering more on question than certainty.

Knowing what he meant, Eleanor nodded. "Yes . . . Papa, that's right. And it's only for a short time." She coerced a smile to reinforce the statement, praying the doctor's expectations were correct.

Exactly when her role as daughter had shifted to

that of caretaker, she couldn't say. But as she looked across the carriage at the strapping giant of a man —whom she favored in more ways than was likely best for a daughter to do—a place deep inside her yearned to again be that little girl who, when she looked into her father's warm brown eyes, knew that everything in the world would be right. And safe. And would make sense.

But that little girl was gone. And so was her father.

The carriage slowed, and Eleanor spotted the post office ahead. "Papa, I need to run a quick errand. But I won't be long."

He glanced out the window. "Perhaps I should come with you. I could help—"

"That's not necessary," she said a little too quickly, and regretted it. She reached for his book. "Why not stay here and continue reading where we left off. Then we'll discuss the passage once we're on our way again."

Not looking convinced, he studied the book in his hands, then finally nodded. "You *will* come back . . . won't you?"

"Of course I'll come back, Papa." She squeezed his hand in affirmation, but the guilt already nipping her heels took a firm bite.

The carriage driver opened the door, and Eleanor hurried into the post office. She paused inside and looked back to see her father reading, his lips moving as he did. She hadn't wanted to risk him coming with her, not when considering the spells that frequently overcame him these days. His temperament was so unpredictable.

Patronage was heavier than she'd imagined, and the queue reached almost to the door. She glanced at the chatelaine watch affixed to her bodice. She had a few moments to spare before her father's scheduled appointment, and she *needed* that contract in hand.

The line moved more slowly than she would have liked, and after a couple of moments, she glanced out the front window to the carriage and stilled, not seeing her father anymore.

She craned her neck to one side. Perhaps he'd changed seats. He'd insisted on that twice already on their ride from Murfreesboro that morning, saying it was bad luck to ride in one direction for an entire trip. Then she saw the door.

Ajar.

She raced back outside to find the driver still atop the carriage but the carriage—empty. And her father nowhere in sight.

"Armstead!" she called up, searching the street. "My father. He's gone."

The driver appeared at her side, bewildered. "I'm sorry, Miss Braddock. Last thing I knew he was in here."

"You go that way." She pointed. "And if you find him first, please . . . try not to upset him. We don't want to cause a scene."

"Yes, ma'am!"

Eleanor started in the opposite direction, peering

inside stores and businesses as she went, trying not to think about her father's recent antics or what might happen if someone attempted to confront him and he became upset.

The high-pitched laughter drew her attention first. Then she saw him. Across the street. Peering in the window of a dry-goods store.

Dodging a freight wagon and another carriage, she managed to reach the other side, but not before her father had entered the store and taken a spool of ribbon from the shelf, along with a pair of scissors.

He spotted her. "Eleanor! Isn't it pretty? I thought you would enjoy this. You like wearing ribbons in your hair."

She managed to get the scissors from him, but he stuffed the spool into his pocket.

"Papa, it's lovely but . . . I don't wear ribbons anymore, remember?" Eleanor retrieved the spool and returned it to the shelf. Then she glimpsed a man, presumably the proprietor, headed straight for them. Consternation lined the man's face.

He glared at her father, then her. "May I help you?"

Embarrassed, Eleanor tried not to show it. "We were just looking, sir. And now—" She took her father by the arm. "If you'll excuse us, please."

Feeling the proprietor's attention on her back, Eleanor hurried outside, grateful to see Armstead walking toward them. With his assistance, she managed to get her father back to the carriage without further incident.

"I'll watch him this time, Miss Braddock," the driver insisted. "You go on inside, ma'am, if you want."

Considering what awaited her that afternoon, Eleanor felt she had little choice.

In a hurry, Marcus Geoffrey exhaled, questioning yet again his desire to experience the life of the common man. The queue inside the post office nearly reached the door, and he estimated at least a ten-minute wait. It seemed patience was a virtue he was destined to learn.

The door to the post office opened behind him, and an older woman entered, slightly stooped and tottering. At the same time, the wind gusted and blew the door back. The woman reached for it . . . and stumbled. But Marcus caught her and stopped the door before it slammed back against the wall.

"Oh, thank you, sir." She covered his hand on her arm, regaining her balance. "I'm not as spry as I used to be."

"Who among us is, madam?"

She gave him an appreciative look, and Marcus —thinking of his own dear mother, gone long before her time—motioned for the woman to move ahead of him in line. He withdrew a pad of paper and pen from his suit-coat pocket and used the opportunity to sketch an idea for the warehouse his crew was renovating. It had come to him earlier that morning and he hadn't yet had time to—

"Yes, that's correct. The gentleman said he

would leave it here for me," a female stated from somewhere in front of him. "Would you mind checking again, please?"

Marcus slowly raised his head, curious about the creature to whom the beguiling voice belonged.

"Yes, sir," she continued. "At least that was my understanding."

Marcus looked toward the counter and spotted the woman—or rather, the explosion of *pink* with a woman swathed somewhere beneath—speaking with the mail clerk. Her voice bore the accent customary to the people of Nashville but had a satisfying, almost sultry, quality to it. Like the touch of a breeze on the back of one's neck on a hot summer day. But the woman's ensemble . . .

Her jacket and skirt, well tailored, stood out in marked contrast to the hues of black, gray, and dark blues worn by most of the other patrons.

"I'm sorry, ma'am, but there's nothing for you here by that description. Nor do we have record of having sent anything like that to Belmont."

She sighed, shoulders sagging.

Even viewing her only from behind and without benefit of an introduction, Marcus knew who she was. Personal business took him to her aunt's estate nearly every day, and he'd overheard Mrs. Adelicia Acklen Cheatham speaking of the woman's arrival, expressing an eagerness for her to make everyone's acquaintance at Belmont.

But having met more than his fair share of wealthy, well-bred, overly eager, husband-seeking women in his life—despite this one being taller than most and the niece of the richest woman in America—he had no intention of pursuing her acquaintance, nor encouraging it in any way.

If she attempted to gain his attention, he would be kind, he decided, even affable—considering Adelicia Acklen Cheatham was his benefactress, of sorts. But beyond that, he would firmly, yet gently, rebuff any flirtations on the young woman's part.

She turned then and headed straight for him.

He summoned an air of practiced nonchalance, the words replaying in his mind . . . *Firmly, but gently.*

The woman didn't so much as *blink* in his direction as she passed.

Feeling aptly put in his place—and not overly fond of the feeling, Marcus watched her exit the post office. He wasn't accustomed to being ignored. Her attention was clearly focused elsewhere. He studied her as she walked toward a waiting carriage, the driver already standing by the door.

Tall and blond, she bore not the slightest resemblance to her aunt, who was a petite brunette. Even at a mature age, Adelicia Cheatham was still a striking dark-haired beauty. This woman, on the other hand, while not *un*attractive, possessed less remarkable features, less delicate, to be sure. Hers held more strength. One might even describe her as handsome. And he suspected she was older than he'd first imagined—

"Sir?"

Marcus turned.

The elderly woman he'd assisted earlier was several feet ahead of him in the queue. She smiled and motioned him forward.

Feeling a little foolish, Marcus moved ahead, then chanced another look back at the window in time to see the woman climb into the waiting carriage.

It had been a long time since he'd noticed a woman who—when in such close proximity—hadn't reciprocated his *noticing*. Of course, he hadn't endeavored to gain her attention. If he had been trying, she would have noticed, he assured himself.

It meant nothing, really. After all, he'd had enough of those kind of women. And the woman he had now, he didn't want. But . . . he blew out a breath. Nothing he did would change that.

Minutes later he reached the counter.

"Good afternoon, Mr. Geoffrey." The mail clerk greeted him, already rising from his stool. "We have something for you, sir. It arrived this morning."

Satisfied, Marcus waited. But when he saw an envelope instead of a box or crate, his satisfaction waned. "Nothing else?" he asked.

The clerk shook his head. "That's it. I'm sorry, sir."

Marcus managed a polite response and stepped to the side, fingering the envelope. The hand-stamp announced the origin of the envelope even before he read the return address. He tore open

29

the flap and found another envelope inside. When he saw the royal wax-embossed seal, he quickly concealed it, even as he felt an unseen noose tightening about his neck.

Never had Uncle Franz written to him, and Marcus knew only too well who had put him up to it. He started to tuck the letter away to read later but thought of his father's tenuous health, and reconsidered. Moving to a quieter section of the busy post office, he opened the letter.

His gaze fell upon the salutation and first lines of the missive, and he swiftly realized his father's health was not the issue. The letter was about something else.

To the Archduke Gerhard Marcus Gottfried von Habsburg . . .

His uncle's use of his formal name and title didn't bode well for the letter's purpose, and Marcus's gratitude for the ocean separating him from what he'd left behind—at least for a little while longer—grew one hundredfold.

His gaze edged downward, past the formal opening.

Come next June, Gerhard, the reprieve granted to you shall have expired. At that time, you shall return home according to our agreement, in order to fulfill your duties to crown and country. Those born to privilege must bear its responsibilities with integrity and honor, despite one's personal feelings and regardless of their . . .

Marcus folded the letter and slipped it back into the envelope, wishing he could dismiss a decree from his uncle—the emperor of Austria—so easily in person. He knew his uncle's speech by heart. It was one he'd heard countless times as a boy when he was third in line to the Austrian throne, behind his father and older brother.

But he'd heard it even more often in the weeks prior to leaving for America when the Austrian newspapers had reported he'd become second in line "through extenuating circumstances."

He'd never sought the throne, nor ever considered that it might someday come to him. He still didn't believe it would happen. Not with his uncle healthy and strong, and still trying for that first son. Marcus hoped—even prayed, on occasion—that the Almighty would make fruitful that royal endeavor.

He could scarcely believe close to a year had passed since he'd left his homeland. He was still somewhat surprised his uncle and father had agreed to his coming to America. But after Rutger's death . . . everything had changed.

He had changed.

Both his uncle and father agreed that time away would be good for him, and good for the House of Habsburg, considering the rumors that were circulating around Rutger's death. "Best you not be seen in public for a while, Gerhard," Uncle

31

Franz had counseled. "Let the scandal calm to a simmer, then slowly dissipate to nothing, as these situations almost always do—given time and something else on which the public can chew. And by all means, if you must sow any last wild oats, do it discreetly. The last thing we need is an *American* scandal on top of this one."

His father's last letter had confirmed that Uncle Franz's prediction had held true. The rumors were subsiding. People were forgetting what had happened.

But forgetting was something Marcus could never do.

If there had been any significant political unrest in the country, his uncle and father would never have allowed him to step foot outside Europe. But with the volatile years of war behind them, and the previous year's compromise of dual monarchy with Hungary accepted, the empire was at peace. The ship was sailing smoothly, as his uncle had stated upon his departure.

Still—Marcus looked at the envelope—apparently Uncle Franz felt the need to remind him of his obligation. As if he could ever forget. He loved his country, and his family, rife with greed and ambition though its members were. It wasn't for lack of affection or honor that he eschewed the crown.

He simply didn't desire to ever rule his country. He'd seen that side of life. Now he wanted to see another.

Out on the street, Marcus breathed in the fresh air, catching a hint of fall on the breeze. He searched the thoroughfare for the carriage—and Mrs. Cheatham's niece—reliving her snub and feeling a tug of humor. Perhaps he was losing his touch with women.

Or more likely, Adelicia's niece bore more resemblance to her aunt than first met the eye. He smiled. Adelicia Cheatham was her own woman in every way. He'd seen her when in town before. She held her head high, looking neither to the right nor the left. She seemed impervious to social pressure.

After an appointment, he was headed to Belmont to check on his plants in the conservatory. Perhaps while there, he would have opportunity to make the acquaintance of Adelicia's niece. Purely for social reasons, of course. International relations, some might say.

He made a quick stop by his room at the boardinghouse and stowed the letter from his uncle in the cedar trunk at the foot of the bed. As he closed the lid, his hand lingered on the artfully carved woodwork. He hadn't brought much in the way of furniture when he left Austria, under-standably. But leaving the trunk behind hadn't been an option.

His maternal grandfather—a humble, unassuming man—had possessed remarkable skill with a blade, a gift Marcus hadn't inherited. He ran a hand along the edges of the trunk, easily distinguishing the artistic work from the lesser-crafted attempts of a nine-year-old boy, treasuring the memory of the man who had prized spending time with his grandson above perfection.

Marcus rose, glad again that he'd brought the trunk with him. It fit well in this setting.

He'd grown accustomed to, even appreciative of, the sparse surroundings of his current living quarters, which were a far cry from the palace and his family's private residence. He could have leased or even purchased a house upon his arrival in Nashville. But that would have gone contrary to the decision he'd made before coming to this country. . . .

He intended to experience how ordinary people lived, and was learning a lot about himself in the process—not all of which he liked.

His uncle had warned him against causing a scandal in this country, but that was the last thing his uncle needed to worry about. Marcus was done with that part of his life. No more pursuing women and no more liquor—at least not in excess. No more wasting his life, as he'd come to realize he'd been doing.

Cordoning off that vein of thought, he strode in the direction of the city's courthouse, mindful of a distant pounding at the back of his head. Too much work perhaps. He was hopeful his crew renovating the textile warehouse across town would maintain their progress. They were a week ahead of schedule, and he wanted to maintain that lead.

As he walked, he searched the endless wash of cloudless blue overhead, then let his gaze trail the lush rolling hills surrounding this city, even while —in his mind's eye—he saw the snowcapped Alps of home.

Looking back over his life, he realized how much time had slipped past him, and how much of his life had been lived by another's dictate. His had been a privileged upbringing, no question, with ample opportunities to study and learn. But also with obligations. Always, always obligations.

America's South was far more devastated from the war and its aftermath than he'd imagined, but his skills were being utilized. It was so different and *freeing* that, in rare moments, he could almost forget the life he'd left behind. He'd wanted to come to America since he was a boy, since first learning about the "thirteen brave little colonies" from his tutor. But it was only when a trusted mentor had introduced him to Luther Burbank's publications and then Marcus had met the botanist in person—and later visited his Boston nursery full of thousands of plants—that his dream had been set in motion.

However short-lived that dream might prove to be.

2

"You know, Eleanor—"

Eleanor watched her father as he leaned forward in the carriage, her frustration with him having faded. But not her frustration over having no contract. She hoped the lack of follow-through on the part of the man who owned the building didn't bode ill for their agreement.

"I think this is a good decision," her father continued. "As you said, it will give me an opportunity to rest and"—a faint smile hinted beneath his silvered-white beard she'd trimmed that morning—"it will allow you the opportunities a young woman such as yourself needs."

Eleanor was tempted to laugh. *"A young woman such as yourself . . ."*

She was twenty-nine and could count on one hand the number of months until her thirtieth birthday. One could hardly describe her as young anymore. Nor did she feel as such.

Her father's comment reminded her of what Mrs. Hodges, the seamstress, had the gall to say to her only days earlier. Eleanor fingered the sleeve of her new jacket, then ran a hand over her skirt, still a little embarrassed by it, and more than a little perturbed at the outcome of her exchange with the woman—and at Mrs. Hodges's meddling.

"That was a delicious dinner you prepared for us

earlier this week," her father continued. "Though I still don't like the idea of your being forced to cook." He grimaced. "Bernice shouldn't have left us for that position with another family. I'm more than a little disappointed in her. The least she could have done is to have given us more notice."

Eleanor regretted her father's resentment toward their former housekeeper and cook, especially since she herself was responsible for Bernice's departure. But to tell him the real reason Bernice had left their employ would wound him too deeply.

So she reached for a brightness she didn't feel and redirected the conversation, a skill she'd finely honed in recent months. "Don't feel badly about me cooking, Father. As I've told you . . . I enjoy it. And besides, you're eating better these days. Your appetite has improved."

His brows shot up. "How could it not with that . . . what do you call it? That fancy egg dish you prepared?"

"A savory custard. I think I finally came upon the right combination of ingredients this time."

"I heartily agree. I hope you kept close account of what you added. I'd like to have that again."

"I did." She kept close account of all her recipes, both those passed down from her precious mother and those she'd devised on her own—and with good reason, considering their present circumstances.

Most of her recipes leaned toward the savory variety, but she shared an affinity for the sweets too.

As they'd traveled on through Nashville, she'd seen a bakery claiming to have the *Best doughnuts in town.* She looked forward to seeing if the message on the sign held true, and also to scouting out her potential "competition."

But that little bakery would only be competition if her plans actually came to pass.

Then it registered with her. . . . How coherent her father sounded, how much like his old self. She looked over at him, questioning yet again if she was doing the right thing. Or if, perhaps, she was acting prematurely.

Usually her father couldn't remember what he'd eaten five minutes ago, much less days earlier. Yet he recalled events from his childhood or early marriage with stunning clarity.

"My only regret"—his expression grew thoughtful—"is that Teddy wasn't there to enjoy the meal with us."

Eleanor felt a twinge at the mention of her brother's name, and at the wistfulness in her father's features.

"He'll enjoy that savory custard, Eleanor. I hope you saved him some." Eyebrows raised, his expression turned conspiratorial. "And those little muffins with the jam. He always likes the sweets, you know."

It was all Eleanor could do to maintain his gaze as down deep another chunk of her heart broke. "Yes," she whispered. "I know."

"Have I shared his latest letter with you?" Her

father patted the left breast pocket of his coat, then the other. "He's doing so well, Eleanor. Which I always knew he would."

Feeling a sickening affirmation of the choice she'd made, she looked out the window as he searched for the letter that wasn't there.

Though still a good distance away, the expansive four-story brick building came into view, and the carriage driver slowed the horses' pace to negotiate the turn onto the long narrow drive. It shamed her to admit it, but Eleanor was relieved no other carriages were in sight.

When she'd first inquired months ago, the institution had been full, with a waiting list. And the only reason they had an opening now, she knew, was due to her aunt's influence, or more specifically, her aunt's husband. Recently retired, he had been director of the institution for years.

Eleanor had been assured of confidentiality, and she was certain they took great care, but if anyone discovered that her father—Garrison Theodore Braddock, once one of the most revered attorneys in the state of Tennessee—was *here,* what thin veneer of honor and respect that still clung to the Braddock family name would be stripped away in a blink.

She motioned out the opposite window, not wanting her father to see the sign marking the entrance of the institution. He only knew he was "going to a nice place to get much needed rest," as the doctor had instructed her to say.

"Look there, Papa." She pointed out the window overlooking a field. "You've always loved cardinals."

The brilliant red bird with its distinctive black markings sat perched on a branch as though heaven itself had willed the diversion. If only she could believe that was true. But heaven and its Maker had never felt so distant. Nor so silent.

The finely appointed carriage they traveled in—far nicer than anything her family could ever have afforded—jostled over the dirt-packed drive, and Eleanor's grip tightened on her reticule as the nerves in her stomach twisted another half turn.

In recent days, she'd managed to sell their family home, the house she'd lived in all her life and where her father had been raised, along with most of the furniture, keeping only a few pieces that would be delivered within the week either here, for her father, or to her "new home"—if she could call it that. She didn't plan to be there long.

Their home's condition had declined over the years, and the meager funds from its sale had gone toward paying off a loan her father had secured years earlier, and for which he'd used the home as collateral. The rest had mostly gone toward her father's treatment. The institution demanded six months' payment in advance, with promise of reimbursement should the patient require less time. She trusted her father would fall into that category, but in any case, she was determined to spend what little money remained as frugally as possible.

Bernice, their cook and housekeeper for twelve years, had been most understanding about the quiet dismissal from service—they simply hadn't been able to pay her any longer. Not since the law firm—a practice her father had built and managed for over twenty-five years—had been forced to close its doors after the war.

She couldn't bring herself to admit the financial devastation to her father. If he knew how far they'd fallen, it would surely push him over the edge.

"Perhaps you could pen a response to Teddy this evening, Eleanor." Her father nodded as though considering the prospect an excellent one. "We could compose it together, following dinner. Likely he's wondering why we haven't written. But . . ." He turned to the satchel on the seat beside him. "Where *is* that letter?" He rummaged through the contents, growing increasingly earnest. "It must be in here somewhere."

Sensing his frustration mount, Eleanor knew better than to disagree with him. Almost four years had passed since Teddy had died in the war, and still there were moments when the ache of loss felt as though they'd gotten the news only yesterday. And that was especially true whenever her father spoke of him in the present tense.

Those occasions, growing more frequent, laid siege to the hope that indeed the doctors were correct about his mental faculties returning.

She'd ceased trying to correct her father's slips in memory some time ago. He became emotional, even agitated when she did. On several occasions his behavior had bordered on violent, and she'd actually begun to fear he might do her harm, however unintentionally. Though she was tall and strong—or *stout,* as her grandmother had once described her as a girl, patting her leg firmly—she was no match for him.

Suddenly, he stilled. He looked over at her.

His eyes narrowed as though he were reading her thoughts, and Eleanor braced herself for what was coming.

"Theodore," he whispered. "Oh, my dear son . . ." His eyes grew moist. His chin shook. "Why, Eleanor? Why did they kill my boy? They—" His voice broke. "They shouldn't have killed my only boy."

Eleanor gave a slow nod, her breath quickening. "I know, Papa. I know . . ." With each tear that disappeared into her father's beard, she sensed his control—and *him*—slipping away again.

This is for his own good, she repeated to herself over and over. *And at the doctor's recommendation.* Yet she couldn't deny the guilt pressing at her from all sides.

The carriage slowed.

She checked the chatelaine watch hooked to her bodice. One o'clock. Precisely when she'd told the director to expect them.

She looked out the window and saw a woman and two men descending the steps of the building ahead. From their manner of clothing—the woman

42

in a dark dress and starched white apron, the men in dark slacks and white vests—she assumed they were employees of the institution.

Her father looked out the window too, then back at her. Slowly, his expression changed from pained to fearful. "Where are we? What is this place?"

She reached out to calm him, but already suspicion darkened his gaze.

"Father, it's going to be all right. Remember what the doctor said about going someplace where you could get some rest. This is—"

"No . . ." He pulled back, shaking his head. "I don't want to be here. I want to go home."

"Papa," she said softly, using a firm but gentle tone. "Listen to me."

His expression hardened. "You *must* take me home, Eleanor!"

"We spoke about this earlier," she continued. "And you said you thought it was a good—"

"Driver!" He pounded on the side of the carriage. "I insist you return us home. This moment!"

He reached for the door handle, the carriage still moving. But Eleanor beat him to it. His hand tightened over hers in a painful grip.

"Take . . . me . . . home," he said low, drawing himself up as he stared down.

His grip excruciating, Eleanor felt her eyes begin to water, as much from grief as from the physical pain.

The carriage stopped, and the two men approached. Though quite short, they were strong, broad shouldered. Their presence communicated anything but welcome. Or comfort.

They had been joined by Dr. Crawford, the director with whom she'd interviewed weeks earlier when she'd toured the facility—what portions of it a family member was permitted to visit.

She looked at them and shook her head, trying to keep them at bay, the pain in her hand nearly unbearable. If only they would give her a few moments, she could calm her father down. She didn't want their first impression of him to be like this.

"Papa . . . the people here are going to help you." She tried to pull her hand from beneath his on the door latch but couldn't. "*Please* let go. You're hurting me!"

"You don't care about me, Eleanor." Accusation weighted each word, his face flush with anger. "If you did, you wouldn't be doing this."

With one last torturous squeeze, he released her hand, flung open the door, and bolted from the carriage.

Powerless to intervene, Eleanor watched as her father—though a foot taller than the men—proved no match for their combined strength. As they forced his arms behind his back and wrestled him into submission, her father's angry screams, then his cries, tore at her heart. And her conscience.

Armstead climbed down from his perch atop the carriage and stood wide-eyed by the door, obviously uncertain what to do next.

Her hand still throbbing, Eleanor climbed out of the carriage, only to be met by Dr. Crawford.

"My apologies, Miss Braddock." He lifted a hand in warning. "Under the circumstances, you won't be able to accompany your father inside today."

"But . . ." Eleanor glanced beyond him to see the men leading—almost dragging—her father up the front steps to the imposing double doors. Each step of the way, he fought them, calling out her name. She forced herself to look away and addressed the doctor. "You said I would be welcome anytime, Dr. Crawford."

"And you will be," he assured, glancing at a young woman standing behind him. "But your presence today"—he shook his head—"would only increase your father's agitation. We'll administer a mild sedative straightaway and—"

"A sedative?"

He nodded. "For his anxiousness."

"Is that necessary? He usually calms down within a few moments."

Dr. Crawford gave her a look, and she remembered the details she'd disclosed during her previous visit. She glanced away and saw Armstead had moved to check on the horses. "Sometimes it *does* take an hour," she admitted softly. "Or more."

"Miss Braddock . . ." Dr. Crawford's voice held compassion. "It's noble, what you've done . . . taking care of your father as you have. And yes," he added quickly, "there are times when he seems almost normal, I know. But as you said yourself, those times are becoming less and less frequent.

"As I stated during our initial meeting, it is imperative that we immerse your father in a carefully controlled environment, one that minimizes confrontation and friction. From what you've told me and . . . frankly, from what I just observed, I believe it would be best for you both if you allow us to proceed as I've recommended."

Eleanor looked from him to the imposing double doors, then back again, not at all inclined to agree, not really knowing what was best.

"If we are to help your father," he continued, "*if* he is capable of being helped"—his pause felt like it went on forever—"then now is the time, Miss Braddock, before his memory loss advances further. And . . . it would be best if you would give us a few days before returning. I'll send word as soon as he's ready to see you."

Everything within her fought the idea of leaving her father alone, and in such a frantic state, much less for days before she returned. But try as she might, she couldn't think of a single argument to refute the doctor's prescription. Her father blamed her for bringing him here and would be upset with her for who knew how long.

Following the incident where he'd lit an oil lamp, then proceeded to set the still-lit match atop a newspaper, she'd confiscated every matchstick in the house. And he hadn't spoken to her for a week. And that had only been over matchsticks.

Finally she gave a small nod.

"Very good," Dr. Crawford said, a touch of relief in his voice. "I assure you, Miss Braddock, this is the best course."

Eleanor glanced back at the building. She'd thought it so stately and regal upon first view. Now it seemed sterile and lonely, almost fore-boding. Not so much a place of healing as one of . . . confinement.

"Before you go, Miss Braddock . . ." The doctor gestured to the woman behind him. "Please allow me to present you to the nurse who will be caring for your father while he's with us." The nurse stepped forward, and Dr. Crawford continued the introductions. "Miss Smith is newly arrived to our fair city but comes with sterling credentials."

The young woman's demeanor could best be described as curious. But her eyes, blue as a robin's egg, seemed kind and open. "It's indeed a *great* honor to make your acquaintance, Miss Braddock." Miss Smith offered a poised and proper curtsy, her crisp British accent suiting her perfectly.

Eleanor lifted a brow, grateful for the generous greeting but more than a little surprised by it. "That's very kind of you, Miss Smith. But the pleasure is mine." She returned the curtsy. "Let me retrieve my father's satchel. It's on the seat inside the—"

"Oh no, ma'am!" Miss Smith practically lunged for the carriage door. "I'll happily retrieve it for you." She did just that and climbed back down, giving the carriage an overlong awe-filled look.

Only then did it occur to Eleanor. . . . Did the woman think *she* owned a carriage so fine? That she was so wealthy, so high and mighty? The thought was laughable, but Eleanor didn't laugh. She gestured to the book in the side pocket of the satchel. "I marked where we left off reading in each of my father's books. I read to him every night before he goes to bed. And sometimes during the afternoon. It calms him."

"Then I shall do the very same, Miss Braddock." With a parting curtsy, Miss Smith turned and disappeared inside the building.

Eleanor thought of the one book she hadn't included in her father's satchel. It was her book, but one they both loved and read from frequently. She would often quiz him about its contents, hoping the ritual would help sharpen his mind. She didn't think he would miss the little volume but knew she would have if she'd left it with him.

She accepted Dr. Crawford's assistance into the carriage, fighting the recurring sense of guilt.

"Miss Braddock . . ."

She looked back, surprised to find him smiling, something she couldn't recall having seen him do before. The gesture erased years from his face. He seemed reluctant to release her hand.

"Once again, ma'am, please allow me to thank you for your trust. I assure you that I, along with my colleagues, will do everything we can for your father. So please"—he gave her hand a gentle squeeze—"try not to worry."

With a doctorly, almost fatherly, nod, he relinquished his hold.

"Thank you, Doctor. While I can't promise I won't worry about my father, I can tell you that I trust your judgment. And I'll do my best to think positively about the outcome of my father's treatment."

"Well spoken, Miss Braddock. Honest and straightforward too." Dr. Crawford nodded and took a step back. "Much like your esteemed aunt, I dare say."

Eleanor felt a twinge of annoyance at his parting comment, but the hint of amusement in his eyes told her he'd intended it as a compliment. She managed a smile and sat back as Armstead climbed atop the carriage and gave the horses a command, but she couldn't help reflecting on her years at the Nashville Female Academy and how that same comparison by professors had plagued her there. *"Your aunt also earned exemplary marks in arithmetic, Miss Braddock, as well as French and German, as have you. Your skills in recitation aren't quite on par with hers, but there's time. She was, however, exceptionally gifted."*

As Armstead maneuvered the carriage about the turnaround, Eleanor sighed and closed her eyes, pushing that memory away, and choosing instead to concentrate on gathering her scattered wits and mentally preparing for the next hurdle—her *esteemed* aunt.

She hadn't seen Adelicia Acklen—Cheatham now, she reminded herself, her aunt having remarried the previous year—since the fall of 1860. Before the war and all it had brought, and taken. Before Joseph, Aunt Adelicia's second husband and Papa's closest cousin, had died.

Eleanor glanced down, hoping again that what she was wearing—her finest ensemble, albeit in her *least* favorite color, pink—would be nice enough. She hadn't purchased anything but day dresses since the war. She hadn't needed to, until now.

Frowning at the gaudy brightness of the material, she recalled her exchange with the seamstress back home. . . .

"A woman such as yourself, Miss Braddock, needs to wear more color. It helps"—the older woman had fluttered her hands—"enhance one's features. And dear, if I might say . . . you could do with a little enhancing."

Mrs. Hodges . . . always honest. But that was all right. Eleanor was too. "While that may be, Mrs. Hodges, I've never been fond of pink. I much prefer sienna, or perhaps a rich brown. Those colors are far more practical. And suitable, considering so many of our friends and family are still in mourning clothes."

"Yes, yes . . ." Mrs. Hodges heaved a sigh, her lips

pinching. "We all lost someone in the war. Or several someones," she said softly, looking away. "I've sewn enough black dresses to last me a lifetime, Miss Braddock. But it's been *three years,* and part of moving on with our lives, and in our hearts"—she inhaled deeply—"lies in choosing how we dress. And as I've always said, the plainer-looking the woman, the more color she should—"

Eleanor held up a hand. "Sienna, *please,* Mrs. Hodges. Or a rich brown."

Mrs. Hodges, a longtime family friend, simply stared, tight-lipped, then whispered something beneath her breath. Eleanor paid no mind at the time, but when she'd returned to the dressmaker's days ago for the fitting of the skirt and jacket, she wished she had.

"I didn't have enough of the sienna or brown, Miss Braddock. So I'm only charging you half the quoted price. And see now," Mrs. Hodges had said, once Eleanor stepped from behind the dressing curtain, "doesn't that look *pretty!* And it makes you look years younger, my dear. Just as I knew it would! Surely you'll attract *some* man's attention."

The rumble of the carriage jostled Eleanor back to the moment, and she glanced again at her skirt and jacket. Feeling like strawberry icing splashed atop a cake, she knew she had a better chance of the carriage sprouting wings and *flying* the five miles back to town than she did of attracting a man's interest.

But she had to admit . . . though she was still

irritated over Mrs. Hodges's intrusion, the discounted price had helped to compensate, given her precarious finances.

But what bothered her even more, at the moment, was that she was worrying over such a thing as clothing. How frivolous so many of the niceties had seemed in the years following the war.

And yet . . .

She needed her aunt's assistance and, therefore, her approval—which, if past experience still held true, wouldn't be easily garnered. How a person dressed mattered greatly to her aunt, so it mattered greatly to her too. *Today.*

Her jitters getting the best of her, Eleanor shifted on the seat as Armstead urged the horses to a faster clip down the drive. Her thoughts turned to the business proposal she'd devised that would surely win Aunt Adelicia over. The plan had *nothing* to do with the war, or death and dying. It would enable her and her father to live independently again, once he was well.

Thinking about the agreement she'd made with the building owner, she hoped her strong convictions hadn't prompted her to make a costly misstep she would regret.

Eleanor leaned her head back on the cushioned velvet seat. So much had happened since she'd last seen her aunt. She felt like a different person on the inside. Yet outwardly . . .

She was still much the same. Plain and tall. No, *taller*.

And she expected Aunt Adelicia was still stunning, still incredibly wealthy, and still the ever-gracious hostess of Belmont, the most exquisite estate in Tennessee—perhaps even in America, if a newspaper article Eleanor had recently read held true.

But one term the journalist had used to describe her aunt—American royalty—felt like too much.

She scoffed. She was grateful for her aunt's kind generosity, but *royalty?* Hardly. But what if her aunt *had* become like one of those spoiled, puffed-up European dukes and duchesses she'd read about in *Harper's Weekly?* The ones who considered themselves to be so much above and better than the rest of the common . . . *ordinary* people.

Eleanor shook her head. Heaven forbid. . . .

As the carriage bounced along the long, narrow drive, Eleanor stared at the empty bench opposite her and could almost hear guilt's silent scolding. How long had it been since she'd left her father for any length of time, much less in the manner she just had? A part of her still couldn't believe she'd done it.

Almost without thinking, she slipped a hand into her skirt pocket and pulled out the handkerchief, the one she'd carried all these years. The material was silky soft between her thumb and forefinger, its familiarity—and history—an inexplicable comfort.

She traced a finger over the embroidered flowers now faded with time and from repeated washings. Despite her best attempts at the outset to remove the bloodstain, a ghost of it remained. She'd tried to find her. The soldier's *Mary girl.*

For two years after the war, she had searched. But her efforts had been like trying to drain the ocean one thimble at a time. Everywhere she looked another wave rose in an endless sea of widows and fatherless children awash in grief. Why she'd ever thought she would find the woman, she couldn't imagine.

No, that wasn't true. She knew from where her hope had issued.

At one time, she'd thought it had been God's design for her to find the woman, to tell her that her husband hadn't died alone, that he'd loved her to the end. Then to tell her what he'd said, and maybe learn what he'd meant. But what a silly, romantic notion that had proven to be.

There was wisdom in knowing when to let go of a dream, and even more, in knowing when it had let go of you.

It was strange, maybe even wrong in a way—Eleanor wasn't sure—but she still carried within her a seed of the love that had poured from the soldier's lips before he died. It lived inside her, its heart still beating. Faintly at times. More steadily at others.

But it wasn't a comforting thing. Quite the contrary. It made her grateful she'd never had opportunity to give her heart to a man. She was one of the fortunate ones, she'd concluded. She'd been spared the grief of loving and losing. After speaking to widow after widow, hearing their all-too-familiar and heart-wrenching stories, she'd decided that, contrary to Tennyson's requiem—a favorite of her father's to quote—it *was* truly better to have never loved at all.

As the carriage neared the main road, she leaned closer to the window for a breath of fresh air and spotted the sign at the entrance. *Tennessee Asylum for the Insane.* She flinched. The letters were carved so grandly into a slab of native limestone, the rock edifice upon which it rested, so proud looking. The irony wasn't lost on her. Neither was the fact that the wisest, wittiest, kindest, and most *practical* man she'd ever known was now at home within the asylum's walls.

A sinking feeling started somewhere around the center of her chest, threatening to pull her under. She sat up straighter, reminding herself of what she'd told Dr. Crawford about determining to think positively about the outcome of her father's treatment.

Hoping for any sign at all, she looked out the window and searched the branches, hoping to see the cardinal again.

But the leafless branches were empty.

Marcus met the man's timid stare with challenge, sensing he was hiding something. No doubt, at the instruction of the employee's superior, the illustrious mayor of Nashville, Augustus E. Adler—a man Marcus was loath to depend upon, much less give answer to someday.

Mr. Barrett, the mayor's nervous little assistant, leaned forward, his hands tightly knotted atop the secretary's desk—a Napoleon-style replica, and a poor one at that. "If you'll allow me to explain, H-Herr . . . Geoffrey."

Barrett stumbled over the title, his Southern way of speech stretching the word into two oddly paired syllables instead of one, and Marcus's already-tried patience further thinned. Whenever certain people—like Mr. Barrett—heard the "European" in his voice, as they called it, it seemed to bring out their "Southern German."

"Mr. Geoffrey will suffice, Mr. Barrett," Marcus said, his tone managing a hint of cordial. "Please continue."

"Oh . . . thank you, *Mr.* Geoffrey. That is most generous of you, sir."

The pounding at the back of Marcus's head ratcheted up another notch at the man's gushing smile.

"May I say, Mr. Geoffrey"—again, that smile—"your English is superb. I wonder, sir, how you manage to speak our language with such a—"

"Mr. Barrett . . ." Marcus leaned forward in his chair and, at the same time, heard the inaudible echo of a warning he'd received often in his childhood—*"The English language isn't spoken with the same guttural force of our language, Your Excellency. Your manner could be . . . misconstrued, if you do. Now, again, please. And this time, with a measure of gentility."* Marcus breathed in, then out.

"All I require from you, Mr. Barrett, is that you tell me whether or not Mayor Adler has reached a decision on this project. Last week he gave his word—to me and the other three contractors—that he would decide by today."

For a few seconds, Barrett's mouth moved but no words came. "I . . . I can explain, sir." His face flushed. "It *was* the mayor's intent to award the contract for the project today. But, unfortunately . . ." Barrett took a breath, as though desperately needing one. "Mayor Adler is still reviewing the various designs, including"—he winced—"a *fifth* bid that was submitted to his office at the last moment."

"A fifth bid?" Marcus frowned, and even from four feet away, he heard Barrett swallow. "Submitted by whom?"

"A . . . local company, sir."

Marcus leveled his gaze, the throb in his head kicking to a steady thrum. If this man only knew to whom he was speaking. "And does this *local company* possess a name, Mr. Barrett?"

"It does, I'm sure." Barrett looked anywhere but across the desk. "But I'm not privy to that information, sir. I give you my word, Mr. Geoffrey."

The silence lengthened, and Marcus let it.

He hadn't trusted Mayor Adler since he'd caught the man in a barefaced lie on their first meeting. He'd called him on it and had been paying the price ever since. Adler had made it clear he "didn't much care for Europeans." Which Marcus found humorous, given the origin of most of America's citizens.

Marcus glanced at the side door leading to the mayor's office, wondering if Adler truly was out of town. He was tempted to barge in and prove the statement false—or true—but taking such action would bring him no closer to building the finest opera house that Nashville, or possibly all of America, had ever seen. Nor would it bring him closer to making a name for himself—a name that didn't rest on a family dynasty, or his father's or uncle's accomplishments, but rather on his own hard work and ingenuity. He could never have achieved that in Europe. But with time and circumstance working against him as they were, it was appearing less and less likely he would achieve success in Nashville either.

A knock on the door drew their attention, and a woman entered.

"Mr. Barrett, I have tea for you," she said, a coyness in her tone. The diminutive brunette shot Marcus a look that lingered. Then she glanced at Barrett and quickly added, "For both of you."

"Thank you, Miss Thornton." Barrett gestured, seeming somewhat relieved by the interruption.

The young woman set the tea service on the desk corner closest to Marcus and poured slowly. Too slowly in Marcus's estimation. But her continued stare in his direction let him know that swiftness wasn't her intention.

She was petite. And pretty. And most of all, she knew it.

He doubted—with his having inherited his parents' tall stature—whether the young woman would reach him midchest, even standing on tiptoe. She was fragile and delicate-looking, much like the fine china she held out to him. And much too much like Baroness Maria Elizabeth Albrecht von Haas.

His mood darkened at the accompanying memory of the baroness and their . . . relationship, if one could call it that, and at the fate awaiting him upon his return to Austria. Extending an empire through marriage had been a long-standing Habsburg family tradition, and he could already hear his uncle redrawing the boundary lines.

Marcus lifted the cup and drank, wishing it were something much stronger than tea—even stout coffee would do.

From a young age, he'd grown accustomed to this kind of attention from women. At first, it had fascinated him, the way they flocked to him. And with little to no effort on his part. As he grew older, that fascination turned into an amusement, even a sport. "The challenge of the quest," as one of his friends used to say.

But after what happened with Rutger—

Marcus saw his brother's face so clearly in his mind, and he swallowed hard, strong-arming emotions to keep them at bay. The way he'd lived his life before *the incident* seemed almost foreign to him now. Yet he couldn't forget. And God help him—if God was still listening, if God gave second chances to men like him. . . .

Keeping his gaze to himself, he did nothing to encourage the attention of the young woman beside him.

Finally she crossed to the door and closed it quietly behind her.

"I feel certain," Barrett continued, "that the mayor will announce his decision no later than this time next week."

"I wish I shared your certainty, Mr. Barrett."

Marcus returned his empty cup to the tray and stood, frustrated with the mayor's delay and eager to be on his way. "When is Mayor Adler scheduled to return?"

"Monday at the latest, sir." A flicker of relief sparked Barrett's expression as he gained his feet. "I'll tell him you stopped by the moment he disembarks the train. And I'll relay your inquiry regarding the status of your company's bid as well."

Marcus crossed to the door. "If you'd also be so kind as to inform the mayor that I, along with the other three firms who placed bids on time and in proper order, will be expecting confirmation that this . . . *anonymous* fifth bidder did the same."

Barrett blinked. "Yes, sir, of course. I'll relay that request to Mayor Adler as well. And may I say with utmost sincerity, Mr. Geoffrey, the mayor would want me to assure you that his office desires to be of assistance in any—"

"Good day to you, Mr. Barrett."

Marcus closed the office door behind him, not caring to hear Barrett's parting insincerities.

Minutes later, as he passed the post office on his way out to Belmont, he wished again that his colleague from Boston, Luther Burbank, would mail the package as promised. He didn't think Burbank was holding out on him.

But given the subject of their collaboration, there was always that possibility.

"Is you sure you want me to drop you off *here,* Miss Braddock? Long way up to the main house, ma'am. And most of it be uphill."

"Yes, I'm certain, Armstead. Thank you."

Eleanor accepted his assistance from the carriage. Having already checked her watch, she knew she was early, despite the tour of the city and country-side Armstead had given her. She'd intended to stay at the asylum to help her father get settled, but since those plans hadn't come to fruition . . . "Mrs. Cheatham isn't expecting me for a while yet. And after all the riding today, I welcome the chance to walk."

She wasn't about to arrive so early for an appointment with her aunt, especially her first in years. She knew how important punctuality was to Adelicia Acklen Cheatham, even if Armstead wasn't aware. Although, seeing Armstead's thoughtful look, she got the inkling he might fully understand.

"Walkin', it's good for a body," he said, a smile lingering in the depths of his voice.

On a playful whim, she glanced from side to side as though worried someone might overhear.

"Though I haven't been here in years, I haven't been gone so long that I've forgotten my aunt's *high* regard for punctuality. I no more want to arrive an hour early at Belmont than I would a minute late."

"Yes, ma'am." A knowing grin creased his face. "The Lady likes ever'thing runnin' on time. That's for sure. She got her schedule, and we best keep to it."

Eleanor smiled, feeling an unexpected kinship with the man, especially considering what he'd witnessed earlier today. "I'll explore the conservatory for a while, then make my way on to the house."

"Yes, ma'am."

"And, Armstead . . ."

He turned back.

"Thank you for understanding about what happened with my father. And for your . . . discretion."

He nodded, taking his time to answer. "We all got our roads to walk, ma'am. Ain't none of 'em pretty all the time."

"No, they're not."

He tipped his hat to leave, then hesitated again. "How 'bout I wait 'til you come up to the house 'fore I tote your luggage in. Make it all proper like."

"That would be much appreciated, Armstead." She smiled in gratitude.

As the carriage pulled away, Eleanor let her focus wander the vast grounds and gardens of the estate, until it finally came to rest on the mansion atop the hill.

The afternoon sun bathed the enormous Italianate-style villa in a warm glow, giving it a ruddy pinkish hue from this distance. Her aunt had appropriately named it Belmont, *Belle Monte* in French. *Beautiful mountain . . .*

Moving her gaze downhill, Eleanor studied the lavish formal gardens in front of the mansion. The gardens were circular in formation—the largest of the three situated nearest the home, its counterparts descending downhill, diminishing in size.

Marble statuary spaced at random intervals—sometimes beside a cast-iron gazebo, other times set apart—stood like silent sentinels watchful over their domain. Flowers bordered endless beds, the fading summer palette of crimsons and saffrons, purples and pinks clinging to their petals—the pink looking far better on them than it did on her.

She scanned the rows of shrubbery, looking for a certain plant, one they'd had in their garden back home. But it was nowhere to be seen. Its flowers, being more common in appearance, were probably not elegant enough for Belmont, but she enjoyed their fragrance.

In the distance, to the west of the mansion, lay an empty plot of ground where she would've sworn another building had stood years earlier. An art gallery, if she remembered correctly. But for whatever reason, it was gone now.

On the east side of the mansion, a new building

was being erected—the brick building twice as long as it was wide, and every bit as stunning as the rest of Belmont.

The estate was more impressive than she remembered.

Feeling very small—and out of place—she sighed and turned to look behind her. The glass-walled conservatory, complete with domed cupola, that housed Aunt Adelicia's prized collections of flowers and trees, shrubs and herbs, appeared to be at least twice the size of the family home Eleanor had recently sold. There was no telling the variety of plants contained within, or their cost.

She followed the walkway leading to the main door of the conservatory but, before entering, paused and lifted her gaze to the nearby water tower.

The brick structure, well over one hundred feet tall, she estimated, reached skyward to the ethereal blue. Her focus trailed to the top, where a windmill turned in the breeze.

As beautiful as Belmont was, she hoped her stay would be brief.

Thinking of the proposal she had for her aunt—the acceptance of which would enable her to make a way, however humble a one, for herself and her father—spawned a thread of anxiousness that worked a stranglehold around her confidence. An odd emotion, since ordinarily she wasn't easily intimidated.

But there was nothing *ordinary* about Adelicia Acklen Cheatham. Or about Belmont.

When visiting in the past, Eleanor had never felt at home. But considering the surroundings, who would? The place was like make-believe—at least in comparison to the world in which she lived.

She opened the door to the conservatory, and a warm *whoosh* of air greeted her. Not surprising in view of the glass ceiling and a full September sun overhead. Within seconds, the heady scent of roses enveloped her and—unprepared for what she saw— she let the door close behind her with a soft thud.

Roses. Pots and pots of roses. Table after table, row after row. Some of them quite tall, obstructing her view to the next aisle, and blossoms in every shade imaginable—from deepest crimson to snowiest white, from golden yellow to palest pink. Some varieties, lower growing and shrubby, huddled together like friendly neighbors over a fence. While others seemed to raise lofty heads in unabashed pride, as if believing themselves more regal.

Hundreds of blooms, perhaps thousands, filled this section of the conservatory. Surely this collection rivaled the very storehouses of heaven.

And yet . . . while she appreciated nature and enjoyed the outdoors, and had even helped her father tend a vegetable garden years earlier, she'd never cared much for flowers. They were beautiful, to be sure, but also frivolous and extravagant. What use had they other than to just look pretty?

She breathed the perfumed air. As much as she hated to admit it, however, the scent was nothing less than enchanting.

Reaching the end of the first aisle, she turned the corner to start down the next when she heard voices and stilled. She cocked her head to listen, but . . . nothing.

Certain she'd heard something, she took a step back and looked down the aisle from whence she'd come.

But again . . . no one.

She made a quick tour of the remaining rose collection, finally skipping the last two aisles, and moved through an open doorway into another section of the greenhouse. This section was filled with tropical plants, but a small grouping of plants in a corner, on a table all their own, immediately caught her attention.

They were some of the ugliest plants she'd ever seen.

Of the cacti family, if her guess was correct, they were tubular and gangly, without a single bloom. She saw a card tacked to the side of the table and leaned down. *Selenicereus grandiflorus.*

Her limited study of Latin combined with her almost nonexistent use of the language since leaving school enabled her to easily pronounce the words, but that was all. She had no idea of their translation, or of the plant's common name.

She did, however, remember her Latin professor. Quite well.

Dr. Carlton Adessa.

Oh, how the girls in school had fawned over him. They'd called him Dr. Adonis behind his back, after the mortal god of beauty in Greek mythology. It still seemed unfair that a man could be so . . . beautiful. Dark-eyed and swarthy, with an air of confidence that both preceded him and followed in his wake. Everything about the man had been attractive. At first.

With painful clarity, she remembered the day Dr. Adessa had passed her in the hallway. She'd just returned from a windy walk and stopped at a mirror to fix her hair. He smiled as he approached, and she nervously wondered if he would remember her name, since she'd earned the highest mark on the last exam.

Eagerly shoving wayward strands of hair into place, she managed a smile. And as he passed, he said, "One cannot make a silk purse from a sow's ear, Miss Braddock. Hurry now, class is beginning."

Eleanor exhaled a humorless laugh at the memory, and recalled how his attractiveness had changed in her eyes. And how the incident had framed how she saw herself too.

Growing up, she'd been called strong, sturdy, even handsome on one occasion. But *pretty* was a word that had never been used to describe her. Taken individually, her features weren't completely without merit. Her eyes were a deeper brown than most. Her blond hair was long but thin, so she braided it into a bun at the base of her neck. Her nose was probably her best feature—similar to that of the *Venus de Milo*, she'd been told.

Of course, she was nearly as tall as the statue of

Venus, which more than offset whatever positive there was in the comparison.

She sighed. She hadn't possessed the courage to offer Dr. Adessa a swift rebuttal back then. As a young woman, she'd been far too eager to please others, to earn affirmation. But somewhere through the years, that had changed. Perhaps because she'd finally learned how impossible a goal it was to earn everyone's approval, especially when the world's criteria for judging stood so widely separate from her own.

She turned her attention back to the cacti and considered the reasons her aunt would have such plants in her collection.

Knowing better but unable to resist, she gently touched a spine on the cactus, then drew her hand back, frowning. It was sharper than she'd imagined. Bringing the tip of her forefinger to her mouth, she soothed the sting, her admiration for the plant edging up a notch. What it lacked in beauty, it made up for in strength, and in its ability to protect itself.

She checked the time again. There was still plenty of time before she was due at the house, so she turned her attention to the tropical plants. Trees that would take many men to move, if they could be moved, stood directly beneath the cupola. As she continued, she passed a cast-iron fountain topped with an equally cast-iron cobra coiled and ready to strike.

A doorway to her left with stairs leading down

intrigued her. But it was dark, so she continued on. While the prospect of exploring underground was appealing, the possibility of appearing before Aunt Adelicia with six inches of mud on her hem was not.

Gazing ahead, she glimpsed yet another room and sighed, shaking her head. The conservatory went on *forever,* much like the mansion did, as she remembered. Such lavishness . . .

By comparison, she pictured her father's former vegetable garden. He'd found such enjoyment and relaxation in tending that small patch of land. She fingered the waxy leaf of a shrub, contemplating. Perhaps the asylum would let him plant some tomato and squash plants. And maybe green beans. He loved those.

She checked the watch hooked to her bodice. A few minutes, and she would need to make her way up to the mansion.

Catching the hint of a familiar scent, she paused. She closed her eyes and breathed deeply, and was carried back to warm summer nights as a little girl, when her bedroom window was open and the heady perfume of lilacs enveloped her room—and her dreams.

A simpler time. One she missed.

When she opened her eyes, the memory faded. Left in its place was a loneliness, keen and sharp-edged, and not at all unfamiliar. Whenever she thought about her father, about what his future— *their* future—might hold, she questioned if this sense of being adrift, orphaned, in a sense, would ever leave.

Knowing what her father would say if he were there, she instinctively straightened, squaring her shoulders. "Be practical," she whispered. "Sensible. Focus on what is before you, Eleanor. Not on what your imagination attempts to convince you is there."

Working like a talisman, the spoken words helped to push the emptiness away. Not banished forever, she knew, but cordoned off . . . for now.

She turned to leave, but her focus fell on a doorway—or more rightly, on something through the doorway.

She stepped closer, listening for movement beyond the threshold, and then knocked. The glass door squeaked open an inch or two more.

"Hello?" Her voice sounded overloud in the silence, her gaze fixed on what appeared to be a surgeon's scalpel on the edge of the table.

She waited. . . .

No answer.

Concerned, but mostly curious, she nudged the door open farther and stepped inside. And quickly wondered whether Aunt Adelicia's gardeners were practicing horticulture . . . or medicine.

Plants that appeared to be . . . bandaged, their roots wrapped in gauzy strips, lined a series of tables on the far wall. Pots of dirt sat behind them, as though someone had left recently and would return soon. Likewise, rows of corked glass bottles, each filled with liquid and labeled in Latin, stood shoulder to shoulder on shelves. Shiny scalpels, even syringes, lay neatly arranged on a cloth.

She frowned. What kind of *gardener* needed all of—

"I asked you to moisten the root base *if* it was required, not *drown* them!"

Eleanor nearly jumped out of her skin at the voice. Turning, she glimpsed two men striding down the aisle toward her. Her first instinct was to hide. But where? She wasn't about to hide in this . . . infirmary. And if she crossed directly in front of them, they would see her.

"The plants will be fine, Mr. Geoffrey, I'm certain. I did as I thought best. After all, I am the head—"

The taller man, still several yards away, stopped abruptly and turned, his back to her. "I know who you are, Mr. Gray. And I'm well aware of your position here." He blew out a breath.

Feeling like a naughty child in danger of being caught, Eleanor did her best to blend in with the greenery, wishing she'd worn anything but pink. She didn't dare move lest the rustle of her skirts give her away.

"Next time," the taller man continued, a foreign accent giving the words an even harsher edge, "do as I instruct, not as you think best. And try it without the bottle. That will help." The man uttered something unintelligible. "Never mind. There won't be a next time. I don't want you touching any of the plants in the—"

The man facing her suddenly raised his hand. And with a shudder Eleanor realized he was looking directly at her.

4

The taller man turned to fully face her and cocked his head as though trying to remember whether they'd met before, which, of course, they hadn't. As if time were bending back upon itself—cruelly so—Eleanor felt herself standing again in the hallway of the Nashville Female Academy, with "Dr. Adonis" staring down.

Only, this man made her former professor look like a pudgy second cousin, twice removed. To say he was handsome was like saying that . . .

She blinked, not meaning to stare but staring all the same. Try as she might, she couldn't think of a comparison that would do him justice. But one thing she swiftly gathered—not only from the way he spoke to Mr. Gray, but from the way he looked down at her—was that he and Dr. Adessa had been cut from the same arrogant cloth.

His gaze briefly moved past her to the open door and then returned, possession in his glance. "May we be of assistance to you, madam?"

His tone, so formal, so measured, answered her question about whose workroom she was standing in, as well as confirming her impression of him. His accent—German, she thought—accounted for his aloof manner, at least in part. They weren't a people known for their warmth and vivacity.

"Yes . . ." Eleanor nodded, hoping her features didn't reveal her thoughts. "I would greatly appreciate that, sir. Thank you." She included the other man with an acknowledging glance. "I need to exit the conservatory, and this door"—she gestured behind her, pleased at how confident she sounded—"obviously did not meet that need."

The man's blue eyes narrowed the slightest bit. The scarcest hint of a smile showed on his mouth. He clearly knew she'd been snooping. "My apologies, madam, that your . . . needs failed to be met in a manner so inconvenient to you. The door you seek would be one of *seven* along the north wall." He gestured, his gaze never leaving hers.

This time, without question, underlying amusement and insinuation colored his tone. If she hadn't been guilty as silently charged, she might have been offended. But as it was, she—

"Oh, for the love of . . ." With a huffing laugh, the second man threw the first a dismissive glance and maneuvered around him, smiling, his own demeanor a marked contrast. "Henry Gray at your service, ma'am," he said, his congeniality making up for the other's lack. "Head gardener here at the Belmont estate. And you must be Miss Braddock."

Eleanor hesitated. "Why . . . yes, that is correct, sir. But how did you—"

"Mrs. Cheatham informed us that a favorite niece would be arriving today, which means we're all to be on our best behavior."

Mr. Gray stood a little straighter and gave his jacket lapels a smart tug. "May I welcome you to Belmont, Miss Braddock. And please . . ." He cast a look over his shoulder. "You must forgive our Mr. Geoffrey here." He winked. "He's out of sorts today. Gets that way when someone interferes with his experiments. Well, actually . . . he's out of sorts most days. So best you simply ignore him altogether."

The mischief in Mr. Gray's voice said he was teasing. Still, a frown flitted across Mr. Geoffrey's features. Seeing it prompted Eleanor to smile. She looked between the two men, still trying to figure them out. Mr. Gray was the head gardener, yet the tone Mr. Geoffrey had taken with him was anything but deferential. Odd behavior for an under gardener.

Despite her lack of enthusiasm for Mr. Geoffrey, she most definitely liked Mr. Gray. Even if she did have to lower her gaze considerably in order to look him in the eye.

"I understand your father has been delayed in joining you, Miss Braddock."

Mr. Gray's question caught her off guard, and she grappled for an answer. "Ah . . . yes. You're correct yet again, Mr. Gray." How to respond to such an observation without revealing the truth? Or lying outright. "My father . . . He is—"

"Seeing to family matters, I understand," Mr.

Gray supplied, his features innocent of further meaning, hidden or otherwise.

She breathed a little easier. Apparently, Aunt Adelicia had anticipated—and circumvented—the topic of her father, and Eleanor felt a special endearment for the woman. "Yes. That's it precisely." She sensed Mr. Geoffrey watching her but kept her focus on his superior. "My father will be joining me as soon as he's able."

Understandably, some of Belmont's servants would remember the distinguished Attorney Garrison Braddock from years previous. It would be naive on her part to assume that no one in Nashville had gotten wind of their financial predicament, or of them losing their home. News of an unfortunate nature always seemed to travel faster than news of good fortune.

Still, she would be prepared the next time someone inquired after her father.

"Mr. Gray, sir!"

Hurried footsteps sounded behind her, and Eleanor turned to see a young Negro boy running full out down the aisle. He skidded to a halt two feet in front of her, breathless and holding his side.

"Mr. Gray"—the boy gulped air by the lungfuls—"Mr. Thatcher . . . needs to speak with you, sir. Right quick too. Up at the"—another deep breath—"new billiard hall. Somethin' 'bout . . . them long windows you all be puttin' in."

Frowning, Henry Gray exchanged a look with Mr. Geoffrey, whose expression altered little.

"Thank you, Zeke." Mr. Gray gave him a nod. "Tell him I'm coming."

Zeke dipped his head and then, to Eleanor's surprise, grinned up at her as he took backward steps. "You Miss Braddock, the Lady's niece."

Eleanor smiled at the certainty in his voice. "That's right, I am. And you must be Zeke."

His brown eyes lit. "Yes, ma'am! If you be needin' a horse, or a pony, or a carriage"—he glanced behind him, then back—"or if you need anythin' at Belmont, you just let me know, ma'am. I know most everythin', and I's here to help."

Eleanor laughed, then quickly realized how foreign the response felt. "Thank you, Zeke. I'll remember."

Eleanor dared glance in Mr. Geoffrey's direction, only to find "Adonis" staring directly at her, his eyes like pieces of blue glass with the sun behind them. The man was absurdly handsome. But she sensed he knew that, which only served to detract from the fact. At least a little.

"It's certainly a pleasure to meet you, Miss Braddock," Mr. Gray said. "And while I apologize for leaving so abruptly, please let me extend an invitation to visit the conservatory anytime. Mr. Geoffrey here will be most happy to escort you outside. And on to the mansion, I'm sure, should you wish."

"Oh no," Eleanor said quickly, seeing Mr. Geoffrey look at his superior, then back at her again. "That won't be necessary."

"Nonsense, Miss Braddock. It would be my pleasure." Mr. Geoffrey's deep voice sounded something akin to velvet, but in his eyes Eleanor read only duty and accommodation. Neither of which she invited.

"Oh, and Mr. Geoffrey . . ." Already halfway down the aisle, Mr. Gray turned back, his tone bordering on patronizing. "Don't forget, Mrs. Cheatham would like to be apprised of the progress on your . . . collaboration."

Mr. Geoffrey frowned. "I have already been quite—"

"First thing in the morning, please, Mr. Geoffrey. She was adamant about it." With raised eyebrows, Mr. Gray looked at the man as though he should have known better than to argue, then hurried on.

Wishing to leave in equal haste, Eleanor was dismayed to find Mr. Geoffrey, long arm extended, gesturing in the opposite direction.

"I'm quite capable, Mr. Geoffrey, of finding my own way. But your *generous* offer is appreciated all the same."

She swept past him, feeling somewhat avenged in the act—until he fell into step behind her.

More than a little irritated, she determined not to acknowledge him and walked on, hastening her steps. Her crinoline underskirts swirled as she swept past table after table, trying not to think of him directly behind her. But to no avail.

"You needn't see me out, Mr. Geoffrey."

"But it's my pleasure to do so, Miss Braddock.

After all, I dare not lose Mrs. Cheatham's favorite niece in the conservatory on her first day. I shiver to think what consequences such an outcome would set in motion."

Eleanor barely resisted the urge to roll her eyes.

Seeing the cast-iron fountain beneath the cupola ahead, she mentally retraced the path she'd taken on her way in.

"You'll turn left up there," he said, "then a right down the third—"

"I *know* where I'm going, Mr. Geoffrey."

"Oh . . . forgive me, madam. I was under the impression you had lost your way."

Eleanor firmed her lips. She would *not* further engage this man. He obviously thought quite highly of himself. And he was purposefully trying to bait her—that much was clear.

She'd done nothing wrong by exploring the "plant infirmary." She hadn't touched anything or moved anything from its place. She'd simply been curious, and curiosity was an excellent catalyst for improving one's intellect. Never mind that it had also landed her in trouble on numerous occasions.

"If you *were* to get lost in here, however," he continued, apparently enjoying the sound of his voice more than she did, "either somewhere amidst the Norfolk pines or the tropical palms . . . or perhaps, let's say, you were lured in by a bunch of carnivorous camellias, rest assured we'd organize a search party straightaway."

She blew out a breath. "Equipped with flares, I

trust." As soon as she said it, she regretted it, and quickened her pace.

He did likewise. "Actually, no. Shooting flares in a structure such as this is somewhat discouraged, as you might guess. Unless of course, you are looking for a way to annihilate every living thing within its glass walls, as well as destroy the structure itself. If that were your purpose, I imagine shooting a flare would rank high at the top of that list."

Hearing the touch of a smile in his voice, she knew—even only having met the man—that he wouldn't be wearing that smile if she were to look back. Which she didn't.

But wait . . .

She slowed, looking around, then stopped. Where was the aisle with the—

"You missed your turn, your ladyship," he whispered from behind, sounding closer than she'd expected him to be. "About fifteen feet back. Perhaps you didn't know your way as well as you thought. . . ."

Her body flushed hot, then cold with embarrassment. His deep voice—and that accent, she admitted, though not wanting to—could have had something to do with it as well. She'd always admired men with accents. But she knew better in this instance. Because even knowing what little she did about him, she knew enough.

And that was exactly what she'd had of him. *Enough.*

She took a step forward before turning, then leveled a stare. "You have made your point, Mr. Geoffrey. Resoundingly so. I admit, you caught me snooping earlier, and . . ."

How could a person's eyes be so *blue?* And—could it be more *unfair?*—thick, dark lashes framed them. Trying not to think of her own pale, blond ones, she refocused.

"I offer you an apology. I don't know why I felt the need to cover my earlier actions. I didn't disturb anything in the room. I give you my word. I was merely curious about something I saw. So . . ." She nodded once. "There we are."

Slowly, as though he were trying the gesture out for the first time, his mouth curved into a smile. His entire countenance changed, and the effect was heady. Much like the scent of roses had been.

"Apology accepted."

She nodded. "Thank y—"

"On one condition."

She frowned. "One cannot accept an apology and then set a condition. If you desired terms of acceptance, you should have stated those conditions at the outset."

He eyed her. "Then I rescind my acceptance."

"One cannot rescind a verbal agreement once it's been adjudicated. By *adjudicated,* I mean—"

"I know what the word means, Miss Braddock." His eyes narrowed a touch. "Let me guess . . . Your father is an attorney."

"He was." She lifted her chin. "One of the most

honored and respected in the State of Tennessee. At least . . . at one time," she added, instantly wishing she hadn't.

She glanced at her watch again and cringed to see the minute hand so closely approaching the twelve. If she was late for her aunt due to this foolishness . . .

"You must excuse me, Mr. Geoffrey. I truly need to be on my way."

Gaining her bearings, she set off. And again, she heard him behind her.

"I'm grafting plants."

She glanced back, not understanding.

"What you saw in the room. You said you were curious. That's what I'm working on. I'm grafting plants to make them stronger, to create more beautiful flowers. And to introduce colors we've not seen before."

"Ah . . . how interesting," she said over her shoulder, then heard him laugh beneath his breath.

"Which is what someone says when they're not really interested but want to appear as though they are."

Spotting the door through which she'd first gained entrance, Eleanor paused and turned back. "Not to be rude, Mr. Geoffrey, but . . ." She glanced around. "I've never been overly fond of flowers. I simply don't see the need."

Disbelief filtered across his expression, and she offered a tiny shrug. "But I'm certain that, whatever it is you're doing, my aunt must be most grateful for your services. And being an under gardener here at the Belmont estate . . . well, that's quite an accomplishment in itself."

"An under gardener," he repeated, his eyes taking on a bemused cast. "Yes, being an under gardener is a very respectable position."

"Indeed, it is."

"You're a person that prizes logic, aren't you, Miss Braddock? And you're quite straight-forward . . . for a woman, I mean."

Eleanor squinted. "I beg your pardon?"

"No, no . . ." His brow furrowed. "I meant it as a compliment . . . your ladyship."

She exhaled, not liking the silly title he'd assigned her. "Then your compliments need work, Mr. Geoffrey. Much like your *Selenicereus grandiflorus*." Enjoying the surprise in his eyes, she gestured to the cactus she'd seen before, then continued toward the door, speaking over her shoulder. "If your determination is to make plants more beautiful, you might want to start there."

She pushed the door open and glanced back to see him watching her. To her surprise, he bowed at the waist.

"It was, indeed, a pleasure, Miss Braddock."

Suddenly all she could picture was him in a black cutaway with tails, complete with tailored vest and trousers that complimented his lean physique. It surprised her how at home he looked in the imaginary garb. And how affected she was by imagining him in it.

She blinked to clear the image, still trying to sort out the man. "Likewise, I'm sure, Mr. Geoffrey." She let the door close behind her and all but ran the entire way to the mansion.

By the time Eleanor scaled the front steps and reached the door, she was winded and perspiring.

A stony-faced housekeeper offered her entrance, and Eleanor stepped inside and introduced herself. Mrs. Routh, the *head*—with strong emphasis—housekeeper, gave her a good looking over, and Eleanor swiftly deduced the woman's opinion of pink.

She was, however, grateful when Mrs. Routh said nothing about her ensemble and gestured for her to follow.

The mansion's interior was even more beautiful than Eleanor remembered. To her immediate left, beautiful in detail and so lifelike beneath a massive portrait of Adelicia and one of her daughters, was an exquisite statuary of two children sleeping. Eleanor didn't remember having seen it before.

But—she slowed, her eyes widening—there was one piece of artwork that most definitely hadn't been here on her last visit. She would have remembered it, for certain.

Situated in the middle of the entrance hall, in front of the marble fireplace, stood a most *evocative* statue issuing a rather bold greeting, and Eleanor couldn't help staring as she passed it. The sculpture was of a woman kneeling down, sheaves of wheat draped across her arm. But it was the artist's rendering of the subject's clothing that drew her attention.

The woman's dress had slipped from her shoulder to reveal—for all who entered the Belmont mansion to see—a rather shapely breast. An interesting choice for an artist to make, most certainly, but even more interesting that Aunt Adelicia chose to display the statue in the front entrance hall.

Eleanor's gaze moved to the mantel clock, and she squeezed her eyes tight. She took a deep breath in an effort to calm a sudden flurry of nerves, then smoothed the wrinkles from the front of her skirt. She never should have stopped by the conservatory.

What she wouldn't have given right then to wring the muscular neck of a certain under gardener.

Spotting Mrs. Routh several paces ahead, Eleanor hurried on.

No matter where she looked—from the richly patterned wallpaper and lavish draperies, to the flowered English Wilton wall-to-wall carpet, to the magnificent bronze chandeliers illuminated by gas-fed flames—beauty reigned supreme. Paintings adorned nearly every inch of wall space. Eleanor wished for more time to view them.

But she had no choice but to hurry and catch up again.

Mrs. Routh rapped softly on the glass pane of the

central parlor door, then turned the knob. "Your niece has arrived, Mrs. Cheatham."

Choosing to ignore the punitive trace in Mrs. Routh's tone, Eleanor gained her first glimpse of her aunt sitting poised on a settee. Aunt Adelicia's dark hair—without any touches of gray as far as she could see—was swept up and gathered in wispy curls. No matter the passage of years, Adelicia Acklen Cheatham was still stunning. No less than Eleanor had expected.

Eleanor's gaze met that of her aunt, and she felt an unexpected rush of emotion as she remembered the last time she'd visited Belmont—with her mother and father and Teddy. Now all of them, including Uncle Joseph, were gone.

Or . . . almost.

"Aunt Adelicia . . ." Eleanor curtsied. "How wonderful to see you again after all these years. Thank you for allowing me to come and live with you. Though, I hope it won't be for too long. I don't want to become a nuisance. I'll work hard to make certain that's not the case."

Realizing she was talking too much, Eleanor literally bit the tip of her tongue.

Aunt Adelicia rose from the settee with beauty and grace, and with an elegance customarily ascribed to . . . *royalty*. Eleanor could not argue with the truth.

Her aunt was so petite, her movements delicate and graceful, couched in femininity yet with undeniable strength, and Eleanor found herself

wishing she were more like that and less like . . .
herself.

Aunt Adelicia inclined her head, her smile ever
radiant. "Welcome to Belmont, Eleanor, my dear.
You're *late*."

Still nursing the slight sting from Aunt Adelicia's
politely framed rebuke, Eleanor took another bite
of creamed sweet potatoes, whipped lighter and
fluffier than she'd ever tasted, and observed the
family interaction around the Cheatham dinner
table.

Six children, ranging in age from eight to
eighteen, including Dr. Cheatham's teenage
daughter and son, chattered away, while Dr.
Cheatham and Aunt Adelicia contributed as well.
Laughter abounded, as did the variety of topics and
tasteful cuisine, and as Eleanor watched her four
younger cousins, who appeared enamored with
their new sister and brother, it was obvious that the
blending of families with Aunt Adelicia's third
marriage was a success.

But despite the warmth and gaiety of the setting,
including the fine scalloped china and crystal goblets filled to the brim with ice and freshly squeezed
lemonade—such a luxury—Eleanor couldn't dispel
the loneliness in the pit of her stomach.

The scene caused her to miss her father even
more.

She wondered how he was, if he was adjusting.
Had he eaten dinner? Sometimes it took some

coaxing for him to eat. *Please, Lord*—she squeezed her eyes tight—*let him get better.*

She was grateful for the time she and Aunt Adelicia had spent together earlier. Although she hadn't had an abundance of her own *pleasantries* to exchange, she'd enjoyed learning what was happening in the Cheatham family.

For all that might be said about her aunt, Adelicia Cheatham was a devoted mother.

Eleanor had hoped the right moment would come to present her idea to her aunt, but it never had. So when dinner drew to a close, she determined to try again.

She accompanied her aunt and Dr. Cheatham into the small study, and was more than a little surprised when Pauline—who'd proudly announced at dinner that she would turn nine soon—snuggled up beside her on the settee.

Eleanor hadn't seen Pauline since the girl was a tiny thing, perhaps a year old. And that had been in Alabama at an Acklen family gathering, after her own mother had died but before the war.

She remembered holding Pauline as a baby and struggling with the desire to have a child of her own. She'd relinquished that hope years ago, or liked to think she had. In moments like this, however, the distant heartbeat of the mother she might have been crept ever closer, pulsing with renewed warmth beneath the surface of her skin.

Pauline looked up and linked her arm through Eleanor's. "Where are *your* children?"

"Pauline!" Aunt Adelicia softly scolded. "That is not a proper question to ask a woman . . . of *any* age."

Scowling, Pauline lowered her head, but Eleanor had to smile. In features and coloring, Pauline was the spitting image of Aunt Adelicia, and had the makings of her mother's boldness as well—though perhaps without the acquired decorum just yet.

"That's all right, Aunt Adelicia. I take no offense." Eleanor looked down and smoothed Pauline's dark hair. "You asked that because it seems as though I'm old enough to be a mother. Is that correct?"

Pauline shot Aunt Adelicia a guarded look, then nodded.

"Well, you're right," Eleanor continued. "I am old enough to have children. But the reason I don't is because I've never married."

Already seeing another question forming in the girl's mind, Eleanor hoped it was one she could answer in mixed company.

"Why *aren't* you married?"

"Pauline Acklen!" This time embarrassment tinged Aunt Adelicia's scolding.

But Eleanor, seeing the question for what it was —innocent curiosity—couldn't blame the child. Not when she possessed the same trait herself. She quietly considered where her own curiosity— albeit, far less innocent—had landed her earlier that very day.

She aimed a look at her aunt and Dr. Cheatham,

silently requesting their permission to proceed. Dr. Cheatham, who was swiftly losing his battle to contain a smile, glanced at his wife, who nodded, her scowl quite pronounced.

"The reason I'm not married, Pauline, is because . . . I've never met a man I've wanted to marry." Even though that was the truth, an underlying and more pronounced truth lingered beneath it, around it. And filled every inch of space in the room. "And it's also due, in part, to the fact that . . ." Eleanor was surprised at the warmth rising to her cheeks, and at how difficult the next words were to say aloud. "I've never had a man ask for my hand in marriage."

Pauline's dark brows pinched together, and Eleanor tried to imagine what question was coming next.

"So . . ." The girl pursed her lips. "The man has to do the asking?"

Grateful for the reprieve from the personal questions, Eleanor gave her cousin's little arm a squeeze. "It's customary, yes. But it's also something that most couples will have discussed, at least to some degree, before the gentleman takes it upon himself to ask the lady. So when it comes your time"—she brushed a kiss to Pauline's brow, tossing a wink in her aunt's direction—"and a young man you love very much asks for your hand in marriage, it shouldn't come as a surprise."

Even as she said it, Eleanor knew she was perpetuating the promise of a reality that didn't come true for every girl, especially in the aftermath of the war, with marriageable men so scarce. But it would come true for Pauline Acklen—pretty, vivacious, and from an enormously wealthy family. Someday Pauline would have her pick of suitors.

Apparently satisfied with the response, Pauline jumped up from the settee, darted for the door, and then turned. "When I grow up," she announced, hand on hip, "and I meet a man I want to marry, if he doesn't ask me first, I'm going to ask *him*."

She closed the door with a thud, her youthful declaration hanging in the stunned silence.

Dr. Cheatham's quiet laughter dispelled it. "Your daughter grows more like you every day, my dear."

Eleanor smiled, especially seeing the droll look Aunt Adelicia shot him.

"You know very well, Dr. Cheatham, that I am a woman who believes most strongly in the traditional and . . ."

Still listening to the conversation, Eleanor's attention was drawn to the open window. Though dusk cast its purplish spell, it was still light outside, and she spotted Mr. Gray and a man she didn't recognize walking in the front gardens. It wasn't until she found herself scanning the remainder of the grounds that she realized who she was looking for—

And quickly stopped.

A brief knock sounded, and Cordina, Belmont's head cook, entered the small study carrying a silver service.

Eleanor remembered the woman's name because she could hardly wait to ask her about the dishes they'd enjoyed at dinner—the smooth-as-silk sweet potatoes, the butter beans so tender without being mushy, and the roasted pork. The meat had practically melted in her mouth.

"Brought you all your evenin' coffee, Mrs. Cheatham. With some of my teacakes, o' course."

"Thank you, Cordina." Aunt Adelicia moved a book from the table. "And again, dinner tonight was delicious."

"Yes," Eleanor added. "It certainly was. When you have time, Cordina, I'd love to know how you get your pork roast so tender."

Cordina beamed as she lowered the laden silver tray to the coffee table. "Oh, it ain't no secret, Miss Braddock. You just got to make sure you let the meat set a while in some spices 'fore you put it to cookin'. Then you cook it long and slow. Rushin' it only make it tough."

Eleanor wished she had paper and pen at hand. "Which spices do you—"

"Cordina"—Aunt Adelicia leaned forward—"you've been so busy today. I think we can serve ourselves this evening."

Smiling, Cordina ducked her head. "Yes, ma'am. Thank you, ma'am."

As the door closed, Eleanor couldn't help but feel as if she'd somehow gotten Cordina in trouble. Surely not by initiating a conversation? Though a war had been fought—and lost, by the

Confederacy—largely over the issue of slavery, she knew some people still preferred the ways of the "old South."

But even in the few hours she'd been back at Belmont, she'd witnessed her aunt conversing freely with the servants—both Negro and white— so she didn't think that was to blame.

Aunt Adelicia served Dr. Cheatham first, then poured a cup of coffee for Eleanor. "Cream and sugar, dear?"

"No, thank you. I prefer it plain."

Sipping, Eleanor silently rehearsed how best to broach her plan with her aunt, preferring Dr. Cheatham not be present when she did. But whatever she said, she needed to deliver the words with confidence and determination, or Aunt Adelicia would never agree to fund the venture.

And she needed that funding. *A loan.* She would pay back every penny. And it would be worth it, because she would finally be doing something with her life, something that mattered. A job that would allow her to be independent, to have a home again. For her and her father.

"So tell me, Miss Braddock"—steam swirled from Dr. Cheatham's cup—"are you prepared for the adventures my wife has planned for you?"

Glancing between the couple, Eleanor met the comment with a raised eyebrow. "I suppose it depends on what those adventures entail."

"Oh, pay him no mind, Eleanor. He's simply trying to stir up trouble." Aunt Adelicia smiled, her delicate pinky extended at a perfect angle as she sipped. "But I *do* have some ideas I'd like to discuss with you. When we have a moment."

Sensing something pass between them, Eleanor felt a little like a beetle about to be pinned to a board. Especially when remembering what Mr. Geoffrey had said to Mr. Gray in the conservatory—*"You said she wanted to discuss an* idea*"*—and how Mr. Gray had looked at him.

"Well," Dr. Cheatham said, rising, "I believe that's my cue, as they say." He winked in Eleanor's direction. "Consider yourself forewarned, Miss Braddock. And as I said at dinner . . ." The creases at the corners of his eyes grew more defined. "Welcome to our home. We're most happy you're here."

"Thank you, Dr. Cheatham." Eleanor set her cup aside. "And thank you for all you're doing for my father." She looked at her aunt. "I'm grateful to you both. I know it's due to your influence and connections that a place opened for him there." Reliving the scene when her father had bolted from the carriage, she felt her throat tighten. "And I'm hopeful for his recovery."

Again, she felt something subtle pass between them.

"Miss Braddock, I'm certain Dr. Crawford told you they'd do everything medically possible to help your father. . . . And I look forward to going by this week and seeing him myself. In the event Dr. Crawford hasn't discussed this with

93

you yet," he continued, "the initial medication they're administering has a sedating effect."

Eleanor nodded. "He did mention that."

"Very good. After the first week or so, depending on the patient's adjustment, the medication is typically decreased, and your father will be encouraged to become more active. So you might give thought to what hobbies he would enjoy pursuing. Something that would give him purpose and provide exercise."

She thought for a moment. "He's always loved tending a vegetable garden. I didn't see sign of a garden while I was there, but perhaps I could help him plant a small herb garden in his room by the window. If his room *has* a window."

"I'm certain it does," her aunt chimed in. "And that's an excellent idea."

"Indeed, it is." Dr. Cheatham's smile held compassion, and gentle warning. "You must not cling too tightly to the hope that he'll fully recover, Miss Braddock. When dementia—*if* that's what it is—begins to manifest itself in a person, the deterioration of the mind rarely reverses course."

Her heart beating harder, Eleanor nodded, appreciating his candor and compassionate manner, even though his words cut her to the quick.

He reached over and took hold of her hand. "One day at a time, my dear," he said softly. "That's all that is given to us. And sometimes"—his own countenance clouded—"even that we must break down into hours. And minutes."

He squeezed her hand, and she squeezed back, grateful for the firmness of his grip, and realizing how long it had been since she'd touched anyone in such a way—*purposefully* holding a hand, giving a hug. Or receiving one. Even today when greeting her aunt, she'd curtsied. And her father had never been a demonstrative man.

Teddy, though . . .

Eleanor felt a knife through her heart, thinking about her younger brother. Teddy had known how to hug. What she wouldn't have done to nestle into one of his hugs again.

Calling upon every ounce of reserve, she thanked Dr. Cheatham again with a smile, not trusting her voice.

No sooner had he opened the door than Richard and William appeared. The two thirteen-year-old boys—brothers since the wedding and thick as thieves—grabbed him by the arm and clamored for him to join them in the billiards room. With a parting glance, Dr. Cheatham peered back into the study, feigning the fear of being kidnapped.

Aunt Adelicia merely smiled and waved.

Eleanor exhaled, part sigh, part amazement. She'd never experienced a home life with such vibrancy of youth. "It seems there is never a dull moment in this house."

"Oh, there's not." Aunt Adelicia laughed. "Especially since we installed the new billiard table off the grand salon. Just until the new billiard hall is completed," she explained. "The boys love it. We moved the schoolroom upstairs for Claude and Pauline. Of course, the older children will be going away to their schools soon. But for now it's quite lively having them all at home. And I wouldn't have it any other way." Her features softened with gratitude. "There's nothing more beautiful than family, harmony, and affection."

Having thought much the same thing moments earlier, only from a different perspective, Eleanor rose to pour herself another cup of coffee. She offered to refill her aunt's first, but she declined.

Thinking it better if she were facing her aunt straight on for this conversation, Eleanor claimed the chair opposite Adelicia's. Only then did she notice the vase of cut roses on a table in the corner. The petals were purest white but for the very tips, which looked as though they'd been painted in the palest shade of pink. Like a sunrise.

She'd never seen anything like them and didn't have to think long to know from where—and from *whom*—they'd come. She recalled Mr. Geoffrey bowing to her, so regal in his bearing. The gesture had seemed second nature to him. Odd for a man in such a position.

The recollection stirred feelings she didn't quite know what to do with. She only knew they were best left unstirred.

Collecting her thoughts, she looked across from her and knew this was the moment she'd been waiting for.

"Aunt Adelicia, I—"

"Eleanor, dear, I—"

Having spoken in unison, they laughed.

Eleanor gestured. "Please . . ." But she really wished she could get her part over with first.

Aunt Adelicia offered a conceding tip of her head. "Eleanor, dear . . . as Dr. Cheatham stated so well, we're grateful you've come to live with us, and we want you to feel at home here. Belmont will be your home for as long as you like."

Grateful, Eleanor hoped her expression communicated that.

"After all, your father was my late hus—" Aunt Adelicia's voice caught, and she briefly firmed her lips. "Your father was my late husband's dearest cousin," she finished, her voice softer. "Joseph always spoke so highly of him." She gave a faint laugh, the melancholy in her features lessening. "He told me countless times about all the trouble your father got him into when they were young."

Eleanor smiled, sipping her coffee. "I've heard those same stories too, many times. And each time the risks grew greater."

"And the punishments more severe." Aunt Adelicia sighed, the sound full of memory. "You've done well, Eleanor. With your father, I mean. And taking care of the household, all of the responsibility resting on your shoulders. The past years have been hard . . . I know."

Eleanor fingered the delicate handle of the cup. "It's been . . . a challenge, at times." She knew, too, that—despite the splendor of her current surroundings and the present happiness in this home—her aunt had endured her own weight of grief and responsibility throughout the years.

Aunt Adelicia held her gaze. "I've known you since you were eleven. And you've always been older than your years. You know that, don't you? You were born an old soul, Eleanor. I recognized that in you from the start. Because the same was true for me."

Eleanor bowed her head. "I've been aware of that quality in myself for a very long time. Maybe since childhood." She lifted a shoulder, then let it fall. "I just never realized anyone else saw it."

"I used to give Joseph a hard time about calling you Little Ellie. Especially when he continued it into your teen years."

Eleanor exhaled a laugh. "By then, I was as tall as he was."

"He always meant it as an endearment. I hope you knew that."

"I did. Just as my father did when he too continued using it. But . . . my father hasn't called me that in years. Which is only right, considering." Eleanor smiled, more from a sense of obligation than humor.

She took a sip of coffee, but it had grown lukewarm.

Aunt Adelicia sat straighter. "Enough of this remembering. A little makes one more grateful. An overabundance sows bitterness." She reached for something on the table behind her. "Now . . . I'm especially thrilled at your arrival today, because there's the dearest group of women I want you to meet. We gather once a week for coffee and to chit-chat, and do something special. And tomorrow we're meeting here! I've already told them all about you. You'll adore them, and I know they'll adore you."

Eleanor tried to appear enlivened at the prospect, but seeing what was in Aunt Adelicia's hand made that difficult. That, and the fact she'd never enjoyed making small talk. Especially with people she didn't know.

"Tomorrow we have someone coming to teach us how to make these floral sachets." Aunt Adelicia sniffed the perfumed bag in her hand, then held it out for Eleanor to do the same. The pungent scent caused Eleanor's eyes to water.

"Isn't it beautiful?" Aunt Adelicia beamed. "They're made using crushed flower petals. Two weeks hence, a woman from England will be here to teach us how to make *paper* flowers. She sent me a sample in the mail sometime back."

Her aunt handed her the sachet, then retrieved a long, thin box from the desk drawer and withdrew a flower—a chrysanthemum, Eleanor thought— and handed it to her as well, proudly looking on.

Holding the sachet in one hand and the flower in the other, Eleanor rotated the stem between her thumb and forefinger, not understanding why anyone would go to such great lengths to make something from paper when the real thing could be plucked not twenty feet away outside.

Her aunt moved to stand beside her. "Isn't the detail delightful?"

"Yes. It's . . . quite something."

Aunt Adelicia fingered the trailing scarlet ribbon cinching the top of the sachet. "The ribbons are hand-spun silk from France."

Considering the prospect of a life where hour upon hour would be spent making perfumed sachets, paper flowers, and chitchat, Eleanor found herself wishing for enough silk ribbon to loop around her own neck a few times—before pulling taut.

"Of course, our ladies' group takes part in other pursuits as well. We attend concerts, and the opera. Oh, and the ballet on occasion. So splendid. We also have a contingent—the Nashville Women's League—that meets in town. There are a few women closer to your age in that group, so you would find that beneficial. They participate in . . ."

Listening to the endless activities engaged in by Aunt Adelicia and her friends, not to mention the *league,* Eleanor felt a wall being erected around her at a rapid rate. Her aunt's friends were all married women, and wealthy, judging from their apparent plentitude of leisure time and how they spent it. So very different from her own circumstances.

The term *royalty* came to mind again, and she had to concede . . . the journalist who'd written that article *did* have a point. Her aunt and her aunt's friends lived a charmed life, one her aunt was inviting her to live along with her. But Eleanor couldn't.

Between the perfumed sachet tainting the oxygen around her and already knowing how adamant her aunt could be once her mind was set, she found it impossible to breathe. It felt as if someone had cinched her corset too tight.

". . . and then last year, I conveyed all the ladies to New Orleans, where we took part in the festivities in the city before continuing on to my—"

Eleanor stood abruptly, her thoughts colliding. She deposited the items on the coffee table. "Forgive me for interrupting, Aunt Adelicia. And I know you mean well, but . . ." She took a fortifying breath. How to speak her mind without causing hurt feelings? "But *this* . . ." She motioned to the sachet and the flower. "I'm sorry, but . . . this isn't me."

The surprise in Aunt Adelicia's face slowly melted to compassion. "Oh, my dear . . . I understand." She gave Eleanor's arm a squeeze. "With all you've had to bear, you simply haven't had the same opportunities in life. But don't be intimidated by—"

"No." Eleanor shook her head. "That's not it. I . . ."

She'd been waiting for the right moment, rehearsing it, and now that the moment had arrived, it wasn't unfolding at all the way she'd hoped. Gone was the well-rehearsed speech. Seeing the uncertainty in her aunt's expression, she prayed for the right words.

"I appreciate what you're attempting to do, Aunt Adelicia. Honestly. But the truth is . . . none of those activities appeals to me." Oh, where were the words that would make her aunt understand? "I want to do something useful with my life, Aunt. Something that matters, that helps others. And if you'll allow me, I have a plan I'd like to—"

A single dark eyebrow rose, and Eleanor realized—too late—how her words must have sounded. A cloud moved over Aunt Adelicia's features, and Eleanor braced herself for the storm.

6

"Please forgive me, Aunt Adelicia. That did not come out at all in the way I intended. The meaning I proposed to convey was—"

"I believe you've already conveyed what you *meant,* Eleanor." Aunt Adelicia stared. "Whether or not it came out as intended."

Eleanor felt as though she'd taken something fragile and precious and had carelessly shattered it into a thousand pieces. And she had only herself to blame. "Aunt Adelicia . . ." She sighed and lowered her gaze, that same wave of weariness from earlier in the day sapping her strength. She wanted to sit again but didn't dare while her aunt remained standing.

Keenly aware of her situation and of how truly

at the mercy of her aunt she was—but more so because she truly regretted hurting her—Eleanor lifted her head and met Adelicia's leveled stare.

"Please accept my apologies, Aunt. I did not intend to offend. Nor was it my intent to belittle you or your friends." Thinking again of what she'd said, her face heated. "I've never been good at speaking around issues, Aunt Adelicia. Just as I've never been gifted at pretending I feel one thing when I feel another. It's always seemed easier to simply speak my mind. Though, typically"—her laughter came out flat—"I've managed to communicate with more grace and reserve than was demonstrated just now."

Her aunt regarded her, and Eleanor knew whatever was coming, she likely deserved. Finally Aunt Adelicia sat and folded her hands neatly in her lap.

With a look, she indicated for Eleanor to sit as well. "I, too, Eleanor, have always found that speaking the truth is the shortest route to a resolution."

Hearing that gave Eleanor reason to hope. She opened her mouth to respond, but her aunt raised a single slender forefinger. That tiniest of gestures carried a weight of meaning Eleanor understood completely.

"However," her aunt continued, "that particular route does not always ensure a peaceful end. Nor a satisfying end for either party."

As swiftly as hope had come, it retreated, and

Eleanor waited, knowing better than to try to take the lead again.

"A moment ago, you said you had a plan. And I believe you were about to share that *plan* with me."

Eleanor nodded but discovered her carefully practiced speech was now a jumble in her mind. Perhaps straightforward was best, after all. "I would . . . like a job."

The comment drew another raised eyebrow.

"A job that would eventually allow me to earn enough money to live independently. With my father, of course. Assuming his . . . health improves. All my life, I've . . ." She stopped, realizing she'd misspoken. "For what *feels* like all my life, I've lived by another's by-your-leave. I'm almost thirty years old. I have no prospects of marriage, nor any hope of such on the horizon. And I've accepted that. After all, I'm"—she sighed—"not the kind of woman that men generally consider beautiful."

Generally was a generous term. No man had ever told her she was beautiful. Sensing her aunt's response, she rushed on.

"But I *am* talented . . . and intelligent. I have abilities, and I welcome them being challenged so that I might continue to learn and grow." Eleanor glanced down at her hands. "Even as I hear myself saying this, I realize there's a great chance you may perceive me as being unappreciative. But that isn't the case. I shudder to think about where I, and my father, would be right now"—she looked

up, an uncomfortable tightness in her chest—
"without your kindness."

For the longest time, Aunt Adelicia said nothing.

Seconds ticked past, and from somewhere outside, the low coo of a mourning dove drifted in through the open window.

"I would like to offer you a position, Eleanor, and would if there were anything available . . . and suitable. But I'm afraid I already have a *liaison* . . . an assistant. We employ a tutor for our children, and I have a personal attorney as well as an entire law firm at my disposal. Dr. Cheatham manages the plantations in Louisiana at present. And as long as I have breath in my body, you will *not* be a servant in this home." She started to say something, hesitated, and then smiled. "To be honest, you don't want to work for me. I can sometimes be quite demanding."

Eleanor looked at her aunt seated across from her, and admired her more than she ever had. "Thank you for that, Aunt. But . . ." She chanced a slight wince, trying to signal that what she was about to say was likely not what her aunt expected. "I'm not asking for a job here at Belmont. In fact, I've paid for three months' rent on a building in town. And signed a contract too. I . . . want to start a restaurant. I want to cook."

Aunt Adelicia blinked. Several times. "You . . . want to cook?"

Eleanor nodded. "I want to be a chef, actually. I've been cooking for years, and I'm quite good. Women are starting cafés and restaurants all across the country in cities like New York, Philadelphia, and Atlanta. And they're having great success. The world is changing, and those changes are bringing new opportunities for women."

Catching the faintest flicker of what she felt certain was interest in her aunt's eyes, Eleanor's courage rose. And the spark nudged a memory of something she'd planned to say. "The fourteenth amendment was recently ratified, granting black freedmen the right to vote. Everyone said it would never happen. But it has! And people are already talking about women being granted that right as well. Surely that won't be far off, and there's no telling what doors will be open to us then."

Still staring at her, her aunt frowned. "You want to be a cook. In a restaurant. In town."

It wasn't a question. But again, Eleanor nodded. "The building used to be a small boardinghouse, but with a little renovation, I think it will meet my needs."

She hesitated, not wanting to admit the next part. Even though she'd prayed about her decision before acting on it, she dreaded her aunt's reaction. "I haven't actually *seen* the building yet. But the advertisement in the paper described it in detail, and the proprietor and I have exchanged letters. I reviewed his references and have every reason to believe he's trustworthy."

For a moment, nothing. Then Aunt Adelicia gave a single nod. "Go on." Her voice held neither approval nor disapproval—only command.

"My agreement is only for three months. That's all the money I could comfortably put down after arranging for Father's care. The proprietor wasn't keen on that time frame. He wanted a lengthier agreement and would still like to sell the building. But I convinced him to rent it to me. For the time being, at least."

Eleanor dared to smile, hoping to lighten the moment. But the moment won out, and her smile died.

"What I want to speak to you about, Aunt Adelicia, is . . . I was thinking . . . actually, I was hoping that you, being a business-minded woman—and considering how you sometimes invest in businesses—would be willing to loan me the money to establish my own business and make my way. Of course, I'd pay you back, Aunt. Every penny. With interest."

Eleanor started to say more, but instinct told her she had said enough. From somewhere in the house, a clock chimed. Eight times. And each stroke seemed to last an eternity.

Wordlessly, her aunt rose and crossed to the window. The sun had nearly set, and a breeze ruffled the lace tiering her skirt, bringing with it the sweet scent of late-blooming lavender.

Her aunt stared out into the dusk. "I appreciate your enterprising spirit, Eleanor. I admire it, and even share it to a certain extent. It is . . . intoxicating to think of all that might lie ahead."

Feeling the flutter of what could only be

described as her dream being given life, Eleanor sat straighter.

"Eleanor . . . Elaine . . . Braddock," her aunt said thoughtfully, turning back. The trace of a smile touched her mouth. "You're a Braddock, but your grandmother was an Acklen. Having traced both of those lineages, I know you share the blood of strong, driven people, people who were pioneers and leaders. You hail from a family tree that is revered and that still commands honor and respect in the finest social circles, no matter your present circumstances."

Eleanor could scarcely believe this was happening. After all the planning, the dreaming, the daring to hope. After so much disappointment . . .

"But as you were Joseph's niece before his death, you are therefore . . . my niece. And no niece of mine is going to serve as a *cook*. And certainly not at some . . . common establishment in town. It would be disgraceful, void of propriety . . . for someone of our place in society."

"But . . . you said you admired my spirit. You said—"

"I'll do everything I can to help you make your way, Eleanor. But it will be in a proper manner worthy of the woman you are and the family from which you hail. I cannot sanction a path so contrary to one I believe you should be pursuing. Nor would I, being a business-minded woman, as you stated, ever choose to invest in a venture so fraught with risk and uncertainty."

She exhaled and moved from the window back to the settee but remained standing. "You invested money—even if short term—in a building you've never seen? Trusted the word of a man you've never met?" Aunt Adelicia gave a humorless laugh. "I dare to wonder if the building even exists. More than likely, the man with whom you dealt has long departed from Nashville, taking your contract —and your money—with him."

Eleanor bowed her head, because she couldn't bear to sustain her aunt's gaze, but also because she didn't want Adelicia Acklen Cheatham to see her struggle to contain her emotions.

"Eleanor . . . my dear . . ." Her aunt's tone softened. "I can see how much this prospect means to you. And though I do not wish to argue about it further, I would like to suggest another possibility for your future."

Slowly Eleanor lifted her gaze.

"As you know," her aunt continued, "bonds are forged between families all the time—marriages built on mutual respect, a shared vision for the future, and the security of inherited wealth."

Eleanor listened, not quite following. What did this have to do with her restaurant? Then a sinking feeling formed in the pit of her stomach.

"These unions aren't accidental, of course. This is how posterity is assured and how upstanding families such as ours propagate their wealth." Aunt Adelicia paused, her smile ever radiant. "I trust you're following my thread of thought, Eleanor."

Eleanor rose from the settee, the very act feeling like one of defiance, considering her aunt's height was so much less than her own. "Aunt Adelicia, I'm not interested in . . . propagating wealth. Nor do I wish to marry a man simply for his money. Even if such a man existed who would be interested in me now that the bloom is off the rose."

Adelicia lifted her chin and glared. "Of course you wouldn't marry a man only for his money. I would be ashamed of such a choice on your part if you did. However"—her expression softened—"friendships develop from acquaintances, and over time, those often lead to . . . something more."

Aunt Adelicia smoothed a hand over her skirt, briefly looking away as she did. "Understanding this . . . in recent weeks I have exercised the liberty of making discreet inquiries of a number of our widowed or single gentlemen friends about their . . . personal plans for the future."

Eleanor stifled a groan. "You didn't . . ." But seeing her aunt's nod, she closed her eyes. It took every bit of willpower for her not to grab the silk ribbon from the potpourri and end it all right then.

"I'm sorry to report, however," her aunt continued, "I haven't found a suitable match as of yet. But I haven't exhausted my search, by any means, so I'm confident I will be successful."

Eleanor let out the breath she'd been holding. "I wouldn't cling too closely to that confidence, Aunt Adelicia." Feeling more beaten and bruised by the minute, she tried not to show it. "I gave up on the possibility of my marrying a long time ago."

"Well, I haven't. You're a bright young woman, Eleanor, with much to offer. We simply have to find the right man."

Eleanor couldn't bring herself to respond but noted her aunt's chin lifting ever so slightly. "I take no pleasure in disappointing you this evening, Eleanor, as I so obviously have done. But your request is simply out of the question. I am quite adamant on the matter." Her aunt's voice—steel in velvet—came softly in the silence. "Furthermore, I am not accustomed to having my wishes questioned, nor defied, especially by my own family. So please, my dear . . . do not broach this subject with me again."

Later, in the finest guest quarters of the mansion—or so the young servant girl had said—Eleanor changed into her nightgown. She'd been a little surprised at the location of the suite—located in the east wing, directly off the hallway from the formal and family dining rooms. The views of the estate from her windows were exceptional, even draped in moonlight, and Eleanor was grateful.

She climbed into bed, the sheets cool against her legs, her aunt's warning still echoing in the silence. Wanting the feel of something familiar, she reached for the dog-eared volume on the bedside table, one from which she'd derived much pleasure through the years. The title—*Conversations on Common Things*—was barely legible, and she thumbed to the place marked by the ribbon, then began reading. But the words by Dorothea Dix fell uncommonly flat.

After several attempts, Eleanor finally sighed and returned the book to its place. Simply wanting this day to end, she reached over to turn down the oil lamp . . . and paused.

She pushed the covers back and crossed to the wardrobe on the opposite wall, the Persian rug luxurious beneath her bare feet. By the time she'd been shown to her room, her clothes had all been unpacked, brushed free of dust and dirt, and put neatly in their place. And her extra pair of boots had been polished to a shine.

What a difference from home. *Home.* How far away Murfreesboro seemed. Only a handful of hours by carriage, yet another world away. And gone, forever. She thought of her father, as she'd done countless times throughout the day, and hoped he was resting, adjusting.

She felt guilty living in the luxury of Belmont, when he was alone in the asylum—and even more so for being grateful for the temporary reprieve.

Finding the skirt she'd worn that day, she reached into a pocket but found it empty, and her heart jolted. Quickly, she tried the other pocket, and her eyes closed in relief.

Back in bed, she tucked the covers beneath her chin. *"It does no good to cry, Eleanor,"* her father had said more times than she could count. *"A person held hostage by emotion is a fool indeed, and will be proven such in due time."*

Rolling onto her side, willing the ache in her chest to lessen, she gripped the handkerchief tucked in her palm, and her thoughts turned to that night so long ago, with the soldier, when the world had seemed on the very brink of destruction.

She'd made a promise. Not to him directly. But in a way, it felt as though she had. "I'm sorry," she whispered into the darkness, as she'd done many times before. "I tried to find her. . . ."

When sleep refused to come, she wished she could walk outside in the night air like she used to do in their backyard at home. But being unfamiliar with the rules of her aunt's house, she didn't feel comfortable striking out at this late hour.

Best save the walk until morning. Perhaps at sunrise.

Instead, she walked, in her mind, the hallways of the building she'd rented in town, having imagined the layout from the proprietor's detailed description. Seeing herself through Aunt Adelicia's eyes, she felt every bit the fool she likely was.

And yet, she couldn't deny how *led* she'd felt to take that step in procuring the building. At her earliest opportunity, she planned on finding out if she had indeed been a fool.

Or only a foolish dreamer.

Just after sunrise the next morning, Marcus arrived at Belmont. It was far too early to call at the mansion for the meeting Mrs. Cheatham had requested, but he'd awakened with a nagging suspicion. One that first occurred to him yesterday. . . .

What if Mayor Adler had already decided who would be awarded the contract for Nashville's new opera house but for some reason wasn't announcing it yet?

He reined in at the conservatory and tethered his horse, Regal, to a nearby tree. Despite his lack of desire to rule, there were rare moments, like this one, when he missed how his decisions had been accepted in Austria without argument or question.

Or anonymous fifth bids . . .

No one in Nashville knew his family heritage, including Mrs. Cheatham, which was as he desired it. While on her grand tour of Europe three years earlier, Adelicia had met Emperor Franz Joseph, his uncle, but not the men in line to the throne. And that, as it turned out, had worked to Marcus's benefit.

On the surface, the business arrangement he had with the estate's mistress might appear to some as being fortunate. But good luck and fortune had had nothing to do with it. He had been in audience when Mrs. Cheatham was presented at his uncle's court, and had learned several details about the woman, and her city, that made it an excellent destination for his venture to America.

He had come to Nashville, to the Belmont estate, for a very specific goal, which he was far closer to achieving now than when he'd arrived. Thanks, in part, to the city's sultry summer heat and relentless humidity, odd as that would sound to some. And to the estate's underground irrigation system that the groundskeepers of even the Chateau de Versailles would envy.

He rubbed the muscles knotted at the base of his neck, recognizing the mark of too much work and too little sleep.

First rays of dawn lay like a blanket of jewels over the Belmont estate, causing the drops of dew to shimmer in the light. He'd heard Belmont referred to as a Southern Versailles, and he could understand why. The scene reminded him of the request Mrs. Cheatham had made. Or "collaboration," as Gray had referred to it yesterday.

"I want you to create me a rose, Mr. Geoffrey. Blush pink in color," she'd told him, ever exact a woman in her opinions, and willingness to share them. *"Like that of first dawn, but not too light, and with the slightest hint of purple. But not overly orange. And not too overt."*

He admired the woman but was hopeful that—after months of work—he was close to achieving the exact hue she imagined. Not only so she would be pacified, but so he could focus his attention on something far more important—his primary grafting endeavor.

His gaze trailed upward to the mansion, its pinkish facade almost ethereal in the freshness of morning, and he wondered which room belonged to Mrs. Cheatham's niece. And was she, by chance, an early riser? He smiled, thinking of her thinking of him as an under gardener. Talk about fulfilling his desire to be seen as a commoner. . . .

He couldn't remember the last time he'd met a woman so bent on escaping his company. And that, of course, only made him want to press his company upon her further. He'd always had that orneriness about him. When she'd reacted the way he'd suspected she would, it only made the antagonizing more enjoyable.

And that voice . . . He'd enjoy listening to her read Tennyson aloud. Or perhaps John Donne. Anything, really, so long as she was doing the reading.

Miss Braddock was certainly a woman who made an impression. Though he didn't remember her for the same reasons he usually remembered a woman.

Part of her appeal—and she did have a certain appeal, despite her . . . plainness—was that it appeared she didn't much care whether she made a good impression or not. Which was an intriguing quality when compared with all the women he'd known whose sole purpose—in the way they dressed, in the elaborate contouring of their hair, in their flirtatious manner—was, above all, to be remembered.

Yet Miss Braddock seemed the exact opposite.

Her hair? Plain. Pulled back into a braided bun at the nape of her neck. Her manner? Anything but flirtatious. And her choice in dress? He hadn't seen that much pink since visiting the Jardin des

Tuileries in Paris several springs back. Pink tulips everywhere. And yet she possessed a sharp wit, keen intellect, and a sensibility rarely found in the gentler sex. She was a compelling woman, and . . .

Compelling?

That was a word he hadn't used to describe a woman before. *Interesting* . . . He usually thought of women in very different terms, while focusing on very different attributes. But look where that had gotten him.

And where it had gotten Rutger.

Marcus closed his eyes at the memory of his older brother, which was never far away. Sickening regret took advantage of the moment and overtook his weakened defenses. If only he'd been with Rutger that night. If only his brother had confided in him. Rutger had long been given to bouts of melancholy, but never had the family expected that—

Marcus exhaled a shaky breath, knowing only too well that nothing would be gained from such pondering. So he attempted to turn his thoughts in a different direction. But the path his thoughts took wasn't much better. . . .

What was he doing engaged to a woman he didn't love—much less like? Oh, he had liked her at first. At the time, he was certain he'd never seen a woman more beautiful than Baroness Maria Elizabeth Albrecht von Haas. But how fleeting her beauty had proven to be, even though her countenance hadn't changed.

And yet . . . in his eyes it had.

But Marcus knew there was no use in tugging at this thread of a question either. Because there was no avoiding an arranged marriage when your life was prearranged from birth.

The air inside the conservatory was warm, and the fresh scent of roses mingled with the sweetness of honeysuckle for the perfect blend of richness and simplicity. He made his way to the propagating room, the earlier nagging suspicion returning.

He was all but certain he'd submitted the lowest bid among the four contractors. Or five now. This project wasn't about money for him. He already had money. This was about something far more important, and lasting. Something money couldn't buy.

And something he couldn't accomplish in Austria.

Because an archduke of the House of Habsburg, now *second* in line to the throne, simply didn't build buildings—or "play in the dirt," as his father referred to his study of botany. An archduke spent his life preparing to reign over a kingdom, whether or not he ever got the chance to rule. And whether or not he wanted to.

When he first heard of the mayor's decision to build an opera house, he'd known that was the answer to the second of his aspirations—to put brick and mortar to a long-held dream.

In his mind's eye, he envisioned the opera house he had designed, the perfect blend of form and function. Structure and nature companioned as one.

If given time and opportunity, he would capitalize on the natural beauty of this city and integrate it with the elegant lines and movement of the Neo-Renaissance style. The combined beauty would be something of which America had never seen, and of which Austria would, hopefully, soon read about.

If only his father could see his designs.

Then again, perhaps not.

His father had never shared his love of botany or architecture. Only after serving seven years in the military had Marcus earned the freedom to pursue his studies as well—as long as it hadn't interfered with his other obligations.

But discovering the difference between knowing what you had the ability to do and knowing what you were born to do had been a valuable lesson for him. One he'd never forgotten.

In the propagating room, he examined a whip graft he'd performed earlier in the week, studied the wax-sealed scion and stock—a twig of a Baldwin apple tree grafted on a wild crab apple. He'd wrapped the immediate area in a bandage to give further protection and to hold the scion more firmly in place until the union was accomplished.

Both nature and the grafting wax seemed to be doing their jobs. The only requirements now . . . consistent sunlight, moisture, and time.

He checked the rows of other grafts, making meticulous notes as he went along, then moved outside to the field garden located a stone's throw away behind the conservatory. For almost a year now, this plot of ground had been designated for his experimentation.

Due to the lateness of the growing season, he'd planted his latest outdoor experiment in long wooden troughs that could be moved inside the conservatory when the lingering warmth of summer departed. He had no scientific proof that fresh air made any difference in a plant's development. But it did in people, so he figured, why not keep them outside for as long as possible?

A layer of dew covered the young potato plants, and in the freshness of morning the leaves almost glittered, appearing as beautiful to him as any prized rose. Because within these leaves, which fed the heart of the plant nestled securely in the earth's womb, was the answer.

At least that's what he told himself every time he crossbred a potato—which he'd been doing for the better part of a decade.

He sighed. None of the potatoes he'd seen thus far, in Austria or in America, fully met his idea of what a potato should and *could* be in form, size, color, production, and lasting quality of freshness—the specimens were small and wont to suffer from dry rot.

So much waste, too little production.

He examined each plant, gently lifting the leaves of the Early Rose potatoes, a crossbred variety he'd worked with for years, watchful for dark spots or areas of discoloration. The plants had yet to flower, that stage still a few weeks off.

He'd been only eleven years old when the famine struck Europe twenty-two years ago. Still, he remembered. Starvation and loss had touched every corner of the continent. He shook his head. Though Ireland was most greatly affected, with one million people dead in that country alone, the disease ravaged potato crops throughout Europe.

He checked the last plant. The leaves were hearty. Not a speck of dark on any of them. A good sign—one he'd seen often enough while waiting for the plant to mature . . . only to finally unearth the same ill-shaped, dry-rotting little tubers almost three months later.

But just as he knew he could construct the opera house he'd designed, if given the chance, he knew there was a way—there had to be—to create stronger, more disease-resistant food. Potatoes, specifically. And he was certain he'd be the first to find it.

Although he was equally as certain Luther Burbank would offer a differing opinion. Marcus hoped again that he'd made the right decision in agreeing to share findings with Burbank. After all, they were working toward the same goal.

In the end, as was often the case in science, only one man's name would be remembered for the discovery, and Marcus wanted it to be his own. He wanted to be known for something other than what had been handed him.

He brushed the dirt from his hands and checked his pocket watch, surprised to discover it was later than he'd thought. Pushing himself to his feet, he started toward Regal.

He had a meeting with Mrs. Cheatham, and if luck was on his side, he would have another run-in with Miss Braddock.

7

Minutes later, Marcus dismounted by the front steps of the mansion and, seeing Zeke running straight for him, gathered the reins of the stallion.

"You out here early this mornin', Mr. Geoffrey, sir."

"Yes, I am, Zeke."

The boy reached out as if to take the reins, a gleam in his eyes. And Marcus easily guessed why.

He eyed the boy, then the recently purchased stallion. "Are you certain you can handle him?"

Zeke gave the stallion a look of admiration and puffed out his chest. "Sure I can, sir. I been takin' care of the Lady's horse for a while now."

Following the direction in which Zeke pointed, Marcus spotted a magnificent bay stallion in the corral. He'd seen the horse before, but never being ridden. *That* was Mrs. Cheatham's mount? He found himself surprised by the woman. Yet again.

Marcus handed over the reins. "I entrust Regal to your care, young man."

With cautious respect, Zeke reached up and stroked the stallion's neck. "He's a beauty, sir. Where'd you get him?"

"From Belle Meade Plantation. Not far from here."

"Oh yes, sir. I been over to Belle Meade with Mr. Monroe. That's where the Lady gets all her horses. They got 'em some mighty fine ones, don't they?"

"The best I've seen." He started up the front steps. "I shouldn't be long." At least he hoped not.

Marcus could count on one hand the number of times he'd been invited—or summoned was more like it today—to the mansion. And that was fine by him. The conservatory was where he felt most at home, with nature.

He rapped on the door, and the housekeeper—her name escaped him—gave him entrance. He briefly explained the nature of his visit. "Mr. Gray said Mrs. Cheatham wanted to see me this morning."

She ushered him through the entrance hall, with its statuary and paintings fit for a palace. But it was the expert craftsmanship in the woodwork and marble work of the mansion that drew Marcus's eye.

She paused outside the central parlor. "Please wait in here, Mr. Geoffrey. I'll inform Mrs. Cheatham of your arrival."

When meeting with Mrs. Cheatham before, they'd usually met in a small room off to the right of the entrance hall. The library, they called it. Though, compared to the libraries he was accustomed to back home, the small space reminded him more of a quaint reading room.

A painting on the parlor wall drew his attention, and he took a closer look at the stunning colors and masterful detail. Just as he'd thought—it was Jan van Kessel's work, a Flemish artist whose paintings hung in the palace back home.

From memory of van Kessel's other pieces, he dated the painting to the mid-sixteen hundreds, give or take. Adelicia Cheatham's owning one was impressive.

The next painting that caught his eye earned a near smile—a younger Mrs. Cheatham standing shoulder to shoulder with a bay stallion that looked very much like the one outside. But having seen both the woman and the thoroughbred, Marcus knew that a stool or crate of some sort must have been involved in capturing the image on canvas.

Adelicia Cheatham, petite as she was, would have had to stand on tiptoe for the top of her head to come even close to reaching the thoroughbred's withers. Not so for another woman he'd met only yesterday . . .

He stepped forward and peered into the grand salon, then down both long hallways, admiring the architectural design and wondering, again, in which wing Miss Braddock's room resided. He further wondered whether or not she rode. No dainty pony or delicate mare would suit her—in stature or in temperament. He would gamble—if he still allowed himself that vice—that she was a competitive rider.

He looked back at the portrait of Mrs. Cheatham on the wall, and this time, he thought he caught a glimmer of resemblance between her and her niece. Not in physical appearance so much as the set of the chin, and the direct, uncompromising look in the eyes. He had no idea whether the two women were blood relations, but they most definitely shared the trait of obstinacy. Miss Braddock seemed to have difficulty sustaining a smile, whereas her aunt could command one at will, whether heartfelt or not.

"Bucephalus," a familiar voice announced behind him.

Marcus turned. "Pardon me?"

Mrs. Cheatham smiled. "My stallion's name—Bucephalus."

"Ah, I see." He bowed at the waist. "Good morning, Mrs. Cheatham."

"*Guten Morgen*, Herr Geoffrey," she said pointedly.

"*Guten Morgen*, Frau Cheatham."

"Oh, I adore European accents."

"And I find the accent of the American South especially charming, madam."

She shook her head. "American accents are nothing by comparison. But you are gracious to say as much. I appreciate your coming this morning, as I requested. As Mr. Gray informed you, I'm sure, I had wished to speak to you about the special rose you are grafting for me." She sneaked in a dazzling smile. "But as it turns out, there is an idea I desire to present to you, Mr. Geoffrey. And in that regard, your timing this morning is impeccable. But we mustn't dally. A group of ladies is scheduled to arrive for a meeting shortly. So if you'll join me in the library"—she motioned—"I give you my word, this won't take long."

Marcus followed, his curiosity not so much roused as his guard was raised. It occurred to him that she might ask him to take over the construction of the new billiard hall. But the thought of coming in midstream on a project wasn't enticing. Especially with the setbacks they'd experienced.

She'd admitted to him early on that if he'd arrived before she'd taken bids for the project, he likely would have been chosen for the job. While flattered, to an extent, Marcus was fairly certain he did not want to be in Mrs. Cheatham's direct employ. Designing a flower for her was one thing. Constructing a building to her liking would be another. And her reasoning for having the art gallery torn down nearly a year ago—because it interfered with her view—only confirmed his opinion.

He stepped into the library and was surprised to find Mr. Monroe, Mrs. Cheatham's personal attorney, already there.

Monroe offered his hand. "Mr. Geoffrey, good to see you again."

"You as well, Mr. Monroe." Marcus glanced between him and Mrs. Cheatham, even more curious now about this *idea* she desired to present. Especially if she needed legal counsel present.

Monroe smiled as though reading his thoughts. "Not to worry, Mr. Geoffrey. You're not about to be served with a summons. My being here is strictly coincidental."

"Oh yes, indeed." Mrs. Cheatham claimed her chair behind the desk and indicated for them to sit as well. "Mr. Monroe is helping me stave off the Federal government's excessive taxation of my property." She scoffed softly. "The war is long past, but Washington, D.C., continues to treat some of us as though we're *Southern sympathizers*. I'm afraid the same is true of local government. They're ready to tax or take at every turn." She shook her head. "The North still doesn't trust us."

Monroe gave a brief laugh. "And do you trust them, Mrs. Cheatham?"

"By no means," she quickly countered, then smiled. "But that's different. I'm in the right."

Even Marcus had to smile at that.

Monroe turned to him. "I'm glad our visits happened to coincide this morning, Mr. Geoffrey. I've wanted to thank you for allowing my wife to bring her students to paint some of your recent . . . *creations,* I guess we'd call them. Mrs. Monroe came home raving about the new varieties and colors of roses that now fill the conservatory."

Marcus gave a nod, remembering how he'd purposefully steered Mrs. Monroe and the children away from his grafting room and outdoor garden, not wanting one of the children to accidentally pluck something they shouldn't. "*Creations* is a strong word for what I do. It's more a process of repetition and discovery. I merely take what the Almighty has created and . . . alter it a little."

"Well, well . . ." Mrs. Cheatham smiled. "I didn't realize European men could be so humble, Mr. Geoffrey."

Marcus laughed, despite himself. "Only those who have worked with nature enough to know how truly magnificent and boundless it is in design, and how little we actually understand about it."

Mrs. Cheatham dipped her head in acknowledgment. "Well stated, Mr. Geoffrey. Again, I appreciate your responding so quickly to my request for a visit. Mr. Monroe being here makes it all the easier too. But first, I hope you still find the facilities here at Belmont to your liking. The conservatory, the watering system, the plot of land I've loaned to you at no expense."

Marcus eyed her for a brief second, sensing she was up to something. "Yes, madam. Belmont's facilities are beyond question the finest I could ask for. As is the weather in this part of your lovely country."

She beamed. "While I can't take credit for the weather, I'm so pleased our arrangement continues to remain satisfactory for you. Because it certainly remains so for me."

Marcus knew when he was being set up, even by one as skillful in persuasion as Adelicia Acklen Cheatham.

A quick glance beside him found Mr. Monroe

looking his way, and the faintest grin on the man's face told him that Sutton Monroe not only knew what was going on, but he knew what Marcus was thinking too—which made the situation all the more interesting.

So Marcus settled in for the show. His only question . . .

What could such a woman—whose personal attorney was present and already so well informed —possibly want from him?

The lower the address numbers went, the rougher the neighborhood and its residents became, and the tighter Eleanor clutched her reticule. She didn't have an abundance of money. But what little she had, she had on her person. Which, in hindsight, hadn't been the wisest choice.

She'd slipped from the mansion straightaway after breakfast, not wanting to risk being cornered by the gathering of her aunt's friends. Aunt Adelicia had been civil enough about her not attending the meeting today, though her pensive frown had spoken volumes.

Pedestrians and wagons crowded the streets, along with a surprising number of children, many of them young—and so thin, their eyes large with hunger. Several times, as people passed, they bumped her without so much as a backward glance, much less a *"Pardon me,"* and even in her simple shirtwaist and skirt, Eleanor felt over-dressed.

She heard German and Italian being spoken, and caught several Irish accents coloring the mix. Only one street over, rows of warehouses dwarfed the smaller business establishments, and weathered shingles above the doors made the addresses difficult to read. Many of the buildings weren't numbered at all, which only made the search more challenging.

One-seventeen, one-thirteen . . .

The longer she went without locating the building, the more she feared Aunt Adelicia's prediction about the building owner would prove true. And she loathed the thought of appearing the fool to Adelicia Cheatham.

After an early breakfast, she'd managed to slip away, thankful her aunt understood, or at least accepted, her missing the women's meeting. She hadn't asked what errand sent Eleanor out so early in the morning but, with lingering disapproval, insisted she take a carriage. Eleanor preferred to walk and needed the exertion. She hadn't slept well, and it was only two miles from Belmont into town, but under the circumstances, she'd agreed.

She had, however, instructed Armstead to let her off a few streets away, near the little bakery she'd seen yesterday—Fitch's Bakery. Not only so she could walk, but because she didn't want Armstead knowing where she was going—especially if the building proved to be a rattletrap. Or worse, nonexistent.

Hearing a familiar sound amidst the hubbub of the

city, she paused. The music took her back to a place she didn't want to go. But the melancholy strains of the fiddle refused to be deterred, and before she knew it she was inside the canvas walls of the field hospital again, listening to the soldiers outside the tent as they gathered round the campfires and played, singing sad refrains of home and of loved ones dearly missed.

She breathed in, certain she could smell the acrid smoke.

" 'Black is the color of my true love's hair,' " the man sang in a twangy voice, the roots of his heritage shaping both the notes and their soulfulness. " 'Her cheeks are like the rosy fair . . . The prettiest eyes and daintiest hands . . . I love the ground where on she stands . . .' "

Unable to resist, Eleanor moved closer, peering over the crowd of people gathered to see a ragtag band of musicians. The man singing was an amputee, his empty shirt sleeve tucked into the waist of his trousers. She couldn't help but wonder if she'd been with him when they'd taken his arm. There had been so many . . . too many.

When the song finally ended, the fiddler drew out the final note, its strain bittersweet. Not a person moved. Even the air dared not stir. The singer bowed his head, and for a moment, only the clink of coins in a cup could be heard. Then as quickly as the melancholy strains had laid them all bare, the fiddle came alive again, as did the singer and the other musicians with him.

With the fiddle leading the way, a banjo and zither joined in, then a mouth bow. Eleanor had to laugh when the man who'd been singing started dancing, kicking his legs up and moving faster and with greater dexterity than she would have imagined. His missing arm didn't hinder his balance a bit.

" 'If it hadn't been for cotton-eyed Joe,' " the man sang, the words coming so fast she could scarcely understand them. " 'I'd been married long time ago. Where did you come from? Where did you go? Where did you come from, cotton-eyed Joe?' "

The crowd started clapping. Whoops and hollers went up. Even Eleanor found herself tapping her foot in time to the music and swaying. It was impossible to stay still. Judging by the expressions around her, others felt the same. It was the furthest thing from Mozart or Beethoven, but something about the spirit of this music—the chords, and the tempo—touched her down deep.

This music . . . made people happy.

When the song ended, applause filled the sudden silence. Eleanor worked her way through the crowd and deposited some coins into the cup, nodding to the singer when he thanked her.

Returning to her search, she continued on—heart and steps lighter—peering at the numbers as she went.

Ninety-three, ninety-one . . .

She paused to check the cross street—Dogwood. She had to be close. The building couldn't be much—

"Help you find somethin', sweetheart?"

Eleanor looked in the direction of the voice and saw a man staring at her. Two others alongside him looked on, their sneers anything but friendly.

"No." She squared her shoulders. "That won't be necessary."

"You sure?" He moved toward her, his mouth curving in an unseemly slant. " 'Cause you look lost to me. And ah . . ." He stepped closer. His gaze raked over her body—pausing briefly on her reticule—before meeting her eyes again. "I'm a man who knows his way around a woman, if you get my meanin'."

Getting his meaning as well as a *pungent* idea of the number of weeks since his last bath, Eleanor took a backward step—and met with the brick wall behind her. She glanced past the men, and became keenly aware of how empty the street was. And of how alone they were.

The man staring down at her was massively built, taller than she, and thick through the chest. But it was the desperate look about him that put her most on edge.

Eleanor moved to skirt past him, but he grabbed her upper arm. She jerked back, and he held tight.

"Maybe you didn't understand me," he said, this time looking pointedly at her reticule. "I'm curious to know what you got in there. And"—his eyes narrowed—"what you got in that pocket of yours."

Eleanor stilled, the worn fabric between her fingertips swiftly registering. She withdrew the stained handkerchief from her pocket. With it came memories, and an unexpected spark of courage. "I assisted in a surgical tent in the war. A soldier gave this to me during the Battle of Nashville . . . as I watched him die."

The brazenness in the man's eyes faltered for a second, and that was all she needed.

Wrenching her arm from his grip, she reached for bravado she didn't feel, and leached every trace of kindness from her voice. "So while I understand you quite well, sir . . . perhaps you did not understand me. When I say I do not require your assistance, that is *precisely* what I meant."

Not waiting for his response, she pushed past him and strode on, resisting the urge to look back to see if he was following. She strode to the next block, heart thumping, grateful to see other people ahead, and only then did she glance behind her.

No sign of the men.

She hurried on, reading the addresses but more discreetly this time.

There. Just ahead. That had to be it. Eighty-seven Magnolia Street. The address had sounded so charming in the newspaper advertisement. But as Eleanor approached her destination, she wondered if *87 Selenicereus Grandiflorus* might not have been a better choice.

She was tempted to smile at the memory the comparison stirred, but as she stood in front of the building, all frivolity fled. Mindful of the wagons in the street, she paused to get a better look.

At least the building existed. That much was good.

But it was a far cry from what she'd imagined. It was not the "excellent opportunity for a thriving business or enterprising restaurateur" the advertisement had boasted.

Still, the wood-plank structure wasn't leaning to one side, as were its neighbors, and its large glass windows, though caked in dirt, were intact. Same for the windows on the second floor. The ones she could see, anyway.

She tried the front door but, as she'd expected, found it locked. She sighed and peered through the layers of grime and dirt, and felt a tickle of possibility. Or what might have been a possibility, if things had worked out differently.

The front room would have made a wonderful dining area. She could imagine tables draped in simple red-and-white-checked cloths, and sturdy straight-back chairs. Nothing fancy. That wasn't the point. The point was the food, and cooking, and feeding people, and finding a way to a better life. A life with more meaning and purpose, that would also provide for her and her father.

"Sorry, ma'am, but the building's already rented. That's why there's no sign in the window."

Eleanor straightened and turned.

A stout little man staggered back a step. "*Lawd* have mercy, you're a tall woman!"

Maybe it was due to what had happened a moment earlier or perhaps it was watching her dream fade to nothing through a grimy plate-glass window, but Eleanor found her humor in short supply.

"Yes, sir. I am tall. While you"—she looked him up and down, which didn't take long—"are decidedly not."

He frowned as though shocked at her rebuttal, then let out a barking laugh. "And you're quick too! I like me some sass in a woman. Though, no offense to you, ma'am, I like my women shorter." He waggled his thick gray eyebrows. "Where I can cozy up to 'em better."

Eleanor stared, the pieces falling painfully into place. "Mr. Stover, I presume?"

He frowned again. "Yes, ma'am. But how did . . ." His eyes widened. His gaze slid from hers down to her feet then slowly back up again, not a trace of inappropriateness in the act. "Miss *Braddock?*"

"Yes, sir. Eleanor Braddock. It's a . . . pleasure to meet you, Mr. Stover."

"Well, I'll be—" He clamped his mouth shut, then laughed again. "I gotta give it to you, ma'am. You surprised the daylights outta me. And call me Stub, if you want. Everybody else does. Guess you're here to see your building. Come on in. She's a beaut!"

Eleanor started to correct him about it being *her* building. But seeing that he'd already unlocked the door . . . would it hurt to look around before she explained her situation?

If the man had recognized her last name or knew of her relation to Adelicia Cheatham, he'd never made mention of it. And she wasn't about to make the connection for him.

He gave the door a push and, to her surprise, motioned for her to enter first. Perhaps there was a little gentleman in him, after all. She couldn't help but smile at the pun.

Walking off his frustration, Marcus made his way across town, still coming to grips with what Adelicia Cheatham had asked him to do. And that he'd agreed to do it! It was approaching midmorning, and wagons and carriages clogged the streets, vying for passage at a hasty clip.

He had to admit, the woman was, by far, one of the best negotiators he'd ever had the pleasure— and slight displeasure, at the moment—of meeting.

And her secret—he'd learned too late—was *patience*.

No telling how long she'd been planning this, waiting for the opportune time to spring the idea on him. Although, he reluctantly acknowledged, for months now he'd been getting the better end of their arrangement.

But today all that had changed with her request.

Designing and installing a garden wasn't the main issue. Although designing gardens for rich women wasn't high on his list of priorities, he could easily accomplish the task. And the extra work would present a challenge if his firm was awarded the contract to build the opera house, but his company could handle both projects.

No, the real issue was *where* Mrs. Cheatham wanted the garden designed and installed. He almost laughed thinking of how it would look on his résumé. Or better yet, in *Nashville's Daily Banner*.

He could see the headline now—AUSTRIAN ARCHITECT DESIGNS GARDENS FOR THE INSANE.

He crossed the street, heading in the direction of Foster's Textile Mill, where his crew would already be at work. Determined to put the meeting with Mrs. Cheatham out of his mind, he moved his focus to the day's work. The renovation of the textile mill and warehouse was nearly complete. All they needed to do was install the new front entrance and put up the—

His thoughts broke rein, and he shook his head. *The Tennessee Asylum for the Insane.* Every time he thought of the place Adelicia Cheatham wanted him to construct a garden, he relived the scene in her office. . . .

"I want you to create a beauty spot, Mr. Geoffrey," she'd explained. "That's what my father used to call gardens, God rest him. Every place needs one, and the asylum needs one desperately. Oh, and a small plot for a vegetable garden too. I visited the institution not long ago, and the place is all brick and stone and mortar. Hardly a setting conducive for healing body and soul."

"The . . . asylum?" he'd questioned. "For the *insane?*"

She gave him that cool look. "Do you know of another asylum in the city, Mr. Geoffrey?"

"No, madam, I do not. But—"

"And not everyone there is insane, Mr. Geoffrey. Some of them merely need rest. And . . . quiet." She studied him, a calculating look in her eyes. "Do you not believe in the soothing nature of beauty?"

He looked at her then, knowing he was a goner.

He wasn't certain if Adelicia had a personal connection to the asylum, other than that her husband, Dr. William Cheatham, had once been the asylum's director. But from whatever source her motivation stemmed, he was aggravated with himself for being caught off guard.

The aroma of freshly baked bread caught his attention, followed by the faint but steady pounding at the back of his head. With breakfast far behind him, he needed something to ward off this *schrecklich* headache before it took hold. And he knew just the prescription. He headed in the direction of the yeasty scent.

Intentionally redirecting his thoughts, he studied the structural lines of the buildings he passed and found himself contrasting the differences in architecture and how they flowed together—or didn't.

Clapboard structures neighbored brick, which stood shoulder to shoulder with buildings of cinder block and those of roughhewn pine. The remnants of war still hung over the city like a threadbare cloak. He saw it in the boarded-up buildings dotting the side streets and in the deserted warehouses hulking dark and empty near the river.

But the once-faltering heartbeat of this city was gradually regaining its rhythm, and he was determined to be part of that process.

He spotted the familiar yellow-and-white-striped awning of the bakery ahead and was grateful when he didn't see a line trailing out the door. What awaited inside wasn't his mother's homemade apple strudel, God rest her soul, but it was plenty good.

And the coffee . . .

He liked his coffee hot and strong, and Leonard Fitch always kept a fresh pot matching those expectations.

Inside the bakery, Marcus joined the queue of patrons. The aroma of cinnamon and freshly baked bread whetted his appetite.

As he neared the counter, a boy standing off to the side drew his attention. The boy—perhaps eleven or twelve, of average height but thin, and wearing a *Kippah*—had Fitch engaged in conversation. Or perhaps *negotiation* better described it.

"*Three* doughnuts this time, please, Mr. Fitch. I will do everything you request, *and* sweep out the storeroom *and* haul all the trash out to the back."

Fitch frowned and rubbed his jaw, but Marcus knew the man well enough to know the look was part of the negotiation. He also recognized the boy's accent. Salzburg, perhaps. Or maybe one of its surrounding farming communities.

The boy's English was good, and his balance of respect and cleverness even better. Especially for one so young.

"You drive a hard bargain, Caleb. But . . . I believe we have ourselves a deal." Fitch shook the boy's hand and gave him a subtle wink. "Go on now. Get to work."

The boy didn't wait to be told twice.

Fitch looked up. "*Guten Morgen*, Marcus! I expected to see you a little earlier."

Leonard Fitch was the only person in Nashville —in all of America—who addressed him by his Christian name. But Marcus didn't mind. It felt good to hear his preferred given name spoken aloud every now and then, instead of always Herr or Mr. Geoffrey.

Fitch hadn't a speck of Austrian in him, yet he'd insisted on learning a few German greetings. Marcus recalled the morning he'd stepped into the bakery—his third or fourth visit, if memory served—only to hear a hearty "*Guten Morgen*, Herr Geoffrey" coming from behind the counter. The simple courtesy had connected him to this older gentleman in a way he still found surprising.

Leonard Fitch had proven himself a trustworthy friend, and Marcus had frequented the establishment pretty much every morning since. And since everyone in Nashville addressed the proprietor of the city's best bakery as Fitch, he did the same.

"*Guten Morgen*, Fitch. How is the world treating you this fine day?"

"Pretty fair. 'Bout as good as I've treated it so far, I guess. Coffee?"

"The largest cup you have."

A moment later, Fitch handed him a steaming mug. "Your regular order?"

Marcus nodded and took a sip, relishing the strong brew. He laid his coins on the counter and raised his cup in silent greeting to Mrs. Fitch, whose expression was kind but harried. Then he moved to a vacant table off to the side.

Soon after, Fitch joined him with his own cup of coffee and two fresh doughnuts. He nudged the doughnuts in Marcus's direction.

Marcus bit into one, and the sweetness filled his mouth. *Best doughnuts in town.* That's what the sign above the door said, and it was true. Fitch made them from scratch every morning. And once they were gone, folks were out of luck until the following day.

"You get word?" Fitch asked, eying him over the rim of his cup.

Marcus shook his head, knowing what he was referring to. "Not yet." Both the *Republican Banner* and the *Union and American* newspapers had published the names of the four companies that initially submitted bids, so that was common knowledge. But he'd further confided in Fitch about his specific designs for the opera house, and knew Fitch had glimpsed his passion. "I was told a fifth bid was submitted at the last moment." He shared the outcome of his meeting with Barrett, sparing Fitch the details.

Fitch sipped his coffee. "So now, you wait. Again."

Marcus shrugged. "So it would seem."

As they talked, the queue at the counter gradually lengthened again, and Fitch stood. He retrieved a copy of the *Republican Banner* from a nearby table and plunked it down in front of Marcus, then tapped a side column.

"In case you haven't read today's edition yet."

Midbite, Marcus read the headline, then scanned the article—and looked up.

Fitch raised a brow. "Maybe there's an opportunity there."

Marcus finished chewing. "I desire to build a work of art the beauty of which America has never seen. Not an—"

"I know." Fitch had the look about him that he always did when he thought he was right but didn't want to force the issue. "But there's a lot of money in that group of ladies, Marcus." He tapped the newspaper again. "Their pockets go deep in the midst of what's otherwise a pretty shallow pond right now. So maybe nobody outside of Nashville would ever hear about it. But a lot of local people would, and that might stir up something else that—"

"I appreciate what you're saying. And if my goal were to gain the favor of wealthy females in this city, then perhaps. But my purpose in coming to Nashville is—"

Fitch held up a hand. " 'Nuff said. It was just a thought."

"A passing one, I hope . . . my friend." Marcus raised a brow.

Fitch offered something that resembled a nod but grinned a little as he walked away, which told Marcus the man hoped he would give the topic further consideration. But Fitch would have to be disappointed on that count.

Marcus sipped his coffee, glancing down at the article again—NASHVILLE WOMEN'S LEAGUE TO BUILD NEW TEA HALL. A tea hall. For a group of wealthy women, no less. Mrs. Cheatham's name listed first among them.

He shook his head. Whoever took that job would have at least twenty bosses, all of them wearing skirts, and none of them agreeing on anything.

No, thank you.

He downed the dregs of his mug and spotted the young negotiator returning from his labors, the satisfied swagger of a job well done in the boy's demeanor. Caleb collected his payment and devoured one of the doughnuts before he reached the door.

Something about the scene stirred Marcus.

Though Jews in Austria currently enjoyed an equality of sorts with their fellow countrymen, that hadn't always been the case. He wondered how long Caleb and his family had been in America.

Long enough, obviously, for the youth to have learned English.

Odd, but he found himself a little envious of how at home the boy seemed in his own skin. Here he was a grown man of thirty-three, and he still didn't feel at ease with who he was. Or who he was expected to be.

Marcus stood, not welcoming the path his thoughts had taken. Would he ever truly be the man he wanted to be? Especially when, come next summer, he would leave everything to return to duty, to fulfill the crown's calling.

Part of him answered emphatically, *"Yes!"* but another part of him seemed to hear another voice, and uttered not a word.

He made eye contact with Fitch as he left, only then noticing that his headache was better. Fitch's coffee and doughnuts—or maybe it was the man's company—always seemed to help.

Marcus crossed the busy thoroughfare, then cut down a lesser-used side street. Only a block from the textile mill, the foot traffic thinned, and from somewhere behind him came the sound of scuffling, followed by a groan. He paused, then retraced his steps to the alleyway. . . .

Indignation flooded his chest. His face heated. "Hey!" he called out, and the largest of the four boys—the other three pinning Caleb to the ground—turned his head and looked back. But the boy's feet remained firmly planted, his stance unchanged.

And Marcus quickly realized why.

8

The stench of urine on Caleb's clothes was strong.

The four boys took off running, and Marcus started to give chase, but as soon as the youths reached the street, they split up, and one look at Caleb told Marcus the boy needed his attention. They'd beaten him pretty badly. Multiple cuts and already-purpling bruises marred the boy's face and neck, but what worried him most was the humiliation the boy had suffered.

Little question existed in Marcus's mind about *why* the boys had done it. Hearing the degrading names they'd called Caleb revealed much.

Marcus helped the boy up and over to a bench outside the dry-goods store and sat next to him, looking into eyes that seemed years older than the boy's age.

"Here," he said, pressing his handkerchief to a gash on Caleb's chin to stanch the bleeding. "Hold it there. Apply pressure."

Caleb did as told. "Thank you, sir, for stopping when you did. And for helping me."

Marcus hesitated, already anticipating the answer to his question before he asked it. "This has . . . happened before?"

Caleb bowed his head. "People must be taught to be kind. It is in their nature to be otherwise." He lifted his gaze. "That is what my papa used to say."

"Used to?"

"He died," the boy said softly. "Earlier this year."

The starkness in the youth's voice, the way he stared ahead as though searching for something that wasn't there and never would be again, robbed Marcus of any response, save a roughly whispered "I'm sorry."

Caleb nodded but didn't look up.

"And your mother?" Marcus asked, hoping for the boy's sake she was still living.

"She misses him," Caleb whispered. "Same as me."

The gut-honest reply tugged at Marcus's heart, while also rekindling his anger.

"Do you know the boys who did this?"

Caleb's silence spoke loudly enough.

"Would you be willing to tell the authorities their names?"

Gradually, Caleb lifted his gaze, then slowly shook his head. "People who do things like that will not stop simply because you ask them to . . . sir."

Then it hit Marcus that he hadn't introduced himself yet. He held out his hand. "I'm Marcus Geoffrey."

Caleb's grip was strong and sure. "My name is Caleb Lebenstein."

Marcus raised an eyebrow. "Couldn't hide from that one even if you wanted to."

The boy grinned, apparently understanding. "And you cannot hide either . . . Herr Gottfried."

For a brief second, Marcus thought Caleb was referring to his family's royal lineage. Then he quickly realized the boy was merely referencing their shared heritage, as well as cleverly revealing that he was aware of Marcus's use of the American-sounding version of his family name. Smart lad.

"You're right." Marcus nodded. "We both have things about us that reveal who we are." He was struck by how true that was. Truer than the boy knew.

"My papa said a name is just a name. That it is the man behind the name that makes the man who he really is."

Again Marcus stared. Such an old soul in one so young. "I wish I could have known your father, Caleb."

"I wish you could have too," he acknowledged.

Seeing the crusted blood on Caleb's chin brought Marcus back to the previous conversation. "This country has laws, Caleb. Laws to protect people. If the parents of those boys knew what they'd done, the boys would be punished."

Caleb gave him a doubtful look, then glanced away before turning back again. "Do you know the worst of it?"

Marcus said nothing, but looked down at the boy's coat, able to guess.

"They took my doughnuts."

Marcus had to smile at the unexpected answer and the lopsided grin that followed. "Well . . . I think we can remedy that."

He stood, and Caleb rose with him, but shaking his head.

"I do not have any money, Herr Geoffrey. I—"

"The doughnuts will be a *gift*."

Caleb looked up at him, and blinked.

"*Ein Geschenk*," Marcus repeated, motioning for him to follow.

Caleb fell into step beside him. "*Ja, ich weiß ein Geschenk*. I was surprised by your offer. That is all. *Danke*! Do you think Mr. Fitch will have any left?"

Marcus shrugged, impressed by the boy's ease in alternating between languages. Reminded him of another boy about the same age . . . another lifetime ago. "I don't know. But have you tried the fritters yet?"

Caleb squinted. "What are . . . fritters?"

Marcus laughed softly. "That's precisely what I said when I first heard about them." Seeing the boy's curiosity, he was reminded of how his own Grandfather Marcus, his namesake, had toyed with him in a good-natured way, and how he'd relished it. His maternal grandfather had been able to hold a straight face longer than anyone he'd ever known, even as the promise of a smile lingered at the edges of the old man's voice. And he'd had the strongest grip of any man Marcus had encountered.

"Fritters are a little larger than a mouse," Marcus continued, "but not as fat as a rat." He paused and held his thumb and forefinger apart to indicate the size, and to add a little credence to the story. "They're hard to catch, but once you do, you fry them right up . . ." He made a satisfied sound. "And they're delicious."

Caleb eyed him, cocking his head to one side. Marcus simply waited. Then Caleb began to laugh. A deep, cleansing sound. And though Marcus couldn't be certain, he wondered if that was the first time the boy had really laughed in months. He knew the feeling. It had taken him months following Rutger's death to feel joy or truly laugh. But it was returning again. Slowly.

And it felt good.

As they walked on, Marcus explained what a fritter really was.

"And they are good?" Caleb asked, climbing the stairs to the bakery.

"*Very* good."

"As good as my *Mutter*'s strudel?"

Holding the door open, Marcus paused and stared down. "*Nothing* is ever as good as your *Mutter*'s strudel."

Having seen almost every square inch of the building—except the room she most wanted to see—Eleanor took a moment to size up the front area again, listening as Mr. Stover finished yet another story. A little rough around the edges and with an endless supply of tall tales, he seemed a kind enough man.

Dust covered the floors and walls, even more so in the second-story's bedrooms. But nothing that a good sweeping and mopping wouldn't remedy. She was surprised at how much the thought of cleaning the place appealed to her. She wished she could roll up her sleeves and scrub the building until it shined.

But circumstances quickly reminded her that it wasn't *her* building. Not anymore.

Mr. Stover brought his boot down hard on the floor. "Darn roaches. Wish winter would come and kill 'em all off again."

"Cold weather won't necessarily kill all of them, Mr. Stover. Some species hibernate through the winter, even through the freezing cold. That's why there are so many of them."

He looked at her. "Do tell. You one of them women who went to school and everything?"

She smiled at the quirk of his brow. "Yes, I'm one of those."

He opened his mouth as though to respond, then froze. "The post office!" he said suddenly, rubbing his jaw. "I was supposed to leave the contract there, wasn't I?"

She nodded. Not that it mattered much now. But how to tell him that . . .

"I'll get it to you. But first come on in here, Miss Braddock. I'll show you the kitchen."

Finally, the room she most wanted to see.

She followed him through a doorway and around a corner and was pleasantly surprised to discover sunlight flooding a spacious kitchen. "Whoever designed this had forethought for utilizing natural light."

He squinted. "Say again, ma'am?"

Curbing a grin, she gestured to the bank of windows. "The person who designed this building put windows in all the right places."

"Ah . . ." He nodded. "That *person* would be me."

She stilled. "You built this, Mr. Stover?"

He laughed. "And I didn't go to school or *nothin'*."

She laughed along with him, aware of the extra twang he'd added. For her benefit, no doubt. "School doesn't teach you everything. Sometimes not even the most important things."

She admired the workmanship of the cabinets. The drawers slid easily without sticking. The cabinet doors lay flush and square against the shelving. The kitchen even came furnished with pots and pans, bowls and utensils. Everything she needed. It was perfect for her.

She imagined herself cooking there, baking. The sturdy worktable seemed to beckon for a dusting of flour and a yeasty scrap of dough to be kneaded to a glossy shine on its smooth planks. She could almost feel the suppleness beneath her fingers. Baking bread had been a challenge when she was younger. Now it was therapy, almost an addiction.

But . . . this wasn't meant to be.

"There's a well out back. The hand pump gets stuck every now and then. But give it some elbow grease, and it works right good."

Eleanor took it all in. "You did a fine job, Mr. Stover. And what a nice, large kitchen in which to cook."

His smile dimmed as he looked toward the stove. "My wife always liked it. Made some mighty fine meals in this kitchen."

Catching the past tense, Eleanor trailed his gaze, trying to imagine what he was seeing in his mind's eye. She remembered what he'd written in his letter. "You and your wife ran a boardinghouse together here?"

"She did it mostly. I helped some. Back then I was workin' for the railroad. Then the war came. And she got sick, and . . ."

For a second, it appeared as though he might say more. Then he lowered his head.

Eleanor tried to think of a response, but silence seemed to fit best. Giving him a moment, she continued looking through the kitchen, confronted by the fact that everyone had hurts. No matter who they were, or what kind of home they lived in, or what family they came from, no one was immune.

The thought wasn't new to her. If not for moments like these, there were times when life's hurts became so overwhelming, so blinding, that a person could be lulled into believing that he— or she—was the only one.

"Mrs. Stover, she . . ." He swallowed, the sound audible in the silence. "My wife made a buttermilk pie that could warm your belly like nothin' else. Did it in one of those pans right there." He motioned to iron skillets and pie tins hanging neatly on the wall. "She always had plans to open up a little eatin' place, too. A *café,* she called it.

Out front there. So when I got your letter, Miss Braddock, it just seemed to be the right fit. *And* the right time."

Eleanor looked at him. "Do you mean . . . the building has been empty since . . ." She let the sentence trail off.

He nodded. "She's been gone almost five years now, ma'am. Just didn't feel right at first, openin' up somethin' else when this was hers. But it's time. And if you don't mind me sayin', Miss Braddock . . . I think my sweet Eloise—I always called her Weezie—would welcome you cookin' in her kitchen."

Eleanor felt a pang of regret, stemming both from what he'd said and from dreading what she must tell him.

"Mr. Stover, I need to discuss our agreement. You were kind enough to allow me to sign a lease for three months, a much shorter term than you desired, I know. But . . . I'm afraid I . . ." Her admission was even more difficult in light of what he'd shared. "I find myself without the necessary funding to open my restaurant. I was so certain it would come to fruition. But . . . it didn't. And unfortunately I don't see any immediate solution on the horizon."

He didn't answer right off, just ran his hand along the top of the oak worktable. "So . . . you're sayin' you won't be takin' it after all?"

Eleanor shook her head. "I'm sorry, Mr. Stover. I wish I could." More than she could say. . . .

She felt awkward asking her next question, but in light of her financial situation, she had little choice. "The contract I signed—and that I *will* abide by—stated that my three months' rent was not refundable. I understand that," she hastened to add. "But if you *are* able to rent the space within those three months, would you consider returning whatever portion remains? It would be a great help to me. But again, I recognize you're under no obligation to do so."

He looked at her with something akin to admiration. "My Weezie was a good talker too. Knew how to string words together like you do, so that they all made sense. And yes, ma'am, I'll get the sign back up, and we'll see what comes."

Back in the front room, Eleanor paused, her heart telling her one thing, while her head told her another. Finally, an idea having formed, she found it wouldn't let go.

Key in hand, Mr. Stover looked back from where he stood by the door. "You all right, Miss Braddock?"

Eleanor surveyed the room. "I wonder, Mr. Stover. . . . Would you allow me to make a business proposition? It's something I think might profit us both."

After accompanying Caleb part of the way home, well past the alley where the boys had attacked him, Marcus waved good-bye to the boy. He was grateful Fitch had still had a few doughnuts left.

Turning the corner toward the textile mill, Marcus glanced up, and slowed his pace, his attention drawn to a building across the street, or more rightly, to the woman standing in the open doorway of the building. There was no mistaking who she was. His question centered around what Adelicia Acklen Cheatham's niece was doing in the city's warehouse district. And why, of all the oddities, she would be shaking hands with a man?

He started across the street, his first thought to ensure her safety. But when she looked his way, alarm tightened her features. Then it struck him . . . She hadn't appeared the least distressed—

Until seeing him.

9

By the time Marcus crossed the street, the man was walking away and Miss Braddock stood alone by the closed door. All signs of alarm had been smoothed from her expression, and carefully crafted composure was in its place. He had to hand it to her—she was not a woman ruled by emotion.

He liked that. Along with the fact that she didn't seem particularly fond of him. It was a rare occurrence for him with women—one he found irresistible.

"Mr. Geoffrey!" She managed a smile that almost appeared genuine. "What a coincidence . . . meeting you in town." She slipped something into her pocket. Or tried.

A key landed with a dull thud on the hard-packed dirt.

She bent to retrieve it, but he beat her to it, catching her grimace.

The iron key was heavy and deeply notched, crafted for a substantial lock. Much like the lock on the door behind her.

Marcus glanced down the street. The man she'd been speaking with moments earlier, some distance away now, turned and briefly looked back in their direction. Marcus didn't recognize him.

He turned his attention back. "Good morning, Miss Braddock." Bowing slightly, he held out the key, and she scooped it from his palm, her annoyance clear. "And you're right, it *is* a coincidence. I wasn't expecting to see you either. And certainly not in this particular neighborhood."

"Yes, well . . . I . . ." For an instant, her expression faltered. Then her lips formed a tight curve, and she gripped the key as though imagining it were his throat. "I had business to tend to this morning. As you must surely have for my aunt's estate, Mr. Geoffrey. So please"—she gestured as though admonishing a child to run along—"don't let me detain you."

Not many things tempted Marcus to smile. But she did. He liked that she thought him an under gardener. For the time being, anyway.

He looked at the door behind her, his imagination

running rampant. Whatever *business* drew her here, she didn't want him to know about it. But what would a woman like Miss Braddock want with an old clapboard building when she had the entire Belmont estate at her disposal?

She was formidable when it came to sparring, but that only made the challenge more appealing. And he liked having the upper hand. Especially when remembering how much pleasure she'd taken in putting him in his place yesterday with her comment about his compliments needing work. And about the *Selenicereus grandiflorus.*

"It is most kind of you, Miss Braddock, to concern yourself with my schedule. But I am, in fact, in no particular hurry." He withdrew his pocket watch and checked the time, partly for show, but also mindful of his needing to get to the textile mill. "So . . . your ladyship . . ." He bowed again for show, then closed the watch with a *snap,* aware of the smugness in his tone. And the frown on her face. "You may happily consider me at your disposal."

Looking as though she *would* like to dispose of him, she leveled her gaze, unblinking. Her expression told him she knew exactly what he was doing, which only increased his satisfaction.

He took a step back and pretended to size up the structure. "Don't tell me Mrs. Cheatham has decided to expand her estate and commissioned you as purchaser on her behalf?"

The stone-faced stare the comment earned only spurred him on. "Or better yet, you're looking for a place in the city to escape the ordinariness of Belmont?" He nodded, acting as though he were considering the property. "Very nice choice. Large windows." He peered through the grime. "Spacious front parlor. Excellent location."

Seeing her eyes narrow, he wondered what tack she would take. Would she sidestep the issue and retreat? Or would she confront and defend her ground as before?

He knew which response he hoped for.

"You are correct, Mr. Geoffrey." Her tone was strict, and she squared her shoulders in a gesture he was already coming to recognize. "Unfortunately for me, sir, you have the advantage in this situation, as we are *both* keenly aware."

Marcus didn't dare interrupt, seeing she wasn't finished yet and also sensing victory close at hand.

"While I had hoped to take care of this errand quietly"—she hesitated, seeming to choose her words with care—"I see that fate has robbed me of that blissful opportunity." Her thin smile took on fuller life. "Unfortunately for you, Mr. Geoffrey, I'm not easily coerced or intimidated. So, my *dear* sir . . ." She tugged on the hem of her sleeve, the smugness in her tone reminiscent of his. "If you'll please excuse me."

She stepped back to the door, slid the key into the lock, and turned it. Giving the latch a firm shake, and apparently satisfied, she slipped the key into her skirt pocket and, with a parting glance, turned on her heel and strode away.

Marcus watched her go, feeling strangely denied. Not bothering to check his watch this time, he pursued.

Despite her determined stride, he caught up with her easily. "Though the possibility of Mrs. Cheatham purchasing the building still holds merit, I believe, from your behavior just now, that—"

"My behavior?" she asked, casting him a sideways glance.

"Yes, that's right." He liked the way she lifted her chin ever so slightly when she was on the defensive. "I believe the building holds more of a personal connection for you. My only question is why?"

She smiled. "That's odd . . . I would think your only question *should* be why you're about to run into that wagon."

Turning back, Marcus saw the obstacle just in time and narrowly avoided it. But he didn't miss her satisfied laughter.

Eleanor increased her pace, knowing it would make little difference. Of all the people she could have happened upon in town—and at *that* building—why did it have to be him—this overly confident and most definitely too-high-brow-for-his-own-good under gardener who, for some reason, seemed to take pleasure in annoying her.

And he was good at it too.

When Mr. Geoffrey fell into step beside her again, she looked over at him. "Shouldn't you be off planting a tree or"—she made a face—"making something more beautiful?"

His laughter was deep and punctuated, and could easily become addictive, she decided. Not unlike the man, annoying though he was.

"I'll do that later. But for now, I thought I'd escort you to wherever it is you're going next."

"In the hopes, no doubt, that my next destination will lend a clue to the mystery of my last?"

He nodded. "Precisely."

She laughed. "I hate to disappoint, Mr. Geoffrey, but *that's* where I'm going next." She indicated with a wave of her hand.

He trailed her wave, and a smile reached his eyes even if it didn't alter his mouth. "The sign does not lie, madam. They truly *are* the best in town."

As he opened the door, she noticed how finely tailored his suit was. Whatever appointment he had on behalf of her aunt must be of an important nature. She started to comment on his manner of dress, but caught a whiff of a yeasty aroma coming from within the bakery and all else faded.

She stepped inside and breathed deeply, her mouth watering. The aroma alone was worth the visit.

"*Guten Tag*, Marcus!"

Marcus? Peering over the line of patrons in front of them, Eleanor saw a man behind the counter waving in their direction—at Mr. Geoffrey. Mr. *Marcus* Geoffrey, apparently. She looked beside her. The name suited him.

Mr. Geoffrey returned the gesture. "*Guten Tag*, Fitch."

Eleanor waited a few seconds, then leaned closer, lowering her voice. "Frequent patron, are you . . . Marcus?"

Faced forward, he nodded once, the scarcest hint of a smile showing. "Now that you know *my* given name, Miss Braddock . . . would you do me the honor of telling me yours?"

She liked looking at him from the side. Actually, she liked looking at him from any angle. Although heaven help her if he ever knew. The man's ego practically entered the room before he did.

"Francesca," she answered with some hesitation, then schooled a grin when he turned to look at her.

"I don't think so," he said softly.

She tried to appear affronted, but it didn't work. "When I was growing up, Francesca is the name I always wished my parents had given me. It sounded so . . . elegant and adventuresome."

"But?"

All humor departed. "They named me Eleanor instead."

"Eleanor," he repeated, the name sounding far more enchanting the way he said it. "Much better."

Eleanor stood a little straighter, actually liking her name a little better.

Two patrons ahead of them in line, a young woman turned and looked back at Marcus, then nudged her friend, who also sneaked a none-too-subtle gander. The women giggled like schoolgirls, heads together, whispering.

At first, Eleanor didn't think Marcus noticed. Then a look of crafted nonchalance passed over his face, giving him away. He noticed all right. And further, he seemed accustomed to the attention. But of course he would be, handsome as he was.

Moments passed. The queue moved slowly. And Marcus sighed at least twice, peering over heads. Apparently the man wasn't accustomed to waiting.

She cleared her throat. "From where does the name Geoffrey originate? It doesn't sound very German."

"That's because I'm Austrian."

"Which . . . is German."

He frowned. "The two peoples share a common language but little more. And the family name is actually . . . Gottfried. Geoffrey is the Americanized version."

She nodded, knowing other German immigrants who'd changed their names for various reasons. Though their accents, like his, were impossible to miss.

When they reached the counter, Mr. Geoffrey—Marcus—introduced her to the proprietors and ordered two doughnuts and two coffees. She reached into her reticule.

"No," he said quietly. "Please, allow me."

She pulled out her coin purse. "Thank you, Mr. Geoffrey, but I'm *quite* capable of paying for myself."

He met her gaze. "*That* was never in question, Miss Braddock."

Aware of Mr. and Mrs. Fitch looking on and of

how quiet the patrons around them had grown, Eleanor acquiesced.

Marcus led her to a table by the window but didn't sit. "I'm sorry I can't join you. I need to be on my way." A smile played at the corners of his mouth. "Trees to plant and weeds to pull, you know."

To her surprise, he placed both doughnuts before her.

She frowned. "You're not eating one?"

"I stopped by earlier." A devilish smile swept his face. "I already ate mine."

Despite his brawny confidence, Eleanor didn't wish to appear rude. "Well, thank you for the pastries. And my apologies if I seemed ungrateful just now. That wasn't my intention. I'm . . ." She looked up at him. Why would such a man—even if only an under gardener—take such an interest in her? "I'm unaccustomed to having things done for me." She gestured toward the counter. "Including that."

He leaned down. "Well . . . Eleanor," he whispered, "you'd better *start* growing accustomed to it."

An unaccounted-for shiver passed through her.

"After all," he continued, "you live at the Belmont estate now, and you're the niece of the wealthiest woman in America."

And just like that, the shiver was gone. That was why he was being so kind to her—she was Adelicia Acklen Cheatham's niece. And a *rich* niece in his mind, no doubt. Add to that, he was employed by her aunt. Sadly, discovering his motivation wasn't a big surprise.

Eleanor managed a smile but didn't feel it on the inside.

"Trust me, your ladyship," he continued, a gleam in his eyes, "I *will* figure out why you have a key to that building."

"I'm certain you will, *Marcus.* Though the real reason will pale in comparison to your imagination, I assure you. And I would prefer you not address me as *your ladyship.*"

"And why is that? After all, you *are* the niece of Mrs. Adelicia Acklen Cheatham. Which, if you believe what you read in the newspapers"—amusement lit his expression—"she's American royalty. Which, in turn, makes you—"

"Please." Eleanor held up a hand. "Don't say it."

Her reaction seemed to take him aback. But only for a second or two.

"Does madam feel uncomfortable with the role she's been given to play?"

"Madam," she parroted back, trying not to appear as much out of sorts as she suddenly felt, "does not appreciate being compared to a group of pompous, self-centered people who have no understanding of real life, much less any interest in making a meaningful contribution to the lives of others."

Eleanor blinked. The words had left her tongue effortlessly. She could scarcely believe she'd thought of *precisely* the right thing to say in the very moment she needed to say it. And she'd said it to *him,* no less. It felt good. And yet . . .

Judging from the blank look on Marcus's face, he was equally surprised.

"Well," he said softly. His smile didn't come as easily this time. "I don't wish to wear out my welcome. I hope you enjoy your doughnuts, Miss Braddock. Good day to you, madam."

He downed a quick drink of coffee, then deposited his mug on the counter, waving to Mr. Fitch as he left.

Eleanor peered out the window, watching him until he disappeared from sight, a part of her regretting what she'd said. And yet she didn't know why.

She hoped he wouldn't mention anything to Aunt Adelicia about the building, or her having a key. But then, it was doubtful Adelicia Cheatham was on a first-name basis with any of her under gardeners.

Seeking comfort, she sank her teeth into a warm, sugary fried little piece of heaven.

Closing her eyes, she chewed. And savored.

Delicious didn't begin to describe it. She took another bite. Who needed men when there was such food? She might've smiled at the thought if there'd been the least hope of her dream of owning a restaurant ever coming true.

Finished with the first doughnut, she studied the second, while considering a third. She looked around the bakery. If this was the competition, she might as well go ahead and hang up her pots, pans, and pie tins.

Not that she had any other choice.

● ● ●

Marcus read the headline on Monday morning's *Republican Banner* and, at first, he couldn't believe it. So he read it again—and disappointment hit him square in the chest. Followed swiftly by anger.

He scanned the article beneath the banner— MAYOR AWARDS NEW PROJECT—and his blood began to simmer.

He pushed back from the table and stood. He'd known this was a possibility. Over the past few days, he'd simply come to think that—

Well, it didn't matter now what he'd thought.

"Mr. Geoffrey! How are you this fine . . ." Mrs. Taylor, the proprietress of the boardinghouse, at least twenty years his senior, took a step back. Her eyes widened. "I hope that stormy expression isn't aimed at me, Mr. Geoffrey. Or a reaction to the breakfast served you just now?"

Marcus sighed. "No, madam. Everything was excellent, as always. But if you don't mind"—he held up the newspaper—"I'd like to borrow this for the morning."

"Certainly." She reached to clear his dishes. "Oh! A parcel and a letter arrived for you a moment ago. The parcel came *special delivery*. From Boston, I believe, sir. It's on the bookcase in the hallway."

"Thank you, Mrs. Taylor." Hoping the package contained what Luther Burbank had promised to send him—almost a month ago—Marcus headed for the entrance hall.

The last time he was with the gifted botanist,

Burbank had commented, "Those who are making history, Mr. Geoffrey, seldom have time to record it." And while Marcus agreed that journaling results was tedious work, he was convinced the key to what they were searching for was in the details. Somewhere . . .

As he'd hoped, the package was from Burbank. But the letter—Marcus stiffened as he opened the nondescript outer envelope only to find another sealed envelope within—was from the baroness. Her third in as many weeks. Baroness Albrecht von Haas's missives were becoming more frequent and insistent in tone, always inquisitive as to the exact date of his return, and as to why he didn't respond more promptly to her letters. Especially given, as she phrased it, ". . . *the bliss of our impending nuptials, my darling.*"

The familiar ache in the back of his head began to thrum.

In his room, he quickly set aside the letter, then opened the package and leafed through a notebook containing scribbled captions alongside fairly well-sketched drawings. Thankfully, Burbank's attention to sketching was better than that of note taking, and Marcus looked forward to reviewing the man's findings in greater detail.

But for now, he unfolded the single page of stationery on the top and read the script.

Dear Mr. Geoffrey,

    I received your correspondence dated July 30

and reviewed it with great eagerness. Indeed, your findings regarding the potato grafts are not dissimilar to my own. However, I have every reason to believe that a recent graft I made from two lesser-known varieties will prove most successful, and may very well be the answer for which both of us have been searching.

Enclosed are my own field notes, hastily penned though they are, and in sad condition compared to yours. I will write again with news—hopefully of a celebratory nature—once the plants have matured.

Grateful for our partnership,
Luther Burbank

Marcus stared at the words, and even as he felt a spark of hope over Burbank's promising accomplishment and what it would mean for millions of people around the world, he felt his own hope deflate. First the mayor's announcement in the newspaper, and now this. Were both of his aspirations destined for failure?

Disappointment fueling his frustration, he stowed the collection of field notes in the trunk at the foot of his bed and turned to leave . . . but saw the unopened letter from the baroness on the dresser. He debated, then . . . feeling only the slightest twinge of guilt, he locked the door to the room behind him and headed to the mayor's office seven blocks away.

He'd gone a full two blocks before a thought

occurred to him about Burbank's potential discovery. A thought that both encouraged and shamed him. How many times had he thought he'd found the exact graft that would produce a better, more disease-resistant potato, only to be disappointed when, once the plant matured, he unearthed not what he'd been hoping for, but the same shrunken clusters of blighted tubers instead?

So just because Burbank *thought* he'd found the answer didn't mean he had. Still, the man's instincts when it came to plants were remarkable. He was gifted.

As he walked, Marcus sorted out the twists life had thrown him this morning and tried to focus his thoughts. He found the task helped along by a recurring image of Miss Braddock—*Eleanor*—who had been the subject of many a thought in the handful of days since their chance encounter in town.

He pictured her standing in front of that dreary little clapboard building, stately shoulders back, expression defiant, and he found himself wanting to see her again. Which was precisely why he'd made no attempt to do so.

But he couldn't stop thinking about what she'd said to him before they'd parted ways. It had struck closer to home than she could have imagined. *"Madam does not appreciate being compared to a group of pompous, self-centered people . . ."*

Every word from her lips had sliced. And the knowledge that she didn't know the truth about him made her stated opinion even more painful.

But one thing he knew wasn't true . . .

Contrary to the second half of her statement, he *was* attempting to make a meaningful contribution to others' lives. Albeit he wasn't having great success at the moment. . . .

Whatever her connection to the property, he'd witnessed no change in the building when he'd passed by yesterday afternoon. But perhaps if living at the boardinghouse became unbearable—a trace of humor softened his frustration—he could request she rent a room to him. Imagining her reaction lightened the unseen weight on his shoulders.

He passed the bakery and something else she'd said returned on a whisper. *"Shouldn't you be off planting a tree or making something more beautiful?"* Remembering her sarcastic remark encouraged a smile.

While it also . . . didn't.

He liked being seen as a common man in her eyes, so that wasn't the bothersome part. He also liked that she seemed to be warming to him, at least a little. Or perhaps she was simply being kind to her "aunt's under gardener."

Whichever proved to be the case . . . when the timing was right, when he was through having his fun, he would clear up her little misassumption.

No, what bothered him was the possibility of her discovering who he *really* was, who he *had* been. Not his connection to the House of Habsburg. The title of Archduke would matter little to a woman like Eleanor Braddock in the long run. Oh, she might be impressed at first. Then again, as he recalled what she'd said, likely not.

But when it came to the man he'd been *as* archduke . . .

If she ever learned about his less-than-discreet relationships, if she knew the truth about his . . . "romantic escapades," as the newspaper had phrased it, her opinion of him would be colored. Or more rightly, cast in shadow. And that *did* bother him. To think of her, thinking less of him.

He didn't know Eleanor Braddock well, not as well as he'd like. But—wisest choice or not—he wanted to. Very much.

What was it young Caleb Lebenstein had said? That it was the person behind the name that made the man who he really was. Marcus sighed. If only that would prove true for him.

He paused briefly at the corner and waited for a line of carriages to pass, a thought surfacing that would have been considered traitorous if given voice in Austria. . . .

Could a man who had been defined by his title and family history for the better part of his life have a second chance to make his life—and himself—better without it?

He'd imagined life without the weight of expectation that accompanied being in the lineage of the House of Habsburg, many times. What he'd never considered was that he might actually be a better man without it. That possibility was new to the equation.

Everything had always come so easily for him. Either that, or things had been given to him on a silver platter, as the saying went. But he had a feeling that this unlikely renovation of the man he wanted to be would prove to be more extensive, and costly, than first met the eye.

And it would end up being all for naught once he returned to Vienna in June. To his old life—and new bride.

Spotting the mayor's office ahead, Marcus gathered his wits, framing what he wanted to say to the mayor—*if* he could keep his temper under control.

"Now, ladies, let each of us take the delicate strands of hair and wrap them ever so gently, but firmly, around the piece of wire given you. . . ."

Eleanor sat at her braiding table—one of twelve Aunt Adelicia had purchased for the event—and stared at the gathered strands of hair arranged on the cloth atop the silver tray before her.

Huddled over their own tables placed around Aunt Adelicia's central parlor, the other women giggled like schoolgirls as they attempted to follow Mr. Mark Campbell's tedious—and never-ending—instructions. When did the man breathe?

In addition to the braiding tables, Aunt Adelicia had generously purchased a dozen copies of the gentleman's book, which was succinctly entitled,

Self-Instructor in the Art of Hair Work, Dressing Hair, Making Curls, Switches, Braids, and Hair Jewelry of Every Description, and Mr. Campbell had insisted on signing each one.

"This will form the basis of the square chain braid, my dear ladies," he continued, "which is the easiest braid, and by far the most handsome, if I may say. And one that should be practiced to perfection before trying any other, as it will enable the beginner to execute all others after the first is perfected."

Eleanor looked at the clock on the mantel, more than willing to pluck every strand of hair from her head if her aunt would simply accept that these types of gatherings were not for her.

She sighed.

Aunt Adelicia had spoken with her *again* about joining the Nashville Women's League, the contingent of women that met in town, and Eleanor had finally agreed to visit. Not only to appease her aunt but also to have reason to go into town when the need arose. And the need *would* be presenting itself.

Her gaze wandered out the window to the gardens, and she yearned to see her father again, to hear from him personally. Dr. Cheatham had visited the asylum, as promised, and reported that her father was "coping with his new surroundings as best could be expected."

Not overly promising news.

It hadn't been a full week yet, though, and she hoped any day to hear from Dr. Crawford, granting permission for her to visit.

Her focus moved beyond the gardens in the direction of the conservatory, and she wondered if *he* was there, full well knowing it was best she not wonder about him at all. Still . . .

At her aunt's encouragement, she'd taken a walk every afternoon, and somehow, each time she'd ended up at the conservatory. "I'm simply stepping inside to check the roses," she'd told Zeke when he'd asked. Yet she knew better.

And that was just it, she *did* know better.

She knew Marcus had been there because, when she peeked into his "infirmary," as she thought of it, plants and bottles and whatnot had been moved. And Mr. Gray himself had told her that the room was designated for Marcus's purposes alone.

So he'd been there but had made no attempt to cross paths with her. Not that he should. Or should want to—

"Miss Braddock, are you having some difficulty? I'd be most happy to assist, if that's the case."

Startled, Eleanor looked up to see Mr. Campbell hovering overhead, his thick mustache looming even larger from the low angle. Aware of him looking at something in her lap, only then did she realize she'd withdrawn the worn, stained handkerchief from her pocket. She quickly stuffed it back inside.

"Ah . . . no, sir," she answered, trying to form an intelligible response. She'd been taught to always tell the truth, but at times the truth seemed cruel. Especially when sensing his sincerity. She felt badly now about her earlier thoughts. "I'm sorry,

Mr. Campbell, but . . . I'm afraid I simply don't . . ."

His brow crinkled. The enthusiasm in his face waned. And looking up at him, Eleanor had an epiphany. This man was doing what he truly loved to do. His delight in his work showed in his actions, his speech, in his two-hundred-and-seventy-six-page personally autographed book, and even in the way he moved about the room, almost flitting—in a somewhat manly sort of way—from table to table.

She found herself envious of him.

"I'm afraid, sir," she began again, realizing there was much she could learn from him, even if she cared not one *iota* about the art of hair work, "that my mind wandered for a bit. I'm not quite certain where to begin."

His face positively lit. "Well, my dear Miss Braddock, let me guide you! It's so very easy, even for a beginner such as yourself."

As he outlined the steps, Eleanor felt someone's attention and briefly lifted her gaze. Seated across the room from her, Aunt Adelicia simply smiled.

Eleanor watched Mr. Campbell and caught on quickly. He moved on to the next pupil with a spryer step, and she continued weaving and looping, letting her thoughts do much the same.

Yesterday as they'd returned home from church in town, Eleanor had half expected Aunt Adelicia to inquire about the building she'd rented. But not a word. And *she* wasn't about to broach the subject. With her aunt's ever-full social calendar guiding her days, Eleanor hadn't gotten back into town to fulfill her "business proposition" to Mr. Stover, but she would.

She also wanted to cook in Eloise's, or Weezie's, kitchen . . . at least once. She missed cooking, the comfort and solace it gave her, and didn't think Mr. Stover would mind. She knew just what she would bake for him too.

A knock sounded on the door, and Mrs. Routh entered, envelope in hand. "Pardon me for interrupting, Mrs. Cheatham."

The housekeeper glanced in Eleanor's direction, and Eleanor couldn't keep her hope from rising.

"A letter arrived for Miss Braddock. One for which I believe she's been waiting."

"Miss Thornton, under no circumstances am I to be disturbed today. By *anyone*. Is that clear?"

"Yes, sir. Perfectly, sir."

The door to Mayor Adler's office stood open, and Marcus stood just outside it.

An impatient exhale. "And *where* is my coffee?"

"I'll get it right away, sir."

Hearing the rustle of skirts, Marcus stepped to one side as Miss Thornton exited the office in a rush. Distress lined her features. And more so once she saw him.

Not wanting her to be blamed, Marcus quickly moved inside the office and closed the door. "Mayor Adler, a word with you, sir."

Seated at his desk, the mayor stilled, then slowly

looked up, whispering something unintelligible beneath his breath. "Mr. Geoffrey . . . I expected a visit from you today."

"As I gathered just now when you said you weren't to be disturbed."

Mayor Adler's jaw hardened. "Now, see here, sir! I have every right as mayor of this city to choose the architect who I believe will do the best job."

"Yes, sir, you do." Marcus approached his desk. "But you also had an agreement with the four companies who placed the original bids that they would be notified before the announcement was made public. Professional consideration, you said."

Adler stood. "I cannot be held responsible for a newspaper that publishes a story prematurely."

"Even when you're quoted in that article . . . Mayor?"

Adler's face flushed. He moved from behind his desk. "This is America, Mr. Geoffrey. And I am mayor of this city. I do not answer to you, and I feel no compulsion to offer an explanation in this instance. If you do not like the way business is conducted here, may I suggest there are other cities in which you may seek to build your building with its . . . 'integration of structure and nature.' " He gave a harsh laugh. "And with what you describe as . . . 'tree-like columns.' "

The final three words hit Marcus like a physical blow, and jerked him back to a similar conversation he'd had years ago. With his father. "Your designs, Marcus . . ." His father had taken him by the shoulders. "They're *fantastical,* my son. It cannot be done. Build what you already know, what Austria and all of Europe expects. Then, perhaps, you will earn some respect."

But it could be done. Marcus knew. He'd known it for almost a decade. It simply hadn't been done *yet.*

"I will stay in Nashville, Mayor Adler," he said quietly. "And I will build that building."

Adler laughed, moving back behind his desk. "That may be, Mr. Geoffrey. But you won't do it with my city's money. Which brings me to another issue. How is it that your bid was substantially lower than the rest?" His eyes narrowed. "It makes one wonder if you have other financial backing that you failed to disclose."

"No other financial backing, sir. As I stated in my bid, which included confirmation of deposited funds with a bank in Boston, I simply planned to underwrite a portion of the project myself. It was —and is—that important to me."

"Yes, we confirmed the funds, Mr. Geoffrey. But my question remains . . . *How* do you have the ability to fund such an expenditure? If not for undisclosed investors."

Marcus's mouth curved, no warmth in the gesture. He had no intention of revealing the source of his money to Mayor Adler. Doing so would reveal the ties to his family, which would reveal far too much. "With all respect, Mayor . . ." He paused. "How was it you phrased it? I feel no compulsion to offer an explanation in this instance."

Mayor Adler stared, his displeasure palpable. "Lest I have been unclear . . . your architectural *style* has no place in this city. With the plans I have, Nashville stands to become the cultural focal point of the United States. Someday everyone in America will equate the exquisite beauty of Mozart, Beethoven, Rossini, and Verdi and all their masterful creations with *this* city. *My* city. But you, sir, will have no part in it."

Wishing they were in Austria, Marcus enjoyed a fleeting moment of pleasure as he imagined what he would do to a man like Augustus Adler back home. How would Adler react if Marcus revealed who he really was? Even at such a distance, the House of Habsburg was not without power and influence. But the cost—

Marcus sobered from his imaginings. The cost was far too great. And the pleasure, too momentary. Having had enough, he turned to leave.

"And to confirm, Mr. Geoffrey . . ."

Hand on the latch, Marcus looked back.

"You *have* filed all the necessary permits for the projects your company is currently undertaking, haven't you?"

Hearing the underlying threat, Marcus closed the distance between them again. "I have, Mayor Adler. As you'll see if you take the time to check . . . sir."

"I sincerely hope that's the case." Adler smiled. "Because here in Nashville, we like to do everything by the book."

One last question churning inside him, Marcus knew the mayor would likely sidestep the issue, if not refuse to answer altogether. But he couldn't leave without asking. "Mayor Adler, the article announced the project was awarded to Architectural Associates of Nashville, but it failed to name the owner of the company. I'm curious as to who—"

The side door opened, the door leading to the office of Mr. Barrett, the mayor's assistant. But the much younger man striding into the room, project sketches in hand, wasn't Mr. Barrett.

"Father, I'm wondering about the size of the balcony and whether the supports I've planned will sustain that much—"

"Everett!" Mayor Adler barked. "Not now."

"But I need to know so I can tell the reporter from—"

"*Not . . .* now," Adler repeated, blotches of red mottling his face.

Marcus stared, the pieces jarring into place, their jagged edges cutting as they did. The irony of the situation wasn't lost on him.

Here he was, refusing to reveal the source of his money because he didn't want his family name and influence to have any bearing on his success or failure—when in reality, the money being from his family, part of his inheritance, bore influence over whatever success or failure he had, at least to some extent. Just as Mayor Adler's family had influenced *his* choices.

But Marcus had purposefully worked to keep his family out of the equation—whereas Mayor Adler had intentionally involved his.

At that moment, Everett turned and saw Marcus. The young man scowled. "Who are you?"

Marcus's smile came more genuinely this time. "I'm a man who likes to do everything by the book."

11

Eleanor rose with the sun, dressed quickly, then crept down to the kitchen, and—thanks to Cordina —ate a quick breakfast before the mansion began to stir. She wanted to get into town first thing, preferably without having to explain her destination to her aunt.

Satchel in hand, she felt mischievous as she gripped the knob of the front door and—

The handle turned beneath her palm. Eleanor took a cautious step back as the door opened.

"Oh!" Claire Monroe stopped short. "I'm so sorry, Miss Braddock," the woman whispered. "I wasn't expecting anyone to be up so early."

"No, no, that's fine." Eleanor stepped to the side, keeping her voice low. "Come in, please." She'd met her aunt's liaison days earlier, and had liked her instantly. "I was just heading out before the family members awaken. I have some errands to run in town."

Claire gave her a knowing look, and Eleanor wondered if the woman guessed who she was actually trying to avoid.

Then Claire smiled. "I don't blame you one bit. Once the day starts around here, it's likely to be noon before you're given another chance to get a word in."

Eleanor laughed softly. "Yes, precisely."

Claire Monroe was a natural beauty—much like Aunt Adelicia—who seemed to exude vivacity and charm. Thick auburn curls, swept up and gracefully pinned, framed her face, and she seemed almost to glow from within.

Claire glanced past her, then leaned close. "I haven't had opportunity to mention this to you yet, Miss Braddock, but—"

Eleanor touched her arm. "Eleanor, please."

The young woman's eyebrows raised. "If you'll extend me the same courtesy?"

Eleanor nodded. "Indeed I will . . . Claire."

Claire's expression warmed. "What I wanted to tell you is that . . . as your aunt's liaison, I assist with many of her personal affairs." Compassion laced her features. "I hope you're not upset by this, but . . . I'm aware of where your father is and of his . . . situation. I only share that with you now so you're not surprised by my knowledge if it comes up later. I don't want to appear as if I've been dishonest with you. That's very important to me.

And . . . I want you to know that I'm praying for you, Eleanor." Claire's eyes misted. "Even though I've not walked the exact road you're walking right now, I *do* know what it's like to watch a parent suffer. It's one of the hardest things I've ever done."

Eleanor's eyes filled. Though she'd vowed to do her best to keep her father's whereabouts secret, surprisingly, it didn't bother her that Claire Monroe knew. She didn't know Claire well, but if Aunt Adelicia trusted her . . .

"Thank you for that, Claire. Truly. And . . . thank you for your prayers. They mean so much."

Now, if only God would answer them.

A while later, satchel in her grip, Eleanor slid the key into the lock at 87 Magnolia Street and stepped inside, more excited about her business proposition—cleaning the building—than she thought she'd be. But it wasn't really about the cleaning. And though she did hope to recoup a portion of the rent she'd paid Mr. Stover—*if* he was able to rent the building again, which might happen faster if clean—it wasn't solely about the money either.

Setting the satchel down, she looked around the dusty, dingy quarters.

She thought that God had shown her a purpose. Opening this restaurant had been a step toward pursuing what He had planned for her, or so she'd thought.

Apparently, she'd been mistaken. And slowly, she was reconciling herself to that fact. Just as she was reconciling herself to the other areas of her life that hadn't turned out as she'd thought they would.

But one thing she knew, this building, including the kitchen in back, would sparkle like new once she was finished.

She unpacked her apron and the cleaning supplies she'd purchased earlier that morning at the mercantile—an expense for which she hadn't budgeted. But since coming to Belmont, it was clear she would be paying for very little. Aunt Adelicia wouldn't hear of her spending her own money. So her funds were going to hold out better than she'd expected.

Eleanor smiled again, seeing the purchased packages of seeds tucked inside the satchel. Rosemary, thyme, basil, and oregano. Some of her father's favorites. She could hardly wait to help him plant them.

She needed to mail the letter she'd written him —the second since he'd been at the asylum. He hadn't responded to the first one. But that didn't surprise her.

Yesterday's letter from Dr. Crawford had contained encouraging news, however. Her father was acclimating well, the doctor reported, and he said she could visit as early as the following Monday, scarcely a week away.

A brief visit, he'd warned. But still, a visit.

She planned to go first thing Monday morning. She only hoped her father was as eager to see her as she was him.

Having spotted a broom, mop, and pail on her first visit to the building, Eleanor retrieved those from the kitchen, then wrestled water from the hand pump out back. For a moment, she thought the pump would win. But elbow grease, as Mr. Stover had called it, finally prevailed.

Once the pail was full, she set to work on the front room, sweeping and mopping. In no time, the water in the pail turned to sludgy brown, and she stopped counting the trips made out back to discard the dirty water and start afresh.

After three hours, she'd made meager progress and realized she'd far underestimated the time it would take to clean the front room alone, much less the entire building.

Sighing, she stood and stretched, her back and shoulder muscles aching. That morning, she'd accepted a second biscuit with ham from Cordina, and sat now—resting against the wall—and savored every bite, along with a teacake Cordina had sneaked in as well. *Delicious.*

The woman was so knowledgeable about cooking. Cordina had shared her recipe for the pork roast, but Eleanor sensed her hesitance to share more. Eleanor guessed her hesitance came in knowing that Aunt Adelicia would frown upon their recipe exchange.

Just as Eleanor knew her aunt would frown on what she was doing now.

Still, Adelicia Acklen Cheatham was a generous person at heart. In the past week alone, Eleanor read in a newspaper of her donating a bell to the First Presbyterian Church, and then read of her part in preparations to build a new tea hall for the Nashville Women's League—although the reporter had taken a rather dim view of the project in his summary, subtly questioning the need for such a structure. But in spite of her aunt's philanthropy, it was unlikely she would understand her niece's desire to clean an old building.

Eleanor stood and brushed the crumbs from her skirt, careful the remnants dropped on the section of flooring she hadn't cleaned yet. Through the still-grimy front windows, she could see murky images of people passing but couldn't make out their features, much less tell if it was someone she knew. Although . . .

If Marcus Geoffrey were to pass the door right now, she was certain she'd know him, dirty glass or not. He'd fill the doorway, for one. Second, she'd recognize the confident—and most times, bordering on arrogant—manner in which he carried himself, as though he considered the rest of the world beneath him. Yet, she'd glimpsed moments when he seemed almost kindhearted, with his self-deprecating attitude and ability to draw her in.

She'd seen him from afar yesterday evening, working in a garden behind the conservatory. She hadn't approached him, even though she'd wanted to. Her aunt would surely frown upon the fraternization, but Eleanor welcomed the interaction with someone outside the social sphere of Belmont.

Because in spite of her aunt's efforts, that's where she was, and where she'd always been. Outside the circle.

She decided to clean the kitchen to break up the monotony. And to dream. She worked on the large cast-iron stove and oven, scrubbing and wiping it down until it gleamed.

She couldn't wait to use it. Whipping eggs for a savory custard until they were light and foamy, then folding in the cheese and herbs and tucking it all in a flaky pastry. She breathed deep, smelling only linseed soap and wet plank wood, but she had no trouble imagining the comforting aroma of still-warm buttermilk pie, its crust all flaky and golden, or the yeasty heaven of freshly baked bread. She enjoyed creating pastries, working with dough.

She eyed the iron skillets and pie tins lining the wall. "Your day is coming," she whispered, wondering if she should make something to take to her father as well as cooking something for Mr. Stover.

She checked the watch hooked to her bodice, and found it was later than she'd expected.

She removed her soiled apron and fixed herself up as best she could, regretting now that she'd told Armstead she would walk home. But maybe the walk would help stretch the muscles she'd forgotten she had.

Satchel in hand, she locked the door behind her, frowning at the grimy windows. She needed a stool to clean those properly, and made mental note to bring one with her next time.

At midafternoon the streets weren't as crowded as they'd been that morning. Mostly women and young children milled about now, many looking as though they had no destination. Or if they did, they weren't in a hurry to reach it.

Feeling more at ease in the area, Eleanor decided to walk back a different way.

She passed warehouse after warehouse, many standing silent and empty, their darkened windows a reminder of a city still mending from war.

But when she turned the corner, she spotted one warehouse that was apparently mending quite well. In fact, the business looked as though it were thriving. A crew of workers near the front of the building was constructing a new entrance, and new signage was being installed above the large yet-to-be-stained double doors—*Foster's Textile Mill.*

The pounding of hammers and rhythmic buzz of handsaws sounded almost like music compared to the lonely silence of previous streets. Not to mention the men's banter and laughter as they worked.

Eleanor quickened her pace as she passed the workers. But glimpsing what had been built on either side of the entrance, she slowed again, imagining how much Marcus would approve. The large rectangular boxes were constructed of wood and filled with soil. For plants, no doubt.

Even though she didn't *dis*approve, Eleanor

shook her head. It seemed an odd place for a flower garden. And the time it would take to water and care for it . . . Not very practical here in the middle of the city.

A chorus of voices rose, and she looked down the street to see a group of people gathered around a staircase, a man addressing them from a platform above. She moved to get a closer look.

The group seemed to be made up exclusively of women, and though she couldn't hear what the gentleman was saying, the women responded by raising their hands, many of them pressing toward the stairs, even pushing others out of the way.

An elderly woman was shoved to the side, and she slipped and fell. Eleanor rushed to help her.

"Are you all right, ma'am? Can I—"

"Get your hands off me," the woman snapped, pushing her away and gaining her feet again. "You young ones, always shovin' your way to the front, gettin' the jobs. I can sew circles 'round the lot of you!"

Eleanor stepped back, mindful of other wary looks she was drawing, and of the unrest in the crowd.

The man called out from above, "You women I chose, make your way up the stairs. Mrs. Billings here will give you a thorough checking."

Clutching her satchel, Eleanor stepped to the side, watching as six women climbed the stairs. All younger, just as the older woman had accused. The stern, matronly looking Mrs. Billings stood at the top of the stairs, her hands gloved.

The first young woman stopped just shy of the landing and bowed her head. Eleanor cringed as Mrs. Billings searched the woman's hair, then waved her on through the door behind her.

With the sixth woman, Mrs. Billings paused and stepped back. "Lice!"

"Please," the young woman cried, grabbing hold of Mrs. Billings's skirt. "I have children to feed. I—"

Mrs. Billings stepped back. "I'm sorry," she said stiffly. "There are rules."

The young woman, openly weeping, retraced her steps, pressing a hand to her hair and turning away from the others, barely able to get through the crush of women pressing forward again.

"You!" the man called, pointing.

Another young woman clambered up, her breath coming hard. "I'm clean," she said, bowing her head. "And I'll work hard."

After checking her hair, Mrs. Billings waved her on through.

With that, the door closed, and the crowd began to disperse. But Eleanor couldn't move. A weight held her feet to the patch of earth where she stood as surely as if she'd been planted there.

She exhaled, unaware she'd been holding her breath. *If not for the grace of God . . .* was all she could think.

And yet, God didn't love her any more than He loved these women. And heaven knew, she'd done nothing to deserve her present living situation. *"You live at the Belmont estate now, and you're the niece of the wealthiest woman in America."*

Marcus's words returned with painful clarity as Eleanor watched the women walk away. By God's grace, she was niece to Adelicia Acklen Cheatham. But being the recipient of her aunt's graciousness when confronted by such want and need . . .

She felt a sense of shame—and at the same time, overwhelming gratitude. The two emotions didn't marry well inside her and birthed an unease that reached deep.

She searched for the woman who had been turned away. But she was gone. Only a handful were left, most standing about, speaking ill of the man and Mrs. Billings. Only one woman walked away alone. She had a . . . presence about her. What, Eleanor couldn't describe exactly.

But suddenly, the roots securing her feet to the ground gave release.

Eleanor followed the woman for almost two blocks, trying to work up the nerve to approach her. Her stomach churned. Her thoughts did too. In her mind, she kept hearing the elderly woman's harsh rebuke and didn't wish to repeat that.

She'd helped people before, had volunteered during the war, for heaven's sake. But this was different. This wasn't like binding up a wound or tying a tourniquet. This kind of wound wasn't visible, but it was real, nonetheless.

She saw it in the frail set of the woman's thin shoulders and in the worn dress that hung a little too loosely in all the wrong places.

The woman slowed her pace, and Eleanor did likewise, watching as she paused briefly in front of the fruit stand at the mercantile before continuing on.

Determined, Eleanor maneuvered around passersby, silently rehearsing what she would say. She wanted the words to come out right, not to sound as though her desire to help stemmed from pity. She knew what it was like to receive a gift from someone who felt sorry for her, and it wasn't an experience she was eager to cause.

Closing the distance, she inhaled, trying to calm her nerves, surprised at how jittery she was when she simply wanted to offer—

Just then the woman did an about-face. Eleanor sucked in a breath, and barely managed to keep from plowing right into her.

"May I help you, ma'am?" The woman's voice was soft but direct, and bore a distinct—and familiar—accent.

Feeling off-kilter, Eleanor took a hasty step back, uncertain how to respond. "I . . . I was following you just now."

"Yes, I know. I saw you." The woman didn't appear angry so much as cautiously curious. "First, back at Foster's Mill for the work call. Then"—she gestured with a nod—"in the reflection in the window back there."

Frowning, Eleanor glanced behind her at the mercantile and, sure enough, saw the street mirrored back in the pristine plate glass. She exhaled, feeling more than a little foolish—and also impressed. "I'm sorry if I frightened you. That wasn't my intent."

"You did not frighten me, ma'am. But I am . . . curious as to why you follow me."

"Well, when I saw you back at the mill, I . . ." Eleanor hesitated, trying to read the woman's expression and failing. She finally decided to just state it outright, the words spilling out on top of each other. "I would like to help you, if I can. I don't know what you need. Or if you need anything. But I've been in need before. I know what that feels like, and . . ." Her throat tightened with emotion. "It can be a very lonely time. And overwhelming."

The woman studied her for a moment. "Why me? Out of all those women?"

Eleanor thought about it. "When I looked up, you were the only one walking away alone." Her smile felt timid. "Everyone else I heard was complaining, and . . . I'd already tried to help an elderly woman, but"—she winced—"that attempt didn't fare well."

A trace of humor touched the woman's eyes. "Likely, that was Berta. She is not one to be meddled with. No matter how good your intentions."

"Yes . . ." Eleanor sighed. "I discovered that. But you . . . you didn't seem angry. Or hostile. You seemed . . . resigned." She shook her head. "No. That's not the right word." Almost certain she'd *felt* the word whispered inside her, she finally said, "Reconciled—that's what I sensed when I watched you walk away. And . . . as I've learned from experience, there's a big difference between resigning yourself to something and being reconciled."

The woman bowed her head. When she looked up, her eyes were moist. "Yes, miss, there is. To be reconciled requires hope." Her voice caught. Her smile trembled. "Even if that hope is thin."

More certain than ever that she'd done the right thing in following her instincts, Eleanor had an idea. She surveyed their surroundings and spotted a familiar sign not too far down the street. "This may seem somewhat forward, but . . . would you join me for a meal? I'd be obliged if you would allow me to treat you at the bakery."

The woman appeared to consider the offer, absently chewing the corner of her lip. Then she shook her head. "I am sorry . . . I cannot accept. But if you have work that needs to be done this afternoon, perhaps some washing or ironing. I could do that for you . . . in exchange."

Eleanor's admiration for the woman deepened, and she didn't have to think long about what she wanted to hire her for. "I'm afraid I don't have any ironing or washing, but . . . how are you at cleaning?"

The woman smiled. "I am very good at cleaning, ma'am. And I do not mind hard work."

"Fine, then. We'll start first thing in the morning." Eleanor gestured. "If you'll join me at the bakery now, we can discuss the details."

The woman peered up at her. "I work first, ma'am. Then I get paid."

Eleanor needed to get back to Belmont. And she was on foot, which meant it would take even longer. She tried to think of something the woman could do to earn a little food for the evening meal, but nothing came to—

She'd almost forgotten. She had one more errand to run.

"There *is* something you can do for me today, if you don't mind." Eleanor unlatched her satchel. "And surely this is worth a loaf of bread and some cheese."

What could only be described as *hope* slipped into the woman's eyes. But as Eleanor withdrew the letter she'd written to her father, she stilled when seeing the address on the front.

G. Braddock. Tennessee Asylum for the Insane. Did she really want her father's whereabouts revealed?

Sensing the woman waiting, Eleanor realized the longer she hesitated, the more attention she drew. Grateful her thoughts were hidden, she found herself weighing the cost of others discovering where her father was against the probability that this woman would go hungry tonight.

Aided by the weight of shame, the scales tipped. And Eleanor found she could breathe again.

"I have a letter to be mailed," she continued. "And the post office is several blocks away. I'd be so grateful if you'd see to it for me."

The woman took the envelope, her gaze never leaving Eleanor's. "Thank you, ma'am," she whispered, her chin quivering. "I will do this now."

Eleanor handed her a coin. "For the postage. I'll be waiting for you at the bakery."

The woman nodded, a single tear slipping down her cheek. She turned to leave.

"Oh, before you go!" Eleanor said, waiting for her to turn back. "My name is Eleanor. Eleanor Braddock."

"It is an honor to meet you, Miss Braddock. My name is Naomi." The woman's smile lit her face. "Naomi Lebenstein."

Nearly two hours later, Eleanor passed the outskirts of town, weary in body but with her spirits renewed. Naomi Lebenstein was a dear woman. And she was from Austria, as Eleanor had suspected. She had a son too, and when Naomi spoke about him, her countenance brightened with unabashed pride.

Naomi hadn't shared her full story. But she had said she was a recent widow, among the thousands of others in the city.

The sun sank low on the horizon, and Eleanor increased her pace, eager to get back. Despite her fatigue, she marveled at the wash of color in the sky. Golden orange, pink, and purple, each hue distinct but melding into the others. The scene reminded her of a portrait hanging in the front entrance hall at Belmont entitled *An American Versailles*.

Thinking of Belmont made her ponder what she would say if Aunt Adelicia asked her about being gone all day. Eleanor switched the satchel from one hand to the other, her shoulders tired. Surely she wouldn't be expected to give account for every hour. She was a grown woman, after all.

Hearing a carriage approach from behind, she moved to the edge of the dirt road and glanced over her shoulder, hopeful it would be Armstead, or at least a carriage from Belmont. But it was no one she recognized, and the carriage passed.

She waited for the swirl of dust to clear, then continued on.

A mile down the road, with a mile yet to go and frustrated at being so tired, she debated whether to stop and rest. Her feet ached, as did her back. The cleaning had taken more out of her than she'd expected it to. But she refused to stop. When the day came that she couldn't walk two miles, then—

Hoofbeats sounded some distance behind her, and she moved again to the side for the rider to pass. But when the hoofbeats slowed from a gallop to a canter, then to a walk, she turned.

Seeing who was astride the stallion, she instantly warmed but did her best to keep her pleasure from showing. Her lack of experience with men had, oddly enough, not left her without lessons learned. It was best a man not know what you thought of him until you were more familiar with the man.

"Good evening, Mr. Geoffrey."

He reined in, the pleasure in his own expression going slack. "Mr. *Geoffrey?*" His dark brows drew together. "Please tell me we've not taken a backward step since our last meeting . . . Eleanor. And what are you doing walking all this way? Did you not arrange for a carriage? Or did your driver not return as planned?"

Deciding to ignore his playful reprimand, she went straight to his questions. "Neither, actually. Armstead drove me into town, but I told him I preferred to return on foot."

He leaned forward. "On foot? All that way."

"As you see." She made a sweeping gesture with her arm. "It's only two miles . . . Marcus. It's not that far."

His mouth tipped on one side. Not a smile really, at least not a full one. But it might as well have been for the effect it had on her.

"You're an interesting woman, Eleanor."

She cocked her head. "And again, I must say that your compliments, sir—if that is, indeed, what was intended—need work."

With a laugh, he swung down from his horse. "Duly noted, madam. Now, I ask that you allow me to give you a ride home"—he glanced at the stallion—"if you're willing to brave Regal's fierceness."

"Regal? Quite a name for quite a horse. The name is of your choosing, I suppose?"

"Not at all. He was already named when I purchased him." A glimmer of humor lit his eyes as he held out his hand. "But I admit the name drew me."

Eleanor stroked the thoroughbred's sleek neck. "I love horses, actually. And he's a beauty." She studied Marcus's outstretched hand, then looked back at him. "As much as I adore walking and would customarily decline your polite offer . . . today, I'm most grateful for it."

She set her satchel down, slipped her hand into his, and accepted his assistance onto the horse. Sitting sidesaddle, she arranged her skirts to cover her legs, impressed with his generosity.

"Thank you, Marcus, for giving up your—"

When he swung up behind her—*very* close behind her—Eleanor stiffened. She'd simply assumed that he would—

"You don't mind me riding along with you, do you?" Amusement peppered his deep voice as he handed her the satchel. He reached around her to adjust the reins. "Regal is well capable of carrying us both, and it seems a shame for me to walk when we can ride and . . . visit."

More than a little unnerved at their close proximity, and *feeling* the gleam in the man's eyes, Eleanor determined to keep her focus on the road ahead—but his rolled-up shirtsleeves revealed sinewy forearms brown from the sun, arms now resting on well-muscled thighs.

Having shied away from ever carrying a fancy lace fan—what with all the silly nonsense about signaling romantic cues to a man across the room —she had to admit . . .

What she wouldn't have done at that moment for a slight breeze.

But she wasn't about to let him get the best of her. Not when she knew he was doing this just to get a reaction from her.

"Why, of course I don't mind, Marcus." She smoothed a hand over her skirt. "I simply didn't realize Austrian men suffered from such weak constitutions."

His laughter was immediate, and his breath warmed her cheek, sending shivers skittering from the top of her spine to the tips of her toes. Eleanor took a steadying breath. So much for putting him in his place.

He prodded Regal to a walk, and Eleanor tried in vain not to dwell on the solidness of Marcus's chest, or on how his arms encircled her waist as he held the reins. She noticed everything about him, from the scent of his bay rum and spice cologne to his skill in handling the powerful thoroughbred.

His hands were large, but not as rough and calloused as she'd expected. Nor was there dirt beneath his nails. His fingers were like those of a pianist, and she wondered whether he played. Then remembering his occupation, she realized he'd probably never had opportunity to learn. Though she shouldn't be quick to judge. Aunt Adelicia took pride in hiring her gardeners from the finest garden houses and estates in Europe. Who knew what education the men received in their training?

And based upon what she'd seen of *this* man's skills, she wouldn't be a bit surprised if Marcus Geoffrey executed a flawless sonata.

"So tell me," he said, peering around at her. "What lured you into town today? Anything I might need to know about?"

Humor edged his voice, and she smiled at his feeble attempt to learn more about the building she'd rented. "Oh, this and that. Various errands. I went to the bakery again."

"You didn't."

"I did."

"Without me?"

She nodded, feeling his chin all but resting on the top of her head. "And the doughnuts were even better than the other day."

He laughed again, and she liked the sound of it up close. The resonant rumble in his chest.

The sun wouldn't set for another two hours. But already, to the east, the barest hint of a thumbnail moon graced the horizon, the pale sliver over-eager to begin its nightly trek.

Eleanor had to admit, this was much better than walking, and she liked that Marcus didn't feel compelled to fill the silence.

He guided the horse through the massive columns of chiseled limestone marking the entrance to Belmont, and the peacefulness and beauty of the setting made it feel as though they were entering another world. Which they were in a sense, when contrasted with what she'd seen today.

She thought of Naomi and her son. It hadn't occurred to her to ask how old he was. She hoped the bread and cheese would be enough until morning. And though she hadn't mentioned anything to Naomi, she was already making plans for breakfast and lunch tomorrow.

Marcus shifted behind her, and Eleanor glanced back.

"Are you all right back there? Not about to fall off, are you?"

"I'm fine, madam. I'm simply . . . enjoying the view."

She liked that he wasn't addressing her as "your ladyship" anymore. It proved that, though the man was arrogant, he was teachable. That said a lot.

"Oh!" she whispered, squeezing his arm. "Look!" She nodded toward a doe and two fawns grazing a short distance off the road. The doe raised its head, senses alert, as they passed but didn't bolt. Neither did her young. *Beautiful* . . .

"So," she said, keeping her voice quiet. "What were *you* doing in town today? Another errand for Mrs. Cheatham?"

"I . . . had business to tend to. But I've been eager to get back here. A special flower I grafted is due to bloom any day now. Three plants, actually. With several blooms."

"A flower . . ." She raised an eyebrow. "Grafted how?"

"Your aunt requested a rose in a most . . .

particular color. A blush pink, like that of first dawn," he said, as though repeating instructions verbatim. "But not too light. And with the slightest hint of purple."

Eleanor laughed, knowing whom he was mimicking and able to imagine the inflections in her aunt's voice. But she was also impressed. "You can do that? With flowers, I mean. Create such specific colors?"

"And shapes and sizes of petals, and stems. We can determine whether the blossom will be of a more delicate variety, or heartier. But it follows . . . the heartier it is, typically the less aesthetically pleasing."

Eleanor nodded, the familiar descriptions *handsome* and *sturdy* coming to mind. But what captured her attention most was the passion in his voice.

"It's been a challenge," he continued, "creating a blossom that will be beautiful enough to satisfy Mrs. Cheatham's taste, while also assuring it possesses the traits to endure the elements. She requested that it bloom in the front garden throughout the summer. So, in full sun."

"And how long does it take to . . . *develop* a flower like this?"

"It's taken years, of course, to acquire the knowledge we have thus far, which is considerable. So—"

"So the more you've learned, the faster the process has become."

"You would think so. But that's not necessarily

the case. So many variables influence the outcome of each grafting."

He leaned closer as he spoke, his arms tightening around her. Eleanor guessed it was an unconscious gesture on his part, and couldn't decide whether she was pleased or perturbed that the gesture wasn't more intentional.

"I'm collaborating with a botanist from Massachusetts. We're grafting trees and other plants, and are sharing our findings, which is immensely helpful. Through experimentation, we select the plants that conform to our designs, and then destroy the others. We segregate the chosen ones so their qualities won't be lost in breeding with the mass. The law of heredity—like produces like, if you will—is interwoven inextricably with the law of variation, which proposes that no two organisms are ever exactly alike. We're very close, but we've yet to isolate . . ."

Eleanor smiled, listening to him.

He paused, then peered around at her. "What's wrong?"

"Nothing. Please continue."

"You're laughing at me."

"I'm not laughing at you."

"You're *smiling*."7

Hearing the boyish accusation in his tone *did* tempt her to laugh, and then she couldn't hold back.

"I'm not laughing at you, Marcus. I'm simply moved by how much you seem to love what you do. And you do, don't you?"

His hands briefly tightened on the reins. "Yes . . . I do. Since childhood, I've been fascinated with nature. But grafting, or . . . gardening," he said more pointedly, his tone growing more somber, "is actually only part of what I . . ."

He stopped, and she sensed his hesitance again.

"Honestly, Marcus, I want to hear more about this. I find it—"

"No," he whispered, then pointed ahead. "It's that."

She looked up to see a crowd gathered around the conservatory. Servants and workers, at first glance. But on closer inspection, she spotted Dr. Cheatham among them, along with her aunt, who chose that precise moment to look in their direction, her expression anything but pleased.

Eleanor braced herself for a reprimand—for her having been gone all day, *and* for being with an under gardener, perhaps. Feeling twelve years old again—and resenting it—she accepted Marcus's assistance down from the horse while considering how to respond.

In the same breath, she reminded herself she was a guest at Belmont. Her aunt's concern over her whereabouts was understandable . . . and actually warmed her heart, in a way. How long had it been since someone had worried about *her* instead of the other way around?

"Eleanor, my dear, are you all right?" Her aunt grasped her hands. "When Armstead said you insisted on walking back, I was concerned."

"Yes, Aunt, I'm fine." Eleanor briefly tightened her grip. "I apologize if I worried you. I went into town and—"

Aunt Adelicia held up her forefinger. "One moment, please, dear. I want to hear *all* about your day, but first . . . Mr. Geoffrey, I'm so glad you have returned. I believe your assistance may be required. There's an issue with a water pipe."

"A water pipe?" Marcus secured Regal's reins to a nearby tree. "How might I be of help with that, madam?"

"Workers are here to fix it, but they've mentioned something about a structural issue. Would you be willing to take a look at it? The kitchen no longer has water, and I'm expecting sixteen women tomorrow morning for tea! So please, if you'll simply . . ."

And just like that, they walked away, and Eleanor found herself standing alone. Without reprimand. Without scolding. Without anyone to hear *all* about her day.

Giving a weary but partly humored sigh, she conceded she was of little to no use in this situation. Much like an under gardener would be. So why had her aunt requested Marcus's assistance? Then again, she knew. The man *exuded* confidence. So whether or not he knew anything about the topic at hand— she shook her head—people assumed he did.

She made her way to the mansion, her feet still sore, despite the respite. Almost to the main fountain in the center of the garden, she heard footsteps behind her.

"Eleanor!"

Recognizing the voice, she turned, unexpected anticipation rising inside her. She told herself not to hope, but hope paid her no mind, and when she saw him, she dared imagine that he, too, had felt something similar to what she had on the horseback ride, and was coming to—

"I thought you might need this." He held up her satchel. "I saw it sitting on the ground back there."

She looked at the bag, then at him. She'd *told* herself not to hope. "Thank you, Marcus. That's very kind of you." She took the satchel and glanced beyond him. "It would seem you have a job ahead of you yet tonight."

"It would seem."

He sighed and ran a hand through his hair, rumpling it in a boyish, yet alluring, way. Was there anything about this man that wasn't attractive?

"But I don't mind," he continued. "I've never been bothered by darkness. Or close spaces."

She frowned. "Where will you be going?"

"In the tunnel."

She frowned.

"There are pipes," he said, "that extend from the water tower throughout the estate, including up to the mansion. The pipes run through the basement of the conservatory. And there's a tunnel—a short one—that houses the pipes before they branch out."

With her gaze, she traced a line from the tower uphill. "Can you walk in it?"

"A little ways. Then you have to stoop, then finally crawl. It's really not . . ." He eyed her. "Wait. Don't tell me. . . . You like tunnels?"

"No," she said quickly, then made a face. "I like . . . exploring."

He smiled and looked away, shaking his head. *"Du bist die bezauberndste Frau, die ich kenne."*

Wishing now that she'd taken four years of German instead of only two, Eleanor cleared her throat. "I beg your pardon, but . . . did you just say I'm a *surprising woman?"*

His smile went slack. "You speak German?"

This response she remembered quite well. *"Nur ein wenig."* Only a little.

His blue eyes danced. *"Das wird ein Spaß werden,* Miss Braddock."

She thought fast, working to keep up with him. "Obviously, I know my name. And I think I heard the word for . . . *fun?"*

"You most certainly did, madam."

"But what was the rest of it?"

"You'll find out soon enough." He gestured to her skirt. "But if we go exploring in that tunnel, you might get a little dirty."

She grinned, wishing she knew the German word for *tunnel.* "I've never minded a little dirt."

"Ja," he whispered. "I would have guessed that."

He bowed. "I'd better get back before Mrs. Cheatham comes looking for me." He turned to go, then stopped, his expression more serious. "I meant to ask you earlier . . . Have you heard from your father? About when he might arrive?"

Eleanor felt her smile fade. "No, I haven't. But . . . I'm expecting to hear from him soon."

He held her gaze a little longer than necessary. "Well, I look forward to meeting him when he does." He inclined his head. "Good night, Eleanor."

She offered the semblance of a curtsy, wishing she didn't genuinely like this man as much as she did. "*Gute Nacht*, Marcus."

Later that night a knock sounded on Eleanor's bedroom door.

"Eleanor, dear?" came a soft whisper. "It's Aunt Adelicia. Are you still awake?"

Eleanor laid aside her book, nudged back the bedcovers, and slipped into her robe as she crossed the shadows. The door creaked as she opened it. "Yes, I was just reading. Please . . ." She stepped back. "Come in. Is everything all right?"

Her aunt entered, carrying a lamp, and gently touched her cheek. "I'm sorry to visit so late, and yes, everything is fine. But you disappeared so quickly after dinner, I wanted to make certain *you* were all right."

"Yes, I'm well." Eleanor gestured for her to sit in one of the chairs by the window and then sat opposite her. "I was simply weary after the long day. Retiring early to read proved to be too much of a temptation."

Her aunt nodded. "Quiet moments are to be treasured, and seem to come so infrequently these days." A dark eyebrow shot up. "Especially with all the rigmarole going on down at the water tower."

"Was the leak easily repaired?"

"Thanks to Mr. Geoffrey! I'm beginning to question whether there's anything that man can't do. I'm grateful he's here."

Eleanor smiled, having had much the same thought. On both counts.

"But, dear"—her aunt leaned forward—"I truly want to hear about your day, and learn how you're faring. I do so want you to be happy here with us."

Having had time to reflect on the events of the day, as well as her aunt's generous invitation to live at Belmont, Eleanor knew how she wanted to answer that question. "I actually had a wonderful day today, thank you. And I'd love to share the details with you. But first I need to tell you about the building I rented."

Aunt Adelicia offered a nod, one that was a tad cautious, if Eleanor read her right.

"It *does* exist. Though you were correct, in a way. The property was not as it had been described in the advertisement. The verbiage the proprietor chose was most definitely colored by personal bias."

"The seller's perspective always is, my dear."

"But I've spoken with him about the possibility of my money being returned."

"And?"

"And he agreed that, if he could rent the building within the three-month time frame, he would refund the prorated portion of my payment."

"I admire you for broaching that possibility with him, Eleanor. But I would also warn you not to cast your hope in that corner. Chances are good that anyone else seeking to rent that property will demand to see it first"—Eleanor felt a sting, yet couldn't argue with the truth—"and when they do, I predict they'll take their money elsewhere."

"Which is why," Eleanor quickly added, "I spent a portion of the day interviewing and hiring someone to clean the property." She decided to forego sharing how she'd spent the better part of her day cleaning the building herself. Aunt Adelicia would neither understand nor appreciate that fact.

Aunt Adelicia's brow knit, and Eleanor hurried to offer support for her decision.

"My thought was that if the building were cleaner, more presentable, not layered in dust and grime, the chances of it being quickly rented would be greatly enhanced." Seeing no visible sign of approval in her aunt's expression, she rushed on, intentionally leaving out the building's location. "The structure seems quite sound. None of the windows are broken, and it has a large—"

"Eleanor," her aunt said softly.

Eleanor closed her mouth, resisting the urge to look away. Imagining what lecture was forthcoming, she almost wished now that she'd pretended to be asleep. "Yes, ma'am?"

"Your decision"—Aunt Adelicia regarded her—"shows excellent judgment."

Eleanor blinked, not certain she'd heard correctly.

"Far better to spend a little," her aunt continued, "with the chance of regaining the larger portion, than to certainly lose it all by doing nothing. And if the building doesn't rent, you haven't spent that much. And what's more, you will have left the property better than when you found it. Which is always an admirable goal. Well done, my dear."

Never in a hundred lifetimes could Eleanor have imagined how good it would feel to have Adelicia Acklen Cheatham's approval. She thanked her just as another detail popped into her head. "This will likely necessitate my going into town each day, at least for a while. To . . . supervise. Will that present a problem?"

"Not at all. Simply ask Zeke or Eli to arrange a carriage for you. And do be certain to visit the Nashville Women's League while you're in town. I spoke with the league's chair, Mrs. Holbrook, and she said she didn't think you had been by yet."

"No, I haven't. But I will. Very soon." Especially now that she knew a Mrs. Holbrook was watching for her. "Thank you again, Aunt Adelicia."

"You're most welcome. And now . . ." Her aunt reached into the pocket of her dressing gown and pulled out an envelope. "I have one more thing I need to speak with you about this evening."

Eleanor glanced at the envelope, sensing this was the real reason her aunt had knocked on her door.

"I had planned on telling you about this some-time later, Eleanor, but, I fear—" Aunt Adelicia looked down, fingering the stationery. "Certain events have forced my hand."

Eleanor's heart lurched. "Did Dr. Crawford write you? Is it about Papa?"

Her aunt lifted her gaze, her eyes swiftly widening. "No, no, my dear. It's nothing like that. This isn't about your father. Well . . ." She lifted a hand. "It's not directly about him. Although he *was* the motivation behind the plot, you might say. I think you're going to be quite pleased, though, once you hear what I'm about to tell you."

Though doubting that, Eleanor found her curiosity piqued.

"Over a year ago, your father wrote to me requesting that, when the time was right, I lend my assistance in arranging a secure future for you. I've already stated to you that I'm committed to doing just that."

Eleanor stared, not liking the direction their conversation was taking.

"Considering our close family relations and my long-standing affinity for you, dear . . . I most happily agreed to your father's request. And . . ." Smiling, her aunt reached over and covered her hand. "Within a fortnight, or a month at the most, a very nice gentleman will be calling on you, here, at Belmont. He desires to take you to dinner . . . with the intent of becoming acquainted with you. *Much* better acquainted."

Eleanor winced. "Oh, Aunt Adelicia . . . you didn't."

"I most certainly did. The gentleman's name is Lawrence Hockley, and he's a widower with no children. I've known him for the better part of fifteen years and can speak to his character and steadfastness. I knew his wife too, God rest her soul. She was a kind and quiet woman who died during the war. An illness of some sort, as I remember. Lawrence . . . Mr. *Hockley,* has been in Europe these recent months and wasn't expecting to return until spring. However, business in the States demands his attention, so"—her aunt's eyes sparkled in the glow of lamplight—"he'll be returning soon."

Eleanor opened her mouth to respond, but words failed her. Unable to remain seated, she came to her feet, and the act loosened the lock on her tongue. She heard herself laugh and instantly knew from her aunt's expression that laughter was not the desired response.

"I'm sorry, Aunt Adelicia, but . . ." She briefly closed her eyes. "If I were a young woman in my prime, perhaps this would be different." She stilled. "Does he know about me?"

"*Know* about you?"

Eleanor firmed her lips. "Does he know my age? Does he know my situation?"

"I've told him you're an enormously talented

and accomplished young woman who has faced the challenges of life following the war with grace and—"

Eleanor sighed and shook her head. "So the answer to my question would be *no*."

Her aunt stilled, and Eleanor knew she'd crossed a line.

"My sincere apologies if I've offended you, Aunt Adelicia, but . . . I'm almost thirty years old. I've never had a steady beau in my life, much less a *gentleman caller* who truly desired to become *much* better acquainted. Only two men have ever approached my father about calling on me, and that was years ago. And their interest only stemmed from my family connections." *To you,* Eleanor wanted to add, but didn't.

"This Mr. Lawrence Hockley, whoever he is, and however kind and . . . noble he may be, has— regardless of the most sincere intentions on your part, I am sure—been grossly misled."

Her aunt stared, then finally spoke. "Are you quite done, Eleanor?"

Feeling her spine stiffen even as her pride burned, Eleanor nodded. "Yes, ma'am."

Her aunt sat again and motioned for her to do the same.

"I desire to speak plainly, if I could, Eleanor."

"That would be appreciated, Aunt Adelicia."

Again, a look of warning, but less severe this time. "As you stated before, my dear, you have relinquished hopes of ever marrying."

Hearing the fact spoken aloud was jarring, but Eleanor nodded, matching her aunt's direct gaze.

"You are an intelligent woman, Eleanor. You're polished, refined, and so very . . . common-sensible. You conduct yourself with decorum and integrity, and have done so, I might add, since a young age. In light of this, I believe you'll make an excellent helpmeet for the right man."

While a part of her was flattered, Eleanor couldn't help but think of how cold that list of characteristics sounded when viewed in light of matrimony. "Thank you for that, Aunt, but . . ." She gave a humorless laugh. "Men don't often look for intelligent and *commonsensible* when looking for a wife. They're far more interested in diminutive and pretty."

Judging from her aunt's slight frown, she'd hit a nerve. And gotten her point across.

"You're right. Men do not always show the best judgment in that regard. But there are men who are more practical in nature. Mr. Hockley is one such man. And do not judge yourself so meanly, Eleanor. You are a striking woman."

Finding this entire set of circumstances lending itself more toward the comical than real drama, Eleanor tried to look at the situation practically. If there were such a man out there, as her aunt described, she would be a simpleton not to entertain the possibility of such a match.

And she could scarcely cast such an opportunity aside. However farfetched it seemed.

"Have you forgotten, Aunt, that my father is in an asylum? Even if Mr. Hockley is as practical a man as you claim, as soon as he discovers—"

"He knows about your father."

Eleanor felt her mouth slip open. "You *told* him?"

"Lawrence Hockley is a trustworthy man. And understanding. He—"

"That may be, but that secret was *not* yours to tell!"

"Perhaps not. But in light of the greater good seeking to be accomplished on your behalf, I didn't feel it right to keep that from him. Dr. Cheatham agreed."

"Dr. Cheatham is privy to this as well?"

"Yes. He and Lawrence have been friends for years. He would also defy you to find a more upright and steadfast gentleman."

An ache began to pulse at the base of Eleanor's neck, and she rested her head in her hands.

"Very few marriages, Eleanor, are rooted in the deepest of loves. However, with time, and taking into account the disposition of the man and woman, affection can grow. It's a cruel reality, but"—her aunt's voice changed, grew softer, yet less warm—"life rarely affords the luxury of marrying for love. Especially in our current society. There are scarce few men as it is, much less ones worthy of seeking your hand."

Eleanor swiftly decided it best to keep her thoughts to herself.

"As I've told you before, you are a Braddock

and an Acklen, and with those names come a rich heritage that few women in this society can bring to a marriage. I will not see you marry beneath yourself, Eleanor. While we may not be royalty in the purest sense, our family lines are held in great esteem, and we each have an obligation to preserve that legacy as best we can."

Eleanor lifted her head. "Does he know I have no dowry?"

The look on her aunt's face said it all.

"You didn't tell him."

"As your nearest relatives, Dr. Cheatham and I will have the honor of providing that on your behalf."

And yet you wouldn't give me a loan to start a business, was all Eleanor could think in the moment. She didn't dare say it aloud, but she also couldn't bring herself to thank her aunt.

Aunt Adelicia rose, oil lamp in hand. "It would be in keeping with etiquette for you to write a letter to Mr. Hockley, expressing your gratitude for his attention and invitation." She patted Eleanor's hand. "But we can discuss all this at greater length once we're both rested."

Eleanor accompanied her to the door. Perhaps it was well-entrenched decorum rearing its politely irritating head, but she couldn't let her aunt leave with such tension between them. "I appreciate the thought behind what you're doing, Aunt Adelicia. Or what you're trying to do. But believe me when I say, I will hold no ill will toward you or Dr.

Cheatham when after our dinner Mr. Hockley promptly withdraws his *design* to get to know me better."

In the orange glow of the lamp's flame, her aunt's expression remained unyielding. "I gave your father my word that I would see you married, Eleanor. And married *well*. And I fully intend to keep that promise."

"You made that vow to a feebleminded man who was losing grip on his faculties. One who never should have written that letter."

"No, my dear," her aunt whispered, pressing the letter into her palm. "I made that vow to a father who dearly loves his daughter, and who was looking out for her future even as he saw his own slipping away."

14

Seeing the asylum again, Eleanor felt her stomach churn. Scarcely two weeks had passed since she'd brought her father there, yet it felt like much longer.

She accepted Armstead's assistance from the carriage, then waited as he retrieved her satchel, reminding herself to deliver the envelope Dr. Cheatham had asked her to give to Dr. Crawford. Dr. Cheatham's wise counsel that morning at breakfast still resonated within her. She only hoped the meeting with her father went well enough that she wouldn't have to put it to use.

She was grateful neither Dr. Cheatham nor Aunt Adelicia had broached the subject of Mr. Lawrence Hockley again. She prayed the entire situation would fade to nothing, regardless of her aunt's wishes.

Though powerful and influential, even Adelicia Cheatham had her limits.

Eleanor stared up at the four-story brick building with its rows of windows spaced in perfect symmetry and tried to guess which one belonged to her father, or if his window overlooked a different vista.

She hoped his anger toward her had softened. But if not, maybe the savory custard she'd brought would serve as a peace offering.

Cordina had turned a blind eye to her sneaking into the kitchen earlier that morning. *If* the definition of turning a blind eye included setting out the exact bowls and utensils needed to make the custard, as well as leaving instructions on where to find any forgotten ingredients. *Such a kind woman . . .* And such a delightful place in which to cook.

Beautiful murals adorned the brick walls, lending the space an airy, open feel. She'd noticed them briefly before but hadn't taken the time to really study them until that morning. A person could almost forget they were in the basement. Leave it to Aunt Adelicia to have such masterpieces painted in the kitchen.

When Cordina had told her who was responsible

for the murals, Eleanor had been equally surprised. Claire Monroe, her aunt's liaison, was truly gifted with the ability to paint.

Cooking again, even that little bit, had felt so good, and Eleanor looked forward to the possibility of using the kitchen in Mr. Stover's building a time or two, *if* he approved. Given a few more days and Naomi's assistance in cleaning, she doubted the dear man would even recognize the property.

"Want me to tote the satchel for you, Miss Braddock?"

"No, Armstead, I can manage it from here, but thank you."

He nodded, a knowing look lingering beneath his subtle smile. "I got an errand to do for Mrs. Cheatham, but I be back by noon, ma'am."

Appreciating his quiet support, Eleanor ascended the front steps, satchel in one hand and ham-and-cheese custard in the other. Her heart raced as though she'd run a mile, which made the September sun feel even warmer.

Nearing the entrance, she glimpsed piles of dirt to the side of the building and noticed workers digging and tilling. Of all things . . .

Here she'd brought pots, soil, and seeds with her in the hope of providing her father a bit of enjoyment in gardening, and it would appear someone at the asylum had caught that same vision—except on a *much* grander scale. Walking paths, benches, areas being built up into berms.

She prayed it wouldn't be the case, but if her father were still at the asylum come spring, perhaps she could persuade Dr. Crawford to give him a small patch of ground for vegetables. Her father would love that.

Balancing the cloth-covered casserole—an antique dish that had belonged to her mother—Eleanor opened one of the large wooden doors, and startled when it slammed shut behind her. The next set of doors, which had stood open in welcome upon her first visit, were locked tight.

Through the glass pane, she saw a man headed in her direction—one of the men who had subdued her father, if she wasn't mistaken. Still embarrassed about that incident, she half hoped he wouldn't remember her.

"Miss Braddock," he said as he opened the door and granted her entrance. "Good to see you again, ma'am."

"Thank you." She stepped inside. "You as well, Mr. . . ."

"Jameson, ma'am." He took the satchel from her. "You're here to see your father."

It wasn't a question, but she nodded anyway.

"Come with me, please. I'll escort you to his room."

He opened yet another door and led her into a different wing of the building than she'd visited before. The scent of antiseptic hung heavy but couldn't mask the odor of urine and unwashed bodies.

For a moment, she was back in the surgical tent during the war, the pungent odors exhuming painful memories and images she'd spent years laying to rest. Needing a deep breath, she settled for several small ones instead and hurried to keep up.

Closed doors lined both sides of the hallway, and employees moved about quietly, the women's chatelaine keys jangling from starched white aprons. Through narrow windows in the doors, Eleanor glimpsed patients. Some stared back, expressions blank. Others sat by windows, looking outside, up at the sky.

Her heeled boots echoed in the stairwell as she trailed Mr. Jameson up a flight of stairs to the second floor, trying to stave off a growing sense of unease.

He opened the door, and to her relief, this hallway was absent any distinguishing odor. The entrances to the patient rooms were open too. At least the ones she could see. The quarters were sparsely decorated, but nice, clean looking.

"Your father's room is right here, Miss Braddock." He set the satchel by the partially open door. "I'll be at the desk down the hallway should you require assistance."

"Thank you, Mr. Jameson."

Palms sweaty, Eleanor took a steadying breath, catching a whiff of ham and cheese and reminding herself that the man on the other side of the door was her dear father, not some stranger.

Still, she knocked.

"Hello?"

No answer.

"Father?" She gave the door a push. It opened silently on well-oiled hinges.

Her father was seated by the window, head bowed. At first, she thought he was asleep, then she saw the book in his lap. She stepped inside the room, and he looked up. And squinted.

"Eleanor? Is that you?"

She didn't know why, but she was surprised he sounded so much like himself. And he looked well too—dressed and shaven. "Yes, Papa, it's me. I . . . I brought you your favorite custard." She moved closer.

He laid the book aside but didn't stand. Neither did he smile. "They told me you would come . . . eventually."

His voice held a cynical edge that nudged her guard up a notch. "I came as soon as I could, Papa. As soon as they said it was—"

"Dr. Crawford comes every day. We talk, take walks together. He's such a good man. But my own daughter . . ." He laughed. The sound wasn't pleasant. "She's too busy to visit. And this, after *you* were the one who put me in this godforsaken place, abandoning me like a—"

"Papa . . ."

She set the custard on a side table and went to him. He turned away.

"I *did* want to come before this, but I . . ." It occurred to her then that perhaps Dr. Crawford hadn't shared with her father that it was *he* who had requested she wait, for her father's benefit. The decision before her became clear: Tell her father the truth and risk damaging his relationship with the man responsible for his healing, and the one who'd obviously already won his trust. Or say nothing and bear the brunt of his anger.

She knelt beside his chair, wishing he would look at her, and working to speak past the knot at the base of her throat. "Papa . . . I haven't abandoned you. You're here to get better, remember? And it's only for a short time." She reached for his hand, but he pulled away. She schooled her expression to hide the hurt. "Dr. Crawford tells me you're doing well. That you're making prog—"

"The two of you have spoken?" He turned back, his eyes narrowing. "About *me?*"

Hearing the suspicion in his tone, Eleanor rose, finding herself in familiar—and heart-wrenching —territory. She unwrapped the casserole so he could see it. "Why don't I get some plates, and we'll have the custard I made for you."

"I don't like custards."

"Well, I think you'll like this one." She forced a brightness to her tone. "It's ham and cheese. Your favorite."

"I said . . . I *don't* . . . like . . . custards."

She looked at him but didn't see her father in the eyes looking back. "All right," she whispered. "We don't have to eat it now. That's fine."

Searching for a safe topic, she looked at the book he'd laid aside. "Perhaps I could read to you."

He didn't object, so she took that as a good sign.

She recognized the worn volume. "Tennyson. I've missed reading this with you." An old cigar band marked his place—the same cigar band he'd used in that book for years. When she saw the poem he'd been reading, she looked back at him, his surly disposition making more sense. "You're missing Mother today," she said softly.

"I miss her every day." His voice came out flat, hard. "Just like I miss Teddy." For a brief instant, at the mention of her brother's name, the severity in his features lessened. "I haven't gotten a letter from him in days. Not since you . . ." His jaw tensed. "You *left* me here. He stopped writing because of you, you know." His voice grew louder, more accusing. "He's afraid that if he comes to see me, you're going to do to him what you did to me!"

He shot to his feet, eyes going dark, and Eleanor took a step back.

"Papa!" She firmed her voice, drawing on tactics she'd used in the past. "Don't be angry. We can discuss this, if only you'll—"

He grabbed for her arm, but she jerked away. Should she call for Mr. Jameson? Surely, he would hear.

"I've written my banker instructing him to remove your name from *every* account. You'll not drain one more penny from me, daughter! Not after treating me this way. Teddy—" His breath caught, and he nearly choked on the name this time. "He would never have done this to me." He stilled, his features pinching tight. "If only they hadn't . . ." Tears pooled, and fell. "Why?" he whispered, chin shaking. He gently took hold of her arm. "Why did they kill him, Ellie?"

Her emotions already bruised and tender, Eleanor felt her breath leave in a rush. Hearing *that* name on her father's lips . . . From another lifetime, a better, far sweeter one.

But as swiftly as sorrow came, rage returned.

His grip tightened on her upper arm, and she struggled to break free.

"Mr. Jameson!" she called, certain she'd heard footsteps in the hallway. But when she saw her father raise his hand over his head, something snapped inside her.

Eleanor shoved her father with a strength she didn't know she had, much less thought she'd ever have to use against him. He staggered back a step, eyes seething. Then he reached for the casserole, unmistakable deliberateness in the act, and sent the dish crashing into the wall behind her.

Stunned, her breath coming hard, Eleanor stared at this man she'd known all her life, hearing again what Dr. Cheatham had said to her at breakfast. *"There may be times you'll need to remember . . .*

it's not your father speaking to you, it's the disease."

She struggled to see this moment through the lens of that counsel—but all she saw was that her father, the only family she had left, had become someone she did not know. She could scarcely reconcile that this was the same man who had penned the tenderly worded letter to Aunt Adelicia sharing his desire for his only daughter whom he loved so dearly to marry.

Mr. Jameson appeared and swiftly maneuvered around her to stand between them, then nudged her toward the door.

"Mr. Braddock." Mr. Jameson's voice was kind and steady. "Everything is going to be all right, sir. Dr. Crawford is on his way."

Her father's gaze darted about the room, the look in his eyes frantic, like that of a wounded animal.

Eleanor heard someone behind her, and Miss Smith—the nurse she'd met the first day—swept past her as though the tension in the room were nonexistent.

"Good morning, Theodore!" she said, her voice lyrical, encompassing a smile.

Theodore? Eleanor frowned. Her father hadn't been called by his middle name since he was a boy.

Miss Smith proceeded to smooth the bedcovers and pillows, then moved to the window, her movements measured and routine, her presence bringing calm.

But Eleanor caught an almost imperceptible look the young woman gave Mr. Jameson as she passed.

"Oh, I almost forgot . . ." Miss Smith reached into her pocket and withdrew something.

Eleanor craned her neck to see what it was, noticing her father doing the same. She trusted the staff, but still . . . She hoped this wasn't a ploy of some sort, a way to administer an injection or medication. That seemed cruel, even in light of what had just happened.

A touch on her back, and she turned to see Dr. Crawford. He motioned her into the hallway, then closed the door behind them.

"Miss Braddock," he said, voice low, "though I have yet to be apprised of the details, I assume from present circumstances that your visit did not go as desired."

"No, sir, it did not." Eleanor rubbed her arm, still a little shaken. "He's still so angry with me. Livid, is more like it."

Dr. Crawford's sigh held consideration. "Though your father has been stubborn at times about adhering to schedules and taking his medication, we've witnessed *none* of this anger since—"

"I was here," she supplied, reading the truth in his expression even before he answered.

"Yes, that's correct. But, Miss Braddock, it's quite common for a family member to be the focal point of a patient's anger. After all, in the absence of someone to blame, we often blame those we love." He shrugged. "It doesn't make sense, I realize. But it *is* the case. And you must remember, as frustrating and disturbing as this is for you, imagine what it must be like for your father, especially a man of his intellect. He can quote law briefs from 1853 and remember the most minute details of cases he tried and books he's read, yet he can't recall what he had for lunch. Or what he did an hour ago."

Understanding, and yet also not, Eleanor looked back at the door. "Could it be something I did or said that brought this about?"

"I very much doubt it. But . . . tell me about your visit, from when you entered the room until your father became violent."

She recounted every detail.

Dr. Crawford listened, nodding on occasion. "And when he threw the dish, do you believe you were the intended target?"

She replayed the scene in her mind, still trying to reconcile her father's behavior. "No . . . he threw it well away from me. But I do think he intended to strike me with his hand. And would have, if I hadn't pushed him away."

The door to her father's room opened, and Miss Smith exited. "He's calm now, Doctor. And eager to see you, sir."

"Very good, Miss Smith. Thank you."

"Yes, Miss Smith." Eleanor touched the nurse's arm. "Thank you for coming when you did."

"You're most welcome, Miss Braddock."

"May I ask," Eleanor continued, trying for a casual tone, "what was in your pocket? Back in the room just now."

The nurse shot a look at Dr. Crawford, and Eleanor's heart fell.

Dr. Crawford gestured. "It's all right, Miss Smith. We have no secrets from family members here."

Miss Smith briefly bowed her head. "In getting to know your father, ma'am, I've learned he responds best . . . to these." She reached into her pocket and held out her hand.

Eleanor looked, both puzzled and relieved. "Sugar sticks?"

Miss Smith nodded. "Peppermint is his favorite. So I always keep a supply on hand."

With an appreciative nod, Dr. Crawford dismissed the young woman, then laughed softly. "Not what you expected, Miss Braddock?"

Eleanor shook her head. "I didn't even know he liked them."

"Don't feel badly. Our staff is dedicated to learning what methods and motivations work best for each patient. And it seems your father has an insatiable sweet tooth that has proven most convenient." He smiled. "Now, in light of what happened earlier, I'm recommending a slight change of course. One that's proven successful in situations such as these."

Already sensing she might not like this *change,* Eleanor waited.

"For the next month or so, I suggest you write to your father in lieu of visiting."

She started to object, but he held up his hand.

"You are welcome here anytime, Miss Braddock. You are, after all, paying for your father's treatment. But you're also paying for our expertise. Your father is mentally ill. But he's also grieving, and grief takes many forms. Not the least of which is anger. Letters are an excellent way to communicate while removing the pressure of an immediate response. Your father is struggling with how to respond to his own emotions, much less life and all the changes it has thrust upon him. Both from within and from without."

Eleanor heard the wisdom in his words. It simply wasn't what she *wanted* to hear.

He reached for the doorknob.

"Dr. Crawford, one last question, please."

He paused.

"Nurse Smith addressed my father as Theodore . . ."

"Ah, yes, apparently that was at your father's bidding. I'm not certain why he requested it"—his eyes narrowed—"but one time, when he and I were in my office, he corrected me when I called him Garrison, told me to call him Theodore instead."

"So . . . what do you think that means?"

"It means we're on a road, Miss Braddock, with twists and turns. It's a road I've traveled with many other patients, but never with your father. Take heart that, while the journey is, on one hand, unknown, it's not completely unfamiliar. Your father still knows who he is. That is a very good sign. But I've seen no evidence of the disease waning, a possibility you and I had discussed and hoped for upon your first visit."

"But you said that was a possibility."

Covering her hand, he offered an encouraging look. "All of life is a possibility, Miss Braddock. None of us can predict what will happen tomorrow." He gave her hand a squeeze. "Now, about writing those letters. . . . You don't have to decide right now. Give it some thought. One day at a time, Miss Braddock. That's all we're given."

She nodded, hoping her voice held. "And sometimes . . . even our days must be broken down into hours. And minutes."

Eleanor left the pots, soil, and seeds she'd brought for her father with Nurse Smith, along with strict instructions not to tell him they were from her, lest he dash those against the wall too.

Another nurse escorted her back to the main entry, and Eleanor wasn't halfway down the front steps when she realized she still had the envelope from Dr. Cheatham for Dr. Crawford tucked in the side pocket of the satchel.

She hurried back inside to catch the nurse, but the foyer doors were locked. Peering through the paned glass, she knocked. And knocked again.

But no one came.

She pulled out the oversized envelope and considered leaving it at the door. But she'd assured Dr. Cheatham she would hand deliver it.

Outside, she looked for Armstead, but saw no

sign of the carriage—as she expected, since her visit had been far briefer than planned. Now, how to get this envelope to Dr. Crawford?

The sound of spades shoveling dirt drew her attention, and she peered over the side of the steps. Surely there was another entry into the building. A back way, perhaps. And she wagered one of those men would know where it was.

Leaving her satchel at the bottom of the steps, she picked a path through the freshly turned soil, closer to the workers, so she wouldn't have to raise her voice.

"Excuse me, sirs?"

One of the men stopped midshovel. "Yes, ma'am?" He wiped his brow with his sleeve. "Help you with somethin'?"

"Yes, thank you. I'm wondering if you could tell me where—"

"Miss *Braddock?*"

Eleanor froze at the voice behind her. It couldn't be. And yet—

She turned, his name sticking in her throat. "M-Mr. Geoffrey . . ." A thousand thoughts collided at once, but only one mattered.

How was she going to explain being at the Tennessee Asylum for the Insane?

Marcus couldn't believe it was her. Yet he'd recognized her instantly. That dignified, regal stature, the unassuming grace with which she moved. And that up-until-now-not-fully-appreciated

235

sway of her shapely hips as she turned. How had he missed that about her? But, at the moment, it was the smoky brown eyes staring unblinking into his that rendered him transfixed. Not to mention a little speechless.

Which didn't happen to him with many women. In fact, none that he could remember since he'd passed puberty.

He cleared his throat, brushing the dirt from his hands. "You're the last person in the world I expected to see out here, Miss Braddock."

Her lips moved but no words came at first. "I . . . I was thinking the very same thing about you . . . Mr. Geoffrey."

Aware of listening ears and eager to shed the formalities an audience demanded, Marcus indicated for her to join him near the front steps.

He was surprised to discover a satchel there. And even more surprised when he recognized it as hers. "Don't tell me you've grown weary of Belmont and have decided to take up residence *here?*" He laughed.

She did too. But it wasn't the spontaneous, warm response he'd hoped his comment would elicit.

"No, of course not." Her smile short-lived, she briefly looked away. "I ah . . . told Dr. Cheatham I would deliver a package for him." She held up an envelope. "But the front entry is locked."

"And with good reason." He nodded toward the building. "That isn't a safe place for you to wander around inside. While most of the patients seem docile enough, there *are* some who can be violent." He motioned to the envelope. "Why don't you let me deliver that for you."

She stared for a moment, her expression inscrutable, but leaning toward melancholy. She handed him the envelope. "Thank you. I would appreciate that, Marcus. It's for Dr. Crawford, as you see there." She indicated the name on the front.

He sensed something different about her but couldn't pinpoint what. She was more reticent than the evening he'd escorted her back to Belmont. Remembering how she'd stiffened when he'd first swung up behind her on the horse, and how she'd rallied with a sharply honed response, left him wishing for another such encounter.

And discovering she knew some German, even a little, had pleased him more than he'd let on.

"I'd ask what *you* were doing here . . ." She gestured to where his men were working. "But I think it's rather obvious. I'm glad someone decided to do this. It will be an improvement."

He eyed her. "I thought you didn't like gardens."

"I never said I didn't like gardens. I'm simply not overly fond of flowers."

"I believe your exact words were . . . *'I simply don't see the need.'*"

She raised an eyebrow. "You have a good memory."

"When it serves."

She offered the tiniest of smiles, then moved to retrieve her satchel. He reached it first and, hearing the clomp of horses' hooves, turned to see one of the Belmont carriages. She held out her hand as though to take the bag from him.

He shook his head. "I'll carry it for you."

"Thank you," she whispered, and wasted no time in meeting the carriage. Her gaze flitted from him to the asylum and back again. "How much longer are you here? I mean . . . How long will it take you to put in the garden?"

She seemed almost nervous. Even disturbed. Perhaps he shouldn't have been so honest with her about this place and its patients. "About two weeks or so. Mrs. Cheatham gave specific instructions to—"

"Mrs. Cheatham?" She paused at the edge of the walkway. "My *aunt* is responsible for this?"

He liked the way the space between her brows wrinkled when she disapproved of something. "Yes, madam, she is." Seeing Armstead about to climb down, Marcus waved to the man, indicating he would assist Eleanor himself. "Your aunt . . . now, there's a woman who's fond of flowers."

"Indeed she is," Eleanor said beneath her breath, accepting his hand briefly as she stepped up.

A little *too* briefly for Marcus's taste. In his experience, women often sent him signals through such a supposedly innocent gesture—by gripping his hand overlong or glancing seductively from beneath fluttering lashes. Or, from the more brazen, by leaning forward to afford him an ample view of their . . . womanly assets.

But not *this* woman. She seemed impervious to him. Or at the very least, indifferent.

It had been a long time since he'd looked forward to being in someone's company as much as he did hers. There was something inviting and so . . . unforced about her. To say he found her charm appealing was a gross understatement, which probably should have sent a warning through him.

But it wasn't the first time in his life he'd been attracted to a woman he couldn't have. And he *was* attracted to Eleanor Braddock, despite her dissimilarities to other women he'd pursued. But that was just it. He wasn't going to *pursue* her.

And she'd made it clear she didn't wish to be pursued by him, even if he were free to pursue. Which he wasn't. So . . . that was that.

"Thank you again, Marcus, for delivering the envelope." She glanced past him to the building, trepidation weighing her gaze.

"Eleanor . . ." Holding the carriage door open, he leaned in. "I'm sorry if what I said about this place frightened you. That wasn't my intent, I assure you. It's simply that . . . what's inside those walls is something no lady should have to witness."

She gave a soft, unexpected sigh. Not a laugh really, because there was no humor in it. And again, a sadness slipped in behind her eyes. "I appreciate your concern."

He closed the door but lingered, determined to draw a smile from her. "The roses I told you about, the ones I grafted for your aunt . . . one of the buds bloomed. But it wasn't quite the right color. The others are set to open anytime. You should come by and see them."

She nodded. Hardly the response he desired. Then it came to him . . .

"Don't forget, Eleanor . . ." He leaned in again. "The tunnel is still there, waiting to be explored. I'd be happy to show it to you anytime."

Slowly, her mouth tipped up on one side. And that was enough, for now. The carriage pulled away and he watched it go.

It wasn't until later that night, after a dinner eaten alone at the boardinghouse, that he surmised why his thoughts turned to her with such frequency. For the first time in his adult life, he was actually friends with a woman, with none of the various *strings* otherwise attached.

He liked the thought of simply being friends, strange and unfamiliar though it was to him. And unlikely, based on past experience. But he didn't want to think about his past, or even his future— beyond the next handful of months.

He especially didn't want to think about the *strings* tying him to Austria, or his obligations to the House of Habsburg, or to Baroness Maria Elizabeth Albrecht von Haas.

Retired to his room, he picked up the still unopened letter on the dresser and studied the exaggerated flourish of her script on the front, then slid his finger beneath the closure and opened it.

Multiple pages of stationery. No wonder the envelope felt thick.

Sighing, he sat back on his bed and scanned her always superfluous greeting. The baroness never used five words when she could use thirty.

He skipped on down.

You must know, Gerhard . . .

The baroness addressed him by his proper first name, which suited him fine. Until recently, only his mother had called him Marcus, the name he shared with his maternal grandfather, and that he'd declared as his first when arriving in this country.

I have been reading much about the Americas in your absence, and am quite fascinated with the description of this New World that borders the far side of the Atlantic. I am eager to learn more about its inhabitants—"colonial rustics" as your father describes them. You must find it terribly difficult to abide the smallness of life there among them. Indeed, I mourn the hardship you must be enduring.

Embellishment was her specialty, in so many ways. His sense of justice rose to challenge his frustration. The baroness wasn't an altogether unpleasant person. She simply wasn't the woman he would choose to spend his life with—if he had a choice. Which he didn't.

In her defense, she hadn't chosen him either, so they were in the same wretched boat. Only, judging from the tone and content of her letters—including this one—she didn't share his lack of enthusiasm for their future together. Quite the opposite, in fact.

Yet I realize that your leaving Austria for a time was not wholly of your own choosing. As your uncle predicted, the rumors about your brother have fallen to a hush. Come next summer and our glorious union as man and wife, that dark time will all be behind us. Forgotten forever.

He scoffed. Forgotten by her, perhaps. But never by him.

It hadn't been his choice to tell her the details about Rutger's death, but his father and uncle had insisted. Brides of arranged marriages—at least in the Habsburg monarchy—were schooled in family politics of this nature. They knew how to maneuver among society, how to drop hints, and how to nurture seeds of untruth.

And Baroness Maria Elizabeth Albrecht von Haas was a master of both.

I wish you would abandon this foolish notion with architecture and plants and return to Austria, to me, and to the grand future that awaits us. I often entertain the idea of—

Marcus bolted upright, her next words burning like a brand on his skin. Surely he'd misunderstood. The baroness couldn't seriously be contemplating the idea of . . .

He exhaled, and forced himself to begin the sentences again.

I often entertain the idea of joining you, Gerhard, and of seeing that country for myself. However simple and unrefined it may be. I long to practice my English on the commoners. But I understand it is an arduous voyage, and Vienna—with all its pleasant society—is at its best in fall. We have so much which to—

The mere thought of Maria Elizabeth Albrecht von Haas stepping her dainty little privileged foot onto American soil—much less in the city of Nashville—made him shudder. Suddenly the vast ocean separating them seemed minuscule, then shrank again by half, and he hastily reached for pen and paper to author a prompt reply.

One that would paint a far less fascinating portrait of life in the Americas with its *colonial rustics,* and that would keep his *fiancée* firmly grounded in Vienna.

16

Marcus straddled the thick oak beam, mindful of the height but even more so of the warehouse's three-story ceiling only inches above his head. He hadn't done this kind of work in ages and it felt wonderful. It behooved a man—even *the boss,* as his crew called him—to keep his skills from getting rusty. Climbing was in his blood. He'd been raised scaling heights.

On the opposite end of the support beam, Tom Kender—a compact but powerful man, and one of his finest workers—mirrored Marcus's actions, though with slower progress.

"I hate heights," Kender whispered, more to himself, it seemed, than to Marcus.

"How high you are, Kender"—Marcus inched forward, concentrating on his balance—"doesn't change your talent or your ability. Only your perspective on it."

"Yeah, well . . ." Kender squeezed his eyes tight. "Right now my perspective tells me that if I *do* fall, it *is* gonna matter how high I am. Or was."

Marcus laughed, partly in the hope of easing the man's nerves, but also because Kender's remark sounded much like one he'd uttered himself years earlier. To his grandfather.

His thoughts turned to the man after whom he'd been named. He'd been just a boy when his maternal grandfather had first taken him into the Alps. Little had he known then that those summer trips—time spent climbing the peaks and traversing the heights, quoting Tennyson to each other around the fire at night, and then falling asleep beneath a thick blanket of stars—would so influence the paths he'd taken.

Every brick laid in the foundation of a life, however meaningfully or haphazardly placed, shaped the whole. He could now see that fact borne out in every branch of study, from mathematics to science, from economics to chemistry. Each part of the equation influenced the whole.

If only he'd realized that far-reaching truth as a younger man. He would have been more careful about *every* choice along the way, instead of merely those that had seemed important or self-satisfying at the time.

On the heels of that thought came another, for reasons he understood only too well. He wondered what Eleanor was doing right that moment. He'd seen her briefly at church yesterday, sitting in Mrs. Cheatham's pew.

A few days earlier, he'd happened upon her on the grounds at Belmont, and she'd regaled him, in a rather caustic manner, with step-by-step instructions on how to make potpourri from crushed rose petals. Something she'd apparently been forced to learn during one of Mrs. Cheatham's womanly gatherings, of which Eleanor apparently was not fond—no surprise to him—and he'd enjoyed every minute of her bitter diatribe.

They had plans to explore the tunnel together this Friday evening, and he intended to hold her to that agreement. In the way of *friends,* of course, he reminded himself.

He looked forward to meeting her father when he arrived, and already guessed that Eleanor, with her logic and sensibilities, likely took more after him than—

"You're almost there, sir," Robert Callahan, his foreman, called up from the warehouse floor. "You too, Kender."

Marcus narrowed his thoughts and covered the last few inches to the midpoint on the beam. Positioned below, Callahan and seven other workers secured the ropes that held the new crossbeam suspended near the ceiling.

Marcus repositioned his leather tool belt, making mental note of where the mallet and spikes were so he could retrieve them without having to look down.

He peered across the beam that hung between him and Tom Kender and saw sweat pouring from the man's face.

"You're almost here, Kender. Another couple of feet. Don't look down. Just concentrate on the beam right beneath you. That's all there is right now."

"What I'm concentratin' on, sir"—the man's breath came heavy—"is the big mug of ale I'm gettin' right after work. *If* I live through this."

Smiling to himself, Marcus called down instructions to the workers below as he maneuvered the heavy crossbeam into place.

"We're almost there," he yelled after a moment, estimating the remaining distance from the notching in the crossbeam to the starter holes they'd drilled beforehand for the spikes. "Callahan! Back to the right about six inches." Marcus eyed it. "Kender, you good on your side?"

"Yes, sir. All good."

"Lower it, Callahan! Slow and easy!"

"Slow and easy, sir," Callahan repeated from below.

A trusted foreman was a hard thing to find, and Marcus was grateful to have found Robert Callahan. Callahan demanded the best and was respected by the men, yet could join them after work for an ale and fit right in among them. Something Marcus hadn't quite managed to do yet. He envied that about Callahan.

With a solid *thunk,* the massive traverse beam connected with the support beneath them, and Marcus set to work hammering the spikes into place on his side.

"Life sure looks different from up here, doesn't it, Mr. Geoffrey?"

Marcus looked over to see Kender holding tight to the crossbeam, the man's gaze riveted to the ground below. "Look at me, Kender!" he commanded.

The man lifted his head, his eyes a little dazed.

"*Don't* look down. Keep your eye on the work."

Kender blinked and sat up straighter. "Yes, sir."

Marcus slipped in another spike and positioned the mallet. But he sensed the need to keep the man focused. "So what made you volunteer to come up here today? Someone else could have done it."

Kender exhaled. "If I tell you, sir, you'll think it's daft."

"I doubt it. But if I do"—Marcus paused for effect, not looking up—"I'll be sure not to show it."

Kender laughed beneath his breath. "It's somethin' my papa used to say when I was a boy. I'd practically forgotten it, and . . . I don't know why, but it's come up again. A lot of things from early in life seem to be doin' that these days."

Marcus kept hammering, feeling as though the man had been eavesdropping on his own thoughts. He judged Kender to be a little older than he was, maybe close to forty, but Marcus could relate.

"My papa," Kender continued, "used to always say, 'Tommy, every day, boy, you need to do somethin' that scares you a little. It keeps life fresh, and keeps you grateful.' "

Marcus nodded. "Wise man, your father."

"Yes, sir, he was, in a lot of ways. Anyway . . . that's why I'm up here now. When you asked for a man to join you earlier, I felt my hand go up. Almost like somebody else was raisin' it for me."

Marcus considered that for a moment, then handed Kender the mallet. "I appreciate your courage in seeing it through. And, for what it's worth . . . I think statements like that, things people have said to us, tend to come back when we need to hear them most."

Whether due to lingering nervousness or to the man's strength, Kender hammered the remaining spikes into place in record time, then returned the mallet. "Mind if I ask *you* a question, Mr. Geoffrey?"

"Not at all."

"What are *you* doin' up here, sir? I mean . . . you got men to do this. You own the company. Why did you do it?" He laughed. "You're the *king!*"

Marcus met his stare, that one word reverberating inside him. And like the mountain is clearer to the climber from the valley, so was the life he'd left behind, however temporarily. Might he actually be a better man without that life? And its . . . obligations? The question returned with surprising force.

But ever vigilant, honor and duty swiftly squeezed the life from the doubt and prevented it from taking root. He had no choice. He was a Habsburg. He *had* to return to Austria.

His answer to the man's question came far more easily. "I do it for two reasons. First, I enjoy it. And second . . ." In his mind's eye, he could see his father and uncle so well. "Because I think it's wise for the man who is *king,* as you say, to remember what it's like . . . not to be."

Later that day, Marcus passed by "Eleanor's building," as he thought of it now. He glanced over, half hoping he might see her there. Then slowed his steps.

The windows . . .

Gone were the layers of grime and dirt. He cut a path across the street and through foot traffic to peer inside. He could actually see the interior and could have shaved in the window's reflection, the glass was so pristine.

A *For Rent* sign stood propped in the windowsill. Good decision for the proprietor to clean the place. It should help with getting it rented.

Why Eleanor had a key to this property still baffled him. But in any case, the door was locked tight and the place was empty.

He headed toward the boardinghouse, but dreading another evening alone decided to take a different route back—one that would no doubt prove a little painful and definitely frustrating. But he preferred to see the development in person rather than just read about it in the *Republican Banner* or the *Union and American* newspapers.

Four blocks and five minutes later, he stood in front of the plot of land he knew as well as the back of his hand. Anger and betrayal, stronger than he'd anticipated, gripped him all over again.

The land, once thick with clusters of pine, maple, and birch, had been leveled. *Every* tree gone, every bit of vegetation uprooted. Including the one-hundred-year-old poplar around which he'd proposed a garden be planted.

High above it all, stretched between two metal

poles—both of which leaned to the left—hung a bright red-lettered banner proudly announcing:

COMING: NASHVILLE'S
FINEST OPERA HOUSE
PREMIERE ARCHITECTURAL
ASSOCIATES' NEWEST PROJECT

Marcus blew out a breath. As far as he knew this was the company's *first* and only project.

Remembering the questions Mayor Adler's son—Everett, if memory served—had been asking when he'd entered the mayor's office, Marcus seriously doubted the opera house would ever be completed. Or if it was, whether the structure would stand long. Part of him hoped it wouldn't. While the greater part of him knew that wasn't what he should be hoping.

By nature, he wasn't one who wished ill on others. But when it came to men like Augustus Adler—

"Mr. Geoffrey!"

Hearing his name, Marcus turned and searched the street. "Caleb . . ." He greeted the boy with a handshake, pretending the lad's grip was painful. "*Schön, Sie wieder zu sehen!*"

Grinning, Caleb only squeezed harder. "It is good to see you again too, sir."

He saw Caleb fairly often now. Mainly in the bakery, which—judging by the paper-wrapped loaves of bread he carried under one arm—was probably where the boy had just come from.

Marcus had also seen him at Foster's Textile while his crew was there renovating the building. The boy had been on his way to meet his mother, who he had explained worked there on occasion.

Caleb peered up, *Kippah* atop his head as always. "What are you doing on this side of town, sir?"

"I decided to take a different way back to the boardinghouse tonight."

"I stopped by Foster's Textile yesterday. They said your work there was finished."

"It is. We completed the renovation last week."

"Where are you working now?"

Marcus nodded toward the end of the boulevard. "A few blocks north of here in a factory. Another renovation."

Caleb's shoulders sagged a little. "But you are tired of doing those. You said it yourself."

This time, it was Marcus's turn to smile. "Money's still scarce for most businesses. And it's less expensive to renovate than it is to build something brand new."

Caleb nodded but said nothing. He peered up at the banner rippling in the breeze, then back again, a question in his dark eyes. "Before, when you told me you hoped to build something but did not get the chance . . . is that what you wanted to build? The opera house?"

Feeling "found out," Marcus credited the boy's astuteness, even while not appreciating it at the moment. "It is. But I'll find something else. Don't you worry."

"Oh, I am not worried about you, Mr. Geoffrey. You are a good man. And good men always find their way."

Marcus leveled his gaze. "Something your father used to say?"

Caleb grinned. "No, sir, that was all me."

Laughing, Marcus glanced down the street, an idea coming. "Where are you headed?"

"Home." The boy lifted the bread. "I bought this for dinner. Mama should be there." His expression brightened. "You should come. She would like to meet you. She made *Semmelknoedel* last night. There is enough to share."

Marcus shook his head. "I don't want to impose."

Caleb frowned, eying him like a venerable schoolmaster might have. "*Ein Freund kann niemals eine Zumutung sein.*" Then the boy's expression softened. "Especially one from our homeland, Herr Geoffrey."

More than a little touched, Marcus gripped the boy's shoulder and gave it a squeeze, which earned him another grin.

"*Danke*, my young friend. You're very kind."

Marcus indicated for Caleb to lead the way, then fell into step beside him. "So tell me what you've done today, Caleb."

"Well, as we always do, Mama and I begin with prayer. Then after breakfast, she teaches me from Papa's books before she goes to her work. Then I go out to find what work I can too. I have places I always check, but sometimes they do not need . . ."

The boy's response continued in greater detail than Marcus had imagined, and stretched over six blocks and down an alleyway, until finally Caleb paused before a partially boarded-up two-story building. Not too far from Eleanor's building, Marcus realized. But this property was in even greater disrepair.

Of clapboard construction, the building had an arthritic appearance, its sagging walls and crooked windows having long ago abandoned their original intent. Even the exterior doors—what few remained—leaned like weary soldiers against thresholds whose welcome had been worn thin a lifetime ago.

Across the top of the building, in faded, barely legible capital letters were the words *Maxwell's Haberdashery.*

"This is where you live?" Marcus heard the question in his voice and regretted it.

"Not by ourselves, of course. Other families live here too." If Caleb had taken offense, his tone didn't reveal it. "Mama and I have two rooms instead of just one. Come, let me show you."

Marcus followed him inside, down one narrow hallway, then another. Caleb greeted what few women and children they saw by name. And Marcus soon discovered that the impressions he'd formed about the interior of the building, based on having seen the outside, proved grossly generous.

The once-white-plastered walls now stood dingy gray, stained with time . . . and other things he didn't care to dwell on. The plaster itself had worn so thin in spots, the boards peeked through like aging bones.

"Careful there," Caleb said, pointing.

Marcus stepped over a hole in the plank-wood floor, the board rotted clean through. Some of the other boards beneath him felt none too sturdy.

"Here . . . is where we live." Caleb pulled back a curtain draped across a doorway. "I have my room there—" He gestured to what might have been a storage closet at one time. "And Mama has hers."

Marcus peered inside. "Your mother isn't here?"

"Not yet, I guess."

Staying in the hallway, Marcus surveyed the room. "You and your mother have it arranged very nicely." And they had, with what few possessions there were. Mismatched dishes stacked on a shelf, a few womanly knickknacks beneath. Bedding folded and piled neatly on a straight-back chair in the corner. And books . . . everywhere, stacks of books.

All remnants of a better life.

"There is a kitchen down the hallway. That we all share."

Marcus nodded. "I look forward to meeting your mother. Do you think she'll be here soon?"

Caleb shrugged. "She may be working late. She has to sometimes. But we have the dumplings here in a bowl and then Mr. Fitch's bread."

Marcus heard him, but his attention was fixed on the slits of daylight fingering their way through hairline cracks and warped wood on the outer wall. It wasn't a significant problem now, but come winter . . .

"I have an idea, Caleb." He stepped back. "Why don't you save the dumplings and bread for breakfast, and we'll go get something to eat in town? While we're there"—he attempted to sound conspiratorial, knowing that if Eleanor were there, she would have succeeded masterfully—"we'll get something for your mother too, and you can have it waiting here for her when she gets back. All my treat, of course."

For an instant, the boy's eyes lit. Then his honest, hardworking upbringing seemed to offer challenge, and he shook his head. "You do not have to always buy me things, Mr. Geoffrey. That is not why I—"

"Caleb," Marcus said gently, "I was dreading eating dinner alone again tonight. So . . . you'd actually be doing me a favor. And this would give us time to talk. I have a business proposition for you."

The boy squinted.

"A job opportunity I'd like for you to consider," Marcus explained. "With my company."

The boy's expression sobered. He squared his shoulders.

And Marcus knew he'd won him over.

After dinner, Marcus toyed with the idea of riding out to Belmont. But it was late, the sun's light nearly spent, and the reason he would be going all the way out there would likely already be retired for the evening. So he returned to the boarding-house instead.

A while later, the coolness of the sheets soothed his tired back and leg muscles, and he closed his eyes. He thought again of what Caleb had said to him, before they'd walked to the boy's house.

"A friend can never be an imposition. Especially one from our homeland."

Marcus sighed in the dark, appreciative as other moments from the day replayed in his mind.

One stood out among the rest.

Was he a good man, as Caleb had said? And if he was, why did he feel as though he'd been striving to find his way for years . . . and couldn't? He felt as if he were lost in a fog, partly of his own doing and partly of others.

He'd been so certain he was the man destined to build that opera house, to show the city of Nashville how beautiful the partnership of man's design and nature could be. At least until the fifth bid had entered the equation.

He shifted, trying to get comfortable, well able to imagine his father's and uncle's reactions if they knew he was renovating old warehouses, planting gardens at an insane asylum, and patching up an old shack of a building.

So much for "building something no one had ever built."

He turned onto his side and shoved the second pillow beneath his head. Sleep felt a long way off.

So he did what he always did when the night

stretched on before him. " 'Half a league, half a league, half a league onward,' " he spoke into the darkness, imagining the crackle of a fire among the familiar peaks of home. " 'All in the valley of Death rode the six hundred. Forward, the Light Brigade!' "

The image of his grandfather Marcus wielding a branch like a sword coaxed the memory closer, and he could almost hear the deep baritone of the man's voice reaching across the years, stirring to life lessons of honor and courage bequeathed to a young boy.

"Was there a man dismayed? Not though the soldier knew some one had blundered. Theirs not to make reply, theirs not to reason why. Theirs but to do and die. Into the valley of Death rode the six hundred . . ."

Eleanor scooped a bite of warm buttermilk pie onto a fork, careful to get a fair amount of crust along with the silky, sweet custard. Casting a quick look at Naomi, she handed the fork to Mr. Stover, who slipped the bite into his mouth.

As he chewed, Eleanor sneaked a glance at the watch pinned to her shirtwaist. Almost half past five. She'd told Marcus she would meet him at the conservatory at half past seven tonight to explore the tunnel. She could hardly wait.

She was under no illusion that this invitation was anything other than him being kind to his employer's niece. But still, she sensed he enjoyed her company. And she very much enjoyed his.

Looking at him wasn't too painful either.

She watched Mr. Stover's expression, trying to gauge his reaction to the pie. The dear man had graciously granted permission for her to use his wife's kitchen, and in return she wanted to do something special for him. The recipe was one she'd perfected through the years. She only hoped it was similar enough to his late wife's, and that perhaps the taste, and the memory, would bring him comfort.

Judging from the slow smile spreading across his face, it did.

"Just like my Weezie's," he whispered, then licked his lips. "Tastin' this almost"—his voice broke—"makes me think I could see her walkin' round that corner any minute." He took a breath. "Thank you, Miss Braddock. This was awfully kind of you, ma'am." He pointed to the slice she'd cut for him. "Mind if I finish it *before* dinner?"

Eleanor laughed and nudged the plate forward. "Naomi and I will help you eat the first pie . . . but the second one is for you to take home."

"Would you like me to set the table now, Miss Braddock?"

Eleanor turned. "Yes, please, Naomi. Dinner won't be long. Will your son be joining us, I hope? I'm looking forward to finally meeting him."

"He said he would try. But he should have been here by now. Maybe he is still working. He has a new job working for a man in town." Motherly pride softened Naomi's voice. "If he does not come, Miss Braddock . . . would it be all right for me to take him a plate of food?" She turned to Mr. Stover. "*If* it is all right with you, sir. I will bring the plate back tomorrow morning. I give you my word."

Fork in hand, Mr. Stover nodded. "Don't mind at all, Mrs. Lebenstein. With all you and Miss Braddock have done to this place . . . seems I should be owin' you."

Eleanor put the final touches on dinner as Naomi set the small table Mr. Stover had brought from his house, along with four mismatched chairs. A welcome change from sitting on the floor as they'd been doing.

She thought again of her *appointment* later that evening.

She'd briefly seen Marcus yesterday afternoon as he, along with other men, loaded plants and trees from the conservatory to take to the asylum. Each time she pictured him working there or considered the possibility that he might come into contact with her father, she shuddered. She was thankful when he'd told her the garden was almost finished.

She wondered how her father's window garden was faring, or if he'd even planted the seeds. She'd written him every day since last seeing him. And every day, she hoped to receive a response.

It was difficult, abiding by Dr. Crawford's recommendation to not visit him for now. But if it helped her father get better . . .

In addition to making two buttermilk pies, she'd slow-cooked a beef roast, choosing that over pork in consideration of Naomi and her son, uncertain of their eating restrictions. She'd followed Cordina's cooking instructions to the letter. And even now, the fragrant meat was "resting"—as Cordina called it—on the worktable. *"Let it rest for twenty or thirty minutes, and it'll slice up real nice, Miss Braddock."*

Only vaguely aware of Naomi and Mr. Stover's conversation behind her, Eleanor drank in the homey feel of the kitchen. The "hub of the home," as her dear mother had called it.

She inhaled the comforting blend of aromas— buttery mashed potatoes warming on the stove, field peas Naomi had shelled earlier simmering in a neighboring pot, bits of onion nestled among them. All that remained were the yeast rolls browning in the oven.

This little celebratory dinner was turning out rather nicely. Even if it had cost more than she'd planned. The roast had been a splurge, but a good one. And she'd gone through almost *four* pounds of potatoes just to find enough that weren't spoiled or molding. And she'd bought them only two days ago!

But it was for a special occasion. Mr. Stover's building all but sparkled now and was truly ready to rent. Strangely enough, a part of her hoped it wouldn't rent too soon.

Yes, she could use the money Mr. Stover would return to her if it did rent, but she'd enjoyed cooking today. That enjoyment had been peppered with bittersweet thoughts about what this building could have meant for her—and for her father— had Aunt Adelicia said yes, but . . .

Eleanor smoothed the front of her apron. It was silly to miss something you never had, couldn't have. Best to be grateful for what you *did* have, and move on.

She pulled the pan of rolls from the oven, and in the haze of heat, a memory rose, a memory so vivid it could have been from yesterday. She could see the soldier's face, could feel his blood-slicked grip on her hand. She placed the bread on the stove and reached inside her pocket.

How could a worn handkerchief offer such reassurance? Especially when it represented a promise she hadn't kept. She'd tried, though. She'd spoken to countless widows after the war. Learning their names, listening to their stories, until she wondered how God's heart could possibly hold the flood of their grief, much less how He kept their tears in a bottle, as His Word promised.

As she'd done so many times, she prayed again that the soldier and his Mary girl were, somehow, both at peace.

The creak of the front door drew their collective attention.

"*Mutter, bist du hier?*" a young voice called.

"*Ja.*" Naomi tossed Eleanor a smile. "We are here. In the kitchen."

A young boy rounded the corner, and his smile was the first thing Eleanor noticed. That, and the *Kippah* sitting atop a head of thick dark hair that had a curl to it any woman would envy. He was thin, though not by nature, Eleanor suspected. Much like his mother.

He hugged Naomi tight, as though he hadn't seen her in weeks, and the sweet gesture brought a lump to Eleanor's throat.

"Caleb," Naomi said, voice soft, "may I present Miss Braddock, the lady who gave me the work here. And this is Mr. Stover, the owner of this fine building."

"Very nice to meet you, Miss Braddock." Caleb dipped his head, then offered his hand to Mr. Stover. "Very nice to meet you too, Mr. Stover."

The man's eyebrows shot up. "Well, aren't you just the grown-up one."

Everyone laughed, including Eleanor, but something Naomi had said tempered her humor.

"Caleb." Eleanor briefly touched Naomi's arm. "Your mother has told me all about you. I'm so glad you're able to be with us tonight."

"I am too, ma'am." The boy took a deep breath. "It smells good in here."

As Eleanor served up the plates, she slipped Mr. Stover an extra yeast roll after catching him eying the pan. When it came time to serve Caleb, she read his expression and added an extra dollop of mashed potatoes.

The smile the boy gave her would no doubt slay a young girl's heart someday. If it hadn't already.

As Mr. Stover said grace over the meal, Eleanor bowed her head, keenly aware of the blessing of these unlikely friends, and of how much it meant to her to be sitting with them. She thanked God for each, and then prayed for her father . . .

All while picturing a mysterious dark tunnel and an impossibly handsome man.

After dinner and with hardly a moment to spare, Eleanor closed the door to the building behind her, reticule on her arm and covered plate in hand. She waved good-bye to Naomi and Caleb, still thinking about what Naomi had said in passing.

". . . the lady who gave me the work here."

Eleanor slipped the key into the lock, feeling so foolish. It hadn't occurred to her until hearing that statement that this *celebratory* dinner, as she'd called it, was likely anything but for Naomi. They had finished cleaning the building—all except for whitewashing the walls in the main room, which Mr. Stover said he would pay Naomi for doing. But finishing that meant no more work for her. And therefore no more pay.

"This pie right here is gonna be breakfast, lunch, and dinner for me tomorrow, Miss Braddock."

Eleanor returned the key to her reticule, warmed by Mr. Stover's expression and by how he clutched the pie tin as though someone on the street might try to snatch it from him.

"Mr. Stover, thank you again for giving me permission to cook here on occasion. It means more than you know."

"My pleasure, ma'am. After eatin' your food tonight, I know my Weezie would be pleased too. Best I've had since . . . since I don't remember when."

The softness in his eyes revealed his thoughts, and lingering grief.

Eleanor had intended to send a portion of the remaining dinner home with him as well. But he'd insisted Naomi and Caleb take it. Naomi had graciously accepted, saying she would share it with their neighbors tonight. She possessed a kind and tender heart. As did Caleb.

Naomi hadn't revealed much about her past, yet Eleanor felt a kinship with her. Watching mother and son disappear around the corner, Eleanor imagined that—despite the woman's quiet disposition—if given the right circumstances, Naomi Lebenstein could be a force to be reckoned with.

She liked that.

"You want me to walk you home, Miss Braddock? It's gettin' late fast."

"Oh no, Mr. Stover. I'm fine. There's plenty of light left. But thank you."

In all their conversations, she'd purposefully not mentioned where she lived or whose niece she was, and Mr. Stover had never asked. And though Aunt Adelicia knew about the building, she didn't know the building's location. It still seemed best to keep the two worlds separate.

"For what it's worth, ma'am . . . I think you'd have done a mighty fine job at havin' a restaurant. I wish it could've worked for you."

"Thank you, Mr. Stover." Eleanor glanced back at the darkened building, able to picture imaginary patrons filling tables and chairs. "I wish it could have too."

Maybe she wasn't coming. Perhaps something had detained her or . . . she'd forgotten.

Marcus weighed the possibilities, and even though both outcomes meant he wouldn't see her tonight, he hoped her reason was based on the former rather than the latter.

Even as that thought crystalized inside him, he realized he cared far more than he should have about whether she came or not. Far more than he would for a mere *friend*. Faced with that reality, he found it impossible to ignore the truth.

Eleanor Braddock was no more merely a friend than he was merely an under gardener. And yet she wasn't anything *more* to him either. Not a lover. Not a . . . *paramour*. Not even the potential of either. He laughed without humor.

From every indication she'd given him, her feelings extended only to those of friendship.

Which was where he needed for his own feelings to remain as well. So . . .

All was proper and befitting decorum. He was safe. And so was she.

He planned on telling her tonight that he didn't work for Mrs. Cheatham. It was time she knew the truth. Although he would have been more eager to correct her misassumption if his company had been awarded the contract for the opera house. Renovating warehouses didn't seem nearly as impressive.

It crossed his mind to tell her about his impending departure as well. But—call it selfishness, or maybe wishful thinking—he didn't want to introduce that factor into the equation at present. He liked their relationship, platonic though it was, and how she treated him. As though he were an ordinary man. And he didn't want to do anything to change that.

He checked his pocket watch. A little past eight.

He spied the *Selenicereus grandiflorus* and remembered Eleanor's less than complimentary remark about the cactus. "Don't worry, you grand old madam," he said, fingering a spine, mindful of how sharp they were. "Your day is coming."

And he knew just *who* he wanted there watching with him when it did.

He took a last look through the glass wall of the conservatory to watch the sun as it rested briefly atop the trees in the distance. He stood perfectly still, his gaze fixed upon the highest branch of a colossal cedar silhouetted against the western horizon. And he followed the sun's determined progress as it inched lower . . . lower . . . sinking softly into night. And into day on the other side of the world.

Since leaving Austria, he'd never once been homesick. But he'd also never felt so far from home as he did right in that moment. But it wasn't homesickness he was feeling, There was a difference between the two, he quickly decided, a difference he couldn't define but keenly felt.

He turned to leave, but movement from the corner of his eye drew his focus. He spotted the telling outline of a bell-shaped skirt hurrying by the fountain outside, and would've sworn that—despite approaching dusk—the sun had reversed its course.

"I'm sorry I'm so late, Marcus!"

"You're not *that* late." Marcus opened the door for her, noticing a flush in her cheeks—and the look she gave him. "Well, maybe you are."

"My errands in town took longer than I thought they would. Then I needed to stop by the main house first, and I saw my aunt, and she asked about my day, so we spent a few moments visiting because they leave for Alabama in the morning, and then—"

"Eleanor," he whispered.

"What?" she whispered back, brown eyes widening.

"Take a breath."

She smiled and held out a covered plate. "For you."

"What is it?"

"Open it and see." She winced playfully. "It got a little crushed on the way here, though. So it's not as pretty as it was at first."

He took the dish and removed the flowered cloth. "Pie!"

"But do you know what kind?"

He eyed it. "I can't say that I do. It doesn't resemble anything we have in Austria."

"It's buttermilk pie."

He tried to school his initial reaction. But judging from her frown, he didn't do it swiftly enough.

"Why did you make that face?"

"I'm sorry. I-I'm not overly fond of buttermilk."

She waved a hand. "The pie has buttermilk in it, but it doesn't *taste* like buttermilk. It's sweet and custardy, and you're going to love it."

"Yes, madam." He gave a mock salute. "I trust you completely."

He escorted her to his "surgical wing," as Henry Gray referred to it, and found the closest thing he could to a fork.

"A tongue depressor?" She laughed.

He twiddled the wooden stick in the air. "They serve many purposes."

He managed to take a bite. And she was right. "This is . . . *köstlich*, Eleanor."

She curtsied. "*Danke*, Herr Geoffrey. *Ich bin froh, dass es Ihnen gefällt.*"

Marcus nearly dropped the plate.

She laughed again. "I've been practicing my German at night. Mind you, it took me an entire evening digging through my father's crates of books to find my old German text from school."

"Your father speaks German too?"

An odd look flashed across her face. "No, he . . . he doesn't. The book I was looking for just happened to be packed with all of his, and—" She crossed to the table where he'd placed plants selected for grafting. "I only speak a little of the language, mind you. German was among my studies at the Nashville Female Academy. For only two years, though. I practiced that sentence for *days,* hoping you would like the pie. If you hadn't"—she shrugged, managing to look both charming and alluring at the same time—"I would have improvised."

"I bet you would have." Marcus took another bite, enjoying the pie. And her.

He finished chewing and pointed to the plate, tongue depressor in hand. "This truly is excellent, Eleanor. My compliments to Cordina when you see her next."

Her mouth slipped open. "Cordina? She didn't make it." She raised her chin. "*I* did."

He smiled and waited for her to do the same, knowing she was teasing.

"No, really, Marcus. I baked it. Earlier today."

He searched her gaze. She was serious. "I beg your pardon, I . . ." He knew to phrase an explanation carefully, not wanting to offend. But in his experience, *servants* prepared food. Not rich nieces from well-to-do families. "I didn't realize that women of your . . . social status knew how to cook. Much less like *this*."

To his surprise, her expression softened with gratitude. A far different response from the one he'd feared.

"Thank you." Her voice came softly. "I appreciate that . . . very much."

The utter openness in her eyes—as though he were seeing straight through to her heart—stirred him, and he grew more aware of how alone they were. And of how "not good" that was at the moment.

Silence framed the passing seconds, and though he knew such a thing was out of the question, he wanted to take her in his arms and kiss her, and wondered what her response would be if he did. Even more—this next thought kicked his pulse up a few notches—what would it be like for this woman to *want* him to kiss her? In his past, he hadn't been a patient man in that regard. Granted, the women he'd met as archduke hadn't been the patient type either. They'd had agendas. Aggressive ones. But then, so had he.

Eleanor Braddock, however . . . She was different. She was—

The images of her that filled his head completely

undermined everything he'd told himself earlier. *Friends*. A bitter tang tinged his mouth. She saw him that way, but he couldn't claim the same. And yet he needed to.

She offered the briefest of smiles, then turned to study the plants, which allowed him to study her.

In the eyes of this intriguing, lovely creature, he was an under gardener. But, he reminded himself, if she knew him as Archduke of the House of Habsburg—the man he wanted to leave behind, even as he knew he never could—her opinion of him would certainly not be the same. The irony wasn't lost on him.

What once had been his greatest advantage was now his greatest disadvantage.

She pointed to a bandaged root of a daisy. "What is this?"

Appreciating her interest, he came alongside her. But not too close. No need to tempt fate.

"It's something I've been working on for over a decade. My grandfather had a fondness for flowers. There was a certain wildflower, an oxeye daisy"—he leaned against the table—"that grew under an elm tree in his garden. He used to pick them for my grandmother. She appreciated them, but she was a woman who enjoyed the *finer* things of life, shall we say."

"Like someone else we know?"

"Indeed." He smiled. "My grandmother wished the wildflower was less gangly. Better suited for a garden."

"So you made one that was."

"It wasn't quite that simple. Nor am I that intelligent."

She gave him a look saying she doubted that, which endeared her to him more than any subtle squeeze of a hand could ever have done.

"When I was young," he continued, "I took an interest in botany, then later had the great fortune of being tutored by a scientist whose brilliance in the field of biology is, in my opinion, unsurpassed. He's especially gifted in the studies of heredity, which is what interests me most. Plant *breeding*," he said more delicately, "as it's called by some."

Eleanor nodded, not seeming the least offended by the word.

He sighed. "Unfortunately, the significance of my mentor's work has yet to be recognized by most of his peers."

She studied him. "But you admire him very much."

"I do. Gregor Mendel taught me more than all of my other professors combined. Only last week, I received a letter from him answering more of my questions, in extensive detail, as always. So he continues to teach me, even now."

"And my guess is that you learned to keep extensive notes too." She nodded toward stacks of notebooks on the table, then raised an eyebrow as if to say, *"May I?"*

Marcus nodded.

She picked one up, and as she leafed through it, he briefly considered inviting her to join him outside in the field garden, thinking she might appreciate the significance of what was planted there. But there was nothing impressive about the leaves of a potato plant. What might someday be impressive—once the plants matured, and *if* the grafting proved successful—was still hidden deep in the earth, yet to be seen.

She lifted her gaze. "You are very detailed! 'Diagram of Tree Grafts'," she read aloud. " 'Record of Blooming. Record of *Budding*'?" She looked up. "You keep track of everything."

"I have to. It's the only way to remember all the various combinations of grafts and the out-comes of each."

She tilted the notebook at an angle. "You're also very good at sketching."

"Thank you, madam. I've had a great deal of practice." Already having decided to tell her the truth about his real occupation, he saw his opportunity. "There's something else I'd like to talk to you—"

"Ah!" she said, lifting a hand. She pointed again to the daisy. "Finish telling me the rest of this story first."

He stared, amused at her feistiness. "You came here to see the tunnel, not to talk about plants. Even though I know how interested you are in them."

"I *am* interested."

He leveled a stare, enjoying the way she wrinkled her nose.

"Well, maybe I'm a little more interested in what

you do to the plants to change them and create new ones, rather than just how they look. If that makes sense."

Never before had a woman shown this level of interest in this part of his life. Well, other than his mother. She always had been his greatest advocate. The few times he'd tried to speak with the baroness about it, she'd quickly changed topics, wiping her hands together as though scraping off imaginary dirt.

"After I discussed it with Dr. Mendel, we envisioned the perfect daisy as having larger flowers of purest white, and a longer blooming season. In addition, the flower needed to do well as both a cut flower and a garden flower, so we started first with the *Leucanthemum vulgare*—the oxeye daisy," he added. "And we cross-pollinated it with the English field daisy, *Leucanthemum maximum*, which had larger flowers than the oxeye. We then pollinated the best of these hybrids with pollen from the *Leucanthemum lacustre*, the Portuguese field daisy, and we bred their seedlings selectively for six years."

"Six years?" she repeated.

He nodded. "And they bloomed nicely. But I wanted whiter, larger flowers."

She narrowed her eyes. "Competitive at heart, are you?"

"Maybe a little." He winked. "But the success we'd had merely gave me the desire to succeed again."

"Make the flower stronger, more beautiful."

He looked at her, *really* looked at her, and was glad when she didn't look away. "That's right. But that didn't happen until I arrived here and discovered that Mrs. Cheatham had a *Nipponanthemum nipponicum* in her collection."

Eleanor exhaled a *pfft* sound. "Doesn't everyone have one of those?"

He laughed. "Do you know what it is?"

"I have absolutely no idea."

"It's a Japanese field daisy, a species with small, pure-white flowers. I took the most promising of the triple hybrids and pollinated them with that. And ended up with—"

"The prettiest and strongest flower in the history of the world!"

This woman . . . intelligent, witty, and possessing a beauty he'd failed to truly see—much less fully appreciate—until now.

How could he have ever agreed to share a future with a woman like the Baroness Maria Elizabeth Albrecht von Haas, when there was such a treasure as Eleanor Braddock in the world?

Hesitating for only an instant, he offered his arm, same as he would have done for any other woman. "Allow me to show you the resulting flower, madam? Quickly . . ." He looked up through the glass ceiling to the purpling sky. "While we still have some light left."

She slipped her hand through. "I'd be honored, sir."

He led her past the line of cabinets to a door around the corner.

"Oh," she said, "I didn't see this door when—"

She paused as though having caught herself, and he wasn't about to leave well enough alone.

"When I caught you snooping in my surgical wing?"

She peered up. "That's what you call it?"

"That's what Mr. Gray calls it." He briefly covered her hand on his arm. "*I* call it my haven."

Her eyes warmed. "I can see why."

His hand on the latch, he focused on her, anticipating her reaction when she glimpsed what was beyond the door.

19

Color. Everywhere. Explosions of it. And in hues Eleanor had never seen before, much less in flowers. Tones so rich and vibrant. Others so pure, soft as a whisper. She couldn't decide where to look next or which was more beautiful. Or if the beauty was due, at least in part, to knowing the man responsible for it.

Aware of him watching her, she tried to find the words to describe it but failed. Finally, she exhaled, then drew in a breath—and that's when she smelled the familiar fragrance.

An instant later, she spotted them.

"Peonies!" Gathering her skirt, she maneuvered

down a narrow aisle in order to see them better.

He followed, his laughter hinting at disbelief. "Out of this entire propagating room, humble peonies are what excite you?"

She leaned down and inhaled memories of home. "I looked for these in the gardens the first day I arrived here, but didn't see them anywhere."

"That's because we haven't planted them outside yet. I'm still trying to win Mrs. Cheatham over to them. She said the plant was a little *less grand* than she desired."

Eleanor said nothing but wasn't surprised. "Well, I think they're lovely. Bushy shrub and all."

"I do too. In fact, I . . ."

When he didn't continue, she looked up.

"What?" she said softly, reading his sheepish look.

He fingered one of the leaves, glancing over the room. "I brought these over with me when I came, and have been—"

"You brought these plants all the way from Austria?"

"Many of them, yes." He narrowed his eyes as though debating whether or not to tell her something. "I paid for an extra cabin on the ship and filled it with plants and trees. I'm sure it seems odd, but some of these plants are from grafts and hybrids I've been working with for over fifteen years." His words came faster, as though he were trying to convince her. "I couldn't leave them behind. Not after all that time."

She glanced around the room, taking it in, and imagining what that cabin had looked like. And the expense of such a decision. But fifteen years *was* a long time. . . .

She looked up. "You are a most *interesting* man, Marcus Geoffrey."

"And you, Miss Braddock"—his smile came slowly—"are a most intriguing woman."

The blue of his eyes deepened, rousing an awareness inside her, an anticipation she wasn't prepared for. Part excitement, part fear, it made breathing a challenge. As did the step he took toward her.

He leaned in, deliberateness in the act, and the air around her evaporated. He lowered his face toward hers and—

"This is the flower I wanted to show you," he said, reaching around her.

With his face so close, his body only inches from hers, Eleanor didn't dare move lest they touch. Still, a small part of her wanted to move just so they would.

Heart hammering, she got a much better look at those mesmerizing blue eyes and that solid jaw already dark with tomorrow's beard. Everything about him bespoke strength and masculinity. Even the faint laugh lines framing his mouth and the corners of his eyes only added to his appeal. *Adonis, indeed.*

She caught a whiff of his bay rum and spice cologne, and something else decidedly male, and her gaze went to his mouth, even as her own went dry.

He straightened, seemingly unaffected, while it took her every ounce of her concentration just to draw breath.

Her face heated, and she forced herself to focus, feeling both naive and foolish. What on earth had possessed her to think this man wanted to kiss her? It wasn't as though—

"Eleanor?"

She blinked. "Yes?"

"Are you all right?"

Not eager to meet his gaze, she lifted hers. "Of course." She smiled, wondering if her eyes were as wide as they felt. "I'm fine. Why?"

One side of his mouth tipped ever so slightly, as though he knew a secret she didn't. "Did you hear what I said just now?" His voice came softer this time.

He'd said something?

Then, as if her mind were playing tricks on her, she realized she *had* heard him. What he'd said simply hadn't registered at the time. "Of course I did." She laughed, determined to appear unaffected as well. "You said something regarding what I asked you about earlier. About the daisy."

He nodded, his sigh resembling a laugh. "Close enough." Then he held out his hand.

He cradled a clay pot that contained the most beautiful daisies, their large petals white as snow, their golden middles perfect little drops of sunshine.

She felt a swell of pride. "You did it," she whispered.

"Mendel and I did, years ago."

"And your grandmother?"

"She loved them. This daisy is a descendant from the ones in her garden."

"Hence, why you couldn't leave them behind."

"I'm continuing to perfect it, though, with the help of a botanist in Boston."

"Boston?" She eyed him. "Best not tell my aunt you're getting help from up north. She didn't like it when the Federal Army confiscated her home during the war. And I can tell you with utmost certainty she won't welcome a Northerner's *ways* infiltrating her garden now."

"So I've gathered. But he's brilliant with plants. He's about ten years younger than I am, and about fifty years ahead of his time." He returned the daisy to the table. "One more flower to show you. Your aunt's rose."

She followed him down another aisle, and he stopped by a table brimming with roses in every imaginable shade of pink. No, she corrected herself. That wasn't true. She thought of her pink skirt and jacket. None of *these* pinks were nearly as offensive.

"I don't have the color quite to her liking yet, but—" He picked up a rose whose buds were still closed. "I'm hoping this little beauty will be the one. They should be open in the morning if you want to come back and see."

Sensing he wanted her to, she nodded. "Then I'll be here."

He retrieved a lantern from a nearby table, the vestiges of day nearly spent. He lit the wick, then offered his arm.

"And now, madam . . . your tour awaits."

Beneath the conservatory lay another world, a cozy labyrinth of passages and rooms that Eleanor quickly fell in love with.

She'd always enjoyed the dank smell of earth, equated it, for some reason, with the passage of time. She and Teddy had spent many a childhood afternoon in a cave on their family property, exploring, pretending they were in far-off lands. The memory of her brother tugged at her heart.

Marcus held up the lantern, continuing their tour. "This is where all the bulbs are kept before planting. The area over there is for storage, similar to the one I showed you a moment ago."

"This is larger than I thought it would be." She peered into an adjacent room. "Are those . . . furnaces?"

"Yes, exactly. For winter."

She followed him inside. The walls of the furnace room were brick, and above them, wooden beams supported the ceiling.

"The air is heated down here," he continued, "then travels through pipes and up through vents in the floor of the conservatory. We determine the temperature in each of the rooms by controlling how big the fires are. And also by how far we open the vents."

She sighed. "Truly impressive."

"That's what I thought when I first saw it." He motioned overhead. "Those are the pipes I told you about before." He knocked on one. "Pure lead. They deliver water from the tower throughout the estate. Watch your step through here."

Seeing the tunnel ahead, Eleanor felt a shudder of excitement. And a touch of wariness. It was narrower than she'd anticipated, and very dark, of course. She could see the faint outline of pipes affixed to the ceiling.

"You're not changing your mind, are you?"

"Absolutely not!" She nudged him, grateful they were back to their usual banter.

"Are you ready, then?" He held out his hand. "It won't take us long, but I do have something I want to show you."

She accepted, trying not to dwell on how good her hand felt tucked inside his. Safe. Warm. Protected. She and Teddy used to hold hands in the very darkest part of the cave simply because the one leading had the lantern. But holding hands with Marcus was a far cry different. And it was a difference she liked.

"It's a little muddy through here. You may want to gather your skirt."

She paused and did just that, then quickly slipped her hand into his again.

The walls weren't as slick as the cave from her

childhood. Whoever dug this tunnel had shored up the sides with brick, but left the hard-packed earth on the floor. The path was slippery in spots and inclined slightly, so she stepped carefully.

Tendrils of roots fingered her hair from above, reminding her she was underground. As if she could forget.

The lantern's burnished arc of light bounced from one wall to the other, then back again. With Marcus in front, she couldn't see much before them. And though nothing but hollowed-out earth lay ahead, she was glad he'd gone first instead of—

Her foot slipped. She felt herself falling.

She tried, in vain, to grab hold of the wall for balance, still clinging to Marcus's hand. Then she grimaced, anticipating the pain, and embarrassment, of the inevitable when—

Strong arms encircled her waist, preventing her fall. At the same time, she heard a crash. And the tunnel went black.

"*Vorsicht!*" Marcus whispered, holding her against him. "Are you all right?"

Her body spared from injury, Eleanor couldn't say the same for her pride. She ventured a laugh, his closeness unnerving. But the result came out weak sounding, much like the attempt. "I'm sorry . . . I thought I was watching closely enough."

"No harm done. Not yet anyway," he said, an odd tone in his voice. His arms tightened around her.

Eleanor couldn't see his face, but she felt the warmth of his breath against her cheek and the hard muscle of his chest beneath her palms. The temperature in the tunnel jumped by ten degrees.

She tried to think of something to say—and couldn't.

"You're sure," he whispered, "that you're all right? You're not hurt?"

His voice sounded different—huskier, deeper. His hand moved over her back, slowly, tenderly. And for the first time in her life, Eleanor knew what women meant when they said they went weak in the knees.

"Yes," she said, working to catch her breath, but not from the near fall. "I'm fine. Just . . . embarrassed."

"Don't be." He loosened his hold. "The same thing happened to me not long ago. I still have the bruise."

She smiled in the darkness, grateful he couldn't see her face. Surely she was three shades of red.

"Here." His hand trailed a path down her arm, then he pressed her palm against the brick wall. "You stand right here. No running off now. I'll relight the lantern . . . once I find it. I didn't hear the glass break."

The tunnel muffled their laughter, and she heard him groping around in the darkness, then the telling clink of metal.

"Got it!"

As his footsteps moved behind her, she discovered a new respect for darkness, and a deeper gratitude for light—and the warmth of someone's hand enfolding hers. She shifted her weight, and winced at a twinge in her ankle. But she wasn't about to admit it to him. Not and risk him saying they'd finish the rest of the tunnel some other time.

She would drag her leg behind her, if need be. She wouldn't miss this opportunity to be with him down here.

A moment later, a wash of orangy light cascaded down the tunnel and she happily accepted his hand once again.

They continued on, and after a few steps, he turned. "Here's where it gets interesting. Well, *more* interesting." He smiled. "Most people could continue without stooping. But not us."

True to his word, they both had to stoop as they walked, which made progress more challenging.

"Where was the leak that night? When Aunt Adelicia asked if you would take a look at the damage?"

"Some distance on up, before the tunnel branches out. Oh, be sure and keep your eyes open. I saw a rat in here that night, so—"

Instinctively, she tightened her grip on his hand, and he laughed.

Realizing he was only teasing her, she poked him with her thumbnail. "That was *mean!*"

But she couldn't help smiling in the dark.

They walked—or hobbled—another few steps before he stopped. He gave her hand a squeeze before releasing it, then knelt down and placed the lantern on the ground. She knelt too, grateful for the chance to rest her lower back.

"A fascinating thing about plants," he said, "and nature in general, is what can be accomplished given time, and persistence. And nature has plenty of both. I remind myself of that every now and then, especially when a graft I've worked on for months fails, or a hybrid doesn't bud. Then I see something like this—" he picked up the lantern and shone the light down the tunnel—"and I am reminded, yet again, of how strong nature really is."

Eleanor peered around him, narrowing her eyes in an effort to see better. Something protruded from the wall a few feet ahead, coming right through the brick. "What is it?"

"Remember the oak near the main gazebo?"

She glanced up, imagining the scene above ground. "That's a *root?*"

He nodded. "That tree's well over a hundred years old. And will likely be here long after we're both gone."

"Thank you, sir, for that sobering thought."

He smiled and so did she.

"I want to touch it," she whispered.

"Why does that not surprise me?"

With some maneuvering—and hitting her head once on the overhead pipes—Eleanor moved closer.

She ran a hand across the rough surface, grateful the tree had been spared during the war. "Over a hundred years old. . . . It feels more like rock."

"And yet it's alive, as much as the rest of the

oak. And has as important a role as the leaves and branches."

She tried to wrap both hands around the root, and couldn't. "I've walked by this tree countless times, and never once have I stopped to think about what was beneath."

When he didn't respond, she looked over and read understanding in his expression. And even . . . appreciation. She marked the moment to remember. This man . . .

Adonis, undeniably so. But perhaps there was more to Marcus Geoffrey than met the eye.

Walking beside Marcus back to the mansion, Eleanor found herself admiring him more than she'd ever thought possible based upon their first meeting.

He was quiet. But it was late, and likely he was as tired as she.

With October almost upon them, the night air held a touch of cool. A northern breeze rustled the trees, and Eleanor tucked a wayward strand of hair behind her ear. Her ankle was still a little sore, but she wouldn't have missed tonight for anything.

Like a lighthouse beacon, a three-quarter moon hung over the mansion, spilling its light across the estate and giving the gazebos and marble statuary a silvery, dreamlike cast. How extravagant this estate was—the grounds, the mansion, the conservatory, bowling alley, ice house, and on and on it went. Especially when she compared it to what Naomi and Caleb had. Or didn't have.

Eleanor couldn't begrudge her aunt owning such an estate. Aunt Adelicia was quite generous with her possessions and had opened her home so graciously for a niece by marriage who had nowhere else to go. But . . . Eleanor took in the surroundings. Such extravagance was simply too much for her, personally. She didn't see the need.

She preferred things more practical. After all, the function of a building could lend as much beauty to the structure as did the outward facade, perhaps even more so.

When she and Marcus reached the main fountain, a few yards from the front steps, he briefly touched her arm.

"Eleanor . . ."

She paused.

"I want to thank you for being my guest this evening. It was a pleasure to share those things with you. And to see them through your eyes."

"I'm the one who's grateful, Marcus. Everything was wonderful. The tour, the tunnel, learning more about your responsibilities here. And seeing that daisy and hearing the story behind it. You really are so gifted at what you do." She hesitated, deciding whether she should confess her next thought. "I suppose I can admit something to you now . . . At one time, I considered you to be fortunate to have the opportunity to work here at Belmont. But now . . . I believe my aunt is the fortunate one—to have you in her employ."

He glanced away as though uncomfortable

beneath her praise. "You're kind to say those things, Eleanor. But . . . about my being an under gardener . . ."

He looked back, and though she couldn't see the precise definition of his features, she sensed embarrassment on his part. And after tonight, seeing what an ambitious and intelligent man he was, she thought she knew why.

"Please, don't misunderstand what I'm about to say," he continued. "Being an under gardener is a respectable profession, especially here at Belmont, but I—"

"Of course it is, Marcus. And you should be proud. Look at all you've accomplished. One day, probably very soon"—she hoped he could hear her belief in him—"you'll be the *head* gardener of an estate. But what head gardener, much less an under gardener, has managed to do what you've already done? You're doing what you enjoy. I'd even say . . . what God created you to do. And that's what matters. No matter what anyone else tells you."

He shifted his weight, and although his expression remained lost to the shadows, she could see well enough to know he was looking at her.

"And what is it *you* enjoy doing, Eleanor? That you would say . . . God created you to do?"

Hands laced together at her waist, she heard subtle challenge in his tone. How honest should she be? After all, he already knew about the building in town. But compared with the work he was doing—and was capable of doing—her own little *dashed* dream of opening a restaurant seemed so inconsequential.

Still, considering what he'd done for her tonight . . .

"Do you remember the building in town? Where you saw me that day?"

"Hmmm . . ." He cocked his head. "Would that be the building that goes with your key? And that you've avoided answering my questions about? And that is now clean and has a rental sign in the front window?"

Only mildly surprised at his response, Eleanor couldn't stem a smile. "That would be it."

"Then, yes." A smile tinted his voice. "I think I remember it."

She shook her head. "You've been spying on me, Marcus Geoffrey."

"Not at all, madam. I'm simply observant. And . . . you *did* drop the key that day."

She appreciated his levity. It made what she had to say a little easier. "Earlier tonight, you said you didn't realize women of my . . . *social status* knew how to cook. Well . . ." She lifted a shoulder and let it fall. "That's what I enjoy doing. Cooking."

His silence encouraged her to continue.

"Before my—" She caught herself just in time, not wishing to introduce the subject of her father into the conversation. "Before I moved from Murfreesboro, I read an advertisement in a newspaper about a building for lease, and after exchanging letters with the proprietor, I made the decision to rent it"—saying it aloud, and to him, was harder than she'd thought it would be—"in order to . . . start my own restaurant."

His head tilted as though he hadn't heard her correctly. "A restaurant . . ."

His tone hinted at skepticism, and her guard rose accordingly. Still, she understood why he was surprised. Hers wasn't a conventional choice.

"Yes, that's right. But I wasn't able to secure the capital for the restaurant." She decided to skip the part about having asked Aunt Adelicia for a loan. "So the day you saw me in town, I was meeting with the proprietor to tell him I wouldn't be renting the building after all."

He didn't say anything at first, his nod coming slowly. "I'm sorry the loss of that opportunity was disappointing for you, Eleanor."

"Thank you."

"But I'm wondering . . . if you didn't rent it, who cleaned up the building? It looked like it was ready to be occupied last I saw it."

"Well . . ." She told him about her proposition and about Mr. Stover accepting the terms. "The building hasn't rented yet, of course. But it stands a much better chance *now* than it did."

"That was a very wise move on your part."

"I appreciate that, but . . . in hindsight, I realize I shouldn't have signed that contract sight unseen, or before I had the money to start my business. It was simply too risky."

"Sometimes you have to try, regardless of the risk. Because how else will you ever know?"

The soothing tumble of water from the fountain filled the silence between them, along with the chirrup of crickets bedded down for the night.

The breeze picked up, and Eleanor reached again to tuck that same wayward strand into place. But to her surprise, Marcus beat her to it.

He gently slipped her hair behind her ear, and his hand lingered.

He walked her to the door, the gas lamps that adorned the front of the mansion providing ample light. It occurred to Eleanor then that nearly twelve years had passed since she'd been escorted to the front door by a man. She remembered both times well. She'd been eighteen, and the men—both much older and clearly interested only in her family name and connections—had been nothing like Marcus.

Her father had proven understanding when she'd spoken to him about not wishing to marry either of the men. He'd assured her there would be plenty of time for marriage later. But then . . . her mother had died. And after two years of mourning, the war had come, which had taken most of the men. Except for a very few.

And none of them were anything like the man standing before her now.

Eleanor hesitated, not exactly certain what she should do. The evening hadn't been a formal outing, after all. And Marcus wasn't courting her, by any means. Did she curtsy to him first? Or did he—

He bowed, a touch of mischief in his eyes.

"Thank you, Eleanor, for the pleasure of your company this evening." As he straightened, he leaned forward. "Now," he whispered, "you curtsy, then offer me your hand."

A little embarrassed that her naivety was so obvious, she did as prompted.

He kissed her hand. Not once, but twice.

She slipped inside, grateful to find the entrance hall empty. Just before she closed the door behind her, she glanced back outside and saw Marcus look back at the very same time.

"Remember," he called softly. "In the morning."

She smiled and nodded. Foolish man. . . . As if she could forget.

Later, as she lay in the dark of her bedroom, it occurred to her that Marcus had never finished his thought about being an under gardener at Belmont. It *did* occur to her, however, that perhaps he'd intended to suggest she use her influence with her aunt for the advancement of his position.

But that possibility conflicted with the man she knew. Or thought she knew.

And yet—that familiar voice rose inside—why else would someone like him be interested in someone like her?

She turned onto her side and pulled the covers close beneath her chin. If that *was* Marcus's intent in getting to know her better, then he would be sorely disappointed.

But not nearly as disappointed as she would be.

20

Early the next morning, working in the propagating room, Marcus heard the telling creak of a door. "Good morning!" he called, already knowing who it was. He went to welcome Eleanor. "I was hoping I hadn't kept you out so late last night that you'd—"

He stopped short. "Mrs. Cheatham!"

"And a good morning to you, Mr. Geoffrey." Curiosity laced the woman's expression. "Although . . . I'm fairly confident I am *not* the person you were expecting."

Unaccustomed to being caught off guard, Marcus knew better than to try to bluff his way with Adelicia Cheatham. But neither was he eager to admit who he was expecting, not in light of what he'd just said. He hadn't been a schoolboy in years, yet he remembered well the begrudging apprehension he'd felt when called to give account for his actions.

It wasn't as though he and Eleanor had done anything wrong last night, so why did he suddenly feel as though they had?

"No, madam, you're not." He chanced a look toward the mansion, but the moisture filming the glass walls obscured the view. "But it's always a pleasure to see you, whether by appointment or otherwise."

She smiled. "You, Mr. Geoffrey, are far too kind."

But her guarded expression said she hadn't forgotten his greeting.

Whatever business she had, Marcus knew he needed to get it done swiftly and then see her on her way. "Mr. Gray isn't in yet this morning, madam. But is there a way that I might be of service?"

"Indeed, there is, Mr. Geoffrey. I want to see the progress you've made on my rose before Dr. Cheatham and I leave town. Our plans to take the children to visit family in Alabama have been significantly extended. After receiving a rather heart-tugging letter from Dr. Cheatham's daughter, Mattie, we've decided to surprise her at her school in Maryland. We'll be gone for a month, perhaps a little longer should we decide to stop in New York."

Movement in the gardens behind Mrs. Cheatham drew his attention, and through the clouded glass, he spotted someone making their way toward the conservatory. Definitely female judging by the skirt. *Why* couldn't Eleanor have chosen this time to be late?

"Your rose is right through here, madam." He swiftly ushered Mrs. Cheatham into the propagating room, but she took her time joining him. Was she moving at so leisured a pace by coincidence? Or was she doing it just to spite him?

He wouldn't put the latter past her. Because it was what he would do in the same situation. He didn't like to be coerced. And neither did she.

"This is the latest version of the rose, madam. I hope you're pleased."

He could tell immediately by the quirk in her brow that she was not.

"It's quite an . . . orangy pink, don't you think, Mr. Geoffrey?"

He hadn't heard the sound of a door yet and could only hope Eleanor had seen something outside that would delay her.

"I think it's actually quite nice, Mrs. Cheatham. It has the hue of pink at sunset that—"

"You mean *sunrise,*" she corrected. "I said sunrise in my original description."

"Yes, madam, you are correct. You did. And I meant sun*rise*. But—"

"But just now you said *sunset,* and I'm wondering"—she eyed the flower as though it might respond—"if perhaps that's not why this bud has more orange to it. You thought I said sunset, when, in fact, I said sunrise."

Now she was toying with him. He could tell by the way she kept glancing outside, watching and waiting, just as he was doing.

"Unfortunately, Mr. Geoffrey, I think we still have some distance to cover before we achieve the desired color. But you're doing very fine work, and I appreciate your dedication to the task. Speaking of which . . . in my absence, I would greatly appreciate your keeping a watchful eye on the progress of the billiard hall. I'm not much pleased with the current height nor style of the parapet along the roof, nor the size of the windows. I told the architect to incorporate your recommendations exactly as you drew them for me. They're far better than the original design." She paused, exhaling. "Do you know what I wish, Mr. Geoffrey?"

Marcus thought of several things he would wish for in that moment, but none that he could voice. He simply shook his head.

"I wish *you* were building my billiard hall. It would be completed by now, and would be stunning, I'm sure. Mrs. Foster, wife of the gentleman for whom you did the renovation on the textile mill, went on and on about how pleased her husband was with your improvements. How exacting you were, and detailed."

Now she was simply stalling.

Marcus heard a door open, and his thoughts jumped to how he might salvage the moment since escaping it was impossible.

"Mrs. Cheatham, despite what you may be—"

"Marcus? Are you back there?"

He clenched his jaw, not missing the look Adelicia Cheatham gave him. As though she were thinking, *"Marcus? Instead of Mr. Geoffrey? How interesting . . ."*

"Yes, Miss Braddock. We're back here," he called, hoping she would catch the subtle hint.

"Miss Braddock?" Eleanor's voice carried a smile. "After exploring the depths of a tunnel with someone, I believe you have earned the permanent privilege of—"

Seeing them, Eleanor paused midstride through the doorway, having much the same look on her face that Marcus imagined had been on his moments earlier.

"Aunt Adelicia!" She smiled. "What are you doing down here? I thought you and Dr. Cheatham were already gone."

"We had planned to be, dear. But we got a later start. Dr. Cheatham is having Armstead bring the carriage around, so I decided to walk down here on the off chance of catching Mr. Geoffrey."

Eleanor crossed the room to them. "If I'd known you were coming, we could have walked together."

Not a trace of pretense layered Eleanor's tone, Marcus noted. And surely Mrs. Cheatham did too.

"And pray tell, my dear, what brings you down here so *early* on a Saturday morning?"

Marcus knew he wasn't imagining the faint inflection in her tone.

"*You,* actually, Aunt." Eleanor laughed. "Last night when M . . . Mr. Geoffrey and I were *unearthing* the secrets of the tunnel below—"

The way she scrunched her shoulders when she said it made Marcus smile, but the way Mrs. Cheatham looked at him didn't.

"—he also showed me the roses he's grafted for you. The latest was set to bud this morning, so . . . here I am, anxious to see it in all its splendor."

If he had scripted a response with the hope of allaying Mrs. Cheatham's suspicions, he could not have penned a better one. Eleanor Braddock . . . Open. Honest. Unpretentious.

Mrs. Cheatham's features relaxed. A little.

Marcus stepped forward. "Please allow me to show you the bloom, Miss Braddock. Though, I must warn you"—he slipped Eleanor a discreet wink—"voice your opinion at your own risk, for we have both already expressed ours."

He held up the flower and easily read Eleanor's expression. "Apparently, you share your aunt's opinion, Miss Braddock."

Mrs. Cheatham beamed.

"No, I don't. I . . ." Eleanor flushed. "I mean . . . it's not that I agree or disagree. It's simply that . . ." She winced. "Pink is not a favorite color of mine."

Mrs. Cheatham frowned. "But you adore pink, Eleanor! You have that lovely pink ensemble, which you don't wear often enough, quite frankly."

"Reason being," Eleanor said gently, "I don't like the color."

The rumble of a carriage reached them, and Mrs. Cheatham briefly peered outside, then back at Marcus. If he'd still been a betting man, he would have wagered the whole lot on what she was about to say.

"Eleanor, dear, are you certain you don't want to go with us? Pauline would adore your company, and so would I. We would happily wait while you gather your things."

Having bet right, Marcus felt no victory at the win.

"I appreciate your invitation, Aunt Adelicia. But,

as we discussed . . . I believe it's best I stay here. I have plenty to keep me busy."

Seeming hesitant, Mrs. Cheatham finally nodded. "Quite right, my dear, of course. But promise me you'll write every day."

Eleanor narrowed her eyes playfully. "How about every other?"

Mrs. Cheatham patted her hand in parting but turned when she reached the door. "Be sure, Eleanor, to wear your pink ensemble for your upcoming dinner with Mr. Hockley. He's so looking forward to the two of you getting to know each other better. He said as much in a recent missive to Dr. Cheatham, in which he also shared how much he enjoyed receiving your letter. He said it was most . . . *encouraging*."

Marcus and Eleanor glanced at each other at the same time. Then just as quickly looked away.

"Yes, Aunt, I'll do that. Thank you."

"And please keep working on my rose, Mr. Geoffrey. I'm eager to see its culmination. Preferably before next summer, for *obvious* reasons."

Marcus tensed at the mention of next summer. In the course of their business dealings, he'd made Mrs. Cheatham aware of his scheduled return to Austria, but he hadn't counted on her—

"And please *do* check with the architect on the billiard hall," Mrs. Cheatham continued. "He's expecting your input, Mr. Geoffrey. I trust you'll watch over the project in my absence. Any problems at all, and Mr. Monroe will know where to wire me."

Keenly aware of Eleanor's scrutiny, Marcus managed an informal bow. "It will be my pleasure, Mrs. Cheatham. Safe journey, madam."

As Mrs. Cheatham's footfalls receded, he felt Eleanor's continued attention. No doubt, she was questioning the mention of next summer, and also why her aunt would ask an under gardener to oversee a building project. But he had his own questions, such as who this Hockley fellow might be, and exactly what the nature of the man's interest in Eleanor was.

He looked over at her, knowing he needed to offer explanations and hoping she wouldn't be upset.

But to his surprise . . . she looked as though she was trying not to laugh.

"The *architect* is expecting your input?" Eleanor knew she shouldn't laugh but she couldn't help it. "The look on your face, Marcus, when she asked you to check with him . . ." She shook her head. "My aunt truly *does* think highly of her gardeners, doesn't she?"

She smiled up at him, then paused, noticing he wasn't laughing. "What?" she asked. "What's wrong?"

"Nothing's wrong. But . . . the reason she asked me to check with him is because . . ." His mouth slowly edged up on one side. Amusement lit his eyes. "I *am* an architect."

She stared, then gradually realized what he was up to and decided to play along.

"And I'm an international chef who's been invited to cook for the season in Paris." She struck her best snobbish pose. "But not to worry. I'll still allow you to eat my creations. On occasion."

He laughed, the sound rich and inviting, and the look in his eyes deepened, much like it had last evening in this very room.

"No, Eleanor." His deep voice was soft. "I'm serious. That's what I was trying to tell you last night."

She searched his expression, her humor fading as she caught evidences of truth. "You're not teasing?"

He shook his head. "No, madam. I am not."

"But . . . you *told* me you were an under gardener."

He gave her a look. "When we first met, right out there"—he pointed—"you *assumed* I was an under gardener." He shrugged. "I simply never bothered correcting you."

She thought back—remembering the look on his face at the moment in question, the way he had bowed—and she realized he was right. She *had* made that assumption.

She stepped back and looked at him, trying to

see him for the first time all over again. "*You* . . . are an architect?"

He laughed again. "Is it that difficult to believe?"

"No. And . . . yes. You just seem like a gardener." She waved her arm. "Look at all of this. Look at what you've done."

He fingered the leaf of one of the many *shunned* roses. "I'm an architect who has a passion for botany. Everything I've told you is true, Eleanor." He leaned in. "Except . . . for that day in the bakery, when I had to leave. I didn't really have trees to plant and weeds to pull. I had to get back to the project we were working on at the time."

"We?"

He nodded. "I own a construction company."

She laughed. "Of course you do." But she meant it this time. "What were you working on then?"

"A warehouse downtown. A renovation."

"And what are you working on now?"

A shadow crossed his face. "Another renovation, actually."

"Is that what you like to do most? Renovations?"

"No." His laughter came out flat. "That's merely where the work happens to be available right now. My preference is new construction. I recently submitted bids to design and build two other projects—a photography studio and a library. But I have yet to hear back from them."

"I predict you will. Very soon. And that you'll be awarded the contracts."

He raised an eyebrow. "Then I'll choose to

believe the same." Yet his manner lacked his usual bravado.

"Well . . ." Mindful of the time, Eleanor glanced at the chatelaine watch affixed to her shirtwaist. "I'd best be getting back."

He gestured. "Allow me to see you out."

"Why? Lest I cannot find one of the *seven doors* located along that north wall just there?" She attempted to mimic the same tone he had used with her upon their first meeting here in the conservatory, and was glad when it drew a smile.

"You don't forget much, do you, Miss Braddock?"

"I believe I could say the same of you, Mr. Geoffrey."

She preceded him from the propagating room and back through his *haven,* grateful he hadn't inquired about Mr. Hockley, and still not believing Aunt Adelicia had brought that subject up at such a time. And on purpose, Eleanor knew. The woman never did anything without thinking it through first.

Still two rooms away from the nearest door, Eleanor caught the scent of roses. She glanced back at Marcus. "What would you build if you could build anything you wanted?"

"Hmmm. . . . A building more beautiful, more awe-inspiring than anyone has ever dreamed or imagined, Eleanor Braddock. People will stop on the street just to stare at it." His smile worked like a tonic, drawing her in. "They'll admire the design, the way the structure blends seamlessly with nature. As though all that beauty—the building, the trees and hills surrounding it—had been created for that exact spot on earth. Together, from the very begin-ning."

The way he described it sparked something inside her, like the strike of a match setting flame to a wick. But it also brought to mind what she'd been contemplating last night . . . the extravagance of this estate, and others like it.

She paused by the cast-iron cobra fountain. "But this *more* beautiful, *more* awe-inspiring building, Marcus . . . what would it be for?"

His brow furrowed. "What do you mean?"

"I mean . . . what would be the purpose behind building something"—she tried to smile but couldn't sustain it—"*so* very beautiful. Surely your desire isn't *only* to create something more beautiful so that people will stop to admire it."

He took a moment to answer. "Of course, that's not the only reason. But there's nothing wrong with wanting to create something beautiful." His eyes narrowed the slightest bit. "When you cook, isn't your goal to not only make the food taste good, but also to make it . . . pretty? As you said last night?"

Eleanor had to think back. The slice of buttermilk pie, and how she'd apologized for having crushed it a little in the transport. "Well . . . yes, of course, I do. But . . ." She exhaled. "You can't compare a pie to a *building*."

"*Ja* . . ." He nodded. "Sure, I can. Because we're discussing why to create something more beautiful instead of . . . simply functional. So the comparison is justified."

"The comparison is silly."

He eyed her. "Tell me you don't do your best to make whatever food you cook look appealing."

She huffed. "Well, yes . . . I do. But that's because part of the pleasure in eating is the presentation of the food."

"Ah!" He held up a finger. "But making it beautiful does nothing to actually enhance the flavor of the food, Eleanor. It's strictly *ästhetisch*. Or . . . aesthetic, as you Americans say. Am I correct?"

She pushed his finger aside. "The point I was trying to make is that cooking something with the mere purpose of it being beautiful is *never* my primary motivation. Nor, in my opinion, should it be yours when you're designing a building." Hearing the urgency in her tone, she attempted to soften it, not wanting to sound as perturbed by the discussion as she felt. "Beauty can be found in function, even in simplicity. And in the purpose for which a building is built and how it's used." She met his gaze with challenge. "Not everything has to be *beautiful* to be worthy of admiration, Marcus."

No sooner did the words leave her mouth than she wished she could recall them. Beneath his discerning gaze, she felt exposed. Knowing she wasn't a beautiful woman was one thing. But the possibility of discovering that the man she cared about—*far* more than she should—held a similar opinion, was more than her heart could take.

She cleared her throat, doing her best to sound normal and more confident than she felt. "I hope you get the chance to build your building someday, Marcus."

He looked at her for a long moment, as though weighing his response. "Thank you, Eleanor. I do too."

Again, she heard that thinnest sliver of doubt in his voice. And with uncustomary boldness, she briefly pressed a hand to his chest, thinking of what he'd told her only hours earlier. "Don't give up. Keep trying, regardless of the risk. Because how else will you ever know, if you don't try?"

The blue of his eyes deepened as he moved closer. He slipped his thumb beneath her chin and lifted her face to his. Unable to move, much less form a thought, Eleanor could scarcely breathe.

He pressed a slow, warm kiss to her forehead. "*Danke*," he whispered, lingering, his breath warm on her skin. "*Für die süße Erinnerung.*"

Eleanor closed her eyes, her pulse racing. *Thank you . . . for the sweet reminder.* The nights of reviewing her German textbook were proving helpful. She kept still, wanting to memorize the moment.

Far too soon, he stepped back, looking at her with an intensity that made her face burn.

"I'm sorry to have kept you so long this morning." His voice sounded a little hoarse. "Especially after keeping you out so late last night."

"Yes . . . it was quite the inconvenience, Mr. Geoffrey. And not enjoyable in the least."

Surprised at the control in her own voice, she was even more so at the smirk that tipped his mouth. It was downright roguish, and tempted her thoughts down an enticing path they'd not traveled before.

She didn't know much about the ways of a man with a woman, and her instincts could well be leading her astray. But for the first time in her life, she thought maybe, just maybe, she might be about to learn.

"Leave it to Mrs. Adelicia Cheatham to hire a European architect to design a garden at an asylum."

Marcus looked up from where he was measuring for the statue installation to see Dr. Crawford walking toward him. He quickly recorded the figures in his notebook, then extended his hand. "Good morning, Dr. Crawford. How are you, sir?"

"I'm well, thank you, Mr. Geoffrey. And from the looks of things here, you are too."

Marcus surveyed the landscape along with him, proud of what he and his crew had accomplished. "It's taken a little longer than I thought it would, but we're nearing completion."

"Things often take longer than planned in my line of work too. But working on a Saturday, Mr. Geoffrey. That's dedication."

All week long Marcus had intended to get out here, but with the problems he'd had on the job in town—men being out sick, supplies not being delivered on time, shoddy workmanship from three new hires, whom he'd just as swiftly fired—he hadn't had the opportunity.

Crawford looked over at him. "When Mrs. Cheatham told me she wished to install a *simple* garden"—he laughed under his breath—"this is hardly what I envisioned. What you've done here, Mr. Geoffrey, is nothing short of remarkable. I, along with the other board members, am most grateful to both you and Mrs. Cheatham for your contribution to the asylum."

"It's my pleasure, sir. I'm grateful you're pleased." Marcus gestured. "I think the walking paths turned out especially well. As did the fountain. Unfortunately, the flowers probably won't last much past the first of November. Not with the cooler temperatures we're having now. But at least you can enjoy them throughout the month."

Dr. Crawford pointed. "Some of our patients are already enjoying them."

Marcus turned to see nearly every window on this side of the building filled with faces peering out. Something he'd grown accustomed to. An older woman on the second floor waved, and then the woman beside her did too. Though he felt silly doing it, Marcus waved back. It felt rude not to.

One of the side doors on the building opened, and patients, accompanied by male and female staff, filed outside and into the garden area.

"I hope you don't mind us using this area while

you're here," Dr. Crawford said, consulting his pocket watch. "These are patients from the second floor. Though on occasion, a few of them have exhibited aggressive behavior, generally, they're quite docile. It's important to maintain their schedule, and outdoor recreation on Saturday is always at ten o'clock sharp."

"I don't mind at all, Doctor. I've got a little more work to do, and then I'll be back next week with my men to finish."

Dr. Crawford shook his hand in parting, then approached an older gentleman already seated in one of several arbor swings. The patient's expression was peaceful as he rocked back and forth, back and forth, face tilted toward the sun.

Marcus watched him with a sense of satisfaction.

The swings had been a last-minute addition, and his personal design and contribution. On more than one occasion while working here alone, he'd observed patients milling about, looking at the trees and flowers, or sitting on the occasional bench. But there was something special, something calming about a swing.

He returned to his work, finalizing the measurements for the foundation that would serve as the base for a statue Mrs. Cheatham had purchased. He could have sent one of his workers to do the job, but it was a gorgeous fall morning, and he wanted to review the progress anyway.

He had yet to see the sculpture Mrs. Cheatham had bought. It was still en route from New York

City. But per her description, it would be "something special."

Kneeling in the dirt, he confirmed the measurements a third time, a tedious habit that had saved him countless hours of extra work through the years, not to mention expense. He'd told Caleb as much yesterday when the boy worked alongside him at the warehouse. The boy was proving to be a good worker. Conscientious. And bright. He caught on quickly.

A few of the men on Marcus's crew had jumped at the chance to earn some extra money. So he'd sent them to do the needed repairs on the building Caleb and his mother lived in, before winter set in.

After measuring, Marcus marked the four outside corners using tongue depressors, inserting them into the soil as placeholders for the wooden stakes—and hearing Eleanor's voice as he did. *It's sweet and custardy, and you're going to love it.*

He smiled. He could almost taste that buttermilk pie.

She'd surprised him one night this past week by visiting the conservatory with yet another piece of pie. A different kind. Sweet potato, she'd said. It had practically melted in his mouth. Then she'd rolled up her sleeves and helped him repot camellias.

"Next time," she'd said, giving him a look that brooked no argument, "I want to watch you graft something."

She'd seemed especially happy in recent days,

and while a part of him liked imagining he was somewhat responsible, a greater part didn't. He kept thinking of next summer, and the life waiting for him back in Austria. At least Eleanor hadn't questioned him about what Mrs. Cheatham had said in the conservatory last Saturday about having her rose ready by summer.

He *would* tell her about his planned departure. Soon. But that moment hadn't been the right one.

An image rose in his mind. That of her with her eyes closed, and lips slightly parted . . .

It had taken control he didn't know he possessed to only kiss her on the forehead that day, instead of full on the mouth like he'd wanted to. In that moment, after what she'd said, when he leaned in, his control had wavered.

But it would have been wrong . . . to truly kiss her.

As it was, the kiss he'd given her felt a little like a betrayal. Chaste, yes—outwardly. But inwardly . . . his thoughts had been anything but innocent.

"Not everything has to be beautiful *to be worthy of admiration."*

As long as he lived, he would never forget what she'd said. Or how she'd said it. Eleanor clearly didn't think of herself as a beautiful woman. He exhaled. How he'd wanted to tell her she was wrong. *Show* her she was wrong. But this newer side of him—the man he'd been gradually becoming since his brother's death—had held his old nature in check, keeping rein on his desire for her, which only seemed to increase with time.

He thought about her only half of every waking hour. The other half was spent wondering if she was thinking about him. Marcus shook his head. He was acting like some love-struck schoolboy, when he was anything but.

It didn't help that a few days ago he'd received another letter from the baroness. He hadn't responded to the missive yet, but needed to.

The baroness's letters—always long, detailing recent shopping outings and what she'd purchased, or plays she'd attended and who she'd seen there— came with increasing frequency. As verbose as her letters were, they communicated very little, yet also spoke volumes. About her. About *them* as a couple. About what their life together would be like.

She inquired incessantly, wanting to know what he was doing with his time, what comprised his days. Perhaps if he told her a little, she would be pacified. Sensing a cage closing in on him again, Marcus pushed that part of his life to the furthest corner of his mind. And locked the door.

With the measurements for the base of the statue recorded, he confirmed the distance from all four sides of the rectangle to the outside edges of the area lined with bricks.

He recalled again Mrs. Cheatham's response to finding out about their tour of the tunnel and could understand her perspective. She was simply trying to protect her niece. The woman obviously had plans for Eleanor. He didn't think the fated dinner with Mr. Hockley had taken place, though. He'd made sure he was at Belmont in recent evenings and had kept watch for any strange carriages coming up the lane.

Eleanor deserved a future as fresh and bright as she was—one that *did not* include her working in a restaurant.

He'd been truthful when he said he was sorry the lost opportunity with the restaurant had been a disappointing one for her. But he wasn't sorry it hadn't worked out. His opinion had nothing to do with her intelligence or ability. He, of all people, understood what it was like to pursue a goal you wanted more than anything.

But Eleanor? Running a restaurant? In that ramshackle building? And in that part of town? *Nein, nein* . . . That would never do. What would Adelicia Cheatham say if she knew her niece had attempted such an endeavor? He had no doubt Mrs. Cheatham would disapprove.

He'd chosen not to voice his own disapproval to Eleanor, and with good reason. First, it was a moot point, as the opportunity had passed. Second, it would have ruined one of the most enjoyable evenings he'd ever spent.

He reached for his pack and withdrew a mallet, wooden stakes, some string, and a level, eager to be done so he could ride out to Belmont and check on the maturing potato plants. Or that's what he told himself. . . .

"Give me the string, and I'll tie it around the stakes," a voice said behind him. "It'll be easier with two people."

Marcus looked over his shoulder, surprised to see one of the patients standing over him. The older gentleman from the swing. Marcus glanced around but saw no sign of Dr. Crawford.

Meanwhile, the patient squatted across from him, arm outstretched. The man wiggled his fingers as though impatient to get the task under way.

Marcus hesitated. But what harm could come from letting the old man help? Unless, of course, the man became agitated, lunged for him, and tried to drive a stake through his temple. Chances of that happening were doubtful, he knew. Still, Marcus gripped the mallet a little tighter.

"I'm assuming statuary of some sort will reside in this space?" the man said.

"Yes, sir, that's right." Having heard stories about patients in asylums, Marcus decided to keep his answers brief and to the point. And as lighthearted as possible.

He handed the man the string, keeping the stakes and mallet to himself. Marcus quickly drove the stakes into the ground, then watched, with no small surprise, as the man tied the string to the first stake, pulled it taut—but not overtight, as to disturb the stake's placement—then looped it twice around the next stake, and repeated the process until it was done.

Marcus looked over at him. "I'm impressed."

"Don't be. I was building houses before you were born."

"You're a carpenter?"

The man frowned. "Do I look like a carpenter?"

"Well . . . no, sir, not really. But I—"

"Too much jabbering. Give me the level." He held out his hand. "Let's get this done. I've got other work to do."

Marcus curbed a grin. He couldn't remember if he'd ever been accused of *jabbering*. He wasn't totally certain he even knew what the word meant.

He handed over the level.

The man crouched in the dirt, heedless to all else, and held the level perfectly still above the string, his whitish beard brushing the ground. "Up on my right about a quarter inch."

Looking around to see if anyone else was watching—they weren't—Marcus humored the man by following his instructions.

Finally, the man stood and returned the level. "Check me, if you like. You seem to want to."

Amused but also feeling reprimanded, Marcus did as he directed. Every string . . . perfectly level. He couldn't believe it.

"Just because I'm in this place doesn't mean I'm lame in the head."

Marcus blinked. "No sir, of course not. I never said—"

"No, you didn't say it. But I can see it in your eyes. Eyes don't lie."

Marcus's first instinct was to look away, but then

he figured the man would call him on that too. Remembering how he'd planned on framing his responses, Marcus offered his hand.

"Thank you, sir, for your help today. You did a fine job, and I appreciate it."

The man looked at his hand, then back at him. His chin trembled. Warily, as though he feared it was a trick—and that Marcus might pull his own hand back at any moment—the older man extended his arm.

Marcus winced at his grip. Rock solid. Only one other man in his life had owned a grip like that.

"Will you be out here again?" The man's voice held supplication now.

"Yes, sir. I will."

Eyes moist, the man released his grip. "Maybe I'll have time to see you again, then."

Marcus returned his arm to his side, flexing his hand. "If you're not too busy, sir."

A ringing like that of a school bell—only softer, briefer—pulled the man's focus back to the door.

"I have to go now," he said. "But I'll watch those strings from my room and make sure nobody messes with them."

Marcus nodded.

The man was halfway back to the door when he suddenly turned and ran back. Marcus braced himself, not knowing *which man* was returning.

The man pulled something from his shirt pocket, and for the first time, he smiled. "It's my favorite kind."

Marcus accepted the gift and waited until the door closed behind the last patient before looking at it more closely.

A lint-covered sugar stick.

Later, as Marcus guided Regal back into town, memories of his brother pressed close. He didn't have to question why, or why now. He knew the answer to both. Because he knew the truth.

He thought of the elderly man again and of how threadbare the cord that tethered him to reality seemed to be. Marcus gripped the reins. As embarrassed as he'd been when Adelicia Cheatham asked him to install a garden at the city's insane asylum, he was proud of what he and his men were accomplishing.

But he was even more surprised by how the patients had responded to it.

He enjoyed watching them walk the pathways, stopping to look overlong at the fountain or a tree or a flower, delicately fingering the petals. Or enjoying the peaceful to-and-fro of an arbor swing as the elderly gentleman had done.

But the stigma of such a place was inescapable. What shame and devastation the families of these patients bore. And with good reason. So while he was proud of his work, he still didn't want his name publicly associated with it.

His conscience burned with an increasing awareness as memories of his brother pressed closer still.

Marcus searched the boundless blue overhead, regret welling in his throat. If only he'd known how upset his brother had been, how sad and hopeless he'd felt, he could have talked to him.

As it was, only a handful of people would ever know the truth of what had happened that night. Because *Selbstmord*—Marcus hated even thinking the word—was a coward's way out. And though his family's history was rife with deceit, greed, betrayal, and even murder, suicide was something that didn't occur in the House of Habsburg.

Even when it did.

When Naomi Lebenstein said she didn't mind hard work, Eleanor had believed her. What she hadn't realized was how meticulous Naomi was, or what a difference a coat of properly applied whitewash could make to a room. Not a streak or accidental drop anywhere.

Eleanor turned in circles, taking it in. "Is there anything you cannot do, Naomi? And do to perfection?" She appreciated Mr. Stover giving Naomi the work. It meant steady food on the table for mother and son, which hadn't been the case until recently.

Naomi beamed. "Mr. Stover saw it earlier and has asked me to paint the whole inside of the building now. You do not mind, do you, Miss Braddock?"

"Mind? Why would I mind?" Eleanor continued to the kitchen and placed the crate of groceries on the table, her Saturday shopping complete. "It's *his* property. And the better it looks, the sooner it's likely to rent, which means I stand to at least get a portion of my money back."

She'd confided in Naomi about her original plan for the building, and—contrary to Marcus's tepid response to the idea the night they'd visited the tunnel—Naomi had considered it a wonderful undertaking. Even if a failed one.

"But if he rents it"—Naomi gave her a knowing look—"where will you cook?"

Eleanor shook her head, touched by her friend's concern, especially when considering Naomi's own situation and her husband's passing. Naomi still hadn't shared any details, and Eleanor wasn't about to pry. "I have no idea. But as you've said before, each day comes with trouble all its own. No need to borrow more."

Naomi's smile was bittersweet.

Eleanor started to unpack her purchases. "Besides . . . there are far more troubling things in this world. But what I *do* know"—she reached for her apron hanging on a peg—"is that I'm here right now. And while you continue painting upstairs, I'm going to enjoy making us a delicious dinner."

Eleanor lit the stove, then set to peeling potatoes, feeling quite at home in "Weezie's kitchen." She'd cooked for Mr. Stover, Naomi, and Caleb twice in the past week, dividing the remains among them, and they'd been so appreciative. But she was the one grateful to them.

The pleasure cooking gave her, the joy she took in preparing the meal, was nothing compared to seeing the contented smiles around the table and knowing that, even if only for a while, Naomi's and Caleb's bellies were full and their appetites sated.

Caleb had asked, quite shyly, if he could bring a couple of friends with him to dinner tonight, and she'd said yes without hesitation, eager to meet the boy's companions.

She remembered Teddy and his friends when they were about Caleb's age, how rowdy and boisterous they'd been. Oh, how they could eat after their playful shenanigans! She looked forward to seeing Caleb in that setting and was hopeful that she could stretch the food she'd purchased to curb the hunger of another child or two.

She had a very special dessert in mind too, and since Marcus had enjoyed the sweet potato pie she'd made, she planned on taking him a sampling. The man had an affinity for sweets, which she liked about him.

She paused from peeling. Was there anything she *didn't* like about him?

Her initial opinion of him had changed significantly. She now understood why he sometimes came across as having a superior air—in his tone, other times in an expressed opinion, or a look. It was because of his education. And likely due to his European heritage as well.

But truly . . . an *architect?* She smiled again at how long he'd allowed her to believe he was an under gardener.

Wielding the paring knife like a scalpel, she cut the thinnest potato peel she could manage, remembering the physician's scalpel she'd seen in Marcus's *haven,* as he'd called it.

"Be sure to wear your pink ensemble for your upcoming dinner with Mr. Hockley . . ."

Eleanor tossed the paper-thin peel into the bucket, wishing the dinner was already over and done with.

Mr. Lawrence Hockley . . .

The man had returned from abroad and, according to his elegantly written note, would be "calling upon her person at precisely seven o'clock on the eve of Wednesday next."

Eleanor laughed in the kitchen's silence. Who penned a letter in so formal a fashion anymore? The man must be at least one hundred and two years old. No doubt, he would wear his powdered wig when they went to dinner.

Marcus hadn't said one word to her about it. Not that she expected him to. But part of her liked to think he cared—at least a little—if she went to dinner with a man. If she knew he was having dinner with a woman, she would be interested—too interested.

She slowed her peeling, imagining him asking

someone to dinner like that. It did something funny to her insides, twisted them in a not-so-comfortable knot. It was an undesirable sensation, and she knew what she was feeling.

Which made her like it even less.

Aunt Adelicia had written inquiring if she'd stopped by the Nashville Women's League yet. Eleanor blew a wisp of hair from her eyes. She hadn't but needed to. And *would* . . . before her aunt returned.

She paused. Something familiar niggled at her memory. She couldn't quite think of what it—

The fog cleared, and the memory rose. What had Aunt Adelicia meant when she'd said "Preferably before next summer, for *obvious* reasons" to Marcus, regarding the rose he was cultivating for her?

Eleanor turned the paring knife in her hand. She'd intended to ask him about it the last time they were together. But she'd forgotten.

She slipped the knife beneath the skin of the next potato and felt its flesh give. She sliced it open. *Rotten.* So was the next one. And the next. From the outside, they appeared fine. But by the time she'd finished peeling them, nearly a third of the potatoes resided in the garbage pail—riddled with dry rot.

She had a good mind to take them back and dump them as they were onto Mr. Mulholland's pristine white counter. Either that, or take a knife with her the next time she went shopping for potatoes at his mercantile. Establish a new "slice before you buy" policy.

The mere thought of doing so provided satisfaction.

A while later, with the chunked potatoes waiting in a bowl of water, the chicken frying in an iron skillet, and the dried beans she'd left soaking overnight simmering their way to tender, she mixed together cream, milk, and flour, eager to taste the *au gratin* potato dish again. One of her father's favorites.

She'd finally received a letter from him two days ago. In his own hand. It had been short, all of five sentences. And kind, even if stiltedly so. But at least he'd written and had acknowledged the receipt of her letters.

She couldn't deny, though, it wasn't the outpouring of a father's heart as she'd hoped it would be. Nor did it include the invitation to come and visit him. Reading it had hurt almost more than it had helped.

She removed the browned chicken from the skillet, covered it with a cloth to stay warm, then placed the drained potatoes into a casserole. The creamy cheese sauce, absent of lumps, poured smooth as pudding over the top. Using a cloth, she placed the potatoes in the hot oven.

Needing a lift in her spirits, Eleanor turned to an unfailing remedy. And by the time she'd mixed the dried-peach filling, and kneaded and rolled out the dough, she was already imagining what

Marcus would say when he took his first bite.

She tucked the blanket of dough snug around the edges of the cobbler, as her mother had taught her, giving it a slight crimp. Then she cut slits into the top for the cobbler to *breathe* as it baked.

Into the oven it went, and out came the potatoes. She added the last touches of crushed herbs to those, then returned them to baking, making note of the time. She couldn't wait to sit down and eat. Lunch seemed forever ago.

Hearing footfalls on the stairs, Eleanor turned. "I was just about to call you. Dinner is almost ready. Did you make good progress?"

Naomi breathed deeply. "It smells divine in here, Miss Braddock. And yes, the first coat of white-wash in the smallest bedroom is done."

Naomi, ever observant, pitched right in and seemed to anticipate what needed to be done before Eleanor asked. As they chatted and put the finishing touches on dinner, Eleanor's gaze fell on the frayed edges of Naomi's dress along the sleeves and collar. Even the hem of her skirt too. In Eleanor's memory, Naomi had this dress and one other. She couldn't remember her ever wearing anything else.

Mr. Stover arrived right on time, and as Naomi placed the last tin cup on the table, the door in the front room opened.

"*Guten Tag!*"

Eleanor recognized Caleb's voice, and could hardly wait to see his eager face, along with those of his friends, as they sat down to dinner. But, oddly, she heard none of the boyish rowdiness and laughter she'd expected.

And following Naomi around the corner, she realized why.

Standing hand in hand on both sides of Caleb, children huddled together like baby birds pushed too soon from the nest. Three girls, two boys, their hair matted and unwashed, none of them over the age of seven. The girls' dresses, wrinkled and stained, rose to midcalf and revealed shoes that could barely be called such, they had so little wear left in them. The boys' clothes looked as though they hadn't seen a washing in weeks, their trousers worn through at the knees.

But what Eleanor noticed most about them was the hollowed-out, wounded look in their eyes. The shadow of fear fed by hunger and disappointment, and nurtured by the dread that life promised little more.

Eleanor finally found her voice. "Welcome, children. I'm so glad you're here."

Caleb smiled, but the children immediately looked to Naomi, who spoke to them in German, her voice soft. They nodded, except for the youngest—a little girl who couldn't have been more than four. She all but disappeared behind Caleb, her startlingly blue eyes watchful.

"Mr. Stover"—Naomi dipped her head in deference—"I explained to them that you are the owner of this building, sir. And that this is a safe place for them to be."

Mr. Stover greeted them and, if Eleanor read his expression correctly, was sharing much the same initial reaction as she had.

"And, Miss Braddock," Naomi continued, "I told them you are a kind and generous lady who has prepared a special dinner . . . just for them."

Grateful for Naomi's sensitive nature, Eleanor smiled, wanting the children to feel welcome. It hadn't occurred to her that whoever Caleb brought for dinner might not understand English. "*Willkommen, Kinder*," she offered.

The older children returned the polite gesture. But not little Blue Eyes. The girl frowned, obviously unconvinced.

Caleb looked down the line. "This is Levi and Hutch. And Ruthie and Anja."

The two boys dipped their heads as the older girls stared.

"And this"—Caleb tousled the hair of the little blond beside him—"is Maggie." He grinned. "But we call her Magpie because she does not talk much."

Mr. Stover chuckled, and Caleb glanced at Eleanor as if wanting to make certain she caught his play on words.

Eleanor gave him a wink, then repeated the children's names, smiling at each of them as she did. "Now, shall we eat?"

Caleb ushered the little ones into the kitchen, Mr. Stover following, and Eleanor retrieved plates from the cupboard. With Naomi's assistance, she portioned out the food, hoping she had enough and wishing she'd made more.

Naomi leaned close. "I am sorry, Miss Braddock," she whispered. "I did not realize he had invited so many. These are some of the children who live in our building. We have shared the food you have given us with them. And their *Mutter*s. My son has a kind heart, but sometimes he—"

"No, Naomi. This is fine. *More* than fine." Eleanor coaxed the last of the potatoes from the casserole. "I only wish I'd made extra."

"Whatever these precious children receive from your hand, Miss Braddock . . . be assured, it is more than fills their bellies on other nights."

Eleanor turned to see the children, Caleb included, seated on the floor, forks in hand, filled plates and cups of water before them, all of them staring alternately at the food, then up at her. Waiting.

She joined Mr. Stover and Naomi at the table. Their chairs scraped overloud in the silence. When Mr. Stover bowed his head, everyone else followed suit.

He offered a heartfelt prayer Eleanor knew she'd likely not remember, while at the same time knowing she would never forget the moment, or the tender ache crowding the corners of her heart.

Here she was worried about a restaurant she

would never have, and about having dinner with a man who—despite her flippant thoughts about him earlier—would likely prove to be a very kind gentleman, and all the while, these children, through no fault of their own, went to bed hungry most nights, only to awaken to the same.

She thought again of the women she'd seen clustered outside the textile mill, of how desperate some of them had appeared. And how close she was to being in their same situation. If not for her aunt . . .

How easy it was to slip back into the comfort of one's own life, even into one's own worries and fears, and to unintentionally forget. Tears rose to her eyes. Her throat tightened. *Oh, Lord, forgive me. . . . Help me to be more grateful.*

"Amen," Mr. Stover said, and a hushed echo rose from the children.

Amen. A word that needed no translation.

Eleanor picked up her fork, then paused and looked back to see the children shoveling food into their mouths as quickly as they could, their little jaws working to keep up with their appetites. She glanced across the table at Mr. Stover and Naomi and offered the tiniest smile—before picking up her plate.

They laughed and did the same.

By the time Eleanor scraped the last bite of peach cobbler from the dish—save for the few bites she'd set aside for Marcus—she wondered if this was why God had said no to her restaurant.

Maybe He had something else in mind.

She thought again of a man who carried a rose with him into battle and then carried regret with him into death.

She didn't want that—to have regrets at the end, to look back on things she wished she'd had the courage to do but didn't even try. She didn't want to merely survive this life. She wanted to *live* it.

He was being blackballed. There was no other explanation for it. Marcus crumpled the latest response to a bid and threw it in the post-office waste receptacle. He didn't have to look far to know who was behind the action either. He'd been getting steady work—up until the time he'd confronted Mayor Adler.

On his way out the door, he remembered the letter to Burbank—and a brief one to the baroness —in his coat pocket and returned to the counter.

"Something else for you, Mr. Geoffrey?" the mail clerk asked.

Marcus slid the envelopes toward him. "I need to post these, please. Today, if possible."

"Yes, sir. Wednesday's mail coach leaves in an hour. I'll make sure these are on it."

Marcus handed the clerk a coin. Maybe he should go by the mayor's office and speak to Adler, though he doubted that would help. He had the funds to make payroll for his men. For the time being, anyway. But if business dried up, he would lose his crew. They'd go where there was work. And with no money coming in, he'd have to access his cash reserves, which he was set against doing.

Those funds were earmarked for a special project. *If* it came along in time for him to complete before he returned to Austria. From where he stood, those prospects looked slim.

He had considered moving to another city. Every city needed architects. But it was too late now. Besides, he needed Nashville. More specifically, he needed Belmont and his plants. And with winter coming, the conservatory. But that wasn't all he needed here.

He couldn't imagine leaving *her* behind, never seeing her again. Even if he had no right to think of her in that manner. Which he didn't. Either way, leaving before he absolutely had to wasn't an option.

He'd simply have to continue submitting bids and meeting with city leaders until one of them had the courage to stand up to Augustus E. Adler.

He'd grown so desperate, he'd even checked with the Nashville Women's League about their tea hall—although if Fitch ever found out, he'd deny it with a vengeance. The job had already been awarded to another company, which he'd decided was for the best when he met the woman from the league responsible for overseeing the project. Miss Hillary Stockton Hightower.

To say there wasn't enough money in the world to tempt him to take the job was an understatement.

Everything about her was off-putting: from the delicate way in which she laughed—breathy and practiced—to her carefully arranged blond curls of which she was most proud, judging by the way she tossed her head, to the way she gazed up at him, looking askance and smiling as if on cue.

He hadn't been in the meeting five minutes when she began to speak ill of the architect the organization had contracted. Heaven help that man. . . . The architect hadn't yet begun the project, and Miss Hightower was already displeased.

Marcus couldn't say *auf Wiedersehen* quickly enough.

After a quick lunch in town, Marcus supervised his crew through the afternoon. By day's end, he gauged their progress and estimated another three weeks and they'd be done with this job.

With nothing lined up after it.

Standing at the door of the warehouse and looking down Union Street, he reached into his pocket for a sugar stick, one of several he'd bought after that day at the asylum. But they were all gone. He'd been back to the asylum only once, and hadn't seen the old gentleman.

What he really wanted right now was some of that peach cobbler Eleanor had made on Saturday. Or the chocolate chess pie on Sunday. Or the shortbread on Monday. Or that savory custard with ham and cheese she'd brought him in the conservatory last night. If he couldn't find another job, he might just build the woman a restaurant and set her loose in it.

He smiled at the absurdity of the thought. But considering what he'd eaten in some of the restaurants of Nashville, she'd make a small fortune in no time.

He'd enjoyed walks with her on the Belmont estate nearly every evening since her aunt had left almost two weeks ago. The last two nights Eleanor hadn't met him until it was almost dark. Errands in town, she'd said, appearing exuberant despite the late hour.

Those quiet walks were quickly becoming his favorite part of the day, and he looked forward to seeing her again tonight. He had plans to surprise her with something he hoped she would enjoy.

"Boss, you all right?"

Marcus looked up to see his foreman. "Yes, Callahan. I'm fine."

The rest of the men were gone. He and Callahan were always the last to leave.

"Concerned about the next job, sir?"

Marcus exhaled. "I wasn't until today. I didn't want to say anything while the men were around but . . . you're aware of the bids I submitted for the photograph gallery and the Library Association."

Callahan nodded.

Marcus shook his head. "I got the gallery's rejection yesterday and the Library Association's today."

Callahan frowned. "There's no way anyone could

have underbid us on those. Or proposed a better design."

"I thought so too, but . . . apparently someone did."

While he'd chosen not to relay the details of his last meeting with the mayor to Callahan, he'd made certain his foreman knew that Adler had been terse. And not at all pleased with him.

A moment passed before Callahan spoke again. "Do you think somebody could be behind this, Mr. Geoffrey?"

His tone drew Marcus's attention. "Have you heard something?"

Callahan shrugged, but it was a gesture Marcus recognized. The man had information.

Robert Callahan knew pretty much everyone in Nashville. If anything was being discussed or planned in regard to construction, Callahan knew it. Or would by the time breakfast was over.

"Word has it"—Callahan rubbed the back of his neck—"that Mayor Adler got into a stink with the city council after giving the project for the opera house to his son. And there's more."

Marcus got the feeling he wasn't going to like whatever Callahan said next.

"I heard from someone who should know . . . that we were the city council's first choice. You should've gotten that contract, sir. You should be building that opera house."

Marcus looked over at him. "*We* should be building that opera house, Callahan."

His foreman nodded. "Yes, sir. We should."

Marcus straightened, working the muscles in his shoulders and neck, and determined to sound more optimistic than he felt. "Something will come up, Callahan. It always does."

"Oh, I'm not worried, sir. In all my years in construction, I've never worked with anyone more skilled at this than you are."

Marcus shook his hand. "Thank you, Robert. You're a good man."

"I just call it like I see it, Mr. Geoffrey. Good night, sir."

Marcus grabbed his pack, tucked the set of project sketches under his arm, and closed and locked the door behind him. He needed the warmth of a friend's smile. A beautiful and kindhearted *friend*.

And he knew just where to find it.

"No, sir. She ain't here." Eli, one of the oldest and most trusted servants at Belmont according to Mrs. Cheatham, shook his head. He stepped onto the front porch of the mansion, leaving the door open behind him. "Miss Braddock left nigh on to an hour ago. She be at dinner, Mr. Geoffrey, with a gentleman."

The news hit Marcus square in the chest, and as defeated as he'd felt leaving work earlier, this was even worse. Especially with him standing here with a basket of bread and cheese from Fitch's, along with a bag of doughnuts.

"I appreciate you letting me know, Eli." He

gestured to the man's napkin tucked in his collar. "I'm sorry to have interrupted your dinner."

"Aw, no bother, sir. Just me and Cordina tonight. Down in the kitchen." The man's laughter came easily, as if it was like breathing for him. "She fried up a batch of her chicken, and if I don't wear this thing"—Eli gestured to the napkin—"I be a *fine* mess once I get done."

Marcus smiled and nodded, then turned to head down the steps.

"Mr. Geoffrey?"

Pausing, Marcus looked back.

"We be happy, sir, to have you join us. If you like."

More than a little surprised by the offer, and knowing it showed, Marcus didn't know what to say. He'd spoken to Eli—and Cordina—before. But never more than a few words. And he'd never taken a meal at Belmont. All he could think about was his father and uncle, and what they would say if they knew he'd been invited to dine with a servant and his wife.

"That's very kind of you, Eli." Marcus glanced down at the basket, already having decided he wasn't going back to the boardinghouse to eat alone in the dining room. He'd walk down to the conservatory and eat there instead. "But I'm fine." He patted the basket. "I've got plenty."

Eli's smile just widened. "Warm buttered biscuits," he said slowly, drawing the words out. "Fresh corn done been cut off the cob. A mess of field peas cooked up with bacon. Stewed apples slathered with butter and sugar. Oh . . ." His eyes grew larger. "And for dessert . . . my wife's fresh tea cakes. Pulled 'em out of the oven myself 'fore we sat down to eat."

His mouth watering, Marcus stared up at the man, debating. Dining with servants at Belmont? The archduke in him would have never accepted —which made him certain that accepting was exactly what he should do.

Lawrence Hockley sat across the white linen-draped table from her, the space between them accented with shimmering candlelight, delicate hand-painted Limoges china, wine-filled crystal goblets, and a surprisingly lesser expanse of years than Eleanor had imagined.

He was eleven years her senior, to be exact. Though she would have guessed a few more judging by his mature appearance and disposition. Even knowing him so short a time, she suspected he'd possessed a more formal, reserved temperament all his life. Another *old soul,* it would seem.

The restaurant, *La Bienvenue*, seemed crowded for a weekday evening, although Eleanor scarcely considered herself a good judge of that, never having been there before.

Seated where they were by the window, with a

lovely view of the city and the Cumberland River beyond, they enjoyed a measure of privacy. And conversation between them came more easily than she had expected.

She inhaled, satisfying the need for a deep breath and feeling as though she were interviewing for a position with a company rather than contemplating a potential marriage partner.

In this instance, the two seemed unnervingly similar.

Over the past three hours and the first five courses —comprised of oysters, soup à la Reine, lobster Newburg over toast with cucumber salad, chicken Florentine with rice and vegetables, and frozen ices—they'd spoken at length on a variety of topics ranging from his position as president of the Bank of Nashville, to their childhood, to schooling, to his recent grand tour of Europe. His *fourth,* she'd learned, detecting no trace of vainglory in his tone. He'd stated it matter-of-factly, as he did everything.

With only the green salad and dessert courses remaining to be served, she estimated that by the time the fancy cakes, preserved fruits, and coffee were presented, they would have exhausted every topic known to polite society, and Lawrence Hockley would know more about her and her opinions than most people knew about neighbors beside whom they'd lived all their lives.

"So, Miss Braddock . . ." He sat back in his chair, regarding her with an inscrutable expression. "Tell me more about yourself. Not details I might have surmised from our conversation thus far this evening, or from your letter. But rather, the personal observations a woman might not share with a more casual acquaintance."

"But you *are* a more casual acquaintance, Mr. Hockley." Eleanor framed her honesty with a smile, allowing a hem of truth to show in her eyes.

"Quite right." He nodded, not seeming the least offended. "However, taking into account the purpose of our dinner this evening, I believe we may dispense with the customary sensibilities inherent in society's approach to courtship. *If* you are in agreement."

Eleanor nodded, staring at him from across the table while imagining another man. If Marcus had said something similar to her, the tone in his voice might have sounded much the same—not a trace of humor. But the gleam in Marcus's eyes would have signaled his playful sarcasm and hinted at his truer feelings.

Mr. Hockley, on the other hand was completely serious. Commonsensical to a fault.

"I am wholeheartedly in agreement, sir." And she was. So why was the fact she agreed with this man so bothersome?

She'd opened her mouth to respond to his original question when a server chose that moment to bring the salads. And another to refill their glasses. She was already so full, she doubted whether she could eat much more.

She contrasted the seven-course meal with the

pot of hearty potato soup and loaves of bread she'd made earlier that day for dinner for Mr. Stover, Naomi, Caleb, and the other children Caleb saw fit to invite. Her meals were hardly the cuisine she'd dreamed of creating in a restaurant, and they were nowhere near the culinary experience of this fine eatery. Still . . .

She wished she was there eating with them in a ramshackle building instead of this fine restaurant.

Two nights ago, Caleb had shown up with *nine* children. Two mothers had come as well. Then Tuesday night the number increased by seven. She'd already instructed Naomi to invite them all back on Friday evening. Hopefully, they would return.

Atop the salad were sliced sugared almonds and bits of juicy orange. She could only imagine the cost of this meal. She quickly worked the numbers in her head and estimated she could provide a modest but filling dinner for approximately one hundred people, maybe more, for the same amount.

Mr. Hockley followed the servers' actions, neither smiling nor frowning but simply acknowledging their presence with watchful attention. He was a man of detail, and Eleanor took the opportunity to observe him more closely.

Though she'd feared she would tower over him, as it turned out, he was almost her height. He was absent the imagined powdered wig and walking cane she'd visualized when anticipating this evening in one of her earlier, more pessimistic moments. *Bookish,* is what her father might have called him. He was intelligent, no question. And his sense of humor—

She pondered that for a moment, checking her memory. Had he smiled at her even once during the evening? If so, she couldn't recall.

Precious few strands of once-blond-now-graying hair framed an unremarkable, yet not unpleasant countenance. In that regard, they were very well matched. All in all, he was quite unlike what she'd pictured—which was a relief, in one sense, while a concern in another.

Because if it turned out that Lawrence Hockley *was* interested in pursuing something more with her, the possibility of a future with this man wouldn't be as easily dismissed as she'd first thought. That is . . . if he preferred a woman dressed like a frosted pink *petit four* from a cheap French bakery. Why had she allowed Aunt Adelicia to coerce her into agreeing to wear this ensemble?

Not that she was eager to impress Mr. Hockley. Her honest expectations for this evening remained unchanged from when Aunt Adelicia had first told her about him wanting to meet her. Nothing would come of it.

With the servers departed, Eleanor spoke softly, mindful of patrons at nearby tables. "While I'm uncertain if you would classify these as insightful observations, Mr. Hockley . . ." She inclined her head to one side. "I am a woman who prizes practicality. I have my share of sensibilities, of course, but work to keep them in their proper place. I'm not given to fanciful daydreams but do possess an active imagination and a natural curiosity that finds fulfillment through reading and study. I'm not easily intimidated, but that's not due to a puffed-up estimation of myself, I assure you. I simply do not devote time to dwelling upon what others may think about me. I learned at a young age, and subsequently since, that to do so is to invite disappointment and disenchantment— two foes that I do my best to keep at arm's length." Not customarily so transparent to people she didn't know, Eleanor surprised herself at the length of her answer.

Fork poised midair, Hockley looked at her for a long moment, his features revealing neither satisfaction nor displeasure, and the hushed murmur of conversation in the restaurant inched upward in the silence.

"Dr. and Mrs. Cheatham mentioned your straightforward nature, Miss Braddock."

Eleanor finished chewing, not knowing how to respond. Had he meant the statement as a compliment? She couldn't tell. If Marcus had said the same words, she would have known by the look in his eyes. Or the wry tip of his mouth.

"I esteem frankness in a person," he continued. "For I, too, am practical by nature and have only become more so with age." He sipped his wine, unhurried. "Time has a way of narrowing one's youthful expectations. You make choices along the way, and move on. But as you grow nearer the end of your journey than the beginning, opportunities lost suddenly become more pronounced. To look back over your life, to see what you have accomplished, and what you haven't . . ." He paused. "Those are sobering observations, indeed."

His words struck a chord inside her. Had she not experienced similar moments of reflection?

He lifted his wine glass as though to drink again, then apparently thought better of it. "As I told you in my letter, I am widowed. For almost five years now. My wife, Henrietta, was a good woman. Kind." His brow creased. "Thrifty," he said, nodding thoughtfully. "And clean. We were married for twelve years. I found the arrangement most amiable, and trust that she did as well."

Taken aback by his none-too-intimate summary, Eleanor had to remind herself to nod. Thrifty? *Clean?* This was how he described the woman with whom he'd lived as his wife for twelve years? How would he choose to describe *her* someday, if they were to marry? Strong and sturdy, with good teeth, no doubt.

"I have grieved my wife's passing. However . . . life rarely turns out the way we plan, Miss Braddock. Time moves on, as they say, and forces us to move with it."

Listening, Eleanor glimpsed her own determined, sensible nature in the man. "My condolences, again, Mr. Hockley, on your loss. And—"

"Lawrence, please—seeing as we are dispensing with the usual formalities."

"Thank you . . . Lawrence." The name felt odd on her lips. "And I agree with your general outlook. In my experience, thinking about what might have been has never made it so."

He dabbed his mouth with a napkin. "Well spoken . . . Eleanor."

A server approached with warm yeasty rolls. Pats of sweet creamy butter shaped like rosettes clustered at the edge of the plate. Such artistry in how the food was presented. Exquisite.

"But making it beautiful does nothing to actually enhance the flavor of the food, Eleanor. It's strictly ästhetisch.*"*

Recalling Marcus's comment, Eleanor could well imagine how he would tease her about the *beauty* of this meal if he were here. And she half wished he were. Though Mr. Hockley—Lawrence—would likely object.

She stole a glance across the table and discovered him intent on buttering a roll, in similar fashion to how he'd eaten his dinner. Each food separately, and in specific order. No variation once the pattern was established. He didn't slather butter on the entire piece of bread like she did, so it could melt down into the yeasty crevices. He sliced off a tiny portion of a rosette and carefully laid it atop the bread. Bite by bite.

Calling the man meticulous would have been an understatement. Lawrence Hockley made the hands of a clock look spontaneous. And yet . . .

Such attributes could be seen as a credit to a

man of his profession. Surely, serving as president of the largest bank in Nashville demanded exacting attention. If a woman were to purposefully view such a man in a specific light, she might be persuaded to see these dependable, even predictable, idiosyncrasies as something to be valued. Perhaps even treasured, given time.

Another server approached, but Mr. Hockley kindly, firmly waved him away.

"You are a gracious and intelligent woman, Eleanor, precisely as your aunt described you."

Aunt Adelicia had provided this man a description? That was something Eleanor would've liked to have been privy to.

"You seem quite a disciplined woman, as well," he continued, "respected, and from an established family. One that is still well regarded, despite the challenge of your . . . current circumstances."

His final two words, so succinct and *neat,* encompassed so much that wasn't. Yet Eleanor heard no condemnation in his tone. Only frank pragmatism, which she understood.

He leaned forward. "I am not of a romantic nature. I never have been. Nor do I want to risk a misunderstanding between us in that regard. I have no inclination that ours will be a marriage of the heart—at the outset, at least—should we decide to pursue that course." He hesitated, then sighed. "I'm not even certain there is such a thing. A marriage of the heart, I mean. A man and woman make a decision to wed and then build a life from there. It's hard work, both must sacrifice. It's by no means always enjoyable. But I believe that any man and woman who come together with mutual respect and integrity have as good a chance at happiness as any. Would you not agree?"

"Oh yes," Eleanor answered swiftly, intentionally lowering her voice and wishing he would do the same. She wasn't actually certain she *did* agree with him. At least, not as certain as she might have been at one time, but . . .

Seated one table away, a young woman sneaked furtive glances in their direction, and Eleanor got the distinct impression she was eavesdropping. Or trying to. And this was one conversation Eleanor preferred to keep private.

"At the risk of sounding too forward or indelicate," Mr. Hockley continued, still speaking at normal volume, "I am forty-one years old, considerably wealthy, and I wish to leave a legacy. But in order to do that, I need—"

"Children," Eleanor part whispered, part mouthed, doing her best to signal him with her eyes. But reading signals was apparently not in the banker's repertoire, nor was catching subtleties of any kind.

"An *heir* is what I was going to say. And lest you think I did not spend considerable time contemplating my actions before responding to your aunt, let me assure you I have. I believe we are well suited, Eleanor. I am in need of a wife to give me children, and you are in need of a provider."

Uncomfortable enough, imagining their conversation being overheard, Eleanor felt as though she were looking into a mirror, one that magnified her own sensibilities a thousand times over. And she wasn't certain she liked what she saw.

"Furthermore, I see no benefit to be gained by delaying this decision. Neither of us could be accused of being youthful anymore. Although . . ." The closest thing to a smile she'd seen from him yet touched his mouth. "Admittedly, you certainly fall closer to that category than I."

Eleanor managed a smile at the comment, still aware of the young woman's close attention. On a whim, Eleanor chanced a look in her direction, and the woman immediately averted her eyes, confirming Eleanor's suspicion.

She hadn't seen the woman before, she was certain. She would have remembered her. Pale blond curls artfully arranged beneath a stylish little hat that screamed high society.

"To risk the utmost transparency with you," he continued, "I confide that—"

Eleanor held up a hand. "Lawrence . . ."

Mouth hanging slightly ajar, he stared.

"If we are finished with dinner here . . . might I suggest that we continue this conversation elsewhere." When his blank stare persisted, she smiled. "Perhaps some place . . . less public."

He blinked. "Ah . . . of course, of course. You wish to see my home, to determine what you might well be mistress of."

Eleanor's face heated. "No!" she whispered. "I assure you, sir, I was not implying that I—"

"No, no." He tucked his napkin beside his plate. "I admire you for it. It's most logical and is a necessary requirement for you to make your decision. Home is the woman's domain, after all. Queen of her castle, and all that. Besides, I have reviewed your family history at length, as well as your father's long and illustrious career. Quite impressive, I might add. So it's only fitting that you have opportunity to do the same."

Thoroughly mortified—though also moved by his compliment to her father—Eleanor rose from her seat and smoothed the wrinkles from her skirt. She'd been seated for so long, it took a few seconds to get the feeling back in her legs again. Ever the gentleman, Mr. Hockley offered his arm.

As they passed the table beside them, Eleanor briefly glanced down, but the woman had bowed her head, leaving only her perfect blond curls to shimmer in the candlelight.

"To continue our discussion from the restaurant, Eleanor . . ."

Eleanor accepted the china cup and saucer from the servant and smiled her thanks. She sipped the coffee. Fixed to perfection. Rich flavor, yet not too strong.

"I have not the time nor the inclination to be husband to some young doe-eyed bride with expectations I will never be able to meet. My job is demanding and consumes most of my time. My trips abroad—both for business and pleasure—account for the remainder. And it would be my wish that my wife would accompany me on those journeys."

"Of course," Eleanor responded, knowing some women might have been shocked or even affronted by Lawrence Hockley's directness. But she wasn't.

What he was telling her was nothing she hadn't already considered. This *relationship,* for lack of a better term, would be, at its heart, a business arrangement that had absolutely nothing to do with emotions. At least for him. Her emotions, on the other hand, were currently tied in knots at the mere prospect of making such a commitment.

His house—or estate was more like it—was splendidly appointed. Nothing near the grandeur of Belmont, thank goodness, but lovely. And far beyond anything Eleanor had ever imagined being within her grasp.

And now it was—she realized with a sliver of wonder—within her grasp. If she hadn't personally experienced this evening, she wouldn't have believed it.

Occupying the settee opposite hers, Mr. Hockley leaned forward, his countenance softening with a surprising glimmer of emotion. "My future wife and . . . prayerfully, our children will want for nothing. And . . . as for your father, Eleanor," he said softly, "his every need would be quietly seen to. You would never have cause to worry on that account."

The mention of her father and the promise of his care tugged fiercely at frayed emotions, and—gripping the handkerchief in her pocket—Eleanor struggled to keep the tattered ends from unraveling.

Mr. Hockley eased back, his speech apparently delivered. She needed to respond, but how?

She lifted her coffee cup to her lips and drank, and as the warmth slid down her throat, she looked across at the man who could be the answer to all her prayers. Especially those for her father. And a part of her couldn't help but be amazed.

Lawrence Hockley was the perfect resolution for her circumstances. He was precisely the kind of man she had always pictured for herself . . . before she'd given up hope of ever marrying. And also before . . .

Her heart tightened at the slow-in-coming, but undeniable realization moving over her. He was the kind of man she would have chosen . . . before she'd met and fallen in love with Marcus Geoffrey.

Lawrence Hockley.

No matter how Marcus tried—and he *had* tried —he couldn't get that name out of his mind. Grateful it was Friday, he tucked the project sketches under his arm and left the warehouse.

President of the Bank of Nashville. *Old* money, and plenty of it. From one of the finest families in the city. A widower. No children. And that was only what he'd learned from having dinner two nights ago with Eli and Cordina.

A casual mention of Hockley's name to Robert Callahan, his foreman, yesterday had earned him a little more information. According to Callahan, Lawrence Hockley was a pillar of the community and a "more serious sort of fellow." Apparently, the Bank of Nashville was the only institution willing to loan money to Callahan's brother and sister-in-law for their new business. And that, only after Lawrence Hockley himself had requested a personal meeting with the couple in order to ascertain their character. Marcus sighed.

A gentleman who prized character, who stood up for the little man, and who possessed the means to take care of Eleanor in the manner she deserved. He didn't bother toying with the question of why that discovery didn't give him pleasure. He knew why.

He also knew he had no right to stand in the way of anything that Eleanor Braddock wanted to do and that would bring her happiness. On the contrary, he had an obligation to her—and to his obligations awaiting him back home—to do just the opposite.

So why was he headed in the direction of Belmont? He exhaled again. Because he cared about her, and *for* her. And he enjoyed her company more than a man with a *fiancée* back in Austria should.

The only thing that sated his conscience—even while rankling his pride—was knowing she didn't care for him in a romantic sense. At least she'd never given him reason to think otherwise.

Something else occurred to him. . . .

Eleanor's dinner with Lawrence Hockley had been sanctioned by Adelicia. He knew that from their exchange in the conservatory the morning Adelicia left town. For all he knew, the woman had arranged it all, which didn't help his outlook either. Because what Adelicia Cheatham wanted, she usually got.

Hearing the pattern of his thoughts, he stopped stock-still in the street. *Was machst du?* What was he doing? He and Eleanor were friends. That's all there was. At least that's all he was ever going to act on. So it was fine for them to see each other— on occasion.

But he needed to give her room, and was trying to do just that. He'd wanted to visit the mansion last night when he was at Belmont but hadn't. Just like he wanted to go right now . . . but wouldn't.

Though dreading the loneliness of the boarding-house, he changed course—the effort feeling almost Herculean—and made his way toward the boarding-house. He'd eat a quiet dinner, then try to lose himself in the latest set of notes from Luther Burbank.

He turned the corner, and a cool breeze met him head on. He welcomed it, along with the touches of fall in the burnt orange and reddish leaves on the trees.

One of his greatest joys was helping things grow, so how could fall—when plants and trees went dormant, and annuals died—be a favorite time of year for him?

"Hello, Mr. Geoffrey!"

Hearing his name, Marcus followed the voice and spotted Caleb headed straight for him, a brood of children in tow.

Caleb's grin widened. "Are you on your way home from work?"

Noting the boy was speaking German, Marcus did likewise. "I am. And where are you and your fine young friends headed this evening?"

One of the children with Caleb, a tiny blue-eyed blonde, tugged on the boy's sleeve. Caleb leaned down, and she whispered something in his ear.

Caleb grinned. "She says you ought to come and eat with us, sir. That's a compliment. She rarely says anything about anyone."

Marcus smiled at her, which sent her ducking behind the lad. "I appreciate the invitation, Caleb, but I've got work I need to do."

Caleb nodded, then his eyes narrowed. "Are those the design sketches for the building you're working on now?"

"They are indeed." Marcus knew what was coming next. The boy was fascinated with the intricacies of design, and he had a knack for the details of the process too.

Caleb eyed him. "Are you sure you can't do your work later? You have to eat sometime, sir.

And you're tired of eating alone. You said so yourself."

A darling little face with a pair of striking blue eyes peered around Caleb, and Marcus felt his resolve puddle at his feet.

With a feigned sigh, he fell into step behind the children and listened as they *jabbered*—as his old friend at the asylum had said—to each other in German, which explained Caleb's choice of language.

A young boy pointed to his pack. *"Was willst du da haben?"*

Marcus explained what he had inside his pack as they walked. He wondered where they were going and was surprised when the little entourage turned onto Magnolia Street, where Eleanor's building was located. He hadn't been by there in days.

Her decision to clean the building had been a good one. It showed solid business sense, and he hoped it rented soon so she could move on. He knew only too well how wearing an illusive dream could be. But he wasn't ready to give up his. Not yet.

The boy continued to pepper him with questions, and already weary, Marcus found the lad's enthusiasm a tad daunting. So he was grateful when the children slowed their steps.

But when he looked up, he could hardly believe where they were. Eleanor's building. And there were people inside. A lot of people. Then he noticed—

The *For Rent* sign that had been in the window was gone.

A sense of pride filled him. She'd done it. The building was rented. And due to her industrious efforts, no doubt. He couldn't wait to congratulate her and celebrate the good news the next time he went out to Belmont.

He followed Caleb and the children inside, scarcely able to find room to stand once they'd crossed the threshold. The chatter in the room dropped to a low hum and everywhere he looked, he saw women and children. Not another man in sight. Some were standing, some sitting, but without exception all were staring at him.

Then everyone turned back to what they were doing, and the conversation increased in volume again.

Marcus turned to Caleb and whispered, "This is where you're eating?" But the boy apparently didn't hear. Marcus felt a tug on his trousers and peered down.

The little blue-eyed blonde looked up at him. Her lips moved but he couldn't hear over the noise.

He knelt. "*Was ist es, das Kleine?*"

She touched her tummy. "*Ich bin hungrig.*"

She was hungry. "*Ja . . .*"

He nodded. "*Ich weiß.*"

From where he knelt, he reached for Caleb, about to ask him what everyone was doing here, when the conversation in the room fell away for a second time, and he heard a familiar voice.

● ● ●

"Ich bin so froh, dass Sie heute Abend alle hier sind. Vielen Dank, dass Sie wiedergekommen sind." Eleanor smiled at the women and children, hoping she'd delivered her practiced greeting without any mistakes. Judging from their smiles and nods, she guessed she had. Next, she repeated the welcome in English. "I'm so glad everyone is here tonight. Thank you for coming."

Naomi had told her that most of those gathered were trying to learn the English language. "And repetition helps," she'd said.

The last several meals, Caleb had invited a few of the mothers to join the growing number of children they served, but this was the first evening to offer a meal to any widow or child in need, and the front room was full to overflowing. Judging from the sound of those gathered, most hailed from the German community. Understandable, since Naomi and Caleb had been the ones to spread the word.

Other than knowing how to prepare the food, Eleanor had no earthly idea what she was doing. All she knew was what was happening wasn't by her design. And, strangely, that gave her greater confidence as to where it might lead.

"And now," she continued, glancing at Naomi, "because my German is not very good . . . *yet*"—she smiled—"Mrs. Lebenstein will translate."

Naomi repeated the sentence in German, then paused.

"We've been cooking for the better part of the day," Eleanor continued, "and we have plenty of food. So everyone who is here tonight will get a meal. *No one* will leave hungry."

Eleanor waited for Naomi to translate, watching the children's faces light up as though she'd announced Christmas would come early. But what she found even more touching were the tears that rose to the mothers' eyes when their young ones looked up at them and grinned.

"For those of you who are here for the first time, I'll explain how we'll serve the meal in just a moment. But first . . ."

Eleanor paused as the kindness in Naomi's voice filled the corners of the room.

"As Mrs. Lebenstein and her son, Caleb, told you when you were invited, I want to remind you that we don't ask for or accept any money for these meals. All we ask is that you do something kind for someone else tomorrow, and that you expect nothing in return for that kindness."

When Naomi finished translating, Eleanor leaned forward, affecting a conspiratorial look. "But if some of you children who were here earlier this week would like to tell me a kind act you've done, I'd love to hear it—*after* you've eaten your dinner."

Naomi imitated Eleanor's expression and tone, and the children and mothers alike giggled. Eleanor smiled, grateful beyond words—literally— as several of the children looked at her and nodded.

She'd determined to learn the German language

well enough to be able to converse with these people, and she knew just who she would enlist to teach her.

No matter that she tried to stop, she couldn't help comparing Marcus to Lawrence Hockley. And the comparison always came out grossly one-sided.

She hadn't seen Marcus since Tuesday, and she'd decided she wasn't going to say anything to him about tonight's dinner, or her future plans, for now. He'd clearly lacked enthusiasm over her idea of starting a restaurant, so she'd made up her mind not to share this *venture* with him either.

Which felt odd, since she'd grown accustomed to telling him about almost everything.

She explained to newcomers how the meal, along with cups of water, would be served from the kitchen. Families were encouraged to come through the line together, then could sit wherever they wanted to on the floor. Unfortunately, they only had the original table and four chairs, but Eleanor was working on that too.

As Naomi translated, Eleanor silently counted heads. First, the women . . . twenty-one. And the children . . . thirty-four. Fifty-five, she totaled. Plus herself, Naomi, and Mr. Stover, who was expected anytime. So many. And a crowd of people congregated by the door—Caleb among them—so she might have missed a head or two.

A streak of panic skittered through her. She had assured everyone there would be plenty of food. Now she only hoped there would be.

Footsteps behind her told her Mr. Stover had arrived, and she could tell he was doing something funny again, because the children started snickering.

Smiling, she bowed her head, and the others did likewise. "Our Father, which art in heaven, hallowed be thy name—"

"*Unser Vater, der du bist im Himmel,*" Naomi followed after, a quiet chorus of soft voices joining her. "*Geheiligt werde dein Name.*"

"Thy kingdom come, thy will be done in earth, as it is in heaven."

"*Dein Reich komme, dein Wille geschehe wie im Himmel, so auf Erden.*"

"Give us this day our daily bread . . ."

"*Unser tägliches Brot gib uns heute . . .*"

As Eleanor prayed, eyes closed, she sensed the language barrier lessening somehow. Especially with the final closing.

"*Amen.*"

"And now . . ." she said, loving the phrase a young boy had used a few nights ago, "*guten appetit,* let's eat and drink!"

Children clapped, and she and Naomi went into the kitchen to start dishing up the pie tins. Plates were too expensive, she'd discovered. Metal tins and cups were more practical with children anyway.

Half an hour later, her back beginning to ache from having been on her feet all day, she figured they had to be nearing the end of the line. She glanced at the number of stacked tins left. They'd started with sixty, to be safe. Only eight tins remained. And she'd already served Mr. Stover.

She recognized the next face in line.

"Caleb!" She smiled, glancing at him before taking the metal tin from Naomi. Eleanor added a healthy dollop of mashed potatoes to the side of crowder peas and carrots already nestled against a frugal slice of roast. She tucked a warm piece of corn bread slathered with butter onto the side of the plate. Hardly *La Bienvenue*'s artful culinary presentation, but it was filling.

Thinking of the fancy restaurant made her think of Lawrence Hockley. But she didn't want to think about him—or about the decision he was patiently giving her time to render.

"Thank you, Miss Braddock," Caleb answered, looking at the boy behind him, as if saying, *"That's how to say it in English."*

The younger boy did well. But after serving him, Eleanor found her supply of potatoes exhausted.

"Just one moment," she said over her shoulder. "I have more mashed potatoes keeping warm on the stove. We have plenty, though, so don't worry. You'll not leave hungry."

"Knowing you as I do, Miss Braddock, that's never been a concern."

Eleanor stopped cold. And turned. "Marcus!" She blinked, thrilled to see him but also feeling found out. She spotted Little Magpie beside him, staring up, along with a boy clutching a large leather pack. Two other children flanked him on either side. "I mean, Mr. *Geoffrey,*" she corrected. "What are you—"

He grabbed the tin in her hand, and she looked down to see that the food was about to slide over the edge.

He quickly righted the plate and gave her a wink. "Good evening, Miss Braddock."

Her face heated. She exhaled and tried to pull the tin back.

He wouldn't allow it. "This one can be mine," he said. "It'll give me a jump on digestion."

The twinkle in his blue eyes encouraged her to acquiesce but the *chef* in her wasn't so easily convinced. She shook her head and tugged on the tin. "Not in my kitchen, sir."

He let go, a single dark eyebrow arching. "*Your* kitchen?"

Again, she blushed. "Well, not mine, really. But . . . mine for now."

Under his watchful supervision, she served the remaining portions—scarcely having enough—then joined him, with Naomi and several children, on a vacant space of plank-wood flooring.

Naomi leaned close. "This is so generous of you, Miss Braddock," she whispered, eyes misty. "It is hard for me to put into words what this means to us. These women and children—many of them my friends, who live in our building—would have nothing to eat tonight . . . without this."

Eleanor found herself tearing up at the sweet admission. "It's my pleasure, Naomi. And thank *you* for inviting everyone."

Eleanor made introductions between Naomi and Marcus, surprised when Marcus said he'd looked forward to meeting her.

Naomi glanced across the room to where Caleb was seated with several other children. "My son enjoys working for you, Herr Geoffrey."

Eleanor perked up. "Caleb works for you?" She gave Marcus a discreet look. "In your construction company, I assume."

Marcus nodded, returning the look she'd just given him. "He's a fine boy, Mrs. Lebenstein. You ought to be proud."

Naomi smiled. "I am. Thank you, sir." Her head tilted to one side. "Caleb tells me you are also from Austria."

Marcus didn't answer for a moment, chewing for what seemed like a long time before swallowing. "Yes, madam, I am. And Caleb tells me that you're from a village near Strasbourg, that you were born there."

As Marcus and Naomi visited about their homeland, Eleanor tried her best to coax a smile from Little Magpie. But the girl seemed bent on keeping her at arm's length.

Giving up, for the time being, Eleanor retreated to the kitchen to cut the bread pudding and was grateful to find a majority of the pie tins already washed and waiting, thanks to Marta and Elena, two ladies whose help Naomi had enlisted.

About Eleanor's age, Marta approached, brow knitted. "The . . ." The woman paused as though searching for the right words.

"*Lebensmittel*," Elena supplied from behind, prodding her friend.

But Marta shushed her, whispering, "*Ich möchte es auf Englisch sagen!*" Then she turned back to Eleanor, her countenance determined. "The . . . din-ner," she said slowly, ". . . many good."

Delighted, Eleanor gave her forearm a squeeze. "Thank you, Marta." She pointed to the washed tins, including Elena with a glance. "*Danke für das* . . ." Eleanor paused. What was the word . . . *Oh!* "*Waschen*," she said, waiting to see if she'd gotten it right.

The women clapped. "*Ja! Sehr gut!*"

Eleanor retrieved the bread knife from the drawer, then noticed Marta and Elena had fallen quiet. The women peered over her shoulder with wide eyes, and Eleanor didn't have to guess why. She'd seen that look on many a woman's face when Marcus Geoffrey entered a room.

"I'd be happy to help with something," he said behind her. "If you need me."

Eleanor faced him, knife in hand. "That's a dangerous offer to make in a kitchen, Mr. Geoffrey, if you're not serious."

He looked at the knife, then at her. "If I make an offer, Miss Braddock, always assume I'm serious."

Calling his bluff, she held out the knife, handle first. "I need those five casseroles of bread pudding cut into sixty servings, and then"—wordlessly, he took the knife and promptly began cutting—"we need to spoon a ladle of warm sauce over each one." She laughed softly.

She came alongside him, noticing how perfectly straight his cuts were, and how symmetrical the finished pieces. "Have you done this before?"

"Do you mean have I studied the carefully designed structure of something, measuring its space and allocating its usage based upon the purpose or need at hand?" His delivery, so dry, so succinct, and without a trace of a smile drew one from her.

"Yes," she said. "That's precisely what I mean."

He looked over at her. "Never."

Laughing, she retrieved the sauce pan from the stove. Working together with Marta and Elena, the four of them served dessert in no time.

"Why didn't you say anything?" he asked once they were alone in the kitchen.

Knowing what he meant, she started to shrug, then stopped herself. "Because of how you reacted . . . when I told you about wanting to open a restaurant."

Tin of bread pudding in hand, spoon poised, he stared at her. Then nodded. "Fair enough. But it wasn't because I don't think you can do it. It's because—"

"You don't think I should," she finished for him. "My aunt said much the same thing."

Surprise swept his expression. "She knows about this?"

"Not yet."

He eyed her. "She's going to be back eventually. How will she feel about it?"

"It's difficult to say. . . ."

"I don't think it's that difficult, Eleanor. We both know she'll have plenty to say."

She sighed, not liking the fact he was right. And that he clearly didn't approve either.

"What you're doing here defies common sense, Eleanor," he said quietly. "The expense of the food, the sheer numbers of widows and children in this city, not to mention what others in your social circle would say if they knew . . . all make this a very unwise decision." His gaze moved from her, toward the front room, then back again. "It's also one of the bravest and noblest acts I've ever witnessed. And I'm proud of you."

His praise was so surprising she had to work to take it in. "Thank you, Marcus," she whispered.

He held a bite of bread pudding aloft as if making a toast, the warm cream sauce dripping from his spoon, then he popped the bite into his mouth. He closed his eyes as he chewed.

Eleanor spotted Caleb standing just outside the kitchen, watching. The boy grinned, obviously enjoying Marcus's antics.

"Mmmm . . ." Finally, Marcus looked at her. "Exactly where and when would you like for me to build your restaurant, madam?"

She smiled. And despite the alarms of warning going off inside her, she felt her heart open up a little more to this man.

Caleb joined them, a conspiratorial grin lighting his face. "But, Mr. Geoffrey . . . is it as good as your *Mutter*'s strudel?"

Marcus glanced at Caleb, then back at her, his expression odd. If she didn't know better, she would have thought he was a little embarrassed.

He spooned another bite of the bread pudding. "This is absolutely . . . *delicious*. But . . ." He sighed, his smile resembling Caleb's now. "*Nothing* is ever as good as your *Mutter*'s strudel."

Caleb laughed and nodded as Marcus tousled his hair. And though Eleanor's feelings were anything but hurt by the admission, she did feel a challenge in Marcus's declaration.

And silently accepted it.

Later that evening, Eleanor slipped the key into the keyhole, turned it counterclockwise, and checked the latch, making certain the door was locked.

It was still light out, though barely, and Marcus insisted on walking with her to the bakery, where she'd told Armstead to pick her up.

She had yet to give Armstead the address to Mr. Stover's building, nor had she told him about what she was doing. She always instructed him to leave her and fetch her at the bakery. It wasn't as though she thought she was doing something wrong. But the fewer people at Belmont who knew about these dinners, the better.

She draped her shawl around her shoulders as they walked along, a cool breeze stirring the night air.

"Thank you, again, for your help, Marcus. The children seemed to enjoy you. After watching you with them, I'm guessing you must have younger brothers or sisters."

He shook his head. "No. I'm the youngest, actually."

"Really? How many siblings do you have?"

"Only one." His voice grew quiet. "My brother. He . . . passed away a year ago—last summer."

Eleanor stopped in the street. Marcus did too.

"I'm sorry, Marcus. I . . . I didn't—"

"It's all right." He began walking again, and she joined him.

She waited to see if he would continue. When he didn't, she took the lead.

"I've lost a brother too," she said softly. "My only brother. Younger . . . He was killed in the war."

He slowed his steps, looking over at her. "I'm so sorry, Eleanor. Were the two of you close?"

"Yes . . . very."

"I was close to my brother as well."

Again, she waited, sensing he was going to say something else. But he didn't.

They walked in silence, the air between them anything but tranquil. She felt a restlessness in him. Something she hadn't sensed earlier that evening. And she wondered if he was thinking about his brother, or about his homeland. Perhaps he was missing Austria. Or his family, or—

"I could make you some tables and benches."

So unexpected was his offer, she came to a halt again. He turned and looked back.

"What?" Uncertainty clouded his expression. "Would you rather have chairs? Because I can do that too. But to me, benches make more sense with all the children, and . . ."

She smiled.

He frowned. "You're laughing at me again."

"You are a most surprising man, Marcus."

At his leading, they walked the remaining distance to the bakery. The business was closed, but Armstead was waiting, right on time. Eleanor almost wished she hadn't arranged for a carriage because she thought Marcus might have asked to escort her home otherwise.

But she had, and he hadn't.

"Thank you again for the delicious dinner, Eleanor. And the company. It was a most pleasant evening."

"I'm glad you met up with Caleb and the other children when you did."

"I am too."

She curtsied and offered her hand, remembering the night they'd visited the tunnel. But unlike that time, Marcus grasped her fingertips ever so lightly and his lips barely brushed her skin.

He assisted her into the carriage and closed the door—and then surprised her by leaning close.

"I meant what I said tonight. About being proud of you. You're a good person, Eleanor. Kind. Generous. And . . ." His mouth firmed for an instant. "I'm grateful for the friendship we share."

Eleanor caught the undertone in his voice and felt her spine stiffen against the seat. "Yes," she managed, focusing all her energy on maintaining the brightness in her voice while fully understanding his meaning. "I am too, Marcus."

By the time she returned to Belmont, she had reviewed every look, every conversation and smile, every exchange she'd had with Marcus, and knew she only had herself to blame.

When she climbed into bed and turned down the oil lamp, she realized, again, what a part of her had known all along, had known all her adult life. . . .

To men in general, but especially to men like Marcus, she would only and always ever be . . . a friend. Either that—she hugged her pillow tight—or another line on a banker's ledger.

Eleanor peered from behind the tree, watching her father from a distance as he sat swinging in the garden. She didn't want to disobey Dr. Crawford's orders, but she couldn't stay away any longer. She needed to see him, to make sure he was all right. But also . . .

The part of her that still remembered what it was like to be a young girl wanted to see her daddy again. *Needed* to see him.

In that respect, she wasn't unlike the little boy

who had wrapped his pudgy little arms around her legs after dinner at Mr. Stover's building and had held on tight. That had been two weeks ago, and he'd done the same thing every dinner since.

The boy, Stephan, Naomi told her, was orphaned, having lost both parents to illness after his family's recent arrival to Nashville. With no brothers or sisters, Stephan—four years old—had been found alone in the one-room shack, his parents' bodies on a moldy straw mattress in the corner.

At one time, Eleanor couldn't have imagined such a thing. But now, having met so many of these immigrant widows and children and through hearing their stories—heartbreaking and all too familiar—she could well imagine that happening. But Stephan was fortunate.

A widow had taken him in to raise alongside her children, which often occurred among the community of widows, she discovered. No formal court hearing, no legal rendering of any kind. Simply a child needing a home, and a *home* choosing to love him. Though based on the number of older children Eleanor saw wandering the streets, that wasn't always the case.

She turned her attention back to her father as he swung—back and forth, back and forth—his faced tilted toward the sun. His beard had grown but wasn't unruly. He'd always liked wearing a longer beard.

The garden Marcus had designed boasted a beauty reminiscent of those at Belmont, yet this one had a more welcoming feel. Being smaller in scope aided that, of course. But the meandering stone paths and number of small alcoves claiming either a swing or a bench seemed to beckon the wanderer to sit and partake of the peacefulness.

She'd wondered, at first, why Marcus—an architect—would agree to do this for her aunt. Then she'd thought better of the question. Aunt Adelicia was, after all, a most persuasive woman.

To Eleanor's surprise, Marcus had shown up for a handful of the dinners in the last couple of weeks. He always arrived after it had started, stayed until the end and helped her clean and lock up, then he would leave. Other than that, their paths hadn't crossed. Since she knew he was at Belmont nearly every day, that felt more than a little intentional.

But mostly, it just hurt.

Her father slowed the swing's motion and leaned forward, peering in her direction. Yanked from her musings, Eleanor swiftly stepped behind the tree, wondering if he'd seen her.

Seconds passed, and she peered out again. He was simply sitting there, staring ahead, dazed-looking, hands folded in his lap. And her heart broke a little.

So many needs in the world. How did the Almighty keep up with them all? She felt exhausted just thinking about it. And at times, overwhelmed. But she'd learned something back in the war, back when the world felt as though it was being torn apart at the seams.

She wasn't responsible for seeing to *everyone's* needs. That was *God's* responsibility. Hers was to do what He brought to her attention, what He placed in her path. Whether it was bandaging a wound, making a pot of soup, taking care of her father, or holding the hand of a man as he died.

But the needs within the Nashville community seemed insurmountable. The cost of food for the dinners she provided was ballooning, because with each dinner, more people heard about it and more people came.

She continually looked for ways to stretch her budget and reduce expenses. She cared about nutrition, certainly, but far more about filling empty bellies.

Potatoes, a staple ingredient when feeding so many, was a category of waste she was determined to cull. She'd spoken with Mr. Mulholland, the mercantile owner, but he was unwilling to budge on price. She'd see about that. . . .

She had an appointment tomorrow with a potato farmer on the outskirts of town. Perhaps buying in bulk directly from a supplier would lower her costs.

Ideally, she would like to have offered a meal every night. But after reviewing her finances—and the time it took to shop and prepare the meals— three times a week was all she could manage. And even that, she couldn't do much longer. Not without monetary assistance.

She'd thought about asking Aunt Adelicia for

help, but it was hardly a subject to broach in a letter. Not considering her aunt's response to her first request. What she was undertaking now was a far cry from opening a restaurant, yet this request—if she decided to make it—would require finesse.

Per her aunt's last communiqué, the family was extending its trip and wouldn't be returning for several weeks. Eleanor knew her personal finances wouldn't fund the dinners that long, yet she couldn't bring herself to say anything to Naomi or the other widows. They were always so grateful for the meals, as were their children.

Eleanor watched her father rise from the swing, his tall frame gradually unfolding to its full height. He looked a little thinner through the shoulders, perhaps, but was steady on his feet. He walked toward the door in the side of the building, a worn volume in his hand, and she smiled.

Tennyson, no doubt. His favorite. She wished she could join him for the afternoon and read to him, but—

She was determined to abide by the doctor's wishes, however contrary they were to her own.

"There's nothing I can do about this, Miss Braddock. I've told you before, I get my produce from—"

"I know what you've told me, Mr. Mulholland. But what I'm telling you is that if these potatoes"—she glanced at the two crates at her feet—"are as riddled with dry rot as the others I bought two days ago, I'm taking my business elsewhere.

Yesterday I threw away a third of the potatoes for my potato soup. And that's money I do not have to waste, sir."

Seeing the proprietor's frown, Eleanor felt her own forming.

Her meeting with the potato farmer on Saturday had proven enlightening, though not promising. The cost of purchasing potatoes from him would be considerably less expensive than buying them from Mr. Mulholland. But if she bought the potatoes directly from the farm, there was the fee for transporting them, and she would need to find a place to store them, because the farmer was only willing to sell them to her in the same quantity he sold to anyone else—by the wagonful.

She scarcely had enough room in the kitchen to store the needed supplies for each meal and still have room to cook for the eighty-plus people coming to each dinner. How would she store a wagonload of potatoes? No, there had to be another way to lower her costs.

She rubbed her forehead, aware of Mr. Mulholland watching her.

What had started as a way to help others was quickly turning into a larger-than-she-could-handle operation. And her dinner last evening with Mr. Hockley wasn't helping her nerves. Or her mood.

"Ma'am . . ." Mr. Mulholland shook his head, frustration evident in his tone. "All the stores in the city buy from the same farms around here. It's simply the way of it. Just like corn has earworms and tobacco has hornworms, potatoes have dry rot. That's the way it is. You just have to cut around it."

Knowing the tidy profit he made per pound on the potatoes, even after transportation fees, Eleanor only became more frustrated. "I refuse to buy food that is already rotten, sir." She picked a potato at random from one of the crates, then pulled a paring knife from her reticule. "When did the farm deliver these to your store?"

He eyed her, his expression skeptical. "Yesterday."

"And how long ago were they harvested?"

He looked from the knife to her and then to the knife again. "I wasn't here when they were delivered, so I'm not—"

With a quick flick of her wrist, Eleanor sliced clean through the flesh of the potato. Just as she'd suspected. She held it out, the core blackened with rot.

The proprietor grimaced.

She picked up another and did the same thing. And another. And another. She laid them all on his pristine white counter, rotten side up. "Mr. Mulholland, I'm not trying to be difficult."

The look he shot her held doubt.

"I'm simply trying to spend my very limited funds in the wisest manner possible." She sighed, feeling boxed in and not liking it. Then from nowhere came an image. That of Aunt Adelicia bargaining for twenty-eight hundred bales of cotton during the war, skillfully playing one army against the other to get what she wanted, property that was rightfully hers. And the image gave her fresh courage.

"I understand your predicament, Mr. Mulholland. And I appreciate your time."

He smiled, relief—and victory—lifting his features.

Eleanor studied the crates of potatoes at her feet. "Perhaps I need to start buying my produce directly from the farms. Maybe it would be fresher that way."

She nodded as though thinking the idea through, seeing his frown returning, deeper than before.

"Buying directly from them," she continued, "would be less expensive, I'm sure, though not as convenient for me, admittedly. But that savings could go far toward transportation costs, as well as offsetting the cost of the wasted product that you insist on—"

"Hold on now! Just hold on." Mr. Mulholland held up his hand. "There's no need to do something so drastic. I'm sure we can come to some sort of agreement."

He glanced beyond her, and Eleanor became aware of two female patrons paused in their shopping, staring in their direction.

With a jerk of his head, Mr. Mulholland beckoned Eleanor to join him farther down the counter, where he pulled out a sack and swept the rotten potatoes into it. Then he wiped down the surface with the hem of his apron.

He stared at her, looking none too pleased. "I don't want to lose your business, Miss Braddock. So how about I . . ."

Eleanor listened to his proposition, made some suggestions of her own, and ten minutes later, satisfied with the negotiated terms, she paid her bill.

"I appreciate doing business with you, Mr. Mulholland. I'll return the rotten produce no later than Saturday of each week, then will expect *half* the price per pound I paid to be credited back to my account."

He nodded, all traces of victory long gone. "And don't forget, be sure they're delivered to the back. I don't want crates of those things coming through the front door."

"I won't forget, sir, I assure you."

Grateful she'd thought to negotiate delivery for her groceries too, she smiled as he gave her change. It was only a few blocks from the mercantile to Mr. Stover's building, but transporting the amount of groceries she was buying these days often took two or more trips—even with Naomi's help. She slipped the change into her reticule and turned to go.

"What you're doing, ma'am . . . it's a real good thing."

Eleanor looked back.

Mr. Mulholland stood just where she'd left him.

"Word travels fast here, Miss Braddock. At least with folks living on the street." His exhale came heavy. "I see my share of little urchins every day, trying to steal an apple when they think I'm not looking. Even the widows . . ." He looked past her toward the street. "They come in every day begging for food." He shrugged. "I do what I can. But I'm running a business here, ma'am, not a charity."

Eleanor nodded. "I understand, Mr. Mulholland, which is why I especially appreciate your willingness to work with me on the price."

That earned her a begrudging smile. "Who knows, maybe what I save on apples will make up for the potatoes."

She felt a touch of humor. "Perhaps." His mention of apples reminded her of Marcus's comment about his *Mutter*'s strudel. Though she'd never made a strudel before, she looked forward to the challenge.

"Anyone ever tell you you're a lot like your aunt, Miss Braddock? From what I've heard, and from people who should know . . . she drives an awful hard bargain too."

Eleanor smiled, rather surprised at how much she liked the comparison.

On her way to the post office, Eleanor recalled something Mr. Mulholland had said and slowed her steps. He'd said word travels fast. But . . . *how* fast?

She was losing her anonymity. People were starting to make the connection between her and Aunt Adelicia. Had Aunt Adelicia—though still out of town—gotten word about what she was doing? Surely not. At least Eleanor hoped that wasn't the case.

She doubted her aunt would be pleased with her decision to sponsor the dinners, despite the woman's philanthropic nature. In fact, remembering their conversation upon her first night at Belmont, and what Aunt Adelicia had said—*"No niece of mine is going to serve as a* cook. *And certainly not at some . . . common establishment in town"*—she felt certain her aunt would not approve. Like Marcus had said.

Thankfully, the family wasn't due back until shortly before Thanksgiving. So she still had time to think of a way to present the idea to her aunt in a way she would accept it. If such a way existed.

At the post office, she gave the clerk a letter addressed to her father, along with three pennies for the stamp, then thanked him. She'd written her father every day for nearly a month now. Yet had received only that one oddly worded letter from him in response.

"Miss Braddock?"

Already at the door, her hand on the latch, Eleanor looked back.

The clerk walked around the counter, an envelope in his hand. No, two envelopes. And a small package in his other. "These came for you today. We were about to put them on the mail wagon. But since you're here . . ."

She took them and, recognizing the handwriting on the top envelope, felt a flicker of hope. Then she saw the return address on the package and felt that boxed-in feeling again. "Thank you, sir. Very much."

Outside, she found a bench beneath a tree and tore open the flap of the first envelope, leaving the others for later. Her gaze devoured the brief missive, cherishing every elongated curve and slanted loop of her father's script.

Dear Eleanor,

I am well and hope you are the same. A visit from you in the future would be welcome. If you should choose to bring another savory custard, I pledge to accept it far more graciously than I did the last.

Most sincerely,
Theodore

A soft laugh escaped her. She could imagine the intonation of his voice as though he were standing here, speaking the words aloud. She could also hear Dr. Crawford's—or perhaps Nurse Smith's—gentle coaching as her father had put pen to paper. *In the future . . .* It wasn't the warmest invitation. Yet, it *was* an invitation. What she'd been waiting for.

Theodore, though. Why had he closed the letter with the name Theodore instead of his customary *Your loving father?*

"Good news, I hope?"

Eleanor looked up, already recognizing the voice. But even if she hadn't, and even with the sun in her eyes, the broad shoulders and commanding stance would have eliminated any need to guess.

"Yes, it is," she answered, slipping the letter back into the envelope and both envelopes—the second from her aunt—into her reticule. She placed her reticule strategically atop the small package to mask Mr. Hockley's name and address.

If Marcus remembered Aunt Adelicia's mention of her dinner with Mr. Hockley, he had never let on. Nor had he asked her about it. She'd halfway expected he might—or maybe just hoped.

Marcus gestured. "May I?"

"Of course." She scooted over on the bench.

"I was on my way to see you." He settled beside her.

"You were?" Her tone revealed more delight at that prospect than was likely prudent.

He nodded. "I have something I'd like to show you."

"And . . ." She glanced around. "Where is this something?"

He turned and looked at her, and whether it was his eyes—so blue, like pieces of glass with the sun behind—or the kindness in them that she'd some-how overlooked early on, she thought him the most handsome man she'd ever seen. Which made her think, again, oddly enough, of her dinner with Lawrence last night.

When he had walked her to the door of the mansion, and brought her hand to his lips in a good-night "kiss," not the tiniest hint of attraction had stirred inside her. Though she had to admit she hadn't felt the opposite either. Lawrence Hockley was far from repulsive, after all. He was a little older, yes, and certainly not the most charming man alive. But he was also refined, even dignified. Wealthy, to be sure. And kind. But . . .

He wasn't Marcus Geoffrey.

"Walk with me," Marcus whispered, and stood.

Giving her thoughts a mental shake, Eleanor steeled herself against emotions she knew better than to trust. She rose but checked the watch pinned to her jacket. "I need to get dinner started soon, so—"

"This won't take long. And I promise"—he offered his arm—"it will be worth it."

She tucked her hand inside and walked with him to a warehouse a few streets away.

He paused when they reached a side door. "Close your eyes."

"I'm not fond of surprises, Marcus."

"That's fine. But you need to close your eyes anyway."

She looked at him. "Are you going to surprise me?"

"Yes . . . I am."

"But I just told you, I don't like surprises."

"Which is *why*"—he looked at her as though she were daft—"I just warned you about it. Now, close your eyes, Eleanor."

Trying to hide her grin, and failing miserably, she did as he asked.

He took hold of her hand. "Follow my lead."

Hand tucked in his—and loving the feel of him—she obeyed, her steps timid at first, then growing bolder after the first few. She heard hammering and sawing in the distance.

"There's a step up here. But just one."

She leaned into him, her grip tightening. "I hate surprises," she whispered.

"If only you'd mentioned that before," he whispered back. "Come along. We're almost there."

Finally, he stopped, so she did too, eyes still closed.

"All right . . . Open them."

She did, and blinked. It took a second or two for her eyes to adjust to the dimmer light. Then she saw it. "Oh . . . Marcus . . ." She could scarcely believe it. She ran a hand over the top of the wooden table, then over one of the two benches. "These are wonderful."

"We had some scrap lumber left from the project here. I drew up a design and asked a couple of my men if they'd be willing to help me." His mouth tilted. "We started it over lunch yesterday, and finished it today. It's nothing fancy. And we still need to sand it down and put some finishing touches on it. But it's solid. And will handle those children, for certain."

"And it's a narrow table too, which I like. Very functional."

He nodded. "My thought exactly. It allows enough room for two plates—or tins—right across from each other." He motioned. "But since you serve the food in the kitchen, you don't need all that extra room on the table. Besides, this size allows us to get more tables in the limited space. I estimate eight or nine could fit in there without overcrowding."

Us. Eleanor's heart warmed. He'd said *us.* "It's perfect, Marcus. Just perfect. I . . ." She laughed softly. "I don't quite know what else to say, other than thank you!"

"You're most welcome. But there *might* be another more . . . culinary way to express your gratitude." He rubbed his jaw as though deep in thought. "If only I could think of something."

Eleanor shook her head. "Truly? This is what it's come to?"

His slow grin—part boy, mostly man—acted like hot cocoa on a winter day and threatened to thaw her steeled reserve.

"How about . . . a buttermilk pie?"

"How about . . . I give you, and each of the men who helped you, your very own buttermilk pie."

"*Ja, danke.*" His expression proclaimed victory. And mischief. "*Wir beide haben einen Deal.*"

Knowing he was testing her, she didn't flinch. "*Ja,*" she said, giving the word the accent she'd heard countless times from Naomi and others. "*Wir haben einen sehr guten Deal,*" she said more slowly than she would've liked. *We have a very good deal.*

Pleasure lit his features.

Then something he'd said registered with her.

"From your project here," she repeated, taking in the structure, "is this where you're working?"

He looked around. "Where we're almost *finished* working. We have another week or so, then we'll be done. The men are finishing a storage area in the back of the building." He pointed in the direction of the muffled hammering. "We built a new office for the company's foremen and replaced portions of the roof that were rotting. A common practice these days. Companies are short on capital, and it's cheaper to—"

"Renovate than to build," she finished, catching his inquisitive look. She gave a shrug. "I briefly considered—or dreamed, is more like it—of building a café when I was thinking about opening a restaurant. But I swiftly discovered it was cheaper to buy, or rent, something already established." She looked beyond him to see a room constructed of fresh lumber in the far corner. Centered in one of the walls was a large window allowing full view of the warehouse. "Is that the new office?"

He trailed her gaze. "It is. Would you like to see it?"

She nodded and fell into step beside him.

"The warehouse is closed today, so there shouldn't be anybody here." He knocked on the door, then entered. He offered his hand as she managed the two steps.

Windows had been cut into the two outer walls allowing ample light into the office, which had a higher ceiling than customary. Work surfaces and cabinets gave the room a utilitarian, efficient feel. Perfect for its intended use.

Eleanor breathed in. "I've always loved the smell of freshly cut wood."

He inhaled. "So have I."

She ran a hand along the walls, not a warped or ill-fitting board among them. Same for the flooring. Winter's cold wouldn't dare show its face here. "Very nice work, Marcus."

"Thank you, madam." He gave a slight bow.

An architect's table sat in the corner. "Is that yours?"

"Yes, I brought it over with me. It belonged to my maternal grandfather."

"He was an architect?"

"A builder. And a good one. I learned a great deal from him."

And she was learning a great deal more about this man. She sensed his pride in his work, and with good reason. But she knew this wasn't what he truly wanted to build. She hoped he would some-day get the chance to construct the building he'd told her about—despite her having objected to the way he'd described it, and even her questioning his motivation behind building it. Anything Marcus Geoffrey would build was something she would like to see.

He checked his pocket watch. "Do you need help with dinner tonight?"

She eyed him. "*You* want to help me cook?"

He looked almost affronted. "I'll have you know that I—" the flash in his eyes gave him away— "know absolutely nothing about cooking. But I can provide company and conversation while watching you."

She grinned, thinking of nothing she would like more. "Herr Geoffrey . . . *Wir haben einen Deal.*"

A fountain pen?

Lawrence Hockley had sent her a fountain pen? Seated in the small study later that evening, enjoying a cup of Cordina's spiced tea, Eleanor opened the enclosed note.

Dear Eleanor,

In keeping with the custom of lavishing gifts upon one's future intended, please accept the enclosed token of my gratitude for your kind attention and consideration of my offer.

Eleanor shook her head. *". . . kind attention and consideration of my offer."* It sounded as though she was considering their becoming business partners instead of husband and wife. Merely thinking of making that commitment with him made her shiver. And not in a good way.

She continued reading. . . .

I sincerely beg your pardon but I must cancel our scheduled dinner for this Wednesday evening. Business in New York demands it. I return late Sunday and would appreciate your company for dinner on Monday evening, along with your decision.

Most cordially,
Lawrence D. Hockley

P.S. Lest you infer that I have taken leave of my strongly voiced opinion that we dispense with customary traditions associated with matrimony, please know that my opinion remains unchanged. I merely noted during our last dinner that when you searched your reticule for a pen to make note of a book I recommended, you did not have one in your possession. Now you do.

Eleanor had to smile. Pragmatic though he may be, Lawrence Hockley was apparently not without thoughtfulness. She picked up the pen and turned it in her hand. Then laughed aloud when she saw *Bank of Nashville* engraved on the side. He'd sent her a pen from the bank?

Even as she laughed, something deep inside rose to Lawrence's defense. It *was* a very nice fountain pen, after all. And it demonstrated that the man was observant, at least to some extent. She sighed.

What would it be like to be married to Lawrence Hockley? Predictable. Dependable. Safe. And think of the good she could do in the community. Mr. Hockley was a wealthy man, and from all accounts, he was generous and kindhearted. As she had learned firsthand, taking care of people's needs took money. And she would have money if she married him. Yet things wouldn't be the same.

To think that she could continue cooking for and serving the widows and children of Nashville would be naive. But perhaps if she spoke with Lawrence about it, if she presented the opportunity in the right light, and had time to explain it to him, much like she would do with her aunt, he might be more open to it than she expected. He was, after all, a logical man.

But what would *their* life together be like? As husband and wife? What would—she shifted a little on the settee—sharing an intimate relationship with him be like? If they married, they would likely have children, Lord willing, and that yearning to be a mother that she'd struggled—without success—to fully surrender, would finally be fulfilled. Yet it was the actual . . . coming to be with child—Lawrence Hockley's child—that made her cringe a little.

Her thoughts seemed reluctant to follow that intimate thread, and after a full moment with her imagination not so much as budging, she decided that was enough envisioning for one night. As her mother once told her in an extremely brief conversation when Eleanor was a young girl, "Not to worry, my dear. All of that will take care of itself when the time comes."

Feeling unsettled, Eleanor took a long sip of spiced tea, then looked up, her gaze drawn out the front window to the gardens, then to the conservatory beyond.

This time, she had no trouble at all considering the intimacy between a husband and wife—but with an entirely different man. One she couldn't have. But even more importantly, who wasn't seeking to have her.

All her life, she'd listened to the voice of logic, and could hear it even now. Only recently had the stirrings of her heart been awakened, and they were insistent, persuasive, and counter to those of her nature. So which did she listen to?

If she married Lawrence Hockley, she would never want for anything again. Except for the one thing, the one person, she wanted more than anything else.

Needing a diversion, she remembered and reached for Aunt Adelicia's letter and opened the envelope. Her aunt's descriptions of the family's outings and of humorous things the children had said cheered her. But her aunt's repeated question from previous letters—*Have you visited the Nashville Women's League, as I requested?*—did not.

Eleanor knew she needed to visit soon. But she dreaded it.

Sighing, she turned to the last page—and nearly came off the settee.

She read the words again. Then, frantic, hurriedly flipped back through the stationery, searching for the date on the first page. She'd paid no attention to it when she'd started. But seeing the date the letter was written, she frowned, compared it to the current date, counted, and—

Her exhale came through clenched teeth. Aunt Adelicia had changed her plans yet again and was due home any day!

Eleanor stood outside the imposing two-story brick building, not wanting to go inside, yet knowing she had no choice. The brass plaque to the right of the door caught her eye:

NASHVILLE WOMEN'S LEAGUE,
ESTABLISHED 1820,
WELCOMES WOMEN FROM NASHVILLE'S
FINEST FAMILIES WHO ARE DEDICATED TO
THE SOCIAL BETTERMENT OF THIS CITY AND
ITS GROWING COMMUNITY.

And, after reading it, she resisted the urge to turn and run. *Social betterment* . . . What did that even mean? Eleanor sighed, hand on the latch, eager to get the ordeal over with. She felt as if she were entering the Nashville Women's Academy again, where she would be compared to her aunt at every turn.

The entrance hall of the Nashville Women's League was every bit as ostentatious as she'd imagined. Only with far more lace. It was every-where. Lace draping antique tables and dripping from arms of chairs. Lace even fringed the bright pink floral curtains that contrasted with the deeper mauve floral of the carpet. Absolutely dizzying . . . But at least she knew where to send her pink ensemble for its final resting place when the time came.

"So are you saying you don't think this is a good option for me, Mother?"

"What I am *saying*," a strident voice responded from a side room, "is that the *first* option suits you best. However, if that is no longer available, then you must be willing to accept the second. And you must decide quickly, lest someone beat you to it!"

The conversation coming from the open door on Eleanor's left continued in hushed tones, and she resisted the urge to roll her eyes. She'd just stepped through the door and already there was talk of fashion. Not wishing to eavesdrop further, how-ever unintended, she cleared her throat. "Hello?"

The conversation fell silent.

She'd stepped forward, almost to the door, when movement on her right brought her around.

"Good morning!" A young woman called, turning to close a door behind her. "My apologies I wasn't here to"—her gaze lifted considerably in order to meet Eleanor's, the gesture a comment in itself—"properly welcome you, ma'am. How may I assist you today?"

"Good morning." Eleanor had her little speech

ready. "I recently arrived to Nashville and was encouraged by one of your members to make a visit here." Not revealing her relation to Aunt Adelicia was one way to avoid comparison.

"Ah! How wonderful. I'm Mrs. Daniel Jacobson Smith-Warner, the *third,*" the woman said, giving her a look that seemed intent on conveying shyness, but that did just the opposite. "And you are?"

"Miss Eleanor Elaine Braddock." Eleanor clenched her jaw. *Why* had she used her middle name? How idiotic! Her first and last name had just seemed so small and insignificant venturing into the conversation all by themselves.

The woman's gaze flitted briefly to Eleanor's hair, and Eleanor resisted the urge to smooth the sides. She'd worn it the way she always did— pulled back and knotted at the nape of her neck. Nowhere near as elaborate a style as that of her new *friend.*

"Braddock . . . Braddock," the woman repeated, eying her as though trying to determine if her blood was blue enough. "I don't believe I know that name."

"My family is originally from Murfreesboro," Eleanor offered, and knew immediately by the sideways tilt of the woman's head that her hometown had not impressed.

"I see . . ." The woman continued to stare, tiny lines between her eyebrows telling the true story. "How wonderful for you. But, may I ask . . . *which* member encouraged you to make a visit here?"

Eleanor wished she could turn and leave right then, and never come back. "My aunt . . . Mrs. Adelicia Cheatham."

Eleanor had never witnessed an eclipse of the sun—but she imagined it was something like what she saw. Every trace of skepticism vanished, and Mrs. Daniel Jacobson Smith-Warner, the *third* positively beamed.

"Oh, of course . . . *that* Miss Braddock!" She pressed a hand to her lace-trimmed bodice and her smile spread unnaturally wide. "Oh, my dear, it is a pleasure to meet you. Your aunt told us you would be joining us. But that was weeks ago. We wondered why we never heard from you. . . ."

The woman's words trailed off, signaling Eleanor that an explanation was expected.

"Yes, I'm sorry for the delay. I've been very busy . . . adjusting to life here."

"Well, of course you have. There's so much to do as a"—Mrs. Smith-Warner's smile faltered—"woman such as yourself."

If Eleanor could have blinked in that moment and been anywhere else in the world, she would have. And she would have chosen to be in the kitchen with Naomi, Marta, Elena, and the other widows. Women without a man in their lives, like her.

She felt a bond with them. A kindredness. And a welcome.

Mrs. Smith-Warner looped her arm through Eleanor's. "The first order of business is to introduce you to some of your future fellow magnolias."

Eleanor didn't know whether to laugh or cry. "Fellow magnolias?"

"Oh! You're not supposed to know that until after the initiation. So *shhhh* . . ." She held a finger to her lips, peering up. "Don't tell anyone."

Eleanor smiled. "Not to worry."

"Unfortunately, Miss Braddock, this being Thursday, most of our ladies are at tea in a member's home. But I believe two of our finest members may still be here."

Eleanor followed her across the hallway to the room she'd been about to enter earlier. Bracing herself for a fashion show in progress, she was surprised to see two women seated at a table, their heads bowed together over . . . a newspaper?

"Mrs. Hightower, Miss Hightower," Mrs. Smith-Warner said, at which time the two women turned.

Eleanor's gaze locked with that of the younger woman's. In that instant, she felt a flash of recognition. She'd seen her somewhere before. But *where,* she couldn't quite—

La Bienvenue. Those perfect blond curls.

And perfect they still were, although considerably less shimmery sans candlelight. Miss Hightower's eyes widened slightly before swiftly returning to normal, but that told Eleanor what she wanted to know. The woman recognized her too.

"I'd be honored," Mrs. Smith-Warner continued, directing her attention to Mrs. Hightower, "if you would allow me to introduce a future member to you and your daughter."

"A future member, Mrs. Smith-Warner?" Mrs. Hightower, a stately looking woman, briefly shifted her gaze to Eleanor. Her pointed chin jutted, sharpening what had likely been a beautiful countenance in more youthful years. "I believe, Mrs. Smith-Warner, you mean future *nominee* for membership, do you not?"

"Well, I . . . I simply thought that since she's Mrs. Cheatham's—"

"Because unless every member in this organization has assigned her proxy to you, my dear heart" —Mrs. Hightower smiled, which didn't improve her countenance—"then I believe we may be overstepping our bounds just a little."

Eleanor took an instant disliking to Mrs. Hightower, and already didn't trust her daughter. And even though Mrs. Daniel Jacobson Smith-Warner, the *third,* wasn't high on her list either, she actually felt sorry for the woman.

As introductions were made, Eleanor slipped a glance at the newspaper on the table. It was open to the society page. And here she'd thought the women had been discussing fashion, not future husbands.

"So you're the niece Adelicia has been telling us about." Rivaling Eleanor's height, Mrs. Hightower gave her a quick up-and-down glance. "Your aunt speaks very highly of you."

Eleanor forced a smile. "She was being generous with her praise, no doubt."

"We both know your aunt, Miss Braddock, and

therefore know how unlikely that possibility is."

As Eleanor looked at Mrs. Hightower, *formidable* was the word that came to mind. As did another word she didn't wish to dwell on. Just as she didn't wish to dwell in this moment any longer. Or in this place.

"Thank you, Mrs. Hightower"—Eleanor turned to the woman's daughter—"and *Miss* Hightower, for your kind welcome." She glanced at the woman beside her. "Mrs. Smith-Warner, I appreciate your assistance today as well. Now, if you ladies will please excuse me, I must be on to my next appointment."

Eleanor closed the front door behind her and took a deep breath, grateful to check that dreaded to-do off her list, and ecstatic that her path in life didn't include dealings with Mrs. Hightower or her eavesdropping daughter.

The next morning, Eleanor felt an uneasy sense of *déjà vu* and prayed this visit with her father would go better than the last.

With any luck, the savory custard wrapped in a cloth beside her on the carriage seat wouldn't end up on the wall.

She'd instructed Armstead to stop by the mercantile on their way to the asylum, and it being Friday morning, the streets were busy.

She'd ordered a book for her father last week, and Mr. Mulholland had said she could pick it up today. While there, she would gather the remaining ingredients for tonight's menu, which included chicken and dumplings, stewed apples, corn bread, and molasses cookies for dessert. She wondered if Marcus might show up to help.

She hoped so, even while warning herself not to.

Somewhat to her relief, Aunt Adelicia and the family had yet to return. A flicker of guilt pelted Eleanor's conscience at the thought.

On one hand, she welcomed their homecoming. Yes, she dreaded explaining to her aunt about cooking for the widows and children, but the mansion had been far too quiet and loomed even larger with the family gone, especially in the evenings. And especially since Marcus had been so scarce of late.

But on the other hand, she *had* enjoyed her independence and wasn't overly eager to give that up. More than once in her letters, Aunt Adelicia had expressed an eagerness to hear all about "the wonderful evenings with Mr. Hockley" and the "highly anticipated good news."

Eleanor wouldn't put it past her aunt to have already written the man herself.

The carriage slowed to a crawl and finally stopped. Eleanor peered out the window. Ahead, a freight wagon loading goods from the feed store blocked the left side of the street while other wagons and carriages waited their turn to maneuver around it.

Eleanor felt the carriage dip to one side as Armstead climbed down.

He peered in through the window. "Miss Braddock, I'm sorry, ma'am, but it looks like it could be a while. You all right back here?"

Seizing the opportunity, Eleanor reached for the door handle. "Actually, I think I'll walk the rest of the way."

Armstead assisted her from the carriage even as his expression said he would prefer she stay in it. "You sure you don't wanna wait, ma'am? Mercantile's still a good ways away."

"Yes, I'm sure. I'll enjoy the walk. I'll meet you there."

He nodded. "Yes, ma'am."

She continued on foot, and with each step her thoughts slowed and her concerns faded. What she wouldn't give to be able to spend the day in the kitchen making bread, working the dough until her arm muscles ached, in a good way. Push and roll, push and fold. The kneading process became almost like a dance atop the floured surface. And the aroma of the bread as it rested and rose . . .

There was something comforting about bread needing to be still, needing peace and tranquility in order to become everything it was meant to be. She felt that way sometimes too. Perhaps that's why she enjoyed cooking. It gave her time to "be still" on the inside.

A sign in a window she passed caught her attention, and upon seeing what it advertised, she slowed her pace. *Calico, Simple Prints, and Solid Fabrics on Sale.* The handwriting on the slate board clean and tidy. Right above it painted in plain white stencil letters was the shop's name. *Simply Dresses.* And beneath that: *Made-to-Order Dresses Simply Made Well.*

She peered through the window. It was a tiny shop. Not much to it, really. But she thought of Naomi's two dresses, as well as those of other widows in the close-knit group, and her hand was on the latch before she consciously summoned the act.

A bell jangled overhead when she opened the door.

What the shop lacked in size and elegance, it made up for in neatness and a surprisingly larger selection of inventory than she'd expected. Spools of thread, pin cushions, and seamstress tape, each in their own place, sat atop a small desk in one corner, a dais for alterations beside it.

Almost before the final note from the bell above the door dissolved, a woman appeared through a curtained doorway, smile in place and work in hand.

"Welcome, ma'am. How may I help you?"

Eleanor glanced at her surroundings. "You have a very nice shop here."

"Thank you." The warmth in the woman's expression deepened. "It's not fancy. . . ." She gave a somewhat shy smile. "But neither are the dresses I make. I sew mostly day dresses, ma'am. Also shirtwaists and skirts. I sew them fast but sew them well. I have samples of my work right here. Along with the prices."

Appreciating the woman's candor, Eleanor viewed the dresses hanging on hooks to the side. Simple fabrics, no fancy tapering or scalloped necklines. But the material was thick and well woven, the stitching tight and true, and the buttonholes, even and well spaced. Far nicer than either of Naomi's dresses. And the prices were very reasonable.

Eleanor silently calculated, thinking not only of Naomi but of the other widows. And the children. Her personal funds were already stretched, but at this price, she could manage to help a few. Especially with winter on its way.

"By chance, do you make children's clothes?"

The woman nodded. "I certainly do."

"Well . . ." Eleanor nodded. "You do *fine* work."

"Thank you, Mrs. . . ."

"Oh . . ." Eleanor forced a laugh. "Actually, it's *Miss*. I'm not married."

"I beg your pardon, ma'am." The woman's face flushed. "I simply assumed when you asked about children that—"

"Oh . . ." Eleanor waved the comment away as though it were nothing. "I wasn't referring to my own children, but children in general. No harm done, I assure you."

Eleanor maintained her smile. But deep inside, that distant heartbeat of the mother she might have been rose to a steady thrum. She thought of her upcoming dinner next Monday evening with Mr. Hockley, when he returned from New York, and of the decision she had to make. Her head told her one thing, her heart another.

Seeing the woman shift beside her, Eleanor tucked her thoughts behind an embarrassed expression. "Forgive my manners . . . I'm Miss Eleanor Braddock. And you are?"

The woman gave a brief curtsy, regret lingering in her gaze. "Mrs. Malloy, ma'am. Rebecca Malloy. It's a pleasure to meet you, Miss Braddock."

"The pleasure is mine, Mrs. Malloy." Eleanor eyed the dresses again, *this* decision easily made. "You said you sew fast and sew well. I can clearly see how *well*." Eleanor leaned in as though conspiring. "Now I'd like to see how fast. Shall we?"

Armstead pulled the carriage to a stop outside the mercantile just as Eleanor exited, her father's book in hand. Armstead climbed down to open the carriage door.

"Miss Braddock! Miss Braddock!"

Eleanor turned in the direction of the voice and saw Mr. Stover, short legs churning, waving to her as he crossed the street.

Armstead straightened to his full height beside her, but Eleanor swiftly reassured him. "The gentleman is a friend, but thank you, Armstead."

Armstead dipped his head and moved a few steps away, but he remained watchful.

Mr. Stover stopped before her and worked to catch his breath. "I'm glad I saw you, ma'am. I've got news!"

"From the looks of it, I'm guessing it's exciting news, Mr. Stover."

"Oh, it is, ma'am. It is!" He suddenly looked at the carriage as though just then seeing it and whistled low. "Well, if this ain't fancy enough for Queen Victoria herself."

Eleanor winced, realizing Mr. Stover was still unaware of her connection to her aunt. Feeling as though she owed him an explanation—and guilt prodding her to give him one—she hurried to explain.

"Mr. Stover, this isn't my carriage. It belongs to—"

"Mrs. Adelicia Acklen Cheatham. Your aunt. Yes, ma'am, I know. Everybody in town knows whose buggy this is." He rose on tiptoe and peered through the window, his wheeze of laughter high-pitched. "It's a real beauty, ain't it?"

Eleanor hesitated. "So . . . you've known all along that my aunt is Mrs. Cheatham?"

He grinned. "Not all along, ma'am. But early on. One of the shopkeepers saw you comin' into my place one day and thought I'd done sold the building to Mrs. Cheatham herself." He laughed. "As if she got need for a place like that, I told him."

Eleanor returned his smile, but her conscience wouldn't rest. "I'm sorry, Mr. Stover, for keeping that from you. It's simply that I wanted to—"

"Oh, I think I know, Miss Braddock. You wanted to do this on your own. Stand on your own two feet." He nodded. "You bein' one of them women who went to school and all . . ." He winked. "It added up for me." His expression did another quick turn. "Now, my news! I just met with a man this morning, and I think we got us a renter."

Eleanor heard the words but couldn't believe it. "A renter? For the building?"

"Yes, ma'am!" He beamed. "So you'll be gettin' some of your money back. All of it, if I can swing it, seein' what you've been doin' for everybody else. I met with him at the building about two hours ago. He asked lots of questions too. Was real interested in knowin' how it was bein' used. So I told him all about you and what you were doin'. You better bet I sang your praises, ma'am. And every note was true."

Eleanor tried to appear pleased, knowing this was best for Mr. Stover. But . . . the building. *Her* building. *Rented?* Where would she cook in order to feed all these people? Where would they meet?

Uncertainty crept into Mr. Stover's expression. "You don't seem too happy about it, Miss Braddock. I figured this was what you wanted."

"It was." She managed a nod, then saw the earnestness in his face and realized she was viewing this from a very selfish perspective. "And it is." She gave him what she hoped was a persuasive smile. "You've needed to rent this building for a long time now, so this *is* good news. But you said . . . we *think* we have a renter. So it's not certain yet."

"No, ma'am. But like I said, he seemed real interested. Said I'd know his answer for sure in the morning."

● ● ●

The second-floor hallway of the asylum was unusually quiet, and Eleanor's footsteps echoed down the corridor. Nurses and orderlies passed, greeting her with silent nods and briefly lived smiles. She returned them, wondering what kind of lives these people lived outside these walls and grateful for whatever it was that compelled them to work in an institution like this, caring for people like her father.

Pausing outside his room, she balanced the savory custard in one hand and reached for the latch with the other, all while praying this visit would be worlds different from their last.

She knocked softly and pushed open the door.

Her gaze went first to the chair. But when she found it vacant, she looked at the bed—and saw him curled on his side beneath the covers, his back to her. Concern hastened her steps to him. Was he sick? If so, they should have sent for her.

"Papa?" She set the custard and her reticule aside and rounded the bed, bracing herself. For what, she didn't know. But when she saw the gentle rise and fall of his chest, and heard not a hint of labored breathing or rattle in his lungs—the telltale signs of pneumonia—she began to relax.

His eyes were closed. His hands clutched the blanket beneath his chin. Her mind played a trick on her, and for an instant, she saw Teddy again, as a young boy, curled in that same fetal position, fast asleep. Tears rose to her eyes as she brushed the hair from her father's forehead. The strands felt coarse beneath her fingertips.

"Papa . . . can you hear me?"

Only the sweet unencumbered sound of sleep filled the silence.

The curtains to his room had been pulled half-way closed and dulled the brilliant sunlight of the crisp fall afternoon. She settled herself in his chair, the one they'd brought from home, and leaned back into it, the suppleness of the well-worn leather and the indentation of her father's frame embracing her like an old friend.

Her eyes drifted shut, and she indulged them, the weight of cares and busyness of recent weeks—and months and years—tugging at her like a tide on the shore, and she finally gave in to it.

She awakened to a shuffling sound and looked over to find her father sitting up in bed, a fork in his hand and the casserole containing the savory custard tucked in his lap.

"It's delicious," he whispered, smiling at her.

Eleanor blinked to make sure she wasn't dreaming. But there he was, still eating, still smiling.

She rose and stretched, noting the sun's brilliance had only slightly lessened. She hadn't been asleep long. "How are you, Papa?"

"I'm better now." He held up the casserole. "Ham and cheese. My favorite."

He held out the fork to her, but she shook her head.

"I like watching *you* eat."

Still hesitant to trust the gift of this moment, she moved to sit on the edge of the bed.

"I watched you for a while." He pointed toward the chair. "It was nice, Eleanor. Waking up and seeing you sleeping there. It's been a long time since we've seen you."

The moment quivered, as did her heart. "We?" she asked softly.

He looked at her. "Why . . . your mother and I, of course. She should be back anytime now." He shook his head. "She worries about you volunteering with those wounded soldiers. Being so close to the battle lines. It's not safe for a woman, she says. And I agree."

"Don't you worry about me, Papa. I'm being careful."

"That's what I tell her, but you know your mother." He shoveled in bite after bite.

"Yes," she whispered. "I do."

Remembering the book she'd bought for him, she retrieved it from the side table. "I brought you something. One of our favorites." She handed it to him. "It's your very own copy. The cover looks different because the book has been reprinted recently."

"*Conversations on Common Things* . . . by Dorothea Dix," he read aloud, opening the cover. "Why does this sound so familiar? Have I—" He stilled, then frowned, staring at the page. He shook his head. "No . . . no, no, no, *no, no* . . ."

Over and over he said it. Eleanor leaned closer,

trying to see what he was looking at, what was upsetting him so, when his expression caved.

His mouth moved, but at first no words came. Then finally, "Eighteen . . . sixty-seven," he rasped. "But the war and . . ." He paled. "Your mother . . ."

He looked at her as though searching for an explanation in her features, and in the instant Eleanor realized what was happening, he let out a heartrending cry.

She reached for him, but he curled up on his side again, hands tucked beneath his chin, desperate sobs pouring from him.

Nurse Smith suddenly appeared beside the bed. Eleanor hadn't even heard her come in.

"What happened?" the young woman asked.

"I gave him a book, and he read the title page, and . . ." Eleanor looked at her. "I think it was the date inside."

Her father wept. "Oh, my sweet Anna. My sweet, sweet Anna."

Nurse Smith came alongside her father and put her face close to his. "Theodore, listen to my voice. It's going to be all right. *You're* going to be all right."

But her father's cries all but drowned out the reassurances.

An orderly entered the room, syringe in hand.

"Only half the dose for now," Nurse Smith instructed, still huddled close to her father, arm around his shoulders. She turned to Eleanor as the orderly administered the injection. "This has been happening more frequently. Sometimes multiple times a day. He forgets that"—she whispered the next words—"your mother and brother are gone." Nurse Smith gave a troubled sigh, looking back at him. "And when he remembers, he loses them all over again."

Eleanor's eyes filled. Her father's memory lapses weren't new. They had become more frequent the past two years. But to relive that awful pain of loss *so* often? It was hard enough to endure once. But again and again?

Nurse Smith slipped something from her pocket and when Eleanor saw what it was, she wished she'd thought to bring some with her.

"Here you go, Theodore. Your favorite. Can you take it in your hand, please?"

Between sobs, her father reached for the sugar stick. But he didn't put it in his mouth. He only held it, eyes clenched tight.

Minutes passed, and he began to relax. His breathing evened. His weeping gradually tapered to whimpers, and when he finally opened his eyes again, he looked first at the nurse, then at Eleanor.

"Eleanor," he whispered, relief and gratitude in his eyes. "You're still here with me . . . aren't you . . ."

Speaking past the lump in her throat, Eleanor nodded. "Yes, Papa. I'll always be here. I'll never leave you."

He reached for her hand and brought it to his chest. "Thank you," he whispered over and over, his words growing fainter the closer sleep came. "I don't think I could live . . . if I lost you too."

Feeling Nurse Smith's attention, Eleanor glanced over and found the woman's cheeks wet with tears.

"I love you, Eleanor," her father whispered, his eyes drifting shut.

Eleanor pressed a kiss to his forehead. Then another, and another. "I love you too, Papa. So very much."

The next morning, Eleanor awakened later than planned and had scarcely closed the bedroom door behind her before she heard voices in the family dining room. She froze midstride in the hallway—

But not before a squeaky floorboard gave her away.

"Eleanor? Is that you?"

Recognizing the voice, she clenched her eyes tight.

Not only had she overslept—it was approaching half past ten—but apparently the family had returned home after she'd retired last night. She softly exhaled, yesterday's news about the building and potential renter weighing heavy, and the visit with her father still tugging at her heart.

Wishing for a strong cup of coffee, two of Mr. Fitch's doughnuts—no, *three*—and another lifetime to prepare for this conversation with her aunt, she took a deep breath and rounded the corner.

"Good morning!" She half expected to see the entire family, but only Aunt Adelicia was present. Yet she was certain she'd heard other voices.

Her aunt presided at the foot of the table, a china cup and saucer her only companion. Her smile tight and eyes keen, her aunt's countenance was the definition of composure. And two words entered Eleanor's mind: *She knows.*

But how? A rush of scenarios flitted through her mind but the rule of probability swiftly dismissed each one, and Eleanor finally attributed her suspicion to her own guilty conscience.

She glanced through the entryway on the opposite wall into the library. "I thought I heard voices."

"Good morning, Eleanor. And yes, you did. The children came to see me during their *late* morning break from studies. You just missed them."

Not missing the subtlety of her aunt's insinuation, Eleanor felt the nudge to explain her reason for oversleeping but couldn't without revealing everything. Which she needed to do, but it had to be in the right order.

She'd been so tired upon returning home last night, she'd simply crawled into bed and didn't even remember pulling up the covers. Ninety-six women and children had shown up for the meal last evening. *Ninety-six.* She'd scarcely prepared enough food. She'd trimmed back on the portion size and had foregone eating a meal herself just so they would have enough.

If anyone had ever told her that cooking for widows and fatherless—sometimes parentless—children would have been the answer to her prayers for a restaurant, she would have thought them daft, or at least weak in the head. It demanded most of her time—preparing menus, shopping for ingredients, and then the cooking and cleaning. But providing the meals, and offering encouragement and hope to these widows and their children was more fulfilling and rewarding than she'd ever dreamed.

Her stomach growled. Ravenous, she looked over at the buffet but found it empty. No wonder, considering the hour. She craved a steaming mug of black coffee to bring her back to life. And give her courage. "If you'll excuse me for a moment, Aunt, I'll go downstairs and ask Cordina if—"

"Nonsense." Aunt Adelicia picked up the silver serving bell on the table. "You will be served breakfast here."

The jangle of the bell struck a dissonant chord in the silence, and Eleanor claimed a seat next to her aunt.

A moment later, Cordina appeared with a fresh pot of coffee. She refilled Aunt Adelicia's cup, then poured another for Eleanor. "I bring your breakfast right up, Miss Braddock."

"Thank you, Cordina." Eleanor had grown accustomed to visiting the kitchen and requesting her meal there. She looked at the shiny silver bell atop the table and, for some reason, envisioned the haughty-looking roses she'd seen in the conservatory on her first day.

As Cordina retreated to the kitchen, the clock on the hearth chimed the half hour. Eleanor sipped her coffee, the comforting aroma fortifying her almost as much as the brew itself.

She sneaked a look beside her. "I hope your travels were pleasant, Aunt. Your letters certainly painted lovely pictures."

"Yes, the excursion was most enjoyable. At least at the outset. The children were enjoying exploring the northeastern states, but we decided to return home when my neuralgia took hold."

"Oh . . . I didn't realize. I'm so sorry." Eleanor knew, secondhand, how painful those headaches could be. Her own mother had suffered from them.

"Dr. Cheatham went into town to retrieve powders from Dr. Denard. He should be back anytime. Those offer a measure of relief."

Eleanor nodded. Everything she thought of to say sounded stilted and pretentious. Which it was, compared to what she needed to tell her aunt.

A moment passed, and Aunt Adelicia's gaze came to rest upon hers—unmoving, unblinking— and Eleanor was now certain she knew.

"Aunt Adelicia, I need to tell you something. And I'm relatively sure you're not going to—"

"Here you are, Miss Braddock." Cordina reappeared. "Got you some eggs all scrambled up, two pieces of bacon fried crisp, and a slice of bread with honey and butter, just like you like it."

The food looked—and smelled—more delicious than usual. "Thank you, Cordina."

"You're welcome, ma'am. Mrs. Cheatham, you need anything else?"

"Not at present. Thank you, Cordina. But perhaps some tea later in my room, once Dr. Cheatham returns."

Smiling, Cordina nodded and left the room.

Having gotten to know the woman in recent weeks, Eleanor knew better than to think Cordina wasn't aware of the tension in the room.

Finding herself alone again with her aunt, Eleanor looked longingly at her breakfast, hungrier than ever. But explanations needed to come first. She took a sip of coffee and plunged ahead.

"As I was saying, Aunt Adelicia, I've become involved in something that I didn't actually envision . . . in the sense of what it has become. And I did it"—stating this next part aloud was the most daunting—"even while knowing that you would likely not approve of my actions."

Seeing a single dark eyebrow arch, as if her aunt were thinking, *So why then would you dare do such a thing?* she hastened to add, "It's not that I disregard your opinion . . . or that I'm ungrateful for all you've done for me, *and* my father." She briefly bowed her head. "But I feel so strongly about this. About the rightness of it. Almost as if . . ." She sighed. "This may sound silly, but it's almost as if this was what I was—"

415

"No more, Eleanor, please! I *know* what you've been doing, and it hurts to even hear you speak the words. Especially after I . . ." Aunt Adelicia grimaced, then touched her temple, the muscles in her jaw tightening. "Especially after I made it perfectly clear where I stood on the matter. After we welcomed you into our home, have helped with your father, I . . ."

Eleanor had never seen her aunt cry. And even now, she wasn't certain whether what she was seeing was the start of tears or a rage.

Her aunt exhaled. Her hands shook. "That you would choose to blatantly go behind my back and against my wishes, and would open up such an . . . *establishment* is beyond the pale, Eleanor. And for this behavior to come from a family member is—"

The front door opened and closed. Aunt Adelicia fell silent, and only in the resulting deafening silence did Eleanor realize how loud her aunt's voice had become. And how far-reaching her own decision had been.

Soft footfalls sounded on the plush carpet, and Dr. Cheatham appeared in the doorway of the dining room, newspaper in hand.

He stopped short, his cheeks flushed. "Ladies," he said tentatively, eying his wife. "I take it the subject has been broached."

Eleanor felt the hot prick of tears and bowed her head, knowing the question wasn't directed at her.

Aunt Adelicia took a deep breath, then gave it

416

slow release. "Yes, I was expressing my disappointment to my niece about her decision—against my expressed wishes—to open a . . . restaurant."

Eleanor's head came up. *A restaurant?* She looked between them. "But I'm not—"

"Would you allow me to do the honors, Miss Braddock?" Dr. Cheatham approached, unfolding the newspaper as he did. He laid it before Aunt Adelicia, her expression wary, his bemused. "It would seem, my dear, that your source of gossip was mistaken, greatly so. However"—a glint of mischief lit his eyes—"there is one point in which they were correct. . . . Your dear niece and, henceforth, *you,* are most definitely the talk of the town!"

Marcus stared at the newspaper heading and laughed, wondering if Eleanor had seen it yet. He ought to ride out to Belmont later and show it to her. After his appointment at the asylum.

He finished his coffee, waved at Fitch for two more doughnuts, which Fitch served up with a joke on the side, and then made his way to the livery.

He folded the newspaper and stuck it in his saddlebag along with the pastries. Eleanor had only been in Nashville for two months, and already she'd turned the city on its ear. What would her aunt think about all this . . . ?

Eleanor had told him her aunt was due home any day, so they shouldn't have to wait long to find out. He laughed again, wishing he could be a fly on the wall in the Belmont mansion. If this didn't win Adelicia Cheatham over to Eleanor's way of thinking, nothing would.

The article was detailed. The reporter had done his snooping. He'd written the piece with an obvious slant toward scandal—WEALTHY NIECE OF ADELICIA CHEATHAM EXPOSED AS COOK. But it was the reaction the article drew from patrons in the bakery just now that Marcus found most telling.

He'd overheard a couple of women, similar to Adelicia Cheatham in age and social strata, not two tables away, whispering in disapproving tones, serious brows knit. But the majority of the bakery's patrons—colonial rustics, as his father called them—heartily approved of what Eleanor was doing and weren't shy to admit it.

So while the reporter had intended to expose a rich niece and her aunt to ridicule and controversy—and there would certainly be backlash, Marcus knew, at least from some—what the journalist had unknowingly done was pave the way for Eleanor Braddock's dream—or at least a version of it—to come true.

He only hoped he was in Nashville long enough to see it.

That thought was sobering. Come next summer, he would return to Austria. How could something he tried so hard not to think about occupy so large a portion of his thoughts? He felt the clock constantly ticking inside him. At work, in the conservatory at Belmont, but mostly, when he was with Eleanor.

He was so proud of her. Yes, she was wealthy—she was Adelicia's niece, after all—so she had the money to be generous. Still, he couldn't think of any other person in her position who would humble themselves to do such a thing.

On a far different note, he'd finally responded to the baroness's latest letter with a one-page reply. He'd received a tome in exchange. It consisted of mostly negligible information, but one remark in her letter had stayed with him. *"The court rumbles with rumors of war with Russia . . ."*

The baroness was prone to exaggeration. Nonetheless, he'd written his father immediately and still awaited his reply. Daily he scanned the newspapers for word. But nothing.

He'd been just a boy at the time, but he remembered only too well his country at war with the Ottomans, and the devastation that had wrought. A declaration of war would mandate his immediate return home.

Marcus mounted his horse. Regal seemed antsy, ready to run, just like him. So as soon as they cleared town, Marcus gave the horse his head, and the thoroughbred flew over the dusty back roads leading to the asylum.

The air held a chill, and the countryside, clinging to remnants of an all-too-swift fall, passed in a blur. If only he could feel this free on the inside—instead of shackled to a future he didn't want that was taking him away from the woman he did.

Seeing the asylum in the distance, he reined in,

his breath coming hard. He *wanted* Eleanor Braddock. He'd held back from fully admitting that, even to himself. But it was true. He thought of her constantly. When they were together, and when they weren't. She was a friend, yes. Yet he wanted her to be so much more.

But apparently, so did Lawrence Hockley.

Marcus hadn't inquired to Eleanor about her relationship with Mr. Hockley. And had no right to. *Friends,* he reminded himself. He and Eleanor were friends.

Winded but revitalized, he dismounted, studying the asylum garden from a distance. A freight wagon covered with a tarp sat off to the side, four delivery men waiting with it. He checked his pocket watch. They were early.

The statue Mrs. Cheatham had ordered was to be installed today, and he'd made it clear he wanted to be there when the workers unloaded it and set it on its foundation. He still had no idea what the statue was or who had carved it, only that Mrs. Cheatham said it was beyond exquisite and—

"Ahoy there!"

Marcus paused, looking around for the voice's owner, thinking it might have been one of the delivery men calling to him. But none of them even looked in his direction. A handful of patients strolled the garden, but, again, their attention was focused elsewhere.

"*Pssst!* Take heed, friend, lest you be seen! They may be the enemy!"

Marcus followed the voice this time and spotted a wild tuft of white hair bobbing behind a laurel. And he didn't have to wonder for long about the man it belonged to.

"To the left about two inches." His focus riveted, the elderly gentleman barked instructions to the delivery men as though the statue were from his own private collection. "Almost there. Careful now, careful . . ."

Silently, Marcus supervised from the side. He didn't have the heart to step in and take over. Besides, the man was correct. The statue *did* need to come left about two inches.

The marble sculpture, still wrapped in blankets and bound with rope, was about his own height and measured thirty inches from side to side. A perfect fit for the foundation.

Nearby, a cluster of patients gathered, both men and women, their stares curious.

"Want us to unwrap it for you, Mr. Geoffrey?" one of the workers asked. "Before we leave?"

Marcus nodded. "Yes, that would be—"

"No." The elderly gentleman held up a hand. "Your work here is done, sirs. You may go. We will have the unveiling shortly."

Marcus smiled at the guarded looks the four men gave him, then gave his friend. "On second thought, gentlemen, we'll handle that ourselves." He counted out a few bills and handed them to the foreman. "Thank you. I'll contact the gallery if there are any issues."

As the wagon pulled away, Marcus retrieved the pocketknife from his pack and glanced beside him. "Are we ready now?"

The older man looked from him to the group gathered nearby, then back at the building. Marcus trailed his gaze and saw the windows full of eager faces, patients with childlike expressions, their hands pressed to the glass.

"All right." The elderly man turned. "Now we're ready."

Marcus opened the pocketknife. "How about I cut the ropes and you remove the blankets?"

"Yes, that will work nicely." The man leaned close. "They don't like for me to have sharp things, Mr. Geoffrey," he whispered, his tone secretive.

Marcus attempted to look surprised, as though that revelation were new to him. "Then you're right, this works out nicely, Mr. . . ."

"Theodore."

Marcus extended his hand. "Pleasure to formally meet you, Mr. Theodore."

The man's grip tightened. "No!" The muscles in his neck bulged. "It's simply . . . Theodore."

"Theodore, then," Marcus swiftly corrected, recalling how the gentleman could become agitated. It felt odd to be calling a man so senior in years by his Christian name. But eager to retain the use of his right hand, Marcus complied.

"All right, then." Theodore gestured, eyes bright once more. "Enough of this. Let's get to it." In a blink, his mood had altered. "The people are waiting."

Cautious but also a little bemused, Marcus slit the ropes and pulled them clear, careful to leave the blankets in place. Then, with the flourish of a museum curator, Theodore stepped up, gripped the blankets, and pulled.

A chorus of soft gasps sounded from behind, accompanied by muted applause and rhythmic taps on windowpanes.

Marcus's gaze moved over the marble sculpture. He was certain he'd never seen it before. But what Mrs. Cheatham said about it was true. The sculpture was exquisite.

"Are you familiar with the piece?" Theodore said beside him.

Marcus looked over, hearing a touch of sanity in his friend's voice that, oddly enough, he found disturbing. "No, sir." He frowned. "Are you?"

Theodore gave a pitying scoff. "It's *The Prodigal Son*," he said quietly. "The work of Joseph Mozier, based on the parable in the New Testament." He squinted. "Sculpted in . . . eighteen fifty-seven, I believe. I may be off by a year, but I don't think so."

Marcus stared, which in turn earned him a surprisingly droll look from Theodore, one similar to what Eleanor gave him on occasion.

"I may be in an asylum, Mr. Geoffrey, but as I told you before, I'm not lame in the head."

Marcus smiled this time. He couldn't help it. And Theodore did too.

Recalling something, Marcus reached into his shirt pocket. "Here. For you."

Theodore studied the sugar stick before accepting it. "You remembered," he whispered.

"Of course . . . I've been enjoying them nearly every day at work."

Theodore stuck the candy in his mouth, swirling it between his lips, then turned abruptly and walked to an arbor swing. The same swing Marcus had seen him in that first day.

Marcus followed and sat beside him, noticing a book on the seat between them. Theodore picked it up and held the book close, as though fearing Marcus might take it. The cover was worn and the pages frayed, signs of a book well loved.

Marcus settled back and let the older man set the pace, enjoying the gliding motion.

"And what is it you do when you aren't here, Mr. Geoffrey?"

"You can call me Marcus, sir, if you'd like."

Theodore shook his head. "I prefer Mr. Geoffrey."

"Fair enough." Marcus pulled a second sugar stick from his pocket, growing accustomed to the man's frankness. "I'm an architect. I build things."

Theodore slowed from his swinging. "I assumed you were a gardener."

Marcus laughed. "You're not the first, sir."

Several of the patients stood around the statue, their expressions revealing the same appreciation, even awe, Marcus felt as he took it in. The two figures chiseled from marble looked so lifelike, he half expected to see the rise and fall of their chests as they breathed.

He knew the parable. A wayward son demanding his inheritance and leaving home, only to return a beggar, broken and penniless, without birthright or honor, without any expectation of acceptance. And yet . . .

When the father sees him, from a long way off, he runs to him. *Runs* to his dishonored son.

Marcus lowered his gaze and studied the sugar stick in his hand. *"We will never speak of this again, Marcus."* His father's voice was clear in his memory. *"No one can ever know the dishonor your brother has brought to this family. No one in this family will ever speak his name again. You will take your brother's place in succession to the throne. You will restore the honor and trust my eldest son betrayed."*

Marcus lifted his head and stared into the sightless eyes of the prodigal's father, then at the upturned face of the son who had been lost, and yet was found, upon returning home.

Home . . .

He swallowed. If he returned home, what would he find? The man he wanted to be? He would have a life there, certainly, but not one he desired. But if he stayed here, if he defied his father and uncle, defied the House of Habsburg and the very throne of Austria . . .

A quick intake of breath drew his attention, and he looked beside him. To his surprise, he found Theodore's eyes awash in tears.

"Are you all right, sir?" he asked softly.

Theodore nodded, his white beard trembling. "I wish my son were here. But . . . he's gone away. And"—he swallowed—"he won't be coming back. My daughter . . ." His voice hardened. "She's made certain of that."

Not knowing whether the man spoke from a right mind or from an imagination twisted by some unseen, diseased hand, Marcus was nevertheless moved. "I'm sorry, Theodore. I know you must miss him." Yet he also knew the disgrace that accompanied being in an asylum.

According to Dr. Crawford, some people— perhaps like Theodore's daughter—admitted their family member to the institution and never returned. And though it shamed him, Marcus could understand, at least in part. Hadn't he shared a similar opinion? Before coming to this place. Before meeting Theodore.

"I enjoy our visits, Mr. Geoffrey."

"So do I, Theodore."

A bell clanged, and the patients began to make their way toward a side door. Marcus rose, and Theodore rose with him, book clutched to his chest.

Theodore took a few steps, then paused, his back

to Marcus. "Will you come again?" So soft was his voice, Marcus barely made out the words.

"Yes, sir. If you'd like for me to."

Theodore turned back. "Next time we'll read a book, and discuss it. Germans do like to read, don't they?"

Marcus laughed. "Very much, sir. In fact, the next time I come, I'll bring you one of my books." Marcus knew exactly which one he'd choose. "A book I believe you'll enjoy."

Theodore smiled. "Very good, then." Yet he didn't move. He just stood there, gripping the book.

The bell clanged again, the woman at the door looking their way.

Marcus studied him. "Is something wrong, Theodore?"

He shook his head and frowned, then with a determined stride, walked back and held out the book. "You *will* come again."

It was a question, cloaked in a statement, wrapped in a plea, and Marcus felt as though he were looking at a boy instead of a man. He accepted the book. "Yes, Theodore, I *will*. I promise."

Theodore nodded, eyes misty. "Then, I'll see you soon . . . Marcus. And we'll speak together again."

Marcus waited until the side door closed, just in case Theodore turned to wave, but he didn't.

He strode to the tree where he'd tethered his horse, the enormity of the man's trust sinking in. It was just a book. But it also wasn't. It represented so much more. Regal snorted and pawed the ground at his approach, and Marcus gave the thoroughbred's neck a good rub.

If the front of the book had once borne a title, that day was long past. Marcus lifted the cover and it opened right to the title page. He stared, unable to believe it.

The Collected Works of Lord Alfred Tennyson. He couldn't resist . . .

He thumbed the pages until he found the familiar poem, the one he and his grandfather had reenacted so many times. "The Charge of the Light Brigade." To his delight, that section was especially well worn. Something slipped from between the pages and fluttered to the ground. He picked it up. An old cigar band. Very old from the look of it.

Marcus opened the book again to return the marker to its place when writing on the inside cover snagged his attention. A name. Which he read. Then read again. It couldn't be . . .

He looked back at the asylum, then back at the name, remembering the day he'd seen Eleanor out here. And while everything in him told him it was impossible, the name staring back at him— Garrison Theodore Braddock—told him it was not.

"Giving to those less fortunate is one thing, Eleanor. That's a very right and noble thing to do. But *working* in a kitchen, cooking for them, is another." Color had returned to Aunt Adelicia's face in the past hour, and reserve to her demeanor. But a tension still hovered in the dining room. "Have you given any thought at all about how this . . . *incident* will likely affect your future with Mr. Hockley?"

Eleanor fingered the rim of the china cup. "First, I never intended for it to be an incident, Aunt. I had planned to speak to him about it, but—"

"But that opportunity is now gone. Just as others may well be."

The gravity of her aunt's expression conveyed how important this potential union was to her. Eleanor searched for the words to help her understand why she'd done what she'd done, growing more aware by the minute of how dependent she was upon her aunt's charity.

She looked at the newspaper heading again, her gaze hovering on the word *wealthy*. She'd already deduced where the reporter had gotten his information, however inaccurate in parts. Yet her frustration at Mr. Stover's gullibility was all but dispelled when she realized there was no potential renter. It had all been a ruse by the reporter to persuade him to talk.

Once Aunt Adelicia had read the article and realized the *establishment* wasn't a restaurant, the tone of the conversation calmed to a degree, and Eleanor had explained everything to her and Dr. Cheatham. Starting with how she and Naomi had cleaned the building, to the night Caleb had brought the children for dinner, to the first night they'd served the widows and children.

But nothing she'd said thus far seemed to persuade her aunt. Dr. Cheatham—who she was fairly certain was on her side—had taken his leave a while ago, claiming another appointment. Eleanor envied him, wishing she could do the same.

"I have the utmost respect for what you're attempting to do, Eleanor. But it's simply not an appropriate choice for a woman of your distinction and upbringing. This has likely cost us both *dearly*. I hope you realize that."

Lifting her gaze, Eleanor met her aunt's steady stare, and—for better or worse—she spoke from the heart. "I have the utmost esteem for you, too, Aunt Adelicia. I value your opinions, your courage, your . . . steadfastness. I'm grateful for all you've done for me, *and* for my father. And I would never do anything to intentionally embarrass you or bring shame upon your family. But . . . I must ask you to consider that the life you have in mind for me might not be the life I'm intended to live. Nor . . . the life I want to live."

"But, my dear . . ." Aunt Adelicia placed a hand over hers. "You must know that the likelihood of ever receiving an offer like the one from Mr. Hockley is narrow at best. *Not* because of anything you lack, but because there simply are so few men left. Much less men who have retained their wealth and who could offer you the stability you need. And deserve. You must think of this practically, Eleanor." She exhaled. "Decisions of the heart, I've learned at great cost, are best made with one's head. If you can manage it."

"And that's precisely what I'm trying to do."

Eleanor searched her aunt's gaze. "These women and children I feed have lost everything. Their husbands, their sons, their homes. The widow's pension they receive from the government, those few who are entitled to it, is paltry compared to their needs."

Her aunt started to speak, but Eleanor beat her to it, feeling a rogue surge of courage.

"I would think that you of all women, Aunt, would understand what I'm trying to do. When you believe something is right, you act on it. Regardless of what others may think." Eleanor glanced at the newspaper. "I remember reading an article written about you not that long ago. . . ." She shook her head. "I don't know if I would've had the courage to do what you did with the cotton in Louisiana—to face both armies like that—but I hope I would have."

A flicker of understanding—or was it anger?— flashed in her aunt's eyes.

Eleanor continued, "As for Mr. Hockley, I *do* owe him an explanation, I realize that. And I'll offer that explanation when I see him next week for dinner. At which time . . . he is expecting my answer to his proposal.

"However, as you have stated so succinctly, that opportunity may be gone. If that's the case, then . . ." Did she dare say this? But did she dare not? "While I realize the fault will be mine alone, I also believe that, given the circumstance, it says an awful lot about a man who would choose not to marry a woman

431

simply because she's helping others in this way."

She took a deep breath. It had felt so good to say the words out loud, but now they seemed to hang in the air, suspended like tiny daggers waiting to fall. And seeing the inexplicable expression on her aunt's face, Eleanor questioned whether that had been rogue courage she'd felt a moment earlier, or complete and utter stupidity.

A knock sounded on the front door, and Mrs. Routh's stoic tones soon drifted in through the partially open door, along with a murmur of voices.

"Is there anything *else* you wish to say to me," her aunt said softly. Too softly.

Eleanor swallowed, wishing Cordina would return with more coffee. But if she were Cordina, she wouldn't come back either.

"Excuse me, Mrs. Cheatham." Mrs. Routh stood in the entryway of the dining room. "Mrs. Holbrook and two of the other ladies from the Nashville Women's League are here to see you, ma'am. They say it's most urgent. I've installed them in the tête-à-tête room."

Aunt Adelicia applied pressure to her temple. "Thank you . . . Mrs. Routh."

Seeing her aunt peer through the front window, Eleanor did the same, and spotted a carriage pulling up to the front door—right beside two other carriages already there. She didn't know what her aunt's league friends were doing here on a morning when no event was planned.

She only knew it couldn't be good.

30

Eleanor kneaded the dough with fierceness. Beneath her hands, the mixture of flour, yeast, water, and salt became smooth and supple and turned into a living thing. She blew a strand of hair from her eyes and continued the therapeutic rhythm—*push, fold, push, turn*—that was as familiar to her as breathing, and almost as vital. Especially in the aftermath of what happened at the mansion that morning.

The somber look Aunt Adelicia had given her—part disappointment, part consternation—prior to closing the door to the central parlor was one she wouldn't soon forget. Despite not caring what most people thought about her, she did care what her aunt thought.

More than she'd realized.

She oiled the mound of dough, placed it in a bowl and covered it to rest, then dusted the worktable with flour and started kneading the next batch.

More than anything, she wanted to talk to Marcus. She'd looked for him at the bakery, the livery, then finally at the warehouse where he'd taken her the other day. She hadn't found him, but had met Mr. Callahan, his foreman. Callahan seemed like a very nice man who thought quite highly of his employer, regardless of having no idea of his whereabouts.

It occurred to her then that—in a lovely yet

lonely way—Marcus was her closest confidant. She shared a special relationship with Naomi, as she did with some of the other widows, but she didn't feel comfortable sharing the specifics of this particular struggle with them. But with Marcus she could recount every single nuance, and he would listen without interruption or judgment.

But he was nowhere to be found.

She worked the batches of dough until her fingers and shoulders ached, making more bread than usual due to the article in the newspaper. No telling how many women and children would show up tonight. She arched her back and stared out the window at the gray skies building in the west. Feeding so many people was becoming too much.

And though she hated to admit it, part of her was embarrassed to admit defeat—in front of her aunt, Marcus . . . and the entire town now. But mostly it pained her to let down the widows and children.

She enjoyed providing for them. She enjoyed the cooking, the nurturing. It filled a place within her she'd once thought could only be filled by becoming a mother, or—when that hadn't happened —by starting a restaurant.

Funny how often something she'd been so certain she needed turned out not to be a need at all, but a want—when the real *need* was something else entirely. Something that could only be gained by giving, not by getting.

When Naomi arrived, they started on the potato soup and stewed apples, a favorite dinner among the gathering, and one of the easiest to stretch and least expensive—which was an ever-increasing necessity as her funds dwindled.

Naomi was quiet, and Eleanor wondered if she'd read the newspaper that morning, or had heard whispers on the streets.

Peeling her third potato, Eleanor felt its flesh give. She sliced into it, and grimaced. Rotten. Into the crate it went to be taken back to the mercantile. Men had figured out how to graft flowers and trees to make them stronger or various selected colors. But could they create a potato that didn't have dry rot? She shook her head. Apparently not. She would have to speak to Marcus about that.

She still intended to ask Aunt Adelicia if she would be willing to help sponsor these meals. But their last conversation somehow hadn't seemed like the best time to pose that question.

She stole a glance at Naomi across the growing pile of potato peels, unable to keep silent any longer. "Did you read the article?" she asked softly.

Naomi kept focused on her task, then slowly nodded. "The newspaper was wrong to print those words. They make it sound like what you do here is wrong, or . . . that you should be ashamed." Naomi lifted her face, her eyes darkening. "*They* are the ones who should be ashamed. You are doing *good,* Miss Braddock." A pained look crossed her face. "But I am sorry I did not know you were such an important lady."

Eleanor laughed. "Oh, I'm not. Not at all. My *aunt* is the important lady. I'm merely Mrs. Adelicia Cheatham's niece."

Naomi paused from peeling. "Before this"—she gestured to the kitchen—"every night, women and children in my building went to bed hungry. Then woke up with bellies sore from lack of food. Now . . . three nights every week, they come here and eat your food. And not only that, they are fed in their spirits. They laugh, they share. We have all been reminded, Miss Braddock, that we are part of a larger family. And you . . ." Her eyes misted. "You have done this. And that makes you *very* important in their eyes. And in mine."

Seeing the gratitude and trust in Naomi's expression warmed Eleanor's heart, while also compelling her to admit the truth—that she only had enough money left to cover a handful of meals, depending on how many people showed up. But . . . she couldn't say the words.

Not only because she didn't want to see the disappointment in her friend's eyes, along with the fear of where the next meal would come from, but also because she couldn't begin to imagine her life without these people, and all they offered her. Which was *far* more than she'd ever given to them.

Marta, Elena, and the other women arrived as scheduled, and with their assistance, dinner was soon ready. When the front door was opened, women and children started crowding in, and kept

436

coming. And coming. Many of the faces were familiar to Eleanor, though some were not.

She visited with them, listening to their stories of how they'd "passed on the kindness" as she always asked them to do, while also trying to keep an eye on those still entering.

Finally, she raised her hand, the signal for conversation to quiet and for them to take a seat on the floor. Marcus had told her the tables and benches he'd promised were nearly finished, and while she was eager to put them to use, she hated for him and his men to have gone to so much trouble for the scant use the furniture would receive now.

"Welcome to everyone, I'm so grateful you've come and . . ." As she greeted everyone in English, pausing briefly to allow Naomi to translate, she peered past those seated and those few people crowded around the door, and—in a flash of panic—she saw a crowd still waiting to enter. In fact, the street outside was *full* of women and children.

"For those w-who . . . who have been . . ." Every thought left her head, save one. They didn't have enough food.

Somehow she muddled through the welcome, aware of Naomi watching her. Eleanor indicated for Mr. Stover to step forward and offer a blessing for the food and hoped he would pray as long as he usually did.

Meanwhile, she discreetly signaled Naomi to join her in the kitchen.

Once around the corner, Eleanor kept her voice low. "I counted more than seventy in the front room, and at least that many waiting outside. We don't have enough food for that many people." She exhaled. "And I've always told them no one would leave here hungry."

Naomi glanced at the pots of soup. "Maybe there is something else we can put with the dinner?"

They both started searching the cabinets, but all their effort earned them was a ten-pound bag of dried beans and meager staples such as flour, cornmeal, and odd spices left in the kitchen between meal preparations. Nothing that would effectively bolster the supper.

"Well . . ." Eleanor reached for a pitcher of water, pained by what she had to do next, especially after working so hard to make the soup taste so good. "I'll start watering down the pots."

Naomi nodded, then held up a hand. "Oh!" she whispered. "What about this?" She grabbed the stack of metal bowls they'd laid out for serving and placed them on a back table. She reached for the metal cups by the pitchers of water. "What the eyes don't see, the mind won't tell the stomach to miss."

It occurred to Eleanor what she was suggesting. "We'll serve the soup in cups instead of bowls."

"I have done this with Caleb before." Naomi's expression turned sheepish. "When food was scarce."

"Did it work?"

She hesitated. "For a moment, your cup is full." She smiled. "And that is a picture the mind does not soon forget."

As they worked to make the changes, Eleanor was reminded of another time she had relied on the potency of suggestion in a dire circumstance. No matter how many years passed, she would always wonder what that soldier had wished he'd done for his Mary girl.

She reached for the bread knife. "We'll do the same with the bread. That's one thing we have plenty of." She cut the thick slices down the middle. "Everyone will still get a whole piece, but we'll stack it beside their cup. Oh!" She raced to the icebox, which was empty—except for a large crock of butter she'd been saving to portion out over the next few meals. She turned and held it up.

Naomi nodded. "We'll put extra butter on each slice!"

"No," Eleanor whispered, feeling almost wanton. "We'll let everyone put their *own* butter on tonight!"

Naomi's eyes widened. Then she covered her mouth and giggled like a schoolgirl. "Caleb will not believe it! He *loves* butter."

"Who doesn't!" Eleanor skirted around the table as the telling shuffle of feet and excited voices indicated that Mr. Stover had more than amply blessed the food.

Eleanor greeted the first few in line, knowing them by name since they'd been coming all along.

Though they said nothing when they saw the soup being ladled into cups instead of bowls, something in their eyes caused Eleanor's heart to wrench, and it was all she could do not to apologize.

She served the cups of soup with a smile. "And please help yourself to the butter tonight. It's down on the end."

When the first pot of soup was empty, Naomi brought the second of four, leaning close to whisper in Eleanor's ear. "I told Marta to count how many are left."

Eleanor nodded. "Very good. You might want to water down the remaining pots a little more."

"We already have," Naomi whispered.

Next in line came Little Magpie, the girl's blue eyes wide and watchful, with her mother, Gretchen. Eleanor guessed Gretchen to be in her early to midtwenties. But the dark circles beneath the woman's eyes and her stooped shoulders—helped along by the burdensome weight of her unborn child—gave her an older, more worn look.

"Good . . . evening, Miss Braddock," Gretchen said with deliberate enunciation, her German accent heavy.

"Good evening, Gretchen. How are you feeling?" Eleanor ladled the soup into the first cup, then the second, noticing the mixture was already tepid due to the water they'd added.

"Big," she said, barely smiling. "And . . ." She frowned as though searching for the word. "Needing . . . bed."

"Weary," Eleanor supplied, handing both cups to her while noticing how little Maggie's eyes widened. The girl loved potato soup and had come back for seconds on earlier visits. But there would be no seconds tonight.

Maggie had yet to fully open up to Eleanor, but Eleanor was still working on her. She slipped the girl a wink, and Little Magpie smiled before catching herself and going cautious again.

Eleanor smiled. "How much longer until the baby comes, Gretchen?"

"Mmmm . . . *sechs*?"

"*Six* weeks? That's not long. Be sure to let me know if there's anything I can do for you or Maggie."

"Thank . . . you, Miss Braddock." Gretchen nodded and moved on down the line, gesturing for her daughter to get the bread.

But Maggie shook her head and pointed to one of the cups in her mother's hand. "*Ich will die Tasse nehmen.*"

"*Nein.*" Gretchen sighed and pointed again to the bread. "*Ich nehme die Tasse. Du nimmst das Brot.*"

Eleanor served those next in line, watching Maggie's frown escalate to a scowl at her mother's comment. *I'll take the cup. You take the bread,* if Eleanor translated it correctly. Gretchen turned to go sit down, but Maggie grabbed at one of the cups. It was on the tip of Eleanor's tongue to warn the young mother, but it was too late.

The tin cup clattered to the floor, spilling soup onto the dusty plank wood. Chatter in the room fell silent, all eyes turned, and Eleanor's heart wrenched when she saw Maggie's face crumple. Maggie dropped to her knees and began sopping up the soup with her bread. Gretchen, tears welling, gently pulled her daughter up by the arm, whispering in hushed tones as the little girl cried soft, hiccupping sobs.

Eleanor's vision blurred as she swallowed back the knifing pain in her throat and continued to serve those waiting. Conversation in the room gradually edged up again. But not enough to cover Maggie's quiet sobs from the corner.

By the time Eleanor said good night to Naomi and Caleb, it was a little past nine and she was long past exhausted.

Key in the lock, she paused and looked back at the darkened front room, then at the corner in which Maggie and Gretchen had sat. When mother and daughter had left, the little girl's eyes had been puffy and swollen.

Everyone who had come tonight had been served a cup of soup, but only because—with Naomi's discreet assistance—the last two pots of soup had been watered down. *Three* times. Eleanor had foregone eating anything, and saw Naomi drink only half of her cup before giving the rest of hers to Caleb. Every crumb of bread and speck of butter had been devoured.

For a long time to come, Eleanor would

remember Maggie's soft cries, and the pain etched in Gretchen's face.

She inhaled, then let out a shaky breath, wiping away the tears she'd fought so hard to keep inside earlier, and feeling almost blasphemous at the thoughts she was having.

She believed God saw every hurt, every tear, that He knew the intimate details of every life. Believing in His sovereignty and power wasn't an issue for her. Not anymore. He'd proven that to her time and time again. What she couldn't understand was how He could see those hurts, those tears, the excruciating pain of lives broken and torn apart —and yet chose not to act on their behalf. At least not the way she would have, if she were God.

Her chin shook, both from crying and from knowing that, even now, the Lord heard *every* accusing thought in her head. "I trust you," she whispered, wishing she trusted Him more. "I just don't understand you."

As confident as she was that He had led her to this juncture in her life, she couldn't fight reality. Unless Aunt Adelicia—or someone else—supported her in providing these meals, she was all but finished. Perhaps this idea had been doomed from the start, and in her exuberance, or maybe her pride, she simply hadn't seen it. Until now.

"Focus only upon what is before you. What you can see, Eleanor. Not on what your imagination attempts to convince you is there."

Oh, Papa . . . If only it were that easy.

If only her father were still with her. Oh, he was, in a sense. But so much of their relationship had been lost. And she feared it would never be regained. Would he have to live in the asylum for the rest of his life? That thought alone was daunting. But the financial cost it would demand was even more staggering. How could she possibly ever pay for it? She couldn't.

That reality forced another decision to the forefront of her mind. A decision she needed to give to Lawrence Hockley. It was unsettling, realizing how much time she spent thinking about the decision she had to make regarding the man, rather than the man himself.

She'd been telling herself she was simply weighing all the variables, but her lack of eagerness to give him an answer wasn't due to her not knowing her response. She knew her decision. In light of her alternatives, there was only *one answer* she could give Lawrence Hockley.

Her struggle lay in reconciling her heart to that answer, and that was especially hard since her heart felt reconciled to another man.

She closed the door and locked it behind her.

The street was dark and empty. A gusty wind carrying more winter than autumn knifed through her shawl.

With no reason to keep the building a secret any longer, she'd had Armstead drive her to the building earlier that day, and he'd promised to be back by nine. But . . .

She peered down the road, frowning. He was late. Which was odd, because Armstead was always so—

"Need a ride home, madam?"

She jumped at the familiar voice and turned. "Marcus!" She exhaled, heart thudding yet also pining a little at the sight of him. "You scared me." She popped him in the chest like she used to do her brother, but the gesture felt far more intimate with Marcus. The faint flicker of a gas streetlamp illuminated his smile. "While I appreciate your offer," she continued, wishing she could accept, especially seeing he was on horseback, "I'm waiting for Armstead."

"Which creates a problem . . . since I met him as he was coming from Belmont and told him not to come."

She stared, curious. "Why would you do that?"

"Because it's been a while since I've seen you." He gave a one-shouldered shrug that was distinctly male. "And I wanted to congratulate you on your debut in the *Republican Banner*."

While the first part of his comment tempted her to smile, the second part didn't. Especially after tonight. She briefly bowed her head. "Oh, Marcus, my conversation with my aunt did *not* go well. She and the family returned sometime during the night. And as soon as I left my bedroom this morning, she was there, in the dining room, and we—"

He put a finger to her lips. "I want to hear every single word, but after we're on our way. I'm guessing you've had a very long day, Eleanor. And I . . ." He paused as though about to say something else, then pulled something from behind his back. "I've brought fortification."

He unwrapped the paper, and she smelled them before she saw them.

Her eyes watered. "You got me doughnuts?"

"I did. This morning. I was on my way to see you then, but . . . the day got away from me."

"And you didn't eat them?"

He frowned. "I told you I got them for you."

"Yes, but"—she laughed, hoping to offset a reprisal of tears—"saving doughnuts all day long isn't for the faint of heart."

"Neither is cooking for all these women and children."

She sniffed. "True enough."

"Which reminds me . . . We're nearly finished with your tables and benches. The men and I will bring them by first of next week. I think you're going to be very pleased."

Oh, this man . . . Eleanor was glad her face was partially shadowed. "I'm sure I will be," she whispered. "Thank you, Marcus, for"—her voice caught—"doing that for me. And for them."

He cocked his head and leaned down a little. "Are you all right?"

"Yes. And no . . ." She blew out a breath. "We had a *multitude* of people show up tonight, and we all but ran out of food. Then . . ." She thought of little Maggie again and knew if she said anything else she wouldn't be able to hold her emotions in check. "I'm mostly just tired, I guess."

"Well . . . let's get you home, then." He extended his arm. "Shall we?"

She accepted his help onto the horse and arranged her skirt over her legs as he eased into the saddle behind her. He reached around her for the reins—did she imagine his brief pause when their faces nearly touched?—and she found herself trying to memorize what being close to him felt like. The warmth from his body chased away her chill, not only outwardly but on the inside too. And as they made their way south of town—the cadence of the thoroughbred's stride a lulling metronome inside her—she soon discovered the desperate *what if*s of moments earlier all but silenced.

What she wouldn't give to have a man like Marcus—

No, not a man *like* Marcus, but to have *Marcus* care about her the way a man cared for a woman. Logic reminded her of the nature of their friendship, and she told herself she could be satisfied with that. That it would be enough. But her thoughts and emotions betrayed her reasoning and refused to toe the line.

And the lie.

Despite saying she was tired, Eleanor talked most of the way back to Belmont—between bites of doughnuts. Details of her day poured from her. Marcus listened, having his own questions he wanted to pose but willing to be patient. Especially when it meant he could listen to her voice—the rhythm of her sentences, the rise and fall of her tone—as she shared personal insights he sensed she wouldn't tell just anyone.

Maybe not even Lawrence Hockley.

And the way the curves of her body fit against him—like Eve fashioned just for Adam in the garden—wasn't too bothersome either. He smiled. Though the ride into town had been chilly—the wind kicking up, bringing the cold with it—there was nothing chilly about him now. Quite the opposite.

If not for his pledge to Armstead to deliver Eleanor directly back to Belmont in keeping with "Mrs. Cheatham's *firm* request," he would've been tempted to keep riding.

But when the turnoff for Belmont came, he took it.

Nestled warm against him, Eleanor grew quiet, and a minute later, her head lulled forward before she snapped it back again. She took a deep breath and shifted positions, and Marcus gently tightened his arms about her waist.

He thought again about the book in his satchel, as he'd done throughout the day, and about how she had responded to his questions about her father in the past. She hadn't lied to him. She'd simply . . . evaded the issue. A practice he was quite familiar with and couldn't fault her for. Not without sentencing himself to the same guilty verdict.

Theodore had commented so negatively about his daughter that morning. Was Eleanor the type of daughter who would leave her father at an asylum and never return? Marcus had a hard time reconciling that behavior with the woman in his arms right now. Yet, the antagonism Theodore displayed had been unmistakable.

On the other hand, Theodore Garrison Braddock was hardly a man in his right mind—at least for some of the time.

Marcus guided the thoroughbred down the winding lane toward the mansion, weighing the possibilities. He and Eleanor *both* had their secrets, and he knew whose were worse.

They rounded the last curve leading by the conservatory, and moonlight fell across the road like a silver ribbon unfurling in the breeze. The chirrup of crickets abed in the brush blended with the soothing coo of mourning doves in the perfect lullaby. In fact—

"Eleanor?" he whispered.

Her head tucked beneath his chin, she didn't answer. She didn't move. Telling himself she would have allowed him this privilege if she were awake, and acting quickly before chivalry counseled otherwise, he leaned down and pressed a kiss to her forehead, the feel of her skin soft against his lips.

So soft, in fact, he chanced another. But when she stirred, he quickly straightened, the chaste kisses worth every bit of scolding she would dole out if she'd caught him.

She yawned, stretching. "Oh . . . I'm sorry, Marcus," she whispered. "I fell asleep for a minute."

He smiled. "No harm done." *At least not much.*

She took a deep breath, then exhaled.

He heard more weariness of heart than of body in the act, and gently squeezed her hand. "Are you certain you're all right, Eleanor?"

She said nothing for a moment, then took his hand in hers. Her shoulders started shaking, and her quiet cries awakened a protectiveness within him to shield her. He reined in and touched her shoulder, encouraging her to look at him.

"What's wrong?" he whispered.

She bowed her head. "Something happened tonight . . . with little Maggie."

"Is . . . is she all right?" His mind raced, thinking of the sweet little girl.

"She was so hungry, Marcus. I could see it in her eyes." She shook her head. "Then . . . she dropped her cup of soup. The whole thing."

"Couldn't you give her more?"

A soft strangled sound. "There wasn't enough," she whispered, voice weak. "She started sopping it up off the floor with her bread, and—"

He pulled her closer and kissed the crown of her head, telling himself the gesture was more casual than it felt to him. "I'm sure her mother will take care of her." But even as he said it, he thought of the recently widowed young woman, well along in her pregnancy and overworked as it was—and he wondered. "You can make more food next time. You'll be better prepared."

She shook her head again. "You don't understand."

"I think I do. You had no way of knowing how many people would come tonight. Especially after that . . . silly article today. Next time, you'll simply be—"

"I'm out of money, Marcus." She looked up at him, her brown eyes glistening in the moonlight. "I only have enough for one, maybe two, more meals."

Out of money? He eyed her. "But . . . you're Adelicia Acklen Cheatham's niece. I thought you—"

"I know what you thought." She sniffed. "The same thing everyone else thinks. But my personal finances are in ruin." She blew out a breath. "So, contrary to what you read in the newspapers"— she gave a humorless laugh—"I am *not* the *wealthy* niece of Adelicia Cheatham. I am the all-but-destitute-if-not-for-her-Aunt-Adelicia niece."

Marcus didn't know what to say. He thought back to the few times he'd attended the dinners in recent weeks. He'd assumed she was covering the expenses from the abundance of her wealth—not from more meager coffers.

"So . . . why did you do it?" he asked, the question out before he realized how revealing it was about himself. And though her expression conveyed no judgment, his own conscience declared him guilty.

"Because," she said softly, "they were hungry." She lifted a shoulder and let it fall. "I'd prayed about what steps to take next. I thought it was what the Lord was leading me to do. I was certain of it. And it's funny—I still am certain, but . . ."

Hearing her sincerity, he nodded, while at the same time sincerely doubting the Almighty had been behind that orchestration. He'd seen too many people die of hunger to believe that. No, it was up to mankind—working with what God had created long ago—to provide an answer. To *be* the answer. It was this woman's own loving heart that had been the motivation behind the dinners. He knew that full well.

She looked back at him then, her face pale in the moonlight. "There's something else, Marcus."

Her father. So she was going to share that with him, after all. He wouldn't have to bring it up. But how would he react? As though he didn't already know? No, he couldn't do that, not with her. He'd have to tell her what had happened today, and would show her the book. In fact—he reached into the saddlebag behind him—maybe it would help if he broached the subject first.

Judging by the worry in her expression, he would be saving her some unease. Though there was little he could do to lessen the embarrassment. "Eleanor, I think I can help put your—"

"I've received an offer of marriage."

Marcus stilled—and let the book slide back into the saddlebag. "An offer of *marriage?*"

She laughed softly. "Believe me, I was as surprised as you are."

"No," he said quickly. "I didn't mean it that way. I—"

"It's all right." She laughed again, but it didn't sound genuine. "I know I may seem naive, and I guess I am in some ways. But . . . I've experienced enough of life to know the likelihood of certain events happening. And my receiving a proposal at my age is highly unlikely." She smiled up at him, the waver in her lips making the gesture suspect. "I simply . . . wanted you to know."

Rarely was he at such a loss for words. "I . . . I appreciate that."

"The gentleman's name is—"

"Lawrence Hockley." He said the name out loud before he'd thought the response through.

Her eyebrows shot up. "Yes." She searched his face. "But how did you—"

"A guess." His smile felt tight. "I was there that day your aunt mentioned your dinner with him, remember?"

She blinked slowly—once, twice—as he imagined she might do when first waking in the morning, still trying to see through the warm haze of sleep.

"Yes, I remember," she said softly. "I didn't think you did."

"I remember everything about you, Eleanor Braddock" is what he wanted to say—but didn't. Because while it would have been true, it wouldn't have been fair. He'd committed to wanting the

best for her, and if Lawrence Hockley was best—which still remained to be seen—then Lawrence Hockley was who she should have. Regardless of how much *he* wanted her, right now, in this moment. But not only for this moment.

Her gaze dropped from his eyes to his mouth, and lingered, and Marcus felt his blood quicken with desire. He'd been seduced by women before. He knew the difference between coy and innocent. And the untainted sweetness of this woman, her loveliness and strength, who she was, how she cared about people—not to mention the shapely curve of her waist beneath his hand—filled his head with imaginings. The sweetness of her mouth, the soft hollow at the base of her throat, her—

"Marcus," she whispered, her voice earnest, tender.

"Yes?" he answered, sudden hope overshadowing every reason behind why taking her in his arms and kissing her breathless wasn't a good idea.

"Look at the house," she said, her gaze moving beyond him.

Glad his own face was cast in shadow to hide his disappointment, Marcus breathed in the cool night air, his body still yearning for the kiss that wasn't coming. Nor was it his to take. He followed her line of vision up the hill toward the mansion and recalled Armstead's insistence that Eleanor be brought home promptly.

"Look at the carriages." Moonlight played across her slight frown.

As she'd said, carriages lined the circular drive—ten, at least—and lamplight illuminated the windows of the main floor. "Is your aunt hosting a party?"

"Not that I know of. I think she would have mentioned it. And knowing how she adores music, there would be a stringed quartet on the front lawn if she were." She turned and looked at him. "Do you think I'm in trouble?"

"I don't know." But one thing was certain. . . . He needed to get off this horse and put some distance between them, or he would likely end up doing something he would regret. Because if he kissed her, that would change things between them. And he wasn't willing to risk losing Eleanor Braddock being in his life. Even if only for a few more months.

"The only thing Armstead told me when I asked him if I could pick you up from town was that I needed to bring you home promptly." He snapped the reins, knowing she wasn't going to like what he said next. "At your aunt's *firm* request."

"You have greatly disappointed me, Eleanor, and have placed me in a most embarrassing situation. Henceforth, you must leave Belmont immediately. Likewise, your father will no longer be welcome at the asylum and . . ."

The imagined response from her aunt played over and over in Eleanor's mind, each time louder than the last. As the mansion drew near and the possible consequences for her involvement with the widows and children took frenzied shape in her mind, Eleanor stubbornly chose to listen to the more practical voice. It was foolish to borrow trouble. This gathering didn't need to be about her. Her aunt could well be hosting an impromptu party after having been gone so long, or maybe a club meeting that had absolutely nothing to do with the newspaper article that had so thoroughly embarrassed her that morning. And yet . . .

Why had Aunt Adelicia instructed Armstead to bring her directly home?

Marcus reined in, and Eleanor stifled a groan, wishing she could tell him to keep riding.

Hands braced on his shoulders, she accepted his assistance from the horse and tried not to dwell on how wonderful his hands felt spanning her waist, or on the telling quiver inside as her body brushed his. Everything about this man drew her in. A moment ago, when she'd told him about Mr. Hockley's offer of marriage, he'd acted startled. Which hadn't surprised her. What had surprised her, though, was that he didn't ask whether she'd accepted the offer. He hadn't said a thing. He'd only stared as if not believing something like that could be true for her. Which had been all too revealing.

Still, for a second or two, she'd dared hope. It occurred to her then . . .

Why was a man like Marcus Geoffrey—successful, charming, kind, and most assuredly handsome—still unmarried? Everywhere he went, he turned heads. He could have his choice of any woman. So why was he not—

The front entry opened, and Mrs. Routh appeared in the doorway, hand on hip. Lamplight spilled from behind the woman onto the front porch, followed by a cacophony of female voices, one of them rising over the others, strident and angry sounding.

The practical voice within swiftly fading, Eleanor glanced over at Marcus. "That doesn't sound promising," she whispered.

He winked. "Would you prefer I wait for you?"

"*Wait* for me?" She looked at him, disbelieving. "If I have to go in there, so do you!"

He gave her the smile that all too often made her knees forget their purpose. "I'm quite certain I am not on the guest list, Eleanor."

She slipped her arm through his. "*Sie sind jetzt,* Herr Geoffrey," she said with a German accent. And a rather good one, she thought.

His laughter accompanied her up the stairs.

As Mrs. Routh closed the door behind them and promptly took her leave, that same strident voice from moments earlier carried over the chatter, and Eleanor paused outside the central parlor to peer through the open doorway.

When she saw who was speaking, she cringed.

"As the last founding member of this league, I *insist* on restating my opinion in this matter!"

457

Mrs. Hightower. The woman she'd met at the Nashville Women's League. And judging by the color in her cheeks, the woman was on a rampage.

Over a dozen women were gathered inside, discussion thick among them. And heated. Mrs. Hightower stood amongst her seated peers, her shoulders squared as though she anticipated a fight.

"I do *not* adhere to this notion," the woman continued, each word a bullet silencing the conversation around her. "To abandon the idea of the tea hall is absurd! We are entitled to a suitable location in which to gather for our meetings, where we can discuss the important work we *already* contribute to this community."

Having expended her breath, the matriarch drew in another just as the woman seated beside Aunt Adelicia rose, hand upheld in quiet but assuming authority.

"Mrs. Hightower, your opinion on the matter is greatly appreciated and duly noted. And may I, as president of the Nashville Women's League, assure you . . . we are not *abandoning* the plans for the tea hall." With a subtle but telling glance at the other women in the room, she added quickly, "Which we can never forget, stemmed from your excellent proposal and most generous donation, as well as the work of your daughter."

Hushed murmurs of agreement accompanied understanding nods and seemed to appease Mrs. Hightower to a degree. But her daughter remained stoic, though still lovely.

The silence in the room lengthened.

Sensing the right timing, if there was such a thing, Eleanor glanced behind her to Marcus, who simply nodded, as if saying, *"Best to get it over with."* Wishing she knew what to pray for, she simply asked for God's presence and smoothed the front of her day dress. She grimaced at the splatters of the night's dinner that had somehow sneaked past her apron, then nudged the door farther open.

All eyes moved to her, then quickly skipped beyond to Marcus. And lingered there. Even Aunt Adelicia seemed to sit a little straighter. Eleanor sneaked a look behind her to gauge Marcus's reaction. But he was looking only at her.

She found the discovery sweet. And surprising.

"Ah! Miss Braddock . . ."

Eleanor turned to see the league president approaching.

"The very woman for whom we've been waiting, and"—the board member glanced at Aunt Adelicia—"the reason behind our impromptu meeting this evening. I'm Mrs. Holcomb, president of the Nashville Women's League, and these are our current board members."

As Mrs. Holcomb introduced the women, each nodded in turn. Eleanor had met a few of them before, at her aunt's gatherings, but she didn't bother pointing that out.

"Finally, may I introduce Mrs. Agnetta Hanson Hightower, the last *founding* member of our

459

organization. She is also a highly revered member of the Nashville—"

"Miss Braddock and I have already had occasion to be introduced, Madam President." Mrs. Hightower's tone revealed not a trace of pleasure. "She visited the league house one afternoon when my daughter and I were present."

"Oh . . . indeed?" Mrs. Holcomb nodded thoughtfully.

Eleanor appreciated the adept manner in which Mrs. Holcomb handled the interruption, and found it revealing. Not only about Mrs. Holcomb, whom she swiftly decided she would like very much under different circumstances, but also about Mrs. Hightower, whom Eleanor had already decided she didn't like much at all.

"I will assume then, Miss Braddock," Mrs. Holcomb continued, "that you have also met *Miss* Hightower."

"Yes, ma'am, I have."

"Very good, then." Mrs. Holcomb glanced over at the stoic mother and daughter. "Miss Hillary Stockton Hightower isn't a board member but she often accompanies her mother to the meetings. Which is always a delight."

Again, Eleanor detected subtle meaning in Mrs. Holcomb's tone, even as she noticed Miss Hightower focusing past her, to Marcus. The young woman's eyes brightened with pleasure—and recognition, it seemed. Did Miss Hightower already know Marcus?

Eleanor pretended not to feel the spark of jealousy striking like a hot match inside her. "It's a pleasure both to see you again, Mrs. Hightower, Miss Hightower . . . and to meet the rest of you ladies as well."

Subdued welcomes and the occasional smile issued from the board members, with the exception of Mrs. Hightower and her daughter, who shared similar glares. Although Eleanor was eager to know the purpose of the meeting, she decided that since she hadn't been formally invited, it was best she not inquire.

Only then did she realize she was being remiss in her manners. She gestured to Marcus. "Please allow me to introduce the gentleman with me. This is Mr. Marcus Geoffrey, a . . . friend. He's an esteemed architect from Austria"—she glanced back at him—"and a gifted botanist as well."

Marcus bowed on cue and, as he looked up, shot Eleanor a discreet look she was certain would melt chocolate.

"Ladies . . . it's indeed a pleasure."

"The pleasure is ours, Mr. Geoffrey," Mrs. Holcomb offered, glancing back at Eleanor. "But we are already quite familiar with his talents, Miss Braddock. Mrs. Cheatham has seen to that. I am grateful you're here with us tonight, Mr. Geoffrey. Your presence is most . . . fortuitous, sir.

"But for the moment, *you,* Miss Braddock, are the person with whom we would like to speak." Mrs. Holcomb indicated for Eleanor to sit. "Frankly"—

she laughed, yet there was a hint of gravity to it—"you've caused us quite a bit of trouble these last few hours."

Eleanor stiffened, wishing she could see Marcus in order to read his expression, but he was behind her. Even Aunt Adelicia's countenance was shuttered. And it didn't help to have every board member of the Nashville Women's League staring at her.

Mrs. Holcomb took her seat again. "Miss Braddock, you have acted in a most, shall we say . . . unconventional manner in recent weeks. Not only have you set propriety for a woman of your status at naught, but as a future member of the Nashville Women's League, you have opened the league to ridicule and, well . . . frankly, embarrassment."

Eleanor's face went warm. Now she wished she'd let Marcus wait outside. Dare she attempt to defend herself to these ladies? But how could she not? Heart pounding, she sat straighter. "If you would allow me to—"

Mrs. Holcomb raised a hand, her sigh holding truce as well as consternation. "And yet, Miss Braddock, you have single-handedly done what we, as an organization, have attempted to do since the war concluded. We exist to do good within this community. Time and time again, we have invited less fortunate women to come to the league's building in town for a meal on Saturday mornings. We provide the finest food. Many of the ladies here have donated their own family china, table linens, and crystal. We wanted the experience to be one that makes the women feel special, that makes them feel welcome."

"We've passed the word through neighbors and friends," another woman said. "But only a handful of women ever attend."

"And most times they ask to take the meal with them," yet another woman volunteered. "Then they leave, quickly as they came. And rarely do they return."

"Even though we know they could benefit from the assistance," a third woman added.

Eleanor recalled the wording of the plaque that hung beside the front door of the league building. *". . . women from Nashville's finest families . . . dedicated to social betterment . . ."* No wonder the widows hadn't felt comfortable visiting there. She hadn't either.

She listened as the women continued to lay out their *complaint.* And, gradually, she realized they didn't sound angry with her so much as confounded as to why she'd succeeded at something when they had failed. And slowly, understanding dawned. . . .

She wasn't in trouble. At least not in the sense she'd initially thought. She looked around the room. All of the women were dressed in the finest, most fashionable garments. Jewels on their fingers and dangling from their earlobes, hair neatly arranged, not a thread out of place. Then she glanced down at her own state of dress and—oddly—wasn't bothered by it anymore. Because she knew in that moment that she'd happened upon something more valuable, more precious than anything money could buy. Even though—the irony of her next thought tempted her to smile—it *did* take money to do what she was doing. And these women had *that* in abundance. They had the heart to help too. They simply didn't know how. But neither had she. Until God had shown her, in a very roundabout way—one she never could have anticipated.

She'd wanted to open a restaurant. And, instead, God had opened her life. Her *heart*.

She slipped a hand into her skirt pocket and felt the soft, worn cotton between her fingertips, and thought again about Mary girl. Wherever she was, whatever had happened to her, Eleanor prayed someone was taking care of her . . . the way she sought to take care of Nashville's widows and children.

"As I'm sure you've gathered by now, Miss Braddock"—hearing Mrs. Holcomb's voice, Eleanor refocused—"we have invited you to meet with us for a purpose. After reading the newspaper article this morning, we immediately came to consult with your aunt about it. Following a lively discussion, and after your aunt shed insight on the intentions behind your actions"—Mrs. Holcomb's air of formality seemed to soften—"we came to an agreement. And your aunt graciously invited us all back here this evening to discuss a possibility with you."

Wavering between feeling thoroughly chastised yet also complimented, Eleanor waited.

Mrs. Holcomb continued, "As you may be aware, we had planned . . . and *still* plan, in the future," she added, tossing a perfunctory nod to a stoic Mrs. Hightower, "to build a new tea hall. But after a less than enthusiastic response from the community, we have decided to put that project aside for the time being and instead, sow our resources in more . . . *philanthropic* soil."

For the first time, Mrs. Holcomb smiled, and Eleanor was certain her earlier prediction about liking the woman would hold true.

"Miss Braddock, we would very much like to partner with you in caring for the widows and their children."

Radiant. That's the only word Marcus could think of to describe Eleanor in that moment. Well, that and *sprachlos*, or *dumbstruck* as Americans termed it. Drinking her in from his position at one side of the room, he could see the sheen of tears in her eyes, tears she was doing her best to hide.

"Y-you want to partner with *me?*" Eleanor whispered. The crackle of the fire in the hearth filled the silence. "You want to help feed these women and children?"

"Oh my . . ." Mrs. Holcomb's hesitant laughter was telling. "If you're this taken aback by our proposal, Miss Braddock, I fear that we, as a league, have a great deal of work to do in fulfilling our mission in this town."

"No, no," Eleanor said quickly. "I wasn't suggesting you lacked the desire to help, Mrs. Holcomb. It's just that I came in here with the expectation of . . ."

"Being scolded?" Mrs. Holcomb supplied.

Eleanor hesitated, then nodded.

"Yes, I can see why you might have expected that. However, that's not the case. I assure you."

The league president shot a look at Mrs. Cheatham. Marcus noted the silent exchange, and suddenly the *fortuitous* comment made earlier by Mrs. Holcomb took on new meaning. His thoughts jumped ahead. It occurred to him what Adelicia Cheatham might be about to propose, and even more, what his role in such a proposal might be. Already, his mind stirred with possibilities. He only hoped he was right.

Adelicia rose from her seat like a queen from her throne, and Marcus quelled a smile. Watching her brought Aunt Sisi, Uncle Franz's wife, to mind. And he knew that, given the opportunity, the two women would become fast friends.

"Eleanor, my dear . . ." Adelicia moved nearer the hearth. "The Nashville Women's League would like to do more than simply partner with you to feed the widows and children of this city. Much more."

When Adelicia looked in his direction, Marcus was certain he'd guessed correctly.

"We want to build a home for them," Adelicia continued. "A place where they would not only take their meals but would live in safety with one another. And we believe it would be best if you, Eleanor, facilitated the project, since you're the one who's had such success in helping them."

Already watching Eleanor, Marcus felt a measure of pleasure when she sought out his gaze. The tender hope in her eyes nurtured the seed of it in his own chest.

She didn't speak immediately, and if he hadn't known her so well, he might have guessed she was searching for the right words to say. As it was, he knew she was struggling to contain her emotions. She was a private person, not comfortable with showing her feelings. Something else they had in common.

Finally, she smiled. "I would be honored to undertake the project." A rush of breath left her. Half laugh, half sigh. "And I'm so grateful, ladies . . . more than you can know, for your partnership."

A ripple of excitement skittered through the women in the room. All but two of them, Marcus noticed. The young Miss Hightower, whom he'd met prior to this evening at the Nashville Women's League building, and her mother. The pair looked as though they'd been chewing on rancid lemons. Heaven help the man who married into *that*.

Miss Hightower chose that moment to look in his direction and flashed him a smile before he could look away. He returned the gesture, kindly but swiftly, and engaged his attention elsewhere, careful not to make that mistake again.

Spontaneous chatter grew to a steady hum, and he marveled at the sheer volume of it. These women would use more words in one evening than he'd likely use in a lifetime. How "Queen Adelicia" would ever regain control, he didn't know. But he enjoyed watching the scene, especially with Eleanor at the center of it all.

He was so proud of her. Her love and dedication for the people she cooked for still amazed him. They loved her with equal fervor, and not only because of her benevolence. He'd been there, had watched her serving them. It hadn't felt like charity. It had felt like family.

"I've received an offer of marriage."

He'd failed to ask if she'd accepted the offer. But he doubted whether she had. She would have told him. Wouldn't she have?

After a few moments, Adelicia raised a delicate hand, forefinger slightly extended, and a hush fell over the room.

Marcus made note. So that's how it was done.

"I know the hour is late . . ." Adelicia glanced at the clock on the mantel. "But I have one more thing, ladies, before we adjourn. We discussed a general budget earlier, but now we must each confirm our own donations as well as contact the members on our individual lists to confirm theirs.

"Let's work to have that completed by the end

of the week at the latest. We must have a solid projection of available funds before we can move forward. And knowing my niece as I do"— Adelicia's tone held unmistakable pride—"she'll want to get started on this as soon as possible.

"Speaking of which . . . Mr. Geoffrey . . ." Adelicia gestured for him to join her.

Not really wanting to, Marcus did as bade. Though having been the focus of attention all his life—and enjoying it then—he'd come to prefer the relative anonymity of his new situation. It had been oddly freeing, in a sense.

Besides, as he'd already learned, he was never quite certain what Mrs. Cheatham was going to say. Which made him a little nervous even now.

Adelicia nodded toward the league president. "As Mrs. Holcomb stated earlier, your presence here this evening was a fortuitous coincidence, Mr. Geoffrey. Because only this afternoon, I recommended we seek your services in this venture. *If* your schedule allows, of course, and"—a trickle of humor laced her voice—"granted you gain my niece's approval."

The women laughed, and he did too. "Then I'll simply have to make Miss Braddock an offer she won't be able to refuse."

That prompted even more laughter. But the twinkle in Eleanor's eyes was his true reward.

As the ladies took their leave, he stood in the front hall beside Eleanor, speaking to each of them as they passed while itching for a pencil and pad of paper, eager to start drawing up plans.

"Can you believe this?" Eleanor whispered to him between bidding the board members good night.

He enjoyed seeing her so happy. Especially with the knowledge he had about her father.

"Mr. Geoffrey . . ." Miss Hightower extended her hand to him in exaggerated fashion as though she were offering a rare jewel. "What a pleasure to see you this evening, sir."

Aware of Eleanor's attention, Marcus kissed Miss Hightower's hand, the woman's fingers tightening around his before he let go. "Likewise, Miss Hightower."

"We've been considering adding a wing onto our family home. Perhaps you could stop by and . . . give me a bid?" Her smile turned overtly impish, something the woman considered attractive, no doubt.

"I'll be happy to do that, Miss Hightower. I'll ask my foreman to stop by this week."

Her gaze cooled even as her smile remained perfectly in place. "Yes, you do that, Mr. Geoffrey. And we'll see what comes."

Marcus dipped his head, not looking at her again. *That* type of woman he knew well . . . and had once actually preferred. Though he couldn't for the life of him imagine doing so now.

"Mr. Geoffrey . . ." The last to leave, Mrs. Holcomb paused on her way out. "This is all so exciting, isn't it?"

"Indeed, madam, it is."

"And you, Miss Braddock"—Mrs. Holcomb grasped Eleanor's hand—"are a most impressive woman. And the perfect person for such a mission. Thank you for agreeing to help with this."

"Thank *you,* Mrs. Holcomb. I'm so grateful for the opportunity. The need is monumental, and at times overwhelming, I'll admit. But together, we can accomplish much, I know."

"I'm certain we can as well, Miss Braddock. Now to get it done before Mr. Geoffrey returns to Austria next summer."

The words sliced the moment with painful precision, the air around them pulsing with it. Marcus looked over at Eleanor and read the disbelief in her eyes, the questioning.

But it was the shadow of betrayal that wounded him most. Especially knowing how deserved it was.

"Yes, of course, we must," Eleanor said quickly, scarcely missing a beat. She broke his gaze and turned back to their guest. "We'll simply have to work extra hard to make that happen."

Mrs. Holcomb moved to speak with Adelicia at the door, and Marcus seized the moment, keeping his voice low. "Eleanor, I had intended to tell you about my departure, but—"

"It's all right, Marcus." She put on a smile that didn't suit her. "You don't owe me an explanation. Now, if you'll excuse me, I—"

Marcus gently took hold of her arm and steered her into the library, then pushed the door all but closed. Lamplight on the desk cast a halo of yellow-orange about the room.

"But I do owe you an explanation, Eleanor." He searched her eyes. "At least, I would hope you think I do."

She stared up at him, the contrived smile gone. "Has this been your plan all along?"

If he'd anticipated this reaction and the look in her eyes—the sadness, disappointment—he would have told her weeks ago. Better yet, he would never have allowed himself to become so close to her. He'd thought it had only been his heart he was risking. Not hers. But now, he wondered. "Yes. I've always known I must return to Vienna."

She nodded, then lowered her eyes. Seconds ticked past.

"I'm sorry, Eleanor." And he was. But for so much more than what he could put into words. He waited for her to lift her head, to respond. And when she didn't, he gently urged her chin upward.

Tears traced her cheeks, and what he read in her eyes, in the way she gripped his forearm even now, answered the question he'd pondered a moment earlier. It wasn't *only* his heart . . .

His lips were on hers—and the kiss deepened—before the part of him that knew better could warn otherwise. But it was when she slipped her arms around his neck and pulled him closer, then rose on tiptoe to better meet his kiss that Marcus felt a yearning more powerfully tender than he'd ever known. Her lips seemed at once both hesitant and insistent. Which made him wonder . . . was this kiss her first?

If it was—*oh,* the sweetness of her mouth—then he couldn't begin to fathom what—

"Eleanor?"

Steps sounded in the hallway outside.

Heart thundering, Marcus drew back. Breathing heavily, her eyes wide, Eleanor looked up at him as though questioning whether they'd really done what they'd just done. Tempted to smile at her reaction, he heard the steps coming closer.

"I appreciate you sharing your concerns with me, Miss Braddock." He spoke at normal volume, but it sounded overloud in the silence, almost harsh in comparison to seconds earlier.

He gestured to her to respond, but she looked at him, confused.

"Oh . . ." She blinked. "Yes, of course, *Mr. Geoffrey,*" she said with a bit too much emphasis. But he granted her points for trying.

"So," he continued, "we'll meet later in the week to discuss—"

A knock sounded on the library door.

Marcus opened it immediately. "Mrs. Cheatham." His shirt collar shrank two sizes beneath the woman's appraising gaze.

"Mr. Geoffrey . . ." Adelicia said it slowly, a dark brow arching as her gaze moved to take in her niece who—to Marcus's pained discovery—looked a great deal like a woman who had just been thoroughly kissed. And who—much to his delight—had thoroughly enjoyed it.

Still, at the moment, the first discovery out-weighed the second, and it fell to him to say something—anything—to encourage Mrs. Cheatham's acceptance of doubt over the evidence at hand.

"Tomorrow I'll begin drawing up preliminary designs of the building." He directed the comment to them both. "Then we'll meet again once the budget is approved."

"Yes, I appreciate that." Eleanor's voice held only the slightest waver. "Thank you again for explaining everything in such detail just now."

"It was my pleasure." Unable to give Eleanor any type of communiqué without her aunt witnessing, Marcus simply nodded to Adelicia as he took his leave. "Good night, Mrs. Cheatham."

"Good night . . . Mr. Geoffrey."

Throughout the day Sunday, then into Monday, as Marcus supervised his crew, all he could think about was Eleanor. He'd seen her at church yesterday but only from afar. He'd relived that moment with her in the library over and over and didn't want to think about it as having been a mistake—because it certainly hadn't felt like one. But how could it be anything else? Where did they go from here? Nowhere. Because in June, he was going back home. But what if . . .

What if he didn't go back?

That thought kept pushing to the forefront of his

mind, no matter how many times he dismissed it as ludicrous. Even treasonous, in a sense. At least that's how his father and uncle would view it.

But . . .what if there was a way for him to stay in Nashville? Would he do it if he could? It was one thing to come to this country for a few months, to try his hand at living among the "common, everyday rustics." But would he give up everything, including the security and wealth of the Habsburg dynasty?

He was more than happy to give up an arranged marriage he'd never wanted, in exchange for a chance at one he did. And for a woman who had a far greater hold on his heart, on him, than she likely knew.

Of course, that woman had a standing offer of marriage from another man—which he still didn't know whether she'd accepted or not. But after that night in the library, how she'd responded to him. . . . A woman like Eleanor couldn't kiss like that— wouldn't kiss like that—unless it was genuine.

Oh, God, what am I to do?

Standing at his drafting table in the warehouse office, pencil in hand, he stilled, hearing that last thought return to him. Only, it wasn't so much a thought, as it was . . . a prayer. He sighed. If only God *did* care about the tiny bits and pieces of lives. But He didn't. Marcus knew the truth about kings and commoners. Neither Uncle Franz nor any of the past emperors took interest in the everyday lives of their subjects. They were *kings,* after all.

Likewise, the Almighty ruled from on high, from a distance, and Marcus had learned from youth not to bother Him with the petty, inconsequential ramblings stemming from a young boy's worries and wants. The Most High was busy enough reigning over the universe.

Marcus studied the drawings on the drafting table, the preliminary plans for the widows' and children's home. He'd worked on them every spare minute since Saturday night, and it was going to be magnificent. No doubt the women's league would be generous, and he was ready to put their money to work. He would build a stunningly beautiful home for the widows and children. One worthy of the love Eleanor had for them.

"I'd prayed about what steps to take next. I thought it was what the Lord was leading me to do. I was certain of it . . ."

Eleanor's comment returned as though she were standing there next to him. He could hear her voice so clearly in his mind. She obviously believed God concerned himself with the details of people's lives—and look what was happening in her life now. And in *his*.

Coincidence? He sighed. Or outcome?

A measurement he'd written caught his eye, and frowning, he looked more closely at the building plans, silently calculating. Then he reached for an eraser. The placement of one of the structural walls was correct, but the dimensions he'd written below it were off by a decimal place. How had he missed that? Miscalculate at the planning stage and pay for it double as you're building.

He made the correction, then rubbed his tired eyes.

As his eyesight refocused, the sketch of the building moved from blurry to crisp again, the tiniest measurements and lines all in proper place, all with purpose, and all there . . . by design.

Marcus felt a tingling on the back of his neck and slowly straightened. As an architect, he cared about every inch of this design, every nook and cranny, because it was *his*. He would never build—or even associate his name with—something unless he knew it inside and out. Unless he'd guided every step of its development. So . . .

Could it be that God, the creator of heaven and earth—and of man and woman—thought the same?

Quietly, reverently, Marcus laid his pencil aside and looked about the small office, perfectly alone, yet feeling anything but. At odds with what he was about to do, he couldn't deny the sense of rightness that accompanied it.

"All right, Lord," he whispered, then bowed his head almost as an afterthought. "I'm listening." He glanced up. "If you are too . . . then, please . . . tell me what it is I'm to do."

32

The letter came Monday at noon, delivered during lunch. When Mrs. Routh handed it to her, Eleanor thought it might be from her father. Or perhaps, she hoped, from Marcus. But no.

She instantly recognized Lawrence Hockley's distinctive script and could guess without reading it what the letter contained. She could only imagine what his reaction had been to reading the newspaper article upon his return from New York last evening.

She'd planned to speak to him about this weekend's events during their dinner tonight. But if this letter contained what she thought it did, there would be no more dinners. No more proposal. And the decision—regardless of what *she'd* decided—would be made.

"Excuse me, please." She rose from the table.

Dr. Cheatham and her aunt looked on in silence while the children chattered away.

Eleanor slipped through the library, briefly closing her eyes as she passed the spot where Marcus had drawn her to him and—

Oh, memory was both a blessing and a curse. Every time she thought about that kiss, she got a . . . She didn't know quite what to call it. A feeling, perhaps, but it went deeper than that. It felt as if he'd awakened something inside her she hadn't even known lay dormant. Yet having been stirred, it wasn't eager to be buried and forgotten again.

She'd never dreamed a kiss could deliver such . . . pleasure. She couldn't stop thinking about him, even though she knew she should. Because he was leaving.

It still angered her that he hadn't told her before then. But even worse, she'd read the look in his eyes, just after he'd kissed her—that what-on-earth-have-I-done look that her own curiosity had led her to experience countless times.

He'd immediately regretted the impulsive act. But she hadn't. Would someone born deaf, after being given a brief chance to hear, ever wish to erase the memory of hearing that loved one's voice, or the stringed crescendo of Mozart or Beethoven? Would they choose to wipe clean from their memory the laughter of children or nature's symphony of wind through the trees? Never. At least not that she could imagine.

"I've always known I must return to Vienna."

Must return, he'd said. As though something—or someone—awaited him there. A thousand possibilities rushed in to answer the question, but only one arrowed straight through her. A wife? A family? No . . . Marcus wasn't that kind of man.

Which left her no closer to knowing . . . why had he kissed her?

Regardless of the reason—and despite the persuasive nature of his kiss—learning he was leaving had made her decision about Mr. Hockley easier to make. Though she still had moments of vacillation.

But at the present, she wasn't sure her decision even mattered anymore.

She opened the door to the small study, then closed it behind her. A fire burned low and steady in the hearth, chasing away November's chill. She perched on the edge of the settee, nerves growing more taut by the second.

She fingered the wax seal on the back of the envelope, unable to deny an immense sense of relief, while also experiencing a keen—and unexpected—sense of loss. The security and certainty that could have been hers was gone. Just like that. For her father too.

Her nerves twisted tighter as she withdrew a single sheet of stationery from the envelope. . . .

Dear Eleanor,

    In light of your affinity for straightforwardness, imagine my surprise this morning upon opening Saturday's paper only to see your name therein. As well as to learn about the circumstances that placed it there. Quite a shock, I can tell you. I assume you have reason as to why you have not shared this particular venture with me before now. I greatly anticipate your enlightening me as to those reasons this evening.

                Yours most sincerely,
                Lawrence D. Hockley

She stared. So . . . he *still* wanted to have dinner with her?

A soft knock sounded at the door.

"Come in." Seeing her aunt, she held out the letter.

Aunt Adelicia read the note twice—judging by her patient perusal—then handed it back. A brightness shone in her aunt's expression that not even her practiced reserve could disguise. "Well, it would seem Mr. Hockley is more forgiving than we thought."

Eleanor heard the hopeful lilt in her tone, even as she felt her own sense of relief start to wane. "Yes, so it would seem."

"You sound less than enthused, Eleanor."

"Not at all, I . . ."

Knowing her aunt well, and the reciprocal being just as true, Eleanor knew better than to try to play this game. "As I'm certain you know, this decision regarding Mr. Hockley is not one of the heart for me."

"Not in the romantic sense, perhaps." Aunt Adelicia studied her closely. "But don't fool yourself, Eleanor. Your heart is influencing your decision. Or trying to." Her aunt's expression grew discerning. "I see it in your eyes now. And I saw it in your face . . . the other night, in the library."

Eleanor bowed her head. She'd sensed her aunt waiting for the right moment to broach the subject of finding her and Marcus in the library, and it appeared that moment had arrived.

"Following your heart, Eleanor, is a brave thing to do."

Eleanor lifted her gaze, surprised at the comment.

"But doing so leaves you vulnerable, and often comes at a steep cost. Mr. Geoffrey, who seems to be a decent man—what little we know of him—will be leaving in a matter of months. I know men, Eleanor. And he is not the right kind of man for you, my dear."

"I know that," Eleanor whispered.

"Do you?" Aunt Adelicia moved closer.

Eleanor nodded, forcing a courageous smile.

Aunt Adelicia's eyes softened, and with a wistful expression, she brushed the hair back from Eleanor's temple, much like Eleanor's own mother had done another lifetime ago.

"Men like Marcus Geoffrey"—her aunt's sigh came softly—"handsome, charming . . . *foreign*." She smiled. "They're wonderfully exciting creatures. But take heed, dearest. . . . They are ever so fickle. It's rare for such a man to recognize the truest, most precious kind of beauty, and rarer still when such a man chooses to pursue it."

On the verge of tears, yet knowing what her aunt said was true, Eleanor grew eager to move off the subject. "I'm curious, Aunt Adelicia." She cleared her throat. "Why are you so supportive of me facilitating this building project when you're obviously set on my marrying Mr. Hockley?"

"I don't believe the two are mutually exclusive, my dear. Build this home for the widows and children, under the oversight of the Nashville Women's League, and once you're married, you'll have that accomplishment to look back on and appreciate. Not to mention a legacy that will live on."

"To look back on and appreciate . . ." Eleanor caught the not-so-subtle insinuation, which, in turn, shed light on her aunt's motives. It was a compromise, of sorts, with little-to-no room for negotiation. Aunt Adelicia knew she would never refuse the opportunity to help build a home for the widows and children. Likewise, her aunt had also determined that marriage to Lawrence Hockley was the wisest option. So this was her way of *encouraging* that to happen, while also saving face in a public sense.

Of course Eleanor had heard about her aunt's persuasive nature, but to personally experience its unfolding . . . She didn't know whether to be impressed or livid.

As it was, her own choices were narrow. If she said yes to Lawrence Hockley, once the home was completed, so would be her direct involvement in what had been, thus far, the most fulfilling work she'd ever done.

If she said no to his offer of marriage, though she likely would still be allowed to help facilitate the construction of the building, once that was done —having gone against her aunt's wishes—Eleanor knew her welcome at Belmont would be worn to the nub. And what then? How would she support herself?

But more importantly, how would she provide for the care her father needed?

Still thinking about what her aunt had said earlier, Eleanor looked across the dining room table at Lawrence Hockley, then back at the near-life-size portrait of his late wife hanging above the hearth. She had been a plain-looking woman, with a pleasant countenance. Yet there was something about her that tugged at the heart. Something that—

"So please continue, Eleanor. . . . You said the Nashville Women's League requested that you facilitate a building project. What precisely will that entail?"

She relayed what had been discussed. "We should know our budget by the end of the week and then can proceed from there."

Thus far, Mr. Hockley had treated her no differently than he had during their earlier dinners. He'd given no indication of being angry, although his list of questions seemed unending. Except for one . . .

He hadn't asked for her answer yet.

"And what is the projected date for the building's completion?"

"We don't have the plans yet, but the architect assures us he can be done by June."

He chewed the tender steak filet slowly, methodically, before swallowing. "An aggressive schedule, to be sure. But I'm assuming the building will be basic, functional in nature, so therefore swifter to construct. Whether the weather cooperates or not will also play a factor."

Eleanor nodded as she sliced another portion of her filet, but her appetite gone, she moved it to the side.

"And who is the architect the league has procured?"

Goblet poised to drink, Eleanor hesitated. "Mr. Marcus Geoffrey."

He frowned. "Geoffrey, Geoffrey . . ." The shadow in his expression suddenly cleared. "German fellow. The one who's responsible for so many of the warehouse renovations lately."

Eleanor's grip tightened on the glass. "Yes, that's right. He's from Austria. You've met him?"

"No. But I'm on the city council, and Mr. Geoffrey was one of several architects who submitted plans for the new opera house."

Eleanor set her glass down. "Really? He sub-mitted a bid for that? And didn't get the contract?"

Mr. Hockley leaned back in his chair. "Custom-arily, I would refrain from speaking of private council matters. But seeing as you and I are working toward a mutual goal . . ."

He smiled at her as though he'd said something endearing. Which, for him, that qualified, she guessed. So she smiled in return.

"Mr. Geoffrey's design," he continued, "was, by far, the most inspired. Exceptionally intriguing. And the council was rather up in arms when the mayor awarded the contract to his own son. But as it turned out, Mayor Adler later confided that Mr. Geoffrey's firm was experiencing serious financial trouble and, due to such, would likely not have been able to complete the project anyway. So I suppose it all worked out in the end."

His brow knitted. "But part of the reason I share this with you now is this. . . . Before any money exchanges hands, before you agree on a contract, it would behoove you to confirm that his company is, indeed, solvent. Ask him to provide a financial portfolio for the past five years. Longer, if he has it. In fact, if you'd like, I'll enlist my attorney to contact him on your behalf."

"No," Eleanor said a little too quickly. "That . . . won't be necessary. I'm comfortable addressing the matter." Though she wasn't exactly sure how to go about it.

Marcus had given no indication that his firm was in financial trouble. But remembering how embarrassed her father had been regarding their own financial demise, she doubted Marcus would be eager to speak of such things. He *did* have an air of pride about him.

Following dinner, she accompanied Lawrence into the small study off the main entrance, where a servant soon arrived with coffee and shortcake. The room was sparsely decorated, quite the opposite of Belmont, and had a somewhat sad, even forsaken feel. Still, Lawrence had a handsome home. One of the finest in Nashville. Far nicer than she'd ever dreamed of living in.

"May I ask you a question . . . Lawrence?" Though she'd used his given name on occasion, it had yet to roll off her tongue.

"Of course."

"How is it you're so . . . accepting of my cooking for the widows and their children? I'm grateful for your understanding, no mistake. But my aunt and most of the women's league were not so obliging at first."

"It's quite simple, actually . . ." He took a sip of coffee before speaking again. "I was very much surprised when I first read the article, as I indicated in my letter. But it rarely benefits one to jump to conclusions. Better first to gather the facts. After hearing from you this evening, my suspicions were, in part, confirmed. The article was written, at its heart, for the purpose of maligning your aunt's name. She had much more to lose, you see, due to her elevated social status and your own lesser one."

Eleanor smarted a little at the truth and at how he stated it so matter-of-factly.

"You're a kindhearted person, Eleanor. That you cared enough to want to help the less fortunate speaks most highly of your character."

She smiled, genuinely appreciating the compliment.

"However, that you actually did the work yourself shows a surprising lack of judgment for a woman of your years, as well as a disregard for behavior deemed acceptable within our community, specifically within our own social circle."

Her smile quickly fading, Eleanor's guard rose in its place. "But surely you would agree that if acceptable behavior prohibits a person from doing good, then perhaps the definition of *acceptable* should be reconsidered."

"I don't agree. A person could still accomplish the same good, Eleanor, but through a different avenue. One that's congruent with his or her station in life. For instance, you could have gone to your aunt, or to the Nashville Women's League, and requested they partner with you to meet the needs of those women and children."

"But they wouldn't have done it. Not in a way that would have been successful. That's why I—"

His eyes widened. "That's a rather bold statement on your part. And one, I fear, will have to remain unsubstantiated, seeing as you acted without benefit of my counsel or anyone else's before proceeding. However, I do not wish to dwell on this, Eleanor. It is done, and it was done from a kind heart. And in light of that, I am more than willing to indulge this . . . womanly, philanthropic endeavor with the clear understanding that this will not be customary once we are wed."

He picked up a newspaper, unfolded it, situated it just so, and proceeded to read.

It was all Eleanor could do not to implode.

The heat in her face was nothing compared to the thumping of her heart. It took everything within her to stay seated across from him as he so casually said such a thing, then moved on. To have a man speak to her that way, with such assumption and—

She breathed in through her nose and out through her mouth. She then drank sips of hot, black coffee, trying to burn away the responses that sprang to her tongue with frightening intensity. None of which would serve her well if voiced aloud.

The crackle of flame consuming logs in the hearth was oddly comforting and ushered the moments past. Her silence didn't seem to deter Lawrence Hockley in the least. He read the newspaper first, then a book, leaving her to sit there, trying to envision a world in which she didn't have to marry this man in order to care for the most important person in the world to her.

When enough time had passed that she could leave without appearing rude, she rose from the settee. "Thank you . . . Lawrence, for dinner this evening."

He rose as well, his countenance smoothed of any trace of frustration. "The pleasure was all mine. I'll ask Hilda to get your coat and gloves and see that the carriage is brought around."

Eleanor waited in the entrance hall. He'd failed to ask for her answer, and she was in no mood to broach the subject.

Flickering light from the candelabra in the dining room spilled a soft glow into the hallway, beckoning her in. She followed and caught sight again of the portrait above the hearth in the dining room and stepped in that direction. She stared up, remembering the late Mrs. Hockley's name. *Henrietta*. Plain, practical. It suited the woman. Much as Eleanor knew her own name suited her.

Something in Henrietta's gaze drew her. Perhaps it was the way the artist—Washington Cooper, the signature told her—had captured both the natural light of her eyes, and yet also an empty, almost absent look. Though the woman's expression wasn't severe, neither would it be described as warm.

The corners of her mouth were upturned the tiniest bit, as though someone had reminded her to smile, but everything else about her—including the sadness in her eyes, the way her hands were knotted tightly in her lap, even the rounded, slightly hunched curve of her shoulders—suggested the greater truth of who Henrietta Hockley had been.

And who, Eleanor feared, she herself would become if she chose a similar path.

"Here you are, Eleanor." Lawrence reappeared with her coat and gloves, his own already on. "It's raining, I'm afraid."

Neither spoke on the way back to Belmont, but the rain amply filled the silence, which was Eleanor's preference. As the carriage passed the conservatory, she saw lamplight coming from within and wondered if Marcus was there. She knew then that every time she passed that conservatory, no matter how often in coming years, she would always think of him. And remember.

As Lawrence walked her to the door, tears waiting for release burned her eyes and throat. Again, thinking of Marcus, she offered her gloved hand.

Upon it, Lawrence placed a perfunctory kiss. "I'm most encouraged by our exchange this evening, Eleanor. I believe our pragmatic natures are more than compatible. Would you not agree?"

Unable to deny it, Eleanor nodded.

"And I'm assuming, since I requested as much, that you have made your decision?"

"I have," she said softly.

"And your answer is . . . ?"

For some reason, the image of little Maggie sopping up spilled soup from the plank-wood floor rose in her mind, and Eleanor searched the memory, trying to understand why it would return at that moment. All she could see was that room full of women and children, most of whom had nothing and no one to take care of them. But she had someone. She only had to choose. Perhaps he would not care for her—or she for him—in the way she desired, but Lawrence Hockley was a wealthy man. And he was generous, in his own way.

As his wife, she wouldn't be allowed to live the life she wanted, but she could still live one that mattered. She could see to it that the home always had the funding it required, and she could guarantee that her father would have what he needed for the remainder of his life.

It was logical. It made perfect sense. So why did that *something* deep inside that Marcus had awakened within her let out a silent, deafening scream when she whispered, "Yes."

· · ·

"We have two days of work left here in the warehouse, Mr. Geoffrey. Maybe three, if we stretch it."

Marcus nodded, hearing the concern in his foreman's tone. "That's what I'd estimated as well."

"The men have been asking what job is next. I've told them it's still being finalized. But . . . they have families to feed, Mr. Geoffrey."

"As do you, I realize, Callahan. I should know something this week. And I'll push to know as soon as possible."

"Sounds good, sir." Callahan gestured to the plans on the table. "If I'm not mistaken, I think I see a little bit of your opera house in this design. This is gonna be the nicest widows' and children's home in the state of Tennessee."

It was Marcus's turn to smile. "And here I was aiming for the entire country." He held out his hand. "I appreciate your loyalty, Callahan. And that of the men too. Tell them if we have to go without work for a day or two, I'll pay them anyway, just to keep them on."

"If it comes to that, Mr. Geoffrey, I'll make the offer. But the men . . . They appreciate working for you, sir. They respect you. Not many bosses will scale the rafters with them. Tom Kender's still talking about that."

Marcus laughed. "Kender's a good man. Just the other day, he—"

"Sir," Callahan interrupted, looking past him. "I think you may have a visitor."

Marcus turned and could scarcely believe his eyes. It had only been four days since he'd seen her, since that night in the library. But it felt like much longer.

"Eleanor . . ." He hurried to meet her, offering his hand as she maneuvered around stacks of freshly cut planks. "Good morning. What brings you out here? And so early?" His first thought went to her father. Not that he was supposed to know about him. However, he *was* planning on visiting the asylum later that week. He'd made a promise to the man, after all. "Everyone in your world is all right, I hope?"

"Yes, everyone's fine. And good morning to you, as well."

Formality not usually present graced her tone, but he didn't find that wholly unexpected. Not when considering he'd kissed her breathless the last time he'd seen her, then left without further exchange.

He lightly squeezed her hand before letting go, and when she returned the tiny but telling gesture, he looked at her and wondered what it would be like to grow old with this woman—to get to know the feel of her hand in his like a second skin, to know her habits, her likes and dislikes, what she thought about just before drifting off to sleep, and then again upon awakening.

"I'm sorry to bother you here, Marcus. I considered waiting, but . . . under the circumstances, I thought it best not to."

"Whatever it is, I'm glad you came. It's nice to

see you again." He caught a sparkle in her eyes that did his heart good.

"You as well," she said softly.

"While you're here," he gestured, "perhaps I can show you the designs for the building. I've been working on them day and night. I think you'll be pleased."

It might have been his imagination, but the glint in her eyes seemed to fade by a degree.

"I'm eager to see them, Marcus, but I think it would be best if I showed you something first."

Trying to mask his frustration, Marcus stood back and surveyed the three-story monstrosity of a brick building that took up nearly half a city block. He felt Eleanor watching him, no doubt trying to gauge his reaction.

When he'd gotten into the carriage with her a while earlier, he'd discovered her aunt and another woman from the Nashville Women's League waiting—along with an agenda.

"So . . ." Eleanor's tone was carefully neutral, but the spark of possibility in her expression was not. "Take your time. Look at it. Then tell me . . . what's your initial impression?"

"That this cumbersome brick-and-mortar box should be put out of its misery" came to mind, but he doubted she would welcome his humor. He

was a great admirer of old buildings, of which Europe boasted many. Most dating back to the fourteenth century or earlier. The soaring heights of Vienna's St. Stephen's Cathedral came to mind, and of course the Hofburg Palace. Masterful examples of art and architecture crafted from limestone that had more than simply withstood the weight of time. They had reigned over it.

But this building . . .

He grimaced at the lack of artistry in design and at the mortar already cracked and chipping. Americans didn't seem to build with the goal of withstanding the test of time as much as they built racing against the clock. Of course, he was not one to criticize in that regard when faced with a looming deadline. . . .

He chose his words carefully. "I think Mrs. Bennett and her husband are a most generous couple. Their desire to donate this . . . imposing piece of property says a great deal about them both." He glanced behind them to where Adelicia and Mrs. Bennett stood speaking beyond earshot and with unmistakable exuberance. "Yet its condition is greatly compromised, to say the least. Renovating such a building might be a challenge I'd welcome . . . if not for the specific needs that a widows' and children's home demands. For instance, in my plans I've included—"

"But you haven't even seen the inside of this building yet." She gave him a look he knew only too well.

"That's true . . . but I'm familiar enough with this type of building to have a good idea of what's inside. Don't forget, Eleanor, I've renovated a lot of buildings in this town."

"Which is all the more reason, *Marcus,* to consider this one. Especially since it would be donated."

Hearing that *steel* velvet in her voice, similar to that he'd often heard in her aunt's, Marcus knew better than to push. For now, anyway.

"Have they approved a budget yet?"

She slipped an envelope from her reticule. "I was given it this morning."

He reached for it, but she pulled it back, giving him the faintest smile.

"I want the estimate on your design *and* on the renovation of this building before I share this with you."

He eyed her, proud of her beyond words while also wishing he could throttle her just a little. For a few days he'd let himself believe the chance to build something notable was finally in his grasp. . . . And it still was. He just needed to convince her his way was best.

"Mr. Geoffrey . . ." Adelicia's voice came from behind. "I look forward to hearing your assessment once we've toured the building."

"Yes, madam. I'm certain that will give us all a clearer perspective on the project." He caught Eleanor's sideways glance and returned it.

She shielded her eyes from the sun and peered

up. "It's a handsome property, Mrs. Bennett."

"Thank you, Miss Braddock. It's quite special to my husband. Mr. Bennett visits here nearly every week. The flooring and staircases are sound, he said. But the building *is* in need of repair."

Marcus stared up at the redbrick albatross. Broken windows, like black eyes, dotted the three-story structure. Chunks of brick and mortar were missing, likely due to rifle fire, or a cannon blast. The arched detail work around the windows —which, granted, was a nice addition—was partially missing here and there and only served to whisper of better times long past.

But it *was* still standing, which he guessed said something.

"When Mayor Adler took office," Mrs. Bennett continued, "he immediately ordered that a new courthouse be built." Her tone wistful, she lifted a shoulder, then let it fall. "I suppose this one wasn't grand enough anymore. It was not nearly as ornate as the one the mayor had constructed." Her smile held shades of memory. "My husband and his father built this building when he was little more than a boy, so . . . my husband will be thrilled and honored should you find it worthy of renovation for our project, Mr. Geoffrey."

Feeling adequately chastised, Marcus nodded, but the very mention of Mayor Adler further soured his perspective on the place. He certainly didn't want that man's hand-me-downs. All he could think about was the opera house the mayor's son was building. He knew life wasn't fair, but this outcome seemed especially unjust.

With a proud smile, Mrs. Bennett withdrew a key from her reticule and handed it to him. "Since my husband couldn't be here, would you do the honors, Mr. Geoffrey?"

"With pleasure, madam." Marcus bowed, halfway praying the walls of the building would collapse in on themselves with the turn of the key. That would solve his problem entirely.

To his surprise, the cylinders in the lock clicked with well-oiled precision and the door opened with scarcely a squeak. Not a wall wavered.

He waited as the women preceded him through the doorway. The last to enter before him, Eleanor leaned close as she passed and whispered, "Work to keep an open mind, *Herr Geoffrey,* or I might have to hire myself another architect." She winked and walked on.

Marcus smiled. Apparently he hadn't masked the truth of his feelings as well as he'd thought. He allowed himself the privilege of watching her—all of her—unhindered. He had a feeling that reporting to Eleanor Braddock was going to be an experience he wouldn't soon forget.

Especially when forgetting her was the last thing on earth he wanted to do.

Everywhere Eleanor looked, she saw potential. She couldn't follow one idea through to completion before the next presented itself. Dust motes hovered in shafts of sunlight piercing the windows, and the crisscross pattern of light gave the space an almost dreamlike quality.

The air smelled of dust and disuse, like something set aside and forgotten, similar to the tunnel she and Marcus had visited together. Still, she breathed it in and caught the scent of a dream, but watching Marcus beside her, she doubted whether he would say the same.

She didn't think her aunt or Mrs. Bennett had picked up on his bias, but she had. And she understood. He wanted to build a building *"more beautiful, more awe-inspiring than anyone has ever dreamed or imagined."* She remembered his words verbatim.

The only problem . . .

The budget she'd been given, while generous, had to cover so much more than the building. It had to cover the allowance for food, furniture for rooms, bedding, hiring of staff. A kitchen! She kept a notebook with her and constantly made additions.

Aunt Adelicia's and Mrs. Bennett's hushed voices wafted toward them from a room off the foyer, and the occasional scurry of what Eleanor hoped were only mice scuttling in the ceiling. Mice, she could handle. Rats were another issue altogether.

The foyer was larger than she'd expected, and she pictured it arranged in a way to welcome newcomers. Tables and chairs to encourage visiting in front of the expansive stone hearth, perhaps. Hooks to hang coats and scarves on. Shelves lined with books for the older children could fit perfectly along the wall to her right. And to the left, a large woven rug and wooden boxes containing toys for the younger ones would be a nice addition.

Slowly, she released the breath she'd been holding, as if exhaling all at once might cause the images to disappear. "It has potential," she whispered, then glanced beside her when Marcus didn't respond. She gave him a nudge. "I said . . . it has potential."

Jaw firm, he scanned the ceiling overhead. "Don't make too swift a judgment. You haven't seen anything but the foyer yet."

"Neither have you." She frowned, not caring for the negative bent of his tone.

He tilted her chin upward. "See the dark stains along those support beams?"

Not wanting to, she nodded.

"Water damage. And rot. The roof probably needs replacing, which means a portion of the flooring will likely need it too."

"But Mr. Bennett said the stairs and flooring are sound. And besides, don't your men know how to do that?"

A scowl clouded his handsome face. "Of course we do, but that's not the issue."

"You being from Europe, I thought you would appreciate stately buildings of old such as this."

"I *do* appreciate old buildings, Eleanor, but this"—he glanced beyond her to the room where her aunt and Mrs. Bennett were speaking—"hardly qualifies as stately. We have to be mindful of the cost of repairs for this building. We don't want to spend so much money that we end up spending almost what a new building would have cost. And if we build from the ground up, I can build precisely to suit your needs. Exactly what you want."

She raised an eyebrow. "But I thought that renovating is less expensive than building, and that's why so many companies were choosing that route instead of the other."

He stared at her. "Do you not forget anything, Eleanor?"

"Never." She smiled as sweetly as she could, knowing it would likely irritate him.

Seeing him again hadn't been as awkward as she'd anticipated. He acted as if nothing had happened between them, which was as he wanted it, she guessed. He ran a hand along a wall, knocking occasionally, listening for . . . what, she didn't know. But she enjoyed watching him. Which she probably shouldn't, considering she was—

She even had trouble thinking the word. She was an *engaged* woman. No ring yet. No announcement. No wedding date set either. Lawrence had said they would wait until after the widows' and children's home was completed. And that suited her just fine.

Aunt Adelicia had been thrilled at the news. That made one of them.

"Customarily, yes," Marcus continued, standing on tiptoe to check out the beams overhead, "renovating is cheaper. But sometimes, when the building is as large as this one, and in such a state of disrepair, the cost of repairs can add up. I simply want you to be mindful of that possibility."

"And I want us to be mindful of the budget they've given us. It's generous. And while I'll share it with you later"—she held up a hand when he started to interrupt—"I've learned that the money always spends more quickly than I think it will."

His sigh held concession. "That's always the case."

They joined Aunt Adelicia and Mrs. Bennett and toured the main floor of the old courthouse. For the most part, the interior walls were intact. But in some of the former offices, it looked as though an ax had been used to chop rudimentary passageways between rooms.

Finding herself alone in one of the rooms with Marcus, Eleanor couldn't stop a recurring question from coming. "You said you've always known you must return to Vienna. What did you mean?"

His back to her, he bowed his head, and every second that passed before he answered seemed to squeeze the air from the room.

He turned and looked at her. "I have obligations to my family. To my uncle and father," he added quickly as though reading her thoughts. "It's those obligations that mandate my return."

She clearly heard what he hadn't said. That he didn't want to go into detail. She understood. She'd been grateful the other night when he hadn't pressed her about Mr. Hockley's offer of marriage.

"When will you . . ." The rest of the sentence stayed poised on the tip of her tongue, refusing to obey.

"June at the latest. But I *will* get this done, Eleanor. Either way. Don't worry about that. My men are very good. I only hire the best."

"Why does that not surprise me?"

He took a step toward her . . . and stopped. The look in his eyes was much like it had been that night in the library, and the newly roused stirrings inside her responded to him just as they had then. Yet neither of them moved. They just . . . stared.

"Are you ready to see the other floors?" he finally whispered, voice hoarse.

She nodded. "Yes. Thank you."

He led the way upstairs and she followed, Aunt Adelicia and Mrs. Bennett in tow.

Climbing the staircase, Eleanor admired the woodwork. "The craftsmanship on the banisters is exquisite, Mrs. Bennett. Similar to the mantel downstairs."

"Oh, thank you, Miss Braddock. My father-in-law adored woodworking. It was his hobby, you might say. He was an attorney by day and a craftsman by night. Once he retired from the law firm, construction consumed most of his time." She paused on the second-story landing. "He once told me that if he had a chance to live life over again, he would build things for a living instead of litigating them to death."

Aunt Adelicia laughed softly, running a hand over

the railing. "I wouldn't be surprised to hear many attorneys agree with him. But this was more than a mere hobby for your dear father-in-law, Mrs. Bennett. This building was truly his *gift*."

Marcus, unusually quiet, Eleanor noted, simply nodded in agreement and continued down the corridor.

To her dismay, a thorough perusal of the second floor proved correct his predictions about the water damage. And by the time they finished touring the third floor, she found herself over-whelmed by all the repairs the building would need in order to be inhabitable, much less functional.

Marcus found access to the roof and climbed the ladder, the rungs creaking with his ascent.

"Be careful," Eleanor warned.

He leaned back down and gave a smart salute, leaving her feeling a little foolish. It was some-thing her father or Teddy might have done.

She hoped her father was feeling better this morning. She'd visited the asylum yesterday, and though he'd appeared content for the most part, he'd twice wept for reasons he couldn't seem to explain. Deep, gut-wrenching sobs that broke her heart. As she'd tucked him into bed before she left, he asked if she would make corn bread with butter and honey *"like your mother used to make."* She'd stayed until he fell asleep.

After visiting him, she'd met with the board of the Nashville Women's League, at which time she was formally appointed to facilitate the building project.

She'd been so excited, it was all she could do not to tell Naomi, Marta, Elena, and the rest of the women about it last night at the dinner. But it had been decided—and she agreed—that it was best to wait until plans were finalized.

Her appointment as facilitator had disappointed one Miss Hillary Stockton Hightower, whose mother had nominated *her* for the position, then as co-facilitator when that met defeat. But the second motion was denied as well, much to Eleanor's relief. She didn't think she and Miss Hightower would see eye to eye on much, if anything.

With the board's overwhelming support, she was determined to not only provide for the needs of the widows and children *and* stay within the proposed budget, but also to make Aunt Adelicia proud.

"This building," Mrs. Bennett said, "was used as a barracks for the Union soldiers during the war." She sighed. "I'm afraid it suffered more damage than I realized. Both inside and out."

Aunt Adelicia gave Mrs. Bennett's arm a squeeze. "I'm certain Mr. Geoffrey will make a sound assessment. And when Miss Braddock weighs the options and makes her final decision, it will in no way—regardless of the direction we take—diminish the depth of your family's generosity, Mrs. Bennett."

"When Miss Braddock makes her final decision . . ."

Hearing Aunt Adelicia state it so confidently only made Eleanor more nervous. She'd not considered how it might affect Mrs. Bennett were they to reject the gift—or propose to raze the building and erect the new structure on this land.

Minutes later, Marcus descended the ladder, expression somber. "Well, I discovered where our leaks are coming from. But we can fix them . . . by replacing the entire roof. Portions of the parapet are either loose or missing as well."

Mrs. Bennett looked crestfallen.

"It's by no means an insurmountable task," Marcus added hurriedly. "But it represents a sizable expense. This is a large building and . . . the necessary repairs are numerous."

The silence lengthened, and Eleanor sensed the three of them waiting on her for direction. "Thank you, Mr. Geoffrey." She nodded with borrowed confidence. "The next step, then, will be for you to submit a list of needed repairs as well as a firm estimate for the renovation. Then together we'll look at both the design and expense of a new building. That will enable us to compare the two and make the final decision. For many reasons, time is of the essence, so the sooner we can meet, the better."

"My foreman and I will come back this afternoon and get started right away. I'll have both estimates for you before the week is out, Miss Braddock."

As they turned to make their way back downstairs, Eleanor caught Marcus looking at her. He didn't wink, he didn't smile, but an endearing emotion passed over his face just the same, and seeing it caused her heart to squeeze tight.

34

Friday morning, arriving at the asylum later than she'd planned, Eleanor knocked on the door of her father's room. A meeting with Marcus at the old courthouse earlier had taken longer than expected. He'd said he would have the final costs on the renovation as well as comparative costs for a new building ready by that evening. She prayed, as she'd done often in recent days, that her decision would be a clear one.

"Enter," a familiar voice answered.

She pushed open the door and found her father sitting in his chair by the window, clean shaven, hair brushed, glasses perched on his nose, and attention aimed at the heart of a book. She smiled at the scene, and it occurred to her then that when he was gone—prayerfully, a long time from now—*this* was the image she would carry in her heart.

"Papa?"

He peered up and blinked as though not seeing her well. Then resignation pinched his features and he lowered his book. "Eleanor."

Though she didn't hear explicit welcome in his voice, neither did she hear anger or agitation.

She stepped inside his room. "May I come in?"

"I believe you already have."

She was tempted to smile, thinking of how often

he'd said something humorous like that in the past with the goal of drawing a chuckle from her. But he wasn't smiling now.

She held out the covered plate. "I brought you corn bread slathered with butter and honey."

"No savory custard?"

She set the plate on a side table and removed her shawl. "You said you wanted corn bread, remember?"

"I said no such thing."

She smiled. "When I was here on Tuesday—"

"You haven't been here in *weeks*. I keep track of it all." He held up a pad of paper, blank, save for series of marks made at odd angles all over the page.

She said nothing, only smiled, thinking that might help. But the sharp planes of his face only grew more so.

She pulled the cloth back, the bread beneath still warm. "Would you care for a piece now? Or would you rather wait?"

"Wait," he said, voice curt. Then he firmed his lips and added, "Thank you," as though he'd been coached to do so.

She left the corn bread uncovered, hoping the scent might tempt him. "So, tell me"—she settled in the chair opposite him—"how have you been feeling?"

"Fine, thank you." He stared out the window.

Only three days since she'd last seen him, yet he seemed older somehow, more frail. But perhaps it was the sunlight highlighting the touches of time that wreathed his eyes and mouth.

Her gaze fell to a stack of books on the side table. "You've been reading some of our favorites."

"Nurse Smith is reading them to me now—since you don't anymore."

The barbed comment found its mark. But determined to keep their visit civil, Eleanor hid the hurt and looked for his favorite volume. *Hmmm.* It wasn't in the stack. Nor on the shelf.

"Where is Tennyson, Papa?"

His jaw edged up. "I loaned it to a friend."

That, she found surprising. For years, he'd carried that volume with him everywhere. She hated to think he'd loaned it out only to have it lost. "What friend? Is it someone you met here?"

"You don't know him."

She smiled. "I might." It occurred to her then that this *friend* might be a figment of her father's imagination. "Perhaps I could meet him . . . if you'd introduce me."

"He's my friend. Not yours. And it's *my* book!"

Deciding it best to move on, she picked up a treasured edition of poems by John Donne and opened it. "It's been a while since I've read this one."

"You can't take it." He reached for it. "It belongs to me."

She quickly relinquished the book. "Of course, it does, Papa. I only thought I might read a portion of it aloud while I'm—"

"I told you . . . Nurse Smith does that now!" Clutching the book against his chest, he returned his gaze to the window.

Knowing better than to push the subject, Eleanor decided to try another. "You remember how I've always liked to cook, Papa?" She wasn't surprised when he didn't respond. "Well, I have a job now. I prepare dinners for a group of . . ."

She caught herself and decided not to mention widows or fatherless children or anything that might remind him of the war. Or Teddy. "I've been cooking for a group of people. And I enjoy it very much." She wished he would acknowledge that he heard her. "We're actually building a home where these people can live." She prayed he would look at her. *See* her. "Maybe one evening, Papa . . . once you're feeling better, you could come with me, and meet some of my friends. Have dinner with us, perhaps."

Nothing. Just the occasional blink of his eyes as he stared out the window.

She sat up a little straighter and followed his line of sight. *The garden.* An idea forming, she touched his hand. But he drew back as if she held a lit match.

A moment passed before she trusted her voice again. "Would you like to go down there, Papa? To the garden? I'll take you."

"We can't go now. It's not time."

She smiled. "I bet I can convince Dr. Crawford to let us—"

"I said it's not time!" The muscles in his neck

corded tight. "We have *rules* here, Ellie, and"—he cursed beneath his breath—"you *will* obey them or you'll get the strap, you ungrateful child. Do you hear me?"

Stunned, she stared, wordless. It wasn't the first time in recent weeks that he'd called her by her childhood name. But never in her youth, not once, had he taken the strap to her—or Teddy. Or even threatened to. And *never* had she heard those vulgar words from her father's lips.

"I said"—eyes dark, spittle flew from his lips—"do you . . . *hear me!*"

"Yes, sir," she answered softly, deciding it best to play the role. "I hear you."

A knock sounded on the door, and Nurse Smith swiftly entered, her ready smile in place, signaling Eleanor that the nurse's timing was no accident.

"Theodore," she said, her voice a cool breeze on a sweltering day, "everything is going to be all right." Compassion softened the nurse's gaze as the young woman held her father's hand, stroking his hair as a mother would a child. And he clung to her as though she were life and breath itself.

"It's all right, Theodore. You're safe. Everything is going to be fine. You'll see."

Eleanor watched in disbelief as, in a blink, her father went from grown man to frightened child, and heaved deep, ragged sobs. From nowhere, her own tears spilled down her cheeks.

Nurse Smith's eyes misted as she mouthed, *"Give it time."*

Eleanor nodded, trying to catch her breath even as she felt a rending deep inside her.

A moment passed, and sensing a tenderness in her father's expression, she knelt before him. "Papa, I love you so much." Tentative, she placed a hand on his knee. "I'm so sorry this is—"

He shoved her with a force that sent her sprawling. His face twisted in simultaneous rage and fear. "Who are you? Why are you here?"

Eleanor gained her feet. "P-Papa, it's me. It's Eleanor."

She tried again to come close, but her father screamed and pressed back into his chair, crying and clinging to the nurse.

Eleanor felt a vise around her upper arm and turned to see a male orderly.

"Miss Braddock, it's best if you leave now, ma'am."

When his words finally registered, she nodded, tears blurring the image of her father as he stared up, eyes wide with fear. Numb, yet feeling as though her heart had been ripped from her chest, she retrieved her shawl and reticule and did as he asked, not looking back.

35

Marcus studied Eleanor as she reviewed the financial proposal he'd stayed up most of Friday night to finish. He knew she had no idea how lovely she looked standing there in the morning light, the sun streaming in through the glass panels of the conservatory. And he had no business thinking what he was thinking, much less doing what he was about to do.

But whether inspired by her studiously pensive look as she read, or the feeling that he was finally about to build what he'd dreamed of building all these years, he did it anyway.

He leaned close, watching her mouth, her lips moving silently as she considered the numbers, but all *he* could consider were the seconds until he tasted the sweetness of her kiss again. At the touch of his hand on her cheek, she looked up, and the answer was clear in her eyes. He pulled her into his arms and kissed her full on the mouth. Her arms came around his neck and pulled him closer, closer. Then *she* deepened their kiss, urging him on in a way he'd scarcely allowed himself to dream much less imagine. He traced the curve of her back and felt the comely shape of her—

"Marcus?"

He blinked.

"So what do you think? I'm not sure about the cost comparisons in these two columns."

Closing and opening his eyes again, Marcus looked at her standing at the table beside him, his mouth dry, his arms disappointingly empty, and his thoughts on anything but budgets.

Concern creased her brow. "If you're too tired to do this right now, we can—"

"*Nein, ich bin in Ordnung*—" He sighed, managing a smile. "I mean . . . I'm fine. Let's continue. This way, you'll have everything you need to make your decision this weekend."

He combed a hand through his hair, weary from too little sleep, too many calculations, and uneasy over a letter he'd received from his father in response to the one he'd written nearly a month ago. His father had a way of phrasing things that always made him feel lesser somehow.

Marcus pointed to the columns in question, working to see past the images of Eleanor still so fresh and vivid in his mind. "On this page, I listed straight comparison costs for every step of both projects."

Over the next two hours, they reviewed every item on every page, line by line, and he answered all her questions.

To construct the building he'd designed would cost more than the renovation, which hadn't been surprising. The Bennetts—following persuasion from women in the league—had finally agreed that if the decision was made to go with the new building, the old courthouse would be razed, and they would donate the land. Marcus would've preferred a woodsy acreage elsewhere but the budget didn't allow for such.

A major portion of the cost of the new construction was labor. Because in order to complete the project by the May deadline, he would have to triple his work force. And the first order of business? Demolish the old courthouse. But that's what his cash reserves were for. And he was more than willing to fund that portion of the project.

He'd adjusted the bid accordingly, considering it a donation to the widows' and children's home, as well as his last chance to put brick and mortar to his dream.

Once they finished, Eleanor stood and arched her back, then rubbed her neck and shoulders. "You are a very thorough man, Marcus Geoffrey. Everything in such detail." She moved back to the table where he'd laid the designs for the new building. "Aunt Adelicia said you shared these with her yesterday."

Marcus joined her. "She requested that I bring them by. I think she was pleased."

"Pleased?" Eleanor scoffed. "It's all she could talk about this morning at breakfast. That, and how she wished you'd designed and built her new billiard hall. So yes, I'd say she was somewhat pleased."

He smiled at the compliment. If Adelicia was on his side, the question of which building Eleanor would choose was all but answered.

He studied her profile as she looked at the design sketches again. If she had accepted Lawrence Hockley's proposal, he felt certain she would have admitted as much the other night when she'd told him about the offer of marriage. But just in case . . .

"Eleanor, I—"

"What are *these?*" She tapped the page. "On this portion of the roof right here."

He looked to where she pointed, then smiled, having wondered when she would ask. "Those, madam . . . are roof lanterns."

"I beg your pardon?"

"Roof lanterns. They're windows that are installed on the roof, much like a regular window with glass and panes. They serve several purposes. First, they allow more light into the space, which saves on lamp oil. Second, they allow in the sunlight's warmth, which helps to heat the room. But, most importantly"—he glanced up at the glass panels of the conservatory above them— "the sunlight enables you to grow flowers and plants. *Indoors.*"

She looked at him. "Grow flowers and plants indoors. You mean, as in a conservatory?"

"Similar, but not exactly. We'll have actual flower beds in the lobby entrance, and even a small tree or two. The whole thought behind this building is to bring nature inside, to incorporate the beauty of creation with the beauty and functionality of man's design."

Holding his gaze, she nodded slowly, then

returned her focus to the designs. "I appreciate your love of flowers, Marcus. I appreciate nature too." She looked up. "But how much would these windows cost? Not only in materials but in time to install them?"

"Not as much as you'd—"

"And what if they leak? Water will be everywhere. Or what about hail? One good storm, and glass could come raining down on the children. And wouldn't installing those on the roof mandate cutting through other floors? Think of the living space that would be sacrificed." She frowned. "I've never heard of . . . *roof lanterns*. Is it something from *Europe?*" She said it as if that might be a bad thing.

"Do you have any more questions, Eleanor? Because if you do, go ahead and ask them so I can answer them all at once."

She winced. "I'm sorry. But I'm worried about going over budget. Aunt Adelicia has been very specific about that. And I . . ." She sighed. "I don't want to do anything that will cause her to regret having given me this project."

Marcus heard what she wasn't saying. She wanted Adelicia to be proud of her. Which was something he understood. He thought of his father's letter again and wished he could speak to him. As it was, he pushed it from his mind for the moment.

"The roof lanterns aren't nearly as costly as you might think, and they're already included in the bid. I guarantee you we won't go over budget. I give you my solemn word on that. Now . . . to answer your other questions, I've already considered the issues you raised. We're installing doors, similar to shutters that will protect the windows in stormy weather."

"And just who will go up on the roof to close those doors every time it threatens rain?"

"The windows will seal tight. Same as ordinary windows. Not a drop of rain will get through. The doors are for when it storms."

Saying nothing, she went back to studying the designs. "Another thought to consider if we choose the old courthouse . . ."

Marcus bristled at the thought.

"With winter coming, and so many of the women and children without adequate housing, we might be able to finish a section and allow a portion of them to move in even as we're completing the renovation project. I know it wouldn't be ideal but—"

"That would be *far* from ideal, Eleanor. Children and construction do not mix."

"Neither do children being on the streets, or children bedding down on a cold wooden floor with the wind coming through the walls."

They stared at each other for a moment, and he thought of Caleb's building. He'd sent a few of his men over to work on it weeks ago. Callahan reported that they'd repaired the holes in the floor and sealed the cracks in the walls. He'd said the women and children were grateful. Marcus hadn't been back to see what they'd done. And right now, looking into Eleanor's eyes, he wished he had.

"But," she said softly, "we must also look beyond the urgent. A new building will serve the need very well, perhaps even better in some ways. If we're to encourage members of the community to volunteer down the line, which I hope to, then a new building, one that's attractive and that makes people *'stop on the street just to stare at it'*"—she arched an eyebrow—"will be a wonderful way to entice them inside."

Hearing her tout the advantages of new construction near elated him. Or would have, if hearing his own words parroted back to him hadn't been so unpleasant. He recalled saying that phrase. But it sounded so much more . . . self-centered than he'd realized. Which didn't sit well with him in light of the project's goal. Which seemed to be expanding . . .

"What do you mean when you say you want to encourage members of the community to volunteer?"

Warmth deepened her brown eyes. "Last night, after dinner, one of the children brought me a book and asked me to read to them. So we had a story time. It was wonderful. And that set me to thinking. . . . What if we made a little library? And what if we provided reading classes for the children who don't know how to read? Or for those who need to learn English so they can read the signs in stores and on the streets. Oh!" She touched his arm. "You've met Mrs. Claire Monroe?"

He nodded, enjoying her enthusiasm.

"I've spoken with her, and she's willing to come and teach the children how to paint. Then there's Mrs. Malloy, who has made dresses for some of the ladies. She's agreed to teach the women how to sew. I think it's important that we not only feed their bodies but also their . . ."

A touch of color rose in her cheeks. "I'm sorry, Marcus. I'm talking too much."

"No," he said quickly. "Not at all. Besides, I'd love to listen to you read."

Her smile—something he'd seen little of that morning—was a thing of beauty.

She turned again to his sketches for the new building and ran a hand along the graduated roofline. "What you've designed is stunning, Marcus. Truly stunning."

"I live to serve, madam."

She cut her eyes at him. "Which is precisely the impression I got the first time I saw you."

He feigned being hurt but was also curious. "What *did* you think the first time you saw me? I wager it wasn't a favorable opinion."

"Let's just say . . ." She hesitated. "I was fairly convinced that you thought quite highly of yourself."

"And me being a lowly under gardener, no less."

She grimaced. "I still can't believe you allowed me to think that of you for so long."

"Would it have mattered to you if it had been true?"

"If you'd been an under gardener?"

He nodded.

"Of course not." She met his gaze. "Would it have mattered to you if you'd known I wasn't the *wealthy* niece of Adelicia Cheatham, but rather an all-but-destitute relative who came to live at Belmont"—her voice softened to a near whisper —"because she had nowhere else to go?"

In the fragile silence following, Marcus sensed her vulnerability, and yet her strength too. And resilience that—unlike the simpering nature of so many women he'd met in his life—made her attractive in ways more than only physical. And that was saying a great deal. Because he'd lived the majority of his adult life pursuing pleasure.

But Eleanor made him want to be a better man. No. Not just *better*. She inspired him to be the best he could be. By offering the same of herself. No matter who she was with. No matter if she was cooking in a kitchen in a rundown shack or speaking with a gathering of Nashville's finest.

"No," he whispered, realizing they weren't talking only about their first meeting anymore. "It wouldn't have mattered to me either."

He wished he could have captured her image in a portrait in that moment. One he could carry with him in his pocket for the day he would no longer actually look into her eyes. The sunlight shining on her hair, her playful yet somewhat serious expression. He'd asked the Lord several times since that day in the warehouse to show him what he should do next. But so far, the Lord had remained silent.

Marcus was reluctant to admit it, even to himself, but maybe his initial belief about the Almighty's interest in the details of people's lives had been more accurate than Eleanor's.

Or perhaps . . . it was just *his* life the Almighty found unworthy of closer attention.

"But I no longer hold that view of you, Marcus." Her voice came tenderly, drawing him back. "You are a kind, talented, and very generous man. As evidenced, among other ways, by the tables and benches your men delivered yesterday. The women and children love them. No more sitting on the floor for meals.

"Oh! Which reminds me . . ." She reached into her reticule. "I meant to give this to you earlier." She placed the small cloth-wrapped bundle in his hand.

"What is it?"

"Open it and find out."

He did, and when he realized what he was holding, the same tingling sensation he'd experienced in the warehouse days earlier worked its way up the back of his neck. "This is a—"

"*Kaiser* roll. Naomi shared the recipe with me. We made them for dinner last night. She said they're very popular in Austria, and are named in honor of your *emperor.*" She said the word with an uppity tone, then her eyes narrowed. "Kaiser . . ."

Marcus's grip tightened around the bread. "Franz Joseph," he said quietly.

"Yes, that's it. You're familiar with the rolls, then."

"Oh yes." He nodded. "Quite familiar." If he didn't know better—he looked at her again, just to be sure—he would have thought she was baiting him. But . . . no.

She gestured. "Go ahead and taste. See what you think."

Accustomed to her watching him eat the creations she brought, he took a bite, and closed his eyes as his mouth watered at the familiar taste of home, of a distant but cherished childhood, and of memories from another lifetime. Memories when his mother and grandfather were still alive. And something occurred to him . . .

His thoughts flew back over the years. Since the death of his mother, then his grandfather, he couldn't remember ever being *truly* happy—experiencing that rare contentment you feel with someone you know cares about you without question, and who you cared about just the same—until now.

He looked across the room. Eleanor was gathering the proposal, working to get the pages stacked evenly, and he couldn't help asking . . . "When is the last time you heard from your father?"

Her hands stilled. Her head came up.

He didn't want to make her uncomfortable. But he knew, only too well, the burdensome weight a secret added to a person's heart.

"I-I've actually heard from him recently."

He didn't want to force her into telling him about her father before she was ready, nor did he wish to push her into a lie. He only wanted to help bear the burden, if she'd let him. "And how is he?"

Gaze lowering, she shook her head. "Not well. It will likely be a long time before he's able to join me." She inhaled, then released her breath in a rush, as if forcing out the words. "But he's with people who are taking good care of him. So . . ." She nodded, then cleared her throat. "You don't mind if I take these, do you? To review over the week-end?"

"Not at all. Let me know if you have any more questions. And, Eleanor . . . when the time comes, I look forward to you introducing me to your father."

She held his gaze for the longest time. Then finally, she nodded. "He would enjoy knowing you, Marcus."

He followed her out, and they were nearly to the door when she stopped in the aisle. Right beside the *Selenicereus grandiflorus*.

"I see you've not had any luck *beautifying* that one."

"It doesn't need beautifying. I think it's the most beautiful thing in here."

She shook her head as she leaned closer. "It's growing"—she frowned—"new *things*."

He laughed, seeing what she was referring to. "Most plants do. Over time." Not wanting her to look much closer at those new things, at least not yet, he picked up a recent success he'd had in grafting. "Have you ever seen this color in a rose before?"

She turned and looked at it . . . then at him. "It's pink."

"It's *coral*."

"Which is really pink."

"No. Which is really a combination of pink and *orange*. I had to graft the plants five times before it took. And the blooms proved to be fuller too."

Appearing quite unimpressed by his explanation, she pinned him with a look. "If you want to impress me, Marcus Geoffrey . . . then graft a potato that isn't rotten when you pull it from the ground. Now *that's* something that would impress me!"

She turned on her heel, and—a little dumbstruck—Marcus watched her sashay her pretty little posterior toward the door. He caught up with her before she opened it.

"A potato?" he said, more pleased than she could have ever imagined.

"Yes, a potato. Even with the return agreement I have with Mr. Mulholland at the mercantile, I still pay too much for too little!"

"The *return* agreement?"

She looked away, as though embarrassed, then explained to him about a *deal* she'd arranged with Mr. Mulholland. As Marcus listened to her spirited diatribe, he felt himself falling a little more in love with her, even as he hoped God was listening to her request too.

Because if God *and* Eleanor got involved, that practically guaranteed success with the potatoes.

They stepped outside only to discover the temperature had dropped considerably during the day. Marcus guessed it to be in the midfifties, maybe colder.

According to the almanac, the first frost wasn't due for another two weeks, but he'd already moved the two troughs of potato plants from the field into the conservatory. As soon as the plants flowered and then the leaves started wilting—two to three weeks at the most—they'd be ready for harvesting. It took every bit of his patience at this stage not to dig up at least one just to check its progress.

But he'd gone through this cycle enough times to know that trying to hurry nature along was like trying to tell the sun when to rise.

He offered his arm. "Allow me to accompany you to the mansion?"

She slipped her arm through his, then just as quickly removed it. "Marcus . . . I need to ask you a question."

"All right."

"This is uncomfortable for me, so I hope you'll understand."

"My imagination is running rampant." He smiled.

She didn't. "It's about your company's solvency. I . . ." She hesitated. "I need assurance on your part that once you start the project—whether we renovate or build—you *will* be able to complete it."

More than a little surprised by her query, he paused. "Without question I'll be able to complete it. And on time. You have my word."

She looked up at him, then briefly away. "If it were up to me alone, your word would be ample. But . . . since this project involves other people's investments, I need to request a financial history of your company. For the past five years."

"You . . . want me to provide a portfolio?"

She nodded.

It wasn't that he couldn't do it. In fact, he'd provided his financial information when he'd submitted a bid for the opera house months ago. He was simply surprised she'd asked for it. Then again, he had a feeling this was coming from someone other than her.

"Certainly, I can do that. It'll take me a couple of days to update it, but—"

"A couple of days is fine." Relief flooded her expression. "As long as I have it by Tuesday."

"Consider it done. But I can only provide it for the past year or so. Since I've been in this country."

"Oh . . ." Her expression clouded. "I suppose you could include the years you were working in Austria, then."

Again, though Marcus was certain she wasn't, it felt as though she was fishing for information. "Unfortunately, I didn't own my own company back in Austria. So I'm afraid my company's history here will have to suffice."

He could see her reasoning things out.

"So . . . if you didn't work as an architect back in Austria, what did you do?"

On impulse, he laughed, but not from humor. He attributed it more to the directness of her question and to his utter inability to answer it. "Would you believe me if I told you I was an under gardener?"

She looked at him in all seriousness, then a twinkle lit her eyes and she laughed too.

He continued quickly. "So don't give another thought to the portfolio. I'll get that to you by the first of the week. Along with my bank's guarantee of deposit for my company's cash reserves. Will that suffice?"

She smiled up at him. "Thank you, Marcus. That will be sufficient, I'm sure."

"Good, then. Now . . . about those potatoes."

Her expression perked up.

"If you'd like to join me one afternoon in the next couple of weeks, I'd love to talk to you more about that."

"Are you serious? You would consider trying that?"

He offered her his arm. "I most definitely would, madam. Now, may I escort you back to the mansion?"

"No." Her smile flattened. "But you may escort me to the carriage house. Armstead is waiting to take me into town. I need to start cooking!"

They walked arm in arm through the gardens in the direction of the carriage house, and he sensed the opportunity to ask what he'd tried to ask a while earlier. Even though he wasn't sure he wanted to hear the answer.

"Eleanor, you said something to me the other night, about . . . an offer of marriage." He felt her tense and looked over at her.

She kept her gaze forward, and though her arm was linked through his and he could feel the warmth of her body, a gulf seemed to open between them.

He paused on the path. She did as well, her head bowed. And he sensed her answer even before he asked the question.

"So," he whispered, "you"—he had trouble even thinking the words, much less saying them aloud —"*accepted* . . . Mr. Hockley's offer?"

A cool breeze stirred wisps of hair at her temples.

"Yes," she said, so softly he almost didn't hear. Then she took a deep breath and lifted her gaze. "Yes," she said again, louder this time, with determination in her voice and a smile that started to fade almost before it had bloomed. "I was planning on telling you, Marcus. But . . ." Her laughter came out breathy, nervous sounding. "It's all happened rather quickly. I only gave him my answer Monday night."

The weight of her response slowly settled over him, and Marcus gently released her arm. *Monday night* . . . He could scarcely make himself nod much less form a reply. That was after he'd kissed her in the library. And here he'd been thinking that . . . well, it didn't much matter what he'd been thinking. He'd been a fool. Yet he'd been so certain that—

In a wave, a wash of memories—of *voices*—rushed over him. *"I thought our evening together meant something, Gerhard . . ." "I waited to hear from you, Gerhard, but you never . . ."*

Over and over the voices came, and the irony wasn't lost on him.

Looking into Eleanor's eyes, he felt as though a mirror were being held up before him, and he didn't like what he saw—any more than she would, if she knew the truth about him.

Knowing he needed to say something, he reached for bravado that had seen him through more awkward situations than this one. But no matter his command, the familiar boldness wouldn't come. And all he could do was lift her hand to his lips.

"May I offer my sincerest congratulations, Eleanor. Lawrence Hockley is, indeed, a *most* fortunate man."

Seated directly opposite Lawrence Hockley in Belmont's formal dining room, Eleanor looked across the table at her future, then down at her nearly full plate, finding neither appealing at the moment.

Following church that morning, Aunt Adelicia had invited Mr. Hockley to join them for lunch.

Though Eleanor hated to admit it, every time she was with the man a knot formed in the pit of her stomach. She wished she could blame it on the afore-wedding dithers of a not-so-young bride to be. But she knew better and could scarcely wait for him to take his leave.

She hadn't seen Marcus at church, and she'd looked for him. She was glad, in a way, that he'd asked about Mr. Hockley. It was easier with him knowing. Or at least, she had thought it would be.

Laughter from the children eating in the next room filtered through the closed doorway, making the already sedate mood at this table seem even more so.

"So how was your trip abroad this season, Mr. Hockley?" Aunt Adelicia glanced in Cordina's direction, a subtle signal to begin plating dessert.

"Oh, much like the last ones. Hectic. Mostly business. I've seen all that London has to offer, what little there is, and have endured the grand tour thrice now. Personally, I don't understand the affinity that some in our circle have for that continent."

If Aunt Adelicia had been chewing something, Eleanor was certain she would have choked on it.

"But what about Italy, Mr. Hockley? Austria? France?" Her aunt's eyes lit. "Surely the museums and cathedrals, the timeless works of art, appeal to a man of your culture and standing?"

Working to balance the very last pea on his fork, Mr. Hockley took his time to respond. "I have toured museums and cathedrals enough to last a lifetime. And as for timeless works of art . . ." He cast her a look. "You have seen my home, Mrs. Cheatham. *And* my office. I have little interest in such things. Except in rare cases, when one may purchase them with a measurable guarantee of return on his investment. But even then, there are surer ways to secure one's financial future."

Eleanor's gaze swung from her aunt back to Mr. Hockley, who seemed completely oblivious to the silence in the room and the tight-lipped smile of his hostess. Even Dr. Cheatham, seated at the head of the table, seemed slightly taken aback by the man's frankness.

The knot in Eleanor's stomach cinched tighter.

Pound cake with fresh cream was served and eaten in relative silence. Eleanor took two bites of hers before the *knot* told her that wasn't the wisest choice on her part. She set her fork aside.

"Come spring, Dr. and Mrs. Cheatham"—at Lawrence's voice, all heads came up—"Miss Braddock and I will herald our pending nuptials, then be married in June. I have given some thought as to the date of the wedding, and also to the destination of our honeymoon, but haven't yet made my decision. I will relay that information in ample time for plans to be set and announced accordingly. May I confirm that the wedding will take place here, as you have so generously offered, Mrs. Cheatham?"

Grateful she was sitting down, Eleanor blinked

to make certain she wasn't in some horrible dream. He'd stated his decree as though she wasn't sitting in the chair directly across from him. Not only had he not spoken with her beforehand about any of the arrangements, he hadn't so much as looked her way as he'd made the announcement.

She stared, watching him cut his cake into even little squares and then eat it in much the same way—in quick, efficient little bites. A flash of pain that she was certain showed in her expression suddenly registered, and she consciously unclenched her jaw, still working to hold in the emotion.

Feeling someone's attention, she turned to see her aunt watching her.

"Yes," Aunt Adelicia said quietly, an emotion passing across her face. A silent admonition, perhaps? Or maybe a warning? "That's correct, Mr. Hockley. The wedding will be at Belmont."

Eleanor bowed her head, feeling almost as if she were dying on the inside. In her mind, she pictured her father. She was doing this for him. And not only for him, but for the widows and children. But until the day she died . . .

She had a feeling she would die a little, day after day after day.

Later that night in the kitchen, Eleanor looked at the pitiful excuse for a strudel and didn't know whether to laugh, or throw the dish across the room.

Baking usually helped her to breathe on the inside, to think more logically, see things more clearly. It was therapeutic. And she needed that tonight, of all nights. Because tomorrow she had to present her decision regarding the widows' and children's home to the Women's League. And though she *thought* she knew, she still questioned which option would be best.

She knew what her aunt wanted. What Marcus wanted. Without question, she knew Mrs. Bennett's desire. She knew what most of the women on the board preferred too. But what she didn't know was . . .

What was the better choice? She frowned at the soupy mess in the dish. She apparently didn't know how to make apple strudel either. Her second failed attempt. In one evening!

It was already past midnight, with Sunday put to bed and Monday stirring. She needed to admit defeat, clean up, and set the kitchen to rights for Cordina and the other cooks.

"Nothing is ever as good as your Mutter's *strudel."*

She let out a sigh, hearing Marcus's voice even now. "That may be true, Herr Geoffrey," she whispered aloud. "But I'm going to make a strudel as good as your *Mutter*'s if it kills me."

"*Lawd,* ma'am, I tell ya. . . . You start talkin' to yourself and it's the beginnin' of the end!"

Startled, Eleanor turned to see Cordina standing in the doorway. "Oh, Cordina, I'm so sorry." Eleanor quickly situated herself in front of the strudels. She might not be a head cook or fancy chef, but she still had her pride. "I hope I didn't wake you . . ."

"Lawd, no, Miss Braddock. Me and Eli, we got us a cabin out back. Just the two of us." She smiled. "Eli, he got a hankerin' for some iced lemonade, so that's what I come for. How's that fancy dessert you makin' comin' along?"

The woman tried to peer over Eleanor's shoulder, but Eleanor again moved to block her view, which drew a chuckle from Cordina. And then from Eleanor too.

"I'm guessin' it ain't turnin' out too well, ma'am."

Eleanor slumped her shoulders. "Both attempts were disasters." She stepped to one side.

"Mmm-hmm" was all Cordina said as she looked between the dishes. "Mind if I get a taste?"

Eleanor hesitated, then shook her head. "But you'll need a spoon. I cut the apples too thin in this one." She gestured. "Then too thick in the other. I tore holes in the dough as I was trying to stretch it. I mended them, then they promptly split open again as I tried to roll it up."

Cordina tasted the first one. "A bit grainy, them apples, aren't they?"

"A bit?" Eleanor rolled her eyes.

Chuckling again, Cordina tasted the second. "Soupy, but better." Then she paused. "The dough on this one, it got . . . a little hard. *Chewy.*"

"That's because I added more flour so the dough wouldn't split in the stretching. It didn't work."

Cordina patted her shoulder. "Makin' them fancy

pastries takes time, and lots of doin'. You get it right, Miss Braddock. Give it time."

Give it time. . . . Exactly what Nurse Smith had said about her father. But the way he'd looked at her . . . scared, angry. She didn't think she'd ever forget that moment. "I appreciate that, Cordina. Thank you for letting me use your kitchen."

"Anytime, Miss Braddock. Who you makin' this for anyway, ma'am? Surely you ain't tryin' to bake somethin' like this for all them women and children?"

"Oh, gracious no. I'm . . . making it for a friend. And I promise, I'll clean everything up before I go to bed."

"You want some help? I be happy to do it."

"No, thank you. I'll be fine. You take Eli his lemonade and get some rest."

"All right, then. Good night, ma'am."

Eleanor scraped both strudels into the scrap bucket, feeling sorry for whatever animal would have to eat it, then proceeded to clean and wipe down tabletops.

Nearly an hour later, bone weary and with nothing to show for her effort, she crawled into bed. She started out on her left side but couldn't get comfortable, so turned onto her right.

She didn't even know Lawrence Hockley's favorite dessert. Nor did she really even care to. She turned onto her back and stared up at the ceiling, her lack of feeling for the man gnawing at her. *Lord, I don't think I can do this.*

Tears slid from the corners of her eyes, and she reminded herself, yet again, of how fortunate she was. Especially when she compared her situation to that of the widows she helped.

She blotted tears from her temples and turned onto her side again, images circulating through her mind—of unsightly strudels, lovely coral roses, and of a building unlike any she'd ever seen. And her prayer was a simple one. *Lord, show me what's best.*

She cradled the pillow against her cheek, and finally, finally sleep claimed her.

As her eyes drifted shut, she felt a featherlight kiss on her forehead, then heard a distant, familiar, yet no longer feeble voice. "I love you, Eleanor." Part of her knew she was dreaming, while another part clung to the hope that she wasn't.

And she whispered back, "I love you too, Papa."

Books in hand, Marcus looked first in the garden at the asylum but didn't see anyone. Not surprising. It was a chilly morning. He walked around to the front entrance and knocked, knowing from experience the door would be locked.

A moment later an orderly appeared and opened it. "Mr. Geoffrey, good to see you again, sir." He motioned Marcus inside. "Are you here to see Dr. Crawford?"

"No. Actually I'm . . . here to visit a friend. Mr. Theodore Braddock."

A shadow crossed the man's face. Marcus started to explain how he and Theodore had become acquainted, but the orderly turned away.

"I'll accompany you to his room."

Marcus followed, somewhat familiar with the layout of the building from his meetings with Dr. Crawford. He trailed the gentleman's path up the stairwell and down a hallway, the sound of their footfalls hollow on the tile and the scent of antiseptic heavy in the air.

Something about that smell had always put his senses on alert. The reminder of its purpose, perhaps—to prevent decay, to oppose the natural order of things. Just as fall, with its beauty, had brought brilliant color to trees and shrubs otherwise mutely green, it had also thieved the vibrancy of summer. Death, decay, was part of life. He'd been introduced to that truth as a young boy, then had learned it anew as a grown man.

But it hadn't made it any easier to accept.

He checked his pocket watch. A little after nine thirty. He had less than an hour for his visit. The board of the women's league convened at eleven to hear Eleanor's decision. He was invited, of course, and wouldn't miss it. He'd sent the financial reports to Belmont via courier Tuesday morning, as Eleanor had requested.

Lying awake last night, waiting for sleep to come, he'd replayed the scene in his mind from the garden Saturday afternoon. She was marrying Lawrence Hockley. She'd confirmed it. So why was it still so hard for him to accept?

In thinking about the upcoming meeting, he'd

tried to calculate the odds of her choosing the old courthouse versus his design. Without question, the majority of the women's league wanted the new construction, including Adelicia. And Eleanor knew how much a new construction project meant to him. Yet Marcus also knew she wasn't a woman easily swayed by sentiment. Something he'd admired about her from the outset. Now, however, that attribute might not play in his favor.

The orderly paused. "This is Mr. Braddock's room, Mr. Geoffrey. Have you . . . visited with him recently, sir?"

"A little over a week ago. I meant to return earlier, but with work and other responsibilities . . ."

"I understand, sir. But you need to be aware that the disease is progressing rather rapidly."

He stared. "The disease."

"That's impacting his memory."

Marcus nodded, the news of failing memory not coming as a shock. But the term *rapidly* gave him pause, especially as he thought of Eleanor. "I see."

"He's having increasing difficulty remembering people, sir. And even when he does remember, it can trigger an emotional and sometimes violent reaction."

Marcus recalled the times Theodore had grown frustrated with him. He'd seen firsthand how the man's mood could alter without warning. "I understand and will tread carefully."

Hand on the latch, Marcus couldn't deny he

was a little nervous, wondering if his visit would help or harm. And also wondering what Eleanor would think if she knew he was visiting her father. But a promise was a promise. . . .

He pushed open the door and saw her father standing by the window, one hand pressed flat against the glass pane.

"Theodore?" Marcus said quietly, finding it difficult to use the man's given name now that he knew who he was.

Mr. Braddock didn't turn. Didn't move. Simply stared out the window as though in a trance.

Mindful of the orderly's warning and remembering the strength of the man's grip, Marcus chanced a step closer. "Theodore . . . I'm returning your book."

Still nothing.

Finally, Marcus cleared his throat and spoke in full voice. "Excuse me, sir, but I'm returning your copy of Tennyson."

As though the spell had been broken, Mr. Braddock slowly turned, blinked. His gaze went first to the books Marcus held, then to Marcus himself.

Mr. Braddock's countenance crumpled with emotion. "I knew you would come," he whispered. "She thinks you stole my book, I can tell. But I knew you didn't." His face split into a grin. "Because I know you." In three long strides, he brooked the distance between them and gripped Marcus by the hand. "How are you, Marcus!"

So much for lapses in the man's memory. "I'm well, sir. And how are you?"

Mr. Braddock frowned. "What is this *sir* business? We are friends, you and I. Are we not?"

"Of course we are . . . Theodore."

"Come, come . . ." Mr. Braddock motioned. "Sit and let us speak to one another."

The older man reached for his book, and Marcus surrendered it.

Mr. Braddock held the volume tenderly, then pressed it to his chest, closing his eyes. "Welcome home, my dear, old friend." In a quick turn, his eyes popped open. "Did you read it?"

Smiling, Marcus held out one of the other two books he'd brought. "I have that exact volume in my collection. I know many of the poems by heart."

Mr. Braddock's eyes lit with challenge. " 'Come, my friends,' " he said in a deeply resonant voice. " ' 'Tis not too late to seek a newer world. . . .' "

Marcus leaned forward in his chair. " 'Push off, and sitting well in order, *smite* the sounding furrows, for my purpose holds . . .' "

" 'To sail beyond the sunset' "—Mr. Braddock jumped in, his expression softening, as did his voice—" 'and the baths of all the western stars . . . until I die,' " he finished in a whisper.

Marcus applauded. "Well done, Theodore."

The man took a mock bow from his chair. "Now you take a turn!"

Marcus didn't have to think long. " 'Half a league, half a league, half a league onward . . .' "

"Mmmm . . ." Mr. Braddock's eyes glistened. " 'All in the valley of Death rode the six hundred. Forward, the Light Brigade!' " his rich baritone boomed.

" 'Was there a man dismayed?' " Marcus quoted, seeing his grandfather's face even as he watched Mr. Braddock.

" 'Not though the soldier knew someone had blundered.' " Mr. Braddock raised a forefinger in feigned warning. " 'Theirs not to make reply . . .' "

" 'Theirs not to reason why,' " Marcus said.

" 'Theirs but to do . . . and die.' "

" 'Into the valley of Death rode the six hundred,' " they finished in unison.

Mr. Braddock clapped, his laughter full and deep. "Oh, how I miss that. My son, Teddy, and I used to read verse together." Eyebrows shooting up, he glanced toward the door. "He was here just a while earlier. You might have seen him on his way out?"

Marcus stared, then shook his head.

"Ah, well . . . perhaps next time."

Marcus listened as the man spoke about his son, remembering only too well Eleanor telling him that her brother—her *only* brother—had died in the war.

"He's such a good boy, Marcus. A fine young man. Kind, generous. I couldn't ask for a better son."

"I'm certain, Theodore, that your son . . . feels the same about you."

Marcus's thoughts turned to his father's recent

letter, and he wished he hadn't relayed to the baroness what he was doing in Nashville. Because she'd gone directly to his father. Marcus had read the letter several times. Especially his father's closing paragraph. Words that, he knew, were intended as *royal* counsel. When in reality, each was a knife gouging a lifetime's old wound.

In closing, your absence has served the crown well, Gerhard. The unfortunate incident of last summer has been all but erased from the people's minds. But take heed . . . You must be done with the foolishness about which the baroness informed me. Your mother, God rest her soul, indulged your childhood fantasies. As did her father. And they did so to your detriment. Upon your return, you will wed, then assume your new commission with the royal army. I am yet determined to see you become the son I still believe you can be.

Never once in his letters had his father said that he missed him. But truthfully, it had been a long, long time since Marcus had *missed* his father. It was hard to miss someone who constantly reminded you that you weren't what they wanted you to be.

And when he compared his father's comments— *and* their relationship—to the praise, so heartfelt and tender, from Mr. Braddock for his deceased son, he was cut to the quick.

Sadness shadowed Mr. Braddock's slow-coming

smile. "I only wish Teddy came to visit more often than he does. But . . . that *woman* is to blame. I know she is." His pleasant countenance faded. "She tells him not to come. Keeps him away from me. She's selfish that way."

"That woman?" Marcus asked gently, aware of the man's change in mood.

"The tall one. The one that put me in here." Mr. Braddock leaned closer, his gaze conspiratorial. "She comes sometimes," he whispered. "Creates trouble. Tries to take me outside when it's not time, takes my things when she thinks I'm not looking. She thinks you stole my book, you know. But don't you worry, no one here thinks you did. I've told them about her." He gave an assuring look. "They know the truth."

Marcus nodded, not so much in agreement as to avoid a potential conflict. It didn't take any guessing to know who Mr. Braddock was referring to. What he couldn't reconcile was the woman he knew with the woman the older man described.

A knock sounded on the door, and a nurse entered, tray in hand. "Good morning, Theodore. I've got your medication." She paused. "Mr. Geoffrey! How nice to see you again, sir."

Marcus rose from his chair, not remembering having met the woman. "Good morning, madam."

She smiled. "My apologies, Mr. Geoffrey, for assuming an acquaintance. We haven't been introduced before, sir. I'm Nurse Smith. But I— along with everyone else here—am so grateful for the work you and your men did on the garden. It's making such a difference in the lives of the patients. And the employees."

"It was our pleasure, madam. But we merely designed and installed it. It was Mrs. Adelicia Cheatham who commissioned it." He gestured to Mr. Braddock. "And I couldn't have done it without my faithful friend here. Theodore assisted me in installing the statue."

"It's quite true." Mr. Braddock nodded. "I did."

Nurse Smith grinned. "Well, I'm grateful to you both, then." She set the tray on a table. "Now, Theodore, it's almost time for lunch, which means you need to take your next medications."

Lunch? Marcus pulled out his pocket watch. *Five after eleven?* The meeting! It had already started.

He took hold of Mr. Braddock's hand. "Theodore, I have thoroughly enjoyed our time together. But I'm sorry . . . I must take my leave. I'm late for an appointment."

"You have to go?" The man's face fell. "Now?"

"I do." Marcus knelt beside Mr. Braddock's chair. "But I *will* be back. I promise."

Mr. Braddock looked at him as though weighing whether to believe him or not. Then finally, he nodded. "I know you will." He held up the book. "Because you keep your promises."

"Yes, I do. Speaking of which . . ." He held out the third book he'd brought, one he'd ordered through the mercantile, his own copy being in German.

"It's a favorite of mine. And a gift for you, if you'd like to read it."

Mr. Braddock took the book, gently lifted the cover, and drew in a breath. " 'Nor, what may count itself as blest . . . the heart that never plighted troth. But stagnates in the weeds of sloth, nor any want-begotten rest.' " He looked at Marcus, hopeful.

Feeling the seconds tick past, Marcus smiled. " 'I hold it true, whate'er befall. I *feel* it, when I sorrow most.' " The next verse in the stanza had gained new meaning in recent weeks—painfully so—even as her face came clearly in his mind. " ' 'Tis better to have loved and lost . . . than never to have loved at all.' "

Mr. Braddock's eyes filled. "Truer words never penned," he whispered. "But oh . . . how cruel when made to live out day by day."

Marcus reached over and gripped his hand. "Until next time . . . Mr. Braddock."

The older man's smile trembled. "Until next time . . . my young friend."

Faithful to the thoroughbred heritage pumping through the horse's veins, Regal thundered over the dusty roads to town, and Marcus gave the animal its head. The horse's hooves seemed to barely graze the earth as the miles disappeared behind them.

Upon reaching the outskirts of town, Marcus slowed the horse to a canter, then reined in sharply in front of the league building, sending rocks and pebbles flying.

Breath coming heavy, Marcus checked the time. Almost a quarter 'til twelve. He grimaced. He'd wanted to hear the announcement himself, instead of being told.

He reached the door and heard a flurry of conversation coming from the other side. The meeting was already over. Sighing, he knocked twice for the sake of politeness, then walked in.

The first face he saw from across the room was Mrs. Bennett's, and judging by her teary countenance, he knew which choice Eleanor had made.

She had chosen to build. Marcus felt a weight lift from his shoulders that he hadn't even known was there. Time slowed to a crawl as he looked about the room.

Although he regretted Mrs. Bennett's disappointment and understood her and her husband's attachment to the old courthouse, he couldn't deny his own sense of exhilaration. It was finally happening. A building constructed with the goal of blending nature and architectural design. *His* design. Something accomplished on his own. Without the Habsburg name or influence.

His father and uncle would scoff. Such petty nonsense to them. Because why would the man second in line to the throne of the Hungarian-

Austrian Empire want to embark on such an inconsequential undertaking? But it wasn't inconsequential. Not to him. Not to Eleanor. And certainly not to the women and children she was helping.

They were helping.

Several of the league board members glanced in Marcus's direction, then quickly averted their gazes. Understandable, considering the circumstances. Now wasn't the time to celebrate. They were hurting for their friend.

Eleanor, apparently not having seen him yet, approached Mrs. Bennett and whispered something to her. The woman bowed her head and nodded.

As the pair embraced, Marcus made his way toward them, nodding to some of the other ladies. He wanted to express his gratitude to Mrs. Bennett and her husband for the land, to assure her he would build something worthy of their generosity. He even planned on salvaging what stair rails and mantels were serviceable and then incorporating them into the new building in honor of the woman's late father-in-law.

He didn't like to think about his life after leaving America. Just like he didn't want to think about Eleanor being with Lawrence Hockley—or any other man, for that matter. Yet she *would* marry. As would he. But in the time he had remaining in Nashville, he planned to do everything he could to build the best widows' and children's home for her that he could. And with a kitchen beyond the woman's wildest imagination, which was well within his power.

Eleanor patted the woman's shoulder, then looked up. Her gaze connected with his. Her expression was joyful, and Marcus responded in kind. Then —in a blink—her smile fell away. Her hands, formerly at her sides, were now knotted at her waist. And in the swing of a pendulum, the mood in the room shifted. Or more rightly, came into clearer focus for him. And he realized . . .

The women weren't seeking to console Mrs. Bennett. They were celebrating with her.

Eleanor closed the drawing room door behind her, knowing she was responsible for Marcus's disappointment. Yet also knowing there was nothing she could do to change it.

Marcus stood before the cold, unlit hearth, his back to her.

A single oil lamp illuminated the room, the shadows in the corners in no danger of being overtaken. Muffled conversation and laughter from the women outside in the hallway drifted into the room, forming a dissonant backdrop for this conversation. But this was the only place Eleanor could find where they could speak privately.

"Marcus, I want you to know that I—"

"You made your decision, Eleanor. And I respect that."

He turned, that confident expression she knew

so well back in place. But for a moment, outside, she'd seen what constructing the new building had truly meant to him. She'd thought she understood. But she hadn't. How much more difficult would her decision have been if she had.

"My crews are ready to begin immediately. So tomorrow morning we'll start early, and—"

"Marcus," she said softly. "Please, can we talk about this?"

"Certainly, if you'd like. But . . . what else is there to talk about?"

His voice—though even-toned and friendly—didn't sound like him.

"Well, for instance, all the reasons I outlined at the meeting earlier supporting my decision to renovate instead of build. A meeting I *thought* you were planning to attend."

"I was. But . . . I was delayed."

"We waited for ten minutes before we finally commenced."

He looked at her. "I'm sorry, Eleanor. As I said . . . I was delayed."

She heard a definite abruptness in his tone, so moved on. "Would you like to know my reasons for renovating?"

"Honestly?"

He smiled but it wasn't the easy gesture she was accustomed to. Still, she nodded.

"No. I wouldn't. Because right now, in this moment, it doesn't matter. All that matters is the decision you made."

The glimmer of hurt and disappointment she'd seen before returned, and he looked away.

"Would it help, Marcus, to know I believe, with all my heart, that this is the decision God was leading me to make?"

His smile was disarmingly handsome, yet without a trace of humor in it. "Actually, no," he said quietly. "That's the one thing you could say to me now that would make this choice even more difficult to accept."

"These three ladies have my full authority to sign on the mercantile account, Mr. Mulholland." Eleanor glanced at Naomi, Marta, and Elena, who all looked lovely in their new dresses sewn by Mrs. Malloy—to whom she owed another payment for services well rendered. "I couldn't manage without them. And now that we've begun renovations on the old courthouse, I'm depending on them even more."

Mr. Mulholland printed each of the women's names in the ledger, then turned the book around to face them. "If you three ladies will sign your names right here"—he pointed—"then everything will be in order."

Each of the women signed, seeming to stand a bit taller as they did.

Outside on the street, Eleanor thanked each of

them again. "I couldn't do this without the three of you. I hope you know that."

Marta beamed. "When can we see the building again, Miss Braddock?"

"Is the work going well?" Elena asked.

Eleanor glanced down the street in the direction of the old courthouse. Many of the widows and children had been inside as far as the main floor lobby to view the building before the renovation began two weeks ago. Since then, Marcus had declared it unsafe for women and children.

She wondered if he'd intended for that formal edict to include her too, and simply hadn't admitted as much. She knew that her decision had hurt him, but since the night of the meeting, he'd acted nothing less than the perfect gentleman. And that was the problem. . . .

He was acting. He wasn't being the friend she hoped he still was—and needed him to be.

"Yesterday, when I was there, Mr. Geoffrey said he and his men are making good progress. He also said that if they can maintain this pace over the next five weeks, then"—Eleanor offered a cautiously optimistic smile—"we might be able to host Christmas dinner there together, instead of eating in shifts like we're doing now, and like we'll do next week for Thanksgiving."

"Oh . . ." Elena beamed. "Christmas together would be *wunderbar*. We could decorate a Yule-tree, *ja*? And maybe *Christkindl* would bring gifts for the children."

Marta nodded. "It is a hard time of year for so many." She cast a glance at Naomi, her own smile lessening. "Even more for some."

Naomi lowered her eyes, but not before Eleanor caught the look the three women exchanged. Naomi had been especially quiet in recent days, but Eleanor had attributed her silence to fatigue and to the long hours they'd both been working. Since the newspaper reported the renovation of the old courthouse, word about the meals—and the home—had spread, and each night dinner was served, more widows and children showed up. Naomi was helping her implement a procedure in which all the names and birthdays of every woman and child were recorded, along with their specific needs.

But Eleanor wondered now if her friend's silence was due to something else.

"We are going to meet our daughters at Mr. Stover's building, Miss Braddock," Marta offered. "And will start dinner for tonight. But first, we will stop to see Gretchen. Three weeks until her baby comes, but already she has pain."

"Does she need a doctor?" Eleanor asked, alarmed. "There's a physician in town who has cared for some of the women and children."

Elena shook her head. "She needs rest, ma'am. But she must keep working."

"Because if she doesn't work," Eleanor continued, having heard the same words from so many of the widows, "she can't afford to pay rent. And she has not only herself to think about, and the baby, but precious Maggie as well."

"Naomi has been caring for the little girl at night." Elena ducked her head when Naomi threw her a look.

"Is that true?" Eleanor glanced beside her.

"She is no trouble, Miss Braddock," Naomi said softly. "She is a sweet child. And follows Caleb around like a little duckling. But . . . sometimes at night she has trouble sleeping. She is afraid."

"Afraid of what?" Eleanor asked.

"Of being left alone. Bad dreams come and bring thoughts of her mother dying . . . like her father did."

Well able to imagine the child's fear of losing a remaining parent, especially at so young an age, Eleanor hurt for Maggie all the more.

The wind gusted, and Eleanor tugged the front of her coat closed. "Naomi and I will join you shortly. We need to pay Mrs. Malloy a visit to pick up another order of dresses, then stop by the bakery for any day-old bread Mr. Fitch may have. But we'll be there as soon as we can."

Marta and Elena linked arms, as was the custom among the German women, and headed down the street. Eleanor and Naomi continued on to the dress shop, which wasn't far from the old courthouse.

Fall was already giving way to winter, and though she customarily looked forward to the change in seasons, she worried about how these dear women and their children would keep warm.

Earlier in the week, she'd been to see her father but hadn't gone any farther than the doorway of his room. He hadn't even seen her. He'd been standing at the window, hand pressed against the pane when Nurse Smith had come along quietly beside her. *"It's not been a good day today, Miss Braddock,"* she'd whispered. *"You might wish to come back later this week."*

Sometimes Eleanor wondered if there would ever again be good days for her father.

She sneaked glances at Naomi walking beside her. "What they said about Maggie . . . Is that why you've been so tired lately?"

"It is no bother, Miss Braddock. You know how dear our Maggie is."

Eleanor nodded. "Perhaps . . . if you think she would, she could stay with me for a night or two. Or more, if that would help."

Naomi smiled. "You are a kind woman, Miss Braddock. But I believe Caleb and I can—"

Naomi's pace slowed, and a wary look came over her. Eleanor turned to see what she was staring at . . . and felt as though she'd tripped headlong from one world into another.

"Good day to you, Miss Braddock!"

Tongue-tied, it took Eleanor a moment to react. "Mr. Hockley! W-what a surprise to see you." Realizing that wasn't the warmest of welcomes, she tried again. "How are you today?"

"I am quite well, Miss Braddock. And you?"

"I am quite well also, thank you." If only she

could breathe past the knotted tangle at her midsection. She'd had dinner with him twice in as many weeks, but to see him out and about in the world—in *her* world—was jarring.

Remembering her manners, she made introductions, grateful when he tipped his hat to Naomi.

"Pleasure to meet you, Mrs. Lebenstein."

"You as well, Mr. Hockley."

Eleanor didn't miss Naomi's quizzical look. "Mrs. Lebenstein is not only a co-worker, Mr. Hockley, she's also a dear friend. She's been most instrumental in coordinating the meals for the widows and children. I couldn't be facilitating this without her."

Gratitude softened Naomi's gaze.

"Excellent to know that, Miss Braddock. It's wise to have a replacement trained and waiting in the wings."

Seeing Naomi look at her, Eleanor quickly moved to change the subject. "So what brings you into this part of town, Mr. Hockley?"

"Business, of course. Yours, actually."

"Mine?" Eleanor didn't even try to hide her surprise.

"Yes, I was at the old courthouse visiting with your architect, Mr. Geoffrey."

"You . . . *met* with Mr. Geoffrey?"

"Indeed. Nice fellow. Runs a tight ship. I like that."

"What were you meeting with him about?" Too late, she heard how insistent that had sounded.

But apparently, Mr. Hockley hadn't taken it as such.

"The building beside the old courthouse. The one he purchased last week."

"Mr. Geoffrey purchased a building?" Eleanor realized she kept repeating what he'd said, but she couldn't believe it. She knew the building. An old one of plank-wood construction. "For what purpose did he buy it?"

"Frankly, I didn't ask him. The building itself is worth very little. He told me it was the land he wanted. Something to do with the new home."

"I see." But Eleanor didn't *see* at all. Marcus hadn't mentioned one word of this to her. If she went over budget because of this . . .

Much to her relief, Mr. Hockley seemed as eager to be on his way as she was to send him, and she and Naomi continued to the dress shop around the corner.

It was all Eleanor could do not to march over to the new home right that minute and ask Marcus what on *earth* he thought he was doing purchasing land. But she couldn't leave all the errands to Naomi—who had sneaked more than one look in her direction in recent minutes.

Hoping to avoid that conversation for as long as possible, Eleanor opened the door to the dress shop, the bell jangling overhead.

"Miss Braddock, Mrs. Lebenstein . . ." Rebecca Malloy stepped from behind the counter, her smile communicating she was happy to see them. "Good day to you, ladies."

"Good day, Mrs. Malloy!" Eleanor withdrew the envelope from her reticule, doing her best to keep her frustration to herself. "We've stopped by to pick up the new order of dresses and"—she held out the payment—"to give you this."

Mrs. Malloy accepted the envelope, fingering it thoughtfully before looking back at Eleanor. "I can't thank you enough, Miss Braddock, for bringing me this work. Business was so slow for a while, I was afraid I would have to close my shop. But, thanks to you, my days are full and productive again. And word is spreading among the women on this side of town."

Eleanor briefly touched her hand. "It's we who are grateful to you, Mrs. Malloy."

"Yes," Naomi chimed in, opening her coat to show off her new dress. "It is so many years since I have a dress so nice."

Mrs. Malloy beamed, then held up a hand. "I have your next order ready. Give me a moment to wrap it, and I'll be right back."

As soon as Mrs. Malloy disappeared into the back room, Eleanor checked her chatelaine watch affixed to her waistband, hoping Marcus would still be at the old courthouse when she got there, and hearing Aunt Adelicia's voice so clearly in her head. *The league has been most generous, Eleanor. Please be mindful of that generosity and do not exceed the allocated budget.*

Eleanor let out a sigh.

"If you want to go now and speak with him, Miss

Braddock, I can manage the dresses on my own."

Seeing the knowing look on Naomi's face, Eleanor knew better than to try to pretend. "No, I'm fine. I'll stay and help. But if I go over budget on this building, Naomi . . ." She shook her head. "I can't let that happen. I simply can't."

"Mr. Geoffrey, he knows that. He is a man of business, *ja*?"

"*Ja*," Eleanor whispered. "*Und ein sehr guter.*" And a good one.

Naomi raised an approving eyebrow. "Your accent is improving."

Eleanor managed a smile, while realizing Naomi didn't understand how much Marcus had wanted to construct his own building instead of renovating the mayor's old hand-me-downs, as he'd off-handedly commented the other day.

"Mr. Geoffrey, he is also"—Naomi eyed her—"a friend to you, *ja*? A very . . . good friend."

Catching the lilt in Naomi's voice, Eleanor read meaning in her eyes. "No, no." She shook her head. "Mr. Geoffrey and I are simply friends, Naomi. Nothing more."

Naomi pursed her lips. "As my precious husband used to say, "*Beste Freunde machen die besten Liebhaber.*"

It took Eleanor a moment to translate what Naomi had said, but when she did—*Best friends make the best lovers*—her face went warm even as color heightened Naomi's cheeks. They both giggled, but Eleanor quickly sobered.

In light of her rapidly approaching future, she needed to correct her friend's misassumption. "It is not that way with Mr. Geoffrey and me. We *are* friends. *Just* friends."

Naomi's eyes flashed. "For now, maybe. But someday . . ."

"No," Eleanor said softly. "It can never be that way between us."

The light in Naomi's expression dimmed. "I am sorry to hear this. I have seen you together and thought . . . *hoped*"—she smiled—"that maybe there was . . . something more."

From nowhere, tears came, and Eleanor could do nothing to stop them.

"Oh, Miss Braddock . . ." Naomi's eyes widened. "Please forgive me. I have stepped over my place and—"

Eleanor reached into her pocket for the handkerchief, but seeing it only increased the ache in her chest. She blotted her cheeks, then fingered the faded embroidered flowers. So much of what she'd thought her life would be like hadn't turned out at all as she'd planned.

"No, you haven't stepped over your place," she whispered, the phrase endearing Naomi to her even more. "You are my friend." She needed to tell her the truth. But how? Eleanor glanced behind her toward the back room, making sure Mrs. Malloy wasn't on her way out. "Mr. Geoffrey is leaving to go back to Austria in June. After he finishes the home. And as for me . . ." She glanced again at the handkerchief in her grip. "Come June . . . I will marry Mr. Hockley."

The humor drained from Naomi's face. "*Nein . . .*" She looked out the window in the direction they'd come, then back at Eleanor. "The man we met? On the street? He is to be your—"

"Yes," Eleanor said, not wanting her to say the word aloud. "And after that time . . . I won't be working directly with the—"

Footsteps sounded behind them.

Eleanor quickly dabbed her cheeks, slipped the damp handkerchief back in her pocket, and turned, asking God, again, to take her life and not just make *something* of it. But make it what He wanted it to be.

Even if it wasn't what she would have chosen.

Marcus saw her coming in the door and groaned, not wanting to face the woman right now. Or anytime in the near future.

"Yoo-hoo, Mr. Geoffrey!" Miss Hillary Hightower waved a handkerchief in his direction, as though he were high on a mountaintop instead of standing ten feet in front of her.

He excused himself from the workers he was speaking with and met her halfway. But only to prevent her from coming farther inside. "Miss Hightower . . . Good day to you, madam." He held

561

up a hand. "Forgive me, but I must insist you remain in this area. Only workers are allowed beyond this point. For safety reasons." And also, in this particular instance, for his own sanity.

"How kind of you, Mr. Geoffrey, to think of my well-being."

Smiling, she peered at him from the corner of her eye, then dipped her head and traced a forefinger along the lace trim of her gown, drawing attention to her *décolletage*. So demure. So coy. So very contrived . . .

Marcus kept his eyes on hers. No telling how many times she'd stood before a mirror practicing that combination before adding it to her quiver.

"How may I be of service, madam?"

"I'm here on *official business,*" she said, her accent growing more pronounced. "I've been appointed by the league to be your . . . personal *liaison.*"

He blinked slowly. "To be my what?"

"Your liaison to the league. The board felt that with Miss Braddock being as busy as she is, you might benefit from having a more . . . intimate connection to the women of influence in this city."

"I see." Which he did. He also saw Eleanor striding through the door at that very moment.

He knew Eleanor well enough to know when she was upset, and judging by the displeasure in her expression, he gauged her to be right around . . . *livid.*

"Here is my address." Miss Hightower pressed a

calling card into his palm, her hand lingering around his. "Mother would appreciate the opportunity to speak with you at your earliest convenience about the interior design themes planned for this building. Since the league's name is associated with the project, we want to make certain the interior finishings reflect the splendor and taste of its benefactresses. And of course . . . I'll be there for dinner that night as well. So I'm certain we'll have time to—"

The young woman glanced over at Eleanor, who stopped just feet away, off to the side, and Marcus was certain he heard a layer of Hillary Hightower's Southern charm hit the floor with a *splat*.

Eleanor, however, looked only at him. Or glared, was more like it.

"Thank you, Miss Hightower," he said, "for the kind invitation from both you and your mother. My schedule is quite full at present, as I'm certain you realize." He indicated the building around them. "But I'll contact you at my earliest convenience. And will certainly let you know," he added when she started to speak again, "if I have any questions that a . . . *league liaison* might address."

"A league liaison?" Eleanor looked between them.

Miss Hightower—several inches shorter than Eleanor—drew herself to her full height, which made little difference by comparison.

"Yes, that's right, Miss Braddock." Miss Hightower twisted the handkerchief in her hands. "The board decided this morning that it would be of benefit to all for Mr. Geoffrey to have a designated go-between with the league board. Someone to not only answer questions he might have, but who will also lend counsel and approval for interior design plans."

Eleanor's eyes narrowed the slightest bit. "He already has such a person, Miss Hightower," she said evenly. "In me. If you'll recall, I was named chair of this project."

Miss Hightower laughed softly. "Yes, that may be. But upon further reflection, Miss Braddock, the *board* felt that someone more . . . closely focused on the league's purpose—someone who has a long-standing and distinguished family history in the city—should be appointed to assist as well. Especially since you seem quite consumed these days with the business of . . . *cooking* and such."

Marcus had never pictured Eleanor becoming physically violent, but the image of her and Miss Hightower having a good go of it wasn't altogether impossible to imagine. Nor was it completely without appeal. And without question, he knew which woman he would put his money on.

"Miss Hightower . . ." Eleanor's voice, true and strong, was framed in politeness. "Lest there be any confusion on the matter, this building is going to be a comfortable and functional home for widows and children. Not a showplace. And certainly not an extension of the league building."

Miss Hightower's smile thinned. "But we do

want the building to be attractive. Not simply . . . *plain* and ordinary. After all, Miss Braddock, there's nothing wrong with something being beautiful . . . is there?"

The young woman smoothed the front of her gown and glanced in Marcus's direction. But his attention was drawn to Eleanor, whose chin lifted the slightest bit. He smiled to himself, recognizing that look.

"No, Miss Hightower, there's nothing wrong with something being beautiful. Unless that is all the object has to recommend it. If that's the case, then indeed, its beauty is rather diminished by the discovery, would you not agree?"

Miss Hightower's lips firmed. "Well, I must be going." She curtsied in Marcus's direction. "Good day to you both. Mr. Geoffrey, do be in touch."

Miss Hightower took her leave, and no sooner did the door close behind her than Eleanor stepped forward, the displeasure in her expression having deepened. He liked the color of her eyes when she was riled. They went the shade of burnt umber, and the gold flecks in them resembled sparks from a flame.

"You purchased a building, Marcus? And *land?* Without speaking to me about it first?"

Able to guess from whom she'd so quickly heard the news, he refused to be drawn in so easily. "Good afternoon, Eleanor. How are you today?"

His desire to be in her company hadn't diminished in the least since learning of her betrothal, so he had purposefully limited their time together. But it didn't mean he didn't still think about her. Constantly.

She leveled a stare. "Good afternoon, Marcus. You've apparently purchased—"

"No need to repeat yourself. I heard you the first time. And yes, I did."

"And did you purchase the building and land with the intention of it being part of the home?"

"Absolutely, madam."

Her face went three shades of red. "But why?" She moved closer, her voice lowering. "When you know we *can't* go over budget. Every penny is already allocated. Your decision to do this without speaking to me was impulsive and thoughtless and—"

"I paid for the land myself, Eleanor."

She froze, mouth half open, her pretty little tongue loaded with words that had nowhere to go. She stared. Then blinked. Once, twice. "You . . . paid for it yourself? With your own money?"

"That's right."

"But . . ." She searched his eyes. "Why would you do that?"

"Because I needed the land."

"For what purpose?"

"One that I deem important. And when the time is right, I will tell you about it."

"But you said it's for the home."

"It is."

She blew out a breath. "You're purposefully being obtuse, Marcus."

He smiled. "Without question, Eleanor."

At that, the tiniest glimmer of remorse crept across her expression, even as a streak of stubborn pride—something he was well acquainted with himself—drew her shoulders back. "Please forgive my mistaken assumption. I was wrong. And what I said about you being—"

"Thoughtless? Impulsive?"

She grimaced. "That was mean, wasn't it?"

"It wounded me to the core."

Laughter bubbled up her throat. "Somehow, I doubt that."

He staggered back a step, feigning a dagger to the heart, which further encouraged her laughter. *Oh, how he missed her.*

The flowers on the potato plants had started wilting two days ago. It was time to harvest them, to see if this latest graft had taken. But he hadn't dug them up yet because he'd wanted her there with him. Yet it didn't seem right to ask her now. And apparently, she'd forgotten about it anyway. Which was probably for the best.

He gave her a quick tour of what his crews had accomplished that day, ran some ideas by her for the foyer—which, to his delight, she agreed with enthusiastically—and walked her back to the door.

Hand on the latch, she turned. "I know you're busy, Marcus, but . . . have you given any more thought to grafting potatoes? It would mean so much if you could just try. Even if it doesn't work. I'll do whatever I can to help you. Call you names . . . question your loyalty . . ." The smile she gave him shot straight through to the heart.

Try as he might, he couldn't imagine her with Lawrence Hockley. Even more, he couldn't imagine returning to Austria . . . and never seeing her again.

"Sunday afternoon," he said quietly. "I'll meet you in the conservatory."

"I'll bring a treat."

"I'll bring a tongue depressor."

Standing at the window, he watched her until she turned the corner a couple of blocks down. He'd been right about her early on. She was going to be a good friend. The best friend he'd ever had.

Early Friday morning, Marcus met Caleb in front of the bakery, as he did on occasion. The aroma of warm, yeasty dough and strong brewed coffee greeted them as they walked inside.

"*Guten Morgen*, Marcus!" Fitch called from behind the counter. "*Guten Morgen*, Caleb!"

"*Guten Morgen*, Fitch," they answered in unison, then joined the queue.

"What do you have there?" Marcus gestured to a notebook Caleb carried. It looked similar to one he used at work.

"Miss Braddock asked my *Mutter* to write down the names of all the women and children who come for dinner. And where they live in town and their birthdays. But last night, Maggie spilled her drink on it."

Caleb opened the notebook and held it up. The pages inside appeared legible, for the most part, but crinkled.

"I told *Mutter* I would copy it for her again before tonight."

Marcus gave the boy's head a rub. "You're a good son, Caleb."

The boy grinned.

Marcus wondered how he'd managed all the day-to-day details involved in his job without Caleb. The boy knew the name of every man on each crew, and what his specialty was. He made note of inventory that was low or of tools that were worn or broken. He was a quick learner and a natural at reading design sketches. He could drive a nail straight as any man Marcus had ever worked with. Even though, with the boy's slender build, it took a few more hits to get the job done.

Marcus felt an unexpected tug of emotion and looked up at Fitch pouring coffee behind the counter. He would miss so much about this country. Never would he have guessed that people who were once strangers could become so important to him. So much a part of his life.

It came their turn, and he placed his and Caleb's standing order with Mrs. Fitch.

She nodded. "As well as the order you pick up every Friday morning?"

"Yes, madam. That is correct."

He paid, then stepped off to the side.

"Hot coffee, strong and black," Fitch said a moment later, handing him a full mug. "And another hot coffee, strong and black." Then he winked at Caleb, leaning close. "With lots of cream and sugar," he whispered.

The boy grinned as Fitch handed him a mug identical to Marcus's. "Thank you, sir."

Fitch grabbed his own cup he always kept off to the side. "How goes the renovation, Marcus?"

"Quite well, so far. The old courthouse has better bones than I initially thought." Marcus shot Caleb a look. "But don't tell Miss Braddock I said that. I don't want her to say, 'I told you so.' "

Caleb grinned.

Fitch looked at him over the rim of his cup. "You think it's gonna turn out like you want it to?"

Marcus saw the real question his friend was asking. Fitch knew him well. The man had seen him bid on job after job for new construction, only to be passed over. And instead, have to settle for taking something old and trying to breathe new life into it.

"Actually . . ." Marcus sipped his coffee. "I think it is. And better than I thought it would."

With a thoughtful nod, Fitch disappeared into the back, then returned with two large baskets of doughnuts and placed them on the counter. "Don't know where your crews manage to put all these, but the missus and I sure appreciate your regular business."

Marcus glanced at the queue already backed up to the door again. "As if you need more business." He drained his mug and picked up the baskets.

Fitch grinned. "I'm grateful for it all the same. Along with the chance to do what I enjoy." He grabbed a nearby rag and wiped a coffee ring from the counter. "Work is good for a man. Gives him purpose. Reminds him there's a lot more to life and living than just tending his own self."

Later, at the old courthouse, after Caleb had distributed the doughnuts—the boy knowing each man's favorite—Marcus thought again of what Fitch had said about work, and how Fitch was grateful to be doing something he enjoyed.

Marcus looked around at the exposed wooden beams and framed walls absent their plaster, at the stacks of fresh-cut plank wood and piles of Tennessee limestone set to frame the fireplaces, and he thought about how much he enjoyed doing what he was doing right now.

Building a widows' and children's home certainly wasn't anything he'd ever aspired to. Nor would anyone ever look at this building and stop on the street to stare. But it felt right—him being right where he was. Doing exactly what he was doing. And somehow he knew—despite the lack of divine revelation or prickles up the back of his neck—that what he was doing would stand the test of time. Whether or not this building was still standing a hundred years from now or not.

He grabbed his notebook and pen and headed

upstairs to meet with Callahan. But when he opened it, he realized he'd grabbed Caleb's notebook by mistake. As he closed it, a name caught his eye. At the very top of the page. He grinned.

Then followed the line across to the columns containing each woman's address and date of birth, and made special note of February twenty-first.

That afternoon, Marcus visited the Deed and Title Office in the current courthouse, three doors down from the mayor's office. Just passing by Augustus Adler's office felt like a knife in the gut. Marcus hadn't seen the man in weeks, and wanted to keep it that way.

True to Lawrence Hockley's statement days earlier, the clerk had the paper work ready for him.

"Mr. Geoffrey, if you'll just sign right here, sir. This confirms your receipt of the document."

Marcus did as the clerk instructed, then a minute later in the hallway, he stared at the official deed. He now owned a piece of America. Something he'd never expected to own.

He folded the document and slipped it inside his coat pocket. Now, to tear down the old plank-wood building standing—or leaning—on the site, and begin construction on the—

"Well, well . . . if it's not the builder of heretofore unseen designs."

Recognizing the caustic voice behind him, Marcus knew it would be best if he simply walked on and left well enough alone. But he couldn't.

He turned. "Mayor Adler . . ." This was one person in America he *wouldn't* miss.

"Tell me, Mr. Geoffrey . . . what brings you back to this fine *new* courthouse? According to newspaper accounts, you're spending your time across town renovating the old one to be a . . . widows' and children's home, I believe?" Adler's smile said he found the fact amusing. "Not exactly what you had in mind when you first arrived in my fair city, is it, Mr. Geoffrey?"

Marcus itched to wipe the smug look off the man's face.

"I'm certain you've heard," the mayor continued, his tone even more pompous than usual. "We're making excellent progress on the new opera house. Reporters from New York, Boston, and Philadelphia have all penned stories about the building, and have been quite profuse in their praise. They're already touting Nashville as the *musical city of the South.*"

The pleasure of what Marcus was about to say was the only thing that enabled him to smile. "That's good to hear, sir. I take it, then, that your son finally determined how to build the proper supports to sustain the balcony? So he could explain it to the reporter?"

Familiar blotches of red crept up the man's neck. "Careful, Mr. Geoffrey. Renovations have paper work that can go astray, delaying the project for months. If not burying it for years."

Oh, how different this exchange would be if we

were in Austria, Mr. Mayor. As it was, Marcus realized he wasn't completely without defense. "Yes, sir, you do that." He smiled. "And I'll send one Mrs. Agnetta Hanson Hightower, a leading benefactress of the renovation, to speak with you herself. And if that doesn't work"—he leaned closer—"I'll send her daughter too."

Carrying the image of the mayor's slack-jaw expression, Marcus strode down the hallway and was still smiling when he reached the street.

He briefly stopped by the mercantile to check on the order he'd placed for the kitchen ranges and worktables. The kitchen in "the home," as Eleanor and others now referred to it, wouldn't be ready for some time. He'd temporarily boarded up the main entrance and instructed workers to use the door at the back of the building when they needed to access the area. He wanted the new kitchen to be a surprise for Eleanor.

He stopped by the boardinghouse for a late lunch. He hadn't taken time that morning to read the newspaper, so he enjoyed the prospect of doing so. Turning to the second page—not three bites into his meal—he was drawn to a column heading. His heart stuttered a painful rhythm as the words sank in.

Within minutes, he was at the telegraph office, scrawling a message and shoving it across the counter. *"Kontaktieren Sie diesen Mann*—" Seeing the clerk's confusion, he started again. "Wire this man in Boston. Relay to him the message written below. Tell him to wire it to the international address he has on file. *Immediately*."

The clerk looked at the paper then back at him. "This is gonna cost a small—"

Marcus slammed a twenty-dollar note on the counter. "Just send it. *Please*."

As the *click-click-click* of the telegraph spirited his words over miles of wire, for the first time in months, his heart truly turned toward home. Russia had done worse than mere posturing this time. They'd crossed a line, and Austria was at war.

"You have every right to be angry with me, Eleanor. But if what I've told you is true, if the newspaper article is correct"—Marcus felt even worse than he'd thought he would at giving Eleanor the news—"then I have no choice but to leave."

A score of emotions played across her face—first surprise, then disbelief, which swiftly gave way to concern, then disappointment. He hated the prospect of breaking his promise to her and leaving the renovation unfinished. But mostly . . .

Mostly he hated leaving *them* and what they might have been—or what he'd wanted them to be—unfinished.

"War," she whispered, the word heavy even when spoken that softly. "I'm so sorry, Marcus."

He looked at her in the gray half-light of the

propagating room, a chilly Sunday afternoon rain gently pelting the fogged glass panes of the conservatory. The temperature outside had fallen overnight but did nothing to disturb the perpetual summer of the greenhouse.

"So . . . you're saying you have to leave . . . much sooner than you planned?"

"I'm saying it's a possibility. I won't know for certain until I hear from my father, or my uncle. I sent a telegram to them Friday. But still . . . no word."

She nodded. "This is only the second time you've spoken of your father to me. Or of your uncle. What business is your father in?"

He fingered one of the wilted flowers of the potato plants on the table between them, the conversation getting dangerously close to home. "He's in government."

Her eyes widened. "That sounds exciting."

"And I assure you it's not."

She frowned and started to say something else, but he beat her to it.

"I suppose the reason I don't mention them more often is because . . . I'm not close to either of them. I never have been."

"Not like you were with your brother."

The tenderness in her voice touched him.

"Losing Rutger was like losing the last of my family. First my grandfather, then my mother . . . then my brother. Now they're all gone."

The compassion in her eyes threatened to loosen

his tongue further. He should've left well enough alone when it came to her comment about his father and uncle. But he'd been alone within himself for so long, it felt good to talk to someone—no, to talk to *her*—about home. Or what used to be home.

Still, he realized he was walking a fine line. The *pitter-pat* of rain grew louder on the glass panes overhead.

"Your aunt was kind enough to let me read her recent issues of newspapers from other cities in this country, as well as ones she receives from Europe."

Eleanor smiled. "I think she gets half a dozen papers per day. Did you learn anything new?"

"Not much. The articles that did include mention of it did so without using the term *war*. They referred to it as *politically based upheaval* or *escalation of unrest*."

"Perhaps that's all it is, then. Maybe the journalist here in Nashville purposefully chose to present the news in a more . . . sensational manner." She gave him a hopeful look. "It's not as though he hasn't done that before."

He appreciated her outlook, and her desire to put him at ease. "Admittedly, that thought did cross my mind."

"Will you fight? If it comes to that?"

Her question caught him off guard. But not because he didn't know the answer.

"Yes, I would."

The gray of storm clouds overhead seemed to settle around her. "I've seen war," she whispered.

"Enough to last a thousand lifetimes." She looked down at her hands laced together at her waist. "I was a volunteer in the surgical tents . . . near the battlefields. In the recent war."

A moment passed before she spoke again.

She lifted her head. "I've never tried to imagine a world without God. This one seems hard enough as it is." Her laugh held no humor. "But in those moments . . ." She firmed her jaw. "Caring for the wounded, trying to comfort the dying . . ."

Her eyes closed, and he knew firsthand the horrors she must have lived through, and was reliving again. Savagery no woman should ever have to witness, much less carry inside her.

Finally, she looked at him again. "Promise me, Marcus . . . you'll be careful."

He'd thought she would be angry with him over the possibility of his leaving before the renovation was finished, but her first concern was for his safety. It took restraint he didn't know he had to resist circling the table and taking her in his arms. Not in order to kiss her—though he'd welcome that opportunity, had he the right—but to hold her. To chase away the pain in her eyes and the loss she still obviously felt from that time in her life. *God, why did you put this woman in my life . . . if I can't have her?*

The question came so clearly within him, he was almost surprised she hadn't heard it too.

"I promise," he whispered. "I'll be careful. *If* it comes to that."

Her own transparency inspired his, and he found himself wanting to tell her the truth—about who he was, the kind of man he'd been in the past as opposed to who he was now, largely because of knowing her. But the better part of him—or at least the *greater* part—knew better.

Best he leave America—and her—as the man she knew and respected, rather than as the Archduke of the House of Habsburg, whom he knew she wouldn't respect.

He looked down at the potato plants, then back at her, and rallied a change of mood. "Now, Miss Braddock, you asked about grafting potatoes, did you not?"

Following his lead, she smiled. And, in part, the gloom fell away.

"I certainly did, Mr. Geoffrey. And . . ." She walked to where she'd laid a cloth-covered dish and a gunnysack. From the latter, she withdrew a pair of gloves. "I found these at the mercantile. They're a little big." She tried them on, demonstrating. "But they'll work for grafting, I think."

He laughed. "So you've come prepared, have you?"

"Indeed, sir." She held out gloved hands as proof.

"Have you ever planted potatoes before?"

She paused, then shook her head.

"Have you ever planted *anything* before?"

She frowned at him, deservedly so. "I'll have you know that my father"—she faltered, but only for an instant—"has planted many a vegetable garden in his life." She glanced at the gloves again, an embarrassed smile tipping her mouth. "And I, in turn, have sat and read to him for hours on end as he did."

Able to imagine the scene only too well, Marcus laughed hard, glad when she did too. "Well, that explains why you didn't recognize the plants on the table before you."

She looked down, then peered up again. He could see her mind working.

"Those are potato plants?"

"They are."

"And . . . I'm assuming you planted them?"

He nodded.

"But judging by their size, and how they're wilting, I'm guessing you did this long before—"

"I've been grafting far more than just flowers and . . . pink roses for your aunt. I've been working with potato plants for years, Eleanor. And have been collaborating with the botanist I told you about, Luther Burbank, in Boston, who is doing the very same. But before you get excited," he said, already seeing a gleam slip into her eyes, "we have had very little success. The potatoes graft well enough, but none of the combinations have yielded the desired results."

The momentary gleam in her eyes faded. "And you're thinking this time will be no different."

"Not at all. I'm always hopeful that the next time will prove fruitful. If I didn't have that hope, I wouldn't keep trying."

"Of course," she said, apology in her tone. "So . . ." Gloved hands on hips, she stepped forward, looking at him square on. "Where do we begin?"

He held up his bare hands. "We simply start digging. I'll walk you through the first one."

With exuberance, she removed the gloves, tossed them aside, and joined him by the table.

Though not wanting to get ahead of himself, Marcus couldn't deny his own excitement. What if—after such a long time—*this* was the moment he'd been waiting for? And Eleanor was there to share it with him.

"See how I've hilled up the soil around the stem?"

Watching where Marcus pointed, Eleanor nodded while pushing up her sleeves. She wanted to do this right. And to think he'd already been working on grafting potatoes for years . . .

She'd respected his skills before. But now she admired him even more.

"Start first by pulling the soil away from the plant."

She did as he instructed, smoothing it down.

"Good. Now work the plant out of the soil a little, just to loosen things up."

Nervous, Eleanor gave the stem a slight tug.

He laughed. "A little harder than that."

She gripped it and pulled—and the stem lifted, bringing a portion of the root with it.

"Perfect!" He leaned closer, looking more like a boy at Christmas than a botanist or architect.

"Now, take your hand, like this"—he demonstrated, fingers splayed, slightly curled—"and go right down into the soil by the stem."

"Like this?" She slowly pushed her hand down until the cool soil enveloped it.

"Just move your fingers around, nice and gentle. You'll feel it."

She appreciated his enthusiasm and that he'd allowed her to stay and help. Especially after the difficult conversation they'd just had. His leaving early was one thing. But leaving to go fight in a—

"I feel something, Marcus!" She wrapped her fingers around the cool lump, then looked at him for what to do next.

"Simply pull, twisting at the same time, and it should come up—"

She pulled the potato from the deep-sided trough and held the dirt-encased little tuber out to him. But he shook his head, his gaze never leaving her hand.

"Now gently rub the dirt away. Not too hard because you don't want to disturb the skin."

With her clean hand, Eleanor did as he said, trying to brush away the soil, but . . . "I can't get the dirt to come off."

She laid the potato in his palm, and he looked at it up close. Then he reached into the soil, just as she had done, and pulled out another potato, and another, and another, and another.

By the time he'd harvested the first trough, she knew. He didn't have to say anything. The collection of odd-shaped, blemished little tubers piled on the table beside them said it all.

Feeling his disappointment, and sharing it, Eleanor went to work on the second trough. Which yielded the same results.

"I'm sorry, Marcus."

He sighed, wiping his hands on a rag. "So am I."

"What do we do now?" she asked softly.

"We"—his smile was halfhearted at best—"will clean ourselves up and enjoy your latest culinary masterpiece."

"No . . ." She gestured toward the plants. "I meant about the potatoes. You're not giving up." She looked at him. "Are you?"

"No." He exhaled again. "But with the renovation and the possibility of leaving, I—"

"I'll help you. In whatever way I can."

This time his smile was one she recognized.

"Thank you, Eleanor. Before trying another graft, I'll take a brief hiatus, study my notes again, and send my findings to Luther Burbank. Who knows, maybe he's found something that might help us both."

Side by side, they washed their hands in a barrel behind the conservatory, the water ice-cold. Back inside, Eleanor shivered, squeezing her hands to encourage the blood flow.

"What did you make this time?" He started to lift the cloth, but she pretended she was going to smack his hand.

"No peeking!" She laughed at his bewildered look. "This is a special treat."

"Aren't they all?"

"You're very kind, Mr. Geoffrey. But this one has proven quite the challenge. This is my seventh attempt."

He looked at her. "What happened to the other six?"

"You don't want to know." She positioned the dish in front of him. "Are you ready?"

"Whatever it is, I'm certain I'll enjoy it."

She smiled, then whipped the cloth back. *"Ta da!"*

"A strudel!"

"An *apple* strudel," she corrected, reaching for the knife and cutting him a slice. "I remember what you and Caleb said."

Marcus frowned. "What did we say?"

She handed him a piece on a cloth napkin, trying for her best German accent. "That nothing is as *gut* as your *Mutter*'s strudel."

He laughed, but the way he looked at her reminded her that she was a woman engaged to another man. No matter that the other man wasn't the one she loved. Guilt chided her conscience, and she looked away, at the exact same moment he did.

Marcus tasted the strudel, chewed for a moment, and then nodded. "It's very good."

But she knew him better than that. "What's wrong with it?"

"Nothing's wrong with it. It's fine."

"Fine? I've worked on this for hours, made it seven times, and all it's worth is fine?"

"It's good, Eleanor. It's simply . . ." He hesitated, remorse in his expression.

"Not your *Mutter*'s strudel?"

He shook his head. "But it means a great deal to me that you made this for me. *Danke . . . mein lieber Freund.*"

Eleanor smiled her return thanks, then quickly busied herself with putting things away. What he'd said to her was kind, and appropriate. *Thank you, my dear friend.* So why did it hurt so much?

She heard him behind her and turned. He was pulling up each of the potato plants, roots and all, one by one, then dumping them into a bucket. Wordlessly, she joined him.

"You don't have to do this, Eleanor. Your hands are going to get all—"

She'd already pulled up two plants and held them up as if saying, *"Too late."*

He got another bucket, and silently they worked, one on each trough, pulling and dumping. She occasionally unearthed another potato and looked at it carefully before discarding it, just in case.

She pulled the last plant and pressed it down into the overfull bucket when something caught her eye. She knelt down for a closer look. A shiny little round thing. On one of the vines. "Marcus . . . what is this?"

"What is what?" he said from one aisle over.

"What is this little . . . *ball* on one of the plants?"

He peered over the trough.

Not wanting to damage whatever it was, Eleanor retrieved the entire vine and stood to show him. "It's right here." She pointed.

He frowned and laid his bucket aside. "It looks like a seedball. But that's not possible. The Early Rose variety doesn't produce seedballs."

He reached for the vine—and the little ball dropped. And rolled. In her direction, from the faint sound of it.

They stared at each other, and she sensed his excitement by the look on his face. Goose flesh rose on her arms.

"Don't . . . move, Eleanor."

Knowing what he meant, she kept her feet perfectly still. But she looked down, trying to find it. "Where do you think it went?"

Already he was on his knees searching. Slowly, meticulously running his hands over the floor. He crawled under one table, then the next. She wished the sun would come out so he could see better. He was beside her when he stilled.

His breath left him. And tears rose to her eyes.

He stood, cradling the seedball that looked especially tiny in *his* hand. And though he didn't say a word, she read the fire of possibility in his eyes and knew that—if Marcus Geoffrey was given a choice—any possibility of his taking a *brief hiatus* was long gone.

Moments later, Eleanor raced up the front steps of the mansion to the shelter of the porch. She shook the droplets of rain from her parasol, brushed them from her skirt, and stepped inside the entrance hall. Heart heavy and eager for the privacy of her bedroom, she needed time, and quiet, to sort out what Marcus had told her, along with the jumble of her thoughts.

"Eleanor . . . I'd like a word with you, please."

She winced, in no mood for company. Yet she knew better than to refuse her aunt.

She continued around the corner in the direction the voice had come, and found her aunt in the small study, staring out the front window.

"Good afternoon . . ." Eleanor decided not to sit, hoping the visit would be brief. "Enjoying this lovely rain?"

Slowly Aunt Adelicia turned to face her. "Be careful, Eleanor," she said, her tone not the least gentle.

Eleanor stared, feeling as though she'd walked into the middle of a conversation. "I'm afraid I don't know what you mean."

Aunt Adelicia turned and looked back out the window, then at her again. A calculated move, one that took Eleanor only seconds to follow before it dawned on her. Her aunt had watched her hurrying back from the conservatory. And suddenly the pieces fell into place.

"I was simply visiting with Mar—" Eleanor smiled to cover the social misstep. "*Mr.* Geoffrey. He and I are friends, Aunt." Seeing the arch of a dark eyebrow, she added, "Good friends, but only friends."

"Trust my counsel on this, Eleanor. . . . Men are never *good* friends with a woman unless there's something else at play."

Affronted by the remark, and the insinuation, Eleanor forced a laugh. "He's not like that. He's . . . different."

Her aunt's mouth curved in a way that made Eleanor feel like a foolish little child, and—whether roused by the conversation with Marcus, or the stark memories of war, or perhaps the wearing concern about her father, or her utter lack of desire for Lawrence Hockley—her temper rose to compensate.

"I'm telling you, Aunt Adelicia . . . we are *only* friends."

"And *you* are an engaged woman." Despite the directness of her tone, her aunt's voice remained controlled. "Betrothed to one of the most prominent men in the city of Nashville."

"I'm aware of that."

"You have accepted Mr. Hockley's offer of marriage."

"*Again,* Aunt"—a rush of heat filled Eleanor's chest—"I am not ignorant of this fact."

"Then why do you persist in spending time with another man?"

"Your questioning is absurd," Eleanor said beneath her breath. And yet, her own conscience silently pressed the question. Hadn't she—just a while earlier—felt a prick of warning when Marcus had looked at her?

Not wanting her aunt to see she'd struck a chord, Eleanor lowered her eyes. The distant drum of rain on the roof filled the tense space between them.

"Some choices in life, Eleanor, you only get to make once. You *think* there will be other opportunities, but they never come."

Eleanor lifted her gaze. "Don't you think a woman like me knows about choices that never come?"

Aunt Adelicia blinked, her expression showing the barest hint of surprise.

"The only reason I'm marrying Lawrence Hockley is because of you."

"The *reason* you are marrying Lawrence Hockley is because you love your father, Eleanor. And you realize it's the right thing to do. For him and for you." Aunt Adelicia moved closer. "People of integrity do the right thing. No matter how difficult. No matter the cost to them personally. And everything comes with a cost, Eleanor. Don't let anyone ever tell you differently."

The room grew quiet.

Eleanor looked out the front window in the direction of the conservatory, then back at her aunt. "You say some choices come only once. It's the same with our lives. We're only given this one. I simply wish I could live mine the way I choose —not the way others choose for me."

A muscle twitched in her aunt's delicate jawline. "I trust that will be your last word on this subject."

Eleanor took a deep breath, her lungs feeling deprived of air and her spirit of strength. She crossed to the door.

"Eleanor."

She turned.

"Mr. Hockley has requested a meeting with Dr. Cheatham about your dowry. That conversation will take place two weeks hence."

The comment landed like a blow to her midsection. Her aunt's intention, no doubt.

Torn between the compulsion to apologize and the urge to continue with the litany of reasons she shouldn't marry Lawrence Hockley, Eleanor left the room.

Eleanor opened the door to the mercantile and stepped inside, grateful to be out of December's chill and cold. Three weeks had come and gone, and *still* no word from Marcus's father or uncle. She knew worrying about the situation wouldn't change a thing, but that didn't keep her from testing the theory.

Thinking about Marcus going to war . . . She would miss him terribly in any case, but his leaving under that condition would make it far worse.

She made her way down the center aisle toward the glass containers lining the shelves on the back wall, her thoughts careening like a runaway train. If he did have to leave soon, and he couldn't finish the renovation, then who would? And what if his replacement wanted to charge more than the original bid?

Then there was the building about which he was

being so secretive. She'd tried to get more information from him, but he remained tight-lipped. The crews had torn down the old plank-wood building the week before, and had begun laying brick. But she had no idea of Marcus's plan.

"He's in government," he'd said about his father. The more she'd considered his response, the more it made sense that Marcus hailed from an important family. The manner in which he carried himself. His education. She pictured Marcus some twenty years older and fancied his father resembling that image. A very handsome man, indeed.

"Miss Braddock, how may I help you today?"

The girl, Mr. Mulholland's youngest—thirteen, maybe fourteen years old, Eleanor thought—had her father's businesslike manner about her.

"I'd like a bag of peppermint sugar sticks, please."

"Oh, I'm sorry, but a gentleman came in not an hour ago and bought every last one. What about another confection? Ginger drops, perhaps? We also have licorice." She pointed. "Or maybe a bag of penny candies?"

Eleanor sighed. She'd wanted to take her father his favorite. She scanned the containers. "I'll have a bag of lemon drops, please."

Back outside, she walked to the corner where Armstead had agreed to meet her. And there he was, right on time.

As Armstead guided the carriage through the city, Eleanor watched *life* pass by outside the window—all the different people, coming and going, living their lives. *How does God keep up with us all?*

And yet she trusted that, somehow, He did.

With Thanksgiving behind them, Christmas only two weeks away, and the renovation well under way, she had more tasks on her list than hours in each day to complete them.

Yet as the weeks passed, she grew more certain that her work with the widows and children was what she was meant to do. So why, given that certainty, did she feel so at odds in every other area?

What she wouldn't give for someone to tell her that everything was going to be all right.

Twice a week she went to the asylum. But like some no-account lurker, she kept to the hallway, fearing what would happen if her father saw her again.

Only once had she ventured inside his room since that day he hadn't known her. He was asleep in his chair, and she'd sat for a full half hour, watching him, loving him for the father he'd once been, and clinging to the hope that, one day, he would open his eyes and know her again.

Looming on the corner ahead, a large, prestigious, redbrick building drew her attention. The Bank of Nashville. She knew she should view the building—and the president somewhere within—as an answer to prayer.

But whenever she was with Lawrence Hockley, she either wanted to shake the man senseless until he realized she was there—with a *voice* and an *opinion*—or just shake him senseless and be done with it. Yet Lawrence seemed oblivious to her frustration.

She leaned her head back against the velvet cushion, willing the steady jostle of the carriage to soothe her nerves.

She'd heard more than one wife speak about her husband being in the same room, and the wife saying something, yet the man claiming never to have heard. Eleanor knew now how those women felt. And yet, she also didn't.

Because she and Lawrence Hockley weren't yet married, and they certainly weren't living together as husband and wife—a thought that caused the knot in the pit of her stomach to graduate to a dull ache in the center of her chest.

The recent conversation with her aunt returned in full voice, but she silenced it.

If only there was a way for her to provide for her father's care without going through with this marriage. . . .

The carriage slowed, and she opened her eyes.

The asylum itself no longer held the foreboding quality it once had. But she still wasn't eager for anyone to know her father was there. Especially Marcus.

That day in the conservatory when she and Marcus had reviewed the bids for the home, she'd been tempted to tell him about her father. But considering what he'd said about the asylum early on, and knowing he was leaving, she'd decided it best to leave things as they were.

Still . . . she'd spoken the truth that day when she'd told him her father would have enjoyed knowing him.

An orderly allowed her entrance, and she followed him on the familiar route, bag of lemon drops in hand. When she reached her father's room, she found his door partially open—and heard his voice.

She peeked around the corner.

Seated in his chair, her father was reading. Aloud. Like they used to do together. Wanting to see if anyone was with him, she gave the door a gentle push—and the hinges, once so amiable, betrayed her with a loud creak.

His head whipped in her direction, and Eleanor froze, not wanting to relive what had happened on that awful, awful day. Yet, she missed him so much.

He stared at her over the rim of his glasses.

She stepped into the room, tentative, as though testing to make sure the floor would hold. "Hello," she said softly.

No response.

The bag of candy crinkled in her grip, and he looked down at it, then back up at her.

"Is that for me?" he asked, his tone more hopeful than cautious.

"Yes." She chanced a smile. "It is."

She moved closer and handed it to him, but he didn't look at the bag. He just kept looking at her. She edged toward the chair opposite his, afraid any sudden movement might trigger a reaction.

"Would you mind"—she motioned behind her—"if I sit down so we can—"

"*No!* You can't sit there!"

Eleanor hastened a backward step and nearly tripped in the process, taking the frustration in his voice as a warning.

"My *friend* is sitting there. We're reading a book together."

Heart thudding, she looked at the empty chair, then back at her father. He sounded so logical, so normal. So like his old self. And yet, the chair . . . *was* empty. But what was worse, it was clear he didn't recognize her. His own daughter. She searched his gaze, hoping, praying, willing him to remember. But . . .

She detected not the slightest trace of comprehension.

Tears welled in her throat. Her chin shook. "I'm sorry," she whispered, backing toward the door, her father's face blurring in her vision. "I didn't realize that your friend—"

"Eleanor . . ."

She stilled at the voice behind her, knowing it so well. But also knowing . . . the owner of that voice didn't belong in this part of her world. Her mind spinning, working to think of a way to explain all this to him, she turned—and saw him holding two cups of coffee.

She looked from the coffee back to him. "Marcus?"

"I can explain," he said softly.

She exhaled, remembering not only what her father had said a moment earlier, but weeks ago as well. "You're . . . the *friend?*"

Marcus just smiled.

"But . . ." She shook her head. "He said he was reading to someone, and . . . when I saw the empty chair, I thought . . ." She briefly closed her eyes. "So . . . my father's not—"

"No. At least, not in that regard, Eleanor." He glanced beyond her to her father, who was ferreting through the bag of lemon drops. "Come," he whispered. "Allow me to reintroduce you to someone very special."

The tenderness in his tone, the confidence in his manner, his utter lack of hesitance, gave Eleanor strength in that moment she would never have had on her own.

She followed him back to stand before her father. Marcus placed the coffee on the table—beside a bag of peppermint sugar sticks—then held out his hand to her.

It felt warm and sure around hers.

"Theodore?" Marcus said quietly.

Her father looked up, then glanced between the two of them.

"I'd like you to meet a very dear friend of mine." Marcus squeezed her hand. "Her name . . ."

Eleanor braced for her father's reaction. *Lord, please, please . . .*

". . . is Ellie."

Hearing that name from Marcus was nearly her

undoing. Her father peered up, a frown forming, and she felt the air being siphoned from the room.

Then he smiled, his brown eyes warm and caring. "Nice to meet you, Ellie." He held out the bag of candy. "Care for a lemon drop?"

Marcus stood outside the old courthouse on Christmas Day, welcoming the women and children arriving for the noon dinner and doing his best to seem "of good cheer."

"Merry Christmas, Mr. Geoffrey!"

"*Frohe Weihnachten*, Herr Geoffrey!"

He returned their greetings, but since losing his mother and grandfather—and especially with Rutger so recently gone—he wasn't particularly fond of this holiday. It only served to remind him that the family members he'd loved most were gone. And that the people he cared about so deeply now—he looked inside to see Eleanor greeting the new arrivals—would also soon be gone from his life.

Still no word from his father or uncle, which concerned him, yet also gave him hope. The last mention in a newspaper had been a week ago, and included the words "continued unrest." Surely if the situation in Austria were dire, his father would have found a way to get word to him.

At least that's what Marcus told himself in the absence of news.

Even his communication with the baroness had fallen off. He hadn't received a letter from her in nearly two weeks. But he wasn't complaining on that count.

Aromas of turkey and ham and other food both savory and sweet wafted toward him from inside, causing his mouth to water. Familiar strains of music drifted to him, but familiar only in the sense that he'd heard *the music* before on the streets. Not on any streets in Boston or New York, however. This sound was distinctly Nashville.

Eleanor said she'd hired the former soldiers to play for the event after hearing them on the street herself. The group of men played the banjos and violin—or fiddle, as one man called it—as if the instruments were born to them. Although the tunes weren't any Marcus recognized—and were *far* from those of Vienna's own proud son, Wolfgang Amadeus Mozart—they did have a certain charm, and a way of getting inside a person.

He thought about Mayor Adler's comment from months back and doubted, with this type of music so engrained among the people of this region, that Nashville would ever become the classical focal point of the country, as the mayor desired. If Marcus had to guess, this type of . . . *Southern opera* was what would take root and grow.

Knowing that was in direct opposition to what Mayor Adler wanted, Marcus found himself tapping his foot and silently cheering the musicians along.

"*Frohe Weihnachten*, Herr Geoffrey," came a faint whisper.

Marcus looked down to see a pair of big blue eyes peering up. "Little Magpie!" Her grin melted him, and he scooped the little girl up into his arms. His throat tightened when she hugged his neck.

Marta, who had apparently escorted the girl there, smiled at the scene. "All the way from home she has talked of you. I think she is more excited about seeing *you* than even *Sankt Nikolaus*."

Marcus caught the teasing gleam in Marta's eyes and knew that she and Eleanor had been speaking about events yet to come that evening. "Miss Braddock can be far too persuasive at times," he said softly, mindful of the child in his arms and the others filing past into the building.

Marta laughed. "But when she has so kind a heart, Herr Geoffrey, how can you say no?"

If the woman only knew how true that is . . . He nodded, the ache of loneliness ticking up a notch. "How is her mother?" he mouthed, pointing to Maggie.

"Elena and a midwife are with her now," Marta whispered.

Marcus gave her a questioning look.

She nodded. "We're hoping tonight. For Gretchen's sake."

Marcus brushed a kiss to Maggie's head before setting her down, adding the precious child to the list of people he would miss.

Those arriving went on in, but he waited for a

couple of minutes, watching for stragglers before joining everyone in the gathering room. He scanned the crowd. Had to be upwards of two hundred, at least.

Midday sun streamed in the windows, and nearly fifty pots of red and white camellias from Adelicia's conservatory dotted the room, giving it a festive touch. Eleanor and the women had worked from dawn till dusk for the past two weeks getting everything ready.

After all their hard work, he hoped the celebration went just as they'd planned.

Because the kitchen here, still boarded off, wasn't nearly ready yet, the women had cooked the meal at Stover's place, then brought it over in a wagon. But at least they had a spacious hearth.

He'd modeled the fireplace in the main gathering area after an enormous one in the entry hall of the palace back home. Except instead of polished marble and a hand-carved mantel, he'd followed Eleanor's guidelines of "homey, not fancy," and had used Tennessee limestone and a roughhewn beam. He had to admit, it had turned out nicely. Had a warm, rustic charm to it, and the fire, blazing strong, heated the room well.

He wasn't surprised to find Eleanor in complete charge as she offered the welcome—in English *and* in German. She glanced at him, more than once, as she did, and he thought again of how tightly she'd held his hand that day in her father's room. He would never forget sharing that moment with her.

They'd spoken with Dr. Crawford about her father's condition, and the physician offered little hope that Mr. Braddock would ever return to himself. But he'd also added that physicians still knew so little about how the mind worked.

Marcus could tell Eleanor had taken hope in that statement. He only hoped she hadn't taken too much.

Mr. Stover led the prayer for the meal, and then the serving commenced. Considering the bounty of food on the tables and the gifts stuffed beneath the candle-lit Yule-tree, no child's wish would go unmet today.

Marcus stayed off to the side, waiting until everyone else had gone through the line. Then he saw Eleanor smiling at him.

"It's your turn, Mr. Geoffrey," she mouthed.

He cut a path through the rows of tables and benches his workers had brought from Stover's building. Nearly everyone in the room had a seat because, unbeknownst to him until yesterday, a few of his men had gotten together after hours and made more tables and benches, donating the materials and their time. And judging from nearby laughter, the few children who congregated in circles on the floor didn't seem to care that they didn't have a place at the tables.

Eleanor handed him a plate laden with foods he now loved as much as he did his favorites from home. Which reminded him of the strudel she'd made for him. *Seven* times. *This woman . . .*

How he wished their paths in life had crossed

before now. Before the Baroness Maria Elizabeth Albrecht von Haas, and before Lawrence Hockley.

"It's your turn, kind sir." The smile in her eyes lessened a little. "Any news?" she whispered.

Knowing what she referred to, he shook his head. "I went by both the post and telegraph offices before they closed. Nothing."

"I know you're worried, Marcus. But . . . perhaps not hearing anything is good news."

He loved the way compassion lit her eyes when she truly cared about something. "Thank you, Eleanor. I had that very same thought earlier."

She made herself a plate, and they—along with Naomi and the others serving—claimed the last table and benches. It was a tight squeeze for them all to fit, and Eleanor gave him a brief, almost apologetic, look when she sat much closer to him than she customarily would have.

Marcus, on the other hand, wished they could start eating like this every night.

Quiet conversation encircled the table as they ate, quieter than he would've guessed for such a festive occasion.

Finally, Marta sighed, taking in the room. "It is good to have everyone together for this meal."

The women at the table nodded.

"But it is still so difficult," Marta continued, "to believe this building is going to be our home. That we will live in such a palace as this!"

Marcus looked up, his conscience pricked.

He'd spent most of his life never thinking twice

about all he owned and all that his future as archduke guaranteed. How odd that now, after so many years of searching for happiness and fulfillment amidst such wealth and privilege, he would find the seed of it here—in a city devastated by war and loss, and among people who had so little, yet were grateful for so much.

Never having been one to swoon over a man, Eleanor had difficulty accounting for the flush she felt when Marcus's thigh brushed hers beneath the table. He seemed unaffected by it, while it was all she could do not to melt right then and there.

Either that, or combust. And he smelled so good . . . like something woodsy with a hint of sunshine thrown in.

She sneaked a look at him as he engaged in conversation around the table. He could talk to anyone, whether highborn, like her aunt and the ladies in the league, or more common, like her and the others in the room. Likely, his father's career in government had facilitated that.

All the women listened to him with rapt attention. All except Naomi, who had seemed distant in recent days. Eleanor was beginning to think it wasn't due only to little Maggie staying with her at night. Perhaps she was concerned, as they all were, about Gretchen being in labor, but Eleanor had an inkling it was something more than that.

Naomi had been upset when learning of her plans to marry Mr. Hockley and became even more so when Eleanor shared that the marriage would preclude her working with the home thereafter. Maybe that was contributing to her friend's reticence.

Eleanor looked at her forkful of whipped sweet potatoes, her father's Christmas favorite, and thought of him.

She'd been to see him yesterday, and like other recent visits, their conversation had been pleasant. No angry outburst, no tense moments. But also no recognition of her. Not even the slightest hint of fatherly affection in his gaze. And that made this time of year, when memories of her mother and Teddy pressed especially close, even lonelier.

But she had so much for which to be thankful. It was far better to focus on that instead. Which is precisely what her father would have said to her, if he could still remember who she was.

Marcus turned in her direction, the others at the table involved in quiet conversation. "Dinner was delicious," he whispered. "Well done."

"Thank you. I'm glad you enjoyed it." Why did his praise always mean a little bit more than that of others? "I've been meaning to ask you, have you planted the seedball yet?"

"No. But don't worry, I'm keeping it safe. I don't want to plant it"—his voice lowered, his tone going sober—"until I know without question that I'll be here to watch it grow. Which . . . I hope I will be."

She nodded, hoping the same thing. "Please let

me know when you do plant it. I'd like to be there. To make certain you do it right, of course."

He smiled. "Of course."

"So"—she attempted a serious expression—"when are you submitting plans for the building you're constructing next door?"

His smile turned downright devilish, stoking her former flush into a flame. "As soon as you approve the roof lanterns I wanted to install in this building."

She laughed but felt a flicker of regret at having dashed his hopes in that regard. "I see you've boarded up the windows—so I can't see inside, I assume."

"Very astute, madam."

After leveling the existing plank-wood building, his crew had laid a new foundation, then swiftly begun construction on a brick building that would boast oversized windows—if the boarded-up openings were any indication.

"You wouldn't, by any chance, be building a small conservatory, would you, Mr. Geoffrey?"

His blue eyes warmed. "With brick walls, Miss Braddock? To inhibit the sunlight? And without a furnace system beneath the floor to warm the plants during the winter?" He tilted his head. "But that's a very nice try."

She held back a laugh. "You're not going to tell me, are you."

He just stared, his eyes saying *no,* while also enticing her to guess again. Which, on the grounds of pride alone, she refused to do.

"Are you ready for what's coming next?" she asked.

He groaned. "Do you know how out of character this is for me?"

"Do you know how much the children are going to love it?"

He sighed, his expression inscrutable. "In the event I forget to tell you this later, Eleanor . . ." He looked around the room, then back at her. "It's truly amazing what you've done here. The good you're doing. I'm grateful to be a part of it."

"Thank you, Marcus. But I can't take credit for this. I simply started out wanting to open a—"

He reached over and gave her hand a brief squeeze. "I *know* what you started out wanting. But when that door closed, you said yes to those that followed. When most people wouldn't have."

"Thank you," she whispered. "I'm grateful for the opportunity." She scanned the room. "Looking at how everything has come together, there's no way I could have orchestrated this on my own. I had asked God to open a door. I just never, in a thousand lifetimes, would have imagined it to be this one. And I couldn't be doing this without your help, Marcus. So thank *you* for all you're doing as well." She grinned. "Especially for what's coming next."

His expression turning sheepish, and he shook his head.

"Would you like dessert now or after?"

"After. I'll enjoy it more once this is over."

Still smiling, she excused herself to help serve dessert.

As she ladled warm chocolate sauce over the bread pudding—a favorite of the children's—she caught Naomi wiping away a tear.

Eleanor leaned close. "Are you all right?" she whispered.

Teary, her friend nodded and handed her another bowl of bread pudding. "I am fine, Miss Braddock," she whispered. "I am missing my sweet Viktor. That is all. It is coming up on a year that he . . ." She bit her lower lip. "He was taken from us almost a year ago."

Seeing the pain lining Naomi's expression, "I'm so sorry" was all Eleanor could manage to say. But that felt like too little. Naomi, a very private person—as many of these women were, she'd learned—had never mentioned her husband's name before, or how he'd died.

Aware of those waiting, Eleanor ladled the sauce and presented the bowl to the next child in line. But she glanced back at Naomi, telling her with a look that she was loved. And that they could talk more later.

Eleanor didn't recognize the next woman in line, nor the little boy with her. But she was certain the Negro woman—tall and slender, stately looking, with flawless skin and discerning eyes—hadn't been to Mr. Stover's building for a meal before. She would have remembered her. *And* her small son.

"Welcome to you both, ma'am. I'm Eleanor

Braddock, facilitator of the home we're building here."

The woman dipped her head in greeting. "I'm Belle Birch, Miss Braddock. *Mrs.* Belle Birch. And this is my son, Elijah."

Hearing her speak, Eleanor felt an immediate and unexpected kinship with the woman. Her voice was deep, wonderfully so, and oak-tree strong. And her son, five or six years old at the most—a beautiful boy with skin a few shades lighter than his mother's—smiled up at her, his striking green eyes watchful and alert, and all but confirming the truth of his lineage. A disturbing truth. One that didn't change Eleanor's feeling about the child or his mother, but that she knew might affect others' feelings toward them.

The boy grinned when she handed him a bowl of bread pudding.

"This is your first time with us, I believe, Mrs. Birch." Did she imagine the flicker of uncertainty in the woman's expression?

Mrs. Birch nodded. "It is, Miss Braddock."

Eleanor held her gaze as she served her the pudding. "I'm *so* glad you're here, Mrs. Birch. I hope you and your precious son will come again. Often."

Belle Birch smiled, an almost tangible under-standing passing between them, and Eleanor felt the warmth of it in her chest.

As the last few people were being served, excited squeals of children filled the room, and everyone's attention was drawn to the door where *Sankt Nikolaus* himself stood—white-haired and bearded, clothed in the regal white robe of a bishop with a scarlet cloak draped behind him. In his left hand was a pastoral staff, and Eleanor had to blink twice to make sure it was Marcus.

The transformation was remarkable. Rebecca Malloy had outdone herself with the costume she'd sewn. It was perfect. Even more, Marcus was perfect. The air about him, the regal quality, was remarkable. The man knew how to play a part.

More squeals and laughter as *Sankt Nikolaus* moved among the children, visiting with them, asking some to say a verse, others to sing a song.

Eleanor caught Marcus looking her way and laughed, shaking her head. Since the majority of children were German and the idea of Kris Kringle had originated in Germany, they'd decided to present *Sankt Nikolaus* at the celebration today. But in deference to American tradition—and at the request of some of the mothers—Marcus planned to read a poem well known to American children. Albeit a day late, in one respect.

All the children—Eleanor had counted well over a hundred—gathered around him, and he motioned for them to be seated.

"How wonderful it is to see everyone today," he said, his voice lower than normal and slightly disguised. "*Wie schön zu sehen, alle heute*," he repeated for the German children.

As Marcus spoke, Eleanor looked out over the

crowd and then at the room around them—that would fit at least ten of Mr. Stover's front room—and felt a rush of pleasure. She also felt a pang of remorse when considering that, come summer, her involvement would be over.

"Everything comes with a cost, Eleanor. Don't let anyone ever tell you differently." Aunt Adelicia's words returned with unwelcome clarity, as did the remembrance of last night's dinner with Lawrence at his home. But this being Christmas, Eleanor firmly put both memories to the side—along with her remorse.

Nothing was going to ruin this day.

The children laughed at something Marcus said. Then, having their full attention, he proceeded to tell them about the birth of the Christ child. Without the notes Eleanor had written. Then, following an equally smooth transition, he began reading the poem one of the mothers had provided.

" ' 'Twas the night before Christmas,' " he read in a voice that hushed every other in the room, " 'and all through the house, not a creature was stirring' "—he leaned forward, pausing for effect—" 'not even a mouse,' " he finished in a stage whisper, and the children giggled.

He repeated the phrase in German, drawing the same reaction.

By the time he reached the end of the poem, some of the children were saying it from memory along with him. " 'But I heard him exclaim, ere he drove out of sight, "Happy Christmas to all, and to all a good night!" ' " Again, Marcus repeated the phrase in German, then took a kingly bow before swiftly taking his leave.

Next came the presents, distributed by Marta and some of the older children. Eleanor sat with Naomi and a cluster of women off to the side, watching. New gloves, hats, and socks for every woman and child.

Naomi looked over. "From your Mr. Hockley?" she mouthed.

Eleanor nodded. "And the Bank of Nashville." She'd asked Lawrence for a donation to cover the gifts, and he'd written a bank note without hesitation. Shades of a future she had determined not to think about today.

"Miss Braddock!" One of the women, Sally, touched her arm and nodded toward the front door, where Elena and Marta were embracing.

Eleanor thought of Gretchen, and for a moment, her breath caught—until she saw Marta's smile.

"Good news!" Marta called out, racing toward them. "Gretchen had a boy. And both are doing well!"

Word spread quickly among the gathering, as it always did. At Eleanor's encouragement, and with plenty of food, Elena and Marta took Maggie home to see her new brother.

Nearly two hours later, the room that had been abuzz with life and laughter was once again quiet and calm, and—with everyone's help—relatively straightened. Now only Eleanor, Naomi, Caleb, and Marcus—his *Sankt Nikolaus* costume safely stowed upstairs—remained.

Eleanor stacked the last of the dishes on a table, her apron bearing remnants of everything they'd served that day. "Let's leave these until tomorrow. Mr. Stover said he'd bring his wagon for them."

Naomi wiped down the last of the worktables. "That is good to me."

Across the room, Marcus and Caleb moved the tables and benches to the side, talking and laughing as they did.

"Well, Naomi . . ." Eleanor gave a weary sigh, noticing the light outside fading as afternoon slowly gave way to eve. Armstead would be arriving for her soon. "I've said this countless times, but I could not have done this without you."

When Naomi didn't respond, Eleanor looked over to see her eyes pooling with unshed tears.

"It is me, Miss Braddock"—Naomi took in a shuddering breath—"who is thanking you. You have given me . . . and Caleb . . . life again." She shook her head. "The first months without Viktor, they were so hard. Some mornings," she whispered, "I would open my eyes, reach for my husband in the empty place beside me, and . . ." Her tears spilled over. "I did not think I would make it through that day. Not only from grief, but also . . . from having so little to eat. And seeing Caleb go hungry . . ." Naomi glanced across the room to where the boy worked with Marcus. "Then I met you." Naomi's smile trembled. "That day is . . ."

Eleanor's throat ached as she listened.

"That is when our world changed."

In an uncommon show of affection, Naomi wrapped her arms around Eleanor, who returned the embrace.

"His heart just . . . stopped," Naomi whispered. "We did not get to say good-bye."

Words failing her, Eleanor simply held her friend until Naomi's breathing finally evened. Naomi stepped back just as Marcus and Caleb joined them, concern lining their faces.

As if already knowing what was wrong, Caleb came alongside his mother and slipped his arm through hers. Naomi kissed the top of his head— something that in a year or two, Eleanor guessed, gauging from the boy's height, she'd no longer be able to do.

"Are you ladies ready?" Marcus asked quietly.

Eleanor nodded. "I believe so." She glanced around. "Except for your . . ." She caught herself before she said it and looked at Caleb, who offered a conspiratorial grin, as though reading her mind.

"I know," the boy said softly, his dark eyes sparkling. "And I knew it was him. But I don't think any of the other children did. Even the older ones."

Relieved she hadn't spoiled anything for him, Eleanor nodded. "Your talents, Mr. Geoffrey, never cease to amaze. You certainly know how to embrace a role. If ever you tire of designing buildings, you might seek the stage."

Marcus offered a grand bow, but Eleanor just shook her head.

"You can leave the costume here," she said. "I'll get it tomorrow."

"*Oh* no . . ." Marcus held up a hand. "That's the last thing I need my crews to come in and see. I'd never hear the end of it."

Naomi and Caleb laughed.

Marcus winked. "It's upstairs. I'll be right back."

Eleanor watched him go, then heard the sound of the front door opening. Hoping it wasn't anyone arriving late for the meal, she went to meet them—

And came to an abrupt halt, seeing a woman, and two others behind her, standing just inside the door. The woman looked as if she was debating whether to enter or not. While the other two were undoubtedly waiting on her decision.

To say the woman was beautiful didn't even come close. Eleanor wondered if she'd ever seen a woman so perfect. Her hair the color of summer wheat, her gown a rich burgundy silk with no telling how many layers of lace. And the manner in which she carried herself . . . Everything about her spoke perfection.

"May . . . I help you?" Eleanor asked.

The woman cast her gaze about the floor as though suspecting something foul might lie in her path. Then she cast a similar eye at Eleanor, her disapproving gaze dropping to the soiled apron.

"*Ja,* you may. I am told I will find Archduke Gerhard of the House of Habsburg here."

The woman spoke so *quickly,* her German accent so thick, Eleanor caught only a fraction of the name. "I'm sorry, but there's no Gerhard here."

The woman's countenance—already displeased—turned three shades more so as she stepped forward. "You *will* inform Archduke Gerhard Marcus Gottfried von Habsburg that Baroness Maria Elizabeth Albrecht von Haas is here to see him."

Still struggling to understand the woman's accent, Eleanor had definitely heard one name she recognized. *Marcus.* But the others . . . "You'd like me to tell Marcus that . . . *who* wants to see him?"

The woman scoffed, looking her up and down, then said something in German beneath her breath. "Simply tell him his *fiancée* has arrived!"

Marcus's . . . *fiancée?*

Eleanor looked at the woman glaring at her, certain she'd understood *that* word correctly. Yet her mind kept trying—and failing—to match what the woman had said with what Eleanor knew to be true. Which, she quickly realized with a jolt, likely meant it wasn't.

"You are . . . Marcus's *fiancée?*"

The woman's eyes narrowed. "What is your station"—disfavor punctuated each syllable—"that *you* would address an archduke of Austria in so informal a manner?"

This time, Eleanor understood every word—and heard footsteps coming down the stairs behind her. She turned just as Marcus came around the corner carrying the costume.

His gaze fell first to her, then moved beyond. "Baroness . . ." The word left him in a rush, like a confession begging to be absolved. The utter shock in his expression gave way to recognition, then dread.

"Your Highness!" The baroness swept past Eleanor, turning her head slightly as though not wishing to be sullied by the sight of her. Then with a flourish that would have impressed even Aunt Adelicia, the woman made a sweeping curtsy before Marcus, bowing her head low, the train of her gown falling in perfect folds behind her. The other two women did the same from where they waited by the door.

Glued to where she stood, Eleanor watched the scene, knowing she wouldn't have believed it had she not seen it for herself. *Marcus* . . . an archduke? She almost wanted to laugh, and might have . . .

If not for the small voice inside her that brought to mind all the questions she'd had about him from the beginning, and that kept whispering even now. *You knew something was different about him.* She turned to see Naomi and Caleb standing behind her, chins tucked, gazes averted.

But it was looking into Marcus's eyes that finally removed every last trace of doubt.

"Gerhard . . ." The baroness pressed close to him. "Are you not pleased to see me?" she whispered in German.

In the small receiving room of the boarding-house, Marcus put some distance between them, the pages of his father's letter in hand, his mind still filled with Eleanor . . . and the way she'd looked at him an hour earlier when Armstead had closed the door to the carriage and pulled away.

"Your visit was unexpected, Baroness. Why did you not write to tell me you were coming?"

"I wanted it to be a surprise." Ever persistent, Maria lessened the space separating them and wove her arms around his neck. "I remember you once liked my surprises." She traced a finger along his jawline. "I have missed you, Gerhard. Have you not also missed me?"

She brushed her lips against his in a way that had once stirred his blood but that now left him cold and indifferent. As if sensing his lack of response, she grew impatient and stepped back— his desire from the outset.

"How did you know where to find me, Maria?"

She gave a haughty laugh. "In your last letter you wrote of building a . . . home for widows and children." She said it with distaste. "I had only to inquire of a porter at the train station and he knew the location."

"You didn't tell him who you were, or who I—"

"No. Your father instructed me to travel *quietly*." She scoffed. "Although I do not understand why." Her expression turned petulant. "Why have you not written me? Why do you leave me waiting for you, when you are here"—her gaze swept the room, her frown denouncing her surroundings—"in this . . . *place*."

"I have work to finish in this city, Maria, before I—"

"Work . . . ?" She scoffed. "You came here to escape. But only for a time. Your work is in Austria. Where your life is. Where *I* am."

As if hearing the strident tone of her own voice, she softened, affecting a look he knew only too well.

"We will be such a pair, Gerhard, you and I, once we are wed."

Marcus looked again at the letter his father sent via the baroness. *"Peace is tenuous, but negotiations continue. There is hope."* He let the words sink in. They were as much an answer to his prayer for his home country as they were for himself.

Not peace unconditionally. But at least it wasn't war. And it opened the door for him.

"Baroness," he said as he turned to face her, "I will return as I promised my uncle and father . . . and you. But"—he steeled himself with the memories, and love, of his mother and grandfather, and of the dream they'd instilled in him so long ago—"I will not seek a life in the palace. We will live outside of that scope. We will seek a country-side dwelling where I can continue my grafting, where I can design and—"

Her laughter cut him short. "Grafting? Designing? Oh, Gerhard . . ." She touched his face as though attempting to hush the silly murmurings of a child. "Those are words of a common man. Something you were never born to be."

He brushed her hand aside. "What I was not born to be, Maria, is king. I have never sought the throne, nor do I seek it now. And if it were to come to me, I would renounce it."

She looked as if he'd struck her. "You do not mean it. You cannot."

"As surely as my uncle's contract with your father guarantees my return to Vienna, I pledge to you now that we will never seek a public life in the House of Habsburg."

The narrowing of her eyes told him his words had hit their mark.

She smiled at him again but without the least warmth. "I hope that, while here, Gerhard, you have kept your . . . *playful* indiscretions to yourself. More so than you—or your brother—did in Vienna."

Marcus flinched.

She fluttered a hand. "Don't think I didn't notice the way the woman looked at you earlier." She laughed. "They do grow them tall here in America, don't they? And rather . . . commonplace, wouldn't you say?"

"I'd say you're overstepping your boundaries,

Baroness. And I would advise you to hold your tongue."

She pressed a hand to her bodice, her expression one of dismay. "Is that the common man speaking? Or the archduke? Pray, my lord, I cannot tell."

Marcus leveled a stare, to which she gave a pitying laugh.

"Do not think you are the first to seek the *prosaic* for amusement, Gerhard. Every man in your position has done it. Even I grow bored of dining on the king's fare, and, on occasion"—she met his gaze unabashedly—"seek a pastry in the marketplace."

In the space of a heartbeat, every nuance of Marcus's old life rushed back at him, the force of it hitting him squarely in the chest, all but stealing his breath. He saw so clearly, through the eyes of the woman before him, who he had once been.

Yet he could also see the image of the man he wanted to be, and—picturing eyes so warm a brown, so true in conviction—that he believed he still could be. Given the chance.

If only there were a way for that to happen while also allowing Austria—and his uncle, father, and the House of Habsburg—to save face. While he did not aspire to the Austrian throne, he also could not knowingly do anything to weaken it.

Not now, at so critical a juncture. They were, after all, his family.

He focused again on the baroness, unable to imagine living out his life with a woman like her.

Glancing back in his direction, she smiled coyly, apparently mistaking his attention.

"Gerhard," she purred, slipping her arm through his, "I do not like it when we quarrel. Unless, of course"—she ran a hand over his chest—"it means you will come to see me in the night to soothe the sting between us." She laughed in a manner she likely thought becoming. "Your father has great plans for you. As does your uncle. I have heard them speaking. You will be the most celebrated archduke the House of Habsburg has ever known. And perhaps, one day soon, if fate smiles on us both . . . emperor."

Did the woman not realize what she'd just said? That she considered his uncle and father dying premature deaths as fate smiling on them?

Knowing she no more cared about him than he did her, Marcus could see what she was doing. It was what she had always done. She was buying herself a crown. And he was merely her ticket.

Listening to her simper and scheme, he thought of the phrase "killing two birds with one stone" and wondered if a single letter could accomplish the same goal. He smiled at her, the gesture taking greater effort than he'd thought. "I will pen a letter to my father tonight. You will take it with you on the morning train when you depart."

She pouted. "But I'm not departing on the morrow. I've decided I want to see more of this quaint little country. And its . . . common, everyday rustics."

Marcus stepped close, and for an instant her composure wavered. "You are mistaken, Baroness. You and your maids must rest well, for tomorrow I will escort you to the train myself and you *will* return to Austria posthaste."

She scoffed. "But that is not—"

"For there is no time to waste. You must personally deliver to my father and uncle my wishes in detail for our future. This way, there will be no misunderstanding, and my future with the House of Habsburg—*and* yours—will be guaranteed."

Eleanor usually considered the rhythmic ticking of a clock rather soothing. But right now, seated in the *tête-à-tête* room—waiting for Lawrence Hockley and Dr. Cheatham to finish their *discussion* about her dowry in the library—the constant back-and-forth, back-and-forth of the pendulum made her want to scream. And having Aunt Adelicia staring at her didn't help.

She didn't want to think about how much this wedding would cost her aunt. Not the ceremony, *per se*, but the union. How much was Aunt Adelicia *paying* Lawrence Hockley, in effect, to marry her? And was there anything Eleanor could pay—or do—to change her mind?

"Are you certain you're all right, Eleanor? You've seemed . . . tense recently."

"I'm fine, Aunt. Thank you for asking."

"The Christmas dinner at the home went well?"

"Very well . . . as I've said before." *At least four times.*

Tick . . . tock.

Tick . . . tock.

Tick . . . tock.

"And the renovation, my dear. That is coming along well, too, I take it?"

"Yes, Aunt. Everything is moving along very nicely."

"Oh, that's wonderful to hear."

Eleanor looked down at her fingers knotted in her lap, then thought of the portrait of Henrietta Hockley and quickly pressed her palms flat on the arms of the chair. Outside, the workmen constructing the billiard hall provided ambient noise, the ring of their hammers a cacophonous companion to the ticking clock—and to the pounding in her head.

The door opened, and Eleanor started to rise. Then she saw it was Mrs. Routh, not the men, and settled back.

The housekeeper stepped inside and closed the door behind her. "Mrs. Cheatham," she whispered, then glanced at Eleanor. "Mr. Geoffrey is here, ma'am. For . . . Miss Braddock."

Eleanor shot a look at her aunt, determined to keep her none the wiser about what had happened Christmas Day. She didn't need Aunt Adelicia telling her "I told you so," and certainly didn't welcome her silent scolding. Or her pity, which would be even worse.

"Mrs. Routh," she began, trying not to imagine Marcus standing on the other side of the wall, just feet away. "Please tell Mr. Geoffrey I'm not available for guests at this time."

Mrs. Routh, usually a stickler for decorum, hesitated, and Eleanor felt her precariously stacked house of cards about to crumble.

"But . . . Miss Braddock, this is the third time he's called on you in as many days."

From her peripheral vision, Eleanor saw her aunt look her way and briefly closed her eyes. "Eleanor, my dear, what if it's about the home? The renovation? You need to—"

"It's not about the renovation, Aunt."

"But how do you—"

"Because I *know*," Eleanor said, turning to her.

Just as she'd predicted, understanding filtered into her aunt's expression, followed by a look that made the words "I told you so" seem almost syrupy sweet.

But it was the nearly imperceptible shake of her aunt's head that stung Eleanor most.

Mrs. Routh nodded and left the room, closing the door behind her.

The noise of the carpenters next door nearly drowned out the opening and closing of the front door, and Eleanor forced herself not to look toward the front window.

Then, counting the seconds, she waited . . . and

waited for it to come. Though not for the *ticktock* of the clock this time.

"I see you have discovered I was correct," Aunt Adelicia said softly.

Fifty-two seconds. Eleanor nearly smiled. She'd wagered under a minute. "I would rather not discuss it. Please, Aunt Adelicia."

"Wisdom always comes at—"

"A price. Yes, I know, Aunt. But please . . . suffice it to say I have paid the price in full this time, and"—she took a needed breath—"I am all the wiser for it."

Swallowing back tears, Eleanor knew she could never explain the course of events to her aunt. It had taken her three days to sort out her own feelings. Learning Marcus was engaged wasn't what bothered her most. She hadn't lost *her man*. He'd never been hers, in that way, to lose.

Although, she had to admit, it hadn't felt good learning about his engagement in such a way.

It was more that she'd thought she'd known him. And that he'd known her. That they were friends. Good friends. *Dear* friends.

Archduke of the House of Habsburg. Part of her was still inclined to laugh, while the greater part couldn't.

She and Naomi had agreed not to tell anyone what had happened. It was best for the sake of the renovation of the home if things continued as they had, at least until the project was completed. If word got out that Marcus was an archduke, it would create a spectacle and shift the focus from where it needed to remain—on helping the widows and children.

Naomi assured her that Caleb could keep a secret, and Eleanor had no reason to doubt that.

Eleanor again pictured herself standing before the baroness in that filthy apron, and her face heated with shame as she relived the scene. She'd felt so out of place and more than a little foolish. But what had wounded her most was that she'd felt so very, very common, and plain by comparison.

Not only to Marcus's *fiancée*, but to *him*. In every way.

It had felt like looking at herself through the eyes of Dr. Adonis all over again. And she was certain she'd read the same—was it contempt?—in Marcus's eyes.

The door opened, and this time it was Dr. Cheatham and Lawrence. Eleanor rose, feeling the knot within her twist a little tighter.

"We have finished our negotiations," Lawrence announced. "And they are quite amiable for all involved. But especially . . . for me." He laughed as if he'd told a joke, though no one else did. "The only detail you need trouble yourself with, Miss Braddock, is that I have decided we will formally announce our engagement in April, one month earlier than planned. All other necessities, you may rest assured, are under my control."

As they walked around the corner to the front entrance hall, Eleanor caught the swift but severe look Aunt Adelicia gave Dr. Cheatham. But it was the raised eyebrow he directed back to her aunt that most earned Eleanor's curiosity. Yet when it came to saying good-byes, the couple was all smiles and graciousness.

Eleanor accompanied Lawrence outside and down the steps, welcoming the cold and chill. As his carriage drove away, she pulled the air into her lungs, then expelled it—in and out, in and out—until her lungs burned. Perhaps marrying someone you weren't in love with wasn't all bad. . . .

She thought of Naomi and Rebecca, and so many other widows who still mourned their men. Men they'd loved. *Still* loved, even in death.

Eleanor pulled her shawl closer about her shoulders. If the *loss* she felt over Marcus hurt—and it did—she couldn't imagine the pain of losing a man you'd shared your heart, life, body, and soul with. Her breath puffed white about her face as she watched the carriage maneuver the final curve. Yes, maybe this arrangement was for the best, after all.

Turning to go back inside, movement down the hill, near the conservatory, drew her attention, and as soon as she looked, she knew she shouldn't have.

Marcus. Standing there. Watching her.

She retraced her steps to the front porch, feeling his gaze on her back. She needed to talk to him, and would. Eventually. It would be easy enough, after their conversation, to limit their time together. She simply wouldn't go to the home as frequently. She opened the front door and stepped inside.

Then come summer, the renovation would be done, Marcus would be gone, and she would be married. As would he, apparently. It was quite simple, really. Although, at the moment it felt anything but.

She turned to close the door behind her—*Do not look back at him. Do* not *look back*—and, head bowed, gave it a firm push.

The next evening brought gray skies and spitting snow, and Eleanor, along with Naomi and the others, hurried to put finishing touches on the corn chowder, stewed cinnamon apples, and corn bread.

After hosting the Christmas dinner in the new home, its gathering area so large and spacious, the front room in Mr. Stover's building felt especially cramped. But it would do—it would *have* to— until May. As Marcus had said early on, *"children and construction do not mix."*

Marcus . . . The more she determined not to think about him, the more she did.

Naomi set the crock of butter on the end of the serving table. "Have you spoken to him yet?" she whispered.

Eleanor shook her head. "He's tried, but . . ." She shrugged, a little embarrassed.

It had been awkward enough explaining their *friendship* to Naomi that day in the dress shop, when she'd told her about Lawrence Hockley. Eleanor had sensed then, and still did, that Naomi knew her feelings for Marcus stretched beyond friendship. And knowing who Marcus really was made his friendship with someone like her seem even more unlikely. Almost like charity, in a sense, and she hated feeling that way.

Naomi looked as though she might say something else, but she didn't.

Eleanor gave each of the seven pots of corn chowder a last stir and tasting, then added salt to them all. Earlier that morning, she'd *discreetly* borrowed a book about European history from Aunt Adelicia's library. The House of Habsburg had a colorful, and tragic, past. As much as she tried to imagine the Marcus she knew coming from that lineage, she couldn't. He seemed so different.

She returned her attention to the present and, noticing the crowd of people gathered outside, opened the doors. The snow was falling harder, and she and Naomi encouraged the women and children to come inside.

"Please fill up the benches first," Eleanor instructed. Naomi repeated the instructions in German. "When those are full, please find seats on the floor. Those of you who can climb stairs, go on up to the second floor and have a seat in one of the empty rooms. You'll be served dinner just like everyone else. *No one* will go away hungry."

When Eleanor said the last phrase, she glanced over at Naomi to find her smiling. Prayerfully, their days of watering down soup to next to nothing were over.

To Eleanor's delight, she looked up to see Belle

Birch and her son, Elijah, walk through the doorway. She directed them to a table near the front window. With every face she met, Eleanor half expected to look up and see Marcus standing there, smiling like he always did. But he wasn't there.

And neither was Mr. Stover, which was odd. He rarely missed a night.

Even filling the building to capacity, Eleanor knew there wouldn't be enough room. At least four dozen women and children would have to wait outside while the first shift ate. The group was accustomed to this routine, but not in the freezing snow.

"We'll serve these people quickly and then get you right in," she assured.

She shut the door, but no sooner had the latch clicked, than an elderly woman began beating on the window. "Let us in! It ain't right those of us from round here got to wait outside while them that are foreign—"

Eleanor opened the door and grabbed the scrappy little woman's arm, fearing the woman would break Mr. Stover's window and slice her arm to ribbons.

"Madam!" Eleanor stood a good foot taller and used every inch of it to intimidate. "You will refrain from beating the window."

The woman yanked her arm back. "We ought to get to come in first, instead of them—"

"Every widow in this city, along with her children, is welcome within these walls. No matter what country they're from, what language they speak, or what color their skin. But you *will* wait your turn, or I will ask you to leave."

"You young ones," the elderly woman snapped, "so high and mighty. Thinkin' just 'cuz I'm poor and up in years that I'm good for nothin'. Well, I can tell you . . ."

Then it dawned on Eleanor who the woman was. That day . . . so long ago. Standing outside the textile mill. Eleanor opened her mouth to respond when a voice came from behind.

"Miss Berta?"

The little woman fell silent, and Eleanor turned to see Caleb. She glanced beyond him to where Naomi stood watching with a puzzled look on her face.

"Miss Berta." Caleb stepped forward. "You can have my place, ma'am. I will wait."

Certain the older woman would throw the offer back in Caleb's face, Eleanor was shocked when Berta's wizened countenance softened.

"Well . . ." Berta blew out a breath. "Finally, a young man who's got some manners. Even if you do talk funny!"

Eleanor gritted her teeth as Caleb showed the woman to her seat, then took his place outside with the others.

"Thank you, Caleb," she whispered.

He just smiled and shrugged. "Someone did something nice for me not long ago, and I will never forget it."

631

Eleanor closed the door, hoping Berta would never forget it either.

The meal of corn chowder, stewed cinnamon apples, and corn bread was served and consumed quickly, and the next group was ushered in.

A while later, as they hurried to clean up, the snow coming down harder, the heavy footfall of boots sounded in the front room, and Eleanor paused in her drying to peer around the corner.

"*Hello* the kitchen!" Mr. Stover sang out, his cheeks rosy from the cold, his eyes even brighter than usual.

"Good evening, Mr. Stover." Naomi gestured. "We saved you dinner, sir. If you are hungry."

"Oh, I'm always hungry. But first things first." He slapped an envelope on the counter in front of Eleanor. "Here you go, Miss Braddock. A deal's a deal."

Eleanor looked at the envelope, then at him, not following.

He grinned. "Open it."

She did and, seeing the thickness of bills inside, her mouth slipped open.

"It's the three months of rent you paid me, ma'am. Just like we shook on."

"But . . . I don't understand. The three months have long passed, and—"

"I sold the building, Miss Braddock. For sure, this time. Just a while ago."

Eleanor looked at Naomi, who looked as surprised as she felt.

"And I got exactly what I was askin'," Mr. Stover continued. "All because of you, Miss Braddock." He leaned in. "So I put a little extra in there for you."

"Thank you, Mr. Stover. But . . ." A hundred questions swirled in her mind. Eleanor chose one. "Why do you say all because of me?"

"Because you've made this here little buildin' the talk of the town—that's why. The buyer and his wife want to open up a café. And what better place than here, they said, 'where Miss Braddock already got the idea going.' "

Eleanor looked again at the money, then a second question came. "When does the couple want the building?"

"Oh, don't worry about that. We got a whole *week* before they want to start fixin' up the place to move in."

Early the next morning, the New Year nearly upon them, Eleanor climbed into the carriage. "Thank you, Armstead."

"You welcome, Miss Braddock." He closed the door and paused beside the front step of the mansion.

Eleanor peered out. "Is something wrong?"

"No, ma'am, I . . ." He shook his head. "I jus' . . ."

She waited, seeing the disquiet in his expression. "We are friends, Armstead. Whatever is on your mind, you can say it to me."

He glanced back toward the house. "I thought you might want to know, ma'am, that . . . people are talkin'."

Her heart fell. Somehow the word about Marcus must have gotten out. Then it occurred to her that Armstead might be referring to her father being in the asylum. Considering the aspects of her life she preferred to keep private, she decided it was in her best interest not to make a guess.

She looked at him pointedly.

"They talkin' about . . . you marryin' the bank president, ma'am."

Eleanor let out a breath. "I see . . . ." The one aspect of her life she hadn't considered gossip worthy. "And what are they saying?"

"Just that you gonna marry him, ma'am."

His eyes narrowed, and though, to his credit, he didn't voice the question *"Are you?"* she read it in his demeanor and in the silence following. But, for some reason, she didn't want to answer.

"Thank you, Armstead. I appreciate you telling me that."

Acknowledgment flashed in his eyes, and he dipped his head. "Just thought you be wantin' to know, ma'am." He gave the rim of his hat a brief tug before climbing to the driver's seat.

A snap of the reins, and the team of horses responded.

The chill of winter swept through the window openings. But bundled in a coat, with scarf and gloves, Eleanor didn't mind. Aunt Adelicia had wanted her to take the glass-enclosed carriage, but Eleanor preferred this one. It was less conspicuous. And more . . . *her*.

She'd stayed up last night and counted—*three* times—the money Mr. Stover had so graciously returned to her. Three months' rent, plus an extra forty dollars. It felt like a fortune. It felt like *freedom*.

And would have been, if not for two things— the expense of her father's care and the lack of a way to provide for herself. She didn't begrudge paying the cost of the asylum. Not when she saw how content her father finally seemed. She only wished she could find a way to provide for him— and for herself—on her own.

Only a dusting of last night's snow remained on the ground, and as they passed the conservatory, she looked for Regal near the tree where Marcus usually tied the thoroughbred. But no horse. Marcus must be in town. Just as well.

She faced forward, the carriage jostling over the hard-packed dirt.

Armstead guided the conveyance onto the main road that spanned the two miles to Nashville, and Eleanor's thoughts unfurled like the ribbon of road before them.

She would go by the home first and speak with Marcus about Mr. Stover selling the building. That news couldn't wait. And . . . it would be good to get their first meeting over with. She dreaded the few moments of awkwardness when the words she'd practiced last night would inevitably escape her and she'd be left to—

The carriage suddenly dipped to one side.

Eleanor grabbed hold of the seat to steady herself when she saw a hand reach through the window and lift up the latch. The door flew open, and the next thing she knew, Marcus was seated on the bench opposite her, handsomely windblown and smiling his smile.

"What on earth do you think you're doing!" Eleanor peered out the window, then back at Marcus, the countryside passing in a blur.

Grinning, he raked a hand through his hair. "I've always wanted to do that!"

"Do what? Nearly get yourself killed?"

He laughed. "And this from a woman who loves tunnels."

Feeling herself warming to him—despite what had happened and what she knew—she told herself not to surrender a smile just because his charm all but commanded it. Seeing him again gave her pleasure she had no right to feel, and fearing those feelings were written all over her face, she drew her sense of reserve about her like a protective cloak.

"What are you doing here, Marcus?"

He met her gaze straight on, his own unflinching. "Commandeering your carriage seemed to be all that was left to me, since I apparently cannot persuade you to speak with me otherwise."

With a dip of her head, she acknowledged the truth, then noticed the horses had slowed. The carriage came to a stop, and again, the conveyance dipped to one side.

"Miss Braddock! You all right, ma'am?" Seconds later, Armstead peered through the window. "Don't know what happened back there, but—" He saw Marcus, and his eyes widened. "What you doin' in there, sir?"

"I'm speaking to Miss Braddock." All traces of humor were gone. "*If* she'll grant permission for me to stay."

Both men looked at her. Marcus, with cautious hope. Armstead, with confusion and a touch of concern.

Finally, Eleanor nodded. "Continue on to the widows' and children's home, please, Armstead." Seeing his hesitation, she gave him a reassuring look.

Armstead returned to his post, gave the command, and the horses walked on.

Eleanor looked out the window and glimpsed Regal some distance back. "What about *your* horse?"

Marcus put his fingers to his lips and whistled.

A minute later, Eleanor heard the gallop of hooves closely matching those of the horses pulling the carriage. She smiled and shook her head. "I suppose you're accustomed to people doing your bidding as well?"

Marcus regarded her. "For most of my life, yes."

"How hard it must have been for you to come here."

"Quite the contrary. It felt like . . ." He looked out the window for the longest time. "It felt like the first clean breath I'd taken in thirty some odd years." He leaned forward, forearms resting on his thighs. "I'm sorry, Eleanor . . . for not being honest with you. My coming to America was rooted in somewhat . . . troubling circumstances."

She was tempted to poke fun at what *a royal* might consider troubling, but the bleakness in his eyes kept her from it.

"I told you my older brother died last year. But . . . that wasn't the complete truth. Rutger"—he bowed his head, then slowly looked up again— "took his own life. We don't know why. I guess we never will. . . ."

He sighed, and Eleanor heard a weariness in him she knew only too well.

"But the blow of Rutger's death came on the heels of an uncle being executed in Mexico a short while earlier. Maximilian, father's younger brother—" He paused. "I am assuming here, Eleanor, knowing you as I do, that you may have done some . . . light reading on my family history in recent days."

Embarrassed to admit the truth, Eleanor nodded.

He smiled, though only briefly. "I would have done the same thing." He glanced down at his hands clasped loosely before him. "Maximilian was in league—foolishly so, in my opinion—with Napoleon the third to seize Mexico."

Eleanor held up a hand. "Mexico . . . as in . . . the entire country?"

Again, that smile. "I come from a rather ambitious family."

"I would say so. Please . . . continue."

"Needless to say, the efforts of my uncle and Napoleon were soundly thwarted. Napoleon withdrew his armies, and shortly thereafter, my uncle was captured and executed."

"I'm so sorry, Marcus."

"Thank you, Eleanor, but . . ." His eyes narrowed. "At the risk of seeming unconscionably cruel, especially in light of what you know about my relationship with my uncle, the emperor, and my father, I was never close to Maximilian. So his death—while tragic—was not something I personally grieved. Not like Rutger's," he said softly, lowering his gaze.

Eleanor watched him, finding herself looking upon him one minute as the friend she'd known, only to have the image thrust aside by that of an archduke of the House of Habsburg. For some reason, she could not marry the two.

But she could see, quite clearly, why this man before her would not have been close to such an uncle as he had described just now. Equally, she could understand how the same might be true of his relationship with his father and his uncle Franz Joseph, *the Emperor of Austria.*

"Following Maximilian's death," Marcus continued, "my aunt Carlota, his wife, suffered a swift but severe mental decline. Which, of course, is not allowed for members of the House of Habsburg." His laughter was dark, and embarrassment and shame riddled his handsome countenance. "She is now hidden away, residing in an . . ."

"Asylum," Eleanor whispered, surprising herself by saying it aloud.

He nodded. "Which, as we both know, only too well, is not a subject about which families speak, much less of which they are proud."

"And yet . . . you befriended my father."

Marcus smiled. "Actually, he befriended me."

She shook her head. "Friendship takes two, Marcus."

He looked at her, his gaze moving over her face. "And yours, Eleanor . . . has been one of the most important of my life."

She wanted to believe that, because the same was true for her. But the bruised parts of her heart weren't quite so willing to trust again yet. "What happened to the baroness?"

The care and compassion in his expression bled away. "The baroness is gone. She departed on a train the morning after she arrived."

But not, Eleanor wagered, of the baroness's own volition. The image of such a woman being forced into a decision not of her own choosing tempted her to smile. Until she realized that, in essence, she was that woman too.

"It's a political marriage," he said after a long silence, the four words summing up so much.

Seeing the outskirts of town from the window, Eleanor sensed an opening. "Mr. Stover's building has sold, Marcus."

His head came up. "Sold? As in—"

"As in we have a week before the new owners take possession. And you'll enjoy this. The buyers are starting . . . a café."

In a single glance, he shared the irony of the situation with her and made the moment all the richer somehow.

"Where will you host the dinners?" he asked.

She smiled. "In our new home."

He shook his head. "It won't work. We're not ready."

"We will make it work, despite not being ready. We have no choice. I will not cease caring for those women and children. We can cook over the hearth. Perhaps we can cook at Belmont and then transport the food, if necessary."

"You never give in. I like that about you. It's one of the many things that first drew me to—"

He stopped abruptly, then rapped sharply on the ceiling of the carriage indicating for Armstead to stop. But he never looked away from her. "You would not have liked the man I was. I certainly didn't." His brow furrowed. "For a while, after we first met, I actually began to like the man I was. Or . . . was becoming. But then, I realized . . ." A moment passed, his jaw like granite. "I realized I was only that man because of you."

"No," Eleanor whispered. "You *are* that man, Marcus. I know it. I can see it in you. Even if you can't."

The carriage stopped, and his smile came slowly. Not the dashing, offhanded gesture she'd seen from him often enough, the smile that could slay a woman's heart. But the steady, true, loyal smile of a friend.

He opened the door to the carriage and stepped out. "For the better part of my life, I was not a man who kept my word." His gaze grew earnest. "But I *will* keep my vow to you. I will finish the renovation before I leave."

She nodded, the mere thought of not seeing him once the renovation was finished felt like a vise around her windpipe. "Yes, you will," she whispered, then took a steadying breath. "Naomi and Caleb," she managed, then shook her head. "They won't tell anyone either."

Understanding deepened his eyes. He turned to go, then looked back. "May I still visit your father, Eleanor? If you say no, I'll honor your wish."

Swallowing past the ache lodged at the base of her throat, Eleanor prayed her voice would hold. "Of course, Marcus. You're his friend."

"And he is mine."

The carriage pulled away, and Eleanor dug her fingernails into the seat cushion—counting to ten, making sure he was gone—before she gave in to the heartbreak clawing its way to the surface.

46

"What about the staff for the home, Miss Braddock? Have you commenced with hiring?"

"Not just yet, Mrs. Holcomb. But I will very soon." Eleanor appreciated the league board's invitation to attend their meeting and to provide an update on the renovation. But the afternoon was wearing on, and she needed to get back to work.

Moments before the meeting began, Marcus had sent word through Caleb that he needed her at the home as soon as possible to discuss a problem that had arisen. Eleanor couldn't imagine what it might be. But the last four weeks had taken its toll on them all.

They'd alternated between cooking the meals over the large fireplace in the gathering room of the home, and cooking them at Belmont and transporting them into town. Either way, the food was always cold by the time it was served. With the record chill and snowfall, there had been days when she hadn't been able to make it into town, and she'd worried about the women and children having food. The inclement weather had also delayed the arrival of building materials. Which, in turn, meant they were behind schedule. Marcus had assured her he could make up the time.

The numbers of women and children attending the dinners continued to increase, and there were days when Eleanor wished for the simplicity and quaintness of Mr. Stover's little kitchen again.

Even more, she missed the easy back-and-forth she and Marcus had once shared. She'd been avoiding him for the most part, uneasy around him, while also knowing she needed to move past that. And would, in time.

"Regarding the hiring of staff, Miss Braddock—" Mrs. Agnetta Hightower's voice rang out with authority. "I believe that you should begin interviewing immediately. Take my counsel to heart on this matter. . . . Acquiring credentialed staff takes time. You will need a head cook, as well as experienced cooking staff. Maids for cleaning. A head housekeeper is essential to keep such a facility in proper order. And, of course, the head housekeeper will require her own staff who—"

"Please forgive me, Mrs. Hightower." Eleanor raised her hand to soften the interruption. "But this is a widows' and children's home, not a personal estate." She smiled to ease the correction, not surprised when a frown darkened Mrs. Hightower's countenance. "There will be a director of the home. A position that includes room and board, and a very modest compensation. Each wing of the three floors will also have a woman assigned who will serve as a manageress for the rooms in her area. Someone to help with the day-to-day needs. But the bulk of the work will be done by the women and children living in the home. In that respect, it will function much like a family. A very *large* family."

All the women laughed. All except Mrs. and Miss Hightower.

"Everyone will have a job and will be expected to do their part. Working will be a requirement for living in the home. The women must either work in one of the services the home will provide to the community—such as cleaning, sewing, or knitting. Or they must seek employment elsewhere."

Mrs. Hightower huffed. "But what about the children?"

"We will have classes for the children, which will be taught by the women in the home who are capable of teaching."

"And if there are no such women, Miss Braddock?" Miss Hightower asked, her strident tone identical to her mother's.

"Then, Miss Hightower, I will see to it that they are taught . . . so that they may, in turn, *teach*."

Eleanor happened to look in her aunt's direction and saw the tiniest smile tip Aunt Adelicia's mouth. But when her aunt's gaze met hers, the smile was gone.

Likewise, neither of the Hightowers were smiling. But thinking about whatever problem awaited her at the home, Eleanor found the mother and daughter the lesser of her two concerns.

Mrs. Holcomb stood where she was seated. "Once you have the staff selected, Miss Braddock, please present the list of names to the board for final approval."

"Of course, Mrs. Holcomb."

After the meeting adjourned, Eleanor slipped on her coat and scarf.

"Miss Braddock . . ." Mrs. Bennett approached. "I won't keep you long. I simply want to tell you how pleased my husband and I are with the changes that are being made in the old courthouse."

"You mean in the *new home,*" Eleanor said with a teasing smile.

Mrs. Bennett beamed. "Yes, of course, the new home. I love the sound of that." She glanced about them, then gently urged Eleanor into the hallway. "A quick word, if I may," she whispered. "Before a public announcement is made, I wanted to tell you about"—her eyes positively sparkled—"the café I'll be opening soon."

Eleanor felt her expression go slack. "*You* bought the building?" she whispered.

Mrs. Bennett squeezed her arm. "Can you believe it! I'm so excited. And, Miss Braddock, I have you to thank. I would never have considered doing something like this if not for watching you, and seeing what you've accomplished. To that end"—her smile turned conspiratorial—"I believe I have an offer that will interest you greatly."

Before that moment, Eleanor could not have described what it felt like to have new life breathed into a discarded dream. But reading the question in Mrs. Bennett's eyes, knowing what the woman was about to propose, she could now. Because she felt the flutter in her chest and fresh hope in her heart.

"Mr. Bennett and I would very much like to secure your services, Miss Braddock, to train my niece, who will be managing and operating the café. It'll only be for a short time. I know you're terribly busy, but . . ."

Still listening, or trying to, Eleanor didn't know which was worse—having a dream die a second time, or being asked to help someone else live your dream. The excitement and emotion knotting her throat only seconds earlier landed with a dull thud in the pit of her stomach.

". . . Hazel is unmarried," Mrs. Bennett continued, "and a little older. Quite an . . . unconventional woman, you might say. Both of her parents are deceased, bless her. And William—Mr. Bennett—wants to give his niece this opportunity so she can make her own way. 'Have some meaning and security in her life,' as she says."

From the corner of her eye, Eleanor saw Aunt Adelicia leaving with Mrs. Holcomb, chatting and laughing. "That is a very kind and generous gift on the part of both you and your husband, Mrs. Bennett."

"And again, Miss Braddock, *you* are the inspiration behind it." She linked arms with Eleanor, and they walked to the front door. "I hope you don't think it's beneath you, what I've proposed. Mr. Bennett will compensate you, of course. I simply know how much you enjoy helping others. How dedicated you are to improving the lives of women in this community. I've written

Hazel about you, and she can scarcely wait to make your acquaintance."

"I'm honored to help, Mrs. Bennett. And please, tell Hazel I feel the *very* same."

Eleanor opened the door, and a blast of late January cold nearly took her breath away. She snuggled deeper into her coat and saw Mrs. Bennett do the same.

Mrs. Bennett pulled her scarf up about her face. "When the time comes, I'll be in touch about the café, Miss Braddock," she said, her voice muffled. "And though I know it's quite impossible, considering your station *and* your relations"—she looked in the direction of Aunt Adelicia's carriage—"I believe you would have made a wonderful director for the home."

Watching Mrs. Bennett walk away, Eleanor nodded, the thought lingering. *I think I would have too.*

Caleb gave a whistle, and Marcus—hammer in hand—looked around the corner.

"You see her coming?"

Caleb nodded. "And she is walking fast, sir."

Marcus removed the last nail holding the final piece of plank wood in place, then set the board aside before joining Caleb by the window. "Remember, let me do the talking. If she happens to get angry, I don't want her angry with you."

The boy nodded again.

Marcus spotted her, and Caleb was right. Eleanor

was either cold or angry—or both. She was a ways down the street yet but was covering ground.

Their time together in recent weeks had narrowed considerably. Despite her being at the construction site nearly every day, she somehow managed to avoid him. Which was probably for the best. Fairly soon, though, one of nature's greatest events would be occurring, and he wanted to share it with her. So he needed to smooth things out between them, and today was the day.

Feeling Caleb's close attention, Marcus looked over at him.

The boy's expression had grown somber. "Should I be bowing to you now?"

Marcus laughed out loud, then gave the boy's hair a good tousle. "I'll buy you an extra fritter next time if you *don't*."

Caleb grinned.

"How long have you been wanting to ask me that?"

"Since the day the baroness came."

At the mention of Maria, Marcus sobered. Not one word from her in the month since she'd left Nashville and sailed for Europe a week later. No letter. No telegram. No word from his father either. But he reminded himself to be patient.

He only hoped Baroness Maria Elizabeth Albrecht von Haas proved to be the woman he thought her to be—and that his father's absolute allegiance to the crown was as unwavering as it had always been.

Sensing Caleb's desire for a more thorough answer, Marcus shook his head. "No, Caleb. You don't need to bow to me."

"But you're an archduke," he whispered.

Marcus glanced out the window, checking Eleanor's progress. She'd gotten caught on an adjacent street corner, waiting for a line of carriages to pass. "The first day we met, Caleb, you told me something. Something that's stayed with me, that I've thought of many times. You said that a name is just a name. That it's the man behind the name that makes the man who he really is."

"My papa used to say that."

"And he was right." Marcus sighed. "I just wish I'd learned that earlier in life. But . . . I know it now, and I'm determined to be the man that *some* people think I already am. The man I want to be. Which isn't . . . an archduke."

A look of understanding, one beyond the boy's years, shone in his expression. Caleb's gaze shifted toward the window. "Sir! Here she comes!"

As the boy headed for the back, Marcus went to intercept Eleanor in the lobby—and swiftly discovered he'd guessed correctly when he'd speculated about her being both cold *and* angry.

Her cheeks rosy and breath coming hard, Eleanor looked at him through a scowl. "Please tell me it's nothing serious, Marcus. That we're not *another* week and a half behind schedule and that you haven't found another leak somewhere."

Why was it his first inclination was to kiss this

650

woman? "I hate to be the bearer of bad news, Eleanor . . ." He briefly bowed his head. "But it's worse than that, I'm afraid."

She pressed a gloved hand against her temple. "And here I just presented a *glowing* report to the league board."

"Before you panic, let me give you the worst news first. Or better yet, I might as well show you."

Chin rising slightly, she nodded and followed him. He saw the glimmer of emotion in her eyes and almost regretted what he was about to do. *Almost.*

"We had some issues with the kitchen, I'm afraid."

She exhaled. "Not the kitchen, Marcus."

He led her to the doorway that had been boarded up, then stepped aside, wanting a good view of her face.

Euphorisch. That's the word that came to Marcus's mind as he watched the sun rise in Eleanor's eyes even as she clamped a hand over her mouth to stifle a sob.

"Oh . . ." She shook her head, both laughing and crying, and looked from him, to the bank of gleaming new cast-iron ranges lining the outer wall, then back to him again. "It's . . . so . . ." She reached over and swatted him hard. "You had me worried sick!"

He laughed, and she did too.

"Marcus, this is . . ." She wiped beneath her eyes. "It's the most beautiful thing I've ever seen." She swiftly sobered. "But the cost. I *know* the money for this wasn't included in the original bid."

"Don't worry about that, Eleanor. We're still on budget."

She frowned. "You're certain? Because I—"

"Stop worrying about that." He softened his tone with a smile. "Just appreciate your new kitchen!"

She stepped inside and walked the length of the room, running a hand over the solid oak worktables and around the edges of the wash basins. She paused and looked up at the rectangular windows running the upper length of the outer wall, then stood, hands on hip, staring out the large plate-glass window that faced *his* building.

She threw him a questioning look, to which he answered, "Not yet."

Seeming not the least bit perturbed at being put off again, she eyed the pots hanging from the racks above the center worktables. "You bought cooking pots too?"

"If you don't like them, Mr. Mulholland says he'll exchange them for you."

She looked at him as though he'd grown a third eye.

She opened every cupboard door—*twice*—chuckling each time. "Just wait until Naomi and the others see." She looked back as if to ask if they had.

He shook his head. "I wanted you to be the first. Which reminds me . . ." He motioned for her to follow him.

He led her around the corner and down a short hallway. "This, madam"—he paused beside a closed door—"is your pantry." He opened it wide and bowed like a footman as she entered the room before him.

She turned in circles amidst the shelving, rectangular windows identical to the ones in the other room providing an abundance of light. "I think this is bigger than my bedroom at Belmont." She glanced at him. "But please don't tell my aunt I said that."

He winked. "Your secret is safe with me."

She grew quiet after a moment and walked to the far side of the room, keeping her back to him.

"Eleanor?"

"I'm fine," she whispered, not turning.

He went to her. "Eleanor," he said again softly, wanting to touch her, but knowing he shouldn't.

She finally turned. "All of this, Marcus . . ." She looked around. "I don't know what to say. How to thank you for all you've done, and *are* doing for these women and children."

A few ideas came to him, but Marcus knew better than to share them, even in jest. "I wish I could allow you to leave here today thinking I have such a kind and philanthropic heart, as you suggest. But the truth is, Eleanor . . . I did this for you."

She stared for the longest moment, then stepped

close, lifted her face to his, and kissed his cheek. "Thank you," she whispered, her breath warm, her nearness intoxicating.

A creak sounded somewhere behind him, and she took a hasty step back. Marcus turned to see Caleb standing by the door, smiling.

"I guess she likes it, Mr. Geoffrey."

Marcus looked back at her. "I guess she does."

Eleanor awakened the next morning after a fitful night. A thought kept running through her mind that wouldn't let her rest. Something Lawrence had mentioned to her months ago, and she *had* to question Marcus about it, despite feeling like an ingrate as she did.

She arrived at the home earlier than usual and found Marcus meeting with his foreman and two other workers in a room on the main floor, not far from the kitchen.

The kitchen. She felt her heart sigh a little.

She'd lain awake most of the night thinking about it. She'd been so overcome with emotion and gratitude, the other side of the reality hadn't hit her until later. But when it had—sleep had fled.

She waited outside the room, and when Marcus saw her, he quickly ended the conversation.

He motioned her inside. "My office is your office."

Eleanor stepped inside, nodding to Mr. Callahan, Marcus's foreman, and the other two men as they left. "Marcus . . ." How to phrase her concern in a manner in which he wouldn't take offense? "I need to speak with you about something."

"Good morning to you too, Eleanor." He smiled and pulled two sugar sticks from his pocket. He offered her one.

She shook her head. "No, thank you. And I'm sorry. . . . Good morning." She managed a partial smile.

"Whatever it is, go ahead and ask me before you burst from trying to hold it in."

He swirled the candy between his lips. Lips she remembered only too well.

She pulled her thoughts back. "I need you to assure me that we're still on budget, Marcus."

He eyed her. "As I told you yesterday, we *are*." He laid the candy aside. "So I'm wondering . . . Why do you feel the need to ask me that again?"

"Because . . ."

"Go ahead," he gently urged.

Asking made her feel so ungrateful, especially after all he'd done. Done *for her,* as he'd said last night. "Because of the money we spent on the kitchen. It's beautiful, Marcus," she said quickly. "Finer than anything I'd ever dreamed of for this building. For *any* kitchen, but—"

"You think I overspent."

"Not intentionally. I don't think you would ever do that. It's more . . ."

"That I mismanaged the money, then."

Seeing, and hearing, his frustration, she almost wished she hadn't said anything. But she couldn't live with that option either. "Marcus . . ." She sighed, glancing away. She hated even thinking this, much less saying it aloud. And to a man like *him*. Archduke of the House of Habsburg.

As soon as she thought it, she knew his title—however *royal*—made no difference. Not in this situation. Archduke or not, this man was responsible for a project for which she was accountable. *She* would have to answer to the women's league and, more importantly, to her aunt if they went over budget. Not him.

He shifted his weight. "For being such a straightforward woman, Eleanor, it's taking an awfully long time for you to get to the point."

She met his gaze, the comment stirring her dander. "I know what happened before, with your bid for the opera house. How the city council thought your design was best, but then how the mayor chose his own son's bid over yours. And then later, how . . ." Seeing his eyes darken, she faltered. But only for a second. "I know about your company having been in financial trouble, and how you likely wouldn't have been able to finish the project even if it had been given to you."

"Who told you this?"

"That doesn't matter, I simply need your reassurance that—"

"I've given you my reassurance on this subject before. And I'm standing here now, Eleanor, looking you in the eye . . ."

She felt a tiny shudder as he did just that.

". . . and I'm giving you my word again. But I want to know . . . *who* told you this?"

She swallowed. "Lawrence Hockley."

He smiled, but it wasn't friendly. "I see. And when did he tell you this?"

She started to look away, but the intensity in his expression wouldn't allow it. "Before I asked you for your company's financial portfolio."

He didn't say anything for a moment. "So you knew this, or thought you knew, before you hired me?"

She nodded.

"And yet you hired me anyway."

"Because I believed you. And . . . I still do. But when I started thinking about that kitchen last night and"—she exhaled, looking down—"after seeing how *marvelous* it is, I knew it was far beyond what was included in the original plans. And then I started thinking . . ."

He touched her chin and urged her gaze upward. "You think about a great deal, do you not?"

"More than I should, I know. I blame it on my father." She wanted to avert her gaze, but his fingertips held her face inches from his.

He smiled, nodding thoughtfully. "You're right, Eleanor. About the kitchen. Finishing it cost considerably more than what I had included in the budget. And since it's come to this . . ." He firmed his mouth. "I paid for the overage myself, out of my personal funds."

Eleanor wanted to respond, but the warmth of

his hand on her face pushed every last thought from her head.

He traced the curve of her cheek with his thumb, his gaze dropping from her eyes to her mouth, and she became aware of him moving closer. But it wasn't until he whispered her name—"Eleanor . . ."—that she realized *he* wasn't closing the distance between them. It was *her*.

Breath trapped in her chest, she froze, their lips so close she could almost taste the peppermint on his breath on her own tongue. Embarrassment trickled through her—first hot, then cold. *What am I doing?* She backed away.

"I'm sorry," she whispered, unable to look at him.

"No, don't be," he said quickly, his voice soft. "If only we—"

She put up a hand, not wanting him to say something only to spare her feelings. But he took hold of her hand, brought it to his lips, and kissed it—once, twice—just as he'd done that night standing on the front porch.

"Eleanor, if circumstances between us had been different . . . perhaps we—"

"Please, there's no need to explain." Scraping the dregs of courage and pride, she tugged her hand from his and dared look at him again. And this time, she could see it so clearly. In his stance, his bearing, in the regal set of his jaw. He was *royalty*. And she was—

"Late. I'm . . . I'm late. For an appointment." She hurried to the door, then briefly looked back, feeling the solid beat of her heart throughout every inch of her body. "Thank you again, Marcus, for the gift of the kitchen. I'll never forget your generosity."

"Eleanor, can't we—"

She left as quickly as she'd come, knowing she would have to face him again. And soon. But also knowing she would never forget the look of pity— or was it regret?—in his eyes.

She pushed through the front door and the freezing chill of winter met her head on. She buttoned her coat, pulled her scarf about her face, and started walking, her lingering desire for him still a formidable force.

She walked down one street and then another, finding the brisk air and walk helped to slow the rapid pace of her heart—and her thoughts. What had gotten into her back there? She didn't know.

But then, she'd never been so drawn to anyone as she was to Marcus Geoffrey. And it frightened her.

The faces of her widowed friends—Naomi, Marta, Elena, Gretchen, Rebecca—passed before her as clearly as did the street signs and carriages. All of those women had loved . . . and lost. She didn't envy the grief they carried with them.

The image of Marcus's face rose in her mind— his laughter, the way his eyes glinted when his wit turned wonderfully sharp—and she wondered if in ten, twenty years from now, she would still remember him with such clarity.

Tears rose in her eyes, as did the answer from deep inside.

But he was marrying someone else. As was she.

She buried her hands in her pockets. She'd tried to convince herself that marrying Lawrence was the safer choice. And it was, in many ways. But it also frightened her to think of what she might become in a marriage without humor or feeling. Without love. Without *desire*.

And she knew what she had to do.

It wasn't the same as braving the Confederate and Union armies to save twenty-eight hundred bales of cotton during the midst of a war. But it was the right thing to do. She knew it. No matter how difficult. No matter the cost to her personally.

Backlit by the sun, the title *Bank President* etched in the glass of the mahogany door gleamed like a beacon of hope. Hand on the latch, Eleanor hesitated, staring through the capital letters to the inner office beyond.

The certainty of the decision she'd made yesterday had only grown stronger with the sun's rising. And even more so after her visit to the asylum earlier that morning. Her father—Theodore, as she was growing accustomed to calling him—was growing kinder and gentler in spirit, even as his body grew more frail.

She didn't know what her own future held, but her father's coming months were secure. A meeting with Dr. Crawford had gently but firmly encouraged her not to look too far beyond that, to take one day at a time. And from somewhere within, as Armstead had guided the carriage down the long, narrow drive, she'd heard a still, small whisper echoing that same counsel for her own life. And drawing courage from the memory, she opened the door.

The secretary behind the desk looked up. "May I help you, ma'am?"

"Yes, please." Eleanor gripped her reticule. "I'm here to see Mr. Hockley."

The woman glanced down at the ledger lying open on her desk, then up again. "Do you have an appointment?"

"No, ma'am, I do not." Sensing the woman about to brush her aside, she continued. "But if you would please inform him that Miss Braddock is here, I believe he will be amenable to a brief visit."

The woman scrutinized her. "And what may I tell him is the nature of your visit this morning, Miss Braddock?"

Eleanor thought for a moment, then smiled. "You may tell him . . . I'm here to close an account."

"You did *what?*" Aunt Adelicia's voice heightened an octave. The color drained from her face as she shot up from the settee in the winter parlor. "And you did this without speaking to me first?"

"I didn't do it to spite you, Aunt. I promise." Eleanor had dreaded this conversation all day. Finally, after dinner, she'd managed to find her aunt alone. She'd expected her to be upset, but this . . .

"I simply decided that—"

"You have not the least understanding of what you have done, Eleanor." Anger harshened her aunt's tone. "I gave your father my *word,* my solemn vow, that I would see you married well. With a fortune to secure your future and that of your children. That is what he wanted for you." Aunt Adelicia pressed her fingertips to her temples. "Exactly how did you break the engagement with Mr. Hockley? Perhaps it is yet still mendable."

"I assure you, Aunt," Eleanor said quietly from where she sat, "it is not."

Lawrence had reacted in precisely the manner in which Eleanor had expected—from his studious stare, to the thin, flat line of his lips, to what he'd said in response. "You *do* realize, Miss Braddock, how impractical a decision this is on your part. The chances of your making such an advantageous match with anyone equal to my social standing and comparative wealth is infinitesimal. Especially considering your age and—"

"I'm well aware of that, Mr. Hockley."

He'd continued to stare. "I find this exceptionally unusual behavior. And quite frankly, Miss Braddock, it reeks of feminine sensibilities, something I would never have attributed to you. I assumed you to be far more pragmatic."

Just thinking of it again tempted Eleanor to smile. That was the point in the conversation when the knot in the pit of her stomach that had bound her almost since the first day she'd set foot on the Belmont Estate again, had slowly, but most certainly, begun to unfurl.

And it felt . . . wonderful.

Freeing didn't even come close to describing it. It was a feeling she wanted to cling to—and she knew the recipe for doing just that. Although she'd suspected her aunt was going to like that news even less than she had this.

"Have you forgotten," Aunt Adelicia said, bringing the present into focus again, "one vital consideration in your union with Mr. Hockley, the marriage you so hastily cast aside?" Her tone turned less accusing, more concerned. "What of the provision of your father's care?"

"I haven't forgotten, Aunt. Mr. Stover recently sold his building. And even though he was under no obligation to do so, he returned my three months' rent. I put that toward Papa's care."

Her aunt's expression held surprise. "That was most kind of Mr. Stover. But those funds can't have covered a great length of time."

"I still have some time left on my initial payment, and the additional amount covers enough to give me opportunity to . . . seek employment."

Dark brows slowly rose over questioning blue eyes.

"Lest you think, Aunt Adelicia, that I am now

planning to rely on your kind generosity indefinitely, I assure you I am working to make a way for myself. And for the first director of the Nashville Widows' and Children's Home."

Her aunt looked beyond her to the door, then back at Eleanor, her features not altering in the least. "I suppose you're referring to yourself?"

"Yes, I am."

A deep, ponderous sigh. "And I suppose there is nothing I can do to talk you out of this . . . *lark?*"

Eleanor shook her head, then paused. "Mrs. Bennett is the one who first brought up the idea."

Her aunt frowned. "Matilda Bennett has always been a bit of an . . . instigator."

Eleanor smiled, quickly deciding not to tell her aunt about Mrs. Bennett's latest *instigation,* nor of the woman's offer to hire her, however temporarily. "If that's the case, then I would think you and she have much in common."

Not the least hint of humor was apparent in Aunt Adelicia's demeanor. "Do any of the board members know about your plans?"

Eleanor's courage slipped. "No, ma'am. I was hoping I might gain your support . . . before I turn in the list of staff for final approval."

The leveled stare Aunt Adelicia gave her said the chances of that happening were remote.

Saturday morning, Marcus was in his makeshift office—the future quarters of the director for the home—when he looked up to see Caleb walking in with a basket of doughnuts.

Marcus had to think twice. "This is Saturday, not Friday."

"I know." Caleb set the basket on a table. "Mr. Fitch said these were on the house."

"That was awfully nice of him."

"He also said that you work too much."

Marcus laughed and grabbed a doughnut, then returned to modifying the design sketches for the building next door. The beams were proving to be more of a challenge than he'd thought in theory, as were the—

"His wife says you should get married."

Marcus lifted his gaze. "I beg your pardon?"

Caleb shrugged. "Mrs. Fitch said that . . . at your age and with your success," he said, as though quoting, "you should be married. But then Mr. Fitch said that not every successful man needs a wife."

Marcus smiled, able to hear the couple even now. "To which Mrs. Fitch replied?"

Caleb grinned. "That successful men do not know what they need. Until a woman tells them."

Marcus laughed again, then looked back to his work. "What else have you heard lately?"

"That Miss Braddock wants to be the director for the home."

Marcus's head came up again. "*Was war das?*"

Caleb nodded. "*Fräulein Braddock will der Direktor für zu Hause sein.*"

Marcus put down his pencil. "She wants to be the director? Who did you hear that from?"

"My *Mutter* and Miss Braddock. They were talking in the kitchen yesterday." A slow grin pulled at the corners of the boy's mouth. "Sometimes people who are grown do not see people who are younger."

Marcus's mind raced. How was Eleanor planning on being the director of this home when she was marrying Lawrence Hockley? Surely, a man like Hockley wouldn't allow his wife to work in such a position. Unless Eleanor and Hockley were no longer—

"Oh! This came for you, sir." Caleb laid an envelope on the table and picked up the basket of doughnuts. "I stopped by the post office like you asked me to."

Marcus took one look at the return address and tore open the letter, only half aware of Caleb leaving the room.

His father's handwriting was thicker than usual, as though the pen had been pressed hard to the page. The ink had bled through to the other side.

His father, never one for pleasantries, cut swiftly to the heart of the matter.

Dear Gerhard,

I did not think it possible to be even more disappointed in a son, but you have proven me wrong. Your letter showed me how deeply divided you and I are at heart, and how corrupt your allegiance to family and honor that you would forfeit the God-given path of your birth and ancestry. I cannot begin to fathom why you would willingly choose such a life as you described. . . .

Marcus read each word describing his father's disappointment in him. All the words familiar, yet cutting just the same. He thought again of the letter he'd penned to him late on Christmas night, the letter he'd sent with the baroness. He'd chosen his words well, their intent undeniable.

He'd told his father what he wanted to do with his life, though not about his desire to stay in America. That he'd held back.

Wondering if his letter had served its purpose, he turned the page and continued reading.

You were insistent in your letter that you would honor your marriage to Baroness Maria Elizabeth Albrecht von Haas. At least in this, you have conducted yourself like a Habsburg. However, it befalls me to inform you that, in your prolonged absence, the baroness has developed feelings for another. Her father has recently informed your uncle of the transfer of her affections from you to your cousin, Stephen. They are to be wed this summer.

Marcus shook his head. Stephen was in line to the throne—right behind him. The baroness was, indeed, *precisely* the woman he'd thought she was. Even as he had sealed the letter, he'd imagined her slowly warming the wax until the seal gave, reading every word, then sealing it again.

The baroness's father conveyed that his daughter's own keen sense of loyalty battled her emotions at every turn. But she has made her choice. And since the outcome of either marriage is the same for our family, your uncle has agreed to the match.

Keen sense of loyalty. Marcus couldn't believe his father was that gullible. But perhaps his father's own biases got in the way of the truth.

I cannot say I anticipate your return, Gerhard. Not with the path you have chosen. You have been given every opportunity and have squandered it. Though I accept I may never know the answer, I have often wondered why the son of my heart chose to break it, even as the son left to me seems bent on crushing the remains.

Marcus folded the stationery and slipped the pages back into the envelope, aware that his letter had achieved its purpose. The baroness was marrying someone else, and his father knew the true desires of his heart. Yet he didn't feel the sense of freedom he'd expected.

He'd always known Rutger was his father's favorite. For a parent to show that favoritism was one thing. A boy could explain it away, at least in part, until he'd grown old enough to accept the painful reality. But to *pen* the words on paper to be read again and again was another.

Marcus walked outside to the back of the building, the air brisk and cool on his cheeks. He struck a match, held it to the letter, and watched it burn, convinced now, more than ever, that he'd chosen the right path for his life.

Now to determine whether the woman he loved, loved him in return. Her recent behavior—and her *near* kiss—made him all but certain she did. Yet did *she* realize it? He thought of that day in the carriage with her. He'd told her then that he was from an ambitious family.

Eleanor Braddock was about to discover just how ambitious a Habsburg could be.

"Thank you again, Miss Braddock . . . Naomi." Gretchen, holding precious little Hans, named after his father, hugged them both. As did Maggie, who insisted on carrying the tin containing two extra pieces of chocolate custard pie. "The dinner was so very *gut* tonight, ladies," Gretchen continued. "A *gut* way to begin the week."

Smiling her thanks, Eleanor caught the young mother's wistful glance back at the gathering area where the tables and benches were all but empty. And where the fire in the hearth—that Marcus had graciously built before leaving tonight—was slowly dying down.

They'd had a large attendance for a Monday night, and several of the mothers and children had stayed to visit.

Gretchen smoothed a hand over her son's head. "My dear Hans always said"—she deepened her voice as though quoting him, emotion tendering her words—" 'You wait and see. We will live in a *fine* big house in America.' I am guessing he was right." She kissed her son's cheek. "But I would rather live in a shack . . . and have my Hans still with me."

Naomi hugged her again, and Eleanor found herself praying, as she often did, that God would heal the holes left in these women's lives as they grieved the men they loved. And, secretly—doing her best not to picture a pair of blue eyes like pieces of glass with the sun behind—she thanked God she would be spared that pain.

Because Lawrence Hockley had been right about one thing. Her chances of ever marrying *were* infinitesimal. Especially with her thirtieth birthday just around the corner. Yet she was accepting that truth, again, in her life, even as she was anticipating what her own future held.

Over the past several days, she'd managed to avoid speaking to Marcus. Even with both of them working in the same building, it hadn't been hard. The home was enormous, with three floors and endless rooms. And for the greater part of the week, he'd been working in *his* building out back, which was still forbidden territory for her. But . . . of which she had a perfect view from her kitchen.

Oh, that kitchen . . .

If ever there was a heaven on earth, it was cooking in that kitchen. All the women who assisted with preparation and serving—and who had already been half in love with Marcus—were now fully infatuated due to the kitchen amenities alone.

Later, in her room at the mansion, feeling more like a guest all the time, she picked up her well-used copy of *Conversations on Common Things*. At half past ten, she found herself tired, but not yet sleepy, so she read awhile, taking comfort in the familiar words of Dorothea Dix.

She wished Miss Dix—an advocate for the down-trodden and mentally ill—could see the home they were building, that she could know what inspiration Eleanor had gained from watching her life from afar. Then a thought occurred. . . .

Eleanor sat straighter in the chair. What if they were to host an open house and invite—

A rustling noise beyond the door that led to her balcony drew her attention. Too loud to be the wind. Unless the wind was *only* blowing on the front side of the house. And only by that door.

Eleanor turned down the lamp, inviting darkness from the corners of the room. She rose from the chair and—

There it was again. She stilled. Then instinctively

looked for something to use as a weapon. Her hand closed around a marble statue on the side table—surprisingly heavy in her grip—and she almost chuckled at her actions.

This was *Belmont*. Adelicia Cheatham's home. And the family was only—

An entire floor away. Asleep. Her grip tightened on the cool marble.

She wished now that she'd closed her curtains. But not having changed for bed yet, she hadn't—

Sucking in a breath, she pressed back against the wall.

A shadow. Of a man. Just outside. And he was scaling the balcony railing! Never mind the marble statue. Dr. Cheatham had a Winchester and was an excellent shot.

She was halfway to the bedroom door when she heard a brusque whisper.

"Eleanor!" Then a soft rapping on the glass pane.

She paused and looked back. *No . . .* It couldn't be.

She crept back, keeping to the wall, and peered around the edge of the door. *It was.*

"Eleanor."

Wanting to give back as good as the man gave, she jumped in front of the glass door, brandishing the statue, and Marcus stumbled back, falling against the railing. She laughed so hard she thought she might wake the family.

Still giggling, she opened the door, and the cold night air rushed in. "What are you doing out there?" she whispered, setting the statue aside.

"What are *you* doing in there?" he countered, a frustrated edge to his voice.

"You scared me, Marcus. I didn't know it was you."

"Who else would it be?" Then he paused and looked at her as if wishing he hadn't said that. "Are you dressed?"

She cocked her head. "Would I have opened the door if I wasn't?"

"Excellent point. Put on your coat. I want to show you something."

"Marcus, it's late."

"I know. I had to wait for the family to extinguish their lamps. So hurry, we don't have long."

Hand on hip, she looked at him, all but forgetting about being embarrassed over their *almost kiss*. "We don't have long until what?"

"Eleanor. Would you please trust me. Put on your coat, and I'll help you climb over the balcony."

Already having decided she was going when he asked her the first time, she did as he said.

49

Holding her hand, Marcus led Eleanor at a steady clip through the moonlit garden down to the conservatory, hoping they hadn't missed the start of *the show* yet.

"Why are we in such a hurry?" she said, breathless.

"First, because it's freezing."

She answered with a sharp thumbnail to his palm.

"And second . . . you'll see."

She laughed.

He'd been surprised when he'd stopped by the conservatory earlier. He'd thought—hoped—"the event" wasn't set to happen for another two or three nights. But the Night-blooming Cereus indeed had a mind of its own. Much like the woman beside him.

He opened the door, the warm air from within warding off the chill, and he inhaled. Then he let his breath out, relieved.

"What?" she said beside him, the collar of her coat pulled up about her neck.

"I was checking to make sure the show hadn't started yet."

She looked around. "The show?"

He smiled and gestured for her to follow, remembering the nights he had done this with his family while growing up. But never with his father. His father had always been much too busy for *such foolishness*. He forced thoughts of his father aside, seeing the ashes from the letter in his mind.

Moonlight shone through the glass canopy above them, but Marcus had also lit several lamps so they wouldn't miss anything.

He stopped just before they reached the end of the aisle. "Close your eyes."

"Marcus, you know I don't—"

"Now."

She squeezed her eyes tight and held out her hand, smiling.

He led her around the corner. "All right . . . Open!"

She blinked a few times, looked at the two chairs and the basket sitting between them, then at the *Selenicereus grandiflorus*, then back at him. Her expression clearly saying she was confused.

She bit her lower lip. "We're . . . going to sit and watch the cactus?"

He laughed. "You never have liked that plant. Why not?"

"I *do* like it. It's strong. And formidable. I just don't understand why my aunt, who loves *beautiful* things, has it in her collection."

"Fair enough. We'll see what you think when she's done."

"When *who's* done?" She eyed him.

"The Queen . . . of the Night," he said, bowing in the direction of the cactus, while catching the blank look on Eleanor's face. "You have to bow," he whispered. "Or in your case, curtsy. It's tradition."

She gave him a wary smile, for which he couldn't blame her.

"This takes me back to when I was a boy. My grandmother had a *Selenicereus grandiflorus*. Each year, for one night, and only one night, the cactus blooms. On those nights, Rutger and . . ." Saying his brother's name brought a rush of memories. But most of them sweet this time. "Rutger and I, along with my mother and grandparents, would do as you and I are doing now, and wait to watch her bloom."

Eleanor's features, already soft in the silvery light, grew more so. She looked at the cactus and back at him. Then she removed her coat, handed it to him, and with the sweetest smile, swept her skirt wide, elegant arm extended, and curtsied as though being presented to Empress Sisi herself.

He showed her to her seat and claimed his. Then served her a doughnut and poured cups of coffee for them both.

"Compliments of Leonard Fitch," he said.

She raised the pastry as though making a toast. "The best in town!"

He touched his doughnut to hers. "Long live Leonard Fitch."

She laughed softly, then leaned forward, her gaze riveted to one of nineteen tubular buds set to bloom. "Did you see that?" she whispered. "It *moved*."

"Just wait. It gets better."

As time passed, midnight slowly gave way to one o'clock then two, and gradually, with a patience known only to nature, the blooms began their brief but extraordinary lives. Then released their full fragrance.

"*Oh . . .*" Eleanor closed her eyes and breathed deeply, again and again. "It's so beautiful. *They're* so beautiful."

As they talked through the night—about their

childhoods, and memories neither of them had thought about in years—Marcus wanted to tell her how glad he was they were on speaking terms again. But doing so would have only reminded her of that near kiss, and he knew she wanted to forget it. Even though he didn't.

"What is it," he asked, "that you most appreciate about doing what you do?"

"With the widows and children, you mean."

He nodded.

She stared at the open blooms. "Watching them leave after dinner with stomachs and hearts full." She closed her eyes, a slight frown forming. "And . . . witnessing their courage. Every day. Even as they carry a weight of grief and pain. I never knew any of their husbands, and yet . . . sometimes I feel as though I did. Or do. Because, despite having departed this world, they're still here, in so many ways. I can't imagine what it's like to live with that grief." She turned to him briefly. "And, in a way, I'm glad I won't ever have to."

Not the answer he was expecting, Marcus didn't have a ready response, and he pondered her meaning.

Shortly before sunrise, he walked her back to the mansion, scaled the balcony, then pulled her up beside him. Apparently pulling a little too hard. She fell against him, and he caught her. For a second, she didn't try to move away.

Then, as if realizing how close they were—the curves of her body fitting his better than was likely wise for a man and woman not betrothed—she moved away. Already regretting it, he let her go.

"Eleanor," he whispered, needing an answer to the question plaguing him.

"What?" Her voice gained a nervous edge he hadn't heard all night.

"Are you still marrying Lawrence Hockley?"

She looked at him, then slowly shook her head. "No."

He reached out to touch her hand, and she let him. But this time—unlike earlier, when it was playful—she tensed a little. And rightfully so, on her part, he knew. She still thought he was engaged to the baroness, and leaving come summer. Tempted to show her all of his cards at once, he'd played enough poker—and won—to know better.

"I think that's fairly important news, Eleanor. And you and I are fairly good friends. When were you going to tell me?"

She raised a shoulder, then let it fall, and his resolve to patiently win her heart fell a little further too.

"I'm sorry if you were hurt in the process."

Another shake of her head. "I wasn't. Mr. Hockley and I were . . ." She took a deep breath. "We weren't a good match. Regardless of what my aunt thought."

That told him plenty. And confirmed what he'd guessed about her aunt's involvement.

The creak of a door breached the hush of morning, and Marcus tugged Eleanor toward the house, not wanting to be seen. They had done nothing wrong, but his presence on her balcony could certainly give the impression they had.

Though he couldn't see Cordina as she moved around on the front porch, he recognized the head cook's soft humming, then heard what he thought were rugs being shaken.

Marcus opened the door leading to Eleanor's bedroom, and she slipped inside.

"Thank you, Eleanor, for joining me tonight. And may I wish you . . . an early happy birthday."

Surprise lit her expression, followed by her appreciation. "Thank *you*, Marcus," she whispered, "for sharing 'the queen's' performance with me. I can't think of a nicer birthday gift, or evening I've spent with anyone in a long, long time."

He smiled, knowing that was a pretty good start. He walked to the stable and saddled Regal, and by the time he returned to the boardinghouse well after sunrise, he knew he needed to win her heart slowly, along with her trust, so as not to scare her away.

But how to do that with a woman who was no stranger to loss, or to saying slow, painful good-byes to people she loved?

Over the next week, at the oddest times, Eleanor caught the fragrance of the flowers on the clothes she'd worn that night with Marcus. The scent wafted toward her in the mercantile when she reached for potatoes, rose to her face when she hugged her father in his room at the asylum, and greeted her yet again when she served the women and children at dinner.

But true to Marcus's word, by the time she'd returned to the conservatory the next morning, the blooms were wilted, their lives passing so quickly. Not to be seen for another year.

But it was a night—and a memory—she would carry with her forever.

Something about being with Marcus that night had been different. She couldn't put her finger on it, but when he'd caught her and held her for that instant, she'd wanted to stay there in his arms forever, even as she'd wanted to turn and run.

"Miss Braddock," Naomi whispered beside her.

Eleanor looked up from the serving line to see a young woman staring back, eyes full of loss and pain as clear as any she'd ever seen. "I beg your pardon, ma'am," she said softly. "I was gone there for a minute."

"I know the way of that." A lilt in her voice, the woman smiled. But it didn't lessen the heaviness in her gaze. "Sometimes I don't know why my body's still kickin' when my heart was ferried away so long ago."

Eleanor handed her a plate, not remembering her having visited before. "My name is Miss Braddock."

The young woman offered a curtsy. "Mary O'Connell, ma'am."

Eleanor stared, grateful the woman had already taken the plate. *Mary* . . . And that lilt in her voice. Eleanor followed her progress through the line and noted where she sat, not wanting her to get away before she had the chance to visit with her.

After everyone was served, Eleanor found her at a table near the fireplace. No children. At least not in her company. "May I join you?"

Mary looked up and nodded. "I'd be honored, Miss Braddock."

Eleanor set her plate down and began to eat, telling herself not to get her hopes up. Chances of this being the soldier's *Mary girl* were next to impossible. But just as she had so many times before, she had to try.

"So tell me your story, Mary. Are you new to Nashville?"

"Yes, ma'am. Just came here lookin' for my husband. Or . . . where he was laid to rest. We lived in South Carolina. I had no money, so it took me a while to save to come."

Eleanor put her fork down, knowing there was no use. "You lost him in the war?"

"I did." The shadows in the woman's eyes lightened a shade. "If I didn't know better, I'd be thinkin' you were one of them mind readers." She smiled sadly and looked around. "But I'm guessin' the better part of the women in this room lost their men in the war."

Eleanor nodded. "Yes, they have." Not wanting to press, she knew what questions to ask. She'd asked them countless times before. "Do you know where your husband died, Mary?"

Without warning, the woman's eyes filled. "I do.

I was out there just today, visitin' his grave. A place called Carnton. The woman there—Mrs. McGavock, such a nice lady—she tends the graves. Told me to come back as often as I want. Or to write." A tear slipped down her cheek. "She said she would take my letters to my husband's restin' place and would read them over him. Is that not a kind soul, Miss Braddock?"

Eleanor smiled. "Yes, she is. I've met Mrs. McGavock once before, when I was at Carnton." Taking a deep breath, she pulled the handkerchief from her pocket. "By chance, Mary, does this mean anything to you?"

She held out the handkerchief, and Mary took it. Seeing the tears slipping down the woman's cheeks, Eleanor felt a weight lifting inside her— one she'd been carrying for so long it had all but become a part of her.

"It's beautiful, Miss Braddock." Mary sniffed. "So pretty with the stitches. Did you make this for your man?"

Eleanor shook her head. "No, I . . ." How quickly hope could flee. "I thought you might have. I was a volunteer during the war, in the surgical tents." She told Mary the story, watching understanding slip into her eyes.

Mary shook her head. "It wasn't my Thomas you held as he was dyin', Miss Braddock." Fresh tears fell. "But I've prayed, many a time, ma'am, that he had someone like you with him there at the last." She pressed the handkerchief back into Eleanor's hand. "I hope you find his Mary girl, wherever she is."

Tears clouding her own eyes, Eleanor nodded. She then spotted Marcus eating with Caleb and some of the other boys at a table on the far side of the room. He must have come in after she'd stepped away from the serving line.

He'd surprised her with the loveliest basket of goodies the other day. Doughnuts, of course, and some chocolates. And even some sugar sticks. But it was the book he'd loaned her two days ago—one by John Donne, in German, Marcus's personal copy, no less—that she loved best of all. Such insight into a person could be gained from reading a book they'd read and underlined.

Mary stood, and Eleanor followed suit.

"I need to be goin', Miss Braddock. But I thank you for dinner, and for what you're doin' here. It's good to have souls who understand your grief. Don't make it lighter, really. But it helps to know you're not alone."

They embraced, and Eleanor slipped the handkerchief back into her pocket.

Feeling someone's attention, she found Marcus staring at her, concern in his eyes. She smiled and waved to indicate she was fine, then headed back to the kitchen.

Not that she was being given the chance. . . . But if she ever allowed herself to fall in love with that man—not just a little, but in the way she knew she would if given a spark of opportunity—her heart would be his. Fully, without reservation. The realization was sobering. Because she'd watched countless women whose husbands had taken half their hearts to the grave, and yet somehow those women had continued on, living with heartache.

The problem was . . . she didn't want to be one of them.

A few days later, while chopping vegetables in the kitchen, Eleanor opened a side cabinet to retrieve a dish and paused, seeing a pretty—but unfamiliar —blue glass bowl tucked inside.

She picked it up and found an envelope within— with her first name on the front. She glanced back toward the gathering room, then opened the envelope to find a drawing inside, and smiled.

A *Selenicereus grandiflorus* in full bloom. She brushed a strand of hair from her face, certain she caught scent of the blooms from the Queen of the Night. Marcus had signed in the corner, *"For the moments in life worth waiting for, Marcus."*

And he'd drawn this for her . . .

Reaching a milestone in the renovation during the past week—half of the project completed—was having quite a positive effect on the man. She'd heard him *whistling* the other day as she'd toured the home with Naomi, deciding how to assign the rooms on each floor. She'd never heard him whistle before.

And although the sound had been a happy one, she hadn't been happy to hear it. She'd thought about what he'd said regarding being a different man back in Austria. But she still couldn't imagine him with a woman like the baroness. Perhaps the old Marcus might have desired a woman like the baroness.

But the Marcus she knew? Never.

She glanced out the window to where she'd seen him an hour or so ago, and saw the door to "his building" standing open. She debated with herself, insisted it was his secret to share when he was ready, but curiosity got the best of her.

She laid her knife aside and slipped out the door.

At a meeting with the league board days earlier, several of the women had inquired about the building he was constructing—about its purpose and function in relation to the home. Eleanor had kindly explained that both the land and the structure being built belonged to Marcus, and that they could direct their inquiries to him.

She grinned as she imagined him being cornered by Mrs. Hightower and her daughter.

Though the temperature was chilling, a brilliant March sun reigned overhead in a cloudless wash of blue. She wished she'd thought to grab her coat. No doubt, the interior of the building, whatever it held, would be—

"Some people simply cannot be trusted."

Cringing, Eleanor paused and turned to see Marcus striding toward her.

"I'm disappointed in you, Miss Braddock."

"I'm disappointed in me too. I should have

come out here five minutes ago, when I first had the thought."

He laughed, then looked beyond her and nodded once.

Eleanor glanced over her shoulder to see a member of his crew closing the door. She gave a dramatic sigh. "Only yards away from discovery and having *all* my questions answered."

He smirked. "My heart bleeds for you, madam."

She leveled a stare meant to intimidate, but his smile said it hadn't worked. The stubble along his jawline told her he'd gone without shaving that morning. And the look suited him. "Thank you for the lovely bowl, *and* the picture you drew. They're both beautiful. But . . . what's the occasion?"

His gaze warmed. "No occasion. I simply wanted you to know I was thinking about you."

She stared, a tad taken aback and thinking he would say more. When he didn't, she rushed to fill the silence. "Oh . . . well . . . that's very nice. Thank you, Marcus."

"My pleasure, Eleanor." He tipped an imaginary hat.

Curious about his behavior, she turned to go back inside, then remembered something. "I've been intending to ask you . . ."

He hadn't moved.

"When will you plant the seedball? I'd love to be there and help, if I could."

He gave her an odd look. "I'm sorry, but . . . I planted the seeds about a month ago. After I knew, for sure, that I was staying to finish the project. If I didn't, I was afraid they would die."

"Oh . . ." She forced a smile, trying not to let her disappointment show. "I see."

"I would have asked you to help, Eleanor. But . . . you and I weren't seeing much of each other during that time."

She recognized his delicate way of saying she had avoided him for a while after learning about the baroness. The baroness . . .

Marcus hadn't said one word about her since that day in the carriage. Of course, she wouldn't have told him about her broken engagement to Lawrence Hockley had he not asked. Yet, his was a completely different arrangement, and she didn't feel as free to ask him as he had her.

Exactly what would she say to him once he said, *"Yes, I'm still marrying Baroness Maria . . . with forty-seven names."* She would feel awkward, and somehow sadder for having inquired.

"Well," she said, aware of him waiting for a response, "what matters is that the seeds are planted. When will the plants be ready for harvest?"

"Another eight to ten weeks, or so. Close to the time my next graft for your aunt's rose should bloom. Lord, help me," he said beneath his breath, a boyish grin tipping his mouth. "I've presented well over a hundred unique blooms to that dear woman since I've been here, but not one has passed muster, as you Americans say."

"Be careful. She may not let you return to Austria without having that done."

His eyes sparkled. "That would be a pity, wouldn't it?"

Eleanor laughed, but only because it was expected.

His smile dimmed. "The breed of potato plant the seedball came from isn't known for producing them, so who knows what we'll get. Or when. But one thing is for certain. . . . If we get anything, Eleanor, it will be because of you. I don't think I would have ever noticed it."

"Oh, I'm certain you would have. I know you, and you're very observant."

He smiled again, a look in his eyes she knew, and yet also didn't.

"You'd be surprised what things are right in front of you, madam, that you sometimes miss."

"The renovation is running two weeks *ahead* of schedule now," Eleanor proudly announced, trying to gauge the expressions on the faces of the league board members—especially that of her aunt, who was seated near the end of a row, between Mrs. Holcomb and Mrs. Bennett—but to no avail.

Over the past two weeks, she'd tried speaking to Aunt Adelicia about the vote taking place this morning, but her aunt had avoided the conversation.

She continued, "Mr. Geoffrey and his crews have completed the renovation of the entire first floor *and* a good deal of the second. So over half the project is behind us with almost three months remaining. I'm thrilled to share that all of the woodwork crafted in the old courthouse by Mrs. Bennett's late father-in-law"—she caught Mrs. Bennett's radiant smile—"has been restored and is now a permanent part of the home."

Applause along with whispered affirmations rose from the ladies.

"And if you haven't yet stopped by to see the new kitchen, please do. I'd love to show it to you. Mr. Geoffrey designed it himself. And we have the latest in stoves and cookware. Compliments of Mr. Geoffrey, I must add. He most graciously went far above and beyond the plans we originally had for that area, covering that cost himself."

Again, the women applauded, and judging by their eager expressions, Eleanor was certain some were making mental notes to speak to Marcus about doing the same for their kitchens.

She picked up the list of staff she'd submitted for final approval and saw Mrs. Holcomb rise from her chair. "And now I'll turn the meeting back over to Madam President."

"Thank you, Miss Braddock. As always, that was a splendid report. Thorough and well presented."

Eleanor thanked her and took a seat to the side of the board members, not only because she wasn't one, but also so she could study them better.

Aunt Adelicia didn't so much as look her way. But Mrs. Hightower and her daughter did, and their gazes were anything but supportive.

"Now, ladies, we have before us the list of staff Miss Braddock interviewed and believes will best serve the needs of the . . ."

Eleanor almost wished she'd insisted on leaving the room during the voting. But Mrs. Holcomb had objected to the idea, saying it was best Eleanor stayed, since she was, after all, a league member now—much to Eleanor's lack of enthusiasm over having joined—and in case anyone had questions.

Eleanor reached into her pocket, the silky, well-worn cotton of the handkerchief reminding her that there were many other things far more important than getting enough votes to be the director of the home.

But getting that position represented security in the form of room and board, and a steady salary—albeit a small one—that, over time and with other jobs, would pay for her father's care. It also represented being part of a family she'd grown to cherish in recent months.

So this vote was *very* important. At least to her.

Mrs. Holcomb went line by line through the staff recommendations, reading aloud each position and name of the chosen applicant—along with the notes Eleanor had penned summarizing each person's qualifications—then calling for brief discussion before taking a vote and continuing to the next. Until finally, she reached the director's position.

"The next name is, of course, one that is familiar to us all."

Eleanor kept her gaze lowered as Mrs. Holcomb paid her very kind and generous compliments.

"Before calling for a vote, I'd like to invite discussion. Bearing in mind, of course, that Miss Braddock is in the room with us." Her tone was the definition of decorum. "So if there is a concern, ladies, please let us express it with—"

"I do *not* believe Miss Braddock is well suited for this position! And furthermore, she most certainly is *not* garnering my vote."

Eleanor didn't have to look up to know who had spoken.

"Mrs. Hightower," Mrs. Holcomb said, her tone having shed a layer of warmth, "would you care to elaborate on your concerns? And please, madam," she added, leaving Mrs. Hightower's mouth half engaged in a reply, "remember to do so with kindness and gentility."

Mrs. Hightower huffed. "I am always genteel in my speech, Madam President. But I am also forthright. And I take severe umbrage at the notion that one of *our* members, albeit one of lesser standing due to certain *familial* connections"—she glared in Eleanor's direction—"would think it acceptable to hire herself out like some commoner."

Eleanor froze. *My father.* How had this woman found out about him? Only a handful of people knew.

"There is a fine line," Mrs. Hightower continued, "between philanthropy and publicly disgracing

691

oneself, and I believe she is crossing that line. I *also* believe—"

Eleanor felt the heat rising to her face. She couldn't bear to look up. What Aunt Adelicia must be thinking right now . . .

"—that we, as an organization, should not continue to sanction behavior that falls outside the realm of what is acceptable for a woman. We should embrace the womanly virtues given to us by God, instead of conducting business as though we wear trousers rather than skirts, as some in our number do. Not to mention how this person *traipsed* about the country unescorted in the middle of a war, consorting with the enemy and selling cotton in backroom deals in which no respectable woman would ever have engaged."

Eleanor slowly lifted her head, her thoughts skidding to a halt in the sudden silence, and slamming one into the other. She looked first at Mrs. Hightower, whose face was beet red, and then to Aunt Adelicia, whose countenance was as smooth and serene as glass.

50

The room was in an uproar. Women talking over one another. And not in "proper league" voices.

Two sat wide-eyed, handkerchiefs clutched against their mouths, while another three huddled together, whispering behind their hands. The pounding of a gavel rang out.

"Order!" Mrs. Holcomb practically screamed to be heard over the ruckus. "The board will come to order!"

Stunned, Eleanor watched the mayhem, grateful she'd sat off to the side. It appeared that the issue with the Hightowers hadn't been about her at all. Although something told her they didn't consider her their favorite person, it wasn't so much that they disliked her. They disliked Aunt Adelicia.

Finally, Mrs. Holcomb regained control of the meeting. "Everyone will sit down, please. Immediately!" She gave a quick tug on her jacket sleeves. "I believe," she said, reaching for an air of propriety set at naught moments earlier, "that we have heard enough discussion on this topic. So I will call for a vote."

A hand shot up.

"Please, Mrs. Pate, I said *no* more discussion," Mrs. Holcomb warned.

The woman lowered her hand.

"Now . . ." Mrs. Holcomb smoothed the sides of her hair. "I will call roll, and you will simply state *yay,* indicating you approve Miss Braddock to serve as director, or *nay,* indicating you do not." She cleared her throat. "Mrs. Matilda Bennett."

"Yay."

"Mrs. Loretta Brown."

"Nay."

"Mrs. Adelicia Cheatham."

"I abstain"—Eleanor's hope sank. Her own aunt wasn't even voting for her—"on the grounds that Miss Braddock is my niece."

Mrs. Holcomb nodded before continuing. "Mrs. Laura Hall."

"Yay."

"Mrs. Agnetta Hightower."

"Nay!"

"Mrs. Sandra Lundy."

"Yay."

"Mrs. Ramona Nolen."

"Yay."

"Mrs. Nadine Pate."

"Nay."

"Mrs. Clara Nell Petree."

"Yay."

Mrs. Holcomb called for votes from three more members. One *yay.* Two *nay*s. Which placed *yay*s in the lead, six to five.

Hands slick, Eleanor could scarcely breathe. If Mrs. Holcomb voted *yay,* she would be the director. If *nay,* it would be a tie. Then what would they do?

She looked over at her aunt. If only she hadn't abstained. Then again, how would her aunt have voted?

"And now to cast my ballot." Mrs. Holcomb looked at Eleanor, then back to the board. "I vote . . ."

All eyes on Mrs. Holcomb. No one moved.

"Nay."

Eleanor's lungs emptied. Mrs. Holcomb's lack of confidence hurt more than all the others combined.

"Which now brings the vote," Mrs. Holcomb continued, "to a tie. According to the bylaws of the Nashville Women's League, in the event of a tie vote, any member present who has chosen to abstain *must* cast their ballot. Which means the board strikes Mrs. Cheatham's abstaining vote from the record"—she nodded to the board's secretary taking notes—"and requires that she vote either *yay* or *nay*."

Eleanor looked one last time at her aunt, whose gaze never left Mrs. Holcomb's.

"Mrs. Adelicia Cheatham, would you please cast your ballot?"

Eleanor bowed her head, already knowing what her aunt's response was going to be. Once again, trying to follow where she thought God was leading in her life, she'd been so certain the position of director was something she was supposed to—

"Yay."

The word ringing in the silence, Eleanor looked up, uncertain she'd heard correctly. Aunt Adelicia's smooth countenance revealed nothing. But Mrs. Hightower's stormy frown did.

"The *yay*s have it," Mrs. Holcomb said quickly. "Congratulations, Miss Braddock. You are the first director of the Nashville Widows' and Children's Home, and this meeting is now adjourned." Fast as lightning, she brought the gavel down.

Eleanor rose and responded to repeated congratulations with thanks, some of the members seeming more enthusiastic than others. But when Aunt

Adelicia approached, she felt a special weight of gratitude. And also uncertainty.

"Well done, Eleanor," her aunt said, the picture of composure. "I'm certain you'll fulfill your duties as director with the same excellence with which you've met the challenges of facilitating the renovation."

"Thank you, Aunt Adelicia," she said, aware of others listening. "I appreciate your confidence."

A moment later, to Eleanor's surprise, she saw Mrs. Holcomb discreetly motioning her into the hallway.

"Miss Braddock," the league president whispered, out of earshot of others. "Very quickly—" She peered over Eleanor's shoulder back into the meeting room. "Please realize that when I voted 'nay' just now, I wasn't truly voting *against* you. You see . . . Mrs. Hightower is a very influential—and wealthy—member of this community."

Eleanor nodded. "I think I understand, Mrs. Holcomb."

"No, I don't believe you do."

Eleanor waited.

"If Mrs. Hightower were to perceive that the majority of the board—and the league *president*—was against her, she might well withdraw her membership, and all the philanthropic good she does in this city."

Women began to exit the room behind them, and Mrs. Holcomb gave her hand a quick squeeze.

"Suffice it to say, Miss Braddock, one thing I've

learned in my life is that it's best to keep on amiable terms with those who oppose you, rather than fight at all costs to win every battle." She winked, then stepped away.

Pondering what she'd said, Eleanor spoke with a few other members, then hurried outside in time to see Armstead assisting Aunt Adelicia into the carriage. Eleanor cut a path across the street.

"Aunt Adelicia?"

Her aunt turned, her expression showing a tad more wear than it had a moment earlier. "Would you like to share the carriage home, Eleanor?"

"Oh no. Thank you. I still have work to do here in town. I simply wanted to say that . . . I'm sorry for what happened in there, with Mrs. Hightower."

"You did nothing to provoke that." Her aunt glanced toward the league house. "That's a very old wound, to which I have become accustomed. For the most part."

"I had no idea she felt that way about you."

Aunt Adelicia looked at her askance. "Truly?" She sighed. "And all this time, I thought it was so obvious to anyone looking on." She arranged the folds of her skirt just so-so. "Don't ever let anyone dissuade you from doing what you believe you've been called to do, Eleanor." The natural keenness in her eyes sharpened. "There's nothing more satisfying than knowing you've done all you can to reach a goal set before you." Her gaze dulled. "And nothing more heartbreaking than looking back on an opportunity lost. One that will never return."

Eleanor nodded and started to step back, then paused. "Aunt, I'm wondering . . ." She wanted her question to have a casual air but knew before asking that it wouldn't. "Would you still have voted for me . . . if the situation had been different?"

Aunt Adelicia briefly covered Eleanor's hand on the door, her smile taking on an almost motherly quality. "I guess we'll never know now, will we?"

A few mornings later, Eleanor arrived very early at the home, and as though the quiet beckoned with a voice unheard, she answered, and took a few moments to walk the main floor before starting to work.

She peeked inside the rooms, taking inventory of the spaces ready to welcome the women and children. She closed her eyes in the long hallway and easily imagined the rowdy laughter of boys, the soft whispers of conversation among the mothers, and the giggles of little girls.

All sounds she heard—and cherished—every evening they hosted a dinner.

The wooden floors, newly sanded and refinished smelled of promise and possibility, and she vowed never to complain once the scuff of little feet had worn away the sheen. Because that would mean the building was being used and well loved. And what was the good in having something if you weren't going to use it?

She climbed the stairs to the second floor, running her hand along the woodwork, and then paused—

hearing the sound of footsteps. She tilted her head to one side, certain she'd heard something. But whatever it was, was gone.

After a moment, she continued on.

Marcus and his men had done a remarkable job thus far. She'd seen potential in the building the first time she'd viewed it. But this . . .

The building exuded warmth she doubted it ever possessed before. Not with lawyers and attorneys—and Mayor Adler—residing in it.

Mayor Adler. She still felt badly over questioning Marcus about the solvency of his company. She should have known better. But it hadn't seemed to bother him. At least not for long. In fact, the more time that passed, the happier he seemed.

Perhaps it was because he would be returning to Austria soon, which she didn't even want to think about. They saw each other every day—several times, some days—mainly because he came by the kitchen.

In addition to the bowl he'd given her, he'd left a set of spoons she'd admired at the mercantile on a worktable. It was almost as if he was trying to make certain she would miss him once he was gone. The man had absolutely nothing to worry about.

In the same breath, she recognized she had the life she'd always known, somehow, that she would have. Only, far richer. No children of her own—regret struck a familiar chord at the thought—and yet a houseful of children. No husband, but a life full of purpose. And one without the all-but-guaranteed loss and grief upon which this home had been founded.

Yes . . . She sighed, smoothing the front of her skirt. She was grateful. And determined to be more so.

She walked the second floor, seeing touches of work still needing to be finished, then continued to the third, praying as she walked up the staircase for the families who would live there one day soon, and also for herself, that she would oversee the home with fairness and efficiency.

Furniture for the bedrooms, including her quarters, was set to arrive at the end of April, scarcely six weeks away. So much to be done before then.

No sooner had her foot touched the third story landing, than she heard footsteps again. She stopped, peered down the hallway, first one way, then another, certain she'd heard them.

"Hello?" Her voice was overloud in the silence, and she wished the hair on the back of her neck wasn't standing on end. Not one usually given to such silliness, she almost turned and went back downstairs.

But this was her building. Her *home*. And it was likely just a member of one of the crews arriving early to work, same as her. Still, she grabbed the remnant end of a plank-wood board from nearby. Not exactly a Winchester, but it would inflict damage if the situation warranted.

She investigated—more than toured—the third

floor, watchful. At the end of the hallway, she turned back, then heard a distinct *clunk.*

Right above her head. *On the roof.*

A sense of ownership driving her forward, she strode down the hallway and found the door in the ceiling leading to the roof was wide open, with a ladder leaning against the opening.

She'd visited up there early on, but only once. Then the crews had begun replacing the roof in sections, so it hadn't been safe to return. But now . . .

Having climbed trees with Teddy in younger years, Eleanor gave the ladder a withering stare, then gathered her skirt, pulled it up from behind, and tucked it into her waistband. If the ladder supported Marcus and his men, it would certainly hold her.

She managed the ladder with relative ease, considering what she was wearing. What she hadn't counted on was seeing what was on the roof of Marcus's building next door—and the arms of steel that locked around her from behind.

"Can you not take no for an answer, Madam Director?" Marcus whispered from behind. "My building is to be unveiled at your open house in May. And no sooner."

Loving the name he'd given her in recent days,

Eleanor enjoyed being this close to him, while also knowing she shouldn't. Even if this closeness meant nothing to him, it did to her. And while she hadn't cared for the baroness, and didn't know how betrothals worked in Austria, she wouldn't appreciate someone else enjoying this intimacy with Marcus if he were *hers*.

His grip loosened and she turned, knowing her cheeks were flushed.

"I didn't come up here to see *your* building, Marcus." She casually put some distance between them. "I came up here to make sure *my* building wasn't being ransacked."

He laughed. "Yes, thieves often come up to roofs to ransack buildings."

"If you don't want anyone coming up here, you should have locked the door. That way, I wouldn't have seen"—she let her grin come—"the roof lanterns on your building!"

He exhaled a breath, and she laughed.

"They're beautiful, Marcus." She walked to the edge of the roof and peered over.

He joined her. "I didn't think you liked them."

"I never said I didn't like them. I simply thought they were impractical for our needs."

He laughed again. "Always forthcoming, aren't you?"

"I try to be. Most of the time," she added, the look in his eyes seeming to challenge her statement.

He moved closer. "Good. Because I'd like to

know your thoughts on my intent to court you, Miss Braddock."

She blinked. "I beg your pardon?" Needing support, she reached for the waist-high wall bordering the roof.

His expression took on a look she remembered, if only briefly, from that day in the library. But remembering what *that* had led to, she felt herself responding to him. And he hadn't even touched her. Mindful of the roof's boundaries, she took a step back.

He made up the distance between them, and then some. "My future has changed irrevocably, Eleanor. Two things you need to know, and please allow me to finish before responding."

Too late, she wanted to say. But she nodded instead.

"The Baroness Maria Elizabeth Albrecht von Haas"—he said the name with the haughty tone such a name deserved—"has transferred her feelings to someone else. Hence, she will be marrying another man. Instead of me."

Eleanor felt her mouth slip open. He closed it for her.

"The not-so-lucky man is my cousin, in fact. A boorish, selfish soul whom she more than deserves. The lovely couple is being wed with my extreme pleasure and my grateful prayer for having escaped that personal and political noose."

"But, how did you—"

"Ah . . . ah." He touched her lips, staring at

them for a beat before his gaze met hers again. "No talking until I'm done. Now . . ." He smiled that devilish smile. "You need to know that the Gerhard Marcus Gottfried who will be pursuing you at all costs and with little patience for rebuttal, and none for refusal"—the look he gave her both thrilled her and scared her to death—"is no longer an archduke in the House of Habsburg. Neither in title nor, prayerfully, in the man I am." He cupped her face in his palm. "I have you to thank for that, Eleanor Braddock. And I intend to spend the rest of my life doing just that."

Instinctively, she backed up another step and met the brick wall this time. He grabbed her arm to steady her and didn't let go.

"Now," he said, moving closer again. "Any questions?"

"Yes!" She took a breath, the morning air cold. Not that she cared at the moment. "Why . . . all of this? Now? Up here?"

He smiled. "Because last night as I watched you reading that story to the children—the one they always ask you to read . . ."

She nodded, loving that story.

"I decided I was tired of waiting. And I told myself the next time I saw you, whenever, wherever that was, I was going to tell you. So be grateful it wasn't during a dinner downstairs." He grinned. "Or at church in your aunt's pew."

Her mind spinning, Eleanor was glad he was still

holding her arm. "When did you learn about the baroness?"

For the first time, his confidence seemed to waver. "Shortly before our evening together in the conservatory."

"But that was well over a month ago. Why did you wait to say anything?"

His hand tightened on her arm, not painfully, but more in a . . . possessive sort of way. "Because I know you, Eleanor. You're a practical, levelheaded woman who knows what she wants in life and isn't afraid to pursue it. I also know you're scared."

He moved in, touching her face, the blue of his eyes deepening, and her heart squeezed tight with simultaneous pleasure and panic.

"I can see the fear in your eyes right now. If you'd known for the past few weeks that I wasn't engaged anymore, you wouldn't have allowed me to show you how much I love you. And I do love you, Eleanor Braddock. I think I have since . . ." His eyes narrowed. "Since you mistook me for an under gardener."

She couldn't help but laugh.

"One more thing," he whispered, trailing his hand from her face, down to the high collar of her shirt-waist. "I'd like your forthright response to this."

He took her in his arms and kissed her, like he'd done before, only slower this time, his arms holding her as though they were made to do just that. He drew back slightly, and she thought they were done. But she was wrong.

He kissed her mouth again, then her cheek. With one arm, he held her, his hand spanning the small of her back, while the other explored the curve of her shoulder, her collarbone, then—her heart leapt to her throat—back up to her neckline again.

"Eleanor," he whispered against her mouth.

Eyes still closed, her composure in a puddle at his feet, she took a breath. "Yes?"

"Will you marry me?"

In a blink, she was back. And looked up at him. "W-what did you say?"

"You heard me." He nuzzled her neck. "I want you to marry me. Soon. I don't want to wait. I've already waited half of my life for you."

"But . . ." The strangest feeling—part wonder and excitement, part terror and dread—chased the desire coursing through her. "We don't—"

"We don't what?"

"We don't . . . know each other well enough. Not . . . like that."

His hands on her shoulders, he looked her square on. "You and I know each other better than a lot of couples married for half their lives do."

Knowing he was right, yet feeling an inexplicable fear fanning out inside her, she couldn't bring herself to look at him.

"I know you love me, Eleanor. Seven strudels? *Seven?*"

She winced. "Thirteen. Still, none of them good."

He urged her chin upward, and she glimpsed a confidence in him she wanted to have but didn't.

Not when remembering how much it had hurt to learn of his initial plans to return to Austria. That had been hard enough. But growing even closer to him, allowing herself to love him like she knew she could—and would, if given the chance—then losing him . . . like so many of the women she knew who had lost their husbands . . . That would be too much.

The sting of losing her mother, and then Teddy, was never far away. She'd witnessed the changes in her father, had seen what grief could do to a person. Then there was the soldier that night so long ago . . . the regret he'd borne, the pain in his eyes in those final moments.

Loving someone came at too high a cost, a cost Eleanor didn't think she could—No, she knew she couldn't bear it.

"Marry me," Marcus whispered again, his voice husky.

Already feeling a sense of loss, she shook her head. "I can't."

The ardor in his gaze dimmed. "You're afraid I'll leave you. But I never will, Eleanor."

How did he know her so well? Her throat ached with love for him. "You won't mean to. But you will . . . someday."

"Years from now, maybe," he whispered. "After a full life lived together."

Tears welled in her eyes. "You don't know that for sure."

"And neither do you," he countered softly, then

707

kissed her again, gently, with a tenderness that belied his stature and strength, and that almost persuaded her.

But in the end, the fear in her heart won out. "I can't," she whispered. Then, needing the reassurance of his arms even if she couldn't say yes, she gave him a brief but tight hug before heading downstairs.

Over the next weeks, as the remnant of March slipped into April, then April readied for May, the daylight hours lengthened. Yet the days themselves seemed to grow shorter. Everywhere Eleanor looked there was work to do for the home, for the open house, for the classes they would offer, for the skills they would teach the women and the children, and for Hazel, Mrs. Bennett's niece, starting the café, which Marta and Elena were helping with as well.

And . . . there was Marcus.

He'd asked her twice again to marry him. And twice again she'd said no. She sensed his impatience with her growing and almost wished he'd stop asking. But then, she also didn't. Because she wished she had the courage to say yes.

He'd argued she could keep her position as director if they married, telling her they would work something out regarding the living accommodations, understanding that a man couldn't exactly live in the home. He shared about his own struggle to forge a path for the life he wanted, instead of the life chosen for him. He'd told her about his father's last letter, and she was glad he'd burned it instead of reading those words again and again.

Every argument she put forth, he'd thought of and solved before she could scarcely give it voice.

After dinner one night, she looked at him across the gathering room working on the special reading corner she'd requested he design. His crews had built it to his specifications, and it was perfect—a slightly raised platform with bookcases behind it where volumes already lined the shelves. Rebecca Malloy was working with some of the women to make cushions upon which the children would sit.

As though feeling her thinking about him, Marcus turned and looked back, but his smile lacked its usual enthusiasm.

"Miss Braddock," Naomi said behind her. "A quick question for you."

Telling herself she was making the right choice, Eleanor joined Naomi and several other ladies at a table, their young daughters sitting nearby.

Marta leaned over, excited. "Rebecca is sewing us new dresses for the open house! Fancier even than the ones she has made before."

Eleanor looked across the table. "You are far too generous, Mrs. Malloy. Aren't you busy enough with everything else?"

Rebecca made a sweet grimace. "I have an ulterior motive, Miss Braddock. I'm hoping that when some of the women from the league see my work, they might be interested in using my services."

"Very good thinking." Eleanor grinned, then saw Marcus gesturing for her to join him. "I'll be sure to list your name in the program." She stood.

"But you need to choose *your* dress, Miss Braddock," Naomi said, welcoming little Maggie, who climbed up in her lap.

"Anything is fine, honestly," Eleanor said, seeing Marcus waiting.

"Can I choose your dress?" Maggie piped up.

Eleanor placed a kiss on Maggie's head. "You certainly may. You and Mrs. Malloy together." She winked in Rebecca's direction.

"Is everything all right?" she asked Marcus, seeing an emotion in his expression she couldn't define.

"Would you walk outside with me?"

"Of course."

He led her through the kitchen and out back, and she got excited.

"Are you going to show me the building?"

He laughed softly. "Yes, at the open house, like I've always said."

She threw him a playful frown. Less than a month until the open house. In one sense, it felt like a blink, there was so much left to do. But in terms of finally seeing what was inside his secret building, it felt like an eternity.

"I need to go away for a few days," he said quietly. "And I need to ask you a special favor."

Her frown came genuinely this time. "Where are you going?"

"That's not the point." He smiled. "The point is . . . I need you to water the potato plants while I'm gone. Every day, just like I showed you."

"Oh, Marcus, what if I—"

"I don't want Gray or any of the other gardeners doing it. They always overwater. And I don't want to take any chances."

She nodded. "I'll do it, but please don't blame me if anything happens to them."

"Nothing's going to happen. Other than in the next two weeks you and I are going to be digging up some potatoes. And no peeking at either the potatoes or the building while I'm gone."

"You know I wouldn't."

"I know. Or . . . I think I do."

He drew her into an embrace, and she slipped her arms about his waist, loving the solid feel of his chest and the strong, steady drum of his heart.

He kissed the crown of her head. "I love you, Eleanor."

She tightened her hold on him, the words *I love you too* on the tip of her tongue, begging to be said. But if she said them, that would take her one step closer to losing her heart to him completely.

And she couldn't go there. Not yet. If ever.

Eleanor picked up the card lying by the half dozen purple peonies in a vase in the kitchen of the home.

"Dearest Eleanor,

Though you have all of my love, there are only half a dozen peonies, because I only know you half as well as I'd like. Marcus."

Her heart melting a little more, she glanced out the window toward the building, so grateful to discover he was back. She smelled the peonies. Her favorite. But the new apron beside the flowers made her suspicious.

She looked over at Naomi, remembering her comment to Naomi last week about needing a new one. "How did Marcus know to get me an apron?"

Naomi never looked up from scrubbing potatoes. "Austrian men. Very insightful."

Eleanor heard the faintest grin in her friend's voice. "You're supposed to be on *my* side."

Naomi lifted her gaze, a smile ghosting her face. "And who says I am not?"

Looking out the window, Eleanor saw Marcus come from the building and hurried to meet him.

"Welcome home!" she said and hugged him.

He didn't let her go. "I missed you," he whispered against her hair.

"I missed you too." She drew back slightly. "Where did you say you went again?"

He shook his head. "Nice try, Madam Director."

He kissed her on the mouth—a sweet, chaste kiss—and she sensed his restraint, which only served to stir up whatever it was that had already been stirring inside her in his absence. She also sensed something else in him. Hesitance? Or disappointment, maybe?

"Will you come by the propagating room later?"

She nodded, eager to check the potatoes, but right now, trying to sort out his kiss, and his mood. "I need to stop by Mrs. Malloy's first, but I'll come by right afterward. Are you still hopeful about what we'll find?"

"Hope is such a tenuous word." His gaze held hers. "But yes, I still am."

A short while later, Eleanor welcomed the opportunity to walk, the smell of spring in the air, the flowers and trees having awakened from their slumber. Yet her emotions still felt tender when she opened the door to the dress shop, the bell jingling overhead.

She *did* love Marcus. That wasn't it. And she wanted to be with him. But the thought of giving herself so completely to him frightened her more than she could put into words. But the way he'd kissed her upon his return . . .

She closed her eyes, feeling the sting of tears. He hadn't kissed her the way he'd wanted to, which— for some reason she couldn't fathom—had made her desire him all the more.

While he'd been gone, she'd imagined her life without him, and had never felt so empty and alone.

"Miss Braddock, I heard the bell. I'm so glad

you're—" Rebecca Malloy paused in the curtained doorway. "Are you all right, ma'am?"

Eleanor nodded, brushing her cheeks. "I'm fine. Just . . . emotional today, I think."

Embarrassed, she attempted to set aside the turmoil within her. But when Rebecca placed a hand on her shoulder, the caring gesture only encouraged Eleanor's tears.

"I'm so sorry, Mrs. Malloy." Eleanor pulled the handkerchief from her pocket. "I suppose I have more on my mind than I thought." She dabbed her cheeks, then refolded the handkerchief. "What with all the goings on at the home and then—"

Rebecca drew in a quick breath. "W-wh—" Her voice faltered. Her face went pale. "Where did you get that?" she whispered.

Eleanor looked at the handkerchief clutched in her own hand, then back at her friend. "From a soldier," she whispered. "In the war."

Rebecca reached for it, her hand shaking. "This was mine"—she ran her fingers over the embroidered flowers—"another lifetime ago."

Watching Rebecca's expression, seeing her fingers tremble as she held the handkerchief, Eleanor felt the weight of years—from that one in the field hospital so long ago, to this—fall away. She couldn't stem the tears, and didn't even try.

"I gave this to Patrick," Rebecca cried, "before he left for the war."

Eleanor covered her hand. "And he carried it with him . . . until the day he died."

"You were *there?*" she asked in a broken whisper.

Eleanor nodded, seeing the soldier—*Patrick*—so clearly in her memory. "I worked in a surgical tent. Your husband was brave, Rebecca, up to the very end."

Rebecca took a shuttered breath. "All I've ever known is that he died . . . at the Battle of Nashville."

Eleanor told her about seeing her husband for the first time and how he'd been wounded. "There was nothing the doctor could do, Rebecca. I . . ." She hesitated, remembering what she'd done in the absence of medicine. "I made him as comfortable as I could, and then stayed with him. He spoke of you."

Rebecca smiled through her tears.

"He told me he'd been carrying the handkerchief just like you'd asked him to. And he said he couldn't believe you were his or that you'd said yes 'to the likes of him.' "

"Oh . . ." Rebecca held the handkerchief to her chest. "That sounds just like him. He always used to say that to me."

"Close to the end," Eleanor continued, her voice shaky, "as I held his hand, I knew it wasn't me he was seeing anymore. He was seeing you, Rebecca. He thought he was talking to you."

Rebecca squeezed her hand tight.

"So I leaned down, and I told him . . ." Eleanor closed her eyes, and she was back in that tent, cannon fire blasting, the earth shaking beneath her feet. "I said 'I'm proud to be yours and always have been.' "

Rebecca's sobs came softly. "So many times I've wished I could have told him that, just once more. That I was so grateful he chose *me*."

They hugged each other, Eleanor just letting her cry. Finally, Rebecca straightened and wiped her face.

"There's one more thing," Eleanor said, hoping this wouldn't bring Rebecca pain. "He kept repeating how he wished he'd done something for you. Before he left. He said he knew it was too late, but if he'd had another chance, he would have done it. But . . . he never said what it was."

A smile so sweet and tender bloomed in Rebecca's expression. "Come with me."

Eleanor followed her through the curtained doorway to her sewing room, then beyond to the private quarters in the back, and then outside, to a tiny patch of yard shaded by a dogwood tree. But there, in the sliver of sun-drenched earth off to the side, was a flower bed—full of gorgeous red roses.

"Patrick always promised he would plant me roses where I could see them from the kitchen window." Rebecca pointed behind her to an open window. "It's just as he promised."

Minutes later, as they walked back inside, Rebecca paused. "Miss Braddock, would you like a cup of tea?"

"I would love one." Eleanor smiled. "But please, no more Miss Braddock. Call me Eleanor."

They talked for the next hour, Rebecca sharing memories of her husband and their seven years of marriage, and Eleanor telling her about all the times she'd gained strength from carrying the handkerchief with her, and of what she'd done to try and find the soldier's widow through the years.

"But Patrick kept calling you his Mary girl. So for all these years, I've been looking for a woman named Mary."

Memory warmed Rebecca's expression. "Patrick was from Ireland. His family came over when he was just a boy. When he first started courting me, he called me his American girl." She touched a picture of him in a frame on the table for two in the tiny kitchen. "Over the years, it simply became Mary girl."

When they rose from the table, Eleanor looked again at the picture of Patrick—so handsome and full of health—and felt such grief.

"I'm so sorry for your loss, Rebecca. And for all you've endured." She sighed. "Sometimes I wonder. . . . Might it be better never to have loved at all."

Rebecca's expression turned pain-stricken. "If I've given you the impression, Eleanor, that if I could I would turn back the clock and never have met Patrick, then please forgive me. That could not be more wrong. Yes, I miss him dearly. Not a day goes by that I don't want him back with me.

But the years we had together were the happiest of my life. And even now the memory of that happiness—what I learned from Patrick, the way his love changed me, changed how I look at life, at how I've lived my life since then—all of those things sustain me. The memories give me strength I'd *never* have had without him."

Tears Eleanor thought she'd put away threatened to return.

Rebecca studied her. "Is there someone in your life? Someone you love? And . . . who loves you?"

Eleanor looked away, then nodded.

"Take my advice for what it is, Eleanor. *My* advice only. Don't let fear rob you of life. If my sweet Patrick were here, he wou—" Her voice caught. "He would tell you that's partly what he fought for. For you—and me—to have the freedom to live life to its fullest. Patrick didn't let his fear keep him from fighting. So I determined, after his death, not to let fear keep me from living."

If Rebecca had dropped a pin in that moment, Eleanor was certain she would have heard it.

Feeling aptly put in her place and by someone who had the right to speak from the place of pain, she nodded in acknowledgment. "I'm sorry if I said anything to offend you, Rebecca."

"Not at all." Rebecca gave a tiny shrug. "Patrick always said I was too outspoken for my own good."

Eleanor laughed softly. "I can relate."

"Oh, before you go," Rebecca said as they passed through the sewing shop. "Let me show you your ensemble. Since you're the director, I thought a skirt and jacket would be more appropriate. They're in the closet right here. You may not have time to try them on now—after we've spent so much time talking. But you can come back any day this week, and I can make the needed adjustments in plenty of time."

Eleanor waited.

A minute later, Rebecca rounded the corner. "I hope you like it." She paused and held it up, draping the full skirt off to one side. "Maggie chose the color, but I think it will be lovely on you. She said it's her favorite. *Rosa!*"

Eleanor took one look at the ensemble and almost laughed. At first she wondered if it was a joke instigated by Marcus. But reading sincerity in Rebecca's expression, she guessed it wasn't. "It's beautiful, Rebecca. Simply beautiful."

Rosa, she thought. German . . . for pink.

Eleanor entered the conservatory, a warm rush of air greeting her. As she passed by the *Selenicereus grandiflorus*, she looked upon the cactus quite differently than she had the first time she'd seen it, and even paused to offer a brief curtsy, knowing Marcus would have been amused had he been there.

What Rebecca Malloy had said played over and over in her mind, both gently scolding her while also shining a light into shadows in her heart left unchallenged for far too long.

She still had trouble believing that, after so many years, God had placed her and the soldier's Mary girl together, and she hadn't even seen it. There were other things she'd missed as well. She knew that now.

A table full of pink roses in every imaginable shade caught her eye—Marcus's repeated attempts to meet her aunt's always exacting expectations. He'd told her he had another batch of grafts set to bloom any day. Hopefully one of those would prove worthy.

She paused briefly to finger one of the flowers, and her focus slipped down the stem to the scar marking the place where Marcus had originally grafted the two flowers together. She knew that, with time, and as the plant grew stronger, the slight *imperfection* would become less noticeable. All of the grafted plants bore scars—evidence of the cutting, and also of the healing around it. But what beauty had come from both.

The door to Marcus's *haven* stood open, so she walked on through to the propagating room—but stopped in the doorway when she saw him.

"Marcus Geoffrey! Are you starting without me?"

His head came up, his arm buried halfway in the dirt by one of the potato plants. He frowned at her. "I *am* waiting on you, Eleanor. I was simply loosening the soil for you. That's all."

Studying his expression just to be sure, Eleanor didn't see any potatoes in sight, so guessed he'd been waiting on her after all. But she sensed he was still in that *mood*. Which was disappointing, considering she'd wanted to tell him about her visit with Rebecca. Later would definitely be best.

She joined him by the trough.

"Ladies first." He gestured with a bow.

She rolled up her sleeves. "Did you notice I *hilled* the plants like you taught me to?"

"I did. And you did a very nice job. Now start digging."

She paused, sensing his impatience. "Are you all right?"

"I'm fine. I'm simply . . . eager to see what the seedball produced."

Knowing which potato plant he wanted her to start with—the one where he'd *loosened* the soil—she intentionally started on the one two down. And ignored the dark look he gave her.

Familiar with what to do, she reached into the soil, fingers splayed, and felt for the little tubers. Her hand closed around one. She looked up at Marcus and seeing the *tenuous* hope in his eyes, she twisted and pulled. . . .

And up came a blackened and pocked potato.

"One down," he said solemnly, making a note in his notebook. "Twenty-two to go."

She worked her way down the row, through the next ten plants. All the same. "Do you want to pull some?"

He shook his head. "Unless you've had enough, then I will."

Feeling for him, especially after how excited

he'd been upon finding the seedball, she knew her disappointment was nothing compared to his.

She moved to the next trough, praying as she groped through the soil, then as she pulled. Another seven plants produced the same blemished potatoes.

He was so quiet beside her. She looked over at him and found him watching her.

"What?" she whispered. "Do I have dirt on my face?"

"You're so beautiful, Eleanor. And the best thing about it is . . . you don't even realize it."

She paused, having difficulty believing he'd said that . . . to her. And yet, the truth of it shone in his eyes, and she knew she'd never forget this moment. Feeling her face grow warm, she smiled. "Are you just saying that so I'll continue digging?"

A slow grin tipped one side of his mouth. "Is it working?"

"Absolutely!" She plunged her hand into the dirt again. Then felt something . . . different. Larger. And . . . harder to pull up. She twisted and . . .

Up came an oversized potato, along with a spray of dirt. "It's huge," she said, turning it over in her hand. But on closer inspection, no matter how impressive the size, it bore the same characteristics as the others.

She laid it aside. Four plants to go. Two in each of the troughs.

Giving him a *here's to hoping* look, she harvested the tubers from the next three plants, saving the first plant—the one he'd wanted her to start with—for last. All three plants produced all the same—tiny little blackened potatoes.

"The last one," he said, sounding more hopeful than she would have expected.

"Just remember," she said, "even if this one isn't it, we can try again."

He nodded.

As the cool soil closed around her hand, then her arm, Eleanor prayed that God would give this man the desire of his heart. He'd worked so hard and so long on grafting. And creating a new potato, one more resistant to rot, would do so much for—

Her knuckles brushed against something. She frowned. It didn't feel round. It felt . . . square. Her hand closed around the object, and she pulled it up.

When she opened her palm, she could only stare. First at the little box, then at Marcus, who had put his notebook aside.

"Eleanor . . . I have been your friend"—he cradled the curve of her cheek—"your confidant, your business associate"—he arched a regal brow—"and your partner in late-night conservatory crime."

She laughed softly.

"But I want to be more than that. I want to be your husband," he whispered, taking the box, "your lover, the one you reach for in the middle of the night, and the one who will reach for you whenever you're near."

He opened the box and held out a beautiful band of gold, just what she would have chosen for herself.

"It's perfect," she whispered, seeing the promise of her answer reflected in his eyes.

"I took the liberty of engraving something on the inside." He turned it in the light so she could read it. *"Beste Freunde machen die besten Liebhaber,"* he whispered.

She warmed at his tone and at the meaning of the phrase. *Best friends make the best lovers.* Naomi had been right.

Eleanor peered up at him. "You knew if I saw you loosening the dirt on that plant that I'd start with another one, didn't you?"

He smiled that smile, then he kissed her. "Yes, I know you, Eleanor," he whispered against her lips. "Now, will you marry me?"

She kissed him again, just because she could. *"Ja,"* she whispered. *"Mein Herz ist deins."* *My heart is yours.* Then she giggled. "I've been practicing."

"I can tell." His voice had taken on a dreamy quality.

He started to put the ring on her finger.

"Not with all this dirt. Let me go wash up." Halfway to the door, she turned back. "I almost forgot to finish."

She walked back to the potato plant where Marcus had hidden the ring, and she plunged her hand deep—and felt a fairly good-sized potato. And at least two others. She looked over at Marcus, whose expression turned keen.

She pulled the first tuber to the surface and

handed it to him, watching his expression instead of looking at the potato.

"I don't believe it," he whispered, turning the potato in his hand, looking at it from all angles. He rubbed it gently with a cloth, and then a smile broke across his face. "It's . . ." He looked up at her. "It has a blemish here and there." He showed to her. "But when compared to the others . . . it's *perfekt*."

She pulled a second and a third. Then a fourth. All *perfekt*, just like he'd said. Just like he was for her.

"When I first received Miss Eleanor Braddock's invitation to join the city of Nashville on this momentous occasion, I must admit, I was skeptical regarding what I would find upon my arrival—"

Miss Dorothea Dix was exactly as Eleanor had imagined from having read her book—the epitome of strength, integrity, and grit all wrapped in a tenacity that warned a person, even upon first meeting the woman, that one should oppose her, and her initiatives, at their own peril.

Eleanor adored her instantly.

"—but when I toured the Nashville Widows' and Children's Home yesterday, then had the inestimable pleasure of taking a meal with the tenants of the home last night, every one of my doubts"—Miss Dix paused, gazing at the overflowing crowd—"based, of course, upon past experience of being told one thing only to find another being true, were proved false. This establishment is without question *precisely* as Miss Braddock described. With one enormous and most glaring exception."

Miss Dix turned to look at Eleanor, as did Aunt Adelicia and other league board members standing close by, and Eleanor felt her chest tighten with uncertainty.

"What Miss Braddock failed to tell me," Miss Dix continued, "is how *her* depth of love, dedication, and hard work have forever changed the lives—and futures—of these brave widows and their children."

Spontaneous applause rose from the crowd, and Eleanor, uncomfortable beneath the praise, was tempted to duck her head. But the honest admiration and womanly courage in Miss Dix's gaze—and in Aunt Adelicia's—wouldn't allow it.

Eleanor placed a hand over her heart and mouthed *"Thank you"* to Miss Dix and those around her, wishing Marcus were there to share the moment. She couldn't have done this without him.

Miss Dix continued just as Eleanor felt the tickle of a whisper in her ear. . . .

"Add my hearty *amen* to Miss Dix's last comment."

She turned to see Marcus beside her, feeling the warmth of his hand on the small of her back.

"I'm sorry I'm late," he said softly. "The discussion ran longer than I anticipated."

She leaned close, eager to discover the outcome

of his meeting with Sutton Monroe, Aunt Adelicia's attorney. "Did he have an answer for you?"

Marcus nodded. "It will all work out in the end," he whispered, then glanced down at her ensemble. "You look lovely . . . in *rosa*."

Sensing evasion in his initial response, Eleanor smiled her thanks, knowing they'd have time to discuss his meeting with Mr. Monroe later. And though she still disliked wearing pink, she'd discovered something of a saving grace about the color an hour earlier. . . .

Maggie and several other little girls had requested that the dresses Rebecca Malloy made them be the exact same color as hers, saying they wanted "to be just like Miss Braddock." Learning that had meant so much. And even softened her animosity toward the color. At least a little.

As Miss Dix spoke, Eleanor looked over the crowd, recognizing far more faces than those she didn't. But wishing one special face was there that wasn't.

She'd wanted her father to be able to attend, but Dr. Crawford dissuaded it. *"So much noise and the size of the gathering might overstimulate him, Miss Braddock. I wouldn't wish to ruin the day for you just as I don't wish to subject your father to the emotional upheaval a setting such as that could cause him. Not when he's been doing so well in recent weeks."*

She understood, of course. But it didn't lessen her desire to share her life with him. After all, she was her father's daughter. And always would be. Whether or not he ever recognized her again.

"One final note on this memorable day, dear friends." Miss Dix's voice carried over the hushed crowd. "It is rare, indeed, for a community to unite for such a humble and often overlooked purpose, but to put such care into restoring a building that was once considered, by some, to have outlived its usefulness is also to be highly commended . . . *Mr. Geoffrey.*"

Miss Dix looked at Marcus then, and he bowed, looking every bit the archduke he was. Or . . . used to be.

Eleanor saw no sign of Mayor Adler, nor did she expect to, not following the recent front-page articles boasting about the renovation of the home and the "forward-thinking" kitchen Marcus had designed. And that every woman on the women's league board now wanted in their own home.

But it was the article scheduled to come out in *tomorrow's* edition of the newspaper that had Eleanor most excited. She'd secretly promised the reporter an interview with the designer of a most intriguing invention in the still-secret building next door.

Applause erupted as Dorothea Dix left the stage and Mrs. Holcomb, the league president, took her place behind the podium. "Thank you again, Miss Dix, for traveling to be with us today. You honor us with your presence. And now, before I invite you all on a tour of the Nashville Widows' and Children's Home, followed by"—Mrs. Holcomb shot a look at Marcus—"the *special* unveiling of the building next door that so many of us have grown curious about . . ." She smiled. "It is my profound pleasure to introduce a woman whose generosity in our city is well noted. Mrs. Agnetta Hightower, who this very morning made a most generous donation that will provide every woman and child in the home with a pair of new shoes."

As Mrs. Hightower strode to the stage, Eleanor caught Mrs. Holcomb's look in her direction and remembered that day in the board meeting when Mrs. Holcomb had voted *against* her. The league president's counsel had been exceedingly wise. It was better to remain peaceable with those who opposed you, rather than fight to win every battle at all costs.

Eleanor smiled. The next time Mayor Adler ran for office, he'd better take note of Mrs. Holcomb. With all the changes happening in the world, surely the women's right to vote—and even a woman in politics—couldn't be that far off.

Listening to Mrs. Hightower's speech, or trying, Eleanor found her attention, and gaze, wandering. But she had to close her eyes and open them again when she saw Miss Hillary Hightower on the arm of . . . Mr. *Hockley?*

Possibly sensing her attention, Lawrence Hockley glanced her way and—in a most characteristic manner—touched the brim of his hat and nodded, then faced forward again, as though they'd never shared more than a casual acquaintance.

Which was true, Eleanor guessed, in one sense.

Hillary Hightower chose that moment to look her way, and Eleanor managed a smile even as the young woman lifted her chin and moved closer to Mr. Hockley's side, as though staking her claim.

Eleanor felt Marcus's fingers thread through her own and looked over at him, aware he'd been watching her.

"I couldn't be happier for them both," he whispered, his thumb drawing feather-soft circles on the underside of her wrist, making her wish for time alone with him, which they hadn't had in the whirlwind of recent days.

At the conclusion of Mrs. Hightower's *few words,* Eleanor started toward the front door of the home but felt a tug of her hand.

"Not just yet, Miss Braddock." Smiling, Marcus glanced beyond her to where Naomi, Marta, Elena, Rebecca, and some other women stood waiting to greet the visitors. "You have another appointment first."

Eleanor caught Naomi's grin, as well as the girlish look between Marta and Elena, and knew the women had been plotting. And loved them for it. Rebecca Malloy simply smiled and slipped her hand into her pocket, and Eleanor knew what she was feeling, at least in one sense.

She'd given Rebecca the rose petals she'd saved for so many years. They were a little worse for wear, but the last time she was at the shop, Eleanor had seen them in a dish by Patrick's picture. Just because a husband—or wife—passed on didn't mean the love they'd shared had died. It lived on in the hearts of the people who still loved them. Good-byes were simply part of this life, as much as Eleanor wished they weren't.

But someday, in Christ, there would be *no* more good-byes. Only *together forevers*. She clung to that promise and determined to view this life through the lens of that hope.

She accepted Marcus's offered arm, then heard *"Mr. Geoffrey"* in a familiar voice and turned to see her aunt approaching.

Aunt Adelicia's gaze briefly dropped to where Eleanor's hand was tucked in the crook of Marcus's arm. Eleanor had told her about accepting his proposal and though her aunt hadn't forbidden the union, by any means, neither had she been overly thrilled. *Accepting* had been a better description of her reaction.

Eleanor knew a way to win her aunt over instantly. Tell her the truth about who Marcus was. But that was Marcus's decision to reveal his heritage, *if* he ever chose to. Personally, Eleanor was glad they'd decided to keep it to themselves for now. But oh . . . she could well imagine her aunt's expression if she ever learned the truth.

"Mr. Geoffrey," her aunt continued, "I'm so glad I caught you. The newest blooms you showed me yesterday . . . I've been living with the colors since then, and—" She sighed. "I fear none of them are yet what I'd envisioned."

Eleanor felt Marcus's arm tense.

"But I thought you said you were pleased, Mrs. Cheatham."

Her aunt held up a hand. "I said I was pleased with your repeated efforts, Mr. Geoffrey. And I am! I also stated I would have to see the roses in the right light to be absolutely certain. And . . ." Her sweet smile belied the gleam in her eyes. "Now that you're going to be staying, and that you're going to be . . . *family*"—she gave Eleanor's shoulder a gentle squeeze—"I'd like to see us continue working together for that one *perfect* rose. Like that of first dawn, if you remember. But not—"

"—too light," Marcus supplied. "And with the slightest hint of purple. But not overly orange. And not too overt. Yes, madam." He smiled. "I remember quite well."

Looking more than pleased, her aunt took her leave, and Marcus exhaled.

"I'll be grafting roses for that woman for the next decade, won't I?"

"And long after . . . your highness," Eleanor said, laughing softly.

She allowed him to lead her around his building and to the door she'd wanted to enter for months now.

"Finally?" she said, looking up at him.

"I hope you consider this worth the wait."

"Without even seeing it, I can already tell you that it is."

He unlocked the door, then waited, watching her. With a feigned sigh of impatience, she closed her eyes. The click of a latch, and he opened the door, then guided her inside.

She heard the soft *whoosh* of water, like rainfall only . . . more so, and a cool breeze accompanied the fresh scent. "I feel as if we've walked into another world," she whispered, her other senses heightened without benefit of sight.

His hand tightened over hers in the crook of his arm. "Only a few more steps. Almost there."

The soft click of her heeled boots betrayed a stone flooring or path of some kind, and a momentary touch of warmth kissed her face— sunshine slanting through the windows, or roof lanterns, perhaps?

"All right." Marcus stopped beside here. "You can look."

Anticipation buzzing through her, she opened her eyes and, in a rush, felt her giddiness succumb to disbelief—and complete enchantment.

"*Oh,* Marcus . . ."

All around her, every place she looked—partially hidden behind trees and shrubs, peeking from behind flower beds—delight drew the eye and fascination waited to be discovered.

Adorning two of the walls, from floor to high ceiling, painted murals brought to life the characters from the stories she and the other women had read to the children in the evenings following dinner. She recognized Red Riding Hood, the young girl who fought the big bad wolf. And the awkward, ugly little duckling and the graceful swan he eventually became. *That* story had a special place in her own heart.

"The murals are works of art," she whispered.

"And are all compliments of Claire Monroe."

Eleanor had known the woman was an artist, but this . . .

Yet it was the other two walls that tugged at her attention, and emotions. "Is that what Austria is like?" she asked, looking at the snow-capped Alps reaching to the ceiling, some of them—spurred by the imagination—soaring beyond the roofline.

"It is," he said, voice soft. "I'll take you there someday, Eleanor. And we'll sleep beneath the stars just like my grandfather and I used to do."

"I'm taking that as a promise, Marcus Geoffrey."

Only then did she see them—huge wooden support beams arching overhead like tree limbs, making her feel as though she were staring up into a canopy in the forest rather than at a ceiling. "How did you *do* that?"

Marcus squeezed her hand. "Years of dreaming and planning, followed by months of failed attempts, then finally . . . a measure of success."

"A *measure?*" She softly scoffed. "Marcus, this is . . . beyond belief."

He squeezed her hand, satisfaction in the gesture. "Follow me. There's something else."

He led her around to various pebble-covered islands where children's A-framed swings and seesaws stood waiting to be discovered. And in the very center of the room . . .

"A merry-go-round," Eleanor whispered, remembering how much she'd enjoyed the ride as a little girl. Taking turns pushing the platform round and round, then jumping on and holding tight as the world flew past in delightfully dizzying circles. "This is paradise . . . through the eyes of a child."

Marcus looked around, the satisfaction on his face briefly dimming. "My father believed playing was of no use to a child." Distant hurt edged his voice. "But my grandfather thought differently. As did my mother." His customary smile found its place once again. "I want the children to have a place to play all year long. No matter if it rains or snows. And I modified the roof lanterns." He pointed up. "They close with louvers now. Just crank them open and shut. Much easier than the big doors I'd first designed. You were right." He smiled. "They were too cumbersome."

Eleanor turned in a circle, wanting to take it all in—when she spotted the waterfall in a back corner of the room.

She started laughing, and couldn't stop. "Every child needs a waterfall, too, I guess."

"Well, of course. You can't have the Alps without a waterfall."

The sound of a door opening somewhere behind them drew her attention, and Eleanor turned. She felt her heart give as she looked back at Marcus, then down the path again at her father toddling through a door with the help of Nurse Smith.

"That's the main reason I was late this morning." Marcus tucked her hand in the crook of his arm and led her down the path toward them. "I explained this setting to Dr. Crawford, told him how much it would mean to you to have your father in attendance, and he gave his whole-hearted blessing."

Eleanor pressed her cheek into his shoulder. "Thank you, Marcus. How did he manage the trip into town?"

Marcus laughed. "He loved it."

Just then, her father looked up. A smile broke across his face. "Ellie! Marcus said you would be joining us."

"Hello, Theodore. How are you?" Wanting to hug him tight, Eleanor instead settled for a quick shake of his hand, which felt so frail and weak.

Thoughts of the future and what it might hold threatened to crowd out her happiness, but she quickly reined in her thoughts and her fears. *The good-byes here are only temporary. Someday there will be only together forevers.*

"I'm quite well, thank you!" her father said, holding on to Nurse Smith. "Though . . ." A frown crept over his face as he looked around. "I don't know where I am."

"You're with *us,* Theodore." Marcus put an arm around her father's shoulders. "And your swing is right over here, just like I promised."

Her father patted Marcus's chest. "You always keep your promises, my young friend."

Marcus led him around a corner to a secluded spot where, sure enough, a swing—just like the ones at the asylum—faithfully waited. Eleanor marveled at how relaxed her father was in Marcus's company, and how good Marcus was with him.

"I love to swing," her father said, easing down with the help of the nurse.

"Thank you," Eleanor whispered to her.

Nurse Smith merely smiled.

The shuffle of footsteps and snatches of excited conversation drifted in through the open windows. *The children . . .*

Eleanor joined Marcus by the main entry, and together they welcomed the mothers and children into the wonderland Marcus had created.

In watching his expression as he watched the children, she glimpsed the tangible definition of what it meant to find fulfillment by bringing someone else happiness, by changing a life. Not by having your name—or building—recognized and admired.

One of the last to enter, the reporter from the newspaper greeted Eleanor by name. "Miss Braddock, how nice to see you again, ma'am. I appreciate your making this opportunity available to me."

"It's my pleasure, sir." Eleanor glanced at Marcus, who motioned behind him.

"There are private quarters in the back." Marcus directed the comment to the reporter. "You can interview Miss Braddock there. I'll show you the way."

"Actually, Mr. Geoffrey"—the reporter glanced between them—"I'm here to interview *you,* sir. About your invention of . . . *roof lanterns.*" The man's gaze wandered the room. "And a whole lot more, from the looks of things."

Eleanor loved watching realization work its way into Marcus's expression.

"Is that so?" Marcus said, grinning. "And I wonder who told you about those?"

The reporter started to respond, but Eleanor beat him to it. "*Perhaps* I mentioned it to him earlier, but"—she did her best to keep a straight face—"I just can't remember for sure."

Later that day, after speaking with every visitor at least five times—or so it felt—Eleanor accompanied Miss Dorothea Dix to the train station, then returned to the home to find dinner prepared. She ate with Marcus and several of the women from the league board and women in leadership positions in the home before slipping back into the kitchen.

She retrieved the dish she'd placed in the icebox earlier that morning and slid it into one of the still-warm ovens, hoping her latest attempt would be the charm.

She returned to find Marcus speaking with Sutton Monroe in hushed tones in the mostly empty gathering hall. Their conversation dropped off when she joined them.

"Well," she said, looking between them. "This isn't awkward, is it?"

Marcus smiled.

Sutton Monroe only bowed slightly. "Thank you, Miss Braddock, for a most enjoyable dinner. You've done a remarkable work here."

"I've had a great deal of help, Mr. Monroe. Including that from your most talented wife. Please give her my thanks again for her murals. I'm sorry she couldn't join us tonight. I hope she's feeling better soon."

A hint of red touched Mr. Monroe's face. "I'm confident she'll be fine, Miss Braddock. In . . . roughly five months," he whispered with a knowing wink.

Eleanor covered her mouth with her hand, thrilled for the couple, and still smiling when Mr. Monroe took his leave.

Marcus gestured to a bench. "Sit with me?"

"My pleasure. My feet are killing me."

Eleanor discovered they were alone in the gathering hall, everyone else having retired.

Marcus took her hand in his and brought it to his lips. "I've missed you."

"I've missed you too. Thank you for seeing my father back safely this afternoon."

"My pleasure. I . . ." He briefly bowed his head. "I wish I could have known the man he was, the man you've known all your life. But I've still grown to love him, Eleanor. And we will always . . . *always* take care of him together. Never doubt that."

739

She scooted closer to him, loving how his arms came around her, pulling her to him. "What did Mr. Monroe tell you?"

Marcus's laughter reverberated in his chest. "So much for a tender moment."

She stared, unwilling to be put off.

"I met with him more as a friend than an attorney. And he said what I thought he'd say. That whatever I decide to do, my developing the new potato on the Belmont estate will have no negative implications on your aunt."

Eleanor laid her hand on his chest. "You've made your decision, haven't you?"

He kissed her forehead. "I have."

"And?"

"And . . . later this summer you and I will travel to Boston, where we'll give Luther Burbank what I hope will be—after we harvest this new crop— the beginnings of a new breed of potato. Which, in turn, he can introduce to the world."

Having discussed the reasoning behind his decision, Eleanor understood, and loved him for it all the more. Still . . . "I wish the situation were different."

He shook his head. "I'm truly fine with it. And believe that"—he shrugged—"for some reason I can't fully explain, but that I trust—"

His gaze held a certainty she understood.

"—I know it's what I'm supposed to do. Talking things through with Sutton helped me see that. I understand the local farmers' hesitation to introduce the new plants into their fields. I'm a foreigner. I have no reputation with them."

"Yes, but for one of them to accuse you of wanting to introduce the same blight that swept through Ireland years ago . . ." She exhaled. "That's ludicrous."

His arms tightened around her, and even though she couldn't see his face, she could feel his smile.

"My uncle could use you when negotiating with Russia."

Tempted to laugh, she couldn't, not when thinking of his strained relationship with his uncle and father. "You said that the House of Habsburg would be *embarrassed* if they got wind of your accomplishment. While that may be true, Marcus"—she looked up at him—"I hope you know that your mother and your grandfather would be thrilled."

He cradled her tight, and they sat like that for several moments, then he sniffed. "What's that smell?"

Oh no. Eleanor jumped up and ran to the kitchen. Heartsick, she grabbed a towel and pulled the apple strudel from the oven and plunked the burned attempt down on the counter.

Marcus encircled her waist from behind. "You made me another strudel."

"Correction. I *tried* to make you another strudel. And charred it."

He reached around her for one of several forks left to dry on the counter. "It's not burned. It looks just right."

She attempted to protest, but he forked a bite, blew on it, and popped it into his mouth. He gave a satisfied groan. "Mmmm . . . delicious. Just like my *Mutter*'s."

"Your mother burned her strudel?"

He turned her in his arms. "My Mutter *never* burned strudel. She always baked it to perfection."

He forked another bite, blew it, and held it to her lips. Readying herself for the taste of overbaked pastry, Eleanor accepted. And quickly realized . . .

"You're right," she whispered, chewing, then she swallowed. "It's—"

"Delicious," he supplied.

"Yes!" She glanced back at the dish. "It must be the way the apples are caramelized on the bottom from the longer baking time. Or maybe it's the—"

He framed her face in his hands and kissed her, slow and long, the sweetness of apples and cinnamon only adding to the pleasure.

"Is there anything you can't do, Eleanor?" he whispered, drawing back.

She ran a hand over his stubbled jawline. "There are too many things to list. What about you?"

"Since you've come into my life, I feel as if I can do anything. As long as you're beside me."

"And just think . . ." She smiled sweetly and ran a hand through his hair, hoping her next comment would earn the response she desired. "You've come such a long way . . . for an under gardener."

She wasn't disappointed.

Discussion Questions

1. Eleanor Braddock is a practical, no-nonsense kind of woman. Could you identify with her character? With how she viewed herself both physically and in relation to others?

2. Adelicia Acklen was a "real" person, meaning that her character in the novel is based on a woman who really lived. Adelicia was an extraordinary, "born before her time" woman. What did you think about her character? About her relationship with Eleanor? Can you sympathize with Adelicia's opinions and her perspective on women's issues and marriage? Why or why not?

3. Eleanor's father struggles with health issues. What would you liken his disease to today, and have you ever witnessed this health struggle firsthand in someone you love? Which scenes between Eleanor and her father touched you most, and why?

4. Tamera uses a lot of garden imagery in this story. Are you a gardener? Did you identify with the imagery on both a literal and spiritual level?

5. Eleanor doesn't see herself as an attractive woman. In a conversation with Marcus, she responds, "Not everything has to be *beautiful* to be worthy of admiration." Discuss why you think she reacted this way and whether or not you've ever shared her feelings, especially in the light of the world's definition of beauty.

6. Do you like to cook and/or bake? At one point, Eleanor describes how cooking and baking allows her to "be still" on the inside. Can you relate?

7. We often seek to be filled and to have our own needs met, when it's something else entirely that we need. Discuss how Eleanor experienced this in her character journey. What was it she needed?

8. We often wonder why God allows such hurt in this life, especially when it involves children. Eleanor has some fairly accusing thoughts about God. Have you ever had similar thoughts? What does the Bible say about God's thoughts and ways (read Isaiah 55:9) and how does that relate to this story?

9. Marcus desires to make a name for himself, to leave his mark on the world. What happens to him in his character journey? How does his perspective change?

10. Before reading this story, had you ever heard of Luther Burbank, Dorothea Dix, or Gregor Mendel? Do you enjoy reading novels that include real people from history?

11. In this story, two characters from the TIMBER RIDGE REFLECTIONS series (*From a Distance, Beyond This Moment, Within My Heart*) share a cameo appearance. Did you catch who they were?

12. What was your favorite scene in *A Beauty So Rare*, and what was your favorite passage? (Write Tamera at Tamera@TameraAlexander.com and tell her, she'd love to know!)

Visit www.TameraAlexander.com for the full Reader Discussion Guide that contains more reading group questions *and* Eleanor's recipes from the novel.

Dear Reader,

Writing historical fiction set against the backdrop of real history is a rewarding undertaking. I gain great pleasure in weaving real bits of history and people into my stories, and this novel is chockfull of both.

The Belmont Estate really did have a conservatory and a water tower as depicted in the novel. Adelicia's conservatory was nicknamed the Crystal Palace and contained plants and trees from all over the world (including a *Selenicereus grandiflorus*). Unfortunately, the conservatory didn't survive time. But the water tower did, and it still stands today as the Bell Tower on the campus of Belmont University which now surrounds the Belmont Mansion itself.

There really was an insane asylum in Nashville as well. And for a time, Dr. William Cheatham (Adelicia's third husband) served as its director. The influx of widows into Nashville following the Civil War is also well documented in history, as is the establishment of a widows' and children's home. Women came from North and South looking for their men. Some of the women knew their husbands had died in battles, others came seeking answers. Still others were new to this country, their husbands having died either on the journey to America or shortly after their arrival. However they arrived, the widows often did not have the means to return home and, hence, were forced to carve out a new life with what little—if anything—they had.

The House of Habsburg (of which Marcus was fictionally archduke) was one of the most important royal houses of Europe whose history reads like a modern-day novel. I took artistic license with the details of this fascinating family and invite you to research more of their intriguing history online.

Luther Burbank (1849–1926) was an American botanist, horticulturist, and a pioneer in agricultural science who fictitiously crossed Marcus's path. However, not so fictitiously, Burbank worked for years grafting potato plants in an effort to create one without blight and rot. Ultimately, he did just that when he created the Russet potato . . . from a *seedball* he found *per chance* one day in his garden. Gregor Mendel (1822–1884), Marcus's mentor, was a German-speaking scientist who gained posthumous fame as the founder of the new science of genetics. Finally, Dorothea Dix (1802–1887) was an American activist who worked tirelessly throughout her life on behalf of the indigent insane. Quite simply, Miss Dix did whatever she could to better the lives of others. And her book, *Conversations on Common Things* (published 1824), is a wonderful read.

The book about the art of hair work mentioned in chapter 10 was originally published in 1867 and is available online through public domain. Entertaining reading, let me tell you! Also, the statue of

The Prodigal Son by Joseph Mozier in chapter 29 is real as well, and is a beautiful depiction of God's unconditional love.

To learn more about the history behind this story and other Belmont Mansion novels, and to view pictures of the estate during Adelicia's day, as well as Eleanor's recipes from the book, visit my website (www.TameraAlexander.com). To schedule a visit to the Belmont Mansion, visit www.BelmontMansion.com or call them at 615-460-5459. Be sure and tell them Tamera sent you!

Thanks for reading, friend. The connections we make are precious to me, and I invite you to contact me through the venues listed on the following pages. Until next time, I hope that—as Marcus and Eleanor cross your mind—you'll remember that you were created in the image of the Author of everlasting beauty. A beauty that doesn't fade with time or age, that neither seeks nor needs the approval of this world, and that graces even the tiniest, often-thought-minute details of your life, and mine. God knows you. He sees you. He adores you, enough to graft you into His family tree—and yes, even *prune* you—all for the hope and blessing of an eternity with Him.

Through the true grapevine and His Father, the gardener . . .

Until next time,
Tamera
John 15:4–5

With Gratitude to . . .

My family . . . quite simply, for loving me no matter what.

Karen Schurrer, Charlene Patterson, my editors at Bethany House Publishers, and to Helen Motter, for your endless support and expertise as I wrote, and wrote, this story.

Natasha Kern, my agent, for sharing your fierce love of the written word and of story with me. You really are my hero.

Deborah Raney, my writing critique partner, for all the oh-so-fun "back and forth" through the years.

Leonard Fitch, of Wilmore, Kentucky, who owns the IGA Foodliner grocery store and who makes the best doughnuts you've ever put in your mouth. But you have to get there early in the morning to get some. Right, Mama Ruth Seamands? Because once they're gone, they're gone!

Lauren Luckhart, for sharing the tale of how your uncle—when courting your aunt—gave her a bouquet of roses, just one shy of a half dozen. And for letting me borrow it!

Mark Brown, Executive Director of the Belmont Mansion, for making Adelicia Acklen's family files and documents so readily available to me, and for making me feel so welcome in Adelicia's home.

My readers, for embracing these characters and settings with a passion that rivals my own. I'm so grateful for you. More than you know.

And to the Lord Jesus, whose beauty and reign knows no end. It's all about You.

About the Author

Tamera Alexander is a *USA Today* bestselling novelist whose deeply drawn characters, thought-provoking plots, and poignant prose resonate with readers worldwide. She and her husband make their home in Nashville, not far from the Belmont Mansion.

Tamera invites you to visit her at:

Her website: www.tameraalexander.com
Her blog: www.tameraalexander.blogspot.com
Twitter: www.twitter.com/tameraalexander
Facebook: www.facebook.com/tamera.alexander
Pinterest: www.pinterest.com/tameraauthor/

Or if you prefer snail mail, please write her at:

Tamera Alexander
P.O. Box 871
Brentwood, TN 37024

Discussion questions for all of Tamera's novels
are available at www.tameraalexander.com,
as are details about Tamera joining
your book club for a virtual visit.

Center Point Large Print
600 Brooks Road / PO Box 1
Thorndike ME 04986-0001 USA

(207) 568-3717

US & Canada:
1 800 929-9108
www.centerpointlargeprint.com

LP
Alexander, Tamera
A Beauty So Rare